The Tale
of the
Bloodline

Le Couer Inspire

Etienne de Mendes

authorHOUSE®

AuthorHouse™
1663 Liberty Drive
Bloomington, IN 47403
www.authorhouse.com
Phone: 1-800-839-8640

First published by AuthorHouse 2/23/2010

ISBN: 978-1-4490-5711-4 (e)
ISBN: 978-1-4490-5709-1 (sc)
ISBN: 978-1-4490-5710-7 (hc)

Library of Congress Control Number: 2009913102

Cover layout by Scott and Mitzvah Williams.

Printed in the United States of America
Bloomington, Indiana

This book is printed on acid-free paper.

A broken heart is a whole heart.
A leaning ladder is a straight ladder.

Menahem Mendel, "The Kotsker"

The Tale of the Bloodline

PROLOGUE

$ummoned. Not invited, not coaxed or cajoled. Actually summoned and at the unconscionable hour of five in the damn morning! Thayer Delaquois, doctor of medicine, respected French neuropsychiatrist, settled back onto the plush leather seat of the Mercedes-Benz Pullman limousine. Sensing the twin-turbo twelve-cylinder engines pick up speed, he anxiously flipped the personalized note card and envelope embossed with the heavy gold crest of the de Chagny's against his palm. *Damn chilly morning to be out scurrying helter-skelter,* he complained mentally. *The sun hasn't even risen.* Bewildered, he continued to fuss with the card. The darkened windows of posh Parisian apartment buildings sped past as the driver started manuvering a route out of the city. Traffic was light, but then again, it was Sunday.

So why do I respond like an obedient schoolboy? I should be curled up beneath the covers next to my sweet Vanessa, afforded the luxury of sleeping in. The answer was obvious. It rested in the *billet-doux* he held in his hands.

He hadn't spoken to the world-renowned Dr. Isidore de Chagny for two decades. No one had. In the classroom de Chagny had been a humorless austere man focused on science, forever uncomfortable in crowds. Now the geneticist no longer made public appearances of any kind. Yet here was Delaquois – flying through the February darkness to his comrade's estate. The passenger smirked; nothing had changed since their days in medical school. He was still the slender, envious friend striving to reach Isidore's lofty mental summits. Everything came so easily to de Chagny. Three years ago he'd won the Nobel Prize in Science for genetically engineering an internationally patented serum. News of the remarkable DNA navigator swept swiftly around the world. Now nearly every country was showing interest in the internal switch that made people fall over dead at the age of eighty-two. Thayer sighed, tapping the seat beside him. *Controls population, limits the expense incurred caring for the elderly, and makes Isidore rich!*

After withdrawing from all public scientific circles, there were rumors that the reclusive, albeit illustrious, Dr. de Chagny had grown

1

paranoid receiving the Nobel. Thayer closed his eyes and ordered his sixty-year-old mind to take a nap. Whatever Isidore required, it was important enough to send for him. *Sufficient cause to draw me from the comfort of my bed.* He was grateful for the chance to renew their earlier friendship.

Half in sleep, Thayer heard the window separating the chauffer from the back seats slide downward. "We're approaching the estate now, Dr. Delaquois."

"Thank you." The sky had grown gray with early light. "What's your name?"

"John Kelly."

"American?"

"Yes, Sir. From the great state of North Carolina."

"Do you know why I've been called upon, John?"

"No, Sir," he lied. The entire household knew why.

The vehicle drove alongside a sobering twelve-foot wall, topped in a running coil of concertina wire. Thayer adjusted his spectacles and looked up as they approached the equally high double-doors of a solid metal gate. Thick gray fog clung tenaciously to the ground. The mist scurried in eddies as the vehicle slowed to a crawl. An armed uniformed guard in a watchtower looked down upon them.

"John, when did all this security get added?"

"Over the last three years we've gradually fortified the place," offered the driver. Swinging the limousine with smooth expertise up to the forbidding gate, John brought the vehicle to a stop. He was listening to directions given into an earpiece he wore. Thayer could hear the faint scratchy squeals.

"Just, the physician and myself," the chauffer responded, looking at their guest through the rearview mirror. "He appears distinguished and wise, has neatly trimmed brown hair, graying at the temples, a kind clean-shaven face, and wears silver rimmed spectacles."

Thayer smiled at John's description; he considered himself still handsome despite the beginning wrinkles of age.

John caught Thayer's gaze. "What was your very first assignment in anatomy class? Sorry to ask, Doctor, but they are requesting the information to clear you."

With his mind still focused on the intimidating fortifications, Thayer stared blankly at the back of the driver's head. "Is the concertina wire electrified?"

"Yes, Sir. There are fanatics who want to see Dr. de Chagny dead. There's a particularly nasty group of militant pro-lifers. He's brilliant and his genetic catalyst, as you know, offers the economically depressed world a chance to define their budgets and prepare for aging populations." There was an uncomfortable pause. "They are waiting for your answer."

Thayer registered the information internally. France was a monetarily burdened country, so much of its populace *en chomage* (unemployment). The premise for instituting DNA coded death was simple. If an individual lived on pensions provided by the state, enjoying all their inherent benefits, the government asserted the reasonable right to dictate the time of that citizen's end. Declaring, with all finality, that the individual no longer contributed to society in a productive way and had enjoyed a sufficient retirement. *Things are worse than I thought; the place looks like a damn fortress…has persecution frightened Isidore so much that he's irrational?* Indignant, he cleared his throat.

"Our first assignment was to go over to McCallum Hall. There we chose a cadaver to dissect and study over the first two semesters. In case the mysterious **they** want to know, my specimen was a forty-year-old woman who died of squamous cell carcinoma of the lung. Is that sufficient to get me in?"

Touching the earpiece with his finger, John paused to listen.

It was then that Thayer identified the small fiber optic camera positioned aside one of the limousine's overhead light fixtures. Some of the speakers in the wall of the car's interior were not speakers at all; they were microphones.

"Have the dictatorial 'they' been looking and listening to me for the entire trip?"

"No, Sir, just since we got close to the estate. Observing your behavior was only a precaution. They're opening the gate now."

1   *OPENING PANDORA'S BOX*

𝔓 inioned reader, heed this warning. Venture no further if you are timid of heart or tend to prudish regulations. Consider that only happenstance brought you here and excuse yourself from traveling onward. Turn back. You have lost nothing. Let those whose allegiance remains undaunted devour the story held within these pages. And know this, stalwart souls, the Phantom knows of you and calls you allies.

As soon as the limousine cleared the gate, the driver brought the car to a second abrupt halt. Only a momentary delay – Dr. Delaquois was informed – as security stepped forward to scan the car for bombs or weapons. In the rapidly advancing daylight, Delaquois saw tall towers of motion sensitive klieg lamps dotting the sides of the wall. Still turned on, they shed a tremendous light on the grounds.

Thayer shifted uneasily in his seat. "Watchtowers, electric razor wire, this place looks more like a dreary prison under guard than a spacious home." *My god, this brain trust of the twenty-first century, this hope for an overcrowded world, lives on a police state!* "I suppose he's welded shut all but one entrance," he muttered.

The chauffer offered no response. At a signal from a uniformed guard standing beside the driver's door, John put the vehicle in gear and drove smoothly forward.

The chateau's signature frontage had certainly changed. Gone were the sylvan landscapes, replaced by a dreary open expanse of rolling winter-brown grass. The limousine veered right to where a healthy apple orchard once stood – every spring its branches so full of promise. Only a few bare fruit trees still remained. These few neglected stragglers stood as evidence against the abrasive winds tormenting their branches. Drawing his tan cashmere overcoat closer about him, Thayer twisted to get a better view of the barren grounds.

High up in one of the mansion's mullioned windows, a rather dull nondescript face watched the car's approach.

"Did you know, John, that these old mansions used to have dirt and gravel driveways? Years ago flagstones and colored cement led up to the frontcourt of the chateau's main entrance. Does it still look the same?"

"The entrance is basically unchanged...and I do know about the chateau's history." John guided the car around a curve. "Off to the left are the stables, still standing next to the pond. They've been renovated into garages and a guardhouse."

Thayer sighed with heavy disappointment. Decades ago the picturesque lower segment of the driveway was redone with asphalt blending into concrete nearer the chateau. Even back then change was dawning. *Tradition sacrificed for a smoother ride. Something is always lost when the new usurps the old.* They crossed an arched bridge made of fieldstone taken from a nearby quarry. Constructed in the 1800's by expert masons working over sturdy wooden forms, at least the bridge still functioned. Thayer, as most French, admired all things lovingly and artistically pieced together. Crossing the granite arch, they spanned a seasonal pond and came to a brief view of the chapel. Speeding past the corbelled structure, they headed for the mansion's circular driveway.

In the early morning light tattered flags with the de Chagny crest, symbols of outdated status, whipped atop the French Renaissance chateau. *Such a proud archaic-looking house of fancy balconies,* Thayer mused. Six non-functioning fountains stood in an ordered line, patiently waiting for the moment when they might again cast brilliant sprays of water into a complex and computerized ballet – one complimented by colored lights and long syncopated stanzas.

The car came sideways before the front steps leading to a formidable ancient door. Surrounded by doubled columns, the carved capitals of which extended loftily beyond the level of the second floor, the entrance seemed strangely morose. No one waited to greet them. Without a word, John opened the passenger door then proceeded up the steps, standing ready to open the main entrance. Thayer slid out, stood, and stretched his back. *Icy fog...breath stealing cold air.* "I hope it's warm inside!"

"It is, Sir. I'll see you later on. I need to park the car. Dr. de Chagny will meet you in a moment."

Inside, the classic interior of the main reception area appeared to be in a moribund state of disuse. It was as if Delaquois had entered the eighteen hundreds, before the time of vacuum cleaners and electric dusters. *Odd, there's no servant approaching to take my coat.* He stood eyeing the grand marbled foyer, waiting patiently. The space had a dreamy, romantic character that played so refreshingly against the rigid formality of the digitalized hospital where he worked. In the dim light of a fabulous Bohemian crystal chandelier, Thayer could see an exquisite Louis XVI side table. On its surface stood a tall Delft porcelain vase containing silk flowers, long stemmed white orchids and red tulips. *Unusual couple to pair together,* he thought.

He took off his leather gloves, smacking them impatiently into his left hand. A grave silence surrounded the hall – in the early half light of dawn, the chandelier's tiny electric bulbs were set on low – a particularly dull light for viewing objects. He wondered again why no staff member hurried to him. "Hello," he shouted. "Dr. Delaquois is in the foyer… **unattended!**"

Standing on an intricately patterned Italian marble floor, Thayer looked upward, past the punctuation of the magnificent crystal chandelier, to a soaring vaulted ceiling. Some talented soul had painted a mural in *trompe l'oeil* fresco on the dome. Above him, in the illusion of a celestial sky filled with clouds, dozens of baby angels played a variety of earthly musical instruments. The painting's objects were depicted with such photographic detail, that their realism misled truth. Deceiving the viewer's visual acuity into believing he'd actually entered some magnificently playful portion of heaven's realm.

Thayer heard his old friend's voice as if it were a Silurian whisper spoken from the paradise displayed on high.

"Welcome…welcome to my home."

Strange that the utterance sounds so weak. His brain flashed on the memory of a medical school classroom where that same voice boomed and commanded the attention of every trembling student in the room. *Isidore was never timid when he had an idea to present!* The sparkle of lights playing off the crystal chandelier blocked his view of the great geneticist. Stepping to his right, he caught a somewhat cryptic vision of his host. De Chagny appeared as a distant figure standing in the shadows of a mezzanine that projected several yards into the space of the great entrance hall. A wraithlike elderly man, a tangled mass of thick white hair wafting about his head, Isidore wore a perfectly tailored sharkskin-gray suit. The most astounding feature of his dress – a plain, bone-white mask that covered his entire face!

Thayer was so startled by his friend's abject appearance that he merely gawked. Eventually he recovered enough to wave, from waist-height, at the keen unsettling eyes staring down at him from the balcony. "It's good to see you, old friend. You've grown gaunt and frail. Isidore... you no longer need to wear glasses?" Thayer mentally slapped himself for sounding presumptuous and strained. He'd expected a more personal greeting. They'd been so very close.

"I'm still spry enough to get about," the subdued voice answered. "Apologies for this creepy mask. I've contracted a non-contagious disorder and this costume," he flicked a fingernail against an immobile cheek, "affords some minimal privacy when dealing with employees." The receding eyes behind the mask stayed fixed on those of his guest. Thayer nodded obligingly in response. "See yourself into that small green parlor. I'm sure you remember where it is. I'll be down there presently."

Thayer frowned in momentary confusion, "By all means, let's confer in the comfort of a room instead of the vacant splendor of the foyer." *Where shall I stick my coat, Lord?* Dutifully, he walked past an oil painting of Bacchus, the Roman god of wine and merriment. Yearning to throw a finger at the mocking god, he restrained himself. For all he knew cameras still watched him.

Turning right, into the southern corridor, he went along a series of closed rooms. About midway down the hall, he opened a large mahogany door and stood scanning what should have been a prestigious area with a breathtaking view of the chateau's posterior gardens. The faded interior of the side-parlor reflected a calmer more genteel time. The furnishings hadn't been reupholstered in four generations. A visitor might easily surmise that the aged room was falling into ruin and neglect, except that there wasn't a speck of dust anywhere. Still occupying their exact same stations: the sofas, chairs, and tables remained, for all intents and purposes, practically untouched. *Not unpleasant.* Except that the smell of furniture polish and the distinct scent of newsprint from stacks of dailies, intermingled with the redolence of dry desiccating fabrics, managed to make his nose itch! Because this was Isidore's private parlor the eccentric interior was perfectly maintained. Thayer could be in a museum.

"Does nothing ever get replaced in here?" He inquired of no one in particular as he took off his overcoat and white Peruvian wool scarf. Draping both over the back of the most immediate chair, the tiny slits in the teal green upholstery offered no answer. Finely crafted velvet green wallpaper ran the gamut of the room from floorboards to cornices. Its pattern of faded realistic leaves provided a backdrop for a number of Impressionist oils depicting various hunting scenes. Standing the test of time, the elegant wallpaper showed no evidence of cracks or signs of peeling, but certainly presented a definite washout of color. Removing any of the gilt framed paintings would be proof enough of that.

He chose a comfortable side chair. Plucking a dainty lace antimacassar off the armrest, he pressed it to his nostrils. *Smells like its just been laundered. Lovely.* Patting the covering back into place, he sat, crossed his legs, and folded his hands on his lap.

Too bad Isidore never married, he mused. *It's 2012 – the new age is upon us and he has no heir to all of this. Women must have remained an issue for him.*

Thayer's thoughts returned to their days at medical school. In their final year, his friend had fallen in love with a nurse from a nearby hospital. *What was her name? Ah, yes, Lisette. So predictable…such a sad history.* After a car accident, she'd been taken to an emergency room where an aging physician failed to take needed precautions. She'd suffered a fat embolus to her brain and Isidore had suffered right alongside his fallen girlfriend. In those grief stricken days following her death, he allowed Thayer to console him. He'd welcomed Delaquois' comforting embraces.

Isidore de Chagny, brilliant with finances and science, developer of genetically coded death and sole owner of the serum's patent was a very obstinate individual. The world was still prejudiced against such homosexual liaisons. Propriety demanded he let go of his only solace. In the aftermath Isidore's grief had doubled, turning despair into burgeoning anger. Lisette had been denied a long and fruitful life. He'd wanted to grow old with her, to have children…that was the normal way. Isidore began to rave that the aged were too heavy a burden on society. He would devise a means to equalize the debt he felt humanity owed him, A Death Serum. Once administered, it locked into DNA codes, waiting to permanently alter the manufacture of certain amino acids, bringing life to an end before aging and disease could completely take hold.

Impatient, Thayer took a ballpoint pen from his pocket and rapidly clicked the implement open and closed, open and closed.

A crippled Isidore, walking with the use of a cane, entered and quietly shut the door behind him. Thayer stood, trying with difficulty to discern if the problem was in his friend's knees or hips. "Isidore!" he exclaimed, stepping forward, hand outstretched. "It's so good to see you. I came the very instant I read your note."

Cool fingers caressed the proffered hand. In disparate contrast to the rest of Isidore's withered form, his fingers were rather young and quite perfect. *Bizarre*, marveled Thayer to himself.

Isidore hobbled painfully to the backrest of the chair holding Thayer's overcoat. "Please, take a seat, my old friend. It's good to see you, too. Thanks for coming so quickly."

Thayer stepped back. "Not exactly how I expected to be greeted after so many years of silence." He promptly retook his seat. Resting his hand on a side table, he pointed to a small frame containing a picture of the two medical students standing side-by-side, smiling. "But I am more than prepared to forget being snubbed for over half a decade, and then summarily summoned on a Sunday morning. Let bygones be bygones, I say. Am I here to assist with this disorder that afflicts you?"

Isidore folded slowly onto the wing chair opposite Thayer. The strange incongruous hands reached for a sturdy Aubusson pillow trimmed with silk tassels. He propped the cushion under one of his arms. "Sometimes I need a little support to sit more comfortably." A short brisk inhalation was the only indication he suffered some discomfort straightening his back, the face behind the mask was unreadable.

Thayer carefully studied his old classmate. It grieved him to see this great man so debilitated. Embarrassed, he let his eyes roam the room.

Almost intuitively, Isidore noted, "You know, I've always tried to preserve my heritage. I've kept a good portion of the above ground chateau in the condition it was in when it passed to me from my father." Isidore was speaking almost in a monotone, as if his jaw or tongue didn't function properly.

"Has a stroke afflicted you?"

Isidore's eyes fell to the silver buckles on his polished, Italian, ostrich-leg loafers.

Thayer tried to lighten the mood. "What period are you shooting for with this decor?"

"Around nineteen hundred or so. But my laboratory, housed in the basements, and the chateau's kitchen are the most modern facilities. Those areas require finesse and the best technology available."

"I see that you're also burdened with the need for high-tech security."

Isidore ignored the testy statement. His expressive fingers gestured toward an old family album laying on an end table. "The photographs in that book tell quite a story. My grandfather, Rupert de Chagny, had only one son, my father Lowell who was born in 1920. In 1938, when Hitler invaded Austria, my father was only eighteen. He went to England to work with the Allies against Germany. He foresaw a terrible storm brewing on the horizon, and stayed single in an effort to remain focused on the war. In late spring of 1944, when France was liberated, he returned to the chateau and sent for an English girl he'd worked with in the intelligence arm of the British government. I wasn't born until 1948. My mother died of pneumonia when I was only one year old… too early…too young. Though he grieved to the point of ruining his health, my father managed to last until I completed university. He sold parts of the estate to put me through school. When you and I met in the medical academy, I never told you how haunted I was by their deaths. One never forgets a loss endured at such a tender age."

Of course, he only alludes to the unspoken tragedy of Lisette's demise. Thayer was familiar with his friend's preoccupation with death. *Perhaps the world should die rendering retribution to Isidore de Chagny. So morbid!* As his friend continued rambling, Thayer found it disheartening that he made no mention of their former relationship.

"At twenty-seven I left clinical medicine and began an earnest study of DNA. Now black marketeers and unscrupulous physicians, in countries where my genetic patent is not protected by established law, try to copy the sequence or alter the predictable effects. It can't be done. But so many are willing to pay to have the code cleansed from their systems. They want to grow old…attain whatever age finally destroys them. Certainly you know that the scientific and theological world is in an uproar, yammering to undo the stabilization I've afforded them. They debate endlessly, hour after hour, the basis of something for which most governments are clamoring."

Thayer personally believed this whole discovery a grand mistake, despite the benefits to population control. *And how, just how, was the loss of two parents more significant than the loss of two sweethearts?* "And you've remained unmarried all these years? Who will succeed you?"

Isidore's shoulders jerked as he indulged an unspoken snicker. He walked the topic sideways. "My ancestors favored gathering in the southern salon, but really..." He paused to suck in a noisy almost asthmatic respiration, "All life centered in the kitchen, just a short way down the hall from the family dining room. Shall I call for coffee, Thayer?"

His guest shook his head negatively.

"Refreshments can be here momentarily," Isidore reassured. "The kitchen and lab are outfitted with state of the art equipment, even though the rest of the house has been left in memoriam. The kitchen has red jasper countertops and deep Italian cabinets." Isidore pointed a delicate finger toward the immense windows. "Do you remember that there used to be ornamental pools and sweeping gardens visible through those panes of glass? They ran the entire length of the chateau's backside...a product of my great-great Grandfather's labors. You could step from the kitchen directly into the spice garden and pick fresh herbs. Butlers and female servants stood ready to serve guests who were being entertained. Those were the grand old days. Now the grounds have shrunk. Metered away by war, government need, and the cry of society to expand and gobble up land for housing. This estate is but a pittance of its former glory. There were acres of pasture and dense woodland, a road leading to an ancestral cemetery to the north. Now that cemetery has been turned into an historical site." He sighed heavily, both hands grasping the carved head of his ebony cane.

"Outside those windows were daffodils, azaleas, rhododendrons, and hydrangeas. I have the pictures in that album to prove it. This was a place of enchantment from April through October. That was the golden era. Inspired! The ambiance of walking paths and flowering gardens, fountains strategically placed to delight the eye. Unfettered time to enjoy them."

Thayer knew the formal gardens were at one time an astonishing interplay of geometric sections. Lawns, flowerbeds and fruit trees all laid-out within the natural boundaries formed by the perpendicular wings of the mansion.

Isidore's next words were spoken so softly that Thayer was forced to lean forward to hear what was scratched forth from an obviously compromised throat.

"Beneath the branches of mature trees, in the shady nooks of natural arbors one could read a book, take a nap, or compromise a girl's virtue." Isidore's head dropped forward in apparent sadness.

Thayer hesitated to mention the memory of Lisette. "How old are you?" asked Thayer. "Sixty-one by my recollections. You could still marry and father a child. What is this disorder that troubles your face and causes you to wear a mask? Please, tell me. I pledge the strictest professional confidence."

"Eh?" Isidore's head jerked upward, the melancholy eyes behind the mask suddenly sharp and alert. "Thayer Delaquois, you still prove yourself quite capable of lapsing into the most baffling role of assumptive idiot. I have not brought you here for me!" All sad reflection, along with any hint of reminiscent mood, vanished from de Chagny's voice. "I have a son, a beautiful handsome son, and you will be well paid for your assistance. He needs your help. I want him placed within your care."

"I didn't know you had a boy. You're not the patient in need of..."

The tip of Isidore's cane rose off the floor in a dramatic arc. Its silver sheathed end, covered in a worn rubber cap, pointed straight at Thayer. Without a blink or any hesitating sign he lacked muscular strength, Isidore interrupted. His words emphatic with conviction, "Nature likes to repeat some patterns, certain others she rejects entirely. We all have a need to procreate...extend the species. My son's providential origins need not be disclosed at this time. Suffice it to say that he is a precious piece of humanity...a person of great promise. You will see and judge for yourself. I've sheltered him from the barbarous manipulations of the outside world – a fortuitous decision considering the threats that have been made against my life. He's honest to a fault, uncontaminated by the negativity rampant in the teeming cities beyond this estate."

Thayer sat back in his chair, astonished. "How old?"

"Fifteen. And as I have grown hideous beyond reason, he has grown only more admirable. He represents a kind of ideal physical beauty. He's tall and muscular, with a straight nose, firm chin, full lips. Pale coloring and the most unusual amber eyes...he walks with a grace uncharacteristic for one his age. He's not lanky or clumsy at all. When he was younger, he wasn't given to exaggerated laughter or self-pitying tears, still he's very sensitive. Always tended to take things rather seriously. Then at the drop of a hat," Isidore tried to snap his fingers, but failed the coordination, "without realizing it was not the perfect moment to do so – he would become informal and sociably delightful. Loves puzzles. He has an astonishing amount of forbearance with others and is notably generous. A person has only to compliment something of Erik's, and he will remove it from his person and hand it to the individual who spoke. He values material things rather minimally. He is not given to zealous ideation or religious mandates, keeps his mind open. Yet here, in the first budding stages of adult life, he has become quite an afflicted young man. One who goes for hours without saying a single word. Given to abrupt bouts of anger...the rage of which drives him into a frenzied activity that alarms me. I don't want him hurting himself, he's too important."

Isidore's chest shuddered with a painful spasm. His fingers scratched at his hairline just above the leather mask. "Oh, how I long for the quieter days when Erik amused himself with card tricks and intricate toys."

"You've summoned me here, before breakfast...on my weekend off, to attend a teenager who has grown sullen and becomes, from time to time, overcome with apparent unfounded rage? What's his testosterone level? And who did you say was the idiot?"

"The way you state it, all concern on my part sounds extraordinarily dramatic. I apologize for my rash words. Please, Thayer, see him...talk with him...do an examination. He needs **your** expertise. He does not suffer simple mood swings, these are borderline psychotic breaks and it kills me, in tiny pieces, to see him like this. After these episodes, my son is pensive and dejected, full of bitter emotion that arises from no experience he has ever undergone. I wish to understand these despondent states and avoid further distress for him. Name your cost. My funds are unlimited. Don't leave without a cursory inspection."

Unknown to Dr. Delaquois, no one in the house had any intention of returning him to Paris until the boy was examined and treated. Coming into the room Isidore had cleverly pocketed Thayer's cell phone.

"All right, I'll oblige you...because it is **you** and we have a history. Besides, I'm already on the premises. Where is this feisty fifteen-year-old?"

"I'll take you to him, help me rise." Isidore watched with satisfaction as Thayer stood and politely offered his hand. "After your interview, we'll discuss a plan of diagnostics and possible treatment." Isidore linked his arm into that of his guest.

"Have you considered the use of a walker?" asked Thayer as they headed toward the door. "I'll see this young man of yours, but I want to give you a physical exam as well. That will be part of the cost of this arrangement between us."

"He's down the hall in a fencing match."

"Saints in heaven, what hour does this household arise?"

"Actually, none of us have been to bed yet."

2 SCORPION VS. GRASSHOPPER

It took awhile, but the geneticist and the neuropsychiatrist managed to make their way down the corridor toward the southeastern wing of the mansion. Without Thayer becoming consciously aware of the change, the vacant solemnity of the house began to soak into his spirit. For the life of him, he couldn't think of a single witty remark that might stimulate his decrepit friend into a series of clever retorts. Informal jests and a dark-hearted teasing used to come so easily to the both of them. Years apart can drain a friendship of its amusements.

Along the trek, Isidore's legs seem to regain a degree of strength. Or perhaps he grew steadier in the comforting assurance rendered by Thayer's presence. Within the pressures of a demanding self-inflicted workload, he'd hardened a very sober approach to life. Now, oppressive worry over his boy only accented this joyless state. Over the last few weeks his ironclad-will had deepened dramatically. Erik needed help, and Isidore could be most aggressive. No manner of coercion, dictated out of sheer necessity, would be neglected.

"If you don't mind my saying so, Isidore, you've become something of a strange old bird."

De Chagny paused and lifted the hand holding the cane. The appendage rose like a helium balloon with a stick tail, wafting back and forth on some imaginary current of air. "Not a bird, I fear, but a defensive hermit crab. Did you know that the international papers call me the Angel of Death? Winged Thanatos harvesting lives in a white lab coat with a bloodied sickle in his hand. I've murdered my twin brother, Hypnos, the Angel of Sleep, and put a desperate planet's sense of morality into a coma. They've proclaimed me ethically deficient, a brilliant audacious killer who sells genetically predictable death to the highest bidder. Ah, here we are at last." They stood before another dark mahogany door, not unlike any number of others running down the hall. "Need I remind you to keep inquisitive probing discrete? You'll see soon enough how badly we need your medical acumen. Go ahead – open it. It's not locked."

Thayer turned the knob, opening the door into a kind of viewing room. A number of comfortably padded folding chairs sat directly behind a floor-to-ceiling length of thick Plexiglas. A window cleaned and polished to crystal clarity. Thayer led de Chagny to a chair and took a seat for himself. Before them, on a hard oak wood floor was an indoor gym with the painted outlines of a basketball court, the center of which was an area marked for fencing. Two males dressed completely in white fencing gear were taking the *en garde* stance. Off to the side John Kelly stood with a whistle in his mouth, his fingers wrapped around an electronic remote control.

"We converted two parlors into this gymnasium for Erik," Isidore's voice beamed with pride. "He uses it almost every day." He pointed to a clock with black Roman numerals sitting on a shelf. The burgundy stained walnut housing embraced a transparent face that allowed the exposure of the fascinating metal gears moving behind it. "Erik likes to define time. He made that clock when he was nine. It's quite unique, unlike any other device of its kind. A series of intricately weighted magnets keeps the gears set in eternal motion. It never needs winding."

"He's smart!"

"Precociously so."

"Which one is he?" Both participants were covered head to toe in appropriately padded outfits. An overhead electronic scoreboard read: SCORPION 5, GRASSHOPPER 8. Intrigued, Thayer asked, "The scoreboard is in riddles?"

"Erik's the thinner one on the right. A little shorter than his opponent, but growing nicely. I estimate he'll be six foot by his sixteenth birthday and grow another few inches after that. He chose these pestiferous nicknames. I've no idea what they mean. He ordered their jackets with the arthropods embroidered on the upper left...over the area of the heart."

"Fencing at this hour! And you said neither of you has been to bed? Whatever his malady, he doesn't lack energy. When do you people sleep?"

"When we feel like it. Neither of us requires a great deal of recuperative rest."

"Can they hear us speaking?"

At that precise moment, John Kelly whispered something into Erik's ear. The two fencers turned simultaneously toward the Plexiglas. Their faces were concealed behind tightly meshed silver masks with padded sideflaps that extended over the ears down to their shoulders, swaddling their anterior necks. Together they raised their rapiers to the grilled cages hiding their expressions and saluted their company with a bow and flourishing downward sweep of the blades.

"They can't hear us unless we push this speaker button on the wall." Isidore waved to the young men, gesturing for them to continue the match.

"Your chauffeur functions as a referee?"

"Oh, yes. John is one of Erik's bodyguards. It seemed fitting to hire men that could fill several roles. Both he and his brother had military training – former American Navy Seals – experts in demolitions and martial arts."

"Pity you couldn't hire both men," Thayer said with an edge of sarcasm.

Isidore eyed his guest disdainfully. "Who said I didn't? Watch the match. We're happy to entertain you."

By way of apology Thayer rolled his hand in front of his face and fastened his gaze on Erik.

Compared to his father, the younger de Chagny's movements were like liquid. He flowed over the fencing strips laid out on the floor. Tall and well proportioned, he was indeed shorter in stature than his opponent, but extremely wiry. The flexible blades slashed through the air in lunge, parry, and riposte – fortunately the two combatants were well protected against any mishap. They wore regulation torso jackets with diagonal front zippers and close fitting pants well padded over the thighs. The pants ended just below the knees. From there, opaque white stockings, fitted tightly over the calves, ran down into durable court shoes. Suede fencing gloves, long at the wrists and designed to allow for maximum flexibility, protected their fingers.

There was nothing casual or unplanned about either participant. With a clean touch to Erik's upper left chest, the next point went to the Grasshopper. Thayer learned he was another bodyguard, this one named Dillard.

"*Touché*," announced John as Erik backed up.

They could see the Scorpion pause, testing the weight of his fencing weapon in his hand. He gallantly took off his glove, one finger at a time, and threw it at his opponent, hitting him center-chest. "*Faire suivre* (have forward), *en garde.*"

Dillard kicked the glove aside and remained focused on the challenger.

Isidore shifted uneasily in his seat. "He has to play the aspiring warrior!"

Erik danced gracefully back and forth, right foot leading, then the left as he repositioned. His opponent came at him with a daring straightforward slice, cutting an arc right at Erik's neck. The boy buckled at the knees. With an uncanny sense of maintaining his balance, he took the pommel of his rapier and soundly punched the advancing Dillard mid solar plexus. Driving his adversary back with a bruising blow, Erik had room to straighten.

"Is this fencing or pugilism?" An alarmed, Thayer leaned forward. "What are the rules of engagement? They don't mean to hurt each other, do they?"

"Shh, the glove is off," responded Isidore. Neither fencer was awarded the point. "You know the biblical story of the great flood when God saved two of every animal? Well, all the fish survived in abundance. They don't gossip and they don't blurt out disruptive questions."

Ah, deep within you a risible streak still exists, Isidore! Thayer was surprised and glad to see it. The squeaking thuds of rubber soles meeting polished court floor, brought Thayer's attention back to the match.

A rich array of weaving tactics and long complex moves followed. Proving the versatility of each combatant. They danced with flying swords in a lovely profusion of aggression and defense. Score *touché* went first to the wily Scorpion then to the athletic Grasshopper in a nearly even progression of points. Strategies for footwork and blade mobility, coupled with self-control and a sense of timed distance allowed for equally repeated successes. The scoreboard read: SCORPION 10, GRASSHOPPER 12.

Back and forth they played off each other, two obviously intelligent fencers. So well matched, that at this juncture it was honestly difficult to decide who had the upper hand. Each confronted the other with a variety of classical techniques executed to create confusion and discourage second-guessing the other's strategic return.

The rhythm of the match started gradually evolving. Cooler heads still prevailed, but Erik appeared to be mentally standing back, almost re-grouping. Exploiting the tactic of passive-alert defense, he appeared to rest. Cautiously twirling the tip of his rapier in the free space, Erik deliberately let Dillard become the aggressor. Allowing him the advantage of viewing his rival's next set of moves. Erik played at the match like a cagey chessman, refraining from exploiting his opponent's weakest areas until Dillard revealed his current plan of attack.

When Erik understood, he glided into the role of flamboyant buffoon, swaying and brandishing his arms between strikes like a mocking Jack-in-the-Box on a spring. In this ludicrous attitude, Erik let every newly discharged flourish proclaim how much the sport exhilarated him. Taunt and retreat, taunt and retreat. At one point he even bent a knee and raising his foot like an awkward egret, humorously hopped about. Deliberately stepping outside the strip, he conceded a point and feigned catching his breath.

Annoyed, Dillard watched with his free hand resting on his hip. When Erik returned to the outlined arena, Dillard attacked, sword extended, threatening. Warning Erik that he needed to concentrate and take the duel more seriously. Dillard's movements weren't punitive, more along the lines of 'brace yourself, I'm your instructor'. From the other side of the glass one could almost feel the rising level of competition developing in the gym. The match was turning earnest.

Abandoning theatrics, Erik became a testy driven locomotive. Drawing from the recuperative strength he'd just amassed, he produced a flurry of parry movements to block the persuasive attack. His blade repeatedly knocked Dillard's rapier off its intended target. Riposte, parry, counter riposte, and the uncanny Erik swiftly took the offensive – the heady advance drove Dillard backward before he could respond with a counterattack.

Unable to track this sudden volley of blade movements, John shrugged and stopped awarding points. This was nothing like the duller matches viewed in the more regulated fencing clubs.

Though both fencers possessed a second nature geared toward strategy and grace, it was Erik who kept accelerating the rhythmic cadence of strikes. Maintaining close proximity to his opponent, he rained down a barrage of thrusts. In an escalating anger, Dillard jerked and grunted, making the erroneous decision not to give way. Slashing at Erik with a chopping motion, slicing repeatedly, Dillard refused to retreat. In this moment of wrath, Dillard's blade made contact with Erik's ungloved hand.

Erik barely glanced at the open gash. With arms held defensively inward, he crouched and spun around – one could almost imagine the swirling fan of a liquid black cape. As he rose upward from this unprecedented position, Dillard barely had time to calculate the new tactic's effect. Standing his ground, the older male managed to successfully block the tricky lunge.

Undeterred, Erik stood erect. His sword flashed forward with deadly accuracy. The two rapiers met with a clang in mid-air, each sliding down the side of the other.

Holding firm at the base of their grips, just behind the hand guards, the two competitors pushed and snorted like rutting bucks. The polished swords gleamed in the electric lights. Almost shoulder-to-shoulder, each man exerted a tense forward press. Large droplets of crimson blood dripped onto the shiny floor, smeared by tight unwavering footsteps, as first one, then the other dug in.

At the sight of the bleeding, Isidore sat forward and jammed his finger onto the button. "End it! End it now and address the wound!"

Ignoring the directive, Erik fully intended to continue the scuffle. He backed off, raising his arms in *en garde*. Dillard responded. Erik brazenly switched hands. Holding the rapier with his afflicted right, he promptly executed a *Balestra*, a jumping lunge. Using the floor as if it were a springboard, he pushed off the balls of both feet simultaneously. The flight of the scorpion! Landing gracefully, he moved through the short distance to his opponent with raw artistic power, each movement bearing the bite of calculated plan and purpose. Vigorously executing an intense fluid attack, the blitz rattled his adversary.

Dillard retreated before the weight of the concerted force – front foot back, next foot following quickly. Clang and grinding scrape! The blades met again and again. The spacing between them was precariously inconsistent, refusing Dillard the ability to smoothly maintain balance.

He knew that stepping out over the posterior strip would forfeit a hit, but Erik continued to relentlessly surge forward.

"Shall we count the strikes to mark the end of constantly readjusting stability?" Erik teased.

Fatigued, Dillard decided to advance and reacquire the attack. Onerous mistake. He stepped forward, lunging the blade recklessly.

Off target, Erik merely raised his arm and let the rapier travel harmlessly through the air, right past him. As Dillard drew the sword back, Erik curled forward in the alarming stance of a predator, almost as if he were a venomous arachnid about to leap again. Moving with predetermined mathematical efficiency, he played out a baffling series of well-executed blows, viciously propelling his fencing opponent into the default zone.

Momentarily confused by the newly defined surge of an obviously skilled aggressor, Dillard watched a series of fighting thrusts he had never seen Erik execute. Tripping on his own feet, he fell backward onto his rump.

Thayer expected the defeated partner to be infuriated. Instead, Dillard just lay there resting on his elbows, vanquished, staring up at the winner.

"Go ahead, challenge me." Everyone recognized a victor in obvious restraint.

"No more! You win," the affable opponent responded.

"Good, man," exclaimed Dr. de Chagny from the Plexiglas room. He'd left the microphone speaker on. Erik's fencing partner lifted his facemask and gawked roguishly at the two spectators.

Blinking, Thayer was shocked, "John Kelly's brother!" Both young Americans had razor close haircuts, almost bald, but Dillard owned a slightly bent nose from a past fracture and a striking crescent shaped scar that parted his right eyebrow and ran down his right cheek almost to his upper lip.

Erik tossed the hilt of his blade into his left hand. His right palm ached from the cut, but he wouldn't suffer leaving his partner on the floor and offered the assistance of his injured hand. Initially rejecting the bloody paw, Dillard laughed, then grasped it and heaved himself to his feet. The match ended with the two fencers bowing to each other, then sliding their blades into belted sheaths. Neither seemed hardly winded.

Isidore grumbled in an aggravated tone, "Get a pressure dressing on that hand and come over here. There's someone I want you to meet."

Still concealed in his headgear, Erik came across the gym in bold decisive steps. Standing on the other side of the window with his arms politely at his sides, his hand still dripped blood.

"That's rather reckless, Erik, get a bandage on the wound. Is it deep?"

Erik confidently lifted his hand toward the window, pressing the bloodied palm against the glass in a grotesque display meant to unnerve his elders. "Only the initial epidermis, the *lucidum* and *granulosum* are affected. Nothing deeper. John will tend to it." The voice was intense and melodic, like some fascinating radio announcer broadcasting mood music.

"This is Dr. Thayer Delaquois. He's a neuropsychiatrist from…"

"I know who he is, Isidore," Erik interrupted. He faced their guest, leaving the bloody print on the glass. "Sir!" He bowed politely. "Your reputation in the medical community precedes you."

Thayer nodded, "I'm pleased to meet you. Very interesting match."

Erik raised his bleeding palm, "We play by somewhat different rules in this chateau."

"So I see."

Isidore issued a directive. "Go get your hand fixed! Forgive me if I don't hazard the upstairs right now…feeling somewhat feeble this morning." He tapped his cane on the floor. "I'll send Dr. Delaquois up to your quarters and allow you to make your own, more informal, introductions."

"Have you eaten, Doctor?" Erik inquired with soft, rather pronounced politeness.

"No, nothing as of yet."

The boy bowed again and asked his father, "May I shower?"

"Of course. The doctor will meet you in your sitting room in about fifteen minutes."

The victor saluted the pair with a silent nod. Turning away, he moved with determined steps toward a door on the opposite wall where John and Dillard stood quietly waiting.

Thayer studied Erik's departure. "Why did he keep his face hidden? He doesn't appear to be rude. Is he suffering the same ailment as you? Some genetically predisposed malady?"

"There is absolutely nothing wrong with his face. Whether his disorder is psychological or physical will be left to your academic prowess."

Erik reached his bodyguards. Ushering them ahead of him, he stood studying Delaquois. The graceful figure backed slowly out the exit. Never removing his gaze from the scientists, he slowly and conspicuously shut the door.

"Did he hear me ask about the headgear?"

Isidore twisted to face his companion. "No, he could not audibly hear our words. I touched the button. My son has made it to fifteen without a major accident or misfortune of any kind. I predict that he will grow old and live a long life in the same fashion, and I mean to see that happen. You will help me deliver him from the peril of these moody preoccupations so that he advances in years more happily. What you know thus far is the obvious. He's physically sound, energetic, and driven. You will soon learn that he's handsome, knowledgeable, intellectually gifted, and oddly unpredictable. He's read the entire library...some books twice...and stuck his nose into most of my medical journals. Follow the specific directions I give you to attain his rooms and do not deviate. There are motion sensors, activated lights, and cameras all along the way."

Thayer brushed his fingers slowly across the stubble growing on his chin. In the rush to get to Isidore he hadn't shaved. "On the drive in I saw the guards and precautions you've taken. Isn't all this security just a little excessive?"

"Unfortunately there exists the very real danger of intruders, enthusiastic criminals who wish to do me harm. The government may have decreed my family's social decline by entailing our property away — they have the right to limit inheritance from one generation to the next — but I am still a very wealthy man and can afford to judiciously protect my son! You may leave here as you wish, come back as you deem necessary, but initially I will require that you remain fixed on my son's condition. As I mentioned, your medical interventions will be handsomely rewarded."

Thayer absorbed these draconian statements and justifiably posed another question. "Is there anything you're not telling me?"

"All in good time. For now, I'd rather you explore his ailment on your own. He needs your assistance. Since he passed puberty, he suffers periodic spells of a particularly morbid nature. Why does he want so desperately to be left alone and avoid my company?"

Thayer's eyes lit up, "Spells? He suffers spells?"

"As I said. I'll let you observe and advise a remedy." Isidore heaved a great sigh. "There are a few rules you must agree to before you interview him. You may only examine him in this house. Diagnosis and treatment will be conducted on these premises. You may not remove him. I have a complete laboratory in the sub-basements of this property. They include an x-ray area, MRI, and facilities for running every test you can request. Erik is most precious, any attempt to take him elsewhere will be considered kidnapping and thwarted by force."

Thayer was absorbing these shocking criteria when a soft knock at the door announced the arrival of John Kelly. Standing in the doorway, the bodyguard could be appreciated for the full weight of his formidable stature. Every muscle on his well-defined physique spoke of potential power. A solid man, he stood about six foot two, polite despite his imposing build.

"I'm free to escort Dr. Delaquois upstairs." A simple nod from Isidore gave him the consent he sought. "Doctor, if you'd please come with me."

"Go with him, Thayer. I'll speak with you after you converse with Erik." Isidore wasn't making a request.

At this point Thayer believed he comprehended the strange opportunity placed before him. In reality, he'd only just begun to formulate a clear understanding of the situation and his host's bizarre idiosyncrasies. Regardless of what ailed the young man showering on the second floor, if Thayer continued to offer his medical expertise, it was with the full acknowledgement that he had entered a place cloistered from the world, a *sanctum sanctorum* tightly braced against invasion.

3   EXAMINING A BREACH OF MIND

𝕹oting the hour, Thayer Delaquois traversed the magnificent front reception hall with John. Together they ascended the sweeping marble staircase fashioned over two hundred years ago from Italian marbles of black, white, and deep greens. He let his hand caress the railings of ornately carved woods and wrought iron decorated with gold leaf. Passing through the mezzanine they headed north, down a dimly lit corridor containing, on either side, another series of more closed doors. Carpeted in an eggplant purple, the hallway was more like a tunnel with elaborate crown molding.

Designed for privacy, not airiness, thought Thayer. His perception that objects were rarely replaced inside the chateau was reaffirmed. Small tears in the brown silk wallpapers – their vibrant colors long faded – lent evidence to the conviction. Yet they served as a dignified background for a dozen stately oil paintings of de Chagny ancestors. In reverent silence he paused to appreciate several of the painstakingly rendered portraits hanging on the walls. The craquelures indicated the oils were centuries old. *Genuinely impressive artistry, antique framing, hand-ground pigments.* His fingers trailed the side of a frame. *Embellished with patient attention given to the minutest detail. Who were these noble people? Centuries of proud de Chagny's in these hallways and not a clue as to the circumstances surrounding their lives. Pity really.*

Still eyeing the portrait of a distinguished well-bosomed dame, Thayer cradled an elbow and let several of his fingers reflectively tap his cheek. "From the back, do people have trouble telling you and your brother apart? The distinctive proboscis and disfiguring scar make the frontal view obvious."

"Yes. Dillard's nasal bone was fractured during a skirmish in Iraq. He refused the cosmetic surgery to have the bone and cartilage realigned. Said he enjoyed finally looking really mean. He's proud of that crescent moon scar. A stray bullet ricocheted off a plug of hematite set in some detrital limestone, tore into his face, nearly grazed his eye. His patrol had paused to rest and he'd taken off his helmet to wipe his head." John watched Thayer's eyes travel upward, spying a system of tiny cameras running down the elegant scroll designed cornice of the ceiling. "You're very perceptive, Doctor. Let me assure you…there are no cameras in the bedrooms. Private domain is still honored."

"Are uniformed guards stationed inside the house?" Thayer waved to one of the cameras. "Enormous men, such as yourself, armed with M16's?"

"We are under guard," John lifted his chin in an affirmative nod.

"Do you like working here?" Thayer wanted to ask if they were also being recorded, but didn't.

"The pay is astonishing. Dr. de Chagny is a generous, but formidable presence.   Normally he receives absolutely no one, not even by appointment. Lets his lawyers and accountants take care of finances and legal documents, but goes over their work like a hawk. I'd say he was an elitist. Even tends to himself medically."

"You have an odd way of describing your employer, John."

"The mark of an honest, but loyal employee. I'm only repeating what I've been told is permissible for you to know. Perhaps you should think of the chateau more as a fortress than a mansion." John paused for a moment, dropping his voice and leaning toward the physician. "The Count's son is ill, very ill, Dr. Delaquois. He definitely needs your services."

"How so?"

"You'll see, all too soon I'm afraid. He's become my friend, not just my assignment."

"And where is your brother?"

"Gone to bed, Sir. He usually works from sunset to sunrise and I take the daylight hours. There's often an overlap, sometimes we switch shifts." They had come to another dark doorway. Different from the other entrances, this one was painted in the deepest shade of crimson enamel.

"A red door?"

"You'll have to ask him about the color. Are you familiar with Proxemics, Doctor?"

"Please, call me Thayer. And the answer is 'yes' – it's the psychological study of spatial distances required by humans and the effects of population density on behavior and social interaction."

"Good. Erik doesn't like people coming too close to him. Favors keeping others at a distance until he gets to know them. Go where he indicates until you've come to an agreement about space."

"What?" Thayer was astonished once again. "Explain, please. He does shake hands, correct?"

John paused, a frown crossing his face. "Don't offer your hand. Let Erik indicate how far apart you need to be to engage in conversation. The distance may vary with his mood. Believe me, he'll let you know the degree of comfort he's experiencing…in a most direct manner. The playfulness you saw for a few moments down in the gym was a calculated interlude." John pushed a buzzer next to an elaborate brass key plate. A moment later they heard the lock release. "Admission here is ironically like entering that high-end jewelry store Boucheron's on the *Place Vendome.*"

And so I go to meet another aristocrat, mused Thayer, *someone else taught from birth to set himself apart from the common man.* John showed him into a sitting room almost devoid of light. Somewhere a CD provided a relaxing background of rain and thunder, hauntingly beautiful nature. Entering behind him, the bodyguard shut the door.

Delaquois' vision adjusted slowly, revealing he stood in a space of aging red and gold fabrics and more mahogany furniture. The room smelled of a thousand sooty fires from a well-used fireplace, co-mingled with the scent of lemon wood polish applied to the furniture. He walked forward almost timidly. To his left, visible through an opened arch of ornately carved cherry wood, was a large four-poster bed. He could smell the fragrance of clean linens just laid down. To his right, what should have been a spacious sunny room was left in deep shadow. Dark wood paneled the walls from floor to cornice. The ceiling was a molded relief of *fleurs-de-lis* and flowered medallions. Covering the windows, a heavy set of burgundy-red drapes hung from impressive medieval iron rods. The curtains were so generous in length, their hems pooled on the deeply carpeted floor. From their center, a precious inch of morning sunlight played into the room, a ribbon-like beacon that attracted the eye away from the dreary interior. The somber effect of the room's nearly absent light spoke of privacy and morose secrecy. *Thank the gods, the architects of these old homes thought to utilize grand windows on the outer walls to train sunlight inward!*

John motioned their guest to an old comfortable wing chair and matching footrest. He bowed almost formally. "I'll leave you now," and exited through the area of the bed.

Coughing nervously to clear his throat, Thayer straightening his jacket and sat down. His eyes roamed the room. Some teenage boys preferred rather Spartan 'digs', this one evidenced a good deal of culture.

Pressed to the wall beside the drapes sat a *Confiturier Valmont*, originally a high chest with legs for the storage of homemade jams. Its cover was open, exposing several packages of dehydrated fruits and meats. Apparently Erik used this treasured piece of dated furniture to store a ready supply of healthy snacks. On the mantel sat a valuable eighteenth century French pendulum clock. It's white porcelain face, framed in a ring of solid bronze, depicted an elaborate multi-colored floral basket. An ochre and ruby striped sofa opposite him stood on some interesting cabriole legs and boasted a long scalloped hardwood apron. Several embroidered silk pillows sat on the couch. Set specifically upright and clear of each other, they offered differing eclectic versions of the seventeenth century Jacobean Tree of Life, a long heralded symbol of longevity. On one of the end tables sat a delicate vase containing a dozen white roses. Next to the flowers, a porcelain figurine depicted the provincial theme of a man in a garden, hat in hand, declaring his love to a lady. Thayer tried to picture the occupant of these particularly moody rooms lying down on the sofa from time to time – to think or take a nap.

The doctor twisted in his seat to see what the person reclining on the couch might view. His eyes widened as they took in a strangely decorated wall. About two-dozen handmade masks hung in a stunning, if not bizarre collection. Everything from a Venetian crow detailed with feathers and sequins to a plain simple white kidskin to cover only the upper right quadrant of a man's face. Beneath the collection sat a computer desk. The central processing unit rested to the right of the kneehole on a set of sturdy antique pewter shelves. Along with the sound of raindrops, Thayer could hear a mild humming from the fan in the computer – keeping the unit cool. Feeling more like an intruder than a physician on a house call, he continued his quiet observations: *Color laser printer neatly stocked with paper, twenty-two inch dual monitors, and a forty-two inch plasma flat-panel television. An intelligent and obviously inquisitive young man...I wonder, what he searches for out on the Internet?* Anxious to get the interview over and return home to enjoy the rest of his weekend, he turned back around.

A blurry shadow rushed past his eyes. It shimmered like a distorted mirror. His throat tensed and constricted. Leaving him with the uneasy feeling that he'd almost been touched by something extremely cold and quite powerful.

Whipping his eyes from side to side, Thayer blew out several short breaths and nervously tried to swallow. Whatever was there was gone. He lifted his nose trying to smell. Nothing came to him but the odors he'd appreciated upon entering. He'd had the distinct impression that the 'thing' wanted to taste him. *How ridiculous!* He chuckled and checked his Rolex.

With the hour of nine fast approaching, the sun (if it had managed to eat through the fog), would be mounting the mansion. Bright light would move in ever-stronger beams through the panes of glass covered by the drapes. Telling himself that the windows probably offered an airy and uninterrupted view of the eastern grounds, the doctor rose to take in a view of the outside. Drinking in the advancing light would lift the pensive mood of waiting and banish his silly fears.

Before he reached the curtains a soft smooth voice spoke from the shadows at the far end of the room. An area Thayer's eyes hadn't explored yet.

"The entire property, including those windows, is riddled with motion sensors." Shrewd amber eyes watched the doctor jump and turn. "If you decide to stroll these grounds, I'd take great care to ask for an escort. All the guards are armed and paid not to hesitate employing their weapons."

Indignant, Thayer retorted, "Considering the threats made to your father's life, it's nice to know we're so safe. Forgive me. I thought myself alone!" His eyes were struggling to readjust. When they failed to penetrate the deep obscurity surrounding his new patient, his hand automatically opened the drape an inch more just to enhance sight.

"Do you mind closing that? I don't care for the light. Foggy days, or better yet...rainy ones, are the best. I like the air thick and moist."

Peering into the darkness, Thayer let the curtain close. He saw a long white hand emerge from the gloom. A tapered finger passed before a red LED light. It must have pressed a button, the backdrop of pelting rain ceased. Struggling to see, he discerned a faint silhouette stepping forward. Outlined against the dark wall paneling, it barely took shape. "Do you know why I'm here?" he stammered. *Merde, how I hate being caught off guard!*

"Apparently I'm ill."

"Your father is worried about you. He rushed me here to perform a kind of impromptu examination."

"The renown Isidore de Chagny is worried. Shall we alert the media?"

Craning his head and squinting, Thayer studied the image before him. The figure was taking on better definition. "Why do you call your father Isidore?"

The question went unanswered as the young man approached. The subtle scents of herbal bath soap and shampoo reached Thayer's nose. A tall, almost unnaturally pale, young man – with an obvious stock of black loosely curled hair, still wet from the shower – emerged from the shadows. Coming to the side of the drape, he halted.

Setting the exceptional context of their meeting aside, Thayer took in the extraordinary continuity of the young nobleman's features. Before him stood a teenager with a strong masculine face: intense gold-colored eyes, a defined chin, steady open nostrils, and the suggestion of a strange inner excitement rippling through his lean body. Thayer felt as if he'd just stepped backwards into the remote centuries of the aristocracy and was on the verge of addressing one of history's engineers. *Darwin was correct, so little changes among the finest of our race. What is most attractive strays so little from perfection.*

Erik waited for the physician to stop mentally congratulating himself. "I told you I enjoy the dark." Long sculpted fingers reached for a set of unseen cords. In one swift movement he completely tightened the closure, deliberately denying the room the slightest glimmer of hopeful sunlight. Forcing darkness and total seclusion to absorb them, he asked, "Shall we sit?"

"At least turn on a light. This is a very melodramatic scene."

Erik went to a Tiffany stained-glass floor lamp and pulled a chain. They were bathed in the muted glow of a single frosted twenty-five watt bulb. Thayer's subject took to the couch and gestured Delaquois toward the formerly occupied wing chair. Dressed in indigo jeans and a long sleeved black silk shirt, opened at the upper front, the young man ran his fingers through his hair, ruffling it to speed the drying. He wore no visible jewelry and his dark pants were neatly tucked into black leather boots that came to just below his knees. His form evidenced an elegant symmetry – subtle tapering neck, perfectly proportioned limbs. The quintessential offspring of handsome well-fed generations, ready to unpin a female's heart and divest her of a resistance to mate – should he choose to do so.

Thayer was extremely relieved to see he wasn't in a mask. Taking his seat, he asked, "Did you ever use the masks hanging over there?"

"When I was younger I enjoyed them. They enhanced my games."

"Most youngsters enjoy dressing up in costumes."

"Childhood exploits."

"Yes."

Erik stayed quiet. He appeared more than ready to simply observe. Thayer cursed himself for not asking more open-ended questions. He knew he had to draw his client into conversation. "You are quite a capable fencer. How do you stay so physically fit?"

"Swim, run, play racket ball to increase stamina. I avoid the guards. They all have guns and I secretly hope they'll never use them. The blasts...disturb."

Thayer was grateful for the burgeoning confidence. "I'd probably jump right out of my skin. I've only heard gunfire in movies and even that's too much."

The physician smiled at the vision of a human minus his derma, something akin to an animated medical chart running away from a conflict. He heard Erik make a soft snort. *He couldn't see what my mind projected...he's alert, intelligent, if not unnerving. Those fiery eyes study me from beneath a set of very thick eyelashes – wonderfully long for a boy! How they captivate!* His patient's face was smooth and white, chiseled high cheekbones, well-defined brow – *such ascetic features.* Thayer still couldn't get over the perfect ratios. *A strong, almost angelic face. His skin suggests anemia – if nothing else a lack of sunlight. Despite the coolness of his stare, dark semicircles beneath the ocular orbits can't conceal the fact that appropriate amounts of sleep are an issue. All too typical in teenagers.*

"You sustained a rather nasty cut in your opponent's last attack. Did it require stitches?"

Erik shirked, his eyes glancing briefly at the simple gauze dressing wrapped around his right hand. "No."

"Is it all right that I've been brought here?" Thayer's client offered no reply, simply opened his undamaged hand in acceptance of the situation. He seemed amiable, not affronted. "Of course anything we discuss will be held in the strictest confidence."

Erik visibly tensed. He knew that to be an all-encompassing lie. Nothing much escaped Isidore de Chagny.

"You seem well-mannered. There's no reason we shouldn't get along."

"And you seem like a highly trained professional, more than capable of assessing a neuropsychiatric problem."

"Do you get outside much?"

"Only at night."

"Most fifteen year olds want to be out and about, exploring, discovering the world. It's hard to hold them close to home."

"I must be the exception that proves the rule," Erik added dryly.

"You don't like to go into the city?"

"I don't care for the cacophony of noise. There's a rancid stench in most of the gutters. Nauseates."

"You speak like a young man who's well read." Thayer thought the cool patrician stare quite disconcerting coming from one so inexperienced... *or maybe it's simply that he's like all youth...eternally rebellious.*

Erik's face was neutral, but not vacant. His elegant figure sat straight and dignified. *I wish I were simple...like an apple...fruit, seeds, peel, hard stem.* "So is this initial period of social banter between doctor and patient common? Seems logical."

"Why do you call your father Isidore?" The question went unanswered for a second time as an unannounced John entered with a tray of food. He set a small wooden folding table in front of Thayer, and with a white cotton napkin to protect him from the heat, lifted the silver dome off the plate.

"You've already met John Kelly, my daytime compatriot. You haven't eaten, Doctor. I took the liberty of ordering a *petit dejeuner* (snack) for you. You prefer blintzes. I believe they're your breakfast food of choice." Erik's voice carried an almost jovial, commercially persuasive undertone.

"Yes, I am rather hungry." The delicate smell of cheese stuffed crepes covered in sugared cherries wafted up to his nose. "But how did you know they are my favorites?"

"We are not without inventive wherewithal, Dr. Delaquois. A simple phone call to your wife, Vanessa, gave us the information. John will play butler for you. Would you prefer coffee or tea?"

"How very resourceful. Coffee, thanks. It smells delicious." Thayer spooned dollop after dollop of sour cream atop the cherries as John poured. His first bite was extraordinary – warm cheesy sweetness. Thayer smiled broadly, giving in to the experience with almost child-like joy. "This is as good as any I've ever tasted, as good as my mother made for me when I was little and always underfoot. You're not eating?"

"No, I hope to retire in a short while."

John stood discretely behind the doctor's chair, ready to attend to his needs. "Do you have everything you require, Doctor? I can fetch anything you request."

"Like a hoodwinking wizard? Pay no attention to the man behind the drape!" Thayer answered, half in jest. "Nothing for the present. Thank you."

For a brief moment Erik's mouth half-smiled, "I think Delaquois would like to talk to me alone."

"Please, call me Thayer," another bite of blintz made its way into his mouth – sheer oral happiness. "Pity you have not a plate of this for yourself."

Erik dismissed his bodyguard with a gentle wave of his hand. "I ate with Count Isidore earlier this morning. We are a very small tight-knit family."

John placed a glass of ice water on a table near Erik and left. The drink sat on a coaster beside an impressive slice of polished Brazilian agate. The stone's original edges were left rough, still intact.

"Does the agate please you?" The voice was mellow, engaging. "Concentrate on the stone, Thayer. It's a piece of history." Erik held the translucent slice up before the single light. "It's an exquisite sample. Long millennia in the making. Sleepy liquids flowed through lava holes, depositing silica to create the beauty of a quartz deposit…luminescent crystals merged…sparkles of gray and white, prisms of every imaginable color germinated in the earth. Imagine what it was like to be this rarity, growing sedately in the folds of centuries, floating in the waters of time. Washed in endless comfort." Thayer felt himself rise to the suggestion. It seemed so natural to be the embodiment of the stone, resting in the peaceful creation of eons past. "We will speak honestly with each other," Erik's tone was so pleasant, so appealing. He could have been speaking through the sky to the lovely agate forming below. "What childhood memory lingers most emphatically in your mind?"

"What stands out in yours?"

Erik's shoulders lifted in a congenial shrug, "I asked first."

Thayer accepted one of the decorative pillows from Erik and began absent-mindedly fingering one of its corded tassels. *What an odd twist,* he thought. The doctor had the strange, but not unpleasant realization that the child who loved blintzes might be the subject of the interview. *Doesn't matter.* He felt exceptional, something akin to honey, thick and relaxed. "Not much," he replied, playing contently with the pillow. "A few motion pictures – *The King and I* with Yul Brynner – my dog Daisy, several of the more spectacular Christmas trees we decorated, and the smell of my grandmother's pork roasts."

"Exactly," Erik praised him. "Brief tidbits. Certainly not a vivid moment by moment recollection – as if someone played a movie, froze the action, and physically dropped you into the scene. I'm literally reliving another childhood…one so horrific that I am forever suppressing the urge to scream so vociferously that I pop a blood vessel and die of an aneurysm."

Thayer listened to the euphonic ambassador speaking from the sky with every auditory nerve he possessed.

Erik continued. "I'm constantly surprising myself with fluency in a foreign language, or an understanding of some peculiar feature about this house. It started last October. I woke up knowing exactly how to make my voice come from different directions and in many forms…a ventriloquist's sport…as in the fashion of children. I made the lion emerge from a non-existent forest, then a lamb from a field, sparrows in the trees, lots of sounds. Anything I desired."

His client made the noise of a door creaking open and the psychiatrist looked right to address – *no one.* The entrance was closed. Delaquois turned back. "What a candid disclosure. Please tell me more." Secretly desirous, Thayer wished that Erik would just keep talking...*on any subject...just speak!* The precise, well-mannered vocalizations, smooth and melodic, swam over his ears in such delightful waves. But Erik grew silent and the doctor grew impatient for the calming utterance. "Do you have any pets?"

"Some feisty terrier or furry cat to entertain me? No."

Ah, the intonations of that voice, that lovely voice. "What a shame. Life is to be relished. It has so many wonderful things to offer, and pets are a comfort."

"Some of us have to disregard common enticements and go on about the business of defining what it is to be alive."

"Cynicism? When your whole life lays before you? Troubled thoughts can be a fixation. Deplete you of hope. Stick you in a rut. I'll find the cause and make everything all right." *Platitudes? I'm offering platitudes?* "Do you believe in anything?"

Erik leaned forward, studying his guest intensely. "A wholehearted allegiance to survival. No specific theology or loyalties...other than to Isidore and his work."

"Who schooled you? How have you been trained?"

"I've had many private tutors."

"Where was your classroom?"

"I rather like the attic, it smells of dry rot and dust. Is that weird?"

Thayer tilted his head. His mind decelerated, it required effort to gather his thoughts. "You are a young man who doesn't appear spoiled, not someone wallowing in the luxury of self-pity. You strike me as somewhat sad. You're speaking truthfully, and I appreciate that. I understand you are relatively untouched by the outside world. You are experiencing something that disturbs you...visions or intuitions of an alternate childhood. They might even be hallucinations. I think you're a loner given very much to your own counsel, but find yourself in the uncomfortable position of needing a stranger's help." Silence was the only response. "Do you know that these are unhealthy, actually rather ominous traits? Don't stay mute, even the young should voice their opinions."

Erik's voice deepened. "You have extraordinary intuition. I don't consider myself sullen, Doctor. Perhaps just lonely. Maybe I don't need your interventions."

"Are you on any medication?" *Why in the world did it take me so long to ask that question?*

"No."

"Isn't there something you'd like to understand? I could help you interpret the pictures you see."

"I'd like to know what started these episodes...let's call them dreams...and why have they intensified?"

"It's a natural process to have adventures while you sleep. Everyone has disturbing dreams."

"But not everyone gains knowledge during sleep."

"Some gain insights. Remember, we're only conducting the initial interview. It's always a little tense. Takes time to build nuggets of trust."

Erik's hand reached up, pushing a lock of hair away from his forehead. He contemplated the darkened interior with satisfaction. "Is loyalty to be prized above all else?"

"Yes, I suppose so...that and an insight into one's health...and companionship. Humans have a need to sound ideas off others."

"To whom are you most loyal, Isidore de Chagny or your patient?"

Thayer was astonished. A little forewarning that Erik was this insightful would have helped. "To my patient, of course. Given time I will prove myself."

"Given time," Erik repeated slowly. "You'd risk the omnipotent geneticist's wrath?"

"Absolutely. My loyalties are to you. I've been assigned to your care."

Deep in consternation, Erik made a tent of his fingers, bringing his lips down to their tips.

Odd motion for an adolescent, thought Thayer.

"See the stitches on that pillow, so precise, so endearing."

Thayer felt like a boat set adrift. *Is my mind wandering?* Gazing down he found himself hugging an unfamiliar pillow decorated with a flowered tree. The embroidered wool boucle of turquoise, shades of dark berries, and citron was certainly harmonious, the most pleasant he'd ever seen. Looking to his patient, Erik's amber irises seemed touched with an uncommon radiance. They shone with the lights of faceted sapphires.

"I know I am in trouble," Erik conceded. "With great reluctance I accept your help. The wise and intrepid Isidore is facially and morally deformed...he continues to deteriorate, but perhaps I can be salvaged."

"Listening to your locution is like listening to a man from another era."

"Continue eating. You're letting the food get cold, Thayer. I can't have my physician going hungry," the agreeable voice had become barely a whisper.

"Thank...," Thayer paused mid-courteous response. The next tasty forkful of blintz stayed suspended in the air directly in front of his waiting mouth.

Something peculiar stole the gem-like gleam from Erik's eyes. He frowned, and for a few brief seconds his neck muscles strained painfully, as if he tried to resist some force and keep his head held up.

For the space of a few heartbeats, disbelief put Thayer in denial. *Here is an old soul with a solemn turn to his mouth and the incongruous knowledge of a more experienced man.* His eyes widened as his patient slumped back into the chair.

Erik's expression seemed to freeze; indeed his entire body was suddenly caste into a quickly hardening wax. Vacant eyes stared out past the top of the neuropsychiatrist's head. The young man's right arm hung over the sofa's side, his hand lax – long white fingers pointing poetically toward the floor. More than still, more than quiet. Totally immobile. It appeared his subject had morphed into a plastic caricature in an amusement house.

Thayer's fork hit the side of the Odessa Pillivuyt China plate with a distinct clang.

4 *RANK AND SPLENDOR*

$\mathfrak{S}$creaming for John, for anybody, a mounting sense of calamity enveloped Thayer as his more professional side took charge. Erik did not hear the doctor's cries, nor did he hear John burst in, hollering at Delaquois.

"Is there a pulse? Did you check for a pulse?"

The young de Chagny was unaware they slid him gently to the floor. Sucked like a perch down a current, his mind traveled a long black passage, moving further and further away from the reality of the estate. His heart beat to the crackling sparks of a unique synaptic flare. A sudden hot white light burst in all around him, as if he'd crashed through a door, entering another time and place entirely. There was no pain, no exhilaration, only a tremendous sense of apprehension.

He stood now in the courtyard of the khan, a place located just outside the Persian city where travelers and merchants refreshed themselves and safely stored their goods. He waited patiently while inside the *hamam* (bathhouse) the barbers finished administering to the Daroga. He'd risen early from his divan, to wash and dress away from all the others – to hide the iniquity of his face behind the black hood and veil of *hijab* and *niqab*. Their journey from Nizhny Novgorod into the land of the *Parsua* had been a long one. They crossed through a terrain of violent contrasts, one where rocky ice-capped mountains towered over endless deserts. A land where Nature ordained that bitter cold and intense heat must dwell together side-by-side. Their small caravan of police and cooks trudged the ascent, in some places literally pulling the horses forward to levels glittering in crystals of ice and snow. Their descent off the Elburz brought them into vast empty sands where nothing grew and no animal survived without the care of men. Here the air literally scintillated with the dust of the desert. The harshness of this extreme land toughened the spirits of the Persian people, forcing them into frugality and pragmatism. They were hardy and contemplative, almost unreasonably proud. They lived in a place where ancient ancestors warred for the right to sire new civilizations. Here superstitious astrologers sought insight from the heavens, and learned mathematicians unraveled the laws of physics. Skilled architects designed entire cities, and clever engineers plotted waterways. Despite the wealth of their ponderous knowledge, they freely consulted divining mystics and purchased the curious wares of alchemists practicing the darkest arts.

Silent and guarded, Erik moved toward the stables. Totally covered in black cloth and leather, every part of his body was hidden except for his eyes. Only those remained visible to the outsiders. He found his horse already bridled, hoof scraping the ground with impatience. The warmth and power of the magnificent creature sent a wave of awe through him. He'd felt this same sense of wonder when the Daroga presented him the stallion. In every greeting it had never changed. Patting the neck of the black Arabian steed, his keen eyes searched every nook and cranny of the courtyard. Here on the outskirts of the city, he listened to the haunting chants of religious criers invade the peace of the morning. Their plaintive vocalizations issued from tall minarets, poured over rooftops, and echoed eerily off walls in a series of chilling pleas. Their lonely entreating called out for the first of five daily prayer sessions.

In this exotic disparate land of the *Parsua*, Muslim law and traditions were valued like breath. Respected and honored to the same degree as the refinements of rhetoric and story telling, the sciences of chemistry, physics, and botany. This was a country seeped in knowledge and culture, yet prone to exacting behavior and explicit cruelty.

He'd learned a great deal traveling with the Daroga's small retinue over the last six weeks. They'd stopped every day before sunset to rest and seek nourishment for themselves and their horses. At the border of the district boasting the Shah's capital, they'd come across a group of Bedouin Arabs who'd pitched their tents near a shallow creek. Hidden behind a rock Erik witnessed those same chieftains holding down a young slave, beating him to death for the simple insult of serving their dinner late. Below the brilliant canopy of a sky darkening from carnelian red to indigo, the Daroga located his charge. Whispered into his ear, "We Persians often say that glory lay over this land from the very beginning of creation. But this place that cradled civilization is the very womb of barbarism. It is the heat that inflames the mind." He calmly directed Erik away from the bloody sight, back to their own campfire where he continued teaching him the constructs of his native tongue.

Standing in the khan's cobble-stoned courtyard, Erik remembered the incident with great clarity. They'd broken camp and moved on hours before the Bedouins discovered their leaders dead on their cushions with their throats slit. Motivated by the need for haste, the Daroga pressed them forward through the lawless frontier districts where caves and rocky outcrops hid brazen thieves and bands of fierce independent hunters.

Closer to the convenience of the city, their trip proved less arduous. Here the populace lived in primitive round huts of baked clay and mortar. They herded flocks of sheep or tilled fields, attended mosques. Their party arrived two days ago. And after the harrows of their journey this inn offered a most welcomed chance to rest. They'd engaged their rooms and sent a runner on ahead to alert the Shah of their presence. Security was tight inside the lodge. Considered a talented and innovative magician, Erik was a prize intended for the regent's entertainment. The only other group sharing the *caravansari* was promptly inspected and found to consist mostly of merchants trading French brocades and Chinese silks for Middle Eastern woods and spices. So, for the modest sum of two dinars per head, they refreshed themselves before entering the city proper. The Daroga's people slept and ate the tasty meals set generously before them. The food was more appetizing than the provisions they'd consumed on the road – there they fed on a steady diet of boiled mutton and barley stew flavored with cardamom and dried cloves.

Their time of recuperation passed all too quickly. This morning they would be escorted through the gates by a *janissary* of the Shah's elite military; from there to the palace and on into the presence of the court. Somehow Erik knew all these details as he studied the tallest towers projecting themselves above the tops of the city's stone walls. Each bore a pennant, left unfurled in the stillness of the air.

Beneath his heavy black robes, he tensed. The clop of horse hooves reached his ears. The khan's stablemen busied themselves with bringing the rest of their horses from the stalls. These slender boys barely nodded to the tall skinny magician as they led the bathed and newly brushed animals to the tethering posts. Erik didn't mind their lack of greeting. Placed under the protection of the nineteen year old Daroga, they feared and respected the stranger. The Frenchman was peculiar, and it was rumored that his guardian, the Head of the Shah's Secret Police, possessed the evil eye. No one knew how many tortured souls lay in the dungeons of the palace. Erik fostered their apprehension and said nothing in the manner of friendly comment – the less exposure the better.

A dozen royal guards mounted on horseback appeared at the gate. The stable boys rushed forward to hold the horses' reins. With the instinct of the desert dwellers, a wordless Erik watched as the captain scanned their surroundings. Like most of his men, the captain had a long high forehead and a distinctive nose – reflecting a lineage mixed with the Mongols and the peoples of the eastern Mediterranean. These Persians, with their fine stalwart builds, were warlike, more dangerous than the Cossacks despite the gay plumes that topped their helmets. Trained for battle, today their metal breastplates and those of their horses were etched with intricate designs accented with emeralds, rubies, and deep blue sapphires.

Erik cleared his mind, making it a vast empty space where everything around him could be absorbed and learned. Behind the men came a covered wagon. The rest of the guard quickly dismounted and began dressing the Daroga's horses with caparisons of golden cloth decorated with diamonds and pearls. A lean man urged another with fat sausage fingers to hurry and place the richest trappings on the Daroga's mount. As they tied down saddles worked with silver and copper inlay and affixed tasseled harnesses, they shot inquisitive glances at the veiled man fresh from the taxing trip over the mountains.

"Today you shall meet your host and benefactor!" The Daroga, dressed in a royal blue tunic-uniform that flaunted a yellow bandolier studded with jeweled medals, strode up behind him. "By the beard of the prophet, why is there no wind in this damnable place?" Indeed, the air was perfectly still and they had yet to contend with the afternoon's heat. Staying indoors was virtually the only way to cope with the oppressive temperatures once they bore down upon the populace.

Leaving the stairs, the Daroga went forward to greet the captain. Pleased with how his horse was attired, he mounted and cantered the gray Arabian, showing off his expertise in horsemanship. Nodding to Erik, the rest mounted and formed a procession of two aside – with the Daroga and the magician near its end. As they exited the khan, their grand escort inflated their chests and raised their rifles. Shooting a salute into the air, they succeeded in startling the horses and heightening Erik's anxiety. Four drummers and a half-dozen musicians, playing oboes and flutes, took up the head of the march.

They passed through the ancient city walls by means of an enormous metal gate. Just inside, at a place where practiced storytellers hawked their recollections for the price of a few coins, another group of colorful musicians waited to join their entourage. These new participants led them over the winding pavement with the added sounds of bells and timbrels. Apparently their passage through the city was to be loudly acclaimed.

People traversing the streets paused respectfully, moving aside to let the column through. The owners of horse-drawn carts laden with spices and fruits pulled their wares forward and clustered together to view the parade. The captain took deliberate detours, snaking their procession through bazaars where dozens of tiny shops extended down narrow alleyways. The Daroga pointed out establishments where one might purchase everything from a variety of Damascus silk and fragrant Arabian coffee, to cashmere shawls and hashish. Past these areas of quiet commerce, they came upon some crowded livestock corrals where men bargained for numerous sheep, goats, and horses. Looking over the heads of these noisy barterers, Erik saw the Persian sun shining brightly on the walls of a brilliant blue-tiled mosque. Washed clean in the recently past spring rains, their decorations appeared glorious to his young eyes. All the colors of the city seemed clearer, contrasts sharper, shadows more somber than elsewhere on their trek. Closer to the palace, the buildings became grandly ornamented affairs created by skillful architects. White two-story houses had street balconies festooned with garlands and silk banners to honor the Daroga's return. Veiled ladies with eyes like dark pools of lampblack watched passively as the cortège rode by. Erik could feel their prying stares searching for an explanation of his acceptance into the Persian court.

He sat atop his horse, his back straight, his hands covered in suede gloves with open grommets exposing his knuckles. The cuffs of the gloves were tied three inches up his forearms with black cowhide laces. Lightly guiding the reins, he bore the affront of this conspicuous public exposure with difficulty.

"Wait until you see the women of this court," cantering his horse beside him, the Daroga tried to sound encouraging.

"I have no interest in women," Erik responded. "They are fickle creatures who consume their hours with the accumulation of adornments."

The Daroga laughed from deep within his chest. "I'll wager that someday you will appreciate the subtle places those trinkets can be affixed!"

"Then how is it you remain unmarried?"

"Unmarried doesn't mean inexperienced. Women who have been shown some degree of culture growing-up only want what is beautiful... and rightly so."

"People are people, Khalil. I'll let you investigate for the both of us."

Just then a flurry of flower petals released from several baskets descended upon their heads. The young women on the balconies above them, giggled to have hit their marks so accurately.

The Daroga waved to the well-wishers. Leaving himself dusted in petals, he chided, "Doesn't rational judgment tell you that this is a step up from the gypsies? Extracting you was a feat of tactful diplomacy. Be grateful."

Erik steered his horse around a ragged pothole, "I've traded mud for heat."

Inside the palace they rode through several barrel-vaulted chambers, enormous domes of rock and clay. Their roofs supported by tall columns, their walls decorated with the painted reliefs of lions, bulls, and flowers. They dismounted in an inner courtyard, and proceeded on foot, still accompanied by the guards.

They were led to the screened-in area of an audience chamber that proved to be a magnificent hall, garish beyond imagination. *So this is Paradise*, mused Erik. The furnishings in the room were of superbly crafted woods, many overlaid in precious metals. Rich mosaics affixed to the ceiling portrayed Persian figures in various battle positions. Elegant geometric borders sectioned the scenes. Massive porcelain vases and torcheres of gold as tall as a man ornamented the room. On the walls hung enormous tapestries, and areas of the marble floor were covered in carpets of the finest wools, gathered from every corner of the Near East and the Orient. Through the screen's latticework, Erik studied the court in session.

On an opalescent throne of jasper and gold sat the Shah, a handsome obviously deliberate man. Not yet in his middle years, his dark eyes possessed a cold penetrating stare that chilled those subservient to him. Erik had no doubt the sovereign could be ruthless. He automatically straightened, widening the stance of his booted feet, refusing to be intimidated. The Shah wore a long sheathed scimitar at his side and a smaller curved dagger thrust through a satin sash at his waist. Clothed in Persian shoes, curled at the toes, blousy purple silk trousers, a vest embroidered with hand-sewn flowers, and a long sleeve shirt of iridescent silvery fabric, he cut quite a figure. Curls of glossy tar-black hair with silver-blue highlights shown beneath the sides of the golden turban atop his head. The headdress was arrayed with a spray of perfect peacock feathers and the largest diamond Erik had ever seen. Immediately behind the throne stood a wondrous wall, plated in solid gold and studded with elaborately worked tendrils of copper and silver leaves. A large Persian flag hung to the side. Ordained since the early 1840's, the red, white and green background bore the symbols of the lion and the sun.

From their place of concealment, where they waited to be announced, Erik saw that beside the Shah, but on a lower level, were a number of bodyguards and a corpulent man the Daroga identified as the Royal Treasurer. On the floor to the side of the throne, on a dozen plump cushions, a group of young girls sat in attendance. Veiled and dressed in tight fitting satin jackets and silken ballooning pants, they were girdled in pieces of polished leather encrusted with jewels. It appeared they did nothing more than listen and please the eyes of the myriad men in the hall.

"Who are these other males?" Erik inquired quietly of the Daroga.

"The Shah surrounds himself with men of knowledge, professionals who can advise with the profoundest wisdom. They are experienced physicians and pharmacists, acclaimed grammarians and rhetoricians, along with a smattering of mathematicians thoroughly accomplished in higher arithmetic, geometry, and algebra. Over there," he pointed to a short man scribbling away in a journal, "is an historian versed in our kingdom's past. Next to him is a refined *moallem* of philosophy and two others who are well instructed in the finer points of all our laws and traditions. In the far corner is a young poet standing beside the

Chief Architect...who is looking rather bored I might add. He may find himself accounting for that yawn later on."

From behind his *niqab*, Erik wished they'd spent more time in the khan. He felt like a strange bug about to be dissected. From deep within he called up a stubborn resolve, a genuine sense of disdain for this pompous court and these self-righteous men who egotistically labeled themselves 'authorities in their fields'. Erik was positive that the more a man knew, the more he understood how much he did not know.

A herald, stationed not too far from their position, announced the next group of persons being brought before the throne. So far, business was conducted with a formal, fairly ostentatious overtone.

"Remember the protocol I've taught you," reminded the Daroga softly. "If it appears that the western custom of offering a hand in greeting is to be followed, never extend the left hand as it is a mark of great ignorance." He paused, allowing Erik to quietly list the proper expressions. "I intend to declare to my cousin, the Shah, that I've taken great care with your education and will ask for permission to continue your instructions."

They paused to watch the Chief Usher bring forward three men, each attended by an officer of the police. After the three bent their knees and prostrated themselves face down on the floor, a list of charges was read against them. Erik strained to hear as a small cluster of witnesses came forward to give testimony and petition the regent. With their backs to the far end of the hall, Erik and Khalil heard practically nothing of their concerns.

Curious to know the crimes of those still prostrate, Erik whispered, "What have they done?"

The Daroga stepped in an oblique line to a man reading quietly from a scroll. Careful not to make any unnecessary sound, he came back to Erik and leaned close to the magician's veiled ear. "Three religious from a local mosque – accused of agitating. Each mosque has an imam who assembles the people of his division at the accustomed hours to join in prayer. He's the one on the left."

The entire hall grew quiet as the Shah eyed with disdain the three lying prostrate on the floor. "One hundred strokes to the sole of each foot so they may digest the fact that it is not their business to disturb and vex others. After the physical punishment, clothe them in rags and seat them on camels with their faces toward the source of dung. They are to be led through the quarters of the city with a crier proclaiming in a loud voice that this is the treatment given those who meddle in the affairs of others. Whoever makes it their business to sow dissension among neighboring families, mischievously causing all manner of strife, shall reap pain and humiliation."

The three policemen placed their hands atop their own heads, signifying that they were ready to execute the Shah's orders and expected decapitation if they failed in any particular point. Behind the members of the mosque, they too prostrated before the throne, then rose, dragging their prisoners away.

As they exited, Erik experienced an optimistic, if not perverse approval. *Perhaps it was not a mistake to come to a nation where a capable ruler castigates those who indulge in gossip and sow dissent.* All too soon, the inconsistencies of punishment rendered by this court would force him to rethink this appraisal.

The Grand Herald tapped the tip of a long ornately carved staff upon a block of ebony. His deep voice bellowed across the hall. "The Daroga Khalil Echad Salim returns with the famed magician, Erik." He pointed toward the lattice expecting the pair to emerge.

"Do not speak first. Do not test the Shah or try him in any way," warned the Daroga. "Here, he is master of the east and the west, the vicar on earth sent from Allah to govern all that surrounds him!"

"The Shahanshah, the king among kings awaits," boomed the Grand Herald.

The Daroga escorted Erik to the base of the stairs leading to the throne. The Royal Treasurer, standing over an enormous chest, reached for a bag of gold coins to reward Khalil. The pair knelt; bending at the middle, their foreheads went to the white marble floor in submission.

"Arise, cousin," the Shah proclaimed cordially. "We wish to greet the wondrous illusionist you have so faithfully brought to us."

They stood. "My Lord, I give you Erik. He is a not a man of pleasant cheerfulness and wit, but a master of the mysterious arts, one who converses with the jinn. His beginning was in France. From there he traveled with a clan of gypsies. He was their star attraction in a most lucrative show, a talented musician and singer, whose wisdom caused him to rise to the position of counselor to their elders. The next segment of his life will be to entertain you, the Defender of the Crescent Moon."

At these excessive declarations, the Shah smiled, "And what shall be his end?"

"Who knows what challenges Allah may deem important for him to pursue."

"Does he understand our language?"

"He understands it imperfectly," the Daroga responded. "I have taught him myself and with your permission will continue his education."

I comprehend more than you will ever guess, Erik brooded.

"Have you seen this fellow perform?" the Shah inquired.

"I have, my Lord."

"This evening over a banquet you will give me a full account of your travels. But first, tell me why he stands veiled before me?"

Stunned, Erik stood perfectly still.

"Show me your face. You are my guest and I shall see it."

Mortified, a reluctance to obey swept over Erik. Desperately wondering what to do, he didn't move. *My face! My face! No one should see my face!*

Coming to the defense of his charge, the Daroga broke with decorum, "Cousin, may I approach?"

The Shah ignored the impertinence. The fingers of his right hand barely lifted from the arm of his throne, impatiently gesturing Khalil forward.

The Daroga knelt directly at the Shah's feet, speaking very softly. "You could have him arrested. I will beat him myself if you will it, but I beg you to weigh the difference between discovering the magician's talents and losing one of such renown so quickly. He hides a deformity given to him by Allah that many, more ignorant than you or I, would declare a providential sign of evil. Your request warrants consideration as I myself have seen the magician unmasked and the sight is most horrific."

"Because you argue so eloquently for him, I shall let a test decide his fate."

Khalil brought his hands to his mouth in gratitude, then touched his forehead, lips and heart in reverent oblation. Stepping backwards he returned to Erik's side.

"Can you make the little Sultana laugh, Magician? My daughter sits just there in the midst of her ladies."

Erik bowed to the Shah and angling only slightly, so that the Shah still had his front, he bowed to the women stationed on the cushions. He straightened out his arms, palms toward the ceiling. In the space above each hand hovered a ball of yellow-white fire. Those in the court who could see *ahh'd* in unison. From above her facial veil, the Sultana's brown eyes watched the balls of light roll to the magician's gloved fingertips. In an instant they traveled toward each other, joining quickly before disappearing in a confined burst of light. After the flash, a yellow canary fluttered, momentarily suspended where the fire had been. The bird spread its wings and flew above those gathered near the throne to the lip of a vase containing lilies.

One of the Sultana's maidens jumped to her feet and chortling to the canary, bid it climb onto her finger. She brought the obedient bird to her mistress, who laughed with delight.

In surprise, the Shah gestured Erik closer. The Daroga leaned into his ear and whispered, "Kneel as I did, repeat my hand movements."

Erik humbly lowered his head. Knowing he had three daggers on him, he prepared to defend his anonymity. *Must I show my face to the entire slobbering court?* In truth, he was confused as to how they might actually react and wanted desperately to never again view the horror registering on another's face.

The Daroga straightened in alarm and the Shah noticed. In a strong authoritative voice the ruler sent forth a directive, "Everyone but the magician is to walk to the other end of the chamber."

After a moment's hesitation, the several dozen confused people in the room began to move. The bodyguards quickly took their spears and backed everyone away from the throne. Even the Royal Treasurer, in his haste to yield to a royal command, was forced to leave the chest of gold rewards unattended.

The Daroga gently put his hand on the middle of Erik's back, urging him to advance. With feet of lead, his charge approached.

"Untie the veil and expose your face to only me, the ruler of this great kingdom."

Erik slowly and very dramatically obeyed. Somehow he was loathsome and impure – he could feel it. Looking upon the magician's face, the Shah, much to his credit, showed absolutely no reaction. Apparently the sole center of government could be benevolent as well as cruel. Erik saw only the monarch's pupils dilate. He was amazed at the regal control evidenced in this man's total calm.

"The little Sultana is the jewel of my heart. In the eighteen months since her mother's death, she has not smiled, much less laughed. You, a stranger, have lightened her heart." In a loud voice, so that even those at the back of the room could hear, he declared. "Before me I recognize a most singular circumstance. One that declares that Allah in all His glorious wisdom decides the fates of men. I decree that no one else shall view the face of my new guest. Furthermore, a helmet of gold, to match the color of his eyes, with a red plume at its top, is to be fashioned for my Royal Magician. He is to wear a veil of chain mail fashioned of silver lying over one of black silk to hide his face. All that shall be viewed of him by this court – and the land entire – is his eyes."

He lowered his voice and spoke directly to Erik. "Have no fear. You may cover your face, son." Then re-addressing those gathered at the back, "This unique and talented treasure shall be known as the Royal Inquiline. He is fatigued and needs time to grow accustomed to us. Have him escorted to the apartment we have prepared for him."

Erik bowed and stepped politely backward away from the dais. A tall muscular black slave, with a weathered face and a very conspicuous gold bangle in his left ear, came before the throne and paid homage.

"This is Heerad," declared the herald. "He is given to you as servant and will guide you to your quarters. You are to appear before the Shah any time of the day or night that he bids you come."

Erik bowed deeply in acceptance, all the while reviewing the weapons on his person. His most accurate dagger he wore in a pectoral sheath.

Outside the audience chamber, the Daroga took his leave. "I'll return to you after I've visited my sister. I know she must be anxious to greet me. Heerad will see you safely to your rooms. Speak to no one until they speak. You are privileged now, under the direct protection of the Shah. You need not answer a single question asked of you."

No sooner was the Daroga out of sight, then three richly dressed young Persians turned the corner and walked boldly straight for the Frenchman and the black slave. They showed no signs of wavering course, so Erik stepped aside to give way. The largest of the trio rudely shoved him, shoulder to shoulder, in a jolt. In the instant of contact, Erik deftly pulled a velvet pouch from the assailant's clothing. There was barely a ripple of cloth – then *voila* – the small sack entered Erik's sleeve not too far from a now empty canister of calcium carbonate.

"Stay out of our way, yellow-eyed infidel." The Persian swore beneath his breath, "Uncouth! You are nothing but a maggot-riddled pile of dung."

Erik straightened, tensing with defiance at the insult. Heerad's hand came to rest upon the forearm of his new master, persuading him to refrain from response.

The three cronies snickered and moved on.

"Incompetent clown," laughed one the ruffians as they sauntered away. "We could so easily throttle you." The click of their metal tipped heels grated Erik's nerves. Here were men who impudently wanted their approach noticed. Even as he knew them to be fools, a wave of disconcerting humiliation washed over him.

As Heerad headed them toward his new apartment, curiosity thwarted any thought of retaliation. His fingers were occupied – puzzling over the strange brass objects he felt hidden within the pilfered pouch.

5 *SANCTIMONIOUS EGOS*

Obelisks, covered in ancient writing, rose and fell in an angry swirling obliteration of crystal sand. Confusing. Choking. Moving his arms in irritation, Erik awoke with a cough, hungering for clean air. He heard John Kelly's voice tell Isidore of his awakening. The aromatic smell of freshly brewed coffee came to him. Eyes closed, he reached for his scalp. Adhered to the skin were a dozen itchy electrodes, plastered down with some kind of sticky paste. His eyes opened. Isidore and Dr. Delaquois sat to his left.

"Where am I?"

"In your bed, dear boy," answered Isidore.

"You've had some kind of spell," interrupted Thayer. "I want to move you to a hospital."

"No hospital," Erik's voice sounded strange even to him. As if he were climbing out of a pit trying to regain reality. "How long was I out?"

"About forty-five minutes," John stood on the opposite side of the bed.

"My head hurts. Turn down the lights and give me a mirror."

Prepared for the latter request, John passed him a hand mirror.

Isidore sighed heavily. "There's nothing wrong with your face, Erik."

The grotesque version he hid in Persia, still inexplicably unseen, made his reflection all the more surreal – it bore some kind of foreboding promise that disfigurement was inevitable. In disbelief the young man studied the concerned face staring back at him through the glass. Whole and appropriate, he looked the same as he remembered. *Why do people fear my countenance? Why do I find them so petty and contemptible?*

"Isidore, send the doctor back to his wife," he said indifferently.

"I've brought him here to help you."

Delaquois leaned in closer to Erik. "The electroencephalogram you're attached to showed massive bursts of accelerated cortical activity. The readings were almost off the charts. You were not in a state of sleep. Non-reactive, certainly…but not asleep."

"The hallucinations are falling out of chronological order. Last week I was in Paris. This morning…Persia."

"You've never been to Iran, son. How could there be any 'order' to them?" Isidore sounded deeply worried.

Erik eyed him with seething aversion. "Sanctimonious skeptic! Tell me, when did I ever lie to you? If I've never been to Persia, listen to this." He started to pronounce a quatrain in perfect Farsi.

> "Of dust and earth and bone I'm made
> I rose and came, when called – obeyed.
> When garbed in naught but night I failed
> You crudely sent me forth – to fade.
>
> What praise is there in disposition
> That lacks all thoughts of shame?
> Unholy trials, I writhe undone.
> Born again to kiss farewell the sun."

His body shuddered, his eyes rolled back into his head. Tumbling through the black recesses, sucked rapidly through time along some neural pathway alight with harsh discordant flashes that startled and dissipated before any part of reality might be identified – their patient slipped away.

"Is he seizing?" John fought the urge to holler Erik's name and return him to consciousness.

"No, this is something else. Not a seizure," Delaquois reached over to the EEG machine, flipping on the power. "Was the digital recorder on, John? Did we catch what he said? If so, we need it translated immediately." From his pocket Thayer withdrew a stopwatch. Their patient grew ominously quiet. *Skin dry and cold, respirations shallow.* Thayer raised Erik's arm and left it standing straight in the air. He clicked on the stopwatch and began to time how long it would take before the arm came to rest once again upon the bed. "We may need to start an intravenous. Dehydration is an issue not to be ignored. He'll need electrolytes. I assume you have the necessary supplies."

Isidore nodded to John. "Fetch, Nyah," the geneticist ordered. "Tell her Erik needs an IV. If she's reluctant to meet Dr. Delaquois, which is probable, have her give you the supplies and we'll start it."

"And who is Nyah?" asked Thayer.

"My first assistant and companion. She's in the lab and will lecture me with articulate vehemence once she knows Erik is in want of something."

Without speaking, Erik and Heerad walked through several corridors beautifully decorated in murals and mosaics. Some with multi-colored *graffito*, others displaying bold reliefs carved in stucco: birds, flowers, intricate geometric patterns that must have taken skilled artisans months to accomplish. The last hallway opened onto a lush well-manicured garden simply a riot with flowers and numerous shaded patios. Apparently Persian royalty had a passionate love for vegetation and fruit trees. Three sides of the perfectly square area bore apartments stacked three levels high. The windows of the inhabited units were covered with thick curtains that could be swept aside when the heat of the day subsided.

Access to the dwellings on the upper floors was achieved through semi-enclosed towers with open-air arches that revealed their inner stairwells. The loggia of each landing provided a place to view the garden or stop and converse with a neighbor. Heerad and Erik climbed two double-backed flights of stairs to reach the uppermost level. There they stood before a large wooden door. Wordless, Heerad waited.

Finally Erik understood and impatiently commanded, "Open the door!"

Heerad obeyed without a murmur.

A tiny slip of a girl stood in the immediate foyer. Though she was respectfully veiled in turquoise silk charmeuse, Erik could tell she was no more than twelve or thirteen, just a little younger than himself. She wore a short tight-fitting jacket that acted like a bustier laced down the front. Fluffy white feathers trimmed the neckline. Instead of ballooning pants she wore a yellow skirt of fine semilustrous crepe that flared in four generous bell-like tiers down to her ankles and yellow curly toed slippers.

"I am Fatima," she pronounced cheerfully. "I am given to you by the Shah to run your household."

Several sticks of cinnamon soaked in vanilla burned in a brass holder on a table just past the entrance. The air was fragrant with their perfume. Erik's eyes sparkled, "I am the Royal Inquiline and performer,

Erik. In my country a gentleman presses a lady's fingers to his lips upon introduction." *You have no idea what the sight of you does to me. How 'given to me' are you?*

Beneath her thin veil she smiled tremulously. "You must not touch the women of this land, Lord. Nor suffer them to touch you in any manner," she added sympathetically. "Please step inside and view your rooms." As he passed through the foyer into the first room, she gazed up at him inquisitively, obviously intrigued by a man concealed in a black hood and veil.

The walls of the apartment were ornamented with vines and foliage painted in azure and gold. Small intricately depicted birds roosted in the leaves. Each diamond-shaped section was defined with a border of mosaic bands. The first room on their right was a sitting area, very neatly furnished and immaculately clean. A sofa covered in the deepest indigo velvet, situated in front of the middle of the far wall, acted as a place of honor, giving the appearance that he could hold court himself. Before the sofa several cushions lay scattered on a deep red Persian carpet. His bedroom, off to the left, was a simple affair: large central bed, two heavy leather chests, and a washstand. In this room he turned to face a curtained window that he knew took in a view of the garden. Heerad drew back the *arras* and Erik obligingly looked outside to a cluster of azalea bushes all bearing large pompoms of white and pink flowers. Several almond trees provided shade over an inlaid patio containing a number of carved stone benches. Yellow and black butterflies flitted from flower to flower as a funny-looking caretaker with a comically small watering can appeared. Walking backwards he tripped several times on his own feet. *Must ask about that gentleman.* He turned to Fatima and Heerad. Neither was smiling.

"Heerad, why does the gardener below walk backwards?"

Heerad bowed deeply.

"Rise and answer," commanded Erik.

"He cannot answer the Royal Inquiline," Fatima responded. Heerad stood tall and straight, his arms folded across his chest. "He has no tongue."

"Why has he no tongue?"

"When he was a boy, he and six of his brothers were given to the Shah as a present, already muted so they might serve in silence. He hears perfectly and will obey all your requests." A protracted moment of uneasiness followed. "The gardener walks backwards because the little Sultana has ordered him to do so for one complete year."

"Why?" Erik was incredulous.

"Her favorite walnut trees died in his care. They were old, but she loved them."

Erik froze in disbelief. *At least the man did not have the soles of his feet beaten...and he managed to keep his head.* How cruel was this princess to issue such a decree to an obviously industrious worker. His instincts told him it was a punishment hatched of capricious wrath. *But then... she's learning from her father.*

"I have set out some clothes for you." Fatima's hand swept toward the bed. "A comfortable *dishdasha* (robe) to wear inside the apartment, and leather socks like those used for Islamic prayers and *dawah* journeys."

"*Dawah?*"

"Missionary work done among the followers of Islam."

"I am **not** a Muslim," Erik said coldly.

"Then I am not misinformed," she replied. "Indoors you need not wear your boots. On the washstand is *halal*, peppermint soap, and *mishwak*, an all-natural toothbrush. You scrape a small amount of bark from the tip and then chew the nub. Al-Bukahri has proclaimed, 'Make a regular practice of *mishwak* for verily it is the purification of the mouth and a means of pleasing Allah.' The pitcher is filled with water and mint leaves." She bowed and Heerad followed suit.

"Take a few moments, Master, and freshen yourself. I have a meal prepared for you."

"I am not hungry." In truth, he was parched and starving, but never ate in front of others.

Fatima bowed in obeisance. Once again Heerad shadowed her movements. "Then just look at the food. That would be the polite action." Both she and Heerad backed out of the room, their faces remaining toward the magician.

In five minutes Erik reappeared in the sitting room, still fully dressed in his black robes and leather boots, but gloveless.

"The Shah has sent you a present; Heerad and I have one for you as well. But first, please sit and allow me to serve the food."

Erik folded onto the couch, never taking his eyes off the pair. Heerad placed a small carved eight-sided table before him, it's legs and top inlaid with an intricate geometric pattern in brass and mother of pearl.

After some rustling in the next room, Heerad spread a piece of lace cloth over the table and Fatima entered with a tray. Initially three dishes were served: a fine capon stuffed with coarse rice and spinach, curried lamb with vegetables, and cubed beef garnished with raisins and apples. The smell alone told him the dishes were well chosen and excellently prepared.

Next she appeared with a pot of Chinese Jasmine tea, "Sweetened with a hint of Turkish honey to offer an exotic welcome. I cannot serve you wine, Lord," she said, pouring the tea into a tall glass with a silver spoon to act as a heat sink. "In this country, those who drink alcohol during the daylight hours are looked upon as dissolute persons. Persons soaked in strong drink never appear openly for they are arrested if the police encounter them. This custom is to be commended, as during the day we require clear heads to transact the kingdom's business."

Erik sat looking at the food, hungry and stubborn, listening to her babble on about customs and prohibitive rules.

"Please, Master. Remove your veil and eat," she was obviously not above pressuring. "You appear to be a person with a good appetite. According to the custom of this country, you should satisfy yourself without speaking. I will not cease to entreat you until you do me the favor of enjoying the food."

Keeping his face hidden behind the *niqab* he lifted a few bites to his lips.

Though she was consumed with curiosity and wanted to question this queer behavior (in this age even women went unveiled within their own apartments), she decided to keep her tongue before the mysterious infidel.

"Leave me in peace," he mumbled. The food was excellent and he wanted to eat it. Without complaint the pair left. When he was done, Fatima took away the dishes and Heerad brought water and a towel that he might wash his hands. As soon as he dried them, she presented a tray of dessert, which consisted of a variety of artfully arranged grapes, peaches, apples, and pears. The entirety surrounded by several kinds of sweet honeyed cakes encrusted with dried almonds.

"May I bring in our present?" she asked.

Erik nodded. He watched suspiciously as she exited this main chamber through an arch leading into an area that later proved to be the kitchen. His eyes grew large with astonished alarm as she returned holding a spitting cat. No, not a cat, a baby black leopard, a panther, contained by a collar of gold affixed to a chain she held in her hand.

"This is Reza," she yanked on his collar, "and he doesn't know manners...yet." She walked to a corner of the room and hooked the chain into an iron ring affixed to the wall. The cat pawed at her and continued to spit. With her patience exhausted, she gave the young leopard several cuffs to the crown of his head. When he quieted, she lovingly coddled him in her lap. At this point, the panther seemed an amiable companion to his charming keeper. "He has been fed. He desires now to be walked. When he comes to know you, he will be most loyal."

Erik swallowed hard. "Where does he sleep?"

"On a pallet I unroll here."

"And you?"

"Heerad and I each have a small compartment off the scullery." Stroking the cat's flank, she pointed toward the archway.

"What do you know of the ruler who has become my benefactor?"

"Good. The Shah you shall entertain has twenty children from eight wives, plus four other wives with whom he has no children. Seven children have died in infancy."

"The children are where?"

"The younger ones are kept under guard in a smaller palace north of this residence."

"I saw dozens of guards today. No doubt they patrol these grounds and are at all the gates?"

"The Shah has a multitude of loyal subjects and some ignominious enemies. There are those who would rob him of his wealth and power. Be careful not to leave the palace with anything that does not belong to you within your pockets. Would you like to know more? I am well-versed in a variety of subjects, including our folklores."

"On the way to these rooms I tasted the bullying of three young Persians."

Fatima looked grave. Beneath her transparent veil she chewed on her lower lip. Glancing toward Heerad, Erik saw the man nod to Fatima in affirmation. He touched two fingers to his shoulder, then sent his hand straight out from his chest. An expression of alarm crested the girl's eyebrows together, and she paused a moment before continuing. "The Shah's second son provokes disharmony," she continued in earnest. "His idea of sport is ridicule. He is never reprimanded, leaving all of us who serve here open to his offenses. Brace yourself for an onslaught of derision if his eyes have already sought you out."

Keenly aware that their duties marked them as a part of his household, Erik responded to her with deep concern. "I am only a guest, a paid entertainer, but I pledge that I will not fail to defend you and Heerad in return for your faithful service. I know a few tricks." He clicked his fingers and a flame appeared above the nail of his extended index finger. His hand opened and in one swift motion the flame turned into two pieces of sesame candy wrapped in thin parchment resting in his palm. He gestured toward Heerad, who smiled openly and stepping forward took the sweets. Like a generous child, he offered one to Fatima.

Her eyes widened to compliment the slave as she accepted. "We have need of a good magician among us. But let me caution you not to brag that you will defend us. Here the very walls have ears and there are few lower in standing than servants and slaves."

Erik could almost palpate her level of paranoia. "People capable of violence?"

She nodded.

The Daroga appeared in the front doorway. Fatima stood and bowed. "A word, Sir." She went to stand before the policeman and whispered softly.

Erik stayed seated, watching, his eyes two cold amber suns. Listening patiently, the Daroga fingered the buttons on the front of a more casual, tan colored tunic. When she finished, the Daroga came in and sat on the sofa beside Erik. Fatima poured a cup of tea for their first guest.

"How are you getting on?" He dismissed the servants with a wave of his hand. "Go eat."

"How unhappy can I be in a country where I am afforded the luxury of wearing pajamas, playing chess, and watching polo players ride the most intelligent magnificent horses?"

"And this very day you shall see the ancient Mongolian game of polo, refined and perfected centuries ago by the Persians. Just as I promised."

Lowering his voice, the Daroga leaned closer and switched from Farsi to French. "These servants will come to accept, even respect, your odd appearance. Word has not reached these two, but the order went out rather quickly that you are to remain veiled. No doubt the rumor mongers will suggest that I dared to bring the very personification of evil into the palace." Khalil observed Erik's motionless state; no reaction could be read in the eyes of gold. "Oh, most will honor the Shah's decree, despite the temptation to inspect you for themselves. Of that you may be certain. Fatima will no doubt become infatuated with the ongoing perplexity of your hidden face. Resolve yourself to the possibility that she will attempt to undermine your camouflage. Never mistake any state of attachment for acceptance. She is as superstitious as the rest, and if she manages to see the deformity will interpret it as a curse from the jinn. So take great precautions to avoid being alone with her and remember that Heerad is here to guard Fatima as well as you."

Erik didn't need to ask what harm could befall a servant girl inside a palace. He'd seen enough in the gypsy camps and European carnivals. Men often behaved like pigs, letting their baser need to copulate rule their heads. "I'm glad superstitious fear of me is already spreading," Erik sounded almost jovial at the opportunity to speak in his mother tongue. "We can use that to our advantage. You have my solemn word; I will not act upon any temptation a Muslim woman sets before me. Even pretty Fatima cannot break a spirit that cannot be broken."

"Take special care when you wash and attend to yourself. She will try to peek. These girls are terribly romantic, easily given to sentimental crazes. Let her only guess at your true countenance. As for the rest in the palace, they may well decide you are cursed without ever viewing you," he added grimly. "To my knowledge, only the Shah and I have seen your face." The Daroga raised his voice to a more audible level and reverted to Farsi. "Bring the Royal Inquiline the Shah's gift, Heerad."

From the kitchen's arch, the man appeared with the helmet of gold the Shah had ordered. As he handed the object to Erik, the Chief of the Secret Police proclaimed, "No one possesses the merits and mystery that we find in you. For locating you and bringing you here, I am now hailed as the most industrious officer in the Shah's service. This country and its people will help define your heart, Erik. Always leave this apartment wearing this helmet, for the Shah has decreed it so." Icy skepticism tinged his tone as he lowered his voice. "All must exist in balance here, and when that balance is broken, it is usually forced to equilibrate very swiftly."

Erik lowered the helmet over the *hijab*. Apparently, his head was in the process of gathering more uncomfortable layers, beneath which he could roast.

The Daroga waved Heerad from the room. Once they were alone, he continued again in French. "Trust me. I know the Shah's most praise worthy attributes and his most duplicitous cruelties. Despite the honesty and industriousness of my entire family, the greater whole is subject to extreme poverty, and I am compelled to work for my cousin – this peacock on a throne." The Daroga's voice took on a degree of greater confidentiality. "My apartment is not too far away, closer to the royal family, of course. I will show you how to get to it. Tomorrow I resume my former duties, but you must always feel free to take a place at my table." His voice deepened to a hollow whisper. "These ruffians you encountered will no doubt challenge you. If they do, you must consent to a match…be discreet or your life may be forfeit. They like to engineer confrontations. It is merely a matter of sport with them, and in my absence their need for it has intensified." He wiped a profuse amount of sweat from his forehead with a handkerchief. "Have you dined enough, my friend? We should go."

"Where?"

"In this palace are a multitude of passageways, above and below ground. I will show you their interiors as rapidly as possible. Whenever feasible, familiarize yourself with their routes and particular attributes. Unfortunately, even before we attend the polo games there is someone you must meet…with the greatest expedition! We shall seek guidance from a knowledgeable source.

"Not to fear, Indra's blessings may well save your scrawny hide if you have already made an enemy of Prince Khusrowshah Mohomet. He's grown into quite a thorn. The Shah no longer favors his mother. She's a bitter turnip whose vision ceased when a thick opacity took her eyes."

"Cataracts?" supplied Erik.

"Yes, that's the word. Despite her blindness, she coddles her son, continually praising his beauty and insisting he stay a noticeable presence within his father's court."

ﬅ indful of the newly acquired clumsiness embracing his head, Erik followed the Daroga. He felt obligated to go wherever Khalil directed, but would have preferred to visit the metal smiths and make adjustments to the helmet. Ignoring his discomfort, he trailed the Persian to a distant corner of the palace; past the kitchens, into the great storehouse of food and supplies consumed in the rooms occupied by the monarchy and their servants. They stopped at a hatch-like trapdoor lying level with the floor. Taking note that no obvious lock or trick undid the entrance, Erik wondered what the Daroga pressed to release the catch. Pausing to light a torch, they peered into the hole. The light revealed a winding flight of stone steps descending deep into the earth. Erik hesitated, his instincts fearing to venture where two sides of stone left no way to flee but up or down.

"Come, my boy," urged Khalil. "Let us meet the Magus Rakesh Mizoram. He's descended from an ancient hereditary class of priests. In times long past, up to this very day, they know no borders. Among those of his order, he is deemed one of the wisest."

Freeing himself of the garish helmet, Erik reluctantly entered. He snaked a hand along the walls, appreciating the stone and counting the number of stairs they tread. Despite the fact they were underground, a chill moved through the air, blowing out their torch.

"Oh, for the sake of sanity, relight the thing…quickly." The Daroga dreaded slipping. A fall could be disastrous.

"No need," Erik's sharp eyes were adjusting. "The dark is our companion. Place your hand on my shoulder and I'll guide us down. The passage seems to curve to our left."

In a minute the dim glow of a fire, the flames not yet visible, appeared on the stones at the base of the stairs. The flickering illumination revealed the lower walls were covered in Mongolian Cyrillic writing and ancient Coptic glyphs. They descended a total of seventy steps into the earth before entering a sparsely furnished chamber. Here, in one of the oldest levels of the buildings, an obscene body odor mingled with tobacco smoke and saturated with the sweet smell of opiate filled the air.

Before the meager blaze of a central fire pit sat a thin nearly naked fellow, bony ribs jutted from beneath the dark brown skin of his chest. Sooty-faced with a short scraggly beard set upon his chin, he sucked on a hookah. His head was bald directly on top. What remained of his straight gray hair was oiled and drawn back, flat at the temples, into a shiny tail that fell along his spine. He favored a sleek greyhound whose crown had been shaved. On the floor beside his hip sat a worn turban with a large central emerald fastened in the yardage of twisted cloth. Not a hint of expression could be viewed on the peaceful face. His eyes were closed as if he rested.

On the wall directly behind the ascetic male was an image painted in bright fluorescent pigments and gilt. The mural depicted a Hindu deity: a barefoot man with four distinct arms and a jeweled pointed hat who rode atop a lavishly draped white pachyderm.

"That is Indra, Vedic god of all the heavens," whispered the Daroga. "Though pragmatics often usurp his role, within the pantheon of religion, Indra's cult still has something of value to offer."

The emaciated little man sitting before the fire yanked the hookah's mouthpiece from his lips and issued a gruff curse at the bowl of stew set before him. "Wretched bowl of eggplant ragout! May the cook who made you and the servant who brought you drown at the bottom of the sea! This is absolutely outrageous," he complained. "I am obliged to eat manure, Khalil." He reached into a bowl of shelled roasted pistachio nuts and threw a handful into his mouth.

Erik pulled on the Daroga's sleeve, his eyes tactfully conveying a quizzical question.

Chuckling, the Daroga responded, "As you observe, our wise old man has a most mercurial temperament. Still he has a great deal of wit and I applaud him for expressing himself with such colorful facility. He is my grandfather and great uncle through marriage to the Shah. Years ago he shunned the pompous court above to live here below ground."

"Why does he encircle his wrists with so many copper bracelets?"

"He's always worn those things, he says..."

"Don't stay so far away from me!" Interrupted the old man, studying the pair standing at the base of the stairs. "There is nothing wrong with my hearing. The bracelets encircling my wrists are full of cosmic energy. Like the phoenix, consumed in the fire of its own immolation, I shall rise from this pit, reborn to a higher level of glorious understanding. From there, I shall continue a perpetual cycle of renewal." The scrawny mystic garrulously stretched his arms high above his head. "Rakesh – Ruler of the Day of the New Moon. As you can plainly see, grandson, I rule over nothing but this pit of charcoal cinders that smolders before me. I am a knot on a log of wood, a wart stationed on the leg of a frog, a tolerated inconvenience to the kitchen staff."

Stepping forward the Daroga bowed and touched his forehead, lips, and chest with the tips of his fingers. Sweeping his arms to encompass the chamber, "You rule a mighty pit indeed! Your influence travels into the ears of the Commander of the Faithful and from there touches all. Forgive my distance. I did not wish to interrupt your meditations and waited to declare myself. May I introduce..."

"Oh, sit down and shut your minted rice hole. Since when have you ever feared to interrupt me? The meal I'm served is rubbish; garbage not fit for the goats...and do not speak the name of your companion. It is a horrid name. It isn't even his real name. It's something he borrowed and assumed. Sit! The both of you!"

Erik and the Daroga situated themselves on short wooden benches to either side of the fire pit while the cantankerous man continued spewing reproaches. "Say nothing for the moment. The pair of you can never keep silent enough. Listen and you will learn. The servants who tend me brought news of your arrival. Their unwashed feet couldn't scurry here fast enough – and the omniscient jinn surrounding me have yet to stop yammering about this young magician. Erik is it? Morose name, no joy whatsoever, but important...yes...very important. Though you can't see it from here, you will affect the ages, not to mention what you will do in the brief two years that you are here among us!" The Daroga opened his mouth. "Shush!" The Magus smacked a finger over his lips. "Our guest is wondering how I know he filched his name, since he never told a soul."

Reaching into a pouch, Rakesh threw some dust upon the sad flames failing in the pit below him. The fire billowed upward. When it settled, the fuel burned more brightly with the unmistakable fragrance of sandalwood. "The spirits enjoy praises and lovely smells. They told me the source of your pseudonym. Hand me something of yours, Erik. I'm really going to have to call you something else, something more appropriate, for you are an honored son in the House of the Dead." He shot a finger toward an alcove where a tall six-foot statue of Anubis stood. The walls to either side of the figure were covered from floor to ceiling with diamond shaped cubby holes filled with tubular scrolls stacked one atop the other.

Impressive, thought Erik as he removed his glove and passed it to the Daroga, who in turn handed it to his grandfather. For a minute, the Magus fingered the item, sighed heavily then passed it back.

"The ignorance of fools plagues me, as well. We have that in common, you and I. You may call me Rakesh, Rakesh Mizoram, for it was the name my indelicate mother fancied for me. Had she been more kind, I might have been dubbed Rakesh the Intimidating or Rakesh the Pervasive. Instead she named me for the province where I was conceived. She was raised in opulence, and opulence teaches nothing. Great wealth is to be shunned; few know how to employ it. I see you removed the golden helmet. A praiseworthy action while in my presence."

The implication that he required a more significant name irritated an emotional sore spot within Erik, so he broke the command for silence. "A clever person seeks a wise teacher who will bestow understanding."

Rakesh's sharp brown eyes fixed Erik with a penetrating stare. "Yes. Thank you for that tedious bit of rambling. Accurate and elegant though it may be," replied the Magus, "it leaves the underlying issues unaddressed. Verbiage rolls off the tongue like urine squirted from infants. Sometimes it spurts, sometimes in comes accompanied by long wailing screams."

For some odd reason, Erik did not feel chided. Instead, he warned himself not to converse through backhanded compliments.

"Smoke?" A gnarly hand offered the mouthpiece to the newly hired magician. Erik raised the palm of his hand in polite refusal.

"I see you value knowledge more than ease. A hunger to learn burns within you like an inferno. You already know the exact number of scrolls on that wall and are itching to read them, and I will let you. I intend to open your mind." The Magus set the mouthpiece aside. "You want to ask why. Not for the jinn I do commit. It's because we were both neglected...almost from the moment we drew our first sticky breaths. Me because I lacked physical strength and beauty. My mother told me I was born a listless hairy monkey. You suffered a similar disgrace, less the fur. We learned to handle abuse and rejection with attitudes that protect us from harm, and in doing so, we saw that there was more to life than the need for human comfort. The hunger to know, to understand, to set emotion aside and comprehend truth runs like a swift current that refuses to let us rest. It is how we are...the intelligent and forsaken. So alike."

"Time spent with one's own thoughts is not a crime," Erik spoke defensively.

"Crucial to your peace of mind, yes? But you are not generous with those thoughts, are you? On the contrary, you are selfish to the point of becoming a walnut! Virtually all time granted to you is for yourself. Spent here," he tapped his temple with a finger smeared with stew, "inside your head. Let's be honest. You have changed your geographic location, given up what little semblance of a family you had among the gypsies, and traveled far in a quest for understanding and an increase in knowledge. The common folk should get out of the way, because Erik is prancing in on his mighty steed. To be pointed and correct, that is perfectly acceptable because I have been waiting for you...to do my part in illuminating your journey. Go about your business in the world above this hole and keep what I teach you to yourself. Tell no one the secrets I show you. The price for sharing what has so faithfully been kept obscure from the common eye will be forfeiture of my head, and my neck is not ready to part with it."

"You have my faithful promise."

"And I know I can rely upon that pledge, you have never broken your word. You are very special. You let all factors exist outside of you. You react only when there is a need to do so. The ultimate truth is that you don't care for others, rocks must fall from heaven before you allow yourself to feel. These unique qualities, along with the joylessness you take from life, will help you immensely in your work. By your very nature you are capable of dealing violence. These traits protect and serve you in dozens of ways, especially since you suffer from no small amount of deformity and are constantly on guard to defend yourself from society. And make no mistake, as the Daroga has explained, the Shah wants you to operate outside the rules of our elitist laws. It is my design to keep both your feet stable. Consider **me** part of your payment. My nephew does not fully comprehend the prize before him. I do!

"Oh, don't straighten your back in a huff. How you look on the outside is nothing to me. I've already seen your countenance." From his pouch he gathered another sprinkling of dust and threw it onto the fire. The flames leapt up. The curling smoke took on the shape of a pointy eared, beak nosed monster – a jinn. "Assume the face," ordered the mystic.

To Erik's horror a gray gaseous face with a battered upper-right quadrant, no right eyebrow, and a missing roof to its right nostril floated above the flames.

"You see, how dear you are to them? The jinn absolutely love you and the jinn are important. For Good to exist and expound upon itself, it needs to define evil, hence the naughty jinn. Reflect deeply and meditate on all I teach you. The art of battle and the skills of subtle retaliation develop with practice. Knowing your enemy, possessing intimate knowledge of his habits is vital. You'll need an array of tricks to confound the persons opposing you. Recognizing the potential attack in every situation, planning for its inevitable execution can save your life. After my lessons you will never again feel helpless, angry, afraid, or even excited – unless you choose to be clothed in such foolishness. Never let any foe know the depth of you. Let those in the palace think you a puppet to be used. In a short time the Shah will send for you, he makes preparations even now. You will constantly be told what to do, you'll miss sleep performing the regent's assignments, but then you are accustomed to that. You've burned the candle at both its ends all your life."

Erik stirred uneasily on his bench. "Let the assignments unfold as they will. Khalil offered me a chance to study firsthand the Persian culture."

"And experience what it means to render retribution. Under the guise of amusing entertainer you shall settle accounts. You are to act as a dealer of death – a tool. Untainted by politics, you have no allegiance except to the Shah. You actually disdain pompous administrators...because you know that people do exactly as they want regardless of the law's dictates! Their only desire is to avoid getting caught. To the Shah you are a clean specimen, made loyal now only to him. His errands will leave you pressured for time, his expectations difficult to meet," Rakesh predicted knowingly. "It will be important to step back, carve out a space for yourself and find, not a degree of joy, but a quantum of tranquility. I will teach you how to control muscle tightness, headaches, backaches, pain of any sort. It is good that you never overeat and drink only a scant amount of alcohol. Had you accepted the hooka's charms, I would have slapped your hand. Smoking opium will dull your senses. Never touch the pipe!"

From a tiny box, Rakesh Mizoram took just a pinch of dust. "Lift your veil and breathe deeply of what comes your way. I am about to bless you with Indra's Kiss."

Erik did as he was directed. When his deformed nose and partially paralyzed lips were exposed, the Magus blew the powder on him. The student opened his mouth and inhaled.

"Fear is a fundamental facet of all men, developed in childhood and expounded on in one way or another." The Magus took a poker and stirred the coals. "To choose between good and evil is **not** the ultimate choice that defines us. No, the ultimate choice is made at the moment we fear the most, when we decide between living and surrendering to death. Fear cripples the will to live. When we embrace terror we pay the cost of pain...the answer is to banish fear and survive. Did you hear me? Choose life despite death's solicitous greeting, but play upon the fear that dwells within your enemy. Learn the context of what he dreads. Old traditions are honored here in this wayward court. We Persians are a mix of warriors and pretentious intellectuals practicing the ways illuminated by our ancestors." He paused to study Erik's reaction to Indra's Kiss. "You're wondering if I'm a prophet? No. But I am given to divinely inspired revelations. A magician not unlike yourself, but with a peculiar twist."

Rakesh pointed toward the Daroga and the ignored policeman finally entered the conversation. Setting his own pace, Khalil rejoined the instruction. "The Magus is wise in the secret sciences, considered proficient in many dark arts...tutored by masters and intuitive in his own merit. You may say the same thing about yourself as you absorb your lessons. The regent who rules above this cavern is supposed to possess absolute power, as did those before him. His ministers bask in the luxury he provides and have forgotten how to constrain their behaviors to protect the greater good. Our coffers are insidiously plundered. The chests of the treasury, filled on the backs of the Persian people, are slowly being robbed. While outside these walls an effort to distract the Shah and everyone else is perpetrated. Lawlessness festers in the countryside. A diversion meant to center all eyes on an insurrection that will ultimately dethrone the one sent by Allah to rule us. Historic places are razed to the ground. The royal sepulchers desecrated by the instigators. Even the steles and stone obelisks placed in testament to our laws are not immune. At night they are hacked with chisels. The way to kill a serpent is to cut off its head, erase its presence in a manner that brings about as few deaths as possible. You will be the cutting edge of the knife, Erik. The unsuspected blade."

"Know this, young student," Rakesh Mizoram took back the instruction. "Should we need to smuggle you quickly from this country it can be done. Over the centuries a secret society has grown round the world. Disguised as religion it is almost anti-religion. Men placed in strategic houses of worship, supposedly to minister to the populace but truthfully to provide refuge to members of their society. In this fraternity, there are those fastened to the ground and those navigating the seas, a clandestine group of land-locked mendicants and a corresponding arm of roaming sailors. Both provide resource and sustenance to the whole. The very word magic comes from the fire-worshipping priests of Persia, the Magi, who attended Xerxes and Darius. They birthed a profound religious order – that of magician. The very utterance of the word thrills man, reinforcing his expectation that he can exert control over the divine."

Erik's body jerked, his bent legs angled to the right as one of his long arms swatted at the air beside his right thigh. "A rat, a rat is attacking me!"

"No, there is no rat," chuckled the Daroga calmly. "Look again. You are under the effects of Indra's Kiss, a hallucinogenic poison. We have shown you your true enemy – the rat who walks on tiny-clawed feet, whose teeth can gnaw disease into your flesh, the vilifier. Let the path the rat takes guide you so you may know where to strike."

From a box resting beside him, the emaciated seer took a parchment covered with mystical signs. "This is Persian script, calligraphy called *Nasta-ligh*, a lighter and more elegant form of *Taligh*. These scrolls, passed among us for thousands of years, carry blessing and reward in their words. Written patiently with a piece of reed trimmed into a pen called *qualam* and carbon ink (*davat*), they speak of protection from dangers and evils. Take it. I will teach you how to read it so you may memorize its lines. Speaking its words at the right moment may prove invaluable."

From another box he produced a phosphorescent globe the size of a grapefruit, a chafing dish, various flammable chemicals, and a copper vessel. From beneath his turban, appeared an arthame, a traditional knife for crafting a spell. "Ahura Mazda, the one uncreated Source – unsoiled by the evil desires of men – blesses you. The sacred art of yoga and meditation will be taught to you. They will lead you deep into your body where the intense energetic fires burn."

Erik felt inexplicably open to these spoken concepts. "I want to learn defense and attack – archery, trickery, science – anything that will help keep my skin. I feel unsafe. I can sense the icy stares of others, even at my back."

"Ignore their eyes. Become the master of the secrets of your quest. Not because you are noble or valiant will the truths be revealed to you. Seek particulars and shun distractions. They produce nothing of merit. Let me be blunt. You are a gifted trickster, but we both know that illusions are only believed by minds open to receiving the deceptions. Revealing the method ruins the observer's susceptibility. Therefore, guard your secrets, unless disclosing them will increase terror. Know that magic is not the answer to the worth of your life's mission. The way lies in the quality of your voice. To be candid, your lonely singing marks the door."

Dazed, Erik made no reply. In the gypsy camps he'd seen the effect of his voice. It could sustain a thrall – suspend the minds of men and women alike. Up until this point he'd considered it only a useful talent, not a faculty indicating higher purpose.

An agitated Rakesh Mizoram rapidly waved the arthame through the air. Interfering with the mystical fog blinding his newly acquired apprentice.

Erik straightened, seeing distinctly what had never occurred to him. Survival was everything, not acceptance, to exist and learn paramount. Rakesh added a tantalizing spice, something to savor. Obviously warming to these ideas, the imperfect Erik sat stunned. "Take me into your confidence."

"Stay supple and strong," Rakesh's eyes brightened. "A resilient struggler will always come back for more. Remember that trauma clarifies a man's beliefs. In the moment of sharp injury no one re-defines faith. They simply rely upon already ingrained tenets. Move in secret through the crisis you create for others. We will teach you to be the sword unleashed. The persona will cloak the truer, more insecure self and give you the peace of privacy you crave."

Erik's imperfect lips smiled for the first time since he'd met the Daroga. "When can we discuss this further?"

"First, a quick lesson in how to bend the Shah's approval. Then, Khalil, you must escort our brother to the regent, the Shah has already summoned him. Bring him back to me after the audience, and this time, curse the cooks as you pass through the kitchens."

In a private audience chamber, Erik prostrated himself before the Shah.

"Rise, Magician."

Coming to his knees, Erik exclaimed, "Oh Commander of the Faithful, may Allah pour upon your majesty all the blessings this life offers. After many long and happy years may you be received into paradise, and may Allah see fit to cast your enemies into the flames of Hell!"

The salutation greatly pleased the Shah, "I see the evidence of Rakesh's instructions. He rants in my cellars. Many think him a deranged ascetic, but they respect him. In reality, what is the core of all the known faiths? Only that they wrestle to contain the arbitrary and impulsive nature of men, while bestowing the hope they will someday witness proof of the divine Entity. Rakesh is a powerful Magus who may one day cause a miraculous event. Please take a seat. Pour yourself some wine. We are quite alone."

Erik had been forewarned he would be tested. "With your Majesty's permission, his servant will refrain."

The Shah pressed the issue, shifting the topic of inebriation onto a more intellectual vein. "A man who restrains himself from wine is simultaneously wise and foolish, for he deprives himself of the pleasurable mood that might be experienced once the cup's contents are drained."

"It is also said that an overly merry disposition is contrived and therefore dishonest. Prudence dictates that I conduct myself with more foresight than is usually practiced by people my age."

The Shah folded his hands in his lap. "Praiseworthy decision, but both our proverbs are true, both given to guide us on life's paths. In general, young adults pay little heed to either maxim, freely giving themselves to intemperance and thoughtless ways."

"How may I be of service, Majesty?"

"Nothing of what I say to you now is to be repeated to anyone but the Daroga and Rakesh. They alone bear my total confidence. As the Daroga learned of your talents, he sent encrypted messages on ahead to me. Because of your youth and thin stature, no one expects you to be a killer. People see what they want to see. You are new to us, still unaccustomed to our ways. They will expect you to busy yourself adjusting to our society and preparing to perform. What other young man can see in the pitch black to slice the throat of another, then stand over his kill without so much as flinching as an odious pool of blood spreads toward his feet? You've passed every test with flying colors – dispatched the Bedouins with vigor. Though it was your choice, Khalil faithfully reported the incident and praised you.

"The Royal Treasurer is my sister's husband and I do not wish her disgraced. She would lose all she possesses, her station, and her houses. My treasurer carries money away from this palace. Unauthorized, he robs me blind. The Grand Viziers governing my provinces send tribute, and this ingrate plunders their taxes like a leech! Greed and egotistical insurgence are my constant enemies. In the streets and squares, the places of public assemblies, my spies have watched him and his porters come and go. No doubt they are laden with pouches and boxes filled with coin. I have other ministers who perform their duties with great exactness, and this lout dares to betray me." The Shah paused and studied the newly arrived visitor. "The helmet suits you well and will protect you in the palace. You appear as a golden-headed raven. No doubt you will soar with your wings spread wide."

Erik's uncomfortable head remained motionless. "Thank you for your generosity, I feel I have yet to deserve it."

"Unfortunately, the act of murdering is accompanied by a discomforting degree of danger. You are a man familiar with illusion, and my uncle – embedded in the earth of his own choosing – will show you many more. I have not uncovered who else assists in the treachery, but there must be others.

"Scouting can be done efficiently if one is disguised and not given to fanfare. If anyone attempts to bribe you, report the circumstance immediately. One of my predecessors made it a custom to go on occasional walks. He visited various sections of the city, each time choosing a different route. You must learn the customs and apparel of these people. Dress yourself as a newly arrived merchant, or a strong and sturdy messenger sent on an errand from Baghdad. Remain composed in the face of any complaints made against you as a stranger. Xenophobia is a stalking lion. Should you ever be detained, no mischief will befall you. As my assassin you enjoy my protection."

Grateful not to have to bargain for impunity, Erik thought to ask for it in writing. Before he could frame the request the Shah rendered the sought after insurance.

"This evening you will receive a scroll bearing the words of a binding royal decree protecting you while operating in my service. Written in tiny letters at the top of the parchment will be the phrase: In the name of Allah the most merciful. This is a formally established expression. Any official reading the scroll will understand that I require the most implicit obedience to its dictates. At the bottom will be affixed my royal seal. Keep this document hidden on your person at all times."

"What honor I may obtain will be in the performance of whatever service your Majesty deems necessary."

"The faithful completion of my dictates will be generously rewarded, your recompense substantial. Spend some part of each day in preparation for your first magic show to be delivered four weeks from today. Have the Royal Treasurer dead before the next new moon. I expect my command to be punctually executed. The Daroga will supply you with anything you require."

"Thank you for allowing me the honor of acting as your executioner."

"No doubt we will both benefit. My eldest son, Prince Fazel Soroush, is greatly vexed with the treasurer's transgressions, but I have assured him I will soon have the thieving under control. With less and less money entrusted to his care, the treasurer has had fewer opportunities to steal, but it must end entirely. His death is not enough. I want him to suffer."

"What does he fear?"

"He allows himself whimsical diversions. Fables amuse and delight him; in the evenings he favors wine. As in any culture, we have our own strange folklore complete with a set of idiosyncratic creatures. According to the Qur'an, only King David's son Solomon was endowed with control over the world of the jinn – the Daroga assures me that through Rakesh you will be conversant with them. Secrets. Yes, there are always secrets. Whatever your abilities, it will help you to know that my spies have learned this wretched thief fears the jinn and the Roc."

"A legendary predator," asserted Erik. "A solitary bird of white, brown, and gray feathers. A creature of enormous size that swoops down and lifts whole sheep within its talons, flies the quarry to the highest mountain cliffs, and there devours the flesh undisturbed."

The Shah smiled. "Go now, do my bidding. You have the picture."

℮ lemental sea sponges offer no resistance to the effects of changing currents. They yield and thrive by allowing essential nutriments to swirl through them. In the absence of predators, this passivity permits them to grow in vast undetected tubular colonies. Like the budding sea sponges, Erik moved around the palace allowing information to flow to him, absorbing all that was presented.

To the court's elite the foreigner seemed laconic and austere. He entered a room in an undemonstrative fashion, remaining reserved, no scent of perfume exuding from his skin. In an eerie way, he always left a room as if he'd never been there – even pausing to turn the cushion upon which he sat. From the folds of his robes he produced flowers and candies. Seemingly manufactured from thin air, these pleasantries appeared miraculously in his hands and were distributed to his recipients by way of passing them to the slaves. Card tricks, intricate riddles, and wooden puzzles that no one could solve came easily to the new magician. Within the pretext of entertainer, he learned all he could about the physical structure of the palace and the character of its occupants.

The time of Ramadan was particularly enlightening. He was told that over those holy days the observant populace fasted during the daylight hours. That at least once in every Muslim's lifetime, they went on a pilgrimage to the hallowed grounds of Mecca; and that at all times charitable contributions to feed and clothe the poor, rules of ritual purity, and rigorous hours of prayer were reverently observed.

To amuse themselves within the codes of stringent Islamic law, the haughty royals watched polo matches and arranged fights. They hired jesters, jugglers, comedians, and storytellers. A performance known as *Ruhowzi* was especially popular. A board was placed over one of the pools of water commonly found in any of the dozens of gardens. Acting on the impromptu stage, hired players engaged in comedic skits and outlandish songs. The most popularly requested theme contrasted a poor rural existence against the life of those privileged by birth to live within the palace. The common people built homes of baked clay, wore robes of coarse simple fabrics, occupied themselves with trades, and the providential whims of Fate. Precious water was rationed by royal officials and provided to the taxed populace for personal and agricultural use by a series of canals with gated dams. The satirical impersonations of the *Ruhowzi* depicted the locals going about their daily business, forced to cope with the unfortunate deprivations of their lives. The royal spectators often participated in the skits by shouting derisions, interjecting loud directives, and exchanging verbal banter with the performers.

Erik regarded these shows with profound interest, marveling that the servants were never uneasy at these arrogant displays. He was amazed at how they labored in the palace with serious, but not unpleasant faces – striving only to please. Everything about their conservative body movements indicated that those attending to the royals functioned with nothing but respect. They merely blended into the environment in as inconspicuous a manner as possible. So profound was their effort to remain unnoticed that dialogue with the domestics was non-existent. Erik simply had no idea who possessed a tongue and who didn't.

The Persians were as equally perplexed by the magician. Since he never laughed, and his eyes were all that could be seen of him, no one knew if he was of an amiable nature. Despite their strange emotionless yellow color, Fatima found something very human in her master's gaze. The fact that inside his apartment he was rarely spontaneous with salutations or candid speech did nothing to dissuade her. Every morning she sat outside his door, waiting for him to rise and complete his toiletries. His appearance brought an anxious half-dozen questions from her lips. Would he return for the mid-day meal? Did he require any special equipment brought to him? Could she plan on preparing an evening's repast? She had arranged for musicians to amuse him, would that be acceptable?

For a time Erik bore her interrogations with the greatest forbearance, but having a woman constantly inching into his ears like a persistent flea brought the ultimate impatient response. He often simply grunted. On one occasion he opted to further define boundaries by speaking his thoughts in a fair non-confrontational tone. "Fatima, I wish you to prize tranquility. Model the other servants working throughout the palace. I shall oblige you to hold your questions in queue – for your first is barely uttered before we jump to the next. The profusion of inquiries generates like rabbits in a hutch. You may ask and I will answer – only one question per meeting. Therefore," he said in a steady tone, "choose the question carefully."

Taken in by the spell of his voice, she did not understand why he couldn't reveal his face or be more generous with his time. She believed her enthusiastic curiosity should flatter him and thought his reticence to respond mere male resistance. She longed to detain him in their quarters, to experience this strange influence he exerted over her for one more minute, and then a further minute after that. Bright and intelligent, she decided to revert to statements. Pointing to his feet, she observed, "I see your boots are polished to the highest sheen. Being pleased with our efforts, you may consider returning to your apartment for your meals today."

Remaining mute, he merely shrugged his shoulders and headed for the door.

Addressing his back, she declared, "We have not concluded your household's business."

Wishing to avoid ill manners, he let go of the latch and turned to face her.

The black-clad, unapproachable, tower of masculine aloofness did not intimidate her. Locked into the contemplative scrutinization of the Sphinx, she started reciting an itemized list of requested supplies.

When she paused to breathe, he inserted, "I have no occasion to be rude to you, Fatima." (She nearly swooned at the euphonic sound of her name.) "But I have no great knowledge of our particular needs."

"I will familiarize you," her hands rolled into stubborn fists and her foot went to tapping.

"Not today. Purchase all that you mentioned and nothing more than what is required. Certainly there is plenty of money in the chest."

"There is," she toned down the impertinence she recognized within her own voice. "But please don't expect me to read your mind. I do not have the capabilities you demonstrate to the nobles. I cannot guess that I have your permission if you keep your wishes private. Tell me what you are thinking about these days that has you so absorbed."

Raising his shoulders in disgust, his hands lifted to express exasperation. "No," he answered testily, and with that he left to take his first meal elsewhere.

If his days were spent in random performances and the seemingly innocent absorption of palace life, his nights were full of carefully executed surveillance. The necessary task of observing the Royal Treasurer proved an interesting obligation. The roofs were dotted with bell-shaped cupolas; spaces that afforded him a view of rooms decorated with stone carvings, lavish furnishings, and painstakingly engineered parquet floors. Since the royals were forced (just like everyone else) to contend with sweltering heat, water shortages, and at times strong winds, they devised ingenious methods to help them cope. Buildings had high walls and arched roofs. Clever wind-catching towers called *badgirs* fed random air currents down ducts to refresh rooms and stir the spaces above underground reservoirs of water, cooling the latter and preventing the foul of stagnation.

On his second official tour, the Daroga brought their Frenchman to a heavy copper and iron-gate, one grown green with age and the weathering wrought by time. Beyond this formidable entrance lay the quarters of the royal administrators. A single guard protected this area of residence. Placed safely within the confines of the palace, this sentry served more as a gate-opener than a protector. Erik saw that scaling the walls from an unseen area off to the side could be easily accomplished, given the use of a rope and a steel grappling hook. Provided, of course, that the guard was distracted long enough for Erik to fling the hook for its spikes to catch accurately. Since no portion of the palace was inaccessible to the Chief of the Secret Police, Khalil was permitted unquestioned admittance. Inside the gate a beautifully tended courtyard punctuated by a multitude of sandalwood and cedar doors greeted them. High walls and the now familiar levels of apartments surrounded this area.

That night and for several nights following, Erik climbed a series of rooftops overgrown with vines, and stationed himself at a vantage point where he could observe the treasurer's rooms and any windows facing the courtyard. From the apex of the structure opposite the money keeper's apartment, he lay flat on his abdomen and studied his assignment's nighttime habits.

Once in position, there was very little to fear, for the guard at the gate sat at a table, occupied with rolling dice and solitary games of *pachisi*. Without a cause to investigate, the watchman rarely entered the courtyard proper. Preferring his own amusements to the inspection of surreptitious lovers meeting in shrubs and bushes. Still, Erik was always cautious regarding the guard's possible approach. Shrouded in shadows, dressed in black, his still form was difficult to perceive. He waited, observing, looking for patterns and a way to inject himself within the money-keeper's quarters. The answer occurred as the evenings wore on. The days were hot and uncomfortable; it took hours for the rooms within to cool. As soon as the sun sank below the horizon, shutters were opened and heavy drapes pushed back and tied in place to allow for the passage of air. The *arras* were closed again only when an evening's festivities in the courtyard below became too noisy.

Small parties on the patios spawned other activities. In some places the buildings jutted out into the courtyard's private gardens, creating achromatic areas of thick foliage. In these cooler spots unsanctioned lovers sought the forbidden touch and the feel of bodies pressed together. Erik watched with amused interest. All the encounters were so passionate and so brief. Nothing of any prolonged fulfillment occurred in the vegetation, but the diversions were most welcomed for the treasurer proved to be a very boring man. Eventually closing his mind to all else but the instructions of the Magus and the undertaking set before him, it took but a few nights to learn all he needed to know. In the evenings, the official sat reclining on a chaise lounge, slowly drinking alcohol he procured from a cabinet in his room. Coffers of gold coins lined the walls. After assuring himself he drank alone, he lifted their lids to enjoy the glittering show of monies and ponder how best to abscond with portions of the Shah's vast storerooms of treasure. He rarely called for anything and retired nightly to his bed in an inebriated haze.

With dawning enthusiasm, Erik saw his method of approach. Protected by the Shah's decree, he suppressed his mirth and calling upon his growing ability to remain calm above all else, jumped lightly to his feet. He knew he possessed the capacity to murder. Existing inside him was a large bitter crater. The throngs of people who shunned him, once they'd viewed his face, deliberately dug its vast emptiness. From the vacuous core of that emotionless graveyard he reached out and killed – as one would crunch a roach. He never sought rejection, but it always, predictably and without fail, occurred. The wide-eyed terror, the disdain, the upturned noses as parents pulled their children away from the shows inside the gypsy camp. Somehow the Shah had masked his contempt, but Erik felt he knew the truth. The ruler had been forewarned in the messages sent by the Daroga from their traveling cohort, and the Shah had responded:

Bring the magician onward.

He'd been hired to serve a purpose – that was the extent of Erik's acceptance. What did he care, as long as he was paid?

During the long hours of the following day he walked through the palace entertaining members of the court with tricks involving slight of hand. He knew full well that late in the darkened hours of evening he would become again the ruthless assassin. That afternoon the Daroga presented him with an Arabian dagger crafted of the finest steel – the hilt bore the carving of a winged rampant lion, its claws bared. The weapon balanced perfectly in his hand.

"Luck for tonight's kill," Khalil confided and Erik reassured him luck would not come into play.

At ten o'clock that night the moderately stooped, heavily whiskered figure of the treasurer left his habitual seat on some fanciful errand. In a few minutes he re-entered with a new goblet and pitcher. Before reaching his chaise, he drank, made a disgusted face and bellowed, "What in the tenth level of Hell is this foul brew?"

With his soft slippered foot he slammed the door against further intrusion from the servants and meandered over to his usual seat. Slumping heavily, he sunk his corpulent body deep into the cushions. Javed Pesar Maraghen-Almani refilled his cup nearly to the brim and set the pitcher aside. Erik counted the number of swallows. He passed the time watching the drops of tallow drip off a candle onto a small brass table near the treasurer's right arm. Settled like a large disgruntled tick, the marked man rested the cup of wine on his protruding abdomen. Still Erik waited. When Javed's heavy eyelids closed against the indulgent effects of the alcohol, the assassin stood. With the gardens below empty of occupants, he took up a bow and carefully aimed a steel arrow attached to a rope. Letting the shaft fly downward toward the upper frame of the treasurer's window, he watched the rope follow. The arrow, tipped with steel barbs like those on a male cat's penis, embedded itself in the wood with a deep defining twang. Working quickly, he drew the rope taut and tied the coiled end lying at his feet securely to the frame of a nearby bell-shaped cupola. Testing the strength of his device, he walked to the edge of the roof and attached a pulley with a two-sided wooden handle to the rope. Kicking off from the building he flew. Knees bent to appear ball-like, he crossed the courtyard toward the treasurer's opened window.

Slightly aroused by the landing of the arrow and more recent sound of the pulley moving closer, Javed cupped his hand to his ear. Dazed with drink, he speculated as to the low pitch of the whirring sound. He'd been lax, off his guard, never suspecting that someone on a roof would bother to watch a trusted servant of their monarch.

"Thief – thief – thief," came a whispered chant on the night's scant breeze. "The Roc comes."

Too late, Javed realized how vulnerable he was in his comfortable spot. He struggled to stand on wobbly feet. He thought to flee. *Why can't I stay up?* Appalled, he saw a dark feathered creature bound in over the windowsill.

Stumbling a few feet into the room (the device worked better than he'd calculated), Erik straightened and turning quickly, closed the drape.

A mythical figure now stood with cool detachment in front of the seated treasurer. The costumed Roc viewed with repugnance the glassy look of panic in the eyes of his rotund quarry. Before the thief could plead for mercy, Erik charged, dagger drawn in an attempt to affect a straight-on attack. *One deep thrust into the man's heart.* He so underestimated his victim's strength.

Javed swatted the oncoming arm aside like a mosquito, forcing the blade to miss its mark…but not before the razor sharp edge, held in the hand of so agile an assailant, neatly sliced open three inches of his upper arm. Javed and the Roc both looked in disbelief at the bleeding wound. Furious, the treasurer tried kicking his attacker away.

Erik deftly jumped to the side. Stomping a foot in impatience, the half-man half-bird jerked forward, playfully faking another lunge. Javed reacted by gasping and rearing back. The strange fowl grabbed both thick ankles and in one swift yank, Javed slipped off the couch, bouncing hard onto his rump. A strong odd smell of blood and alcohol began to permeate the air. Locking his right fist, Erik punched the man nearly senseless. He'd designed a straightforward kill and was amazed that even trembling, the treasurer had managed to make the initial thrust just a glancing blow. In an effort to further disorient Javed and gain an advantageous superior position, Erik hauled the money keeper a full seven feet across the floor. The treasurer went obligingly down onto his back, but managed to surprise him yet again.

Unable to repel the assailant, Javed clutched the leg of the small table, dragging it along with them and sending the still burning candle to the floor. The table's legs made a harsh grating squeal as they scratched the marble. Letting go of the ankles, Erik kicked the table into the air, caught it with his hand and soundlessly tossed it onto the bed, where it could cause no further mischief. "Unfaithful larcenist. There is only one way this will end!"

"Why this punishment?" the tick's gullet waddled with folds of fat.

"Retribution. Your own greed has ensnared you."

Javed's eyes widened with comprehension. In a flash of rising courage his mouth fell open to scream for help.

Taking hold of his victim's oleaginous neck, Erik applied exacting pressure on the larynx with his thumbs, choking off the shrill scream before it gained a second note. With his lungs crying for air, Javed clenched his hands around his adversary's wrists and thrashed, trying to wrest himself free. Beneath his palms Erik felt the man's carotid pulse racing. He tightened his grip, obliterating the sensation, knowing that the heart was now pounding ever so painfully within the obese chest.

Without a moment's hesitation, he released his throttlehold on the offensive oily flesh and stuck the knife deep into the gullet.

Permanently and effectively silenced, Javed grew more terrorized and disoriented as a second area spurted blood. Erik let his prey's sticky fingers clutch at his feathered clothes. The treasurer's fists came away full of turkey plumes. Confused that he could pluck a Roc so easily and unable to speak with blood gurgling from the stab wound, the fat clammy digits opened mid-air, releasing most of the captured feathers around his own head. Erik withdrew Khalil's gift and held the dagger's tip before Javed's bulbous nose. Frantically, the man rolled his head side to side to evade the menacing knife.

Erik didn't want to hack and slash away at his target, but it seemed there would be no choice in the matter. He thought of Indra's Kiss. Too late to employ it's debilitating effects, using the drug would have to wait for another day, another opportunity. Alarmed at the amount of time it was taking to commit this murder, he hissed, "Pardon, have to run and check the chicks." He smirked, realizing he was undergoing a metamorphosis, becoming a murderer with a sense of humor.

He pulled off his head coverings. Full of horror and confusion, stunned by Erik's furious eyes and deformed features, Javed at last knew himself defeated. Surrendering, he laid still on the swirling patterns of the yellow and white floor. A widening pool of clotting blood haloed his neck and cranium. Erik's right arm rose in a poetic cascade of freed feathers, and he neatly sliced the man's left carotid. Arterial blood spurted in a six-foot arc onto the walls, spraying a design of red lines and drops that trailed to the floor in rivulets.

Erik stood and stepping back, coldly watched the blob of flesh as it finished pumping blood. The face went lax, Javed faded into unconsciousness, and his wasted life slipped into death.

No weaklings here! Erik tried to swallow, but his mouth was too dry. He sensed his own heartbeat slow alarmingly. Beneath his outfit there was not a drop of sweat on him. The blood within his veins had turned to ice, even in this incessant penetrating heat. Looking down, he saw that his front was covered in crimson. He reached for the official signet ring. Swollen, the fat finger it encircled refused to give it up. Sighing, Erik sliced the digit off, pocketing the trophy. Walking to one of the cabinets, he thought to communicate that the murder fit the crime. *The very notion that you are in the Shah's debt and owe him loyal service never occurred to you. How could you not guess yourself at risk?* Tossing three gold coins into the air, he caught them all in his left hand, then returning to the corpse shoved them in the treasurer's mouth.

After that bit of pleasantry and without further ado, Erik vaulted to the window. Exiting unseen was the next order of business. His only thoughts were to avoid being hunted and trapped after the discovery of the attack. Holding the rope with his left hand, he cut it free of the arrow and with a rocking motion, pried the slender missile out of the wood. Careful to avoid the nasty barbs, he angled the arrow through his sash. Taking hold of the rope, he swung like a monkey out across the courtyard. Landing about three quarters of the way to the opposite building, his feet lightly touched ground. He ran the last few steps, scaled the wall to the roof, pulled up the rope, stuffed his feathered suit and equipment into a bag, and left.

Once inside, he darted from hallway to hallway. Watching for guards, he believed he'd succeeded in not calling attention to himself. Exhausted, he entered his apartment and flopped onto the sofa, grateful to have made his escape. Gathering a pillow to his face, he screamed into the cushion.

From a darkened corner the Daroga stepped forward, "Control your wailing. You were successful?"

Erik breathed heavily, in and out; the hot air entered his lungs as searing blasts. "Yes! I left him laying in his own thick blood."

"You are covered in quite a bit of it yourself. You were able to use the route you planned?"

Erik nodded and returned his face to the blood-smeared pillow. The Daroga signaled for Heerad to go quickly to the corridor and clean up any drops left on the marble floors. "Look for stray feathers that might lead anyone here."

From the safety of the cushion, Erik moaned, "My first official assignment didn't go well. The man would not die. He was flabby but tough – much stronger than he looked."

The Daroga stood in stony silence. What should have been a rather tame affair – dull except for the dramatic entrance – had, in point of fact, turned into a deluge of blood. "He's dead. He steals no more, and superstitious fools will blame a mythical bird. I am proud of you."

With a growing cold detachment, Erik produced the finger with the signet ring.

8 *NOT INSANE, HAUNTED*

𝕷eaving the past and navigating the way back into present-day was treacherous. Was he on the divan in Persia or his bed at the estate? For this awakening he could not tell. Within the horror of his initial perceptions, he had no sense of time or control over his muscles. Like a ship without an anchor, he drifted where the mind and current directed. Filled with the grotesque images of this botched kill, he conceded to several truths. Somewhere deep inside his psyche, he was a fuming volcano of rage. He knew for certain he could be an assassin; the act was in his blood. Cunning and ruthless, taking a life was like blowing out a flame. Yet there was no satisfaction, no sense of pride in an accomplishment. He needed, most definitely, to become a more efficient killer. For the moment, he lacked the strength to deal with the prickly amputated finger. The thought of it disgusted him. Did it wiggle within his pocket? The trauma of that disturbing image gave Erik the impetus to return to consciousness.

He lay there mute, his eyes closed, feeling a headache start to surface. From the distance, he listened to Isidore's concerned voice.

"*Que fait-il?*" asked Isidore.

Thayer leaned over the bed, studying his patient. "I think he's screaming, silently screaming. His vital signs indicate he's coming around."

Erik was not aware that his mouth lay open and rigid. He felt someone's fingers press his jaw upward, closing his lips.

"Look how his blood pressure and pulse have quickened to within normal ranges," continued Thayer. "He may be fully conscious soon. His state appears almost post-ichtal. Care to re-define the scope of my services?" His tone was devoid of humor. "These spells may be true catatonic episodes. For certain it is not sleep where the muscles are relaxed and there is lack of postural control. He held his arm straight up for an hour. The fingers were like icicles. We were the ones who lowered it to his side to prevent a compromised circulation."

"You will deliver him from these seizures and preserve his sanity."

"This boy needs hospitalization for tests. We should call for an ambulance to transport him. I'll supervise his care. If he's suffering intermittent catatonia the malady could be secondary to a number of very serious mental or physical disorders. Lack of proper treatment could result in his death, Isidore!"

"Whatever you require for him will be done **here**." Upset, he lifted the cane and emphatically drove the tip back down to the floor. "I have a complete laboratory and modern radiological facility below. Erik will not be admitted to any public hospital. I will not hear of it!"

Thayer looked at his colleague in astonishment. "Excuse me? You, of all people, are demonstrating a confounding degree of ignorance. Has the boy ever had repetitive episodes in one day? I cannot impress strongly enough the dire needs of this condition. We are presented with a genuine dilemma. How am I to tell if we are dealing with a somatic or psychic malady? Substance intoxication, depression, schizophrenia, bipolar disorder, autoimmune reaction, neurological lesion, encephalitis...or any combination thereof could be coming into play. His brain function was altered during the episodes. You saw the EEG. He needs to be interviewed in depth and observed for lack of eye contact, violent mood swings, and altered motor activity. At some point he could enter into stupor and never return to you. Think, Isidore!

"You witnessed the *cerea flexibilitas* (waxy flexibility) for yourself. We could have put his arms, or his legs for that matter, into any position we chose and who knows how long he would have remained posed. Sitting in that chair, behind that mask, can you diagnose true catalepsy? How can you deny the boy intervention? Catatonics have been known to hold poses for hours, totally ignorant of external stimuli. There's also the ominous danger of dehydration, electrolyte imbalance, malnourishment. If these episodes continue to accelerate, he may require a feeding tube and quiet isolation. Without therapeutic support and the correct environment, his brain could decelerate from sheer exhaustion."

"If this is catatonia, what treatment do you recommend we initiate immediately?" Isidore planned to stubbornly uphold his dictates.

"If you insist on gambling with the boy's mental faculties, I must press the argument that without a valid diagnosis antipsychotics would be out of the question. They might even worsen the disorder. Benzodiazipines are the traditionally preferred first-line treatment. Rarely do we employ barbiturates, and some patients have responded quickly to electroconvulsive therapy. We could try a test dose of lorazepam or zolpidem. There might be a response within thirty minutes."

"Promising, Thayer, but not good enough."

"No drugs," Erik, gathering a rudimentary control over speech, croaked the words like a muffled frog. Verbal expression was a tad difficult since his mouth felt like he'd been eating sand from the Maranjab.

Thayer and Isidore looked back at him with a start.

"My boy," exclaimed the Count. Grabbing Erik's hand, he stroked it fondly.

"Water...and get this IV out of my arm! How long have I been gone?"

"Eight hours," responded Thayer. "I'm told this is the longest seizure to date. It's alarming you had recurrent episodes in so short a time frame. The condition is undergoing a profound exacerbation and the etiology remains unknown."

"May I please have some water?" All the details of his first royal assassination were there, incorporated into memory, readily available for review. Petrifying. He'd stabbed someone to death and cut off the victim's digit just to get at a signet ring. *What prompted me to hide my face in the pillow? Why do I fear showing emotion? What terrible revelation will follow if I remove the veil and they all see my face?* He looked down, amazed not to find himself covered in blood and feathers. The contrast between that non-electric Persian world and this bedroom where modern computers and digital readouts sat waiting with instantaneous information was disarming. Across the room, directly in line with his feet, he saw the shadows move like liquid.

How can I adequately explain the situation to Delaquois when I barely understand it myself? Talk to me! For the present, he felt too de-energized to press the issue with the entity standing across the room. Returning to 2012 was getting harder and harder. *Don't worry – they can't see you.*

John placed a glass of ice water in his hand.

"We need to call an ambulance and move him," stressed Thayer.

Erik downed the entire glass. "No ambulance! I'm not leaving this house." He managed to assert his opinion decisively, despite his lingering confusion and the dawning migraine.

Isidore smirked. "You see, Thayer. There is no need to argue. Erik agrees. No hospital. Diagnosis and treatment will be conducted down in the lab."

"Help me sit up." John took Erik's right arm and leaning him forward, propped him on several pillows. Without being asked, his bodyguard automatically passed him the hand mirror. Erik stared at his face for a moment, rubbed his right cheek with his fingertips, then in disgust handed the glass back.

"You look like a handsome angel," commented Thayer. "Why are you so concerned about your face? What is all this puzzlement over a hand mirror?"

"What about my face looks angelic?"

"You saw the reflection. Even rumpled your features are striking."

Erik pressed his lips together, furrowing his brow. He looked to be in deep consternation. He tried to still his thoughts, to quiet his inner-self and paint some peaceful picture in his mind, but the vision of the defiled and bloodied treasurer was too intense, too vivid. He felt he could reach out and trail his fingers through the blood, touch the feathers lying all about the floor.

Intuitively, Thayer asked, "What did you see while you were unresponsive?"

Dazed, Erik fought the tightness in his throat and the banging drum inside his skull. This was like being on a different planet. Only here everyone still spoke French and he understood too much for this part to be a dream. He had the strange conviction that he wasn't human – that he didn't belong anywhere. He looked at the wall of masks. *As long as I have my masks I can pretend I'm whole.* He saw the visions as if he were living them, and over time they were becoming clearer. So far, he lacked the courage to look in a mirror during one of the episodes. Every ounce of his being dreaded whatever truth he would behold.

Uncomfortable and reluctant to be analyzed, especially by an outsider, he countered, "Why should I confide in you, Dr. Delaquois?"

"Really Erik, you must allow someone to help you. Your condition borders on crisis."

He wants your trust. Trust in yourself and in all the forms our psyche manifests. The words were sent from an unnoticed pool of shadow sailing around the farthest end of the room.

Erik wanted to send the pool a vulgar hand gesture, but didn't. "In my visions there is a man who isn't brave enough to look into a mirror. With the initial rise of every sun, his thoughts proclaim one continuous clear message: He cannot afford to be seen. I am inside that man. We move around together, but his thoughts are not my thoughts. They are his own."

Thayer responded sympathetically, "Classic detachment. Despite the alarming clarity his insights provide, you are wise enough to know that you're not one melded being. I cannot advise strongly enough that you disassociate from this gloomy person. He is hallucination, a figment born of disturbed synapses in your brain."

"He is real." Erik sounded lost to the fact. "You doubt because you don't understand what's happening. I need answers, not speculations, not platitudes." He turned sarcastic. "We might as well call for the prayers of a religious guru and let him sprinkle holy water all about. A shaman might get closer to the truth than you two. Isidore is ready to poke me with needles and dyes. While his cohort abides the medical abduction of my person, provided he can supervise and control every aspect of the kidnapping. Marital vows might soon be in order, gentlemen."

"Hush!" Thayer blurted the word before he could arrest its utterance. He considered Erik's caustic implication a defensive ploy to set aside problematic issues.

Delaquois' body movements told Erik he'd really hit a nerve.

"Monsieur De Chagny," Thayer was on the defensive. "Your father tells me that from childhood, you've always had a trenchant appreciation of cryptic humor. This is not the time to employ it. I find you charming, intense, and moody...with your long black hair hanging down to your shoulders you seem artistic and studious. I would wager that you tend to think rather deeply about subjects, perhaps too deeply. You are a very promising and very disturbed young man."

"I'm not insane and not hallucinating. Let's be clear about several points. I know what's real and what is not. There are no bogeymen standing behind the drapes over there. During these episodes I am living, really living, on another plane. In that world I function within the life of a monster and he exists." He lightly taped his temple. "He is very lonely and capable of great viciousness. He constantly tries to hide those embarrassing truths from the people around him."

"Vicious in what way?" Thayer cut in.

Erik skirted the question. "He's paranoid. Thinks people will shun him if they see his face. So he treads lightly, like a spider covered in layers of cloth, a mask, and a helmet with chain mail. He'd like to lash out and destroy the world, one degenerate component at a time. If you honestly think you can make one microscopic dent of a difference in that man's hold over me, you are mistaken and egotistical. In some ways, and don't ask me to define them, we are very good together. *Corruptio optimi pessima* – the corruption of what's best is the worst of all."

Isidore produced a painful little moan.

Thayer turned to him, his fingers opening in expressive inquiry. Receiving no response, he focused his attentions back to their patient. "Your eclectic repertoire of words doesn't dissuade me. There are positive aspects to the situation. Your father's laboratory offers privacy. I've been told you take very little alcohol and then only with meals. You don't smoke. You eat healthy. You have a multitude of hobbies and activites that give you pleasure. You're obviously intelligent and enjoy reading. Wouldn't you like us to end these frightful episodes?"

"You have no idea," Erik seemed trully distressed.

"Then let's not barter pessimistically for degrees of cooperation. Let's start by accepting that there are things in life that **can** be changed. Nothing lasts forever, not even stone."

Erik despised his arrogance. "You want me to remember that over time the engravings on solitary headstones fade?"

Thayer remained proactive. "If at the end of my treatment you don't feel healthier and happier, I'll put an apology in writing and your father doesn't have to pay me a *sou*." Knowing that some teenager's preoccupied their thoughts with death, he added, "By the way, the solitude of walking through cemeteries (ancient and new) actually rejuvenates me. I understand your skepticism. Make me your partner, and I'll help you find the answers. Good health and peace of mind are precious." Thayer sighed. This client posed real challenges. "In my experience the hardest patients to care for are those who believe they cannot be assisted. Just being a teenager and standing on the border of adulthood is tremendously stressful."

"Do you know why I'm so closely guarded?" Erik sat dispirited. "Because I am currently the only hope for the de Chagny lineage. I'm Isidore's greatest asset."

Thayer reached into his pocket and withdrew a small plastic bottle of tablets. "Let me offer you some encouragement. Your father loves you. These are tranquilizers, very mild. I take them myself. They will not dispel your troubled thoughts, but may help you relax as they occur."

"What are they?" Isidore interrupted anxiously.

"Valbien."

"Ah!" Isidore leaned back in his chair, nodding. His hand caressed the ceramic pot of an exotic Pitcher plant. By modifying their shape the leaves trapped insects and digested them by means of a liquid they secreted. He'd had this one brought up from the lab just last week.

Erik looked questioningly toward the undiscovered place occupied by the eidolon. (His decrepit father caught the betraying glance and vigorously gestured for him to accept the tablet.) Erik took the white pill and pretending to swallow, cheeked the sedative. "I'm reticent to divulge some aspects. There are events that happen during these episodes… almost inexplicable events. It's as if my life were two or three stories woven together. Each is trying to tell me where I've been – who I am. Warning me about where I'm headed. Some scenes are tightly clustered." He studied Thayer's face and read the expected cynicism. "I'm not a nihilist. These are not hormonally stimulated visions emerging from an overactive post pubescent imagination."

Grasping the furtive offer, Thayer responded, "Is there an aura, a specific group of symptoms preceding a vision? Something that alerts you it's about to commence? These sensations might be important indicators that could help guide us. Identifying the aura would warn you to sit in a chair or lay down – for safety's sake."

Erik frowned. He had no idea how he felt before they started, only that he wanted to claw his way to the edge of the pit before the rising whirlwind sucked him in completely. "If I brought an object back would you believe me? Not a mark or a scar on my body, but something you could actually touch?"

"If you came back with marks on your flesh they'd be psychosomatic."

"My prestigious doctor shouldn't be so cynical. I've never been to Persia, but perhaps you're considering that I learned Farsi in secret. No chemical imbalance or tumor playing havoc in my head prompted me to learn the subject." He went to pass his hand through his hair and felt again the sticky electrodes. He yanked them off in groups, flinging them to the side. "Let's consider...just for the sake of argument, that these are graphic past-life experiences, events that for all their confusion really happened."

Isidore coughed uncomfortably and withdrew a handkerchief from his pocket. Embarrassed, he realized he'd have to lift the mask to wipe his mouth.

Erik recognized the predicament and might have laughed had it been a lighter moment. "I move and interact in these climatic dioramas of horror, aware that what I see is real and has tangible meaning. I've tested the thought that these might be dreams I can control. Nothing works. I'll be at a table and mentally order myself to choose a different food than the one I'm reaching for...let's say it's a piece of chicken and my hand was headed for the curried lamb. Invariably my hand stays its original course. I am powerless to stop it and change events. The bite of curried lamb comes with irrevocable exactness into my mouth."

"Your hand brings the lamb regardless of what your mind directs?"

Erik's head nodded slowly. "As if the scene were pre-prescribed. I see and feel everything and can change nothing. I am being instructed that life is a messy disordered affair." He gazed into Isidore's sad blue eyes. "Since my earliest youth I've been taught the opposite. Nature is the queen of organization, and given the necessary requirements, life proceeds most orderly. Death follows birth, the big fish eat the little fish, everything fits." His fingers interlaced tightly, then opened to form a symbolic emptiness. "The knowledge that an abyss of chaos is one breath away brings me no satisfaction, no sense of surety." The corners of his mouth turned down in a poignant frown. "I find it revolting."

Thayer looked distressed. "You want events to make sense. It's very rare that perceptions in a dream-state would evolve in proper sequence. Things are real enough to the mind's eye, but jumbled and out of chronological order. Skipping around is the standard."

Frustrated, Erik centered on Thayer. "Doctor, within each sequel things move forward in a linear fashion. In that other-world I am me, but different, what happens around me makes sense. It's what I'm capable of doing and my motivations that confuse me. I am the equivalent of a covert..." he struggled to say the word outloud, "assassin...some physically hideous monster that takes satisfaction in draining the life from a target. The timetable of the segments being presented skips around. I can accept that…today I was in Persia. At other times it's the later half of the nineteenth century. Last week my two selves were in the back hallways of an elaborate theater. I seem to know a great deal about the place. For that matter, I'm also learning some very interesting things about this chateau. This house hides a multitude of secrets."

"So the jumbled order of episodes is disconcerting, but you're all right with that. You're upset about your talented inclination to murder. How do you come back to us?"

"I haven't unraveled that yet. I'll have to think about it. Each time seems different. Sometimes I just can't take any more."

Intrigued, Thayer leaned forward. "So you don't think you're imagining, you believe you're reliving."

"A few minutes ago I was inside a Persian palace. Since I know why I'm there and what year it is, and I go around acting as if I've actually traveled by horse in a small caravan to get there, I'm banking that the events have really occurred. Do you want latitude and longitude? I can give them to you. There are no cars, no electricity, but the minutest details are discernable. I believe I was an exile, or a fugitive. I fear what's happening, but pretend an amazing degree of over-confidence. I am knowledgeable in areas I've never explored in this lifetime."

"What do you mean?"

"Hand me something to write on."

Paper and pen were placed in Erik's hands. He wrote furiously for a minute. While he did, the lights dimmed as if power drained from the chateau's solar generated electrical supply. A visible nondescript glowing crossed Erik's face. For a brief moment his features shone of their own accord and the smell of ozone hit the air. Handing the pad to his newly acquired physician, he closed his eyes and the phenomenon ended.

Channeling? Even as he broached the thought, Thayer discredited the idea. Instead of analyzing, he found his mind wandering, wistfully musing. *Look how he bears the benign expression of a contemplative angel. If I were an artist, I'd paint his portrait.*

Thayer took the paper and like a robot came to his feet. Instinctively he took a step back. He was an experienced rational man, yet a trickle of dread raced down his spine. Something calamitous brewed in this place. Something ruinous that ate away at the very fabric of joy. "What are these bizarre scribblings? What is all this?"

Erik opened his eyes. The atmosphere in the room corrected itself. "It's beautiful isn't it? I wish I knew who taught it to me. It might be a Magus named Rakesh. It's *Nasta-ligh,* an ancient form of Persian writing. When the visions first started – I really don't know how to say this – I understood they were more than memories. They were messages – difficult to recapture, illusive. In the beginning they were vague, like indistinct adventures boys optimistically hope will grow sharper. Then I taught myself to concentrate on a specific object and let the action unfold around it: a chair, a birdcage, anything that was stationary. As I cooperated, events became clearer. Now more and more of that life is revealed."

"Go on, go on," Thayer said encouragingly, tapping the pad. "Are you as reclusive in that other life? Shy? Don't embellish, just speak plainly."

"No, not shy, but I am reclusive because my face is somehow drastically deformed. I am ugly almost beyond words. Here." He made a circular motion around the upper right quadrant of his face. "In this area."

Isidore inhaled sharply. Bowing his head a small painful moan escaped his lips again.

"Are you all right, Sir?" John inquired from the sofa.

"Yes. Gas pocket. Please go on Erik."

"As I was saying, sometimes the smallest items in the vision scream the loudest at me." Isidore lifted his artificial chin and shot a glance at Erik to see if he was serious. Erik continued, "It's almost pedantic. I'll focus on some trivial item and the item invites me deeper into that other world. The sugar bowl on your breakfast tray of blintzes made me think of white desert sand, Dr. Delaquois. It was such a tiny small aspect of the dunes, yet the action unfolded from there. I'd just crossed the mountains into Persia. Tired, bone-tired, and thirsty. The place was so arid, the air cried for moisture."

"What else do you remember? What did your mind see?"

Poised and relaxed, Erik again refused to answer the immediate question. "I wish this was just me pretending to be someone else. That other-me is taller and stronger. He secretly wants to be an invincible warrior and a musician of great distinction. He's fiercely protective of his heart, because deep inside, in that private realm that no one ever sees, he's very sensitive." Erik paused and stared off into space. His expression that of someone very aged, an old soul still on a journey. "I'm tired. Do you think I could rest awhile?"

Using his cane Isidore stood on his enfeebled legs. "Shall we have a late dinner together, just the three of us? I'll have Dillard wake you in time for an eight o'clock meal."

"All right. I'll join you downstairs." Erik's eyes studied Thayer; the doctor was watching him with genuine compassion. "So would you still like to remove me from the mansion? Take me out into that conglomerated mass of humanity where they teach each other to be cruel and undercut the next piece of competition that comes down the road? I think I'm in the process of learning that skill from a different source. I'm rational enough to hope I've been made for a different purpose."

Thayer heard a gentle rattling coming from across the room, as if someone vibrated his uvula against the back of his throat. There, once again, was that chilling realization that someone else was present. Some strange intangible force stood close by his patient. No one else seemed affected by the presence. Branding himself as foolish, he addressed Erik. "Whatever path you end up pursuing, you were meant for a singular life, not a perplexing duality. The happy adventures in the decades ahead of you are worth seeking, but to grant you their experiences we must root you securely in the reality of the present. Your father doesn't want your existence marred with confusing seizures, shame, and bouts of depression. He wishes you endless contentment and health, of that I am sure."

Isidore touched Delaquois' arm, "Come, Thayer, we'll let him rest. I'll take you on a tour of another member of our family, the Laboratory. There we do not manufacture death, we explore life." He patted Erik's hand in fatherly consolation, "Don't waste another minute on distress. We'll get to the bottom of things."

9 INTO THE DEVIL'S KITCHEN

Intentions, even well meant, don't guarantee positive results. Fate invariably stacks the odds so that a struggle ensues. Out in the corridor Isidore punched the illuminated elevator button with the tip of his cane while Thayer fidgeted.

Nervously brushing non-existent lint from the front of his jacket, Delaquois was ready to ask if he might inconvenience Isidore by taking the stairs. He could run and meet the car at the appropriate level. He had an aversion to elevators, especially small tight ones with gray metal walls and indirect lighting. Within the constructs of his phobia the devices took on extraordinary dimensions. He considered them yawning caverns with precarious floors set above deep scabrous shafts and felt they should all come with warning signs:

DANGER
SUBJECT TO SUDDEN
NECK SNAPPING JOLTS
ABANDON HOPE

In this case such a sign would have been most helpful.

Waiting for the car, Isidore made small talk. "The laboratory lies beneath the chateau's east side, in a section off the basements I had gutted and excavated. Dug a core three stories deep into the earth, a lovely empty space just crying for a scientific facility. The lab is thoroughly modern in comparison to the rest of the house. You can get to it from any floor by this archaic convenience." He paused to chuckle; some unspoken thought amused him. "We had the second floor entrance to the shaft installed in what used to be a linen closet, and the first floor in a day pantry that abutted the main hallway. When the engineers opened the walls they discovered a passage working its way around the inside of the house. Proved to be an ingenious lover's escape."

"Really," remarked Thayer. The smooth brushed-steel doors slid open. The inner dimensions of the box could easily accommodate a stretcher. *Hopefully, Erik won't resist the procedures I propose. If necessary we could sedate him for transport.*

They stepped inside, Thayer nonchalantly taking hold of a cool metal handrail. Isidore dropped an ingenious padded seat down from the wall – not unlike an old cupboard-hidden ironing board. Apparently someone had considered the weakness of his legs during the ride.

"Another of Erik's inventions." Isidore sat with moderate difficulty; unable to remember when he last slept. *A long harrowing day*, he conceded, punching the bottom button marked C1. He liked to think of himself as impervious, and often overestimated his stamina. This tour was a tedious, but necessary obligation.

"We also discovered a very interesting tunnel off the deepest of the wine cellars. Originally it followed a crack in the bedrock, a natural runoff formed in the last Ice Age when glaciers covered the continent. Shifts in the earth, along with enormous pressure from the ice crystals, created a crevice that eventually widened into a crack. The inevitable melting helped establish a lake on the southeastern side of the chateau. At some point in the past, builders redirected the tunnel's end, pointing it toward the woods instead of the lake. A lover's hatch." He gently rocked his feet, heel to toe, toe to heel. "We also discovered an oubliette. A particularly claustrophobic cell until we invaded it. Some were used as dungeons to squirrel away prisoners, leave them to die of starvation. I believe the original purpose for ours was to store grain. We rebuilt the area of the oubliette into a Panic Room, a hideout in case intruders ever break into the lab. Outfitted it nicely. Shades of Gothic Revival."

"Given your extensive security, it's creepy to think reprobates could get past the front gate!" The ride down, smooth as it was, put Thayer's stomach in a knot.

"A good deal of my laboratory snakes out underground from the cellars, extending well into the eastern meadow. Essentially, it takes up all of what used to be the eastern gardens. We sacrificed the recreational space above, but managed to keep the lab inconspicuous. A huge array of solar panels, affixed to the chateau's east sloping roofs, provide electricity in conjunction with the mansion's ancillary generators. At least they cannot be seen from the front driveway."

The elevator came to an uneventful stop and the doors slid open. For a short distance they traveled a well-lit vaulted corridor, reminiscent of the old wine cellars. Rather quickly they came to a set of impressive metal doors. Before Isidore punched a code into the keypad and submitted to the biometric tests necessary to enter the lab, he paused and looked directly at his guest.

"Follow me closely, Thayer. The quality of genetic work we do here demands that you pay strict attention to the delineated areas where you'll be permitted access. It's a little time-consuming entering you into the biometrically coded alarm system. We'll do it when you're ready. You'll be obliged to submit your ID card, personal code, palm print, and retinal scan for admittance."

Thayer tried to be funny. "Imagine, all this to protect the hereditary basis that defines every creature's life – very impressive since the code is walking around everywhere." His stab at humor was ineffective. Isidore just stared at him without remark. "Don't misunderstand me. You received the Noble for a great body of work. You earned it."

His host turned back to the entry system and completed a set of commands. "This is the only ingress you may use, Thayer."

There were a series of clicks as metal cogs and heavy magnets disengaged. With the hiss and release of pressurized air, dual pneumatic doors receded into side pockets. Stepping over the threshold the doors automatically swooshed shut behind them.

"We're in the initial reception room," Isidore said dryly. They'd entered a comfortable waiting area walled in Brazilian cherry wood and floored with a mottled red blue-veined Chinese marble. Several comfortable couches, upholstered in dyed crimson leather, were set against the walls. The entire setting made reference to the importance of red blood corpuscles – one not too subtle for anyone intuitive enough to make the connection.

The air pressure in the room changed noticeably. "You can always wait in here for someone to join you. You should feel honored. No headhunter from any genetics company trying to court me ever got this far, no matter how determined. I decided, for better or worse, that I could accomplish more on my own."

They opened a side door and entered a locker room where personal clothes were replaced by laboratory outfits: blue polyethylene paper hats with clear plastic facial shields, suits and booties of the same meshed plastic fibers. Thayer was extremely familiar with this concept of cleanliness and took only a few minutes to suit-up in the appropriate gear.

"The entire lab is on a negative air flow system with micron hepa-filters in staged depths. There are clean, ultra-clean, and sterile areas," Isidore explained, "all clearly marked. Exacting computerized sensors scrutinize the divisions. Any inoculating wave of foreign material sets off an alarm."

The next set of pneumatic doors led into the laboratory's initial corridor – a world of polished stainless steel walls and fluorescent lights set behind translucent paneling. A significant contrast existed between the lab's atmosphere and that of the rooms upstairs. This scientific space was a living-breathing organism unto itself. Zen-like in its barrenness, it emitted distinctive sounds, smells, and a perceptible airflow. Parts of it actually hummed and murmured like a child at play.

Apparently this great geneticist walked in two very opposite worlds, and in this underground domain he listened to subdued strains of Bach and Mozart. Thayer's eyes scanned the area, searching for clues, wanting to comprehend the secrets held within this scientific realm of wonder. Several glass-enclosed workrooms were positioned to either side of the hall. Isidore turned to face the dual-paned Plexiglas of the first one on the right. The soft lighting in the room, set to a level of comfort for the eyes, disclosed a number of massive floor-to-ceiling hard drives and several alcoves for filing cabinets. Red, green, and yellow lights flickered in non-rhythmic patterns as information was constantly analyzed, sorted, and stored. A panel on the wall housed climate control sensors, humidity readouts, a seismograph, gas analyzer, and barometric pressure gauges.

In the next room they viewed Nyah's back as she sat at a counter. Her attention fixed, she leaned forward staring into the close-fitting ocular pieces of an electron microscope. Safely tucked beneath a sheer blue-paper cap, her graying brown hair showed the visible outlines of a neat bun. A short woman, she had a rather severe scoliosis of the thoracic spine. Though the back of her padded chair concealed most of it, Thayer knew her entire torso was twisted to the right. The walls directly in front of her were filled with a half dozen white-boards electronically lowered from the ceiling. They were covered in genetic code, little arrows, and side notes. For the moment at least, something very minute had her completely absorbed.

"What is she working on?" asked Thayer.

"A special project of compelling interest to both of us." Isidore shrugged his shoulders. His head and neck evidenced a fine tremor. He was in some degree of pain. "She detests fluorescent lighting. Right now she's concentrating so hard, its disagreeable qualities are lost to her."

She swiveled toward an L shaped appendage of the counter and began to type an observation into a computer. Catching the pair at the window out of the corner of her eye, she rolled her chair to face them. She shook her head 'no'. For all her intense searching the next link had not revealed itself.

Isidore waved goodbye. His tremulous fingers entered a code on a keypad and the slats on a set of louvered blinds, held between the two panes of glass, closed affording her some privacy.

Thayer studied Nyah's solemn expression as she disappeared from sight. "Could she hear us talking?"

"No. Every area is sound proofed from the others. She swears like a storm trooper when she's frustrated. Let's complete the tour. I'll show you one of the rooms where we conduct experiments and separate DNA from the rest of a cell's contents. We use a refined process of polymerase chain reactions. Very powerful and extremely accurate."

"All right."

They moved toward a sterile room containing rows of steel lab benches, shelves of glass beakers and flasks, racks upon racks of clean pipettes, and electronic balances for tiny super-precise weights. Windowed cabinets contained dozens of neatly labeled chemicals and bottles of ultra-pure water. Here, banks of frost-free freezers maintained a constant temperature of −112 degrees Fahrenheit. The freezers stood side-by-side with refrigerators, incubators, autoclaves, thermo-sensitive recyclers, and the most up-to-date DNA sequencers and micron-lasers available. Reputable cellular biologists were fanatics about checking and re-checking their DNA samples to ascertain they were contaminant free. Not a single fleck of extraneous protein could be allowed to exist alongside the fragile genetic strands. Thayer knew about obsessive geneticists and was not surprised that Isidore kept an especially strict environ. Beside every computer keyboard rested a fresh box of disposable gloves. This lab was efficiently designed and well equipped.

"Over there is a restricted greenhouse area where we study a variety of exotic plants," announced Isidore, pointing to a room with muted ultraviolet lamps just across the way.

Thayer peered in and saw a counter of *Symplocarpus foetidus* (skunk cabbage) – a North American plant with a fetid odor – sitting beside a series of gene sequencers. The arm of a digital scanner traveled back and forth over the plants, sending a constant stream of data through a variety of computer run genetic equations. A monitor at the end of the counter displayed the ongoing compilations.

"In spring that plant sends up a cowl-shaped brownish-purple spathe, but there's a Pacific coast variety with a large yellow spathe I find interesting. We're expecting a shipment of it any day now."

"Your interested in non-indigenous vegetation?"

"I'm interested in everything living. Currently Erik's condition has the bulk of my attention. The plant room is a sterile area with restricted admittance. Special suits are donned before entering."

Squinting, Thayer stared deeper into the prohibited space. At the back stood several somber-looking, twelve-foot cylinders. The convex metal doors of these dark green chambers were pulled shut and sealed with biometrical locks. Before Thayer could ask what they held, Isidore tugged gently on his sleeve.

"Over here is my office." Isidore punched in another code, and they passed once again through a set of disengaging pneumatic doors. The predictable hush as they shut was an almost foreboding sound.

The office was one of the strangest rooms yet. Semi-circular in shape, it fanned out before them. On the outer wall, an elongated nearly life-size set of video screens gave a magnificent view of the estate's Ice Age lake and its attendant trees. Despite the absent garden the view was pleasant and soothing. Apparently Isidore's vast wealth allowed for some aesthetics. Still, a vast dichotomy existed between the mansion, its outer natural environment, and this lab.

"That's a real-time high-def digital projection."

In front of the screen sat an S-shaped desk, the entire top of which was highly polished tan agate sliced so thin that a light source from underneath set the entire surface aglow. On a table off to one side rested a flourishing gardener's rectangle of wild California sage. When

Thayer took off his protective cap and mask, the expected dramatic smell invaded him.

"Nyah gave me the first cuttings of those plants. I don't remove them for that very reason. She's more than my chief assistant. She used to be my mistress. At one time her body was very attractive. Our little trysts ended long ago. I'm afraid decay has taken both of us by force, and I blame myself. I chose my own path, believed myself impervious to…" he paused, apparently uncomfortable discussing the etiology of his ailment.

"Nyah's scoliosis came later in life? Is it the result of an accident?"

Isidore nodded.

It seemed obvious to Thayer that the scientist was taking great pains to hide the complete picture. *Just how extraordinary is this mystery*, he wondered. *Smaller than a stove? Larger than a bread box?* An air of gravity was building up between them. Their eyes avoided direct contact.

"A wife is no longer a particularly useful proposition," declared Isidore. "The thought of marriage actually offends me. Don't sit down yet. Let me show you my spa. It's right through this door."

"How incongruous to have a spa in a laboratory office. Where are your other assistants, Isidore? For that matter, where are the servants you employ upstairs? Inside the house I've seen no one but John and Dillard to help you."

"Oh, there are others – be certain on that score. My servants work like the janitorial staff of a bank. They carry out their tasks when the manager is gone for the day…avoiding any immediate area where they might disturb me. And it's not surprising to have a spa in close proximity to an office. I enjoy a hot soak, it helps my bones, benefits the circulation to my joints and muscles. After a relaxing soak I've spent many a night asleep on that couch over there. I am persuaded that time is almost meaningless when one pursues the intriguing path of genetics. It's easy to get overwhelmed…forget to eat…forget the consideration of other needs."

The spa proved to be a room lined in redwood with a cascading waterfall feeding a heated pool of white marble.

"Lovely," offered Thayer. *Money provides amenities.*

"You can take off your paper clothing over there. Please, make yourself comfortable."

Thayer peeled off the protective garments. Unashamed to stand perfectly naked, he breathed in the moist air. The fans controlling the airflow in the office and spa were blessedly different from the negative currents generated in the rest of the facility. He tested the water with his big toe, a perfect 102 degrees, and stepped into the pool. Taking a seat on a contoured stone bench, he stretched his arms over the upper ledge and let the bubbles play at the height of mid-chest.

Isidore grabbed a handrail and leaning heavily on his cane settled onto a wooden bleacher that circled the room. Sighing audibly, he longed to enter the recuperative warmth of the waters, but didn't. He still hadn't removed his mask.

"We need to confer." Thayer was determined to gain whatever insights he needed to protect Erik's health. This was not too bizarre a place to hold a conversation; actually it was rather conducive.

"No one can hear us in here, if you're wondering. I guarantee Erik will prove a most interesting case. Is my boy flirting with insanity?"

"He's socially disengaged, isolated, not always reality-based. You're both exhibiting so many signs of malignant anxiety that I can hardly begin to list them. In extreme cases, high levels of stress can cause loss of brain cells. Just admitting that you're both under tremendous pressures will be half the battle to finding a productive answer. I know you're not telling me everything." *The boy is grappling with something very sinister.* "When are you planning on trusting me?"

Isidore stared at the bubbles rushing through the water. "Don't retreat because I'm reluctant to divulge facts. You can't be faulted for wanting to press forward so urgently. Erik is blameless in all of this."

"Listen, Isidore, without solid test results how much can I resonably detect? He is a lonely boy who spends hours playing around in his own head."

Nodding in agreement, Isidore revealed a little something. "There's almost a lacunae – a blank space or missing segment when he comes out of his 'trips'. For a time he's apathetic toward life in the chateau. An aversion for the outside world intensifies with the episodes."

"It doesn't help to foster this need for isolation from mainstream society." Thayer waited for a response that didn't come. "Let's start by gathering some history shall we? Tell me…" after a sensitive pause he continued, "why the boy doesn't think you're his father?"

"I'm not his biological parent, but I've never told him."

"Then how is he aware of the fact?" Once again only the sound of burbling water filled the room. Thayer sighed heavily. This was like pulling teeth and he was not a dentist. "Who is his father? For that matter, who is his mother? You've remained unmarried. By your own admission, never inclined to take a wife. Yet, here is this young man, bright and obviously talented in a dozen ways. Is he related to you?"

Isidore pointedly refused to answer. "He's a little strange," he conjectured, "but what teenager isn't? He does have an interesting sense of humor."

Thayer didn't push the issue. He'd revisit the point shortly. "Do you know if there's an aura to these spells, or some elemental trigger? Does something precipitate the episodes? This is more than melancholic depression or accentuated anxiety. The stimulus might be as simple as a perfume or the profound unwanted stress of doing something he doesn't want to do. My experience tells me to favor the latter."

Isidore shifted uncomfortably, "I think he's having real visions."

"Like in the Bible? That's a rash assumption. Smacks of parental pride. Damned arrogant in my opinion. You should give me straight forward answers, even if it means your ego ends up a little crushed."

"I need to rest, but I can't. I so wanted to press Erik's hand to my chest before we left his bedside, to kiss it a half dozen times. I desperately need to spend as much time with him as I can during the days that are left to me. With him I have everything and without him – nothing. I'm counting on you. His survival is essential, of great portent."

Extremist sentiment. "Did I not leave everything and come at your first invitation? Let me point out that I have no intention of groveling to accommodate your maudlin parental needs. You've made me the boy's advocate."

"I am grateful. Erik will be a more fascinating patient than I'll ever be." He laughed without emotion, an eerie hollow sound. "*Ca ne fait rien...c'est la vie* (it doesn't matter...that's life), in actuality I fear that nothing will change what's happening to either of us!"

Thayer recognized the cleverly sandwiched hints. "What is all this dramatic secrecy? Who is this boy?"

Isidore slammed the rubberized end of his cane onto the floor, catching the shaft as it bounced upward. "I told you. He is my son!

Nothing will amend that." He was stalling. "Everything else will be revealed in good time. And the more you know, the more determined you will grow...eventually leaving all your reservations behind to suck dry the marrow of our situation. Go. Dart around. Wear yourself out running tests. I await your results with baited breath. I have decided to demand one more thing. During his first sedated procedure, we shall put a GPS locater chip within his derma. I told you he is of great value. He's priceless. Place the chip someplace where he won't be able to cut it out unassisted. That's not a request; I want to know where he is at all times."

Thayer's brain jerked to attention. Despite the water's warmth, his skin crawled with an unnamed dread. The cobra demanded attachment, wanted its fangs set deep within his patient's flesh. A dark anomaly brooded within these walls. Behind his friend's veiled speech, Thayer felt certain that some irrational ego-based sentiment had just reared its ugly head. There were promises gone amuck. Perhaps the tragic events leading up to this point were outlined somewhere in this very innocent looking lab. He summoned his sternest voice, "I've decided to stay. I'll need to call my wife."

Upstairs, a handsome Erik watched as a cloud of black fog shrouded the room. He tried to speak, ordered his lips and tongue to form a cry for assistance, but not a single sound would utter forth. The gloom was all encompassing.

10 ELUSIVE TREASURER

Quivering between what he knew to be real and the brewing aphotic void that beckoned him inward, Erik made a choice. Knowing himself still rational, he surrendered to the murky fabric of the passage. This time he entered the Persian world not as a stranger, but as one who'd seen this palace many times before, yet somehow never seen it at all.

Ruffled but unscathed, he angrily strode the corridor to his personal apartment. In the courtyard adjacent to the armory, Khusrowshah Mohomet and his raw brutish friends had just ambushed him. These small skirmishes between this petty-minded prince and his cronies were becoming all too commonplace. They'd shoved him into a wall and had it not been for the intervention of two guards, would have removed his helmet and veil. Avoiding these rabble-rousers was growing trickier by the day. Apparently they had spies who alerted them whenever the magician exited his quarters. To avoid these confrontations he'd stopped simply strolling the palace. Emerging from his rooms only when scheduled to entertain a party and passing through the halls as discretely as possible. He was learning to move in the wake of a tide of people, relatively invisible. Spending more time within the confines of his domicile had two adverse effects; it aggravated him and greatly pleased Fatima.

Throwing himself onto the divan, he lay on his back, the dorsal surface of a hand resting over the helmet's nose bridge. He'd acquired a multitude of problems. Some of the royal occupants shunned his performances; they considered him too close-mouthed and threatening. Mentally trying to distance his mind, he focused on the sounds around him. He heard the faint pattering of tiny feet scrambling and scratching, mobbing in compact hordes…back and forth, rubbing, chewing. *Rodents inside the walls? They're in some empty space. Large enough for a man? For all practical purposes I need another way out. Can they show me how?*

The sweet smell of patchouli wafted through the veil to his mangled nostrils. He knew instinctively that Fatima stood in the arch leading to the kitchen. Driven by her curiosities, Erik heard her approach ever so softly. Tenuously she leaned over him, testing to see if he slept – unguarded. He didn't need to open his eyes to know how beautiful this female looked in her silken clothes. Designed to attract the eyes of males, the costumes of all the women accentuated the flow of their bodies. How very fortuitous that he was a long way from attraction and an even longer way from wanting to copulate. There were bigger problems to unravel. He sensed her hesitation. *She's weighing the consequences of disobeying the Shah's edict, or perhaps she possesses a healthy fear of me.* Forbidden to touch her, Erik had a few moments to consider his next move. He searched his mind and found no desire to analyze any of these women, he wasn't even curious about their seemingly absent ability to reason. *If they have cogent thoughts, they keep them to themselves.* Just as she was about to lift the edge of the chain mail and peek beneath the veil, he spoke.

"There is a fee of ten French francs a minute for viewing me."

Startled and embarrassed, she straightened. "Where would I acquire the vast sum of ten French francs? I merely wanted to offer you some refreshing orange-flower water." She stood barefoot in a flowing open-cuffed Kashmiri kurta – the pinkish-gold color of sand dunes at sunset. Woven from the most fragile threads, the shimmering veil encompassing her lower face did nothing to hide the determined slant of her mouth. Her almond shaped eyes, framed by the long black hair she'd dyed with the darkest blue indigo tinge, shone out like two inquisitive beacons.

"You wanted to pry like Hajji Baba and stick your nose into a place that should not concern you. How will you explain yourself if I shout for Heerad? Tell me what resourceful bit of wit you would employ to account for such close proximity to an infidel."

"Perhaps I'll extricate myself from dilemma by saying that I only wished to employ the chakra stones to heighten your awareness."

Erik's eyes opened wider. "Chakra stones?" In the palm of her right hand she held a blue iolite cabochon about the size of a half lemon.

"In Eastern philosophy," she offered by way of explanation, "within the body abides seven chakras. Each is a center of spiritual energy. Placing this stone on your forehead would enhance your third all-knowing eye."

His head turned toward the door. "Back away, Fatima. We have no time for stones right now. The Daroga is about to thump his fist on the outside of our door."

A loud pounding proved Erik right. He sat up, planting his booted feet firmly on the floor. Something was amiss. "Hasten to answer," he directed. The Daroga entered, followed by two palace guards – the same two that had intervened in the melee near the armory. *Is there to be an accounting?* Despite his frustration at their appearance, he rose to receive the Daroga's entourage.

"You traverse the palace with an escort and bring guards to frighten my servants?"

Khalil motioned for the pair to wait in the hallway. "I have urgent news, Changeling." The Daroga rather favored this new nickname for the Frenchman. After the incident of the Roc, he'd sent his most trusted men to enter the treasurer's apartment, remove the body, and assess the amount of blood spattered and pooled about the room. They'd left the blood and crimson stained feathers, knowing they would spawn a dozen wild stories.

Fatima re-entered the room bearing a tray with a pot and cups. Bowing deeply, she offered, "Will you have some Chinese jasmine tea, Daroga? I also have orange-flower water prepared." She shot a defiant look at Erik.

"Kindly set it down and leave us. Select a fresh set of clothes for your master."

Dismissed from the room like an errant child, the temperamental Fatima found the Daroga difficult and insensitive to her courtesy. "I so eagerly look forward to attending to the magician's clothes," she scowled.

"Silence," hissed Erik.

The Daroga eyed the girl suspiciously. "There are three types of women in this palace: unmarried royalty, married royalty, and common females who are foolishly unaware how easily their heads might be removed. The wise servant shuns becoming a deleterious example for others, and by her actions shows she respectfully fears reprisals."

On that note, Fatima hurried from the room.

Settling onto a seat, the Daroga drew in a deep breath. "Today trouble is heaped upon us like stones brought to a tomb so that the spirits will not rise and provoke the living. The Shah intends to marry his oldest son, Prince Fazel, to a distant cousin who will arrive shortly from the northern city of Tabriz. He has also proclaimed that my only sister,

Soha Houri, who is barely fourteen, shall wed Prince Khusrowshah. The regent intends to announce these engagements tonight."

"Congratulations, Daroga. Your sister is to be a princess."

"Thank you, but better that you offer consolation. She is not, to put it mildly, enamored in the slightest way with the divisive Khusrowshah. She considers him a savage. Women are dominated in this country. Some are not pleased with the tradition of prescribed matrimony. I think Soha Houri, which means Star Fairy by the way, actually detests the ground her intended walks on. And I have it on good authority that this maligning prince wants between her legs as soon as the wedding can be performed. His proprietary boasting goads me. He's bragging to the court that she will bear him many sons. Our Shah is a man who condones his children at every turn, using the least important reason to avoid providing stricter moral upbringing. Not only that," Khalil's voice rumbled, "the Shah summons us to his private courtyard. You need to change your clothes and freshen yourself."

"Did the execution displease him? Or is it that I compare unfavorably to other magicians?" Erik asked unemotionally.

"On the contrary, you are a surprise a minute."

"Then when the Shah commands me to appear, I will arise, grateful for the opportunity to hasten to him. All is well. I shall personally report my success and receive a generous reward for deportment most becoming a fledgling assassin."

"Don't jump to conclusions." The Daroga swallowed.

"What's wrong? Come, Daroga. Trust me and confide what you know."

"Your confidence sends a giddy rush over me," chided the Daroga half-heatedly. "If I were you I wouldn't gloat over a reward until you receive it. We have a most perplexing predicament, one you need to see for yourself…something more pressing than unwelcomed marriages. If you take anything from this land, Erik, let it be abundant discernment. We have a saying: Be cautious. Never trust, never mock, and never depend upon the Shah. He has extraordinary power and with a single twitch can change his mind and end us both."

Erik poured the Daroga a cup of tea before replying. "In the eloquent words of the ancients: Live simply and erase worry from your mind. Give more of what has been granted to you and expect less in return.

Therein lies the path to happiness. I add to those axioms one of my own: Always have a planned exit and a backup route should the first route be blocked."

"You're learning your lessons well."

Fatima returned to them. Flustered, her brooding eyes revealed that she did not enjoy waiting to be acknowledged. "His clothes are ready."

The Daroga lifted a hand in acknowledgement. "Stay prompt and obedient for it is your place to do so. And you go primp, Erik," he hadn't taken his eyes off Fatima, "...**privately**. I'll wait."

"You should indulge me the use of the chakra stones," Fatima pressed. "He needs blessing."

A singular look of refusal, flashed from cold amber eyes, silenced her. Erik rose to enter the bedroom and change into his finest black-on-black paisley tunic, leggings, and long fringed vest.

On the way to the Shah's private garden they passed two sets of spectacularly carved dual colonnades. Even the drama of palace intrigue could not defuse Erik's enthusiastic admiration. The classic designs of these artisans made a structure gleam like faceted jewels firing off prisms as they basked beneath the sun. At the end of the colonnades, a heavily guarded gate opened onto a vast courtyard. The familiar basically square shape was surrounded by dozens of closed doors made of sandalwood and ebony, fitted with gold. A multitude of magnificent staircases led to upper apartments, which were full of vast treasure and amazing objects sent from around the world to honor the monarch.

Cheerful fountains and dozens of caged birds dotted the courtyard's gardens. The pleasant notes of the warbling fowl intermingled like music with the splashing of water jets that lofted sprays double the height of a man into pools lined with crystal rocks. They walked a path traveling to either side of a parterre whose base and sides were painstakingly enameled with hundreds of brilliant flowers. Softening the air of the garden, beds of roses, jasmine, gardenias, violets, narcissus, hyacinth, anemone, tulips, carnations and tiger lilies were planted in great array to bloom at various times in this wondrous spot. Majestic cedars provided shelter from the hot rays of the sun, and a great number of citrus trees grew in small-contained groves set to embellish secluded areas for relaxation. The branches of the latter were heavy with ripening fruit, the promise of abundance.

Small petulant giggles issuing from the balconies above drew Erik's attention upward. Leaning over the railings, women from the Shah's harem watched the approach of the Daroga and the Royal Inquiline. Their inquiring eyes spoke of a heady level of curiosity and teasing speculation.

The Shah's pavilion rested as a hub in the center of the courtyard with everything in the garden arranged in tasteful symmetry around it. At the corners of the pavilion's base, four enormous silver and copper dragons guarded each of the four directions. Seven blue steps of the purest lapis lazuli raised the dais upward. The latticework walls of the gazebo were solid carved ivory, studded with every color of jewel imaginable. Inside were couches covered with elaborately detailed cushions and a low round table of solid gold made heavier with trays of fruit and sweet breads. Even here in the garden, a seat raised higher than any other afforded a place of prominence for the Shah.

From his regal sofa the contemplative ruler watched them approach. After they prostrated themselves, he bid them rise and take two seats of lesser distinction.

Erik noted ruefully that the wretched Khusrowshah Mohomet sat to his father's left, but on a level lower. Beside her brother sat the henna-decorated little Sultana, seemingly unconcerned that her petty sibling lounged with an air of outright arrogance not too far from their father's feet.

Easily affronted, Khusrowshah's ruinous character projected something quite different from the pleasant demeanor of his diplomatic and accomplished older brother, Fazel. Envy and pride eroded his soul, leaving his character dissolute. Every gesture portrayed a man marred by self-indulgence, privilege, and a lack of restraint. The unavoidable order of birth, having placed Khusrowshah as number two in the line of succession, ate at his insides. To further his degradation, the heir apparent excelled him in all things: archery, mathematics, statesmanship, and on this very day a more prestigious bride.

"You move with remarkable natural ease, Erik – almost like fluid." The Shah proclaimed coolly. "Please take some refreshment. The air in the garden is pleasant this morning." Unfortunately, the jewel-encrusted lattice screened most of the garden's delights from its occupants.

"How does a man of tender years acquaint himself with so much grace?" mocked Khusrowshah. "Speak, Frenchman. We are not so formal here."

"By spending time practicing how to walk, moving lightly from the hips with the back straight, and avoiding stray non-purposeful movements." *You bag of manure*, added Erik mentally. He wondered if the Shah was even aware of the altercation near the armory.

"Disrespectful oaf," Khusrowshah popped a grape into his mouth. "You are no acknowledger of rank. You talk to me as you would a female." *I can see that demonic spirit dwelling in your eyes. He wants to eat into me. Look away!*

"Most unfriendly," interjected the little Sultana, for she prized Erik's amusing magic tricks. "If you scorn our father's malice and are rude to his invited guests you will rise from your cushion reproached and wailing."

Apparently she was aware that her brother was a pretentious insult to the court.

"Silence, ingrate," scolded her brother, snatching a peach from her hand. "Females do not interrupt when men are speaking." They all noticed the pleased expression that crossed the Shah's face. "Your magician likes wearing black, Sire. Rather like a Western funeral director don't you think?" Khusrowshah wanted to be offensive; he wanted to expose the fiend hiding in Erik's eyes. A servant leaned over to pour water and pomegranate juice into goblets. Khusrowshah impatiently waved the white-clad man off the pavilion.

"Here in Persia black is the color of dignity." Heedless of her brother's admonition, the little Sultana addressed the magician directly. "Are there other reasons you prefer the color?"

"Dignity, certainly, and it is the shade that absorbs rather than reflects all spectral light. The color that bears the mark of mystery," asserted Erik. "The semblance of a solemn undertaker appeals to me."

"Ah," replied the Shah, nodding his head knowingly. "I would call for musicians to entertain us, but we have important matters to discuss with the Royal Inquiline."

Khusrowshah glared at Erik, barely concealing his hatred. "Father, who is this foreigner that wears *chador* coverings like a Muslim woman in the public streets? Have you had him checked? Maybe he is a female!" An accelerating wave of mirth, fed by insecurity and deep-seated fear, spread over the scoffing face. "Why doesn't the magician make his clothes invisible? If they disappear we could prove his gender." Despite his father's dictates, he too wanted to peer under Erik's protective headgear.

"Don't turn surly and ruin this meeting," the Shah frowned. His head turned toward Erik. "You have something to communicate, don't you?"

Erik answered in his most mellifluous voice, "The Royal Inquiline is your servant, Lord."

"And mine!" Khusrowshah interjected. The touch of a whine interlaced its way through the arrogance. Erik wanted to get up and smack him.

No, not yours. You are too vile to assist. It is you who should disappear! Erik bowed his head in assent. Silently he vowed that this troublesome excuse for a prince, who constantly challenged and roughed him up, would one day eat his words – *on pieces of poison soaked sponge…one by one.* Turning submissively to the Shah, he murmured, "I have something to present to you."

With an uplift of his head the Shah dismissed his children. "Leave us." They rose reluctantly, but obeyed.

Erik took an empty cushion from his sofa. Placing the signet ring on the pillow, he quickly covered it with a silk flower he produced from his sleeve and offered it to the Shah. He mentioned nothing of having to cut off the treasurer's finger to obtain it.

Taking the ring discretely, the regent studied the signet carefully. "Khusrowshah is not my favorite child and he knows it." He placed the ring within the folds of his garments. "How is the female servant within your quarters and the black slave, Heerad?"

"Industrious. I keep both of them sufficiently occupied."

The Shah motioned for the servants standing in attendance at the foot of the pavilion to back away. When they were out of earshot the Shah lowered his voice. "You did not kill him!"

"I did, Sire." Stunned, Erik's tone was deceptively calm. Inside his viscera rolled.

In a harsh whisper the Shah informed him, "You may not be aware that I have been regent since I was twelve. The smallest of facts concerning my reign are written down that those who follow may approve and wish glory to my name. I have accounted for every lesson any noble teacher imparted to me, every childhood game that amused my quiet hours, all my court decisions, and any piece of tribute laid at my feet. Even the night the heir apparent was conceived is known. I want the world to recognize me as a distinguished competent ruler. How will that description fit if I cannot bring to an end those who steal from me? What chicanery is this ring? Are you a thief as well as a braggart?"

The Daroga visibly stiffened and Erik was at a momentary loss for words. Slipping his hand inside his robe to obviously feel the ring, the Commander of the Faithful hollered, "Send for Javed Pesar Maraghen-Almani and bid my Royal Treasurer bring with him a bag of gold coin. I wish to reward my Illustrious Magician."

"Sire, this is too bizarre," mumbled Erik in protest. "We cannot roll back time and view a dead man walking. The greatest of magi cannot accomplish such a feat."

The Daroga squeezed Erik's fingers. "He walks and talks surprisingly well for one who lies no longer breathing in a room off the Magus's hole. Be patient."

"I dare to flatter myself with the simple ability to recognize my own treasurer," added the Shah.

At Javed's appearance inside a distant gate, Erik experienced a sense of wonderment unlike any he had ever known. The revelation that the greedy tick managed to recover and that the Shah still feigned holding him in favorable esteem faded quickly with the dawning of a dreadful understanding. Applauding himself was certainly unfounded. His reputation as an assassin was in question. Yet he knew the treasurer to be dead. The man he'd left on the floor drew no breath.

As the treasurer crossed one of the intersecting garden paths, the Daroga whispered into Erik's ear. "I myself saw two of my most trusted men roll the carcass in an old carpet and carry it to Rakesh's caverns. By messenger he assures me it is still there. Then early this morning, four sheiks, all old men of established service, appeared before the Shah. Miraculously, without a hint of haughtiness or disdain, the treasurer re-appeared to measure out the coins the sheiks wished to bestow on the Shah in tribute."

At the base of the seven steps the treasurer bowed, waiting for the Shah to gesture him forward. With an agitated flip of his hand the Shah beckoned Javed closer. Silently placing the bag of gold coins on the table, the treasurer deferred the honor of actually placing the reward in Erik's hand to someone else.

"Where is your ring?" inquired the monarch smoothly.

"I'm having it cleaned, Sire. It will be on my finger shortly."

Or maybe, as you speak, a second one is being cast by a jeweler, Erik's utter surprise at seeing the royal treasurer was now absorbed by an intense study of the man's body shape and movements. Leaning forward, elbows braced on his knees, he was enthralled, paying the strictest attention to every detail of the treasurer's speech and actions. Even the muffled chatter of women gossiping above their heads did nothing to distract his concentration.

The Daroga sensed Erik's near loss of respectful control and was actually glad to have his ward's face masked. As if on cue, Erik telepathically listened to the Daroga's silent directive to sit back.

"Leave us," ordered the ruler.

The treasurer backed down the stairs, remarkably agile for one so ponderous.

When the man vacated the garden all together, the Shah turned toward Erik. "He claims a Roc attacked him…because the jinn protect him, he was able to wound it, forcing the bird to fly off." The Shah's fingers rippled, mimicking flight. "He has the bloodied feathers to prove it."

Beneath the veil of chain mail and the silk *niqab* Erik's face turned to stone.

The Shah was clearly annoyed. "Since Khalil pledges with his hand on the Qur'an that he saw the *gushtegâv kham* (raw beef) unmoving on the floor, I will allow you to correct this fruitless errand and bring me explanation. I extend the necessary time to complete the task to two lunar months. Use these funds to help supply your needs. Send Khalil to me if you require more. Emerge victorious, my friends, for the cost of failure will be both your miserable heads."

A spasm of deep melancholy gripped Erik. Without protest, he raised his hand to the crown of his helmet. Careful not to fracture the red plume, he indicated that he was willing to part with his cranium should he fail. *Did Khalil make the same gesture?* "I am reawakened to purpose and will not disappoint the world's most gracious Sovereign."

He seized the purse, bowed low to the floor before the Shah, and let his expressive eyes acknowledge the obligation to correct his error.

Erik and the Daroga formally exited the royal presence. Back at the colonnades, the sight of their hurried departure brought a jubilant gleam to the treasurer's eyes. Shooting sidelong glances, they caught the dawning of Javed's odious sneer.

"Family!" The Daroga hissed the word as a sibilant curse.

11 *DOUBLE THE TROUBLE*

𝕌ndaunted by the accursed treasurer's gloating, the pair of conspirators hastened to the Daroga's private apartment. Shielded within its richly tessellated rooms, where meddlesome spies didn't dare to penetrate, they could plot and devise a way out of their predicament.

"Welcome to my home," Khalil ushered them safely inside.

Erik paused to admire the exquisite yellow and green mosaics of inflorescent flowers adorning the walls. The air was warm and filled with the exotic incense of Bakhour chips burning in a shallow brass bowl – a calming blend of sandalwood, amber, and saffron. The scent was meant to tranquilize the thoughts of the government's most persuasive policeman when he returned from his official duties. Normally a most welcomed adjunct, but not today. Considering what they'd just witnessed, a stiff drink of alcohol was more in order.

"My sister should be with us shortly," the Daroga signaled Erik to a couch. "I must know where she is before we begin." His eyes nervously scanned every corner of their immediate surroundings. "Normally she is a warm and vibrant hostess, but regards coercion into marriage as an insult. The unexpected announcement has greatly affected her demeanor. I've never seen her face so sour."

"I don't care if she never joins us, Daroga. We need to talk. School me at some later date about the imperfections of consigned marriages."

Tall with dark eyes and the characteristic skin tones of the northern Persians, the Chief of the Secret Police paused to set his arms akimbo and stare at his unsympathetic guest. "That's rather callous. You haven't even met her. How very fortunate we are not to have been born female! I give thanks daily."

"And why have you never married, Khalil?" Erik asked, suspecting the cause to be a deep-seated need to remain independent and mobile.

"I'm afraid my brother cannot think in the abstract." The feminine voice that answered came from behind a curtain of variegated crystal beads. "Love does not capture his interest as much as secrets and adventures." A slender hand emerged in the center of the beads, separating the strands. In the space provided a sleek wisp of a girl appeared. She presented quite a contrast to the solidly built Daroga. Erik stood and for the second time today was aware of a disconcerting sense of wonder. Soha Houri wore a printed tunic over modest leggings. The brushwork design of long bamboo shoots accented every fragile curve of her body. Without facial veil or head covering, her black hair and brown eyes glistened. Her tan skin, an inheritance of generations bronzed by the sun, shone with the glow of almond oils. Layers of intricately linked gold chains adorned her neck, but her wrists and fingers were free of jewelry.

"Sit, please. Since I am a female and you already know my name, no introductions are necessary." Her tone was docile, even as she castigated them. "We have a second cousin who has fathered eleven daughters. Khalil does not try to comfort him in his shame. He believes the effort useless. Neither of them can picture that eleven daughters means eleven sons-in-law. That fact fails to bring a sense of pride. Male ignorance confounds the mind."

Wanting to fume, she continued speaking to their guest without trepidation.

"No doubt you are aware that today I have been promised in marriage to Khusrowshah Mohomet. I am still pure and possess a substantial dowry; neither can be used as a bargaining chip to aid my predicament. Once I am his wife I will be fused, without hope of extraction, into a patriarchal system where males dominate exclusively. At family gatherings I will be set apart to eat my meals away from where the men are congregated. Held subservient to my husband, the law dictates that I give myself generously to him on every occasion he demands it. My primary purpose, once the ceremony binding this arranged marriage is completed, will be to serve that reprehensible man and give birth to his children. Like all men, he will explicitly require sons. Islam may give order to our lives, but its traditions drain the enjoyment of every refreshment, even water, from the mouths of women."

Khalil cast his eyes downward, avoiding those of his beautiful, if not frank, sister. It was obvious how precious a treasure she was to him.

Soha Houri clapped her hands. Erik assumed she meant to order a servant to produce food and drink. As they sat, she felt compelled to add, "The first wife of Fazel Soroush will be traveling by procession from Tabriz – no doubt her entourage has already set out upon their pilgrimage to this palace. The week after she is wed, I am to be lost to all independent thought, bound hand and foot to Khusrowshah."

Put into terms that were difficult to overlook, it was easy to see why she was vexed. "I offer my condolences," Erik said with awakening sincerity.

Guessing him maimed by some serious illness or injury, she gazed into his eyes in an effort to search his soul. Unlike so many others, who sought the revelation of his face with brazen inquisitiveness, she evidenced not a hint of morbid fascination with the grotesque. Soha Houri wanted to read his heart. "Thank you," she responded. "There isn't a contemplative pursuit under the sun that could prepare me for the life that lies ahead. But the Shah has issued the *nâmzadi* and I must submit."

"I understand," Erik felt something of her grief. Wasn't he trapped as well?

Turning to Khalil, she changed the subject. "You have another guest, my brother. Our grandfather is here. Actually clothed, but without shoes. Apparently, he feels motivated to climb upward from his tomb of a hole. No doubt the matter is of grave importance for he wishes to be seen by no one else but you. I dismissed our servants for the rest of the morning." Grieved, her delicate fingers unfurled to encompass nothing but air. "Please excuse me. Only the solace of my private chamber offers comfort. Learn your lessons well, Magician. There are many who need the relief of your talents."

Khalil nodded and she quietly left.

Rakesh's gaunt form appeared from behind the beaded curtain. Dressed in a white cotton tunic and trousers, a clean white turban atop his head, it seemed he'd been waiting for his cue. "I have risen from my self-imposed dungeon to hear firsthand of a perplexing riddle: The marvel of a treasurer who breathes and occupies himself with service even beyond death. What is it the proverb says? To everyone is given the key to Heaven, but the same key also opens the gates of Hell. I've lived to see the dead take on the responsibilities of the living."

Erik's teacher came into the room. Occupying only the space of a child, he sat cross-legged in the middle of the floor. Facing them, he yanked at his trousers. Peeved at the cloth's constraint. "You fit into this land quite well, Changeling. It speaks to the core of your soul for this is a place of warriors. An ancient philosopher was once asked if he'd ever met a truly happy man. He replied that he had come across one, a grandfather. After siring five sons, the man lived long enough to see his second generation clustered about him before being wounded in battle and dying gloriously of his injuries. As he took his last breath, honor and the knowledge that his seed would last gave him the greatest satisfaction imaginable. The proud *Sarbazi* received a public funeral in the place where he died. The celebration to honor his life lasted four days. Our fallen treasurer knew no such end. Running the rope with an arrow shot from a roof onto a lower window frame and repelling across the divide was very industrious."

"Not thirty minutes ago I brought the Shah the money keeper's ring," Erik admitted, "and saw with my own eyes that the treasurer still lives."

"May that person never know another day of peace! In every instance that you are employed you must bring the Shah something to prove that you have completed the assignment."

"How does the man live?"

"I too am surprised. The sacred smoke gave me part of the solution and I think you already know the rest. I'll double what my nephew gave you in that pouch of gold coin if you tell me you already know the answer. Trust your eyes. If one studies two eggs closely enough, one will eventually find the difference."

"A brother…a twin."

"The runes tell me the mate was kept well hidden by a mother whose husband was executed by the Shah's father. No doubt the boys were raised poisoned against this house. I am aware that trouble descends upon you from another direction and it seems the winds of storm blow together, not apart. We will discover the implications as the truth unfolds."

Erik straightened, anxious for direction. "Yes, there is another matter. I want your advice about Prince Khusrowshah. How best to squelch, or avoid entirely, his rude assaults. He rallies his cronies, brings slander and mischief against me. At some point they will provoke a response I may not be able to control. I don't want to tangle with them, yet they force my hand…and it may mean my head."

Rakesh took a long reed from inside his sleeve. Smacking Erik sharply on his gloved hand, his voice became a directive. "Calm yourself and let the facts converge. For some time, our second prince has disturbed the quiet functions of this palace. He promotes conflict and ignores that the destruction of peace angers others. Why does he stir up dissension? Banded with his confederates, he makes himself formidable and threatening. See past the behavior! This group of thugs relishes dominance over their neighbors. They desire that each of us should act according to their caprice, while they demonstrate they cannot govern themselves. Khusrowshah is occupied with petty considerations and now has gained the promise of my granddaughter. Why does he aspire cruelty when benevolence is a pleasing alternative?"

"I thought this was a country that punishes those who interfere in the business of others. Where is justice?" Erik pressed.

Rakesh raised the reed, but did not strike. "I asked a question! The path to the river of truth is revealed over time, through observation and thought. Is Allah the only one who can peer into a man's intents? Has he not given you ability to analyze?"

Erik left his hand on his knee where it could be struck. "Khusrowshah's father is lenient and refuses to see his son's desire to take-on the role of master."

"And?"

"Aside from power, the title of regent bestows the vast wealth his father has amassed."

"Yes, understanding greed and the driving need for control opens up possibilities. Allah may choose to guide us to the connections laying hidden from our eyes."

Erik was an avowed atheist. "If Allah can help guide these events, let him show himself. I have greater, more urgent problems than looking for a god who likes to remain invisible."

"For a time I was a *qalander*, a mystic cloaked in asceticism, wandering seeking truth. I saw with my own eyes that uninhabitable mountains and arid deserts comprise over half this land." Rakesh was not to be rushed. "So populations concentrate like insect colonies in relatively small areas. The diffuse variety of cultures and dialects in this capital is staggering… the streets are filled with people of independent spirits, all clinging stubbornly to their territorial identities. One group's social customs – manner of dress and diet – stands in distinct contrast against those of another. Hot violent windstorms whip tempers about, and the people clamor for the most basic needs of food and clothing. Even though dams and irrigation projects allow extensive agriculture, no region prospers well enough to allow the lines of difference to soften. Only our austere uncompromising monotheism, coupled with the rule of one decisive sovereign, serves to bond us in a thin semblance of harmony.

"As rigid as these two governing forces are, the populace foolishly, ruthlessly thrashes against itself. No one – not one soul I encountered – acts from pure altruism. Cruelty comes easier than benevolence. Kindness takes discipline and must be cultivated. Administrative law forces them to function in relative peace, and the dictates of a common religion offers them the satisfaction of honoring festivals and holidays. Of a fashion, this system works. We manage to sustain ourselves, free of interference from foreign powers, and produce a quality of art and science that marvels any found elsewhere in the world."

Erik and Khalil listened intently.

"God's prophets, or messengers, are *rasuls*. The last was Mohammad. The birth of the Qur'an brought a great light. Not to be dismissed. Before the Qur'an the capricious laws of individual city-states and fear of the jinn governed men. The jinn are intelligent spirits whose purpose is to playfully confound our lives. They are outwitted by only the most cunning. In this land, a great trial pits reason against dark magic, and neither exists well without the other. A wise man would outwardly support both influences while secretly expanding his intellect. Khalil will teach you to detect and fight physically, and I will teach you to recognize the effects of both worlds on the minds of men. The runes have shown me that you walk the arena of the living and the dead, to do so you need to maneuver virtually unnoticed. This second treasurer offers us a confounding truth that dies in inches. You want to even the score?"

Erik nodded in solemn affirmation.

"Then we will teach you to kill as a phantom. Close, close to the victim. A wisp of demonic intervention that comes and steals a life… then vanishes without a trace."

The student's eyes widened. "The very idea is wondrous. I detest the sound of guns. How does one kill silently and swiftly? Poison?"

"That's one method. Hand me your glove." Rakesh produced a small purple glass bottle from his tunic. He dumped all but one plum from a platter of fruit and tearing a corner of his tunic, set the small piece of cloth next to the plum. Then he produced, from some hidden pocket within his clothes, a live rat. As soon as he set the creature onto the curved platter, it went to the fruit. As it sniffed and started to gnaw, he poured two drops of clear fluid from the bottle onto the rag. In an instant the rat fell motionless to its side, still breathing. He covered the rag with Erik's glove, and the creature lay undisturbed as if in a profound sleep.

"The rat is unconscious from the liquid's fumes. The ingenious French have discovered a substance that leaves a victim defenseless. They're using this to anesthetize females in the pains of childbirth. Opiates cause drowsiness and sleep. Under their influence, a person does not care what happens around them, but stimulated may rise from stupor. I myself enjoy its benefits. This is chloroform. Carried into the lungs through breath, its intake rushes to fix the brain into a rosy coma. You must be careful not to smell it or you too will fall." He took a long pin from his turban and plunged it into the heart of the rodent. The creature didn't even twitch.

"I hear mice in my walls," Erik reached over and set the platter far to his right.

Rakesh smiled and passed him the entire bottle. "From the dungeons, Khalil and I have discovered three secret passages running through this palace. We have named them the wolf, the owl, and the raven's beak. The wolf, *Vrika* in Sanskrit, passes beside your apartment. When consulted about your perspective quarters, I chose them most pragmatically. Not even the Shah knows of these channels. They must have been created centuries ago, the knowledge of their presence lost with time. If we open some form of deceptive entrance, it will allow you to come and go as you please. Such a door would be worth its weight in gold."

"Yes," Erik whispered softly. "I want to come and go as the breeze. Observe unseen. Kill more bloodlessly. We are but bags of blood."

Rakesh smiled broadly. "Then come with me to the underground. I will show you a chart of the body's major vessels, organs, and muscles. Together we shall dissect the first treasurer's cadaver. And Khalil shall walk the way of the wolf with you. Once you know the route by heart, discuss how best to construct an entrance into your quarters. We shall let the second treasurer have his way for a bit. Allow him to win this first skirmish before you start to follow him. Watching him from a distance as you did his brother."

The next two days were spent down in the coolness of the caverns, tearing apart the cadaver, dissecting organs, learning the path of nerves, and the insertion points of muscles, tendons, and ligaments. A man could be hobbled with one slice of a knife. His brain destroyed if the heel of an assailant's hand applied enough force to the tip of the nose to fracture the nasal bone and drive it back into the gray matter of the brain. When Erik completed his lessons in anatomy, the Daroga lit a torch and took him down a passage. At its end a formidable outcrop of igneous rock jutted into the tunnel. With a little encouragement from Khalil, Erik let his fingers explore the possibilities concealed by the seemingly impassable wall. He discovered that the rock created a false front, like a screen. When he pressed himself into a crevice behind the intrusive stone he found himself in a chamber with three pointed arches, each leading to other passages. A different series of ideograms was carved into the keystones of each.

Joining him, Khalil explained, "The one on the far right is *Vrika*. We gave it that name because it flows like the wolf's hind leg." He pointed to the keystones and confided, "For all his keen intelligence, Rakesh has not been able to decipher the meaning of those symbols or the ideas they may refer to...so ancient is the language they represent."

"Have you ever thought of doing a rubbing? Take thin paper and charcoal, transfer the marks, then turn the page over and read?"

The Daroga stared in disbelief. "Could the obscurity of the messages be that simple to interpret?"

"It might if you were a sultan wanting to keep secrets from those who trespassed."

Prepare to take your boots off, we'll be walking in a two foot deep pool of water in a few minutes."

Shortly after passing through the *Vrika's* entrance, the sides and ceiling of the passage narrowed remarkably. So tight were the dimensions that it forced them to lower their heads and bend at the waist to proceed.

"Constructed for much smaller people," commented the Daroga.

"Pygmies," responded Erik dryly. "What do you think of Rakesh's ability to call up the jinn and control them?"

"It's Chinese smoke and mirrors. The more you sally forth into his irreverent showmanship, the more your eyes will see. Superstition is a powerful, at times paralyzing tool. He knew your face from the descriptions I wrote in my dispatches. The Magus can teach you much, but he cannot teach you everything."

Erik smacked him on the lower back in appreciation for the honesty.

For a space, the floor of the passage deepened. They were obliged to remove their pants and carry their boots beneath their arms for they walked knee deep in water. When they came to a dry area of crumbling stone, Khalil pointed to a ladder. They climbed upward to a level where they could sit and rest. "We are in the walls of your wing," The Daroga informed him. From here the passage goes upward at an angle with several other landings. We will have to sound the walls with one of us on the other side to find your rooms."

"The walls are?"

"Three feet thick blocks of stone, overlaid on the apartment's side with plaster and decorations."

Before they started the project, Erik ordered a craftsman to create a bronze cylinder lock for his private bedroom door. Six discs, beveled with ten outer sides – each containing a different number – spun around the notches and spaces of a stationary inner tube. When the numbers were aligned in the correct order, a rod holding a thumb-operated lever fell into place. Only then could the door be opened. Simply spinning the numbers set the notches out of order and locked the door.

With his room secured from Fatima's prying eyes, they worked at night, sounding the stone, locating the one closest to the floor at the head of Erik's bed. In a few nights they had it loosened and mobile. Set onto a flat track of tiny steel ball bearings, the block slid smoothly, but only inward into the tunnel. It took two more days for Erik to reproduce the decorations on his wall and create a false front to conceal the secret entrance.

The pair waited three days before meeting to formulate the next stage of their investigation. They plotted their strategy over refreshments in Khalil's apartment.

"How is your escape hatch working?" inquired the Daroga.

"I leave the door unlocked during the day to let Fatima order the cleaning as she wishes. As far as I can tell, no one but myself has ventured under the bed. As a general rule, people complain when they have to bend over a little. Makes them unwilling to chase dust balls."

"You know the entire palace is astir with rumors, rumors that raise an unusual type of dread. They whisper that you are such a powerful magician, with so fearfully a distorted visage, that the jinn have embraced you and given you telesthetic powers. Since you've come to our land you've developed the miraculous ability to perceive information from a great distance without the use of the normal senses."

Erik pretended disinterest by fingering the rim of a cup of tea. "No doubt Fatima spreads the falsehoods in an effort to repel others away from the apartment. Finding my bed undisturbed every morning greatly disturbs her equilibrium. She thinks I've discovered the art of transubstantiation."

"You no longer sleep in your bed at all? That explains the increasing levels of terror."

"I do what I need to do. At some point Fatima will figure out how to see me. Despite all my efforts to keep my face hidden – she'll conjure up something. Perhaps one evening she'll slip a potion into a drink so I will sleep soundly. So I thwart her by slipping into the *Vrika*. There I sleep immured within the tomb-like passage, and rise hours before she awakens so that I may dress in private."

"Most ingenious," praised the Daroga.

"Years ago I taught myself to exist for long periods on very little sleep and scant nourishment. Eating and sleeping in safety holds the greatest priority. Protecting myself merits every consideration, every scheme."

"Dedication birthed of necessity. You constantly invent very clever ways to conceal and reveal yourself. Even if it means doing without the comforts most humans crave."

"This bungled murder is evidence aplenty that I must develop my talents. The loss of the treasurer is of questionable value when a successful impersonator still fondles the Shah's coffers. I take the fraud's existence as a personal failure and fully intend to correct the situation."

The Daroga had one other amusing tidbit to explore. "You don't sleep alone in the tunnel, do you?"

Erik's fingers tapped the tabletop. In truth, he had little need for companionship. Ultimately, only survival mattered. "I take Reza in with me. The leopard prowls around and keeps the rats at bay."

"Resourceful." Amused – Khalil leaned back, stretched out his arms, and raised his face toward the ceiling. "That explains the occasional yowling that echoes through the walls of your section of the palace. More than a few residents have reported their nerves set on edge. They attribute these lonely muffled shrieks to the jinn raking through the night air, searching for their favorite magician."

"Their lack of sleep is an unquestionable advantage."

"Precisely."

12 *FAR FROM BLESSING*

Instincts coupled with commonsense dictated that whenever Erik and the Daroga were out in public their movements were watched. This understanding played right into their hands, as their duplicitous treasurer spent his more recent afternoons and evenings in the city. To gain the upper edge, they quit the royal residence before noon. Taking the utmost care to remain conspicuous, they headed for a house Khalil owned just outside the palace walls. From there they exited through a tunnel to the yard of the next house, kept vacant and owned under an assumed name by Rakesh. Disguised as a pair of common tradesman in gray hooded *thobes*, they avoided the spies and moved around the streets as they chose.

The third afternoon of their quest found them in a bazaar where a number of brokers and criers sold slaves. Unhindered, they'd discovered that Javed kept a second house only three blocks away. The dwelling sat on a well-paved street lined on one side with acacia trees. Several times they'd walked before the home, the very balcony of the treasurer's upper rooms hanging above their heads. Now they'd skillfully trailed the counterfeit from his secret house to this very spot. Sipping strong Arabian coffee, they waited at a small table outside a café.

While they scrutinized the area, Khalil sat thoughtfully rubbing his chin with his index finger and thumb. "You grow thinner and thinner, Erik. Perhaps you are overly hard on yourself. You need to eat more."

Indeed, there was a change in their fledgling assassin. Having his life threatened tended to reorder his thinking. Erik heard the words, but his mind was occupied elsewhere. He mulled over the process of executing the treasurer with an exactness much to be admired. This time he haunted the movements of his prey with pedantic determination, examining every detail, placing emphasis on the slightest minutia in an effort to accomplish the goal.

The slave market was about to commence business. A myriad of buyers and sellers, jostling and pushing to gain an advantageous spot, crowded about the square. No surprise as there were two-dozen healthy new arrivals on display to be auctioned.

The Daroga directed Erik's attention to a merchant selling various items of refreshment from an aged cart. Just behind the rickety vehicle was the shop of a dealer whose sign boasted the finest oils made from olives and nuts. The treasurer was inside. "The owner of that establishment is soon to be arrested and his death ordered. His brother acts as one of the purchasers for the Shah's household. Both are secret followers of the *Bab* (Gate). A seditious group of politically motivated religious, one that wastes our time, except for the intriguing associations it presents. The *Bab* awaits the coming of a new *Madhi*, one who will enlighten the world and unite all cultures. Hopefully without squabbling," he stressed.

"Where do I rank among the number of the Shah's expendable subjects?" whispered Erik.

The Daroga gently put his fingers on his confidant's forearm. "The announcement of your death would be carried throughout the palace in a matter of minutes. At the first light of dawn you would be interred, and by the afternoon on the day of your burial – already forgotten."

Carried on the wind, water from a fountain's spray occasionally pelted them. "Pity, I haven't offered my first spectacular show. I was under the impression that if I created sufficient excitement and the royal audience reached a state of avid enthusiasm for my entertainments..." His words trailed off.

The hustle and noise around them rose to a fevered pitch. The auction was about to commence. From within the shadows of the shop its owner and the treasurer emerged. Waiting patiently, the men watched as a line of four docile slaves was led to a platform. Such a strange placid moment occurred as the herder of humans aligned his wares to be sold. When the crier began to address the crowd, a mule burdened with two chests came around the corner of the shop. Erik detected a momentary connection between the fingers of the two men.

"Time enough to pass instructions or some form of payment," Erik mused.

"You are a rare creature, eyes like a soaring hawk."

The treachery went far deeper than they supposed. They had not quite discovered how the money was removed from the palace. "Surely the help of others is tantamount," the Daroga eagerly downed his coffee. Slamming some coins on the wooden tabletop, he stood. "We know the rascal doesn't carry it out on his back."

Erik joined him. "Look how bold he is with this travesty, almost fearless. Perhaps he has a royal confederate we've not yet uncovered."

"Wise observation." The Daroga enjoyed the slightest suggestion that they might delve into further layers of intrigue. He prided himself on unearthing deceptions. "We shall settle these accounts very soon, then the two of us will make a bid for a stronger influence at court. The Shah cannot refuse to reward success. He'll bless us generously – no doubt grant every request we make."

For the present, the prospect of using chloroform excited Erik far more than enhancing their prestige. He knew he didn't have to make this assassination bloody, but was determined to make the manner of Javed's second death poetically fit the threat made to their own lives.

An ominous sign brought the pair to their toes, straining to stay observant of all that surrounded them. A dry errant wind violently whipped the dust of the market floor upward into the air, tossing the canopies of the vendors about, ripping weakened fabric. It was as if someone took a paintbrush and spattered menace all about the square. At the height of the flurry, a short rotund fellow fell backwards (or was pushed) into the fountain's pool. For a comical moment, all eyes turned to a pair of sandals and very pudgy legs stuck awkwardly in the air. The foolish feet wiggled spastically, sending their shoes flying off into the water.

Inside his solidly made boots Erik curled his toes; he wore them no matter what the temperature. "I'll exterminate this imposter away from the palace, inside the house he owns secretly."

"Novel approach," teased Khalil. "In the art of homicide you are deciding to take greater risks and through distance from the palace lower the chance of the act being associated with you."

"I have some very good teachers."

"I need never fear boredom with you. It's amazing that I survived the Persian court before our association," Khalil spoke softly. Neither had taken their gaze from the shop where the treasurer stood. The people pressing forward to laugh at the fountain's occupant temporarily blocked their view. The Daroga cursed and Erik quickly climbed the side of a short wall abutting the café. A brief tunnel formed in the throng of people and for a moment the shop's frontage was unobstructed. The treasurer and the mule were gone. He shook his head negatively at a questioning Khalil.

"Frivolous humor used as a reliable diversion. The man provokes me." Stretched to his full height, the Daroga's eyes searched the crowd. Every time the drenched man tried to climb out of the fountain, people shoved him back into the water. "My grandfather counsels that moral code benefits the masses, but at the slightest provocation, even the virtue of politeness vanishes."

"Seems natural enough," their waiter offered an unsolicited response. Coming stealthfully to the Daroga's side, he extended a plate of honey cake.

Startled, an annoyed Khalil eyed the man. "I did not order that!"

Erik ignored the ploy and shot another quick look around the square. He jumped down when the disgruntled waiter backed away. "The treasurer ventures forth so brazenly because he's protected by commonly dressed guards. A little paranoia serves him well."

The Daroga jabbed a finger in the waiter's direction. "Especially if his other allies are in higher places than this café. I recommend you toy with this deceiver. He toys so cleverly with us." From his pocket he withdrew a pouch of gold coins and passed it to the magician. "Test the waters."

"An inadvertent loss." The shiny coins left Erik's hand. Flying through the air they spun, gleaming in the sunlight, catching the attention of more than a few. They landed with soft thuds in the dust. Looking down, a dozen members of the crowd spotted the shiny discs and started pushing and pecking for them. Only the treasurer's confederates remained standing, their furtive glances spanning all directions for danger.

Erik murmured softly, "The eager worship of money dazzles their eyes, exposing more of the Shah's enemies to you. We'll remember their faces when the time comes to strike."

In the cool of the evening hours, Erik climbed from roof to roof, easily obtaining the second floor balcony of the treasurer's recently discovered house. Taking a small brush he swept away the evidence of his footprints and the marks of his hands in the thick layer of dust left from the day's winds. He ignored the dirt on his clothes; for this evening's performance he could suffer a little imperfection about his person. Earlier observations disclosed a row of rooms on the ground floor surrounding a courtyard where servants wandered freely. This balcony stood just outside the treasurer's upstairs private quarters. Putting aside fear of capture, he focused on his next move. Time and secrecy were precious. Despite the warm evening the drapes were drawn. Slipping quietly over the threshold, Erik entered the room. Stepping to the side, he cut a small hole in the drape with the tip of his dagger. He barely breathed.

Illuminated by a series of golden sconces burning aloe wood and ambergris that left specific plumes of creosote on the walls, the treasure's playroom was lit up as if it were day. The chamber spoke of callous extravagant tastes. In addition to a conglomeration of heavy furnishings that lacked even a mild degree of symmetry, a score of open chests were placed haphazardly about. Piles of faceted gems in every color of the rainbow, gold and silver ingots, red coral in natural branches, coins alongside stacks of paper monies, and heaps of polished jewelry were on display. The larcenist sat in front of the far wall on a particularly splendid chair. Accustomed to sucking loot from the bosom of the palace, the treasurer had grown lax – despite the recent attack of a Roc.

The Shah's assassin would make him pay dearly. He felt no sense of regret or amazement over what he would accomplish in the next few minutes. The fires of a generalized anger aimed at the world-entire fortified his determination. Knowing himself capable, his thoughts were not centered on why he could do this, but how. *Plan and execute, plan and execute...do not allow him to fight back.*

The treasurer clapped his hands and a sumptuous belly dancer swirled into the room. Naked from the waist up, her nipples were the painted yellow centers of a spiraling design of purple asters. The delicate points swelled and bounced provocatively. Her finger cymbals set the pace for the dulcet tones of her accompanying musicians. Three men, slight in stature but swaying pleasantly, entered playing flute, tambourine, and lute. The lithe girl spun and skipped before the man. Impressively acrobatic, she raised her arms in graceful arcs above her head. Then smiling, her hips gyrated first in one direction and then another. Clipped to her hair, above each ear, she wore a spray of fragrant white gardenias intermixed with frangipani. Hidden behind the drape, Erik was able to catch only the briefest whiff of their strong perfume. Collared in gold, a heavy chain of silver snaked its way between her breasts and wrapped around her waist.

From his seat the treasurer laughed and mocked the girl's movements, sliding his hips from side to side on his cushion. After only a minute of watching her pelvis thrust rhythmically forward, the man gestured for the dancer to move closer. Clasping the chain, he yanked, deliberately throwing the girl off balance. Her layered necklaces and chandelier earrings jumped as she sought to maintain some semblance of grace. Tightening his hold, the treasurer brought his property to her knees. Though Erik saw only her posterior, he watched the trapezius muscles of her shoulders and upper back tighten. He sensed the dismay she felt, trapped once again in her private corner of Hell. The musicians, still playing their instruments, quickly exited the room.

At a hushed command the girl scrambled to the bed. The coverlet of which was ornamented with elaborate embroidery. Crawling on all fours, she stifled a disgruntled plea and made for the plumpest pillows. She lay on her back, undoing the closures of her long beaded skirt. Apparently she didn't move fast enough to suit the scoundrel. He rose and reaching to his head, angrily threw his tiger-skinned, black silk tasseled fez to the floor. Coming to the side of the bed, he slapped her mouth so hard Erik's face stung. He expected a stream of protests or some bitter petition to come from the girl. The dancer did neither.

Tears welled up in her eyes. Knees bent, hands clutching the coverlet, she apologized. "Oh my Master, I beg forgiveness for displeasing you."

Throwing open his robe, the treasurer lay on top of her like some fat squishy hog wallowing in its pen. Erik knew from experience he was about to witness a rape. He swiftly abandoned his hiding place. Sprinting across the room, his gloved hands opened a tightly sealed bottle. In less than four steps he had deftly soaked a rag with chloroform. Four more strides and he came up behind the treasurer, he hissed in Persian to the wide-eyed dancer, "Hold your breath."

The corner of the treasurer's eye saw only that the curtains released an emerging black blur. Without a scream or so much as a gurgle, Javed had no time to react. The distinctive smell of solvent entered the air, tweaking his nose – drying his tongue. His brain decelerated rapidly. Unconsciousness took him in the space of a swallow. Guided by Erik's hands, he fell to his stomach alongside the girl.

As soon as the target was overcome, Erik sped the rag back into a tightly sealed leather pouch.

Astonished, the dancer kicked her way to the head of the bed. Her attentive eyes took in her master's body then turned to the motionless assailant dressed in black hooded robes, his face concealed in a lacquered silk mask of the darkest ebony. All she could perceive of him was a set of golden sapphire eyes. They studied her every move.

Since she didn't scream for help, Erik concluded the best way to approach the problem was to negotiate. He raised his fingers to the area of the mask covering his mouth, his other hand gesturing for her to keep her voice low. "I have been sent to end his life and can pay you. Will it raise a question if you slip from the room?"

"Yes, the musicians stand just outside the door. They expect to return, but will not do so until they are called. I cannot leave for some period of time. They are loyal and will sic the chamberlain on me. The chamberlain will call for the guards."

"In that case, can you consider an alternative? Can you witness all that is about to happen and deny that I was here beside you? Tell them a phantom, a dealer in death, entered the room." He picked up each of the treasurer's hands and checked the fat cigar-shaped fingers.

"What have you done to him?" she answered with an inquiry of her own.

"Used anesthetic fumes to put a victim to sleep so I can kill him without a struggle."

"He's not dead?"

"Not yet. I need to look for something he may have received recently. A ring."

"I know of nothing, but all his most precious possessions are in this room."

"Lie still while I search."

She nodded dumbly. No more than twelve, the girl was a child shoved too soon into womanhood. Obviously whatever loyalty she held for the treasurer existed on a spider's slender thread. The girl's eyes tracked him as he made his way around the room. Her face traveled through a series of emotions: surprise, dread, curiosity, back to surprise, and as she realized she was not to be harmed – elation.

Erik registered the evolution of expressions as he opened drawers and peered into cabinets, searching for the possible existence of a second ring. "Pretend I'm playing a game," he directed.

Unable to locate the signet, he came to the girl and touching one of her jeweled toes, had a vision of moldering old bones, whole skeletons looming somewhere in the girl's recent past. *Did she hide in a graveyard before her capture?*

"Has he owned you long?"

"One full cycle of the moon."

He planted his hands on his hips. "His anguish will be brief."

"Too bad," her voice bore a heavy undercurrent of fury. "I know who you are – you're the Frenchman, the Shah's new magician."

So his reputation was spreading.

Coming to her knees on the bed she leaned toward him. "It is rumored your face was ravaged by fire. If I do as you request, may I see the scars?"

Her hand came up and caressed the stiffened cloth covering his left cheek. A simple act of tenderness he'd never experienced. Inwardly, he conceded that regardless of her actions he would not destroy her. Taking hold of her hand, he gently lowered it. "My face, Mademoiselle, is the most astonishing thing in the world. I confess it surpasses my own comprehensions. It cannot be fixed, only covered. You have nothing to fear from me, I will spare your life."

Fueled by bitterness, he was not lost to self-pity. The latter emotion only depleted strength and wasted time. Refusing to revisit the horror reflected over and over in the expressions of pitiless viewers, his momentary compassion evaporated. At the climax of shows in the gypsy camps, females screaming and fainting was a nightly occurrence. Standing on his abbreviated stage, they sometimes fell directly at his feet. He was not about to witness one crumbling to lie beside a fat pig pretending to be some sort of grand caliph.

"Have mercy, Sir. Take me with you," her voice remained low as she bargained. Her hands came together in the Western manner of prayer.

"I cannot, but if you stay quiet and remain where I place you, I shall let you watch his demise."

Thought was awkward for the treasurer as he regained consciousness. His tongue was thick, and though he tried persistently to force his eyelids open, they simply refused to comply. His face was pressed into something warm and not unpleasant. Three times he attempted a complete awakening before successfully managing the feat. He found himself on his knees, bent forward, his arms lashed to a chest of jewelry. Turning his head he saw his attacker sitting beside him on the very chair from which he held court.

Bound like a side of beef, he managed a slurred sentence. "Troublesome magician...I had not thought to encounter you tonight." He worked some saliva into his mouth. "I would rather receive a scourging and the habitat of an iron cage than death at the hand of an infidel."

Perking up, Erik feigned credulity. "You prefer unmerciful torture over an expedient end? Perhaps the Shah is amused at your impudent pranks and only wants to return the favor?" He clucked his tongue. "Not your lucky day. From what I've seen thus far, the regent doesn't send his assassin to express comedic thanks."

The girl sat quietly at the foot of the bed, safely out of the way.

Raw pain was beginning to cruise up the treasurer's arms and down his back. Frustrated, an angry edge entered his voice, "I told them it was over, they didn't believe me."

"Them?" queried Erik. "You wouldn't care to elaborate on 'them' would you?"

The culprit's face twisted in dismay. "I can dole out a thousand ounces of gold and give you a chest, even larger than this, filled with stones the size of eyeballs. We'll bring in the scales and weigh all. The sum shall be a hundred times the amount the Shah will reward you. You'll be rich for life. And if that amount does not suffice, consider what might bring you satisfaction and I will order whatever you wish. Join us and prosper! Declare to the Shah that the jinn still protect me."

"Really, you're quite the jester," Erik answered sarcastically, his arms spreading wide to encompass the booty in the room. "We can't have this level of pilfering go unchecked. It must have taken years to collect all this stuff, the amount is staggering. I'm consumed with glowing admiration for you. You do an excellent job of posing as treasurer."

Javed-the-second strained against the container to which he was lashed. With his own ponderous weight pressing down to work against him, it didn't budge. "That's because I am the treasurer. You killed my brother."

"Ah," Erik's Persian was soft and menacing. "In the case of a twining, with two brothers looking so much alike, any argument over who is really dead is rather a mute point. The vigilant have captured two infamous thieves…an integral piece of the greater 'they'. This is a happy day."

From the floor Javed whined, "Until a man is dead, one should not use the word happy, it is better to only use the word fortunate."

"You Persians love to quote advice. Is there a saying for avarice, wicked man? I too have an affection for philosophers, but unfortunately, no particular love for ostentation. Quite accustomed to deprivations, I don't avoid them. I'm leery of the squalor of a rich life. Do you see how decadence has made you lecherous and put you off guard?" His arm elegantly fanned out toward the girl. "Care to bargain for your dancer's life?"

"Impertinent fellow, I am the Royal Treasurer." The sin of pride made him feel untouchable. "I will pleasure my eyes and deflower any virgin-body I desire."

A sinister flash burned its way across Erik's terrible eyes. An abyss of smoldering fire drove this young man. "You're intent on displeasing me. Why belabor the point when you reek of corruption? Your brother soaked up alcohol like a sponge. You it seems have a different addiction, but prudence would dictate that you swallow at least a dram of humility. I will make your death swift if you disclose the place of the ring. Does it lay within a trick drawer?"

The treasurer sucked in a breath and opened his mouth to scream. Erik stuffed a wad taken from Javed's own robe into the cavern. "This time you will stay dead, unable to resurrect. Never again will you take to flight, like a greedy wave of locust ready to consume." He sounded almost sympathetic.

Too bad he couldn't locate the ring. He'd have to settle for taking Javed's head. He sighed, this time he wanted less blood. As Erik pressed the skull deeper into the jewels, the treasurer shook his head violently. "Time to be somewhat more debonair I think." Erik snorted and lifting his dagger chopped through the posterior neck, hacking through the spine and trachea as if he wielded a cleaver. *Not my most charming moment.* He let the blood flow onto the gems and their gold settings, *a tacky mess for anyone having to account for the lot.* Covering the dripping neck with the fez, he scanned the room, looking for something in which to place the trophy. The chamber looked like the den of Ali Baba and the forty thieves. *Not a small box to be had.*

Trembling and sputtering, the girl stood. Her breaths came out in short frightened bursts. With her wide eyes fastened on the severed head, her right hand rubbed her left arm in agitation. Finding herself alone with a decapitated corpse and a killer, her resolve to remain calm fled. Though her instinct was to scream, she forced her mouth closed. *What a predicament!* She berated herself. Why had she trusted the magician with her safety and paid no attention to the fact that she might be in jeopardy. "It's probably too late to…to…to recant leaving," the girl stuttered stupidly. An idea burst into conscious thought. "Wait," she hissed, "You haven't fleeced his nether regions. Let me."

Erik automatically reared back. That suggestion suited him perfectly. He gestured with his hand for her to continue. Quickly the girl leapt forward and reaching upward through the back of the treasurer's legs, sought the required item. Her fingers groped around the soft sticky genitals and seized on a small pouch. "It's here. Give me a dagger."

Erik moved her aside and finding the object, cut it free. The newly cast ring shone like an old friend in his hand. "No doubt he needed to bang it up a little before wearing it. Make it look more used." He studied the signet. "No, the jeweler has made it too small for his fingers, this one is half the size of the other." He lofted the ring into the air, wondering if the error was intentional. Catching it in his palm, he tucked it into a pocket and started toward the balcony.

"They will kill me when they find him." The girl's words were matter-of-fact, surprising given the situation.

He paused and turned. *Is there no end to the skillful manipulations of these women?* "I am an infidel, forbidden to touch a daughter of Islam."

She went to the floor on her knees, her hands beseeching him. "Our meeting is *qismat* (Kismet). I was raised in a Christian monastery in Turkey. I know only the way of the cross."

He sighed. "I had hoped to leave less encumbered." Stretching out his hand, he accepted the role of rescuer. "This will make for something of a flawed exit." As she ran to him, he ordered, "Place yourself beneath my cloak and jump onto my back."

"Thank you for changing your mind."

She was very light. He doubted she weighed eighty pounds. When he shifted her, pulling her thin legs around his middle, a woman's voice echoed in the room behind him.

"Move, Erik. Move! Move! You're in danger. They'll trap you!"

He spun, his newly acquired baggage giving him the appearance of a hunchback. Momentary confusion flooded his thoughts. He knew that voice. He knew it well.

Floating in the air above the bed a beautifully sensuous blue-tailed devil, with the face of an angel and shapely breasts, urged him out with her hands. "They're coming. You'll be confined. Locked in."

He ordered his immobile hand to reach for the balcony's drape.

"Don't go that way. Not that way," the demon repeated. "Leave by the door to the adjacent room and head for the roof."

"I hear her, too. Listen to what she says," the girl whispered from beneath his cloak. "For it is wisely written: Do not refuse a gift, in this case advice, or you shall be judged ungrateful."

Apparently, even their youth loved spouting adages. Erik moved to the secondary exit strategy and retorted, "Is it not also written: Only the fool disregards the prospect of dying on the day of his enemy's death."

Hours before dawn, he climbed unnoticed down the side of a building three dwellings away – the girl strapped to him like a sack of goat milk. The secret police were finished swarming the treasurer's house. They'd sealed the place, awaiting the Shah's orders, and taken all the servants in a long line to the palace dungeons.

Erik decided to set aside pride and material gain. In place of monetary reward, he would request this girl's freedom. He'd force himself to listen to the Daroga's disapproving lectures. Certainly the Persian would insist that only a novice would smuggle a girl out of the house. Erik would quietly reply that wisdom was learned in degrees. He was still in training.

13 ASCENT FROM THE RIVER OF GRIEF

Delighted at how easily he'd snared Thayer into his web, Isidore announced he wanted to take a nap before dinner. His office couch beckoned. He invited Thayer to enjoy prowling around the laboratory on his own. At this point Delaquois needed information and it was well within the scheme of things to increase the neuropsychiatrist's bank of knowledge by letting him snoop for himself.

"I'll see you in a couple of hours. We can make further decisions over our meal." Isidore seemed less solemn, more cooperative. "Problems appear less taxing on a full stomach. Explore wherever you like. The only area off limits is the sterile section where you saw the plants and larger tanks."

Thayer was grateful. He longed for Isidore's most shrouded secrets. This open-ended degree of trust helped set aside his most craven doubts. He re-suited and entered the genetics lab where DNA was actually extracted and analyzed. Here the smell of astringent was the strongest. Amid the aisles of shiny equipment and the shelves of neatly labeled chemicals, he identified nothing more than an extremely well stocked lab.

Anxious, he entered the section where he'd seen Nyah working. Touching a button, the white message boards dropped back into position. Starting from the extreme left, it appeared that they had constructed an elaborate family tree. Some information was missing, but he was able to hone in on very specific details. They were identifying phenotypes, physical characteristics and emotional traits, transmitted by parents to their offspring. Thayer could tell that Isidore was searching for heredity proclivity, an inclination toward very specific talents and the amber eye-color evidenced in Erik's irises. He inwardly acknowledged that he was looking at highly confidential genealogical information. Then reminded his conscience, he did have permission.

Mountains of geometric patterns covered Nyah's white boards. Hexagons and triangles that linked a specific trait from one family member to that evidenced in another. Extrapolations that worked backward to a single source: Raoul Camille de Chagny, youngest son of Count Philibert and his Comtesse, *nee* de Moerogis La Martyniere. Despite the terrible suspicion that he bordered on the brink of truly evil answers, he recognized a singular opportunity to benefit his patient by digging further.

On the shelves, journal after journal outlined the exact formulas used for identifying specific characteristics found in extracted DNA. In the end, everything in genetics boiled down to the application of mathematics. At last, his rummaging afforded him a particularly interesting stack of volumes, a treatise giving him a surprising insight into the past. Thumping the cover of the oldest log, he smirked, "Science may advance dramatically, but people are still basically egotists."

Spreading out on a counter, Thayer took several transparent overlays that marked very specific locations on chromosomes. Placing them one at a time over the series of loci gave a more complete and rather alarming picture. Added to the clues uncovered in the notes and on the boards, the ideas became clearer. The genetic possibilities were endless. Make several copies of an individual. Reduce the number by killing off all but the most perfect specimen. Cross human intellect with insect facility and compulsion. Give the creation a vegetative ability to communicate with scent and telepathy...like a plant. Heighten the immune system, virtually removing susceptibility to germs and outside agents that might attack the specimen. Taking off his spectacles, he laid them on the counter and rubbed his tired eyes. He was reminded of a passage in the apocalyptic revelation to the Apostle John, the one where wild half-animal men run amuck in city parks.

"Have you made some interesting discoveries?" Isidore stood quietly at his back.

Thayer's mind awakened as if from a dream. He had no idea how long he'd been exploring the data. He'd been so horrified at the prospects of what these projects represented. "I'm disgusted and simultaneously mesmerized! What have you been trying to accomplish?"

"What does it look like?" Hidden behind the mask, Isidore's expression remained unknowable.

"To put my conclusions in as precise a fashion as possible," the answer came with conviction. "It appears you've greedily fed an excessive ego that actually dishonors prescribed ethical boundaries. Without a qualm you've operated outside accepted scientific practice. Played with

Heaven's dictums and are paying the price. You are going to bury your own soul. Dark and complex explorations have brought this boy among us."

This time Erik's vision ended like a wave crashing to the shore. His fingers browsed the silken sheets and he knew without a doubt he'd returned to current-day France. Agitated, he arose from the bed and stumbled a few steps. The scent of gardenias and frangipani in the girl's hair still lingered in his nose. He yearned for a little amnesia. Turning, he grabbed a pillow and punched it so hard the casing ripped. The damaged object flew across the bedcovers, sailing to the floor on the opposite side in a trail of feathers reminiscent of the initial kill.

"Where is the dancer? What became of her? I don't need Isidore's smothering attentions, but a few damn answers would be nice!" He angrily grabbed a carafe of water and would have sent it flying after the pillow, but suddenly felt parched. He drank until there was no more to be had.

He stood motionless, staring blankly, holding the empty glass container. His hearing heightened almost painfully. Faint sounds emanated from other rooms in the house, echoes from corridors far away. *What kind of preternatural hearing is this?* He shook his head and focused on the noises. Somewhere a door opened, a maid was whistling, no, now she was singing in a gentle voice...he heard the patter of little feet following her – his children. His? From somewhere else he swore he heard music, wondrous music. He spun in a slow circle. Nothing came visually, nor was it tentative.

Was he projecting sound? How could his mind do this?

He went to stand before a cheval mirror in the corner. Someone, most likely John, had dressed him in claret-red pajamas. He had a private love of the color. Tall and barefoot, with rumpled hair, he looked a sight. He tilted the glass to view only his upper half and suddenly knew where and when he'd purchased it. The fancy looking thing used to be in Sarah's room. He bought the mirror in the flea market at the *Porte de Montreuil*, springtime 1880. Sucking in a sharp breath, he took an automated step backwards. Watching his reflection, he saw a square glass lantern with a pewter base appear at the tips of his left fingers. He shook his hand, but the portable lamp stayed stationery in the glass. His real fingers reached for a Tiffany floor lamp standing beside him. Still watching his reflection, he pulled the chain, illuminating the dragonfly pattern of stained glass. The pewter lantern miraculously stayed in the reflection.

"These are the rantings of a young man of fifteen," he lectured the image with frustrated words that spilled forth like a spray of needles shot by a porcupine. "One who has strange lapses into unconsciousness while he's actually still awake. So he's positive it's not some fatuous form of dementia. A weird geneticist and his fragile crippled assistant raised him. He knows this house. He's always known this house. He knew it before the fabrics were faded, when he rode horses and felt the wind in his face as he galloped his stallion. There are no horses here now. The empty stables contain fancy cars, and some of the guards have motorcycles. No doubt you've seen them – if they're not hallucination." He pointed to his figure. "They've shown you how to ride the Harleys; how to spin the back tire and spit out gravel. So how is it you know how to ride a horse? There's an old in-home theater directly below this bedroom. Painted all in black, it contains a platform that surrounds an octagonal chamber that rotates on fly-gears. It can actually contract down into a six-sided catoptric cistula, and expand again with the right set of maneuvers. You've never been shown how to operate the thing, but somehow you know the mechanisms."

A high-pitched nullifying squeal that hurt his head ended the tirade. Almost defeated, he plied his fingers through the locks of his thick hair. "You like being alone. Spending time with your own thoughts. Skills come easily to both versions of you. Let's be fair, we are insane. Totally and irrevocably insane – seeing as how we walk in two realities. Yes, there are two. Another male grows right beside me. He is me, yet somehow lived before me. He's teaching me the art of murder and I don't understand his motivation. How could I not understand if he is me? Am I learning or remembering? So many questions go without answers. The solutions are always just out of reach. I tell myself that they'll follow my next meal, or they're lodged in the next textbook, perhaps they'll arrive by courier tomorrow morning. In this life I feel like I'm continually trying to solve a puzzle, and I don't have a clue what the end result is supposed to look like. I've only been shown pieces, scraps, tiny detailed shards. The wonder is that I tolerate this strange predicament without becoming suicidal."

He thought to try an experiment. "I call you forward. Listen to me, Magician. They want to give me tranquilizers now, block these so called symptoms. Eventually they'll succeed. It might be months before the effects wear off," he exaggerated for effect. His hands reached forward. Spreading his arms in a large circle to embrace his pajama-self, he commanded, "Like the Shah of Persia, I summon you forth. Appear!" His fingers curled in a plea. "Stop this folly! Come forth!"

A gust of wind blew across the room – its origin unknown. A blur of dark gray moved at his left. He saw it pass the screen on the plasma television set, the glass of Isidore's framed picture, the face of a mantle clock. With a strange confidence he turned back toward the mirror. His image was gray and blurred. "What do you do when your anger peaks?"

"I murder people," answered the obscurity, "as silently as circumstances will allow. And you?"

Are my lips numb? Did they move? Perturbed, he pulled at them. "I punched a pillow a few minutes ago. Seems mild in comparison. If I remember past sins and murders committed in this body, am I still a killer?"

"Yes, but one with a prettier face."

"Am I sleep-walking?"

"You're no somnambulist." There wasn't an ounce of derision in the voice.

"Show yourself." For a moment the silence was deafening. A nacreous shimmering filled the glass. "Please!"

"Come closer to the mirror." The voice was deeper than his own, steadier, more confident.

Erik moved to within inches of the cold surface, and in doing so turned his head, presenting his profile. Stunned he watched his reflection sharpen. Fitting his profile perfectly, the vision of a white mask appeared before him. He saw the covering with great clarity. One similar to it hung on the wall behind him. Redirecting his eyes he saw them both. He backed up and though he now stood full-face, the new image remained angled and unchanged before him. He appeared to be in some sort of cavern with the lantern now resting at his feet. The new arrival straightened his head and back, then went to sit on a boulder.

He bent a knee, setting the sole of his boot against the stone. With a sympathetic pang, Erik realized he recognized the derelict murderer.

"You like black clothes," he said like an idiot.

The figure dropped his chin, almost chuckling. "As we observed with Khusrowshah, black is the color that absorbs all spectral shades – good for a Changeling who favors prowling at night, dogging the steps of others."

The modern version quivered. He no longer saw anything of himself in red sleepwear. It was as if he'd been muted out. For months he'd attempted speech with this other, and now, for the very first time...

"How did you get here?"

"Well, it wasn't by barouche," confided the image. "Call it genetic imprint. As long as you're here, I'm here. I'm alive only in your mind, but make no mistake...I am alive. It's got something to do with that phenomenal hippocampus in your brain."

"How do I know about your life? Why am I learning you bit by bit? Do you know what I know?"

The masked stranger twirled a finger beside his temple. His voice was Erik's, yet it was so much more mature, mellower. "I wouldn't probe too quickly. I guarantee you won't like what you find."

"I'm not afraid. I want to confront this paradox. You've taken over my life like some ominous thunderstorm. I feel like a trespasser violating your unholy memories. You're some kind of antihero I'm emulating. I try to match your strength, to cognitively echo your dedication. I fail rather consistently."

The image placed an elbow on the thigh of the bent leg, resting its chin on some knuckles. "Even though we share common mental baggage, don't assume you can know me so quickly. And you're the one letting the memories through, not me. You're like a faucet," he made a referencing hand gesture, "turned on full."

"You know about faucets?"

"With great certainty I know about them. Everything you know, I know...and more. I predict that very soon you'll have all the required pieces. Patience."

"Patience! I'm schooled in patience." He trembled so violently it took every ounce of control not to smash the glass into a thousand brilliant slivers. "I'm the grand tenured professor of patience!" Enraged, the physical Erik paced in agitation before the glass. Like a baffled toddler he tried to reconcile the bizarre reflection with the reality of the chateau's room. Nothing he did controlled a single movement of the other. Blinded by wrath, he reached for the Tiffany floor lamp and went to charge the glass like a knight with a colorful, albeit clumsy, lance.

The image jumped to its feet, both gloved hands signaling stop. "No! Don't annihilate the mirror. I'll only appear somewhere else and the other surfaces are smaller. They'll frustrate you even more."

The twenty-first century edition knew the statement to be true. He paused, still holding the lamp's shaft parallel to the floor.

"Believe your eyes, trust what you see." With a pronounced surge of deep satisfaction the image straightened. Stiffening its arms, it took the exact same posture as the genuine male before him – minus the Tiffany floor lamp.

Fully alert, the physical Erik took in the weird mimicry of his own expression and stance. "You're physical," he flung the accusation. "You picked the locks, bypassed security. Somehow you broke in here."

"Good! I need you to be a more suspicious!"

"Did we lose our virginity with the dancer?" Erik heard himself ask the words and could only surmise that he was in shock or truly a maniac.

"No, we dutifully handed her to the Daroga. Who, by the way, thought we were suffering the effects of Indra's Kiss for liberating a slave girl from the treasurer's household. We acquired a voracious appetite for a different female. Well, that's a lie...overtime she acquired a taste for us, but we were none the less enamored of her. We loved her more than breathing: a tall brown haired woman with hazel blue green eyes – graceful obliging limbs, tender mouth."

"She's coming, isn't she? I saw her floating in the air – half demon, half female, blue skin."

"God, I hope so. Though blue with a tail was your interpretation of her. We're far past fortunate if **you** start looking for her. Expecting her to appear around corners or in rooms would be a good start. Of course she won't be there, but your guts will twist you inside out, making you wretched because she hasn't returned. She's an addiction that will make you delirious. You'll turn ice cold, simultaneously nauseated and aroused. Overcome with fright over your own un-dentable weakness, you'll cry. But you must never beg her. She hates men that prostrate at her feet."

"How will I recognize her if she doesn't come equipped with a blue tail?" Erik mocked. He so wanted to punch the image, choke it into silence, but then he'd summoned the creepy thing.

"She doesn't have a tail. The knowledge given to you by your subconscious – granted it's significant – bears interpretation. You have a most discerning eye. Use it! Have you seen blue-tailed women in France?"

"Yes, in a game on the computer."

"Then you added the anomaly. It seems you can interject your history into the experience." The guest returned to his boulder. "Please, set the lamp down. Our arm grows tired and this may prove to be a very long night."

Erik put the floor lamp back in its normal spot. "Are you an apparition?"

"No, more like a projection I think. Be brave and trust your excellent brain. I have to tell you that it's damn unnerving when I watch you speak to others without moving your mouth."

The present-day Erik smiled. "You need the semblance of conversation? Remember Fatima told us that even the walls might have ears. It's the same in this place."

"I remember. I'm the one that showed her to you. By the way, I'm gratified to see that the people of this century are less superstitious. The one I came from practically fed on ritual and folklore. Also, you have cell phones...how inventive."

"Sorry." Erik was in the transition of deciding that this conversation was real and not a fanciful daydream. "Cell phones are more complicated now. They're called ComDevs...communication devices. Where exactly are you?"

"Right here. I was past the River Styx, run-through by the waters of death until your birth. I rather enjoy being called into view to answer your questions. Still, I don't recommend that you learn everything all at once. I won't repeat the error of telling you to be patient. Even though it's a quality that reaps tremendous reward, the context of the word seems to set you off. Let information evolve at a pace you can digest. After the deaths of several people we loved, we went through a very serious despondency. The last of a series of lifelong depressions. You're bordering on one now." The image started taking off his gloves.

"Accepted," responded the modern Erik. "All things will come in good time. We are the same human being – nothing can alter that. Take off the mask!"

Unblinking, the image stared back at him. "Take it off…because you need to see me?"

"Seems a straightforward, completely appropriate, request."

"I'm sorry it took so long to get to this point. Our will is rather strong and you've been, for the most part, busy growing up." Adjusting the light, the former Erik raised the lantern to a position beside his head, so that his countenance could be seen more clearly. "It's all here, like a book waiting to be opened…and there's so much more to read. Together we are…"

"What? Together we are what?"

"Something quite uncommonly unique. Look for yourself and discover if such scars come to a man when he is awake…or when he is asleep and in the clutches of some damnable nightmare." He kept the lantern aloft. His long delicate fingers lifted off the mask and set it in his lap.

While the undeniable hideousness awaited recognition, the pajama-version drew closer consumed with the greatest bewilderment. There were his eyes of gold and pale green, a copper colored ring encircled the edge of each pupil. *Lovely.* But the upper right quarter of his face was a horror, plus he was missing the whole anterior structure of his right nostril. The base of the nasal tube lay open like some cracked sewer pipe ready to leak. Around the inquisitive right eyeball, which somehow managed to maintain the ability to blink, the flesh appeared like clumps of raw ground beef. The affliction spread over the right forehead and across a hollowed out right cheek. Tiny veins, like dozens of fetal snakes, traveled through the thin underlying valleys of nearly translucent skin. He had no right eyebrow, and his right upper lip lacked muscular strength. The margin was pulled slightly upward, leaving the tips of his right incisors and canine teeth exposed.

The figure tried to console him. "You could continue convincing yourself that you are a lunatic and have lost your sense of reality. More is the pity, since you are clever as well as handsome. Or you could accept this aberration as authentic and move on." He patiently let the pupil study the anomalies. "Does the revelation of our face disturb you beyond all response whatsoever?"

In truth he was a mixture of emotions: shock, fear, something akin to acceptance, and from deep within his heart more than a smattering of compassion oozed upward. The face before him **was** his! He reckoned his mind forever lost, and regretted the inability to peel off his features and share them.

"Don't! Don't do that tenderhearted thing. The damage can't be changed." The reflection forced itself to age dramatically, the process all the more grotesque as the abnormal growths bled and dried on the spot. Then with a snap of his fingers, he reverted back to his youth.

The physical Erik blew out a long slow breath, he hadn't realized he'd been holding the air in his lungs.

"Christine used to hate when we did that. Besides, one of the first rules of combat is to breathe."

Registering the female's name, he peered into the mirror and breathed normally, "What are we? What damaged us?" Gingerly, he fingered the area on himself and felt only his own unblemished skin.

"All the answers in good time. Remember? Not to worry, today we have a new face. In our former lifetime a near-normal countenance was an arduous project...one only accomplished with copious amounts of *maquillage de théâtre.*"

Their unified mind drifted off in reverie. He saw a stage, a trapdoor, an enormous Bohemian crystal chandelier crashing down on occupied seats as people ran, screaming in all directions.

"I had a glorious voice, now that you've matured you can start singing with it." Amused he added, "The higher and lower registers will be nothing. Sustaining notes will take that forbearance word we won't repeat." The older Erik snapped his fingers in rapid repetition, wanting to wake the daydreamer. He sounded irritated, "Why are you lounging about? Don't we have a dinner to attend downstairs?"

Erik nodded and turned to prepare. With a start he made a sudden realization – he was younger than the man in the mirror. "I'm here in 2012 and cannot account for how I got here. There are no pictures of my mother. I have no memories of her. Isidore said she died and there was a hurried caesarian section. Very dramatic."

"Don't look for our first mother. You've heard the story of Beauty and the Beast? This one would read more like Beast births Beast."

"Isidore has more of the answers, doesn't he?"

"You can opt for immediate and complete understanding, decide on sweet revenge, or simply throw your lot in with me and accept that we have a second chance…and we're prettier this time around."

As he dressed and prepared for dinner, he moved about the rooms more confident than before. With the migraine miraculously gone, the power gained from knowledge changed him. He knew he wasn't a fractured personality, nor was he inappropriately compartmentalizing. The former and the new were not in conflict. His mind relaxed, became a fallow field to explore. As he tied a black silk tie over a delicate Romanian black silk shirt, he told the mirror. "In my past life, I was a talented scoundrel. Today, I am that and so much more."

A steady mental voice added a thought. *Pay attention to your brother's ideas, he's insightful and in his own particular way very wise.*

14 *LIAR!*

L uggage containing several days clothing and toiletries awaited Thayer's approval in his room in the east wing. Packed by his sweet Vanessa and brought to the estate by one of the Kelly brothers, he would have to thank whoever hauled the bags into his quarters. Taking inventory of the lot, he doubted he'd need all the items his wife sent. After a shower and fresh suit of clothes, he hurried downstairs for eight sharp. The formal dining room was everything Thayer remembered. A massive oval, French baroque table was the room's grand centerpiece. The entire outer wall at the table's head was a semicircle that contained an enormous great window of frosted Italian glass. To either side, heavy honey-colored drapes spilled from ceiling to floor. Deeply embossed Italian wallpaper spread swirling plumes and scalloped ridges all around the room.

On the right an intricate jacquard tapestry displayed an elaborate motif of a bouquet and urn, a symbol carried for centuries on banners in village processionals. Conceived and woven by master weavers, it was fitted through grommets over an iron rod and hung as a noble reminder of the feasts once held in simpler more rural times. Thayer guessed it came from the seventeen hundreds and couldn't begin to estimate its current value.

By comparison, Thayer's apartment in Paris was modest, but he could so easily picture living in surroundings similar to these. *I might enjoy this more if Isidore weren't such an enslaved disciple of Josef Mengele.*

In an effort to promote an intimate dinner among friends, someone prepared only the far end of the table. Two tall silver candelabrums, burning dripless white tapers, flickered and glowed before the focal point of the Italian glass window. The aura of the flames sent the table's crystal stemware to sparkling. Accented with gold and ruby highlights, the goblets encircled settings of stunning porcelain dinner plates. The latter were edged in twenty-four carat gold. Beside the plates rested heavy eighteenth century Swiss made silverware.

Isidore settled onto a chair Thayer politely pulled out for the geneticist. "I hope you have an appetite." He pointed to a Louis XIII *Buffet de Chasse*. With turned pilasters and bun feet, its centered doors were carved in reliefs of pheasants and rushes. The drawer handles on the elaborate piece were bronze, opened-mouthed, fox heads. Resting atop this mahogany sideboard where warming plates covered with trays emitting glorious smells. "We are less formal these days and serve ourselves buffet-style. Take a plate and have a look. If you haven't snacked you must be famished. I'd like to wait for Erik's appearance. Dillard assures me my son is on his way."

Beneath the heated domes Thayer discovered ample amounts of beef tenderloin graced with foie gras, grilled sea-bass swimming in an apple-rhubarb sauce, marinated tiger prawns with chilled lime cream, scallops risotto, green asparagus, and gingered carrots. A lavish spread.

Back in his seat, Thayer sipped some extraordinary Dom Pérignon champagne and wondered why servants failed to appear and assist them. "Where does this food come from?" he asked quietly.

Isidore sat with the handle of his cane braced against the side of his chair. "Paris," he replied.

"What I meant was – how does it arrive here? This tenderloin is delicious!"

"I'm glad you like the food. Please have all you care to consume. It's delivered daily though the front gate."

Thayer swallowed and set his fork down. "That's not what I meant and you know it. Who prepares these dishes? Who sets them out? There's not a spider web or a fleck of dust in any of the upper rooms. Do gremlins fly in when no one is looking and clean the place?"

"My staff takes care of incidentals."

"How is it I never see them? For that matter, the only guards I've seen inside the house are the Kelly's."

Isidore's delicate fingers tapped the damask tablecloth. "I trust very few people inside the house and about our persons. The greatest threat comes from the CLL, The Corps of Life Liberationists."

Thayer managed to gain eye contact with Isidore. "Sorry, I've never heard of them."

"Well, we have. Believe me when I tell you their threats are rather nasty. Genetics is such a complex fast-growing field that many religious splinter groups vehemently object to any manipulation of heredity. They've forced many of us into hiding behind multi-level corporations. Today there are groups of scientists secluded in various corners of the world, working in secret on very specific projects...refusing to share their results with anyone. And why should they when their lives are at stake? Trust me, I have a staff, a trusted staff. They come out discretely, do what needs to be done and vanish. The largest number are involved with security about the grounds."

"I'm sorry to hear of fellow scientists trying to function under such pressures, especially since most seek the good of all humankind. I know these grounds and the chateau are heavily guarded."

"My employees are instructed to keep a low profile and leave me to my thoughts. Even as my declared guest, you must always identify yourself if questioned. I'm sorry that all these precautions are so necessary." Isidore picked up a dinner bell shaped like a leggy egret and rang it soundly. A moment later a perky little blond in a neatly tailored gray dress-suit entered through the butler's pantry. "Let me introduce you to Kathryn Arlington. She's John Kelly's girlfriend and assists me by running the household. She pays the bills and sees to the upkeep of the mansion."

"Do you need anything, Sir?" inquired the efficient American demurely.

"No, just your pretty face to reassure our guest."

Like a gentleman, Thayer set his napkin on the table and rose to his feet. "My pleasure." He bowed politely.

"We might prefer to take desert in the gentlemen's parlor," Isidore informed her, pointing to another piece of furniture.

After-dinner refreshments were already waiting on a cherry wood corner cabinet inlaid with antique mother of pearl designs. Platters of dessert cake and sliced fruit sat next to a stack of fragile green porcelain plates shaped like large maple leaves. Thayer's eyes traveled to the cabinet's ornate brass pulls of oak leaves and acorns, they gave tasteful compliment to the talents of some long deceased cabinetmaker. He wondered about the artisan. Had his work been appreciated?

"The gentlemen's parlor is just off the grand hallway," Kathryn informed him, her distinct southern American drawl politely breaking the reverie. This house cast such a spell.

Isidore interjected, "I had the amenity of a wet bar added to that salon. Men used to congregate in there for private chats – made business decisions over cigars and brandy. Nothing gracious enjoyed by the former generations has been dismissed, only enhanced."

Isidore's domestic administrator had a pleasant friendly air about her. "With your permission, I'll have the chocolate cake and melon montage set up on the credenza in the parlor. Perhaps you'd care for music with your meal? Mozart?" At Isidore's nod she turned, exiting as quickly as she'd appeared.

"There are several delicate needlepoint motifs done by my mother in that parlor. Most depict farm animals wreathed in flowered garlands. She felt intimidated by this chateau and wanted to add something of herself to every room my father frequented. You'll recall that I explained she was Lowell's British bride."

"So you told me. Who is Erik's mother?" Thayer hoped for an honest direct answer. "Is she still alive?" Like a computer patiently waiting for the SAVE INFORMATION directive, Delaquois sat in anticipation of the answer.

Erik arrived in the doorway clean and impeccably well dressed. "My earliest memories are playing around Nyah's legs as she sat at her station in the lab."

"Ah, at last you join us!" Isidore seemed almost jovial. "You dine too frequently alone. It's nice to have you here for our first intimate meal with your physician. I don't like it when you sulk in corners...some days are unbearably worse than others. Sit, please."

"Nice to see you up and about," Thayer added as Erik grabbed two plates and headed for the food.

"Did you know that Thayer thinks you too erudite? He wants to extend your knowledge outside what you've acquired from books. Do you favor savoring the sights of the world?"

Erik set one of the plates before Isidore and took a seat. After cutting a bite, he stared at Isidore with eyes as distant as two cold moons encircled with long black lashes. Void of overt emotion, he knew Isidore would never willingly release him from the mansion.

"Tell me about your affinity for masks," interjected Thayer. "How did the hobby develop?"

"Erik started collecting them at about three years of age," Isidore responded. "None of them occupied his interests for very long. He makes the ones I'm forced to wear." Tension ran like a tight cord beneath the lopsided dinner conversation.

Erik chewed and continued to glare at his parent. After drinking some champagne, he asked, "Why have you stopped the lovely dinner chitchat?"

Ignoring the jibe, Isidore continued, "Later on perhaps Erik will take you for a turn around the chateau. There's nothing much to see in the meadows, but we used to enjoy a stroll after meals. Regrettably the lack of strength in my legs prohibits me from happy promenades. Thank you for leading our investigation into Erik's condition, Thayer. I trust your quarters were adequately prepared. You will be afforded every manner of privacy in your rooms. Cameras only follow movements down the hallways and in the social areas. Please feel free to move about as if you were in your own home." (He failed to mention the thermal imagery in the bedrooms.)

Every one of Isidore's staccato sentences skirted the real issues, only adding to Thayer's perception that deeper entanglements lay shrouded in these genetic mysteries. It was alarming how the subject matter didn't even allude to the blaring truths. What was the nature of the physical ailment troubling Isidore? Who did give birth to Erik? Why wasn't he shown the boy's complete genetic makeup? All this essential information hung in the air – screaming to be disclosed. Despite an increasing level of anxiety, Thayer reminded himself that a neuropsychiatrist worth his salt possessed more than a quantum of intellectual endurance. He was willing to pick apart dualities and innuendos searching for answers. It didn't matter that Isidore's head drifted downward, as it did now, his mind lapsing into a catnap at the table.

Impatient and ready to flare, these delicate niceties were having an opposite effect upon Erik. The indecisive never-ending enigma was driving him to the precipitant edge of crazy. "Doesn't this stream of inane comments strike you as rather odd, Doctor Delaquois? They are as non-productive as the banality of recalling how the estate used to look."

Thayer saw the futility of divertive tactics. The boy wanted to cut to the chase. "No, it doesn't bother me. I have agreed to adhere to your father's criteria for conducting the tests. Hopefully, the results will lead to an appropriate diagnosis. Hurried answers might bring us to erroneous conclusions. Keeping in mind the overall vision of a cure, I would prefer extremely accurate data. At this point, I'm not upset over delays and imperfections. Every last detail need not be disclosed to me over dinner."

Erik tensed. His augmented olfactory senses alerted him to the fine musty scent of Thayer's lies. He was as anxious for answers as his patient. Opting to turn up the heat, he observed, "Details and data. The devil dances in those numbers. Better to confront him head on and have an end to circumvention."

"Don't be so aggressive, Erik. You're already too predictable," Isidore wanted to continue the verbal waltzing. "Look, it's Sunday and you're wearing the same color shirt and tie you always wear. Let me call a tailor and have something made that isn't black. You spend too much time in mourning clothes. Strut around. Act like you own the place. You will one day." Isidore issued a condescending paternal pat on the hand.

"I think you're the one who needs tranquilizers, insomnia makes you babble."

Isidore stared at the facets of a crystal goblet. At the bottom of that tall glass of port lay the kiss of numbness. "I don't want sedatives."

Another lie for the growing pile. Erik quietly ate a few bites before speaking again. "Nothing is certain, nothing is set – except the past. Hard to undo what's already happened. Options are short on that score: forget, fantasize, or fornicate your way into a mangled version of events."

"Believe me, I know the past cannot be altered. There are too many sad unused rooms in this house. Rooms filled with furniture covered in cotton sheets to keep the dust at bay. You could make this family proud, Erik. You are the last. You must survive to carry on the de Chagny name."

"Better that it rots beside you in the grave. I wouldn't shed one tear should you and the de Chagny lineage fall off the earth, hand in hand."

"Now see here," Thayer interrupted. "There is no reasonable excuse for insulting your father. Conduct yourself with decorum or put aside the man's food."

Erik's eyes seared into Thayer's. "I give you permission to impose upon your employer. Demand the answers. My guardian is the one who dragged you here on a Sunday. I'm well aware that money to compensate you for canceling your entire schedule has already exchanged hands. He's bought you, locked you into commitment."

He refocused his attentions toward Isidore. "Today you've been preoccupied with all the precipitant factors that stimulate seizures. You even let Thayer burrow around in the lab. Did he miss the iceberg?" His chin lifted toward Thayer in a quick nod. "Watch. That lab birthed many things. I know. I practically grew up down there. Ask him why I've never been shown my birth certificate. To have the rights of citizenship one needs that document. Ask him why we can't know his real designs?"

"*Sapere aude* – I've dared to be knowledgeable," murmured Isidore.

"And to Hades with the consequences?" Erik shot back, his head jerking toward the ceiling. "You divulge witticisms like you're pleased to dole out lemon tarts. I comprehend a great deal and I am not psychotic. I know the year is 2012. Before I was born your construction people came across a passageway that ran from an outcrop of rocks, passed an oubliette, and entered the northeastern segment of the wine cellars. I could draw a detailed picture of the structure for you; the oubliette is now part of the laboratory, the Panic Room to be precise. I know about it, not because I read an account of the demolition, but because I actually fell into it. I broke my right leg in that pit. Believe me or don't believe me. It happened and I was much older than I am now. How is that possible?"

"Have courage. Don't call for my executioner just yet. Champagne is probably more in order. Let's celebrate your gala première with a toast. I suppose the revelations were inevitable. On some subconscious level I probably wanted the facts exposed, I've born the burden for so long and it's vital you survive."

"Explain! How do I understand what I've never seen, never been taught?"

Isidore grew stern. "To own the truth you must strike a bargain. Will you open up and tell me when these visions occur? Give me more detailed accounts? Take me into the vault of your mind?"

"Yes! If you will answer my questions honestly without sidestepping."

"Then the first order of business is to command you not to take any of Thayer's tranquilizers. We'll require sharp wits as this evolves."

"He may be in desperate need of those sedatives, Isidore!"

Erik's voice dropped. A deep growl came from the back of his throat. "I weary of these hellacious delays. I won't swallow his tranquilizers and you stop pretending you own a shred of ethical prudence. Speak plainly and concede the argument, let me acquire the facts regarding my origins. Life in this chateau seems rather tepid, almost calm in comparison to what goes on in my visions. In that other-world action is explicit, people plot and execute devious intentions. Big-eyed she-monsters whisper to me from over beds. Just this afternoon some blue-tailed woman I used to obsess over helped me escape capture."

"Have you nailed her yet?" inquired Isidore. Even at the cost of an all-out argument, he couldn't resist a needling inquiry.

"Not with a hammer or any part of my body," Erik retorted.

Thayer decided to intercede before Erik took a mallet to his father and closed the door on sharing his hallucinations. "You have a savvy sense of humor, Erik. Your father's appreciation for the spirit of comedy has dried up and blown away! What do you think happened to it? There were times when he used to be a fairly animated fellow. Maybe his disorder eroded the whimsical areas of his brain."

"No one appointed you Grand Inquisitor into my life," Isidore retaliated, reaching for a bottle of wine. He filled his glass to the brim, but was too embarrassed to use the glass straw tucked beneath his napkin.

"Let him see how you eat, Isidore." Erik teased. "Go on. You'll choke on your dinner if you don't remove the mask. Thayer is ready for enlightenment."

"You don't care to save me some grace of station?"

"I don't give a maggot's breath about your embarrassment. Politely coaxing explanations doesn't work. You continually stall and circumvent." Erik tried to take a calming breath, but his self-control snapped. Jumping to his feet, he grabbed Isidore by the lapels and lifted him from his chair. It one swift movement forward, he pressed the elder de Chagny up against the wall, forcing Isidore's spindly legs to dangle and kick in search of a foundation. "Let's dispense with social discourse and bite right into the meat of this – like giant reptiles, shall we? Don't touch that dinner bell, Thayer!"

Thayer's hand stopped, suspended in the air above the silver egret.

"Two carnivorous alligators?" Isidore was atwitter at the thought. "Yes, I rather favor the analogy. To bite from life is to open the mouth wide and rip at the flesh. To taste the blood upon your tongue and roll in the muck with the prey locked between your pointed teeth. You and I are rolling are we not? Two predators writhing down into the silt at the bottom of the swamp, forced to meld in viciousness."

Thayer rushed to stand beside the two men. "Might I suggest that you ease down a bit? You're a good deal stronger than he is, Erik. You could hurt him…he is delicate and brittle."

Isidore reached past Erik's shoulder, snatched Thayer's spectacles, and in the space of one millisecond snapped them with his thumb and index finger. "Physical strength is **not** the issue here!"

Thayer took back his busted glasses. "I'll need tape," he said lamely. "We'll have to send for another pair. I have extras in my Paris apartment." This wasn't the first time his lenses had been broken in the care of a patient.

Isidore stared at Erik, amused. "What is true tonight will be just as true tomorrow. I caused these complications, these unforeseen inherent traits," he whispered. "Rushing ahead rashly has cost me dearly. Jonas Salk didn't pay for experimenting on himself, whereas, I…" he cut off his speech and abruptly changed the subject. He wasn't finished toying. "I have a cramp and need to excuse myself. Let go, son." He turned his shoulders as if trying to leave.

"Colossal liar! Let putrefaction take you!" Flecks of angry spittle hit his captive's mask. "You have a cramp like I have female breasts."

Isidore actually chuckled. "Oh, I'm so afraid. The integrity of a lesser man should be questioned, not that of a scientist of stature and a titled count. I do not lie, I only shade the truth from errant exposure!" Isidore grunted with satisfaction. In a perverse way it seemed best to continue playing with Erik's level of insight. Prolonging the game a minimal few seconds longer. "You are the prefect representation. No. You are better than the man. You are everything he ever aspired to be and more, much more. You're him personified and augmented a hundredfold! **My progeny!**"

"No more terse obscurities! If I move my thumbs onto your larynx I can crack your airway like a chicken bone. I barely understand what's happening. Only that I'm teetering at the point of desperation." Erik lifted Isidore higher up the wall. His skinny captive could have been a bag of crunchy potato chips. "Still think I need diagnosing, Dr. Delaquois? It's Isidore de Chagny who sorely wants for rehabilitation."

"Perhaps Valbien is not the drug of choice for you," stressed Thayer, resisting the desire to touch Erik. Even angry the boy's voice was euphonic. "The drug seems to be intensifying your mood swings…it might even be increasing the frequency of your visions. Listen carefully, what I am about to tell you **is** accurate. Touching people when they're sleepwalking can sharpen the effects of their trance. Stimuli from the outside world heightens confusion and opens the way for agitation. There is a genuine possibility that you are sleepwalking. Physically confronting Isidore could be escalating your malignant behavior."

At this precise moment, Mozart's busy *Rondo Alla Turca* started playing over several speakers affixed in the corners of the ceiling. Was someone in the security monitoring station playing a joke to further ruffle everyone's feathers? None of the three diners felt they could suffer through another bar of the brisk sonata.

"Turn it off!" They hollered in comic unison. The piano piece stopped abruptly.

On a nearby marble pedestal sat a *pot a confit*, an antique ceramic jar from the southwest of France. In earlier centuries, before refrigeration, the container preserved duck or goose cassoulet. The upper half was glazed in royal Provencal blue, while the bottom half was left unglazed so the pot could be buried halfway in the ground, keeping its contents cool. Adrenalin pumped through Erik. He felt wild, reckless to the consequences. Holding onto Isidore with his left hand, he snatched the pot off its base. Threatening to bash Isidore's head with the relic, he vowed, "If you don't hold yourself accountable and give me answers, I'll crush your skull. Then I'll go down to the lab and destroy every chromatograph, every mass spectrometer, every…"

"You wouldn't!" The *pot a confit* rose higher. "All right. All right." Isidore finally surrendered. "Stop! I apologize for these theatrics, Thayer. I'm afraid we have very real problems developing here. *Veritas omnia vincit* – but truth defeats all things."

Erik let Isidore's back slid down the wall, allowing the man's feet to resume his weight. "Truthfully, Isidore. So many genetic projects vie for your attention, tell us which one has priority?"

"You, dear boy. You. My ancestor, Rupert de Chagny, had a grandfather who was a maestro, a man talented at any instrument he undertook, a savant, a virtuoso whose voice carried, into vibrant life, any piece of music he wished to sing."

"And?" Erik's tone told him he would abide nothing but the entire picture.

"I wanted those talents," Isidore's words began to slur. "I received my first inkling that something had gone amiss when I developed no inclination toward music. Prepare yourself, Thayer." He reached up. Easing his facemask downward, he revealed a forehead riddled with pronounced wrinkles. Then two wiry gray-haired eyebrows provided a canopy for the most amazing set of mutating eyes. As they watched a deep iridescent blue emerged, eradicating the blue-green of Isidore's former irises.

The mask continued lower. The face was astonishing. There was no nose, just a hole with only the suggestion of a septum and a small budding promontory of nasal cartilage.

From somewhere deep within his soul, recognition stirred. Erik heard himself say a name. "Julian? Julian?" He had no idea what person the name represented. It boggled the mind, yet in some vague unsubstantiated way he identified with the unmistakable slurred speech and the color of the eyes staring out at him.

"Who is Julian?" inquired Thayer, apprehension creeping discernibly into his voice.

Openly incredulous, Erik warred with a substantial degree of shock. "What did you do, Isidore? Julian had a monstrous tyrannical streak. How many worlds are colliding within these walls?"

Isidore exposed a receding virtually non-existent jaw. The set of thin withdrawn lips trembled. "I guess I am the ultimate hybrid creature. Regrettably, you must accept me for what I am, a combination of both Isidore and Julian. Created two years before your birth, still evolving."

Thayer stood watching in disbelief, his head bobbed back and forth between this unrecognizable man and Erik. Delaquois' body language was anything but tentative as his fingers squeezed into the shoulders of his former classmate. "I said," he was clearly past calm and given to shouting, "who, in all the ignominious layers of Satan's Hell, is **Julian?**"

Erik ripped off Isidore's mask, exposing the rest. The neck that held up the deformed face was incongruously normal.

"How's your appetite now, Thayer?"

15 *SCAVENGER OF THE DEAD*

$\mathfrak{I}$nstantaneous pride took over. Embarrassed at Thayer's bellowed question and gawking eyes, Isidore silently pleaded with Erik for mercy. Failing in the effort, his fists reached up to pound weakly against the young man's chest. The pot dropped. Crashing to the floor, it shattered into a dozen pieces.

In a very telling way, the geneticist was growing more distorted. Erik knew he should allow Isidore some form of modest recovery, but this was the first time he'd actually recognized the underlying personality. Behind him, he reasoned that Thayer must be doing what ninety-nine per cent of humanity does at the sight of a monstrosity: gasp, recoil, leer. While mentally berating himself for not limiting Isidore's degradation, he did nothing to promote charity. His ripened anger refused to allow easing the experience for any of them.

"Hand me a candle," he growled. Snatching the proffered object from Thayer's hand, he shoved it close to Isidore's diminutive chin. In the flickering light Isidore's face appeared more bizarre and threatening. Hollowed cheeks, the twisted bump of the anterior nose shadowing the two cavernous holes, the vibrissae hairs quite visible. De Chagny's wild eyebrows telegraphed together – shooting an apex toward his receding hairline, they sent a renewed plea for leniency.

"Whoever thinks the basic laws of Nature cannot be violated errs in judgment. Her decrees are not irrevocable." Isidore's visibly shaking lips drew back in an asymmetrical grimace.

"Yes, apparently that's true." Thayer studied the abnormalities. "Though the price she extracts may prove quite steep."

"Every manipulation forces a redefinition of the basic ground rules. Well? Are you sufficiently put off by my features?"

Thayer placed his hand gently atop Erik's shoulder. "We've won. Please let him go."

Relaxing his grip, Erik wondered if the disclosure of a countenance so hideous and unreal altered Thayer's concession to cooperate in a cure. *At the very least, he must be questioning our familial propensity toward distortion.* "No stalling, Isidore. This confrontation isn't finished. I want answers. Tell us everything!"

Righting himself, Isidore straightened his jacket. "Let's sit." Following this logical directive, Erik assisted him to a chair. The trio crowded together, intent on a huddle.

The earnestness in Isidore's voice convinced them he was finished playing. His deep-seated interest in the mechanics of DNA seemed to rejuvenate him. "After all these years of not speaking about these matters to you, Erik, what a relief to finally disclose the truth of the mishaps. I have no one to blame but myself."

Here on the edge of knowing, Erik could afford to be a little understanding. "Isidore doesn't like to eat in front of others. His face mortifies him. He will let them carry his food away rather than endure humiliation. We should let him eat something."

The geneticist patted Erik's hand and taking the glass straw sucked up some of the wine.

"DNA can be devilishly pesky material," he began. "Billions upon billions of alleles, tiny spots with a singular message to define the greater whole. During the years of my childhood I'd heard stories about the de Chagny's history. The Golden Era, that one period where the stars showered their brightest blessings upon us, occurred with one distinctive ancestor. The meditative composer and musician I mentioned previously was a genius, an architect, a master trickster. He built a wondrous room of mirrors. It sits directly below Erik's bedroom.

"In my early professional years I spent so much of my time inventing serums that redirected the genetics of others, I forgot how to enjoy a personal life. The initial taste of success with my work, motivated me to turn more of my attentions toward this ancestor. I already had our familial traits laid out. An amazing shift in overall facial features and eye color occurred in the generation of the savant's children. Obviously he was unique. I thought to find the direct source of the DNA, decode the particulars and recycle them. Sharing in the talents of a superior predecessor became my goal, only I thought his name was Raoul. I had the tools of Quantitative Genetics to help me estimate variations of specific traits, and I knew if nothing else, I could be tenacious. Raoul was obviously an augmented individual, intelligent, multi-talented to an almost unheard of degree. If I could pinpoint his uniqueness, dissect his genes; I might be able to augment myself. Family rumors had it that the genius and his wife were interred in a secret crypt in the chapel, but there was a plot in the family cemetery with a headstone engraved Raoul Camille de Chagny. A little confusing, so I started with that common grave. We found some bones in an ossuary, totally useless as a source for DNA."

"Yes," interjected Erik. "He was in the dirt of the wine cellar for years before we moved him to the cemetery."

Isidore's eyes grew round in acknowledgement. "You'll have to tell me the particulars later, they might account for some disparities. The ossuary was only a temporary set back. My father's childhood bedtime stories described our ancestor in a mask. No pictures of Raoul exist, but upstairs in the attic there's an oil painting that once hung in rooms belonging to an old bachelor uncle, Michael de Chagny – a talented sculptor. The portrait was of a man with the lower half of his face masked."

"Why did you want to do this?" interrupted Thayer.

"Let's just say personal gratification, scientific ego. All my life I've had insights, remarkable insights. I was close to giving the world governments the means to control over-population. It was time to do something for me. When I could still father children I wondered what it would be like to regain the mind of another. You've seen the lineal map of my ancestors. I studied the genealogy. Several people after Raoul were talented, but nothing like the man himself. All the DNA sequencing and tissue analysis I could accomplish on my own pointed to that one individual. I felt driven to obtain the pure article. It occurred to me that the bones buried in the cemetery were not the Raoul I sought. The genetics pointed to a newcomer interjecting himself into the familial line. Perhaps the original was murdered for greed or love. Whatever the reason, this outsider might have assumed Raoul's name and placed himself within the family. A peculiar, but undeniable truth was percolating there on the white boards before me.

"We had to find the masked Raoul, the usurper. I reasoned he was the one entombed in the crypt. But I didn't know exactly where the crypt rested, or how to enter it for that matter. I scoured the chapel searching everywhere for the tomb's location. I studied the building like one would a topographical map, letting its layout take me from the highest pinnacle to the lowest corner of the basement. I believed the genius would point the way. I only needed to think like a man who was equal parts magician and musician. Removing the covers from a massive organ housed in the chapel, I hit three distinct notes. Those notes traveled on phenomenal acoustics, bouncing off the walls, reverberating all around me. I turned on the bench to see what the maestro would have seen. My eyes fixed on the star in the center of the chapel's transept.

"Standing in the center of that star I turned to see the three cubbyholes in the middle asp. No one ever understood what they were for, books or papers we reasoned. They provide access to gears that extend three long bars out to a lever hidden in a space within the riser of the first step leading to the dais. The lever is revealed when the heel of a hand pushes on the riser's upper border. On that fateful day my eyes saw all the cleverness of the construction...and I wish to all the Fates I'd left that damnable lever alone. But I was a man close to uncovering secrets hidden for decades. Addicted to a quest. I ripped off the proverbial blindfold of caution and opened the crypt. I found a chamber with two sarcophagi. One held a male with a mask – facially deformed – the other a teenage female. Above their heads, etched into the marble in a beautiful script were the words: *Venisti remanebis donec denuo compeltus sis.*"

"From whence you came, you shall remain, until you are complete again," whispered Thayer.

"Almost poetic," Isidore said with a great sigh. "Almost! Oh, I was on top of the world. Initial work led me to believe that the male's disfigurement was not genetic, not the fluke of recessive traits. I felt falsely reassured. Even if the abnormality had an inherited basis, it had skipped three generations without reoccurrence. When I couldn't identify the disfiguring gene of Treacher Collins Syndrome I thought myself safe in proceeding. Such foolish exuberance!

"Now I'm suffering for those hasty conclusions. I injected myself with his flawed DNA. The first clue was a symptom I'd never experienced – enuresis. In my entire life I'd never wet my bed. When genes are passed on, some are assertive and dominant, while others remain silently recessive. My body tried to accommodate the new information in thousands of ways. Over the following weeks I suffered through bouts of lethargy, vertigo, migraine headaches, shaky hands and tremulous speech patterns. Episodes of low blood sugar, dancing spots before my eyes, sore muscles and joints. A brand new sensitivity to light and sound made me continuously ill. A never ending merry-go-round, and I had not one moment's inkling toward creating a piece of music.

"Test results fluctuated dramatically. Some DNA code was permanently altered, some RNA messaging left unaffected as my body tried to reach a state of equilibrium and stabilize. Pain of one sort or another became my constant companion. Then the facial deformity started to develop and is still progressing. As the muscles atrophy and the bone grows porous and contracts, the areas throb and I am in agony. Except for my arms and hands, which have only grown stronger, I'm like a suppurating carcass that hasn't finished rotting. I wanted to enhance myself, create sperm that would seed the next generation with added talents. My obsession fostered nothing but suffering and as an added bonus, mixing the DNA rendered me sterile. A side effect I had not anticipated. Not a single sperm cell grows within me, and the cause remains unknown."

"I can help you, Isidore," Thayer sounded grieved. "We'll vet you with a complete and thorough examination. Tag the damaged DNA and remove it on a molecular level if necessary."

"Don't you think I've explored every possible solution? Nyah works on the cure night and day, and let me assure you she knows as much as I. The final telltale clue that I'd erred, the *pièce de résistance*, appeared with my chameleon ability to change eye color. Rare eye color appeared in only two other generations. The oil painting of the half-masked male shows he had brilliant, almost iridescent blue eyes. The photographs and sketches of Michael and Sarah de Chagny, Raoul's children, reveal they both had distinctive amber irises. Rare in males, even rarer in females. No generation before or after them evidenced these traits. I scoured every source I could locate.

"Another red herring? No, not when we let genetics provide the answer. When the unfertilized egg and sperm meld, each supplies the tiny new creature they're forming with their half of a complete set of DNA. An independent sorting of new genetic combinations to define the progeny promptly commences. Careful analysis with probabilities proved that in this process of recombination, Michael and Sarah inherited their eye color from one parent alone. This direct parent held the key. I named this individual, parent X. If he wasn't Raoul, then who was he? Michael and Sarah were the youngest and oldest of the three children born to the genius. I am the direct descendent and great grandson of the middle child, Ariel. His branch of the family stayed here on the estate. Imagine my shock, when months later Nyah and I identified the male in the crypt as Michael and Sarah's son. Apparently they suffered Genetic Sexual Attraction (GSA). There is no record of their child anywhere. That's why the portrait never hung in the hall, but was kept to the side in private quarters. Intuitively I knew his name was Julian. Sarah was married off to the son of a baron, a neighbor. Their branch of the family lives down the road. I have distant cousins on that estate, but none of us are particularly close."

He threw his napkin down on the table. "So here we are, Julian and I both sharing this crippled body. Most of the time he is not mentally dominant, but I have more to fear from him than the random threats I receive from the militant pro-lifer community. Julian is in a very special category of unconscionable fundamentalist. To him everything is either black or white...there is no gray. He's ill tempered and dangerous, doesn't like subordination and manipulates for control. As you can see, I am quite rational. So he hasn't succeeded in taking over, not for want of trying, but I digress. Forgive the ranting.

"Angry, sick, ready to lay waste to my entire professional career to regain my former self, I returned to the crypt. I read and re-read the words emblazoned on the wall, overturned vases of flowers I had brought in several times a week to pay homage to the maestro, got drunk over the sarcophagus. One solitary midnight, the truth occurred to me... back to the two Raoul's. How stupid of me not to see the irony of it. I turned the house upside down looking for more clues. I found hints almost everywhere, but the best lay in a letter, just waiting for me, in a remarkable safe in the attic. 'Undone by my own hand,' it read. 'Undone by my own hellish hand!'

"Now I understood the bones in the cemetery. Here was proof to confirm the genetic footprint we uncovered. What a wild goose chase that letter sent us on! Nyah and I tried desperately to find Julian's grandfather, the true savant, and I haven't told you the best of it. In Raoul's letter he knows he's dying and bids his wife's lover come take his place. To emerge from the shadows and caverns under the Paris Opera

House and be a French nobleman. Oh, yes! That letter is the most delightful reading. Facts started tumbling into place. My illustrious whispered-about ancestor was the Phantom of the Opera, the Ghost himself! A most tortured soul." He paused to let his words sink into the gray matter of their brains.

"Nearly frantic, we searched for a remarkable treasure, Erik's true resting place. To find the correct 'Raoul', the supplanter, we had to be better detectives. Leroux's book makes mention of a skeleton found near a well in the theater's underground. We went over the place with cadaver detectors. It was never there. How to find him? A brain focused on a single subject can be a powerful tool, a demented, self-driven engine. There were no pictures, but there were clues. In Gaston Leroux's book, Darius is an old servant tending to a Persian called the Daroga, but if Darius were already dead...perhaps the master of disguises might..." Isidore's mind was racing. "The book alludes several times to a certain degree of loyalty felt for the Ghost by Madame Giry and this Daroga. Reviewing the pages I became increasingly aware of their rather stubborn sense of: We must protect him – stand before him as a shield so that the world will not harm him anymore. I returned to the crypt and read again the Latin phrase, this time not with the sense that it mocked me, but that my ancestor spoke to his concealment from all others. It was bizarre, but if viewed as a directive it seemed he wished to speak to me personally."

Erik got up and pressed his back against the wall. Arms folded across his chest, he bent slightly forward. Now he knew the truth. He just simply knew.

Isidore put his mask back over his face. Security. "My predecessor wanted to attempt something rather grand. A logogram is a letter, a symbol or sign representing an entire word, like an ampersand."

"Yes, go on," Thayer responded, relieved to be temporarily spared the view, but anxious to hear.

"There are two *fleurs-de-lis*, one at the beginning, the other at the end of the phrase. Each is contained within an oval. If you mentally place them side by side and let them touch...they equal the mathematical symbol for infinity."

"Riddles and ideograms?" Thayer was incredulous. "Could the man have known you were coming, Isidore?"

"I think he did," whispered Erik.

"He did indeed, but I'll get to that. Don't rush the telling, I've waited too long to divulge it. Since I couldn't give Nyah children," continued Isidore. "And I couldn't be the maestro, at least I could re-create him. In one of life's greatest paradoxes, make him **my** heir!"

In despair, Erik's back slid down the wall until his butt sat on the floor, knees bent.

"While I scoured the crypt for the way into what surely would be a second chamber, Nyah continued an intense hunt on the cellular and microvascular levels. Looking for patterns to determine heredity, she concluded that the amazing talents of our illusive parent X are recessive." Isidore waved his hands in frustration, his mask still not anchored correctly. "Desperation possessed me. I knew it was much too late for my body and I was so close, so close to seeing our illustrious ancestor with my own eyes. I had all the power necessary to bring him back…to let him live again! What a mad hunt, with me growing more crippled by the day, at times by the hour! My facial deformity progressed, my jaw actually receded."

"Wait," Thayer interrupted. "You said **our** ancestor. I distinctly heard our."

"Nyah is a distant cousin to me. The great-great-granddaughter of Pascale de Grasse. A woman the Phantom knew and impregnated after coming to this estate."

Thayer heaved a great sigh. *How intricately this mesh of intrigue is woven.* "We'll explore that fact later. Tell us, how did you find the second half of the crypt?"

"Permit me a swallow of wine," Isidore reached for his straw.

From his low point on the floor, Erik whispered, "What a mistake!"

"No mistake…too late for me, but not for you. You were and are an exceptionally augmented individual. Senses heightened to the point where stimuli become almost painful. It was as if you drew me back to the crypt, compelling me from beyond the grave to find you. The answer came with re-reading the inscriptions. In my desperate need to find your former body, I'd overlooked the simple picture of infinity. Pressing the two sister *fleurs-de-lis* simultaneously, released a catch holding a revolving door. There were so many marvelous clues, and now I'd hit the mother load. Since that discovery, I've located a letter written in Michael's own hand. He sculpted a sarcophagus for each of his parents and at their deaths hid them in the secret chamber. Now I had not just the coffin with Erik, but his music, including the greatest pieces he ever wrote. In the coffin were his private journals, penned in red ink. Did you know that he added his own blood to many of his missives? He put something of himself in his most important writings. In those journals I read that he knew a witch named Lucretia Sorrel, attended a séance, cavorted with spirits. Lucretia predicted that I would come looking for my ancestor. And he must have believed her, because he was careful to arrange things for the future. The body was hermetically sealed in the coffin. There was viable DNA in both the marrow of the femurs and all the posterior molars."

Erik rose to his feet and came to stand behind Isidore. Leaning into his ear, he hissed, "You stole teeth in the name of scientific achievement! Your injuries may be accidental, the price of an ego run amuck, but my predicament is no accident."

"Don't speak to me as if I'm a criminal," Isidore countered. "What would you attempt given my position? I'm certainly not the only individual wanting to tamper with DNA. Some of today's most heated arguments center on the theory of eugenics – the idea that humans should practice selective reproduction in an effort to improve the species. The tenet that superior intelligence can be manipulated and inherited is still widely held among many in the field. So many couples are requesting designer babies. They want children of a particular sex, hair and eye color, with athletic and intellectual abilities. Making you I told myself repeatedly, 'We cannot fail, failure is not an option.' Yet we failed many times. Certain laws were decided upon in that sludge of prehistoric primordial soup that spawned us – laws written in the microscopic molecular compounds of DNA. Edicts placed within the long spiraling chains of nucleotides composed of deoxyribose, phosphate, and the nitrogen-rich bases of adenine, guanine, cytosine, and thymine. I redistributed some of them for you, Erik. Stacked the odds well in your favor for once."

"What are you rambling about?" Erik wanted to choke something, anything.

"Yes! Explain that last statement," echoed Thayer.

"Mortality is a shark that swims and doesn't care who it bites. I simply engineered things in my child's best interests. He was augmented in his former life and now even more so. Everything is heightened, his immune system, reticular endothelials…I could go on and on. The original Erik had amazing genes – already geared for longevity. By my calculations, my Erik might live at least two hundred years. Barring any accidents claiming him." He motioned for his creation to come around and face him. "I've bestowed on you the wherewithal to accomplish Biblical longevity. You see," his fingers swept through the air, "all I needed was a tiny bit of re-hydrated blood. Three billion genetic codes in one strand of DNA, every blue print necessary for building a living human being! We have yet to see all that you're capable of…you haven't finished maturing! You are him in every way and wondrously personified. The original Erik died in 1918, a victim of the great flu pandemic. Who knows how long he would have lived had a virus not consumed him? I've seen to it that you will never die of the flu again! I've engineered your immune system to withstand a constant barrage. Do you want to learn music, medicine, architecture? Trust me, you could absorb those areas of interest, or any other subject you choose to pursue, with remarkable speed. You have the intellect of a genius."

"You dragged me back into this world, but I brought the past with me. And not the pleasant parts either! The most tarnished evil events have come through first, probably because they made more of an impression on inherent memory. It's as if all the days and nights of torment are storming the shores of my consciousness like an invading army. The inner vision I once held of myself is clouded, only with the help of a mirror can I truly see the current me…and even then…the past vies with the present for control of my brain."

Neither Thayer nor Isidore understood what Erik was talking about.

The young man's face was set toward the floor, eyes closed. His fingers groped the air, searching for some invisible comfort. Tears were close to falling.

Isidore rose, his hands tenderly squeezing the searching fingers. "I'm not a numbskull, nor am I a charlatan. You are a *surhomme*, Erik, a superman. There has never been a creature like you. You've never had a cold or the sniffles. You are immune to every disease known to mankind because I vaccinated you genetically. You will never have tooth decay, or visual problems. Unfortunately I didn't know about the memory patterns."

"Dalliance in genetics has a fee. You scientists are devious, too curious – always proposing the next logical questions and trying to answer them. How much did it cost to make me?"

Consumed with the knowledge he'd never treated a patient like this, Thayer spoke too quickly and too loudly, "God save us from men playing god!"

"God has stepped aside for the moment," responded Erik, lifting his face. "I have no other aspirations tonight but to understand this phenomenon. Thank you for coming here, Dr. Delaquois. You have been the catalyst. Now show me my dead body, Isidore."

16 INVESTIGATING THE CRYPT

𝔉og and drifting mist hovered on the grounds as cooler night air embraced an earth, abandoned hours ago by a fleeting winter sun. Hung in the sky, a strange lonely moon appeared as nothing but a nearly indiscernible, hazy disc. They brought Isidore out in a wheelchair. He'd declared his legs too unstable to walk, a direct result of the evening's stress. Erik became oddly energized by the late night excursion. He didn't say much, but as he guided the chair, his head scanned their surroundings, searching for some unseen companion. The thickening condensation effectively dulled the klieg lamps stationed on the estate's outer walls. In the muted light the pitted stone chapel seemed almost invisible. Surrounded by giant oaks that stood as guardian sentries, the structure was down a walkway and secreted from the chateau proper.

The inside of the dimly lit nave proved a softly echoing space – rather thoughtfully decorated. A serene cavern with a groined ceiling attended by walls of cherry wood giving way to creamy sandstone. Sadly unappreciated for only the rare lonely visitor prayed or meditated here. An arcade of columns ran down either wall creating solemn niches for statues of plump cupids and the marble busts of veiled women. The figures created a mood of reverence for love that did nothing to forestall the sense of dread and grief Isidore experienced.

At the transept, he sensed Erik's fingers fidgeting on the handlebars of the chair, evidence of nervous excitement. The aged geneticist yielded to a lingering hope that he could talk Erik out of this macabre viewing. "I must rest a moment. Don't you think this an interesting place, Thayer?"

"Rather sublime. Non-reflective of any religion, which is unusual, aside from hospital chapels of course." He took a seat on the pew beside Isidore's chair. *Procrastination might work.*

Sitting on the first step of the dais, Erik added, "It's actually several places in one." Directly behind him stood the central asp and a long raised rectangular table covered in pure white damask and elaborate lace. The table had eight legs of polished wood, each a nearly naked carved Greek female figure.

"How so?" asked his physician.

"When I show you, try to keep an open mind about the essential nature of a duplicate. Some knowledge seems intrinsic. I know you still think I'm delusional. Certainly disjointed from a rational sense of self, but we haven't spoken the acrimonious 'clone' word. There, we've finally given voice to the five letters. Shall we let them hang in the air like an occult curse?"

"The search always led back to this chapel," interjected Isidore. He abhorred the word clone. "Looking all over hell and creation did not yield the success that this place surrendered." He took off his mask, rubbed his eyes, and laid the covering on the lap-blanket over his knees. "What a tangled web of human interplay they wove. Erik assuming Raoul's name and title, creating an antechamber for his grandson."

"Where is the crypt?" asked Thayer.

"I think I'm entombed down there." Erik pointed to the marbled star pattern in the middle of the transept. The area lay just in front of his feet. He cast his arms out in a large encompassing circle, fingers flared. "I command thee to open! Open Sesame!"

"Very funny," Isidore said, devoid of humor. "No sense of respect for this hallowed place. Do you understand that geneticists have the unparalleled opportunity of correcting scores of devastating diseases and progressive disorders? We've been altering and replicating DNA since the 1950's. The procedures are routine, quite unremarkable. Your former body carried the gene for Wilson's disease; the defect added a more pronounced copper ring to the outside of your pupils. It exists in you no more. You haven't a trace of it. Let's not open the crypt. You are here, nothing is as important as that." He watched Erik stand. "Wait. Wait! You have to know that I hold only the best intentions for you. I wanted to leave you inscrutable, protected, with all the privacy in the world. It's these catatonic seizures that have forced this investigation." His voice was tinged with genuine regret. "Don't reduce your promising life to the stuff of science fiction."

"I agree," Thayer sounded upbeat, positive. "Perhaps these episodes are only vivid waking dreams. I'll help you get the answers. You needn't go down there."

"Not a convincing argument," responded Erik very politely. "What makes you think I can't come here on my own? With every passing day, I grow more insightful and more unstable."

"The urgency to see your donor's body is not that acute," Thayer lied. "Sit back down and tell me of your other interests."

"I'll be happy to print you a full list tomorrow, Dr. Delaquois. Really, I think you're being paid too much."

"And how do you know what I'm paid?"

"I'll explain that tomorrow, too." Erik's hand gestured toward Isidore. "And now tomb robber, let's see my coffin. I insist."

"I want to leave. I need to retire and get some sleep, so I forbid this morbid viewing." For emphasis Isidore concealed his face behind the mask.

"Show me the crypt, Isidore. No. Better yet, I'll show you. Because you lied about how to enter the chambers."

Isidore was dumfounded, "You've never been down there. How could you have discovered the mechanism?"

"You still don't believe me. I remember it. Perhaps you enhanced the hippocampus in my limbic system too much. After all, we really don't understand how instinctual memory is transferred from one generation of birds to the next, do we? The geared pulleys and bars that open the trapdoor to the crypt run under this entire middle dais. Busting through the three niches provides access to a tightening mechanism should the entrance ever fail and require adjustments." He jumped up and turned the two outer carved women on the sanctuary table so they faced inward toward each other. "This table is bolted to the floor. Its faceplate holds a glass tube. When the meniscus in that tube finds true center, as it's doing now, the pivot is turned and…"

He didn't need to finish. The center of the marble star slid back, leaving a black hole surrounded by something that looked very much like the teeth of a bat.

"Delightful setting. Shall we, gentlemen?" Mocking their combined years of scientific expertise came too easily. "See, it doesn't really matter how I know. We get the same effect."

Isidore sighed and allowed Erik to seize the wheelchair and ease it down one step at a time. "You're laughing in my face, aren't you?"

"Laughing? No. Making you accountable? Yes. It is the world at large that will laugh at the jest of exposing me to life again. People are cruel beyond imagination. Coarse and vulgar with everything that's strange. My new face is whole, but my origins are mired in the grotesque.

You didn't think. I have no legal rights. How will you explain to the authorities where I came from?"

"I'll thank you to speak to me with the utmost civility." The chair bumped on a step, jolting Isidore's head. "You did that on purpose. Need I remind you that everything can be purchased for a price, especially leniency." The chair came to rest on the crypt's floor. "As your parent, I wish you only prosperity and happiness."

The space before them was black as pitch. The air literally filled with an uninviting suspense. Here on the threshold, the two doctors resisted proceeding through the initial compartment. Erik pressed a hand to a wall and let his soulful eyes adjust. The emotional conflict had to be faced.

"For God's sake, someone strike a light," Thayer ordered.

"There are candles in the torcheres," Isidore directed. "Here's a lighter, Erik."

"No electricity! How devilishly primitive!" sputtered Thayer, trembling as a flickering dimness helped them identify objects in the room.

The flames revealed two sarcophagi set to waist height on marble briers. The walls of the antechamber were richly decorated with carvings of palm fronds, laurels and swags of fruit.

"These contain the bodies of Julian and a girl he loved. The journals identify her as a laundress named Sonia," explained Isidore. "Julian committed several criminal acts and paid a dear price. Is it all right if we don't look at him tonight?"

Erik gave him an obligatory nod. Engulfed by a strange insistent grief, he ran his hand across the top of Julian's sarcophagus, disturbing a fine layer of dust with his fingertips. *"Filius meus, mors tua vita mea.* (My son, your death is my life.) Ancient Latin words indicating a battle for survival – in a former century, at the bottom of the oubliette, Erik's life necessitated Julian's defeat." He suddenly realized that Isidore hadn't lied about how to get into the retro chamber. "As in the Egyptian tombs of old, the Pharaoh lies beyond. Come, Thayer. Doesn't this adventure enthrall the hell out of you?"

Delaquois straightened his jacket. "What a privilege to be entertained in the theater of the surreal." A little light was adding to his bravery.

Isidore was mute. Powerless to prevent the inevitable, he watched as the pride of his life pushed on the two *fleurs-de-lis* simultaneously. Inside the wall a hanging hook released a rod and a revolving door spun on its pivot.

Lighting the way, Erik entered the second vault first.

In some respects this crypt mirrored the one before it. The two sarcophagi were raised on briers in a room of continuing white and gray Italian marble. On the far wall, emblazoned in high relief were the words: *Ici immortalize deux âmes qui ont aimé pensée après la raison* (Here immortalized two souls who loved past thought past reason). The elaborate pattern of the intricately interwoven letters spoke of eternal commitment. In a corner, pressed up against the wall stood an upright sarcophagus of Anubis. Strange glyphs – symbols conveying coded information – covered the wall to the left of the jackal-god's head. To the right of Anubis sat an ebony statue of Bastet. In one hand the protective cat-goddess held a ceremonial sistrum and in the other an aegis.

"What are those, decorations?" asked Thayer.

"We identified Anubis as a theater prop. Erik and Christine had a thing for the Conveyer of Souls, the Changeling god of the Egyptians," Isidore offered from just inside the doorway. "Anubis is empty, but Bastet is of solid wood, the finest quality."

Erik set the torchere aside. "He didn't want anyone to find this place but you, Isidore. He knew you were coming."

"He didn't believe the predictions of a witch, did he?" Thayer challenged in an effort to cling to accepted rationality. "There's thirty years between Erik's death in 1918 and Isidore's birth in 1948. He's Isidore's great-great-grandfather, they're three generations apart."

Erik looked directly into his eyes. "He knew the numbers. Lucretia told him. Seventy-eight years lie between his death and 1996, the year Isidore placed his DNA inside some wretched female's genetically obliterated egg. Seven is the number of perfection and eight the symbol of eternity."

All three paused to study the sarcophagi. Two imperial angels carved from white marble reposed on the top of each. The reclining statues were exactly the same except that the one on the left had breasts and a more feminine face. They each held a protective sword, the tip aimed at their feet. A reflection of their readiness to do battle during their tortured lives. The hilts of the swords were a pale yellow alloy of gold and silver known as electrum. Their heads were encircled with halos inlaid with stars of carnelian. A symbolic depiction of celestial wisdom that spoke to the incisive acts of a monster and his bride.

The atmosphere inside the crypt became palpably oppressive as Erik moved to the head of his sarcophagus. He inhaled. Not a single stray odor of rot or mildew, nothing but a trace of dust reached his nose.

Isidore could barely contain his apprehension. "One last time, I'm begging you," setting aside pride he pleaded. "Don't view this terrain of corpses and fossilized hopes. Leave it alone, Erik. Live your life above ground. Spend my money. I'll lavish it on you."

Bending at the waist, Erik stretched his arms down over the front of the male seraph, until his hands came to rest on those that held the hilt of the sword. "Something of great value to us lies in this coffin. How will I know who I am without knowing who I was? Help me slide the lid, Thayer."

As their conscripted guest assisted with sliding the cover and easing its side to the floor, he wondered if Erik voluntarily initiated these catatonic states. Focused concentration on a single object sounded similar to self-hypnosis. Thayer dismissed the thought; that ability didn't explain the other symptoms. *Something drained the electricity.* The object lying inside the stone container took his attention – a polished black and silver coffin decorated with a spray of silver roses.

"You intend to submit yourself to this dreadful discovery?" but even Thayer was curious now. Isidore touched Thayer's forearm, signaling him to step back.

Erik lifted the coffin's lid. There laid the corpse of his former self. Dressed in a black tuxedo and white shirt, a piece of gauzy linen loosely covered the face and another the hands. Viewing his own body with cool disdain, he asked, "May I touch it?"

Nausea rolled over Isidore. Why hadn't he foreseen the genius's intractable curiosity? He gave an obligatory nod, sweeping his hand above the arm of the wheelchair in consent. Erik reached down and touched the anterior chest. He found his body hard and cold, so cold. A flash of great liquid eyes and pale, exceptionally long fingers came to him. He lifted the gauze covering the face and at the last second looked away.

Thayer saw his patient trembling from head to foot. *Even this intense degree of stress doesn't trigger a seizure.*

Erik moved sideways around the coffin. Like an engrossed shark sensing blood in the water, the human flowed on a current thick with expectation. Holding his head forward in line with his body, he viewed the corpse from the corner of his eyes, as one would take in a sight almost too horrific to comprehend. Doubts peeled away. Even with this hindered view, he recognized the cadaverous figure in the coffin as an aged version of himself. The visible 'normal' part of the dead face, covered in powder and touched with rouge, was thankfully emotionless.

"This might seem like something of an ill omen," muttered Thayer hopefully. "Like a groom seeing his bride before the wedding – brings misfortune – but life is what we make of it. This is the old Erik. You have different challenges, different opportunities."

Fascinated, the two doctors watched his reactions.

Detached, the young man faced his deceased predecessor. He'd sought this place where the dead aren't nearly finished. He felt oddly disconnected from this version of the man, yet profoundly respectful. *Shouldn't the sight beg the act of mourning?* His voice bore the frost of winter, "Did anger and hatred define him?"

"No. He loved. By nothing more than mutual consent he was Christine's husband. The only official marital certificate we ever found pledged her to Raoul. So far, we have very little of Erik's history prior to his haunting the Opera House. We don't know his real surname, and Leroux says he only borrowed the first name of Erik by chance. I can picture some official at a border crossing calling it out and when no one stepped forward, our ancestor, parent X, took the absentee's place. Erik's origins are left to providence. Hanging from a chain around his neck, left safely inside his shirt, we found an unusual medieval reliquary. Inside is the nail and distal end of a female's index finger…a memento…a sort of 'Carry your loved ones with you wherever you go'. Perhaps it's a piece of his mother or a close friend. It's not from Christine. She has all of hers. I'm inclined to believe it represents the loyalty the Opera Ghost held for the esteemed Madame Giry."

Erik removed the gauze covering the folded hands. The fingers resembled the shriveled elongated digits of an unfed vampire. Erik touched the slender gold wedding band, remembering that Isidore wore the de Chagny signet ring passed down from generation to generation.

With a sigh of resignation, he removed the mask. The face was gray, cadaverous, yet somehow peaceful with all the trials it had endured concluded. He had expected dead hollow eyes, but the eyelids were sunken down into sockets, which no doubt were empty. This wasn't the man in his visions, or the man who'd spoken to him from the mirror; even two-dimensional that man was alive and passionate. The effect of the pronounced facial deformity began to register.

Isidore's austere voice broke into his thoughts. "I believe that in utero a portion of his face was adhered to the placenta. There was never anything genetically wrong with him other than the predisposition towards Wilson's disease that I mentioned. Attached to the placenta, the labor to birth him would have been arduous, terrifyingly painful for the mother. She must have hemorrhaged trying to deliver the neonate and placenta simultaneously. Probably had a common STD, most likely chlamydia. It's the primary cause of miscarriage, and in a viable pregnancy promotes the formation of adhesions within the amniotic fluid. Look at the extraneous pre-cancerous cellular growths. I feel confident that the anomalous area of his face was adhered. Had a simple regime of antibiotics been given to the pregnant woman, all would have been well. But those drugs were unknown in the world of that day. From the moment of implantation, every animal experiences unique conditions within the womb. Fluctuating hormone levels, exposure to disease during gestation, starvation from the lack of one or more of the proper nutrients can all have profound effects on a developing fetus. He was an exceptionally strong male to survive the rigors of such a delivery."

"One can only marvel at the degree of dedication you give your craft," Erik's hand rested on his chest in an oddly old-fashioned gesture. "You've reanimated death and can speak of him as a specimen. Show me Christine."

Reaching into his pocket to pop another Valbien, Thayer was disgusted, "You're a grave robber, Isidore. No better than Mary Shelley's mythical Doctor Frankenstein. Look at the wreckage you've wrought in this boy's mind." Attempting to hand another pill to Erik, he advised, "Forget about the dead woman laying in this other coffin. You'll have time to address what she meant to you later, after you've had a chance to collect yourself and think."

"How did she die?"

"As near as I can discern, congestive heart failure in 1917 at the age of sixty-three."

Erik signaled to Thayer to help him remove the other cover. "You said you found musical works in the coffin with Erik. May I see them and the journals?"

"Of course," answered Isidore. "You're old enough to digest them."

Erik and Christine lay in almost identical coffins. "After love's poison entered his veins he became obsessed with her. Only one woman and one alone could appease the fires burning within him." Lifting the coffin's lid, he set aside the rectangle of linen over the face and viewed Christine's corpse. Trying to generate some form of emotion, he whispered, "Our consort chose to be interred in a simple blue jumper and white cotton blouse." In her hands rested a piece of Bohemian crystal mounted in silver, the frame of which was engraved with the words: Love, happiness, and victory over perils.

"The glow of youthful health once blessed these cheeks," Erik stroked the paper-like skin, his voice bleak and finally evidencing a degree of distress. "Even dead she is still beautiful to me." At last, he was connecting. "In the corner of my mind, some sad libretto plays for this woman. Certainly no melancholy composition can say enough for what we felt. The bodies moldering here in the stale air of this crypt describe nothing of the life we fashioned. Those times are only recaptured in the mind. I want to clasp her to me, but she smells like death – to hug her and not embrace contagion."

Thayer turned to Isidore, "You insufferable lout!"

Isidore made a sickening impatient groan. "I've tried to protect him from harm, tried to warn him...you're my witness, Thayer. He's the one who insisted on seeing this display of corruption."

"Do us a favor, Isidore, and don't say another word. My ears are tired." Thayer knew this experience would leave an everlasting scar on Erik's subconscious.

"Then you won't be wanting dessert in the gentlemen's parlor will you?" Isidore snapped sarcastically.

Around Christine's neck was a chain and an amulet in solid gold of a raven. Grasped in the forbidding claws a ball of pure carnelian. "He chose carnelian," Erik explained, his voice deepening dramatically, "because the red chalcedony possesses a host of mystical attributes: energy, regeneration, and banishment of fear. To the ancient Egyptians the stone was the blood of Isis, the goddess of Nature. He loved her, but he also wanted to greet the scientist who now stands beside him in the tomb...the herald who bears the power to grant immortality." He looked at Isidore. "What Lucretia Sorrel foretold as prophecy has become reality. These bodies were placed here intentionally. The Count knowingly provided a useable legacy for you, his descendant."

"Remember, that the persona of Raoul de Chagny was only a charade," Isidore could not put off being caustic. "He was Erik somebody. Grafted into the family...I suspect by Christine's conniving at the real Raoul's deathbed. The handwriting on Raoul's last letter is definitely hers! He may have dictated the words to her, but she could have easily invented them. The missive bears the official seal of the de Chagny's, so she certainly got her hands on that."

"You're both speaking gibberish." Thayer pulled out a pocket watch to check the time.

"Are we? Doesn't Isidore stand in his presence once again? This time with an interpreter. If we define insanity as a breach of mind, an inability to discern what is really happening, then Isidore is the one who is insane. My terrible nightmares have drawn him back to this holy ground and neither of you get it." Erik was almost poignantly tender. "We are dealing with new paradigms here. Worlds crossing borders, opening other dimensions. You, of all people, should understand."

"Fight these memories," warned Isidore. "I made you to be your own person. You are not the distrustful misanthrope lying there." He pointed to the coffin containing the male. "Refuse to believe that the travesties that man committed are your acts. You have a completely different set of life experiences. Admit to me that you are not a freak, but an extraordinary compilation of a scientist's desire to win out against death. While others fall prey to a genetic time clock, you'll outlive Methuselah and he lasted nine-hundred sixty-nine years!"

"Memories count, Isidore." Erik was maddeningly patient. "Recalling experiences is a process the mind undergoes – molecular threads imprint images, sounds, tastes right into our genetic code. The former Erik walks around inside me, sends pictures to my conscious thought. He gives me his talents and his obsessions. I know his cravings. You unraveled him like a puzzle ball, set him into a beaker to explore at your ease. You stole from him to make me. How?"

"I told you. I pulled the back molars, then drew a corresponding sample of marrow from his right femur."

"Free of guilt. How much did it cost to carry out this exploit?"

"A king's ransom, and you are worth every cent. Not everything is measured in its relation to money. I felt not the slightest pecuniary restraint giving you life. *Au contraire*, the price was my soul. All along the way I worried over every decision we made. Challenged the most trivial choices. Checked my results a thousand times. Before you were conceived I loved you. If it were feasible, I would have altered myself with a transplanted uterus so that I could carry you through your gestation! Not because I wanted to do away with the natural order of men and women mating, but because you were that precious. Trusting you to a female body was agony."

"Your self-mortification does nothing to strengthen me. I needed the truth months ago. Lack of full disclosure has been crippling. You never sought our consent about anything. So who did bear us into this modern age? What was her name? You told me our mother died minutes before giving birth. That's another lie isn't it?" Erik itched to choke his maker, but the careening emotional roller coaster of finally understanding drove him relentlessly onward.

"Nyah's ovum and her uterus supplied your beginnings. She is the vessel that carried you through a surrogate pregnancy, and she was happy to do so."

"Why the falsity?"

"You need to understand that offspring produced by a single progenitor are a rare commodity. It's not an efficient process. I needed someone genetically compatible to us. Nyah had already searched me out. We had documented proof that she shared some alleles with the family. After we irradiated her DNA and inseminated her eggs with the former Erik's DNA, the number of live *in vitro* fertilized eggs per attempt was very low. Even after implantation, zygotes were rejected as foreign objects. Her immune system didn't recognize the embryos as her own, because they weren't. It ordered the secretion of chemicals designed to destroy them. Antibodies may come in handy when fighting bacteria and viruses, but not with the delicate tissues of a promising child. In the end, the process required suppressing her immune system so that she could carry to term."

"How many attempts failed?"

"What does it matter? We succeeded eventually. I cannot tell you the joy I experienced once your little person-to-be self was safely growing inside Nyah. Nine months later we had this perfect little baby. Pure and untouched. My heir. Not to mention all that you brought with you. Nyah loves us. She willingly gave up any thought of acting as a legal parent so that I might make all the decisions regarding your upbringing. Give yourself the life we both want for you." He pointed toward the sarcophagus. "You have all the talents he had in his past lifetime and more. You could be king of the world, and your children, if you choose to mate wisely, could travel through space and rule the stars."

"I am not legally here. It's against the law to make a clone."

"*Merde!* Unpardonable government squeamishness! Duplicates are never exact one hundred percent copies of their donor organisms. They are unique. Their genes interact with varying intensities to every environment they're confronted with and modify physical qualities accordingly. Even identical mono-zygotic twins have different fingerprints, develop at separate rates, have their own individual preferences, and die on unconnected dates. Genetics doesn't control your destiny, Erik. Your life is your own."

"You have not a shred of shame or regret over what you've done."

"I make no apologies. According to the laws of the state I may be a criminal, but you are blameless. There is not a smudge on your non-existent record. You're genetically perfect, think of yourself as the long overdue link to mankind's future."

"Enough rattling," Erik raised his hand. "Cease!"

"I can see why you people never sleep," Thayer was exhausted. "Let's go back into the house and continue these discussions in the morning."

"I don't want to leave." Growing agitated, Erik went to bar their exit.

"He can't stand in two places at once," Isidore said, half amused. "Anubis is a door opening to a tunnel leading back to the house. Trust me, this tomb doesn't give up its secrets easily. Pull the ring in Bastet's nose, Thayer."

Their guest didn't hesitate to do as directed. "Anubis is a damned doorway?"

Rolling silently away from the wall, the Egyptian god of death left a gapping six-foot black rectangle of space from which a blast of cold air issued forth. The candle flames were immediately extinguished. A shivering Thayer rushed to the torcheres and re-igniting a single wick turned to face the just created exit.

Filling the doorway was a tall broad-shouldered glabrous creature. Rat-like in facial appearance, it rather favored Max Schreck playing Dracula in *Nosferatu*. Over the outside of a long-sleeved black jacket, its chest was covered in some kind of skeletal ribbed bodice. Milky blue, sightless eyes that must have operated on sonar honed in on Erik. Out from behind the creature stepped the hunchbacked Nyah.

"Nyah, don't," screamed Isidore.

Fascinated and scared half out of his mind, Thayer's heartbeat accelerated radically. He let out a high-pitched girlish squeal, "What in God's name is that thing?"

Edging its way into the crypt, the humanoid being unleashed a talent Thayer had never encountered in his entire medical career. Not a moment later, the creature's mouth emitted a powerful low-pitched vibration. The steady sonic quavering condensed and compacted the air. Thayer couldn't breathe. He felt his knees buckling under him. Objects swam before his eyes and he knew beyond a doubt, he was about to faint. Without his knowledge or permission, someone had raised the curtain and placed them in the center of a wildly disturbing horror show. Both his hands grasped the foot of Christine's sarcophagus. He nearly gave himself whiplash trying to get his lungs to suck in a scant breath of air to clear his head.

Both the disagreeable creature and Nyah were totally focused on Erik. It was the woman who spoke in a steady sure command. "Time to leave! Come away from this place willingly, or I'll have Torossian haul you from it. As real and vivid as you think the contents of this tomb, they come at tremendous cost – these remains will eat into your psyche, they'll suck you dry of every glimmer of hope."

"Nyah, stop!" Even sapped of strength, Isidore began protectively rolling his chair toward Erik.

Erik's chest swelled with recognition. *Mother!* His entire body shuttered. He fought to stay conscious and almost managed to do so. He stumbled toward his predecessor's coffin, thinking that with only a little effort he might fall within and die. Drawn irresistibly into the abyss, blackness robbed him of thought.

Painfully thin, except for the broad shoulders and muscled arms, the creature's corpse-like head followed Erik as he started to crumble. It moved as if sight were unnecessary, reacting to the waves of sonar its only requirement to accomplish a rescue. In a blur, he rushed to the handsome young man before his head hit the floor. In a fluid smear of nearly indiscernible action, the entity exited through the tunnel with Erik thrown over its shoulder, arms swaying at its back. The air pressure corrected miraculously.

Nyah still stood in the doorway. Glaring at Isidore with indignation, her fingers pushed a button and Anubis slowly closed. "You promised you'd never to bring him to this tomb!"

Stunned and grateful for breath, Thayer couldn't let go of Christine's sarcophagus.

"Damn you, Nyah!" Isidore screamed at nothing. "Damn you! Quick, Thayer, open Anubis again. She'll take him to the lab. In her ignorance and blind concern she'll over stimulate him." As Thayer made several signs of the cross over himself, Isidore retorted, "Superstitious rubbish! Chop, chop! *Allez rapidement!* Open the door. Nothing on the other side will hurt us. I swear it."

Preparing to exit the detritus of the past and face the furor of whatever awaited them, Thayer experienced a keen sense of renewed terror. Ahead lay a limestone tunnel, it's floor illuminated in Tivoli lights. "So, Anubis is a false front. For what purpose, escape from the house?" He positioned himself behind the wheelchair and started to push.

"I doubt it. I believe it was a route for the former Erik to come to the crypt undetected and cry over Christine."

"Where is its origin?"

"The southern basement, underground level one."

"Dare I ask, Isidore…what was that thing that abducted your boy?"

"He looks like the forsaken undead, doesn't he? He likes to be called the Revenant. It's sort of a joke, but he's deadly serious about the moniker. When they were boys, Erik read him a story about vampires and he thinks he looks like one. I assure you he's very much alive and totally uncontainable."

Still alarmed, Thayer stopped the wheelchair in front of Anubis. Popping his head into the opening, he quickly peered down the tunnel and came back. The way was clear, but that fostered nothing of confidence. "Think it's safe to go?"

"For the sake of all that's precious, will you push before it occurs to Nyah to change the security codes? She's smart. It will take half-an-hour to reenter us biometrically."

Visibly shaken, Thayer's voice quaked. "I don't understand. Lay the groundwork for me."

"Torossian is an unexpected by-product that didn't show up on ultrasound...an undetected fraternal twin. His DNA is similar to Erik's in thousands of ways and yet so very different. Who knows," he simply had to plaster the issue with exaggeration, "perhaps Erik created him in the womb for company."

"That's a joke, right?"

"Gather yourself and push!"

"All right, already! Will this Revenant-person release Erik without a fight? You saw how the boy lost consciousness."

17 *TEMPER, TEMPER*

𝕰ddies of black murky nothingness swam across Erik's brain. He searched for anything of substance to latch onto, the tiniest bit of stimulus to show him the path. A faint repetitive sound was the first echoing perception, growing louder as he attended to it. Somewhere the butt end of a dagger was hammering against wood, demanding... *Demanding what? Admittance?* Glad for a point of focus, Erik's internal mechanisms sent his cognitive mind spiraling back across the Persian sands. It was later – on the same night of mayhem as Javed's final murder.

In answer to the insistent banging, Heerad opened the apartment's door. It was the hour of the second watch. The majority of the palace's occupants were asleep.

With an annoyed sweep of his hand to gesture the slave aside, Khusrowshah stepped into the antechamber and swiftly made his way into the sitting room. At the frame of the open doorway, Heerad spied the lowest tip of a sheathed scimitar belonging to one of the prince's guards. He had no idea the number that stood sentry on the landing, but knew that no one passing in the courtyard would spot these men on the uppermost level. From the arch to the kitchen area a sleepy Fatima prostrated before the prince. Standing, she came to the center of the carpet. A slinky almost sheer fabric draped her body like a moonbeam. Without a hint of propriety, Khusrowshah gawked at her shape as Heerad entered the room.

"Lower your eyes. Neither of you may look at me," Khusrowshah ordered. "Where is your master?"

"No doubt he is on an errand for the Shah," Fatima responded respectfully, eyes cast downward. "We don't know the hour of his return, my Prince." Growing more suspicious by the moment, she speculated that the royal's late night visit was for no good purpose.

"Leave the apartment, Heerad," ordered the haughty prince. "Go to the kitchens on some errand and do not return until instructed to do so. Never tell anyone that you've seen me here."

Fatima caught the eyes of the African as he bowed. Furtively rocking a curled right thumb and first digit as if they held a quill, she sent a message. *He has not forbidden that you write it.* Heerad left Fatima with great reluctance.

"Describe the magician," directed Khusrowshah after listening to the door close.

"He is very considerate of us. When he first learned that we may not eat until he has eaten, he sent us from the room and fed himself from beneath the veil. Instructing Heerad and I to enjoy our meal."

"Tell me what lies beneath his coverings."

"I admit that I am as curious as you, Sire, but I know nothing of his features except his eyes."

"Do you think something is wrong with his face? Something deeply grotesque, Fatima? Surely you've tried to steal a peek. When does he bathe?"

"He washes his body daily and afterwards applies no extra scent. I admit that from a crack in the door I have tried to look. No insult was intended. His back is always to me and from that angle he is as normal a man as there can be. Thin, but rather muscular."

"You seem attached to your master. You must be impatient to have him home that you might behold him again." He turned, showing her his posterior. "Look at me. Am I not as handsome?"

Mortified, she raised her head. "More so, Lord, for you are a Muslim." *Every soul within these palace walls knows of your vanity.*

He faced her. "Do you flatter yourself a worthy slave because your gossip touches so many ears? It was no accident that you were given this assignment. You were chosen because your tongue flaps so freely inside your mouth. Your tales that the magician sleeps invisibly above his bed have occasioned a good deal of wonderment and speculation. Perhaps he floats suspended above his bedcovers at this very moment. How would you tell?"

Left alone with Khusrowshah for this unannounced inspection spelled only the worst of trouble, but he posed an interesting question and it foolishly raised her hopes. Perhaps he only wanted information and she might get away from Khusrowshah unscathed. "You make me want to laugh, Sire. My eyes see only what is real and my master has not entered his chamber to sleep this night. He is neither on or above his bed."

"Has he commanded you to dance for him?"

"Never."

"Why not? Surely the versatility of our maidens quickens him. The dances are very sensuous. All those tinkling bells so painstakingly sewed onto costumes, accentuating every move…and the magician, though feared, is popular and frequently asked to perform. You are just as pretty, just as virginal as any of the others."

The prince's praise failed to elicit even a dram of loyalty. *Wicked, ill-bred tyrant!* "Sire, you are determined to make me laugh. I follow my duties and avoid paying myself compliments. It would be folly to think that I might tempt an honorable man, like the Royal Inquiline, into error. No doubt Erik finds all our women beautiful, but obediently acknowledges that not a single one is his to touch."

Raising his hand with a jerk, Khusrowshah impelled her to step forward. Thirty-six strands of brilliantly polished, tiny, hand-strung beads – three dozen rounds of liquid silver light – flowed in a shimmering cascade around her neck. (A peace offering from the aggravating Frenchman.) The prince lifted the necklaces with his fingers. "As delicate as a spider's web." He touched the earrings of lapis and turquoise dangling from her earlobes. "Has the magician touched you? Has his mouth been here?" His fingers came to rest at the notch between her collarbones.

Fatima knew she was in no position to bargain with Khusrowshah and screaming would avail her nothing. He would simply punch her in the throat to silence her. She focused her eyes on the gold clip acting as a closure and adornment below the collar of his blousy shirt.

Excited, the royal drew in a great breath, flaring his nostrils. She smelled of musk and patchouli. The forbidden nature of his misdeeds only intensified his evil urges.

"Sweet dove, so charming, so innocent – you have not answered my question." The back of his fingers traveled down the lustrous cloth until they came to rest above her navel. "You are so frail, one must be careful not to bruise you." He stepped away and listened to Fatima breathe a sigh of relief. "There is no getting around what will happen here tonight. I'd like to clarify the situation for you. Little chin-wagging girl, so very proud of her master's accomplishments, you only pretend to be terrified of a man who hasn't lifted a finger to deflower you." From his pocket he pulled a velvet pouch. "I cannot find the original set of these items, but no matter. I've had a jeweler cast another pair." He poured two small brass objects from the pouch onto his palm and setting them straight – held the pair out to her. "Choose one, the grasshopper or the scorpion. Both are clever. The grasshopper jumps high to devour the reeds and grass, whereas the scorpion has a sharp sting which brings short-lived, but disabling pain." Again he gestured her toward him.

Anxious, she chose the grasshopper, thinking it less lethal. Clenching the insect in her hand, she pressed her fist against her chest and stepped back. With her other hand she brought a dagger from a sheath at her back. Trembling, the blade came forward, marking the space between them.

"Clever asp. Please Fatima, no histrionics – we're past the appropriate moment for them." He playfully slapped the dagger from her hand. She heard the hilt skid across the floor and land somewhere beneath the divan.

"I do not know how to counter this strange fascination my father has with the magician. With a whole heart the Shah repeatedly welcomes him into the royal presence, while I remain an incidental accompaniment to the court. I'm left with no recourse but to discredit this infidel in the most blasphemous of ways. Call for your master, Fatima. Pray that he will attend to your urgent pleas." She didn't move. "Are you unable to summon the man? Pity. His absence precludes any deliverance from the fate dictated by the grasshopper. Had he come, he might have postponed your trials." He watched her face grow stern and deliberate.

Hunger warmed his blood. He debated between defiling her on the carpet or the couch. He decided on the carpet – more room and the floor was clean. He would force her to surrender long enough to have her branches spread and her fruit plucked. "Enjoy this moment's troubles, Fatima." He slammed the scorpion against the wall and in two steps was to her, his hands tearing at her silken nightdress.

She toppled backward, but didn't scream. Scrabbling wildly to regain something of her coverings, her hands groped about clumsily. The grasshopper fell to the floor beside them. Eyes squeezed shut, her fingers felt the fabric of his silk shirt and she dug in her nails.

Resistance seemed to fuel him. "What is faintheartedness," he whispered, "but the violent instinctual realization that you are about to be taken against your will? You can master cowardice."

"Pig!" Fatima answered belligerently. Raking both sides of his upper chest with her nails, she ripped the fabric.

"Impertinent female! Lie still or I'll bind you hand and foot to prevent you from committing further mischief! At my disposal in the dungeons are chains, shackles, and whips of leather straps tipped in metal. All for the purpose of restraining and educating an insubordinate servant."

Ignoring the threats, she continued struggling in a vain attempt to push him off. In a half-strangled voice, she predicted, "He will kill you for this outrage."

Surrendering to the heights of frenzy, he started to beat her unmercifully with his fists. When she quieted, he grinned maliciously and reaching for her own dagger, splayed her maidenhead like a butcher would a chicken. Pushing himself into her bloodied and now accommodating passage, he threatened, "Let this be a lesson to your magician. No one in this palace is more powerful than me. Not even my father the Shah, who grows more lax with every breath."

He grunted, his body jerking forward in an uncontrolled spasm of culmination – his rod betrayed him, delivering itself too speedily. Angry, he came to his knees. He saw Fatima's eyes already swelling from the blows, her face flooded with tears. Still unsatisfied, he placed his thumbs over the lids and with ferocious savageness pressed down at an angle. Out popped the ocular orbs, like two skinned grapes accompanied by the fanfare of a shearing fractured scream. She was about to awaken every neighbor, so he slit her throat.

Rising to his feet, he carried her, dripping with blood, to Erik's bed and laid her on the covers. In revenge for killing his partners, he planned to have the Frenchman condemned for Fatima's murder. He knew where to point the finger because the treasurer's newest dancer had not kept her promise. As soon as the Daroga freed her, she scurried to Khusrowshah's quarters. Gaining audience and hoping for reward, she'd described Javed's death in detail. Revenge and greed had aligned the twin brothers with the villainous prince. Now Khusrowshah was without associates who enjoyed direct daily access to the Shah's wealth. He'd compensated the dancer by making a gift of her to the guards in the lowest dungeons.

Summoning his personal escort from the hall, he ordered the men to watch for the magician's return. "After his arrival call for the night watch. Tell them you heard screams and order them to search. When he is arrested, confide into his ear that he should have taken the treasurer's offer and become a confederate. Of necessity he must pay for not allowing the vizier to live."

Kneeling at the block that allowed him entrance into his chambers, but still inside the tunnel, Erik took in Khusrowshah's scent...and something else...*blood, fresh blood!* Rolling the stone, he slid out and stood beside his bed. He scarcely recognized the slave girl. Stuffed into the center of the covers, her head rested on one of the embroidered silk pillows. He contemplated the gouged-out ocular orbits and bloodied groin without recoiling. The prince's message was clear: There is no one I cannot destroy.

How delicate are her hands. He adjusted them so they lay perfectly reposed at her sides. In his imagination he listened to Fatima's screams. Pictured the knife spearing the tender flesh of her genitals. Felt the anguished shattering loss as the rapist tore into the body she could not defend. He put his hands to his chest as if to tear his clothes in commiseration with her grief. He was not devoid of feeling, just skilled at hiding his emotions from outsiders. Quivering with rage, he envisioned Fatima on her back, forced to lie beneath the loathsome violator. It was then that he spied the droplets of blood leading from the room.

She believed in me and I wasn't here when I was needed!

He followed the blood trail into the sitting room. There he found the bloodied carpet, her dagger, the brass grasshopper, and its companion the scorpion. *Khusrowshah was in a rush and very neglectful.* Erik placed the two new arthropods with the set already hidden within his clothing. Searching the rest of the apartment, he found no sign of Heerad.

As a silent dark streak he returned to the corpse. *You fought with tenacious pride, didn't you? You showed the malevolent prince that you are not so easily governed. Khusrowshah may have devoured your body, but not your soul. Foul sewer of a man, why molest her?* But he already knew the answer: To belittle him, undermine his position with the Shah, worse yet...to make others blame him for the crime. With a sudden angry insight, he realized the trap that had been laid and a great longing to take the prince's life surged through him. *The dancer failed to keep her promise.* Thrown into a world of self-interest and violence, would he ever stop hoping to discover the good in people? *She must have told the prince who killed the treasurer and Khusrowshah is deeply involved, perhaps the very source of this larcenous plot.*

He set aside the inertia of despair and drew upon an inner strength rising up from deep within him. Wrapping a long silk scarf around her throat, a death rattle issued from her neck. *She isn't finished dying!* As a final few bloody bubbles blew forth from the slit, he realized he was too late to apply a dram of nightshade and ease even one moment of her pain. With his fingers tightened into fists, he vowed revenge, no matter what the cost.

Abandoning hope for his own young life, he promised Fatima, "The one who slaughtered you will pay. Forgive me; I have to move you so that he suffers the recrimination. I know that ultimately you would want Khusrowshah held accountable."

Enveloping her in the softness of the coverlet, he lifted the body and pushed it through the opening into the *Vrika*. Once inside the tunnel, he paused long enough to consider his next moves. By his calculations it was still the time of the second watch. The cub Reza was nowhere in sight.

If assassination was an art form, moving a body around was an even subtler battle of wits. And concealing Fatima's remains until she could be placed beside her murderer – a prized skill. How very fitting that Khusrowshah should awaken to find himself hounded by what he destroyed. With some luck Erik would succeed with this ironic re-positioning.

He moved down the tunnel unaware that he was gradually becoming more dangerous, more unpredictable. Trying to remain human when one is cloaked in misery is difficult, the effort calls for almost unreasonable restraint. The sympathies compelling these bizarre actions, this seeking of retribution that drove him to replace evil with equally repulsive evil, acted like poison within his veins. He didn't care about psychosis – a brand new medical idiom only recently mentioned in the European newspapers. He embraced the word! If vengeance drove him to the brink of insanity, he would claim that the derangement was thrust upon him. He knew the name of his enemy and his foe was not invulnerable.

He wondered if the diseased prince knew the Shah's seal prevented anyone from touching his assassin. Erik had no idea. He stopped to shake his head, re-organize his thoughts. No one was going to thwart his purpose. No moral code other than survival and retaliation governed his actions. In the darkened cellars he moved like an effluent wind, winding from one area of the palace to another in order to reach the prince's quarters.

In the royal's bedchamber, safely sealed from disturbance, the rapist slept like a tired baby. About the bed, smoke curled from a hanging incense burner suspended on chains from a golden ring. Charcoal pellets saturated with the extracts of natural oils and resins burned peppermint and Egyptian musk to sooth his dreams. Born into a lineage centuries old, he'd learned to enjoy luxury and magnificence from the time of his first tentative steps.

Contained in an elaborate metal box, a six-volume set of the Holy Qur'an sat on a shelf not far from his head. A *Kiblah* compass rested beside it – faithfully offering the direction toward Mecca – so the prince might know where to face for prayer. Given the man's recent history, both items smacked of religious hypocrisy.

Erik eased Fatima from the coverlet and placed her alongside the prince. *It is written in the proverbs: One who wastes much and reckons little will one day be a beggar.* Ruined by royal privilege and great extravagances, Khusrowshah would have to part with everything he possessed before he'd regret his ways. Erik's hand opened in a gesture for Fatima to stay.

At the beginning of the third and final watch of the night, two of the prince's cronies, Haroun and Mesrour, dared to enter the bedchamber. Grieved at their failure, they'd come to alert their friend that a thorough search for the magician had produced nothing. The Frenchman was simply nowhere. Quietly approaching the bed, they beheld Fatima's body with disbelief and horror. Frantic and afraid, they shoved the young royal awake.

"Great Prince," their dread filtered through to Khusrowshah's dreams, "We urge you to come away from this loathsome sleep. The *Ruh Marg* (Death Angel) has entered here and left you a present."

At those words Khusrowshah turned his head and with mounting dismay viewed the grizzly sight lying beside him. Springing to his feet, his non-existent virtue deeply offended, his fingers yanked at his hair. "Surely the Frenchman has done this, and if the demon can get in here, he can sneak into any place he wishes!" Agitated, his hands still on his head, he spun around scanning the area for the confounding deliveryman.

Haroun's chin bobbed up and down in agreement. "The royal guards have already given the Shah's favorite illusionist the fearful nickname *Vahshat* (Terror). Truly, he is brother to the ferocious jinn of the *Bab el Mandeb*."

Mesrour was more collected. "Calm yourself, Haroun. Bouncing your head like a ball is of no help. Our Prince has a more urgent matter than considering what power the devil manipulated to enter this room. We must move this body before anyone finds it."

"Return the corpse to the Frenchman's apartment!" Drawing his scimitar, Khusrowshah darted behind a dressing screen, thinking to discover his enemy and slice him through. He emerged disappointed. "I intend to accuse him and make an earnest appeal for decapitation as punishment for her death."

"You know this girl?" asked the still terrified Haroun.

"You idiot, it's the servant girl, Fatima." Every movement of Khusrowshah's head and hands spoke of bewilderment. "So much for my designs!"

The violent injuries Fatima sustained were obvious. "The defilement of a woman is punishable by castration!" As soon as Haroun blurted the words his fingers rushed to conceal his lips – too late to retract his statement! His words hung on the air like an ominous curse.

Faced with what he'd done to make the infidel look vicious, Khusrowshah's chest tightened with a growing apprehension. "Necessity invokes its own laws." Sniffing with visible exaggeration, the prince swelled forward to the bed. "At least the body doesn't reek."

"You could beg the Shah to modify the punishment for such a serious offense," consoled Mesrour.

"If I am held accountable for the damage done this girl, there are those who would press my father to ignore my station and execute the legally prescribed castration. When I am regent, I will decree that the consideration of leniency belongs to me alone. Advisors are a blight. But tonight my father is still Shah, so you have no choice but to assist me... before she grows fetid!"

Mesrour was already calculating, "We are running out of time, the third watch has already begun. Fresh guards patrol the halls and soon the very palace itself will begin to stir. We cannot reach the magician's quarters safely, but these remains should be moved as far away from you as possible."

"Shall we take her to the door of the Royal Apothecary?" suggested Haroun. "He is unbearably pompous, always bragging about his intricate knowledge of the properties of all kinds of plants and drugs. When we are ill he makes us swallow the vilest mixtures. And which of us has felt restored at the end of any of his regimens?"

"Yes! Consuming his potions, especially during sickness, is the most loathsome inconvenience. Accusing him of debauchery and murder would give us immense satisfaction, and his rooms are not so distant," confirmed Mesrour. "It's possible we might traverse the entire space without contacting a single guard."

"Then let the innocent pay for the crime...perhaps I can force my father's hand when the time comes to sort out a culprit." Khusrowshah pronounced his next words with vehement sarcasm. "I have underestimated my enemy. This phantom has more eyes than we."

The pair of friends scurried away on their errand, carrying the body of the girl under the knees and arms, almost as if she were in a semi-sitting position. They placed the remains at the doorway of the nearby apartment, laying her on her back with her arms crossed over her chest. The pharmacist had a custom of rising early and was already drinking tea. When he heard the scuffling at his door, his first thought was that he was needed. With a flare for the dramatic, he threw open the door. Stepping out, his foot inadvertently struck the corpse, sending it rolling to the top of a flight of stone steps. From there momentum caused it to tumble, arms and legs twisting and flying, all the way to the bottom. He gasped in dismay, thinking that someone seeking assistance had collapsed at his threshold and instead of rendering aid, he'd caused a harmful fall. Hurrying down the steps – hoping to hear a moan or view some sign of life, he turned the nearly naked girl over. Horrified, he viewed the smashed face and vacant eye sockets. "Where are the eyes?"

Looking up he spied the Captain of the Guard turning a corner about fifty yards away. Swiftly he latched onto the body's ankles and dragged her back up the stairs. The luckless pharmacist had no choice but to cringe and watch the head bounce off every step along the way. Before the Captain arrived at the base of the stairs, the Royal Apothecary had the body inside his apartment and the door shut.

Perplexed, he stood like a statue staring at the female he'd just deposited in his foyer. The pharmacist's wife was an odious conniving woman who pushed her husband to constantly present his newest concoctions at court. In response, the chemist had produced every cure from impotence to whooping cough.

As she entered the tiny space, her husband announced, "I inadvertently kicked someone down the stairs and cannot identify the individual I've killed."

The wife was very vain about her shoes. Gingerly, she stuck the toe of a slippered foot against the side of the body's chest. "Dead!" She immediately demanded that her husband get rid of the thing. "Toothless old man, why didn't you take more care? Plainly, because you are a clumsy fool! We'll carry the body to the Court Physician. Demand that he rouse her and when he cannot succeed, let him pay the consequences. Whenever someone is ill they call for him first. Declaring there is no need to send for you, he pulls out all his tricks and charms. In doing so he labels you incompetent! Give to him what he has wished for you – dismissal from court."

Frightened and in the habit of bending to his wife's insistent orders, the pharmacist could think of no other alternative. Throwing a cloth sack over the battered head, they proceeded. At the Court Physician's door they found themselves suddenly short on courage and set the girl against the entrance. After banging loudly with their fists to arouse those within, they fled.

The Court Physician and his first assistant were already having breakfast. With their heads bent over, nearly touching, they were studying a medical chart showing the location of the appendix when the urgent pounding commenced. As quickly as it began, it ceased. Signaling the physician to stay seated, the assistant armed himself with a long stick from a pile of wood near the fireplace and went to check the disturbance. When no one answered his inquiries, the assistant opened the door. Finding a half-clad woman sitting in the hall, unresponsive, with a sack over her head, he assumed the person to be drunk. He beat Fatima so fiercely about the head and shoulders that the sack tore, and her skin split in jagged rifts. Only the steady hand of the Court Physician halted the rain of blows.

"Idiot, you haven't a brain in your head. The woman is dead and cannot harm you."

"Let my arm go!" the assistant demanded. "I am not stupid. I thought a drunken prostitute was at our door and disciplined her for trying to offend you."

The idea that the apothecary was the cause of this disconcerting event never occurred to them. Even though they considered the man a charlatan who should be forced to drink his own foul tasting poisons.

"Quickly, bring her in! We must decide what to do," directed the physician.

Examining the corpse, they realized they could not be associated with such a death. After some discussion they agreed to place a robe on the corpse and hang it off their balcony, which was covered from view by the uppermost branches of a mature walnut tree. After lowering it, the assistant would go untie the rope and let some early morning occupant in the garden discover the remains. Disease and cure were their specialties, not knotted ropes. Under the weight, slight though it was, the corpse fell through the limbs of the tree to the gnarled roots below. The same unfortunate gardener Erik viewed upon his arrival, still walking backwards with his watering can, watched in amazement as a person dropped to the ground. He, at last, had the good sense to summon the Captain of the Guard. The latter sent a messenger to the Shah that a terrible deed, a grizzly murder, had occurred within the palace.

It was in this hour that Heerad entered the apartment with two of the prince's men and discovered that Fatima was not there. The returning Reza had eaten the eyeballs and lapped up most of the blood, but the dried circles left upon the floor, indicated that the female servant had been seriously injured. Human nature is what it is. Whenever a shocking mystery presents itself, people surmise the same thing: Evil, rampant evil is the cause. Members of the palace guard, already ill at ease around the magician, even though they joked and laughed at his intriguing illusions, still feared the darkly shrouded man. No one wanted to see Erik up close, much less seize him for questioning.

Scattered throughout the palace were dozens of oil paintings reverently depicting the stately Shah. All these royal portraits were viewed and handled with the greatest respect. From a pile, stacked and ready to give as farewell presents to visiting European and Asian dignitaries, several of the best were chosen to set up a temporary court in one of the Shah's entertainment parlors. Eight slaves held the gilt frames of four pictures at waist height as the body of a girl, covered in a modest drape, was placed on the floor. The Captain of the Guard stood in front of an elaborately carved chair, the pharmacist and his wife to his left, the physician and his assistant on his right.

As the Shah entered and took his seat, all present (except for the human picture hangers), knelt with their foreheads to the marble floor.

"All of you up. Up!" The Shah was agitated and disinclined to suffer through formalities. "So curious is my arousal this morning."

Normally the regent moved around the palace accompanied by a consort of advisers and musicians, but only one aged lawyer was awake and able to respond in minutes to an emergency hearing. This man placed an *Azan* clock (a timepiece used to remind believers when to pray), on the floor before the group of arrested individuals. In an officious voice he advised them, "Remember that from your earliest childhood three tasks have been hammered into your heads: pray daily, honor Allah by the giving of charity, and speak only the truth. The latter is interpreted to mean that you should speak as plainly as the words of the prophet."

He ordered the drape removed from the body's face. At this point the countenance was so demolished that no one recognized the victim. In profound disbelief the Shah heard the testimony of all three men.

The Royal Apothecary admitted to accidentally kicking the body down the stairs and without the slightest hesitation, praised the Shah's discernment and declared himself the culprit. The others present were free of suspicion. He also confessed to a total inability to identify the victim or even venture a guess as to what quarter of the palace had produced her.

The Captain of the Guard started by reciting a proverb, "It is written that whoever talks about what does not concern him, often hears what does not please him. From this truth we may infer that prudence dictates we respect the affairs of others." In his next breath, he declared himself fortunate to serve so fair-minded a ruler. He admitted seeing the pharmacist move a person from the base of the stairs leading to the chemist's apartment. Shaking his head in disbelief, he assumed this some remarkable new treatment – of which he wanted no part. Minding his business, he moved on without question and had no idea the woman had suffered misfortune until his men found a corpse lying face down at the base of a walnut tree. He proclaimed himself lax in his duties, and announced the innocence and good intent of the others involved.

The Court Physician spoke last and began by stating that he was, above all things, a good Muslim. "One unreasonably interrupted while in preparation for his prayers – for no man of Islam would neglect the duty. My assistant discovered a woman gravely ill...to the point of death, lying at their threshold. She died of a high fever. To our regret, her temperature rose so precipitously that it caused a seizure. One so fierce that it popped out her eyes. Look at the evulsion for yourself, Sire. Order her turned over and you will observe that the anal sphincter has ruptured from acute pain. Fear of infection prompted my actions. I had to lower her from my apartment to protect myself and my assistant," he declared. "We were arrested before we could don the proper garments, gather a litter, and carry the corpse to be burned."

The Shah experienced a peculiar and rather intense form of angst. To learn that all who stood before him were involved to some degree with the fate of this woman was dumbfounding. Right down the line they confessed to ill will, stubbornness, a lack of respect for their duties, and an almost obscene contempt for the appropriate use of their authority. Embarrassed to find the Royal Apothecary, the Captain of the Guard, and the Court Physician all involved in treachery, he placed his hands before his face.

"Where is my faithful magician?" he inquired.

"Here, Sire." The Royal Inquiline answered from the far end of the room, ignoring the rule to bow to the floor. He stood with his back against the wall, right knee bent with the sole of his boot flat to the plaster, arms with black gloved hands folded across his chest. No one had seen him enter.

The Shah didn't care that the Frenchman hadn't given official notice of his presence. He only sought some trick to open a path for retreat, "Oh, knowledgeable Magician what say you to these proceedings?"

The details reveal that the selfish intents of these incompetents and their petty altercations broach a serious contempt of this court. Later he would request that only male servants be assigned to his apartment from now on. No more women should be put at risk.

"Only one thing is accurately certain. Precisely, that nothing is certain."

The Shah knew the adage well, and responded, "And if this statement is true?"

"It too is also false!"

Relief that such a simple gate allowed him to spare the lives of these key people, the Shah declared, "I thank Allah for the good fortune sent my way when a stranger of such merit was delivered to me. Send for a chest of gold to be brought to my fine young Frenchman. I confer upon him the honor of taking refreshment with me this morning."

From his position on the wall, Erik announced, "It may be difficult to locate the Royal Treasurer."

"In that case," smiled the Shah, "The Captain is dismissed to fetch the Head Household Purchaser. Impress upon him my command and say to my servant that to disobey a royal order would be to tempt ruin."

Erik thirsted for revenge, but knew to bide his time. He could defer the prince's punishment to another day. The night's events disclosed the sham of honor enveloping those who served this palace. He knew the Shah had skilled torturers in the dungeons below. In this subtle battle of wits, he would not forget Fatima's murder and ill treatment. Unlike the defiant Khusrowshah and his greedy need for excess, Erik had not internalized a taste for rich food or splendor. Instead, he chose to follow mysticism and the strength offered by reliance upon self. If the prince somehow managed to call for his decapitation, he would request to be challenged in the arena, where he could test what talents he had amassed and the wisdom of his few years on Earth. Meanwhile, to distract the Shah from pursuing a mounting string of assassinations, he would outline a chamber of mirrors he had thought up. A pleasant room devised to torture the truth from souls unwilling to volunteer the actual facts.

℡ense and expecting at any point to be pounced upon, Thayer shuttled Isidore through the tunnel as rapidly as his legs and years permitted. Rounding a curve, they came to an area where ultra modern stainless steel walls sat right alongside the aged wine cellars. One of Erik's bodyguards, Dillard by the scar on his face, waited at the lab's pneumatic doors.

"She has him in the recovery area, Sir."

"Out of my way, Dillard! This is only a tiff fueled by ignorance. I need to give her some vital information."

"Allow me, Sir." The ex-Navy Seal punched-in the appropriate codes and the doors slid open.

"Wait outside. Thayer wheel me straight through the locker area."

"What about the sterility issues?"

"Where she has him is only a clean room."

"Aye-aye, Sir." Thayer wondered if he should salute the dictatorial captain of the ship.

The laboratory's main corridor was virtually silent. Cycled into nighttime modes, even the whir of computer hard drives could not be heard through the thick layers of Plexiglas. At a room just down the hall on the left, Isidore raised his hand to stop. He punched in the codes himself. The door opened almost soundlessly. Erik's unconscious form lay on a shiny hospital stretcher, both rails were up. Beside the gurney stood Nyah's hunched and crooked figure. The young man resembled Rembrandt's self-portrait at the tender age of twenty-two. Still in his evening clothes, she hadn't covered him. The room was maintained at a constant seventy-six degrees.

From a corner off to the side came a less demonstrative but distinct growl of warning. There stood the inordinately tall creature that abducted Erik from the crypt. The somewhat sunken globes of the Revenant's opaque blue eyes were almost void of any vitreous juice whatsoever. He didn't blink – apparently insensitive to the lab's florescent lights. With an odd precision the being moved to the foot of the stretcher. In the crypt, this thing grabbed Erik in a blurring dash; now purposefully slower, Thayer saw that its joints articulated somewhat stiffly, like those of a strange crustacean.

An involuntary prickly dread ran through Delaquois' body. In response to the creature's lifeless gaze he felt his veins constrict, his fingers turn to ice. In a false display of bravado, he let go of the wheelchair's handles and rested his hands on his hips. Focusing on the strange skeletal bodice, he let a stream of judgmental thought run through his head. *How appropriate, an outer skeletal shell of protection, like a lobster. Good thing there are no claws for fingers. Very creative accoutrement... eccentric...as if we don't have enough theater here!*

A voice with an almost obscene vibrato left the creature's lips, "Impertinent, unbearable clown. Just my outward appearance has made you so anxious you could urinate in your trousers."

Thayer felt his pelvic muscles tighten to delay the stream. *Powerful, almost hypnotic suggestion! The thing walks, talks **and** has the power of sublime subconscious directives!*

"If I had claws, I'd pluck you from the ocean's floor and examine you before munching on your skull." As it spoke, its eyes shone like vitreous silica – almost white silver. Unnerving in that, like Isidore's mask, they displayed no readable emotion.

Thayer spoke with a quavering high-pitched voice, "You have the advantage here if you are capable of telepathic control."

"Leave us!" Isidore issued an order.

The Revenant looked to Nyah and she nodded assent. A symphony of horror, he withdrew in an almost imperceptible blur. A normal blink would have missed the action. As he slipped around the more human obstacles filling the doorway, Thayer heard him project a threat: *Pompous slime, I could cause you such damage.*

"We agreed never to take Erik to the crypt." Nyah's voice was much stronger than her frail body.

"The boy insisted," Isidore tried soothing placation first.

"He did most emphatically. I stand as witness," added Thayer moving quickly to Erik's bedside. "We both tried to talk him out of the discovery, but he refused. Insisted on full disclosure regarding his origins."

Isidore hadn't budged from the doorway. "Remember he's not your son, Nyah. Don't let some misguided maternal instinct interfere with constructive protocols."

"The discussion of who Erik is to me is finished. You altered our agreement when you took him into that hole. He's too young, too vulnerable. I'll intervene when I think it best."

Isidore was ready for an argument. He knew this woman. "You caused this latest seizure, Nyah. You! You ordered Torossian to highjack Erik and right now physical stimulation is nocuous to him. If part of his condition is somnambulism he must not be handled." Giving voice to her error riled him. "Dr. Delaquois says the perceptions experienced in real time, added to those of his visions may lead to deeper confusion. He might actually retreat from us." He heaved in a great breath. "By the way, Thayer Delaquois, this is Nyah Lascelles. Nyah, this is Dr. Delaquois."

"As you can see, he's resting quietly. I haven't even removed his shoes."

"He can't be too warm or too cool during a seizure," Isidore's voice was weakening.

"A mute point since the ambient temperature is preset," she turned to the neuropsychiatrist. "We're on uncharted ground here, Doctor. We don't understand what memory really is – the mind is a fascinating organic structure, don't you agree? Most humans tend to employ its stored information to resolve problems in a most unproductive manner. They fixate on insignificant details, or have a tendency to let emotions act as an obstruction – they succumb to the power of arrogance. Stuck in the proverbial rut, new interpretations that might possibly produce more rapid reasoning are blocked. Erik is teaching himself, through trial and error, how to avoid hindrance. Apparently he's inherited a neural basis of memory, not unlike natural instincts."

"Nonsense," replied Thayer. "With all due respect, what he has is an overactive imagination. His body receives stimuli through his senses, just like all the rest of us. Those perceptions of sight-touch-sound-taste-smell travel over central nervous system channels and are stored as memories to act as buffers for evaluating future stimuli. Sensory information is passed into short-term memory by the individual's attention, thereby filtering the stimuli to only those that are of interest at any particular moment. Long-term memory, intended for the storage of information over a prolonged period, is best served by repetition, and it represents an area of the brain where there is very little decay. The healthy brain retrieves through the processes of recall and recognition, but information cannot, let me repeat, **cannot** be retrieved after death."

"Granted, those are some of the known aspects of memory," her head tilted toward her abnormally elevated shoulder. "But in creating a clone haven't we leapfrogged over death into re-existing life? When we used the non-invasive technique of Functional Magnetic Resonance Imaging (MRI) on Erik, we found dramatically accelerated and heightened activity in the brain's anterior region, the area where we retrieve previously learned information from memory. In comparison, his posterior hippocampus – where new information is encoded into memory – was almost silent. He's accessing his former life like a person would select a chapter heading in a colorful DVD movie. He simply selects a scene from the menu, clicks on the correct episode and observes the action with whatever degree of interest he decides upon. Hence the ability to read and write in languages he's never learned in this life, but was exposed to in the 1800's."

"Even if that were true, he suffers distortions, vivid imaginative pseudo-memories that he…"

"Intelligently modifies to accurately interpret and enliven. Yes, that seems reasonable…and creative. He is continuing his life. With the study of the mind's faculties still in its infancy, Isidore and I are students right along with him."

"God ordained life, not man. You've trespassed." Thayer did not care one iota for this woman's assertiveness.

"Ah, the old constantly relied upon *cheval de bataille* (favored argument). If that's the case, why did God give us the keys to unlock the code? Rubbish! As scientists we make mistakes, but from those mistakes profound knowledge can be garnered. This glorious boy is no error. He was engineered with the greatest care. He's a genius whose aptitudes will heighten throughout his life. I'm told you're bright, so you'll understand this. Erik has reached an age where he is beginning to direct what he learns from deep brain tissue. It follows the natural order of more sentient beings coming into maturity. In the evolving process, these seizures – as you like to label them – are actually protected states of deep access."

"That statement places you in a quandary, Thayer." Isidore had rejoined the conversation. "As he won't be able to communicate its veracity until he wakes up!"

Erik drifted over a burning wasteland. Passing through shimmering distorted currents of air that lifted off the sweltering sand, his heart ached uncontrollably. Fatima was dead, butchered. This time he wouldn't scream, he'd wait. An extraordinary sense of hearing enabled him to detect the strain in Isidore's vocal pattern. As of late, he could hear everything Isidore chose to say, even if the man was occupied in another part of the mansion. He just had to concentrate. Fighting to come back to the present, his eyes flickered open. Nyah was wearing something from the de Chagny jewels. A simple, but spectacular, ten-carat emerald on a gold snake-chain hung around her neck. The air immediately surrounding Nyah's head took on a strange degree of pale orange. Before tonight he'd never actually seen a color produced by emotion. This was her form of worry. He saw her eyes widen, communicating warning. He closed his eyelids. Taking in a slow draught of welcomed air, he knew instantly that they were in the lab. Like a well-tuned GPS, he calibrated their exact position.

"Remember that you are duty bound not to reveal what you have seen here," Isidore was speaking to Thayer. "We have an unparalleled opportunity, one fraught with life altering perplexities. We haven't even begun a preliminary discussion about Torossian. Technological mishap created a tremendously modified organism, an alternative race, if you will. He won't permit us to test him. Likes to guard his autonomy and only speaks when it suits him. Feel privileged that you heard his voice."

"What you've done could just as easily detract from the world, rather than benefit it. You've crossed too many borders. The miracle is that they live at all."

"Life always seeks a path to survive. We're not through compiling and analyzing data. To expose these experiments to the authorities would be premature."

Thayer wrapped a blood pressure cuff around Erik's upper arm. "For the time being, let's focus on Erik since he's the one losing lucidity. What else did you alter in him? This is not an exact copy of the body he had before."

The geneticist was hesitant. "Yes and no. As I explained, the limits of his strengths and skills remain undocumented. Known infections cannot touch him, memory is troublesome. He's not invulnerable to accidents, not impervious to sharp flying objects."

Thayer inflated the cuff and read the blood pressure, then tightened the device again. "I confess, your engineering...the feats you've accomplished...are nothing short of remarkable. He has astounding sensory perception and intelligence. Volatile emotions, but what teenager doesn't?"

Isidore nodded.

"Most likely a defense," Nyah added. "Leroux wrote that he was an outcast prone to theatrics. Have you ever read the book?"

Erik felt a small-bore needle prick his right antecubital space. Thayer released the cuff very slowly and the sedative traversed his vein, heading straight toward his central nervous system. *Drugs! I don't want drugs!* Powerless to stop the spread of the tranquilizer, a taste of metal entered his mouth. Erik heard his own heavy regular breathing. His brother stood not ten feet outside the pneumatic doors. His mind swam as the chemical crossed the blood-brain barrier.

"Hopefully this sedative will deactivate his current state of 'deep access'...as you like to call it." Thayer's voice echoed down some auditory tunnel leading to the cortex of Erik's brain. "He'll sleep for at least an hour."

GO FIND THE BLUE TAILED GIRL, the Revenant sent such a loud telepathic message that it hurt.

The concept of a girl in his life fascinated him. His intellect reeled in a dimension of soundless wonder, a vacuum of chiaroscuro interplay – dark against luminous light. A place where brilliant dancing orbs became almost lurid in their heightened contrast against the absolute black of outer space. The Void! Frightening in its utter and complete emptiness, it seemed endless. He floated in a dream state, no mental concept of this female coming forth. The search ended when he smelled her. Not the heavy oriental musk of Middle Eastern women, not some deeply sensuous spice favored by the gypsies – the perfume of lavender, the fragrance of home. A dizzy rush of release sent him tumbling downward – hunting, prying.

The orchestra music came in syncopated riffs. Hearing had joined olfactory perception. *Certainly she's here. Year? What year?* Provoked enough to risk exposure, he saw himself as an emaciated wraith, a pale semblance of his robust body. Withdrawn and thin, painfully thin, he stood on a dusty catwalk two levels above the stage. Voices reached him from below – distinct individual voices, cultured and high-spirited. One was a strong *contralto forte*. But the scene, the daydream if that's what it was, came to life in monochrome like an old brown ferrotype. Not a single differing hue helped enliven the vision. *The effect of Thayer's drug,* he concluded.

During the *intermezzo* of their little concert, the impresario sauntered boldly across the boards. He entered the area lit by the stage's blazing floor lamps, obviously indignant. Singers and dancers paused to grumble that the manager should remove himself at once. Not amused, the serious fellow grabbed a young soprano. Clasping her firmly by the shoulders, he spun her so she faced the darkened seats of the auditorium.

"There!" he shouted at the trembling girl. "The company's contracts state that you actually face the audience – even in rehearsals. How can I conduct promotions if I must also correct a performer's orientation?"

In the shadows high above, struggling to grasp the entirety of the discolored memory, Erik stretched out his arm. From this distance his fingertips seemed to glide over the soprano's lips. *Intangible…unreachable.* Healthy, virile male in all attributes other than his face, he wanted her as nothing else. He watched the girl burst into tears and run toward the left tormentor drape. She disappeared. *Shall I wager love against a noose for murder and abduction? Yes, I think I'll brave the risk.*

The theater troupe clucked their tongues at the manager, who retorted, "One of you should have addressed your sister's inclination to turn her derriere to the paid seats. Why do I have to deal with apathy and rampant incompetence?"

Where shall I inquire? The Phantom let go of the ropes.

In the space of a heartbeat he stood – frustrated – on the other side of an enormous mirror. Taller than his own height and just the width of his arm span, the beveled glass bore an antique patina from wear. He knew that on her side, gilded laurel leaves decorated the frame. Candles from two sconces bathed her dressing room in soft diffused light. He saw her throwing up in a basin. She'd eaten an omelet for breakfast. She allowed herself a full minute of crying into a hand towel before moving to the *escritoire* (writing desk). From the middle drawer she grabbed paper, inkpot, and quill. He'd had this vision of her before. She was in misery, an intense degree of emotional pain.

He cocked his head, telling himself to dutifully play his part. *Help her avoid the disaster of a formal resignation.* He whispered, "You must admit, your voice has made progress."

Her head turned toward the mirror, her eyes narrowing. "I'm quitting!"

"Leaving the company?"

"*Oui.* At best, I am mediocre. And after that brutish insult..." Wounded tears filled her eyes again. She seemed childish despite the fact she'd finally reached an age appropriate for marriage.

"Who could blame you?" his voice was like silk rippling through the air. She was openly sobbing. "Hush, now."

Tiny, almost invisible shivers distorted her achromatic frame, and he ordered the recollection to don some color. He focused, willed it, and nothing changed. Everything stayed dull washed-out shades of brown. "You could be a diva, a bright star." Her tears slowed. "Come here," he said with unexpected fierceness.

"To the mirror?"

"Yes."

"I know how tall you are," a simple statement of fact as she cautiously brought a footstool forward. Taking a step up brought her eyes level with his. He poked his finger at the glass. Like swimming through liquid silver, the end of his gloved digit appeared on the other side, stopping short of her nose.

"Don't you ever want to touch me?" she sniffled.

"Touch you?" he choked.

"Yes, touch me," her voice was a soft abbreviated cadenza. "What do I care if my reputation is tarnished by an angel?"

A pang of regret entered his chest. It hurt – better to have a poker shoved into him. The name on the metal shaft was Ruin, but he wanted this little strumpet. He swallowed hard, "Where?"

With the agile balance of a dancer she turned on the stool, until her eyes came back around and met his in the glass. She frowned severely. He'd withdrawn his finger. "Where would you like to touch? You can postpone my leaving. I'm ready, loyal seraph. Please, end this agony of wanting and take me in there." In answer to his silence, she bent over and removing the garter from her stocking, held it up for him to view.

"Quite tedious," he responded. "Ridiculous actually. You cannot bribe me, and most perversely Heaven forbids I bribe you."

She stuck out her tongue and swirled the garter round her finger. "Beg me for this."

Warming to the scene, for it felt so right, he taunted her, "I can make you feel things you never dreamed possible. It is you who will beg me."

"Ah, so the notorious Opera Ghost admits that he is only a love-starved male!"

Alighting from the stool, she pushed on the mirror with a triumphant laugh. He backed himself against the wall, trying to fuse with the brick. In the pitch black of the corridor she stood before him. His nose filled with the scent of her. She laughed again and it sounded like church bells. Adhered, nearly helpless to the wall, he so wanted her to be real.

"Are you the blue tailed demon who whispered warnings to me in the treasurer's house?" He lowered his voice to avoid the echo. "Gave directions that saved my life? Are you? I feel I shall lose my mind if I don't discover the answer to that question."

"Indulgent storyteller, can't you feel my bottom in the dark?" Her hands sought him out, pulling him into her arms. "I have no tail, save in a costume. Search."

"Wait," he cautioned, barely able to speak coherently.

Sounding regretful and profoundly aroused, she whispered, "Are you complaining?" Her brazen hands were busy unbuttoning his trousers.

He was so unacceptably deformed. He thought to hypnotize the girl, erase her memory then have her come and do his bidding. "Let us strike a bargain." Relieved, he felt her pause.

She stood on tiptoe to reach his ear and tease him. "You are no phantom. Your heart and body belong to me. No need to bargain – you are about to ask me not to look at your face." In the colorless dark, her hands caressed his masked and unmasked cheeks. "To me your countenance is one of pristine beauty," she held her mouth aloft for a kiss. "Must you persist in this argument that you are unworthy? Allow me to decide, for I hold a very different opinion."

He put his hands over hers. Indeed, beneath the mask his face seemed healed.

"In the dressing room there is a bureau with three drawers. In the top drawer a brass hand mirror…" he could barely finish, she attacked his pants again, "decorated with silver rosettes."

"Shall I fetch it?" She'd managed to free his manhood.

He froze, fascinated by his heavily aroused body.

"Your passion is a powerful thing to behold," she declared. Her hands slid down the shaft. "The body of your organ feels very natural. It's strong and beautiful. Obviously enthusiastic. Casual rumors in the theater describe all your body parts as distort…"

"Vixen. Minx. I happen to control the Underworld," he brought her hands to a halt.

"But not me," she kissed his chin.

"Your name?" speech was getting more difficult by the moment.

"Wife." The word echoed in the corridor and with that breath she was gone.

Enthralled, he let the impact of his arousal fill the space he occupied – it invaded his body like a welcomed friend.

"If wife you are, come back!" He slammed the back of his fists against the ragged wall.

A wooden cart selling wares was just outside the cemetery's main gate on Tuesdays and Thursdays. He went and stood in front of it. *At last some color!* Armfuls of dried wild flowers, dotted with crepe paper creations, spilled over rows of containers – never fading amaranths, rosemary, lavender, Queen Anne's lace, meadow grass, bachelor's buttons, cornflowers, anemones, and black-eyed Susan.

"Looks like I gathered them just this morning from a local *magasin de fleuriste*," the plump saleswoman greeted him cheerfully. "No need for you to assemble a bouquet, they are all arranged and ready to be taken into the cemetery to bless a tomb. My darlings shall last for weeks without a drop of water."

"I'll take the ones in the ceramic basket," he reached into a pocket and produced some bills.

"Lovely choice, you have an eye about you."

Entering the crypt's attic, he put the flowers on a little stool, took a seat on the side of a rope bed, and waited. He wished he had a *sou* for every minute he spent waiting for her. The ceiling overhead was awash with painted phosphorescent stars.

"I'm told women like to be caressed and prefer to be taken in a slow and steady fashion," he practiced his opening line. He knew himself to be a virgin, yet somehow not a virgin at all. He was becoming more and more aware of everything the former Erik knew. Every inviting detail of a woman's anatomy could be recalled. He sat there picturing her curves, her lovely folds, while he experienced a painfully enormous erection. She was pretty, tall and slender. *A dancer? Yes, but not like the performers in the Shah's palace, something more European. Ballet!*

She materialized straight up out of the floor as if born on some soundless platform elevator. "Do you love me?" she asked in a demure voice.

"I worship you, and it seems you've acquired a taste for me. Please let this be real. I'll swallow awkwardness and use everything I know if you'll step over the barriers and accept me."

"My delicate sensibilities tell me not to be astonished at your presence here in the Void."

He felt a surge of elation. A physical appetite racked his body. A sexual innocent, he had no way of concealing his need from her. "Then it's agreed? You consent?"

She nodded soberly, "It is decided. Sealed between us. But I don't care to become just a pleasant habit."

"Call out at any moment and I will come."

She set the tip of her right index finger into her left palm. "If I call out in the moment of pain, it will always be too late. I must call at the instant of anxiety."

Outside the shadow of passing clouds drained what little sunlight there was to the afternoon. A strange foreboding took his soul. Anticipating the worst, he knew the words he feared would come.

"Don't be afraid for me. We are on friendly ground here in my father's tomb. Beyond this sepulcher you cannot expose yourself and challenge Raoul even if he strikes me."

He pushed unpleasant speculation aside. "A gentleman like Raoul would not hit a woman!"

"But he does…because I always and forever want you."

"Then I will run him through, I've dabbled at swordplay."

"Your willingness to defend me is reassuring but unnecessary since this is a chemically enhanced dream. Let's take the time to redefine our relationship."

"I have already developed a new image. You cannot ask for more," he concluded with finality.

She blew him a kiss. "You are so very wrong. In that other life you seduced me with music, won me with songs and adoration. Have pity on me. My thoughts stand in such disarray. Distraction owns me. Treat me to words of earnestness. Please, my cantankerous ruffian, set me at ease. Have patience."

There was that damnable word again. In his former life he must have had the long-suffering perseverance of a saint! "All right." His voice was low. Earnest was easy, how to phrase the sentiments – a challenge. "I am in the active process of jeopardizing both of us because you are and always will be the epitome of my desire. I would tackle a Mongolian horde to win you, so opposing Raoul equates to nothing but a minor skirmish. I offer you the experience of love, to be cherished for yourself, kissed and fondled until you are content." Unconsciously his right hand came to rest over his heart. "If you accept me, repair the rift."

This she understood. "Afford ourselves another chance? Back then we risked scandal, banishment, possible time in jail for…love."

"For love." He opened his arms wide, curling his fingers in invitation. She moved toward him, pushing him back on the blue velvet coverlet.

Floating about a foot above him, she murmured his name, "Erik. Erik."

His pelvis throbbed with the same aching sensations he'd felt behind the mirror when she'd pressed her body against him. Overwhelmed that this love had endured past decades of time, he urged her on. "Come, lie beneath my body. Stay until the day is finished."

She passed through him, spreading a titillating delight into his core. Rolling onto his abdomen, a sweet generous urgency overtook him. Kicking off his shoes, he managed to delay the act. "Foreplay," he declared, moving alongside her.

Beneath her flowered organza dress she separated her legs. He walked his fingers up her inner thigh until they spread themselves through her mound of curls. His palm and the heel of his hand caressed the floor of her womanhood. His face moved to her ankles. Kissing in inches, his lips journeyed over her legs, fueling her need, driving her. As he traveled, a thumb moved rhythmically in and out of her while other fingers applied a precise pressure. Not a virgin, she closed her eyes and moaned. He placed two fingers within her, then three. Each addition heightened her experience – each slow stroke a satisfaction.

"Tell me what you need," he sounded as if restraint was about to break him.

"I like this feeling."

His tender compulsion to please came through with such intensity. "The best is yet to come. I'm going to place my mouth on you, very slowly."

As his lips and tongue came down on her and he sucked, a rapturous current flowed upward over Christine's back and down her arms and legs. For this man she would gladly leave Paris. He was Heaven's very gate. Her fingers ran through the black wavy hair on his head. "You are magic, my magic."

He hurriedly undid his pants, letting them slip to the floor.

When he returned to her, she ran her hand down along his side and explored his attributes for herself. Under her attentions his pelvis rocked back and forth. She smiled knowing she was stimulating him. "Does Erik want more?" she intoned the offer. "More of this exhilaration?"

Nodding, Erik threw the mask across the garret. Skillfully he lifted her, rolled her on top of him. With his hands to the back of her head, he carried her mouth to his, letting their lips make a receptive pathway into their souls. They lingered in this kiss. Melding, blowing back the doors of time, regaining a sense of that one being they had become in the past. He watched her unbutton his shirt. She was unguarded, smiling. Holding her by the hips, the tips of his fingers pressed rhythmically into her. He guided her back and forth over his manhood without accomplishing penetration. They were exploring – reestablishing familiarity. When her exposed vulva reached over stimulation, her eyes looked pleadingly.

Pausing to position her pelvis, it was his turn to extend an offer. "Shall your lover take the next step?"

She thrust her hips in a most daring invitation and rose up on her knees.

Employing a persistent patient gentleness, he let his rigidity probe the orifice. Stroking, stroking, he entered slowly. He was big, filling her, making her throb almost unbearably. He assessed with satisfaction the expression on her face and let her claim the pace.

"The crisis will come too soon," she moaned. "Please..."

"All right." He could vary the repartee. He withdrew and rolling her away from him, supported her right leg and brought his arm between her thighs until his hand rested on her abdomen. She groaned in disappointment. He placed himself close to her back, kissing her posterior neck and shoulder. "Rock on my arm." He pressed his firm attribute against her buttocks, letting it assure her of his appetite. "Prolong the play," he whispered. "Like it?"

Her silence and rhythmic movements were his answer.

She was a wondrous gift, so honest with her needs. After a minute he sang softly into her ear, "My desire – all passion and all fire, your flames light up the night – the source of heat is you."

"Oh, let me see you."

Passing over her like a dark cloud, he took a position kneeling on the bed between her legs. She pulled him toward her and with very little effort he re-commenced stroking the inside of her silken vault, manipulating what he knew longed to be pleased. Lubricating a finger, he reached around her hips and carefully let the digit enter. She thought she would explode with joy; each rolling, crashing swell took her higher than the one before. He tenderly wiped her forehead. She'd broken out into a sweat.

"Rise with me, sweet mistress, rise on the waves until you can take no more."

"I would happily drown in your love!"

In the throws of passion, one leg drawn over him, her mouth sought his. Sucking and kissing, her insistent grinding hips told him how ravenous she was to continue mating.

Control. Control. He wanted to give her satisfaction above all else.

The span of time they spent in this fashion was undetermined. They were lost in each other until her orgasm exploded within her. She shuddered and squeezed down as hard as she could. He did not follow. Tender hands plied their way all across his body, expressing gratitude for the exultation of release. Her warrior withdrew.

"The next one will be even better. Not so severe, more languid...I promise," Erik consoled.

"There will be another? How soon?" The feminine voice was dreamy.

"Oh yes, there will always be at least two. I pride myself on service, but we have to give your body a few minutes rest." *Why not brag, I can accomplish anything in a sexual fantasy?*

She made a low yowling sound, similar to a cat in estrus. "Look how I am so conveniently and fortuitously disgraced."

There in the strangely lit space above her father's mausoleum, he began almost immediately to grow hard again. "And what is this?" she asked.

"A promotion, my body did not completely finish."

"I've not been pure," she confessed. "Raoul has taken me many..."

"Shh, it doesn't matter, I was the first. I'm going to make you feel things you never feel with him. Carve my love into you until you can no longer bear the deprivation. Late at night you are my dream, Christine. I fought your hold over me with everything I could think of...even the body of another."

"It doesn't matter, I am the only one you loved enough to abduct." She was massaging him. Pressing and releasing up and down the shaft.

"I want you to put me inside you."

"Don't stop until you explode." She guided him within.

In and out in delicious invasion, his body tightened and arched violently. Knowing no one was near; he didn't bother stifling the shout of triumph overtaking his throat. Filled with the transcendent brightness of her, his culmination sent a sweet clean sense of wholeness washing through his brain. Very much a part of her presence, he didn't know if he wanted to laugh or cry. Lying against her, slumped in relief, he felt her rise from beneath him and float off his back. He rolled to face her and raising his arms, wanted to hug her one more time. If only he could keep her from going anywhere.

"Take refuge in a vacancy of thought," she counseled. "A welcomed numbness beyond the pain of conscious preoccupations."

In dismay he watched her image fade. In a matter of seconds she was erased from the scene.

19 *SOUR GRAPES*

But in the vast universe, somewhere in that black void of nothingness, Christine's spirit waited to be recalled. This time Erik found the transition back emotionally shattering. He awoke on the same stretcher, the two doctors asleep on nearby chairs, ready to observe their lab rat. Under the sheet and blanket he was in his underwear. The clock read twenty-two hundred hours. Closing his eyes, he pictured her face. Inconsolable. Broken-hearted. He felt as though he'd lost everything. The gratifying knowledge that he now had some of the answers offered no sense of peace or comfort. Going back and forth between the two lives was much more than an interesting pastime; it was beginning to define him, give him purpose. Lessons stored in his head were a practical education to be applied, not dismissed.

"Erik would like a discrete word with you, Isidore," his voice had matured, taken on a lovely, deeper, more melodious quality.

De Chagny rose from his chair, his legs once again strong enough to support him. With his hands on the cold metal rails, he leaned over the gurney. "What an odd manner of speech. Since when do you speak of yourself in the third person? Has something happened?"

"The smoothness of this parlance is not the result of vocal practice, but it should give you greater proof that you have succeeded."

"Yes, I played God like the devil, but you're an innocent in these matters, the beneficiary of all my energetic genius, an experiment accomplished with profound success. No other interpretations are necessary. You're living proof that the human race can evolve in mental and physical strength, move down paths that astound the most fertile imagination."

"You can't smell the disgust on me, but I can! Immense hurdles block my path. Graphic memories that contrast sharply against the vacuous life of an illegal clone squirreled away on an estate. Erik murders in these visions...with a complete lack of remorse. He has emotions and wants to feel them, but cannot connect. He's so frustrated he wants to rip out the throat of an enemy with his bare teeth. And I understand his anger;

I feel it, too. How many times growing up did I wear a mask when there was absolutely no need for one?"

"Assert your own personality, Erik. Don't blend with his. You're handsome, you could be a seraph. We were extremely careful not to repeat the mistakes of the past while Nyah carried you. Especially after we determined the cause of the facial damage done in utero. Right upper face attached to your original mother's placenta with such gruesome results."

Erik responded with a mirthless, hollow laugh. "I don't want to divorce him. I want to embrace him. He is me."

Thayer sat up, listening quietly.

Isidore squeezed the metal railing, "What must we accomplish to give you a sense of autonomy? I will be proud to take the legal steps and claim you as a son. We simply need a lawyer to draw up the statements. Money buys anything. Nyah has agreed to claim you, as well.

"So Nyah admits she mothered us. Did she breast-feed us, too? My apologies, Nyah, if we ever bit too hard," he spoke to the air above him, knowing full well she was listening from some corner of the lab.

"I've had a dream," Erik sat up. "Lower the rail." As Isidore did so, Erik swept his legs over the side. "Some answers still remain unclear, but I am absolutely positive about one thing. I've discovered that the thrill of loving vicariously is overrated, the subtleties of watching someone else touch romantically is tortuous when my own groins call out for attachment. I'm totally lucid and without a moment's hesitation, I'm telling you that I want you to remake Christine Daae for me."

Isidore's eyes widened in alarm, "Something has happened. Whatever it is, I'm out of the cloning business."

"Oh, no you're not. You remade me – now resurrect Christine. When did I brush my teeth with baking soda and mint? Chew tarragon leaves as a breath freshener? Drink tea with brandy for a cold instead of downing antibiotics? Ten minutes ago! Ten minutes! I have little to no control over those past events. You threw the stone into the pond – don't whine that the ripple effects cannot be contained. The circles are proceeding outward without interruption. Self-preservation motivated me then and it does so now."

From the other side of the stretcher, Thayer added an observation. "The nuclei of most somatic cells contain all the information needed to make an entire organism. Her body is there to harvest. Cells from the female reproductive tract work the best. Very few warm-blooded clones are male! Isidore's success with you is phenomenal."

Isidore glared furiously at Delaquois and Erik grinned, "Then it's decided. Thank you, Doctor. For once you've really been my advocate."

"I'll get you a girl," offered Isidore. "If I pay her enough, she'll do anything you like."

"I don't want a puppy, I want Christine. There's an unforgiving turmoil inside me and she is the cure."

"You're being ridiculously stubborn. What if she doesn't want to come back?"

"Who wouldn't want life over oblivion? Where are my clothes?"

"Trust me, you're fixated. Perhaps it can't be helped. In this test of wills I will emerge the victor! I know what's best for you."

"Do you? You're a blasphemer and I'm a bastard. We'll both be off to Hell, only I'll be glad for the trip. You will make Christine!"

Isidore's body recoiled defensively, "I erred in wanting to be my ancestor. Injecting myself with what I thought was your DNA was unorthodox, foolish." He started sputtering, "I was confused. There were very few clues to go on. Only one oil painting existed of a masked individual. How was I supposed to know it portrayed Julian?"

"Is this fussy dissertation coming to an end? Bravo, you win wordiest zoo keeper of the year." Erik stood. He seemed to have literally grown inches in height. "You arrogant fool, you have no idea how completely incensed I am. Summon all your strongest arguments in an attempt to foil my designs and they will fail. Miserably!"

"I'll be so glad when all of this is over and we can return to our normal life."

"Lying, always lying. There is no normal life here. We are standing in a laboratory designed to engineer cells. It's what you do. We will make her! Nyah is too old to play the roll of suitable hostess, but perhaps Kathryn might lend us an egg or two."

Thayer stood and stretched, "May I make a suggestion? Hire a female willing to take hormone injections and have her eggs harvested. Then dismiss her. We'll eradicate the DNA in her gametocyte and inject the nucleus of Christine's donor cell into the enucleated oocyte. A brief electrical shock to fuse them together will play the part of fertilization and there – *le début de la fille que vous aimez* (the start of the girl you love). It's very similar to what you did before, Isidore. When cell division is well established and the dividing cells are developing into an embryo, implant the little creature into a second female for the remainder of the gestation. You said money was no object, but are you willing to wait until she grows up, Erik?"

"What an excellent point!" Isidore turned back to Erik. "Even if you're willing to put aside your poignant argument that clones cannot decline their consent and withdraw from a genetic experiment...are you ready to spend years watching her pass through all the stages of childhood? Two year olds have terrible tantrums. Consider how little you know of this girl. If you did understand her, you'd realize that she didn't like you very much. I'll toss a copy of Leroux's book your way. Read it!"

"I appreciate the candor. I won her once; I think I can win her again. In the end you will cooperate; so spend some time convincing yourself that this is the only way I'll be happy." Erik suddenly realized he knew exactly where Christine's handwritten journals were stashed. He could picture where they sat. He'd ignore Leroux's book and read them instead.

Isidore rallied, trying to issue a patriarchal order, "Abandon this unbridled hope! I absolutely refuse to comply. Get some control and ask for something else!"

"I will not control myself. I've been denied too much," Erik's voice intensified. "I cannot change my features or my past, but I can alter the present and I will have her, damn it! Within this travesty you've created, you are given another opportunity. Arise from your private egocentric stupor. There are elements throughout the entire world that would like to strip you of every privilege, divest you of every reward you've ever received. I'll go to the police, declare myself an illegal clone. They'll run tests, question you without your mask. They'll take your precious Nobel Prize and revoke your credentials. Who knows, you might even forfeit your title. Which, if truth be told, you keep merely to maintain possession of this chateau." He snapped his fingers for emphasis. "The government could lay claim to it at any moment. The media will declare you an ogre. You'll lose respect and be the laughing stock of the scientific community." Erik rendered these predictive threats knowing full well he played his most potent psychological card.

Steadying himself on the side of the stretcher, Isidore braced before responding, "Your attitude is a bit too unsavory...even for me, though some of the outrageous things you spewed are all too true. Insult me if you must. Act on your threats and reveal yourself. You will be an oddity, too. Torossian will never allow exposure. He'll go berserk if they touch him. Plus you'll crucify any chance for Christine!"

"What's in the room with the plants and the tanks? Sonia yes? Nyah wasn't always a cripple. I know things, Isidore." Erik was about to escalate the confrontation. "Little tacky, intimate details...and how do I know them? I can see a great deal of what you see. Down the hall there's a hermetically sealed room containing the partially decayed body of a woman. I'll show her to you. Her name was Sonia. The part of you that's Julian tried to get her back, didn't he? And you've preserved some of Sonia's cloned DNA at the cost of great reprisals. Should that DNA ever be discovered, it stands as proof that you injected Nyah as well. She's always searching for the cure – for the both of you – isn't she? So since you've destroyed Nyah with Sonia's DNA, it seems only fitting that you reconstruct my bride."

Isidore was astounded that Erik had gotten into one of the safest rooms in the lab. The pneumatic door swooshed open and the Revenant entered with a set of Erik's day clothes.

"Get out of here," shouted Isidore, his mood growing more domineering and foul by the instant. "Your impudent brother isn't going anywhere!"

The Revenant raised a threatening arm and thundered across the room while Thayer cowered.

"Thank you." Erik accepted the clothing. "You will oblige me my request, Isidore." He could see his creator seething. "Follow my instructions to the letter. If you don't do exactly as I demand, we'll convince you by crushing those notorious fingers of yours and publicly streaming the event live over the Internet. Thayer can busy himself resetting your digits."

Thayer was clearly dazed. Not only was the threat obscenely doable, but apparently 'the thing' responded more to Erik than anyone else. In an act of ill-thought-out bravery, Delaquois stepped in front of the door to block Erik's way. The Revenant picked him up under the arms as if he were a feather and set him against the wall.

"What are you, some kind of atavistic Hun? The reoccurrence of long dormant characteristics due to Isidore messing around with molecular recombination?"

Pulling on his jeans and boots, Erik counseled, "Stay more upbeat, Thayer. Think along the lines of ancient alien and you'll have the answers."

Thayer brushed off the arms of his jacket, "Think summer and winter solstices, pagan seasonal rituals with bloody sacrificial altars? Slaves building pyramids so pharaohs can sing to the stars and be reborn with the sun?"

"Don't use linear concepts. Pretend life is a dial, a wheel turning in an ever-widening circle. The galaxies have been recreated in what... seven Great Bangs?"

"Madness. Coincidence rules the universe, unpredictable chaos results in molecular rearrangement," Thayer strained to express his thoughts – the creature still loomed in front of him. He gasped; startled by the thought it might not have been fed.

"Where are you going?" Isidore interrupted.

Rapidly buttoning his shirt, Erik ignored the question, "Why don't you two share a glass of absinthe? Let wormwood's green demon convey you into apathy. My frenzied behavior will be more acceptable." He faced Torossian, gently squeezing his upper arm. "Are we not a circus here? A very expensive circus?"

Torossian responded mentally, *I say we bring out all the jarred unhappy experiments! Where are the hairless cats?*

Isidore moved forward on trembling legs, "You don't have to leave, we can explore the situation right here, discover a solution together."

The Revenant went to restrain him and Erik lifted his hand with a decisive, "Don't bother!" The creature backed away. "Put a lit candle in the window so I can find my way home, all right?"

Donning a waist length leather jacket, Erik stormed out with Torossian at his heels.

By way of explanation, Isidore looked to Thayer, "I didn't manipulate his psychic abilities with Torossian. He has an intuitive heightened telepathy all his own. Erik won't get far. The guards will never open the gates without my permission. Help me follow him. He'll be furious when he can't get out."

Leaving the chateau by the northern kitchen exit, Erik stomped off to the garages. He entered the first open doorway and Dillard approached. "Want my Harley?"

"By all means," Erik yanked some gloves from his jacket pocket and took the helmet Dillard handed him. *There used to be horses in here. A black stallion called Muerto and a chestnut mare Christine liked to ride named Venus.*

"The bike is finally paid for, be careful, all right? No zoning out."

"Don't sulk, I'll be gentle with your baby." He mounted the custom painted silver-blue V-rod Muscle Harley Davidson, hit the ignition and revved the engine, listening to 673 pounds of pure power. *A hundred years ago the horses in here would have shied and reared at this uproar.*

Driving the machine out the open door, he spun the back tire on the cement of the parking area, leaving an arc of rubber just as Isidore emerged from the house.

Watching Erik go through the gears, Thayer acknowledged, "Biking is such a perverse form of amusement. Dangerous." *Lord in Heaven, it feels good to needle Isidore.*

Sitting in the wheelchair, the elder de Chagny crossed his arms. "If I had a chin I'd thrust it out. Why is he so stubborn? I'll admonish him the instant he's off that thing."

"You might want to consider chaining him up. He could have another seizure and do himself some damage." Thayer justified the goading with a smirk.

As if to taunt them, Erik raced the Harley around the circular patio where they waited. Passing the central fountain, he waved gregariously.

Leaning down to Isidore's ear, Thayer said, "You know of course that on December twenty-first there will be a galactic alignment…the sun in Leo, opposite Aquarius. There's been global warming since '98 – every summer gets hotter. The world borders on famine, there's a dramatic decrease in grain production. Political tempers around the world are on a short fuse, ready to explode. With very little provocation we could have global war. In the grander scheme of things this is nothing. Let him spread his wings and expend some energy."

"Oh shut up, Thayer. I have bigger fish to fry than world reconciliation." Still reeling from the shock of Erik's open rebellion, Isidore declared, "That's Dillard's bike, I'll fire the son-of-a-bitch for adding to this conflict."

Erik came around for a second turn, this time flashing his lights. He liked sitting astride the motorcycle, letting the engine's powerful vibration absorb his frustration and fury. He sheered into some dirt, sending an arched spray of dust and pebbles into the air. Regaining control, he drove back onto the pavement and headed down the driveway toward the main gate.

Florid faced, the tower guard opened the gate and waved Erik out, despite Isidore screaming threats through the tiny cell phone hooked in his ear. Sitting cross-legged on the floor at the guard's feet, Torossian retracted a very precise set of fangs and let go of the man's ankle. This was the guard's first encounter with the Revenant – he'd wet the front of his pants.

Enraged, Isidore shouted, "I'll fire you, too!" He clapped the ComDev shut and scowled at Thayer. "The moment his contrary ass is back in here I want that GPS chip put in him."

"He'll return soon, I think." Thayer set the wheelchair toward the chateau. "Let's go in and review his medical record, show me everything you have about this boy…and his fraternal twin. No need to remind me that I'm ethically bound to silence."

Out on the road, the ride away from the claustrophobic confines of the chateau was such an invigorating relief. Erik stood up on the foot posts, daringly gave the engine more gas, and gunned the motor. Set between his legs, the bike hummed, a provocative sexual beast his entire body could enjoy. He leaned confidently into the wind, letting the night dissolve his cares. An independent taste of the contemporary world lay before him.

Trees and driveways sped by. Instinctually he followed the signs pointing the way towards Paris. He'd studied the computer maps a thousand times. Deep into reflection, he shunned a twinge of remorse over disappearing out of Isidore's sight. He'd never been separated from the man, but there was a whole new unexplored life out here. *I am a comet hurling through space, soaring in the outer stratosphere over the earth.*

Only the celestial beings understand the hard unbending truth – my soul is split. Both halves are animated; both are living-breathing things that attest to the same love. Only devil-jinn can build a home on this rock, a home in which two hearts might forge a reality. My past and my future have but one voice, and it lifts in want of Christine. Without her, we are soulless, empty. Until she's back, we stand bereft, waiting, watching for the time when we may attend to her.

Relishing the solitude, he ignored the countryside, missing the signs until the tall buildings of the city were actually upon him. He automatically slowed his speed. He had no license, didn't know the city's rules, better to proceed cautiously.

Modern Paris was a conglomeration of concrete canyons; buildings with thousands of lights formed the sides of steep asphalt-paved valleys. A thing of wonder, he found it difficult to accept that such a transformation could be accomplished in so short a time. It took fortitude to enter the maze. Traffic seemed to be merging from all sides. Instinctively he followed the *Voie Georges Pompidous* along the Seine to the familiar and still recognizable *Hotel de Ville*. Even at this hour a steady river of humanity crowded the sidewalks, flowing endlessly across wide intersections while he idled the bike, waiting for the lights to change. The streams of biped ants, all crisscrossing each other's paths, seemed self-absorbed and determined. Some conversed on cell phones, gesticulating madly to listeners that couldn't see a single movement. Others were tired, heedlessly plowing forward to make their way to unnamed destinations: a bed, a bar, some late night supper. The composite pieces of this throng all had normal life-stories – mothers, fathers, siblings, lovers. None of whom had been produced from an egg injected with manipulated DNA.

His observations were marred by the loud honk of someone's horn. Anxious to proceed and not be cutoff, a silver Saab made its way around him. Cursing, the driver entered the snarl of traffic at the intersection. The four-way was a mess. Shiny painted cars jockeyed for position, honking, everyone demanding the right of way, ready to push an inch forward. He coasted through on the bike and listened to the roar of voices behind him. He had no idea what traffic laws he'd just broken. Turning right, he chose a quieter route and came to an abrupt halt when a sign proclaimed that the cross street was *Rue du Renard*.

A nun rolled by on roller skates. Erik took in the incongruous sight. At the corner, she turned to skate back. A yellow taxicab pulled up beside Erik. The impatient driver shoved a hand out the window, middle finger flipping off the nun. The other hand occupied with repeatedly slamming on the cab's horn. Erik reached over and took the driver by the wrist. A face with thick eyebrows, deeply pitted cheeks and oily skin flung a string of curses at him. A quick insight flashed across Erik's brain: *Moroccan flip-top gaming tables, antique stained glass windows from a cathedral, babies crying.* The man was an Egyptian Muslim, married to a Catholic...three little children, all boys. Shocked, the driver yanked his wrist away.

Erik sat, revving his engine and the nun rolled past a third time. Erik flipped up his visor. She turned to smile and 'she' was actually a man with stubble on his face. *Insane, but very clever, my transvestite friend. Did you know that chromosomes control sex? All invertebrates start out female; hormones secreted at the right hour turn the fetus male...Nature did not breed you deficient.* Erik smelled the gonorrhea on the roller skating puff. *Without treatment you'll pay a stiff price.* He never spoke the words outloud, choosing instead to judiciously mind his own business.

Even here, in a city teeming with life, he felt lonely, devoid of hope – a human wasteland – empty and barren. Oh, his heart beat, but it beat for nothing and no one. Christine did not exist. She lay desiccated, drained of life's humors within a crypt. How could he deal with the crushing possibility that she might remain forever within a coffin? Dispirited, he drove to a nightclub quarter in *Le Marais* and parked the bike. An ephemerae of new and aging posters touting musicians and bands covered most of the sidewalls around him. Taking off his helmet the air smelled of beer and cannabis. Alone, he sat on a stoop. Legs apart, he stared down at the concrete.

What does it mean to be alive in a century you were never intended for? A few feet off to his side, a cat, no a kitten, was crouched behind a bush. He heard it mewing softly, plaintively...asking to be rescued. He walked over to the little life, coaxing it forward with playful fingers. Wary at first, the white ball of fur eventually came to him. *Really Erik, this is not the time for you to become an animal shelter.* Ignoring the inner voice, he picked up the kitten. *No fleas or parasites. Homeless.* He set it inside his jacket. Strange that it should settle in as if it belonged there.

Stroking the tiny creature, he went to the street and stood listening to the techno music pumping from inside a nightclub a few doors down. A crush of people milled around in front of the club's main door – tourists and locals out for a party. As the music ended a cacophony of voices reached him. Laughing and joking, the happy crowd acted as if they had all the time in the world. *How many of you are habitual nocturnal partiers?* He tried to conjure a memory of something like this from his past…nothing came…the thumping music started up again, drowning out any inclination to process recall.

A hand touched the middle of his back. He spun around, eyes widening as he took in the vision of Kathryn Arlington. Dressed in a stretchy oyster-gray top overlaid with silvery sequins, his gaze traveled downward to a scallop-hemmed miniskirt falling happily in three flared tiers that barely covered her crotch and buttocks. She dropped a cigarette from her fingers, crushing it out beneath the sole of a flashy red-beaded pump.

"Imagine meeting you here," he frowned. How did they track him down so quickly? A quick scan in every direction revealed no John or Dillard.

"Want some fun? That place down the street jumps." Her hand passed beneath her breasts, pointing in the direction of the milling crowd forty yards away. The subtlety of the gesture caught him a bit off guard.

"I'm sorely tempted, but I don't really know how to act in such a place."

"Sit and drink. That's pretty easy, huh?" she answered cheerfully. "Good god, Erik, lifting a glass to your lips isn't much of a challenge. How'd you get out of the penitentiary? Never mind, don't tell me. Deliver yourself into my hands. I'll see you enjoy a good time. I'm committed to your welfare, just like everyone else in that damn house. Lock up Dillard's baby."

He zipped up his jacket and shrugged his shoulders. A contented fremitus from the kitten's purring vibrated against his chest. In a few moments they were edging their way through the press of people, Erik following on her heels.

She flirted outrageously with the doorman, trying to convince him to let them in. Turning her back to the guy, she stuck out her rump. "You can touch my ass if you like." A short feel and all difficulties getting in were erased. Erik grinned at the doorman, glad not to be asked for a similar tribute. Kathryn was decidedly vamp-like. The contrast between women in the western world and those of conservative Persia was only superficially significant. *Both sets seem taken with preening – in any century or country, the goal of attracting and manipulating the opposite sex has essentially the same end.*

After a short dark hallway they came into a brick room with blinking green and pink neon lights. The music was louder, the lyrics and beat surprisingly engaging:

> We'll come into your town,
> This time we'll party it down.
> We're an American band.

Still not convinced that she wasn't up to some kind of trick, he tried to anticipate Kathryn's next moves. Ushering him over to the bar, she waved toward a bartender. With his face flushed-red from too many years of imbibing alcohol, the man waved back. "Hey, Joe...where's a table? We need a drink." The man pointed to a corner.

The walls were covered with life-sized posters of young adults posing provocatively in all the latest gear. A dance floor jammed with rowdy dancers dominated the center of the single room.

At the table, Erik pulled out a chair and waited. Kathryn smiled at the unexpected etiquette and smoothing her skit, plopped down. "Not your average male! I like this place. They play a lot of music from the States." Her speech was nearly lost as a DJ in a glass booth cranked up the volume.

"Do you come here often?" Erik shouted, taking a seat.

Kathryn ignored the question. "What are you drinking? I'm up for a gin and tonic with a twist."

"I'll have the same." *What would Christine think of this era?* Scanning the dancers, Erik caught one of the girls out on the dance floor waving vigorously to Kathryn. In an advanced state of pregnancy, she did the bump and grind with her hands clasped together in front of a tiny pleated mini skirt. She'd pulled the skirt down and her knit top up to accentuate her growing abdomen. Under the pressure of her ballooning uterus her naval protruded outward like a lopped off limb. Excitement brimmed in the girl's eyes, as if she were thrilled to draw attention to herself. Ignoring the scornful glances of other females, she shrugged off their judgments and amused her dancing partner by rocking her hips to the 4/4 beat of Grand Funk Railroad.

Kathryn followed his gaze. "That's my friend, Claudia. She's a regular. A little more exertion and she'll go into labor tonight!"

"Gossip is tricky stuff," Erik remarked. He watched Kathryn flush with embarrassment. *Is she faking?* He'd never paid much attention to John's girlfriend.

A petite waitress with a short black skirt took their order.

The instant the music stopped, Kathryn signaled her friend over to their table. Claudia and the lanky boy she'd been dancing with rushed to join them. A calculated skid brought her right up to Erik's side. "Order us a drink," she shouted to her partner. As he turned toward the bar, she placed her hand on Erik's shoulder in a much too familiar way. "Hey, Kathryn! Thanks for your message; I was glad to get out of the apartment. Now I'm really glad. Who is this gorgeous guy?"

"Your presence seems to be giving my friend a thrill. Claudia, this is Erik. Erik, Claudia. Where's Desi?"

"Sprawled out over there." Claudia's head jerked, indicating where a man sat propped up against the wall in a happy drunken stupor. "The baby's father is an *artiste*." She stressed the word, patting her abdomen. "Started drinking early this afternoon. Want to steal a peek? Pregnancy has the added bonus of fabulous breasts." She bent down toward Erik, her breath rank with alcohol, and stuck the hard to miss bosoms in his face.

This can't possibly be an invitation, can it? Erik decided not to touch them, despite the active encouragement to do so. "Let me venture a guess, you envisioned a lifetime of classrooms and lectures. Nixed school because you wanted freedom – decided to roar instead. And now you're bent on enjoying every moment you can before the baby arrives, fully aware it will tame your rebelliousness all too soon."

Claudia didn't bat an eyelash, nor did she withdraw her display of swollen mammary glands. "Didn't mean to impose in your space or anything. Just wanted to know if you were up for a freebie. Care to endanger yourself and blow off some steam out on the dance floor?" She picked up his drink and impolitely downed practically the entire contents. "Thirsty," she offered by way of explanation. Intoxicated, she and the fetus were in for one hell of a headache in the morning.

He wanted a swallow of the tart crisp drink, but wouldn't touch it. Who knew what diseases Claudia carried in her mouth? Trying to figure out what to do with this vulgar, yet somehow enticing tub of womanhood, he asked rather blandly, "What would you do if your water broke during our primitive mating ritual?"

The truth of that mental picture shocked her into speechlessness.

Munching a pretzel, her dancing partner returned to their table with two beers. "Don't mind Claudia," he instructed. "She's trifling with you. Likes to bait any male who'll bother to take a look at those newly inflated boobs. Thinks they're finally suitable for Picasso's attention." He nodded toward the drunken father.

Straightening, Claudia bristled and glared belligerently at him. "What an uncouth thing to say! Give me my beer."

Kathryn interjected sweetly, "Let's have a toast. Applaud some good times."

The dance partner moved in closer to pass the drink. "Here, Claudia, toast everyone's health – including your own," he ordered. The edge in his voice said he was willing to start a quarrel. Erik wondered if he was bored and simply looking for an argument, or actually complaining about sharing Claudia's attentions. *Probably both.* With predictable behavior, the moron set his beer down and twisted Claudia's wrist. "Let's dance!"

"You bozo, get your hands off me. You've made me spill some of my beer and I wanted to talk to Erik!"

Repulsed by the scene, Erik asked, "Am I still a viable candidate for a dance?" *It seems I am to undergo the gamut of every emotion imaginable within one twenty-four hour period. I have to believe there's a purpose, some destiny for me to fulfill. Surely it's more than rescuing kittens and girls out of bars.*

"She's taken, Monsieur. Desi wants me to keep an eye on her."

The DJ was pumping up the music again. "Guess he's right," retorted Claudia. Following the brute out onto the dance floor, she hollered, "You'll wish you'd taken your chance when you had it!" She started gyrating, twisting the upper and lower portions of her body in opposite directions. As soon as her friend's back was turned, she faced Erik. Heedless to the consequences of her wantonness, she lowered the neckline of her abbreviated top. Both round breasts popped out at him, hormonally darkened nipples erect as if they'd been ordered to salute.

"I think she wants you to reconsider," Kathryn chuckled.

Erik stared, frowning in disapproval. Apparently Claudia wouldn't comprehend the consequences of her errant behavior until the unlucky birthing. *Hell, this is Paris…maybe this kind of thing happens everyday.*

"Forgive my impertinence, Erik, but do you know that people often get confused around you?" Kathryn leaned closer. "You're very polite in the chateau, don't get me wrong, but you always seem angry. Would it be an inconvenience to lighten up once in awhile?" Her tone was still friendly. He sensed that she didn't know the full extent of the facts. It always amazed him that practically none of the staff ever saw Torossian, much less the lab.

She shifted her seat closer and he noticed that she never glanced around. *Am I supposed to draw the logical conclusion that we aren't being watched?* He had to admire her control.

"Do you mind if I give you a word of advice?" she was forced into screaming.

"Please do."

"Don't let him get to you. Dr. de Chagny should be less melodramatic, less mysterious, and definitely less sarcastic. I'm glad to see you out and in the city. His control over your activities makes me furious."

"Yes, too much snapping and growling." The waitress handed him a second drink and he tossed a wad of bills onto her tray. "I've grown accustomed to his issuing directives." *These petty squabbles between Isidore and I will be resolved and forgotten soon…or one of us will meet a violent end.*

"He'll never hurt you, he's too controlled. He's just extremely overbearing and doesn't need to be, don't you think?"

"Why do girls paint their lips? Put artificial substances over something naturally pretty?"

Her eyes grew round with wonder. "Exactly how old are you?"

"Fifteen."

"You're a virgin, aren't you?" She inclined a pouting impious mouth toward his ear. "Fifteen is the age of consent in France. I'm twenty-five. Care for a more intimate *soiree*? We could trot off to a hotel and explore some divertive sex. I'm not into exhibitionism like Claudia. There are rooms nearby and I prefer making love in private."

Relieved that Isidore hadn't sent her, Erik listened to the sultry invitation, thinking that he finally had her number. She just wanted a night to unwind. In his mind a dragonfly darted from a cattail to a sunlit lily pad, hovering motionless, it poised in midair as if to penetrate the garden. It would almost be better if he had a mistress, but then he remembered Christine and the cemetery. How shocked and awed he'd been at the gnawing, desperate strength of her hunger. They made love like the parts of that Harley parked outside. Each piece geared and greased to work together.

Kathryn twisted a small advertising billet, a coupon for a free drink on Tuesday nights. Erik made a mental note to be more tolerant. "My apologies, Kathryn. The inclination to amuse myself at **your** expense smacks of opportunistic weakness."

A sheen of moisture broke out upon her brow. "As I said, you've always been a little too distant."

"It's a real temptation, but since you are John's girlfriend the pleasure of our consortia would be squelched by the guilt of cheating on a friend."

Her eyes widened with surprise, he'd used the plural. "I'm your friend, too, and for your information, I'm too fine a catch for him. He doesn't deserve me."

"Oh, I agree." He ran his finger around the inside of his shirt collar; the kitten was asleep.

Kathryn looked determined. This was turning into a trifle more than just a jaunt. She succeeded in releasing the upper button of his shirt before he quieted her fingers. Annoyed, she complained, "Don't ignore me. I'm attracted to you, and I'm not accustomed to seeing you in a nightclub. What does it matter if you're out of the compound?"

Listening to the warnings firing off in his brain, he pictured the quickest way home. He cleared his throat before remarking, "I never noticed brusk tendencies in you before. Do you always get what you want?"

He stood and she didn't try to detain him. He filtered his way through the cloistered groups exchanging conversation around the doorway, nodding to those making way for his passage. Locating the ponderously beautiful Harley, he set his sights for the chateau.

Before leaving the city altogether, he stopped beside a stone revetment anchoring an embankment. His head lowered. His eyes, directed toward the asphalt before the Harley's front tire, remained unfocused. The low lonely rumble of a nearby transit train vibrated the earth around him. Sorely tempted, he was glad that he hadn't acted on Kathryn's invitation. He remembered Christine's legs spreading apart, the feel of her strong thighs cradling him as he entered her sweetness.

He shuddered visibly. In this troubled new world, his heart bore the fruit of a still ripening love.

20 CATERING TO RELENTLESS WANT

S ecrets, their lives fed on monstrous secrets. All the way back he coped with the absurdities. At every curve in the road they rose to squelch more pleasant ruminations. He was young, healthy, and he was whole. If the mountain would not come to the prophet, then the prophet would go to the mountain. Dillard was up in the tower at the front gate. Isidore hadn't dismissed anyone. Smiling broadly at the renegade who'd jumped the reservation, he waved Erik in.

"See! Bike's no worse for wear." Erik's boots hit the pavement, idling the motorcycle.

"Your father is in his private parlor. I'm supposed to call and announce that your wayward and unharmed bottom is at the gate...condition of my continued employment. How'd the hog run?"

"Like a kitten. Call him," Erik flipped the visor down and sped off toward the garages to secure the bike.

He entered the parlor, leaving his jacket buttoned, and took a seat. Not a moment later Torossian came in and passed him a bottled water. *Most enlightening jaunt. I liked the spirit of the pregnant one at the nightclub.*

"Thank you," Erik said, taking off the cap and swallowing. "Where's Delaquois?"

"Thayer retired to his rooms," Isidore answered from a high wing chair. He'd been enjoying a fire and had his back to them. He thumbed his cane. "Our guest said we'd worn him out. I'm glad to see you brought yourself home and that it didn't require force to return you."

"Really? Care to face us so we can enjoy your grim expression of delight? Your body language suggests you're rather chagrined. Trying to cope with losing control over me?" Erik sensed Isidore's relief that his prize creation was unscathed.

"You smell of disgusting cigarette smoke." Torossian turned up his nose.

"Sorry. I wasn't impressed with the little I saw of the world. Decided to rescue myself from debauchery."

Isidore stood; leaning on the walking stick he surveyed the pair. "Listen to me, Erik. No one can fault you for wanting to be off the grounds. But unattended? Unguarded? Very dangerous! I have enemies. Take some good advice..."

"Suffice it to say, I plan on being my own person from this point forward. You are going to make Christine Daae."

Dubious, Isidore snickered. "Exactly how do you plan on compelling me to perform this ludicrous task?"

Erik smiled with satisfaction. "What if I offered you a way to mock the entire world? Expend some of that anger toward Nature you relish so profoundly. Give tit-for-tat since life has robbed you of so much. I wouldn't have to force your hand, not in the sense that you forced me into your life. You'd beg me to deliver that plan to you."

Isidore's eyes belied a growing interest. "Go on."

"Christine won't be carried in a pregnancy as I was, we'll ferment her in a nutritive soup. An environment where low voltage currents can run through the mixture and periodically reset her brainwaves. That way she won't be subject to the same catatonic seizures."

Isidore lowered his head, his mind flying through equations and required medical apparatus. "Let's sleep on this. We'll analyze our options in the morning."

Erik stood and bowed deeply. When he straightened, he scrutinized Isidore's posture. *The seeds are bearing fruit already.* "I'm off to the shower to rid myself of the stench of smoldering tobacco. Don't demote Dillard. It practically broke his heart to lend me the Harley." When Isidore's hands opened in acceptance, Erik headed for the door. Pausing, he turned to remark, "Consider sending Thayer Delaquois away."

"His medical background could prove invaluable. I can attest to his loyalty if he wants to assist us."

"We'll need the strictest privacy. Have someone reinvestigate Kathryn Arlington. She showed up right where I got off the bike to walk around. If you didn't send her, it's too much of a coincidence. And there's one more thing." He paused, "May I have a cat?"

"Torossian says you already have the animal. Keep it upstairs tonight."

He hit the shower, bathed both the kitten and himself, gave her water, and towel dried her fur. He spent about five minutes trying to think up a name. When nothing occurred to him, he vaulted into his bed and slept like the dead for hours. Sometime after dawn, he awoke with a tiny fuzzed-up cotton ball purring and kneading his chest. "Early riser? Good." He dressed and walked his new companion to the kitchen where he put in an order for needed food and cat supplies.

With his new pet catered to, he headed directly to the rooms he now knew to be Christine's former chambers. He wanted her journals. Leroux's book wouldn't tell him her mind, but words penned in her own hand would.

Entering the suite, he found the old curtains drawn and the furniture covered in white sheets. *So many gloomy spaces closed off and shrouded... no one occupying them.* He removed several of the sheets. Under one he discovered a glass cabinet with her collection of porcelain boxes, seashells, and ivory skulls – one for each grave in the de Chagny cemetery at the time. Smiling at the thought of her memorizing names and dates to pass away the hours of his absence, he moved to the stylish repository that was her desk. Rifling through cubbyholes and drawers, he found more odd trinkets and mementos. In her own way, she liked to hoard. The sought-after objects were not there. Rubbing his hands vigorously over the thighs of his jeans, he could see the journals, stacked somewhere, safe and sound. The serving table in her room was an ingenious piece, one side featured nautical hatch doors that flipped open to reveal a storage for bottles and glasses, the other end held a removable serving tray situated above several drawers for linens and extra serving pieces. He suddenly remembered her purchasing the thing, directing a servant where to place it in this very room. In all these years it had never been moved.

"I hope you don't mind," her voice resounded with an echoing tender memory. "I couldn't resist acquiring the piece."

"No, on the contrary," he lied. "It clutters the space in a lovely manner."

"Oh, you," she'd poked him in the side. "Here, let me serve you a glass of Tokay."

A small lamp atop the serving piece caught his eye. It consisted of a simple linen shade atop a cylindrical piece of torqued hand-painted wood. The wood looked to be weathered, and he realized it came from the hunter's cottage where they'd raised Julian. "Perhaps this was at one time the leg to another piece of furniture?" The lamp's shaft was screwed neatly into a brass bottom, the electric cord appeared to be aged and covered in some form of decaying cloth. Curious, he unplugged it and carefully unscrewed the lamp from its base, thinking to see how the wiring had been connected. A roll of parchment appeared in his hand. It contained a poorly written message in red ink and a key.

Temptation's satisfaction oft lay inside the walls.

"Good grief," he chuckled, "a message from the former me. These are really sloppy *t*'s and *i*'s. Bouncing the key in his hand, he scanned the room. His gaze fell upon a frame covered in cloth. Gently removing the piece of sheet revealed an oil painting of a French knight, decked in shiny silver body armor, sitting proudly atop his canopied horse. A jousting lance stood straight up from a leather canister affixed to the knight's saddle. "I always hated this oil." Lifting the painting off the wall revealed a dull brass panel set behind it. The key fit the lock perfectly.

On a recessed shelf inside the wall safe, sat a large sculpted stone box, a *Mortum Amoris*. Used since ancient times by sentimentalists, these containers for keepsakes and writings always bore decorations alluding to the seemingly opposite (yet, oh so similar) emotions accompanying death and love. Some were even in the morbid shape of coffins. This one was rectangular with fancy silver closures. Inlaid into the cover was a tarnished silver skull, grinning as it bit the long stem of a red enameled rose. He hadn't purchased this box. Perhaps one of their children did after their parents' deaths. As he pulled the heavy object out, he felt a tugging on the hem of his jeans. The tiny kitten had managed to trail him. "The marble steps must have been a feat. Shall I call you *Mortum Amoris?* Mort for short, even though you're a female." He went to a chair with the box, and the kitten clawed her way up the leg of his pants.

Inside the container Christine's journals lay in a neat stack, exactly as his mind had pictured them. A stylized *fleur-de-lis* was emblazoned on the front of each. To the back, tucked into a corner sat a brass grasshopper and a scorpion. "These are over one-hundred-sixty years old." He showed them to the kitten, she sniffed politely and preferred curling up next to his thigh.

He started thumbing through the pages. In her rambling diaries Christine covered both the mundane and the more momentous events of their former existence with equal brevity. Inside one he found a picture of their oldest son, Michael. As in the albums downstairs, he wore an old-fashioned tweed suit. The young sculptor favored his father in looks, though this picture showed an older Michael, rougher in appearance when compared to the fifteen-year-old with the budding beard who held the photograph this morning.

"Bloody hell," he sputtered. With unfailing clarity, his mind saw a younger Michael stumbling to the gardens…an area now almost non-existent, but in those days so pristine and well attended. The boy was devastated. In his father's office he'd just received an ultimatum about his sister Sarah that tore his heart apart. Walking to a statue, Michael curled his arms around the immobile feminine form. Crying. Sobbing. He pressed his cheeks against the dusty surface, streaking the marble with his tears.

Modern Erik went to the window and peered out, his mind half-expecting to see the continuation of what his memory just spit into conscious thought. Everything was askew now. The surviving trees were taller, this room closed off and abandoned. *Dead.* "Everyone is dead!" His breath became an evaporating circle of moisture on the glass. "Reminders! Everywhere reminders to jolt my brain." He snapped the journal shut. "I will make sure there are NO memories for you, Christine!"

He left the room. Standing in the hall with several of the journals tucked beneath his arm, he waited as a spectral shape came up from behind. He felt the Revenant's cold breath on the back of his neck.

"You'll bring her back to us? Renew our past emotions? We have instincts for her, uncomfortable cravings. The condition is…"

"Called love. A tad unsatisfying since all we have at the moment are non-corporeal memories, a few pictures, and an empty bedchamber," answered Erik, not bothering to turn around.

"Poor consolation."

"Isidore holds more than the lucrative key to the overpopulation of the planet. Where is he?"

"Readying himself for the next *rencontre*. He's in Nyah's work area of the lab."

Dressed appropriately for the lab, Erik pushed the button outside Nyah's computer area. "May I come in?"

"You look exceedingly fit this dreary morning," praised Nyah.

"No prevailing foul winds?" asked Isidore, buzzing him in. "I see you're prepared to convene a meeting of the minds." Isidore nodded to Torossian. Erik's sibling never suited-up for the lab – an ongoing gesture of extreme defiance. "No doubt we'll need everyone's cooperation."

The Revenant ignored the doctor. Keeping his face set toward Nyah, he stood to the side.

Isidore often wondered if he should do away with the hybrid. The major components to his first successful cloning experiment flew through his mind. *There is no accounting for how Torossian got here. Erik, on the other hand, is the perfect product of an exacting procedure. His more dormant personality is just further along in development than we'd predicted. Unforeseen.*

Erik took a stool. "I found her journals."

Isidore snickered. *To have come this far so fast!* He didn't want the boy confused, but there was nothing to be done about the instinctual overlapping of cellular structure. Nature had its way. "Are you experiencing…"

"Some form of intuition?"

How did the child do that? More and more he finished the doctor's sentences. "You know, other people will not appreciate you concluding their spoken thoughts for them. It's considered rude in most cases."

Erik looked at him thoughtfully. "But you don't." It was a simple statement of fact. "You're running a constant experiment and find this newest aberrancy fascinating. You'd love to stick a probe in my head and see how I'm doing it."

"Do you know?" Nyah inquired quietly.

"It's a recent still-evolving capacity and it started with Torossian. If I'm focused on Isidore or aware he's about to communicate, his thoughts are in my head split seconds before he speaks them."

"That's remarkable," commented Isidore. "They call it…"

"Fondling another's brain? No. Clairvoyant telepathy. We should consider that I might also be adding words to you. Projection."

"Shall we put it to the test?"

"If you'll honor my request, you may conduct all the tests you like, day and night if you prefer. All I require is Christine."

You truly don't require anything that I have not already provided. Isidore was already toying with him, exploring a preliminary way of gauging the new talent.

"You're wondering what, in truth, I could need that you have not already provided."

"Remarkably accurate."

"Make Christine for me. She is my soul and I'm impoverished without her."

Isidore's head jerked toward Nyah.

"Christine de Chagny, *nee* Daae, yes? She's not going to enjoy the trip," Nyah added knowledgeably.

"Only if she has memories and I think we can prevent them," argued Erik. "Once she's here, I'll make her understand."

"Make? Like force?" Nyah interjected. "Evolution is a bizarre twisting affair. Just as there is a fight for survival among the species. A struggle for dominance also exists at the genetic level of DNA. Even if Isidore dictates a specific RNA coded order, sometimes the dominant trait wins out and sometimes it doesn't. Cloning is not precise and exact, but rather unpredictable."

"Do you need me to explain the process?" asked Isidore.

"No, I'll read the rest of your notes."

"Which ones?"

"All of them, most are in your computer files, correct?"

"They're pass-coded and encrypted."

"That will just make them a little more interesting to get into."

"In that case," Nyah was smiling, "who would you like for a surrogate?"

"No one. As I said last night, there is another way to gestate her."

"The fetus will need to hear her mother's heartbeat while she forms. The sound of other bodily functions is as equally important. They will help stabilize her."

"It's all right," reassured Erik. "I'll play her music and we'll tape my inward noises for her to listen to, twenty-four seven, while she develops."

"There is also the real consideration that she won't like you as she matures. It took some time before she found you less than distasteful.

How upset will you be if she doesn't spring from the hatch adoring you?"

"I'll be driven to madness, I'm halfway there already. I made a lot of mistakes before. This time I won't make the same ones."

How much do you remember? Isidore asked telepathically.

Erik responded! *A lot! I'm not sure how much is memory and how much is imagination. She can help me sort some of it out. Is Kathryn here?*

She's coming around eleven, answered Isidore.

Torossian unexpectedly slid into the passageway leading to the computer banks.

A moment later, Thayer stared through the Plexiglas at the congregated group. It was damn eerie. Not a single soul was opening their mouth, yet they appeared to be talking. Nyah looked up and smiled, giving him a shallow wave. Thayer pushed a speaker button, bravely clearing his throat for attention.

Get rid of him! Erik sent an emphatic command to Isidore.

I tried…and as I suspected, he didn't listen.

"I have something pressing to discuss with Erik." Thayer employed his most professional tone to mask a suspicion that the Revenant might be close.

Erik turned to challenge Delaquois. "What could possibly be more pressing than the matter I'm currently involved in?"

"Your catatonic episodes."

"You don't believe they're genuine. You think I'm in a simple process of avoidance, or worse yet, seeking attention…because I'm lonely."

Thayer glanced obliquely down the corridor, nervously assuring himself that he stood alone. "I know you're not a charlatan, Erik. I'm your ally. You're in there discussing another cloning because you're consumed with an overriding obsession to regain your former wife."

Erik's hands went defiantly to his hips. "Give me your word you won't repeat that to another living soul."

"You have my solemn oath. The impact and influence of a tumultuous relationship is something Isidore and Nyah should understand on two levels. Clearly as themselves, and in a sub-context as Julian and…"

"Sonia," finished Nyah.

Erik's brain went through a spasm of violent turmoil. In a series of vehement mental shouts, he told Isidore that if he let Thayer in and the neuropsychiatrist managed, through some form of wheedling, to dissuade him from creating Christine, he'd burn the house and lab into oblivion. All that would be left was a field of brown meadow grass to picnic on.

"Unreasonable and unnecessary! Please, have the dignity to cloak your hysterical theatrics and keep them out of my head." Isidore buzzed Thayer in.

"I am never hysterical."

Isidore hit the button a second time, blocking Thayer's entrance. "If you incinerate the lab where will we grow her?"

Out in the corridor, Thayer's arms spread wide in a frustrated plea for a modicum of courteous sanity. The microphone was still on, "Christine must not remember the children, long dead, the realization might kill her."

Leary, Torossian backed completely out of the room.

Erik eyed Isidore, "The busybody is correct, the grief alone would be too much of a shock. I can prevent her from becoming melancholy over the loss of her children, but what can be worse than discovering that part of Julian is walking around – still scheming, still trying to dominate?"

Isidore, scratching his hairline, decided not to return the insult. "What will you do if I concede to your clamoring and we do **not** have a productive outcome?"

"That is for me to unravel. Not you, old man. Will you do it? Give me your word you'll do it."

"Patience, Erik," Nyah angled her computer screen so that it faced him. "See, we're already planning. But we need the benefit of Thayer's assistance if you want to move rapidly. We can't bring him up to speed while he's stewing out there."

Erik nodded and Isidore finally buzzed Thayer in. "Just kidding around," Isidore explained flatly.

"I was wrong to think that you hadn't a humorous bone left in your body," Thayer walked up to Erik and squeezing his wrist, assessed his radial pulse. "What's the verdict?"

Erik eased his wrist from Thayer's clutches and started taking the psychiatrist's pulse. "That you're complicating the situation." The heartbeat accelerated. "Because of your meddling there are now five in the cabal." The cardiac muscle raced to keep up with a purely non-existent crisis. "Are you enough of a masochist to spend long hours laboring to help us bring Christine into the twenty-first century?" Within the psychologically induced tachycardia, Erik felt the pulse begin to skip, rebound, and skip. He mentally ordered the heart to slow. There was no need to torment the doctor with the painful angina that was about to commence.

"Yes," Thayer's mind drifted back into the lab.

Erik let go of his wrist.

"Fascinating effect! You...?" Isidore broke in, carefully caging his words.

Erik stayed focused on Delaquois' face. The color was returning to his cheeks and earlobes. "I told his adrenal medulla to secrete epinephrine. In the process I learned he has a significant amount of arteriosclerotic hardening of the left anterior descending coronary artery."

Incredulous, Thayer put his fingertips on his own carotid pulse. "The vessel carrying the heart's primary supply of blood...the widow maker?"

Isidore returned to their original more engrossing debate. "Let's say I don't refuse, will you give me your word that as she forms you won't become more withdrawn? Your moodiness will have an effect on her. Burn off your labile emotions in the gym."

"So you agree to help me!"

"Haven't we been discussing that very thing? I have a few added criteria. Your demands will cease and desist. We will work cooperatively... as a team."

"My apologies for calling you sanctimonious. You're right. A house divided cannot stand, much less produce. I should never have threatened to damage your position in the scientific community. A rarified genius that won a Noble should be esteemed and applauded, even if he repeatedly injected himself and his mistress with damaging DNA."

Nyah pushed her glasses further up her nose. "Even if he successfully cloned one individual that produced an unexpected pairing and is about to attempt a second?"

"Yes," Erik's solemn declaration resonated in the room. "Most especially under those circumstances, for I would be stripped of hope and lost without him." Revealing a deeply sentimental facet of his nature, Erik symbolically tapped his left chest. "You both claim more than just an elevated place within my heart. My soul may yearn for Christine, but in this new paradigm you are the captains at the helm."

"Then you have my word, Erik." Isidore's eyes were glassy with tears – at last the acclamation he valued most! "We venture forth under a new banner. Not only do I agree to this outrageous proposition, I fully bless it. My hopes are that through the two of you, we will carry heirs to several generations." He gestured toward Nyah's monitor screen, "Sorry that we inadvertently failed to mention that we were already discussing a schedule for the procedure. Your announcement that you'd discovered her diaries took us aback. Did you like the agate box we ordered for them? Ghoulish, huh?"

Erik smiled, "Some of the clues you found during your searching?"

"Big ones!" Isidore's hands alluded to two balls at the front of his chest.

"Go to the crypt, Erik. Check that things are in order there and try not to get too maudlin," Nyah directed helpfully. "We'll need to move the body over here for awhile. Refuse to let any stray thoughts about her desecration enter your mind. The vast majority of graves on this estate have remained intact and undefiled, but Christine's tomb needs to surrender up what it has to offer. Unfortunately, her coffin was not sealed as tightly as the one containing your former body. Her DNA will be more degraded."

"We'll overcome all the drawbacks," Thayer was surprisingly energetic and positive. "We have more minds stirring the pot."

Erik's chin lifted higher. "Aside from the matter of disturbing memories, there is also the age difference that will lie between us. I'm too impatient to give her a drawn-out childhood. If she remains in the soup longer, can we accelerate her growth?"

Nyah's dainty foot tapped the floor, "The work we do is painstaking methodical science. Remember that Nature does not always comply with the precise formulas we project. Extending her birth date increases the possibilities of other complications – respiratory difficulties for one. We'll have to overcome them."

Thayer raised his hand like a student in a classroom. "Then once she comes out, we'll support her breathing until she effectively accomplishes air exchange on her own."

"You must understand, Erik," Isidore added, "she can develop to a particular physiological age in the birth sack, but once she's free of it, from that point on, she'll age normally. We can't put her back in."

Thayer danced excitedly from foot to foot. "Mice without a functioning telomerase gene age faster than normal mice. Withhold the gene during gestation and give it to her when she's ready to be taken out of the vat."

Nyah turned her computer screen back to its original position. "The logical reversal dictates that telomerase, the enzyme that builds new telomeres using an RNA template during DNA replication, will extend life. We used the principal with Erik." Nyah typed furiously at her keyboard. "Crisscrossing the delicate strands of DNA succeeded in several trial runs."

"What if this crisscrossing caused the mental abilities I exhibit? Will she be capable of them as well?"

Isidore went to watch Nyah's computer screen closely. "I'm not sure. What about giving her a reversible Progeria syndrome? Replace thymine with cytosine causing a mutation on point 1824. Accelerating her growth in the tank will hurt, but she'll have more time to live as an adult."

Nyah didn't look up, didn't miss a keystroke. "Nourishment will be a prime consideration. Enriching the soup will lessen the experience of pain during rapid bone growth. No doubt there will be some adolescent moodiness immediately following her birth. Perhaps early teenage depression as her brain strives to maintain the space created by her expanding skull. Thayer can assist more directly at that stage."

Isidore glanced toward Erik, "Not to fear, every obstacle will be overcome."

Thayer asked, "Do you want me to go with you to the crypt?"

Erik hit the buzzer, "No, stay here. I like your ideas. Help them redefine the paradigm."

Running his hands atop Christine's sarcophagus, he whispered demented words of love, "I've come to visit you, Beloved, show you the way back to me. I am and will ever be, the thief calling your name from the depths of the theater's cellars. The path you must tread is more crooked than ever, fraught with treacherous technicalities. Until you arrive, the sorrow of waiting will eat me alive. You are such sweet succor. A ripe fig I could suck dry and never grow tired of…come to me, Christine. Spread your legs. Entice the monster forth. He wants you."

He thought to push the lid, see her face. All he desired at this point was to caress the corpse of his dead wife. The memory of a particular night in the Opera House came to him. She'd just surprised the critical theater-going world of Paris by rendering a stirring vocal performance at the gala marking the retirement of the two managers, Debienne and Poligny. *Tonight I sang only for you, my Angel of Music.* The older version of Erik used to relive that expressive declaration – over and over.

Two girls, one long dead within this crypt, the other a hidden promise waiting to be awakened in an un-harvested clump of cells. "I can pull two worlds together. This newer Christine will not abandon my heart, my tender heart to torment." He kissed the mouth of the female angel. *So cold, so delightfully cold.* "This time I must repeat the mistake of letting you possess a surname not my own."

Her soul rose in gossamer, nearly unidentifiable filaments. Arched chest first, then her head, neck flexed back. She curled upward through the stone to breathe a sentence to him. "So talented, so unfulfilled." Her voice had a soft reverberation, like the sound of a distant church choir.

"Speak, my Love. Tell me more."

"Vulnerable and kind, your loneliness reaches through the veils to trouble my rest."

Surprised, Erik retreated until his muscular bottom came against his own sarcophagus. "Don't you want to live?"

"Until you revive me – I wait unfulfilled."

Kathryn's voice came from the open doorway to the tunnel. Christine's image dissipated instantaneously. "When we fantasize a great love-experience the reality is never what we anticipated. We're always disappointed."

Merde, woman, that's twice you've shown up unexpectedly. How far do you intend to take these intrusions? But she looked so cute in her chic little gray business suit. Her perfume, Shalimar by Guerlain, was a delight to his nostrils. "Let's not confuse appearances with reality. You are John's girlfriend, not mine. Have you set a date for the wedding?"

"No. I've been indulging a rather obstinate tendency to procrastinate. I can be a little headstrong." She moved around Christine's tomb.

"I might have a flaw or two equal to your own."

"Well, at least you're not boring. She was his wife?" She pointed to the two sarcophagi in succession.

"In many ways, his partner. She could have been a renowned soprano, but she sacrificed herself in an earnest desire to see him survive." *And sate her feminine core with his generous affections,* he added mentally.

"How noble. I've followed you in here on a less honorable obligation. I want to apologize for last night. My aggressive proposition was a turnoff. My only excuse, since I certainly wasn't drunk, is that my offer was probably born of overactive hormones. My friend's pregnancy might have been an encouraging influence." *Plus you are so undeniably gorgeous. What do you feel like, Erik?*

She's about to ovulate! "I can tell you like me. Despite our age difference I have an appeal." He straightened, angling his body so she could see the shadow of the erection he'd experienced over the phantasm.

"Are you suggesting we indulge in a little physical pleasure?" She inched closer, stopping only when she was directly in front of him.

Growing more and more familiar with anatomy, he mentally outlined her secret creative center. Its components lay hidden beneath the skirt of her formal garments, waiting, yearning to be used with the bubbling formation of a child. "I'm saying you're a definite distraction." *What frivolous woman wears a suit these days?*

"I could re-extend last night's offer."

"I'm afraid you're reading me a tad imperfectly. I need your help to launch a project that's very important. All it will cost you is a few hormone injections and a tiny bit of pain from a fiber optic scope. Do you think you could part with a few eggs?"

Ogling the zipper area of his tight jeans, she bit her lower lip. He was generously endowed. "Yes, I think I can do that for you."

21 RECONSTRUCTING A LOVER

ℙarting out of necessity and reluctant to do so, Thayer left that morning. To say the least, he was anxious to begin the second cloning, but there was no circumventing the fact that he had responsibilities to address in the world. Schedules needed realigning and his hospital duties surrendered to other physicians. He planned to see his family and announce that he would be working with Isidore de Chagny on a regular basis and would only return to Paris for emergency consultations. He promised to visit home as often as humanly possible, but when one is granted such a singular opportunity, declining the distinction would be professional folly.

At his departure from the chateau, he reminded Isidore to keep searching for the triggering mechanism that brought on Erik's visions. Discovering the catalyst would point their noses in the right direction.

So Erik won the first round of an enormous war. Left on the estate with Isidore, they were free to pursue the reconstruction of his consort. To that end, they dismissed any and all other activities and spent the greater part of each twenty-four hour period in the laboratory. There the truce between creator and creation endured some ragged moments. The first of which was an angry episode in which Erik complained bitterly that no one could decipher Isidore's handwritten notes. The crisis was relieved with an explanation that Isidore wrote in a boustrophedonic fashion: alternating lines moved in opposite directions (one left to right, the next from right to left), creating a long flowing stream of thoughts and equations upon a page. A habit picked up decades earlier in medical school to protect the originality of his work, and to expedite time lost moving the pen. With that hurdle crossed, they met with Kathryn, and with her written consent, tackled the harvesting of her ovum and the annihilation of the DNA they contained.

Thayer reappeared at the front gate on the third day with two enormous trunks jammed with clothes and personal articles. Joking that both his wife and the hospital were furious, but eventually accepting, he happily claimed his new temporary residence at the chateau. He immediately joined Nyah in the preparation of a clear elastic polymer tank. The vat's multi-layered walls had the combined tensile strength of steel and the muscular flexibility of a uterus.

Erik experienced an intense excitement the day that all three eggs took to their artificial 'fertilization' with Christine's DNA. The results were more than passably fine; it was almost as if she reached through time and space to bless the success of the project. The plan was to proceed with the most promising morula, let it develop and keep the other two in stasis in a canister surrounded by liquid nitrogen. In awe and disbelief, Erik needed almost constant reassurance that under the microscope – Christine began to live. They let her develop *in vitro* before attempting to transplant the tiny structure of cells to their more permanent controlled residence.

Erik's constant attendance in the lab began to worry Isidore. Especially when, while musing over some notes, Erik entered the office with an announcement.

"The artificial womb is ready. Too bad we can't patent this container. Given a few years for the world to develop acceptance of the notion, women would no longer need to act as vessels to bear their young. No female would suffer the pains of childbirth or die from some insidious infection ever again. In my time Childbed Fever was the dreaded plague of maternity."

"I didn't give you life to see you grow so serious. You're ready to take on the ills of the entire world. Now that we have a genuine foothold into forming Christine, I need to remind you to prize your own life a little better. It isn't prudent to spend every waking moment in this lab. If nothing else, your youthful body demands physical exercise. The total exclusion of other diversions fosters depression and ill health."

"I'd tell you if I had another vision. There's been none, and I'm not too absorbed, just enthusiastic. I feel genuinely privileged leaping at this smallest chance to assist." Secretly Erik admitted that he could barely tear his eyes away from the rapidly dividing cells. "You won't live forever, and you're the key to her creation."

After an exhausted sigh, Isidore said bleakly, "Regrettably true. This is how I hoped things would be between us, achieving success side by side. In my earlier days, I enjoyed working in private…didn't have to explain to anyone my ignoble interventions on life's humors."

"You've adapted. All of us are honored that you allowed us into the working-end of your scientific domain," Erik reached across the desk and rubbed his creator's weary hands.

"Confronted with the dynamic force of you, what choice do I really have? Would it be a grievous disappointment if I asked you to take me upstairs and break for lunch together?"

Erik was almost amused. "She's frail, but I think she'll endure us having a meal. She's gone through the initial phases of cell division nicely. We can even send Nyah and Thayer upstairs in a second shift. Would it please you if I arrange my work schedule so that it starts and stops with physical activities?"

"Did I fail to mention that you are an inspiration to me, Erik? When I look at you I don't mind my imploding deformities. The aesthetic surface of your physique, your honest commitment to science…in every specific concrete sense of the word…and your splendid genius is a wondrous thing to behold."

"You tampered with the dictates of Life, mocked Fate to bring me into this world. Now you're trying again. It is your genius that will grant us success."

"Glad that you're so suitably impressed."

The day they moved the fetus to the sturdy structure of the vat was momentous. Inside the nutritive soup, maintained at a constant temperature of 98.6 degrees, the tiny creature floated freely. The bank of computers, supervising every aspect of the watery environ, hummed as sensors closely monitored hundreds of molecular levels: oxygen, human chorionic gonadotropin, progesterone, electrolytes and every mineral needed for growth. Back up generators, running off alternate energy sources, should the main power supply fail, all tested at full capacity. Using a keyboard, Nyah's deft fingers mechanically extended an artificial umbilical cord through the ocean of amniotic liquid. The cord's tip, coated in rapidly moving chorionic villi, approached the tiny clump of cells comprising Christine's germinating placenta. The mutually accepting materials latched onto each other, anchoring themselves as predicted. Tiny fiber optic vessels started pulsating blood through embryonic tissues. The huddled group of scientists watched and waited in wonder as an outer magnification device showed them the little creature moving within the enriched fluid of the flexible polymer canister.

Even curled over like a miniscule letter C, with a pronounced caudal tail and only buds for future fingers, Erik never saw anything so marvelous. At the equivalent of five and a half weeks she had a fluttering heartbeat and at six and a half weeks a set of distinct cardiac tones. They watched this heartbeat carefully. Amazingly, it responded to digitally transmitted 'maternal' body sounds and classical music. When indicators revealed that she had developed functioning brain tissue with cyclic awake and sleep phases, they employed a combination of drugs and timed small low voltage shocks that forced her neurotransmitters to reset and recuperate. Knowing she wouldn't remember him, Erik reluctantly accepted that there would only be 2012 for her, no past. She needed no jarring waves of memory. He had misgivings but never voiced them. When independence and coherent function were obtained, would she bond with him? Express some mild form of curiosity toward his identity? With every passing day he curbed his expectations and his questions only built.

Developing in peaceful tranquility within the constant flow of purified mellifluous fluid, the fetus matured into a female child, suspended in space, occasionally opening her eyes and looking out at the blurry lab around her. To Erik she was never anything but beautiful. Her skin was the color of whipped cream, her hair the lightest shade of brown imaginable. Over the weeks her tresses grew in waves that floated about her head. Fingernails developed, bringing with their length the possibility she might scratch herself, but it couldn't be helped. Though she often kicked and somersaulted within the chamber, no damage actually occurred.

Erik recognized the child Christine as she formed. Everything about her was familiar: her cheekbones and chin, brow, lips that parted occasionally to suck a thumb or actually smile. He transmitted telepathic images to her and sat before a microphone, spending more and more time talking with enormous sincerity to the human drifting before him.

"Everything changed the year I turned fifteen. I started having strange visions. They weren't dreams or hallucinations, more like vivid movies where I was an actual participant. What happened to me in the gypsy camps and later in Persia was not a story. I'm some long-suffering antihero in a Gothic autobiography. The events are real and very confusing because they don't manifest in chronological order. Then someone, you to be precise, took a match and lit a candle in the dark. I saw my way clearly for the first time. How ironic. While other teenagers are bored and grappling with what they want to do for a pastime, I suddenly saw through the upsetting morass to my true purpose. The world's entertainments offer no enticement to me. Nothing really matters but you.

"And now you're coming. Compared to the rest of my history, I remembered you rather quickly. You were a swift dawning of understanding. Yes, you rocked my world from the first moment you appeared: a face, a rather lovely face with a brilliant warm smile and an undertone of sadness. We won't discuss that you were blue with a long swishing tail. I've started sketching you, but you really can't see the drawings very well from in there. Had I known what this year would hold for me, I would have celebrated more appropriately on New Year's Eve. I never really questioned things before the visions started. Up until then, defining my life didn't matter. I had plenty of time to do whatever pleased me. And it pleased me to fence, read, ride motorcycles, and monkey around with my shadowy brother, Torossian. Sounds normal, doesn't it? I've since discovered that things are never normal in this chateau. At least not normal in the way they portray families in the reruns of old American comedies.

"There was never a mother and a father, outings in the park or trips to museums. There was always Isidore and his sweet assistant, Nyah, thousands of tests and hours spent here in the lab unraveling puzzles and learning...always learning. My childhood playmate is a strange creature. We'll introduce the two of you carefully so he doesn't frighten you. He likes to be called the Revenant. Melancholy name don't you think? He wants to be known as a living dead-thing. I'm not even sure where he sleeps these days. Here in this locked-down fortress, I'm wound up so tightly. I'm always on edge and making demands, brain-busy, ready for action. He, on the other hand, is as calm as a flowing river – one with a strong powerful undercurrent ready to suck the unsuspecting off the surface. Since we don't take trips, we've always had a great deal of time to acquire knowledge and grow inside this great hollowness. Nothing we did was judged as good or bad, success or failure. The only parameter was stay here. It's as if we were test subjects and someone forgot to tell us the experimental goals. Considered the specimen with the greatest potential, everything I do or say is monitored. They don't follow Torossian so closely. When we were toddlers they put a headset on him to test his hearing – he snapped the thing like a twig. Since then he doesn't tolerate any of their attempts to study him. Breaks all the equipment he can get his hands on when they try. So our infamous creators focus on me. I'd be a raving maniac if it weren't for you. Now I have hope. Asleep, awake…there is no difference…my life is all about you."

In his office, Isidore listened to these speeches, removed his mask and wept.

"Did you know we knew each other before?" Erik just couldn't resist recalling. "From the time you were seven I stalked you, dogged your footsteps. Freedom from me was a playful illusion you allowed yourself from time to time. You used to tell me that all it would take to leave was a short walk to the front lobby and a quick burst through the main doors to a hired carriage. You would order yourself to flee from the Opera House, board a train for another part of France or another country. I would answer that you knew in your heart I'd search you out. Find you. Because I was an angel, I could travel through the walls of any shelter where you tried to hide. Once there, I would invade your prayers, overwhelm you with my presence. It was insidious how I seeped into your thoughts, endangered the very foundation of your sanity. I persuaded you to yield. So you stayed in the theater, virtually a captive… there in the playhouse of horrors where I dwelt so close…so close in the cellars beneath your feet.

"As you came of age, I watched you call upon your will power, petition God for the added strength to walk out the front door, to turn your back on the insistent being that haunted you. Inflamed, I gripped the walls behind the mirror of your dressing room and sang with all the soul I possessed. I sang as no other on earth, begging you, bending you. Letting those all-invasive notes, uttered so unmercifully, incise your resolve, cut it away from you. I adhered your very soul down into mine. I plagued you almost day and night, until you were addicted to me, and once addicted you surrendered. Back then I centered all my strengths on you, just as they are now. Heaven resides within our union, Christine. Hell takes up the rest of space."

Alone in their section of the laboratory, nearly transported with love, he'd pause to sing to her at the top of his lungs. The action seemed so natural; he felt the sound had to be good for her. The tenor solos from so many operas blossomed from within his throat: *Carmen, Madame Butterfly, Don Giovanni, La Boheme.*

And did she have any choice? She couldn't stray too far. Mesmerized, her body flowed on a buoyant stream of sound and wonder. Enraptured by the songs, she let the tones enfold her – take her, even if she couldn't understand the words. The earnest desires expressed in the sounds awakened un-nameable emotions within her burgeoning awareness. The developing female's comprehension oozed down unidentifiable passageways, summoned toward the dark despair encamped at the console below her enclosure.

He sang *arioso*, knowing the new Christine soared and spun on another plane – falling, hurling, dissolving into the music. He let the fingers of his voice ripple over her without contact. Distant. Unattainable. A disquieting indigent force in need of comfort. His reward came whenever a look of concern or concentration crossed her face, and the occasional brief smile lit up his world.

At the *caesura*, when he paused to rest, a frowning Christine made her way to the inner side of the canister. She came to the wall, pressing her hands to the glass. In shock, he stood – knowing that with every fiber of his being he wanted her and no other. If he placed his lips upon the glass would she copy and join him?

From the doorway, drawn by the magical sound of his voice, Isidore and Nyah watched, mournfully acknowledging the depths of the rising storm.

"Do you know what your melodrama is doing?" Isidore's strained question only emphasized his alarm. "Do you have the patience to grant her the time it takes to develop?"

Erik kept his eyes on Christine. She was watching him. "I think she's asking for more song. You know how to reverse the gene that's giving her this mild case of Progeria, right? The acceleration isn't going to shorten her life?"

"No. When she's pubescent I'll reverse the disorder. Once she's out, she'll age normally...normally in the sense that old age will be postponed for two centuries."

Setting his jaw, Erik demanded to know that all the controlled parameters were functioning precisely. "When do you estimate she can come out of there?"

"This is not one of those endless knotted ropes you like to unravel, Erik. We cannot dictate, only provide. At this point she sets her own pace."

Inside the vat she swayed on a silken rippling current of fluid. Still frowning at the maestro.

"Are we ready to work?" Thayer eased around Isidore and Nyah. "Or is everyone going to stand around staring at each other? It's time to re-calibrate the instruments – it's important."

"I was just asking that same question," replied Erik.

Isidore grunted. "Can you describe the fundamental nature of good and evil, Thayer? Because in this room we've stretched the validity of good intent to its very limits."

"And therein lies the exact definition you seek. All that promotes Life is good." Thayer went to stand beside Erik. "Evil is that which denies Life, everything that negates the creative process."

"You're devastated without her, aren't you?" Nyah understood Erik's motivations.

"I am destroyed until the day she breathes again." He shot an uplifted chin toward Isidore. "He's a jealous critic. One who doesn't try to empathize. A wheedling judge who dispenses with extenuating circumstances as it suits his purpose."

Reacting to the anxious quality of Erik's voice, the unhappy creature inside the tank hit her open hand against the transparent wall. The source of the sweet sounds had forgotten to turn off the microphone.

"You're exhausted, Erik." Thayer's voice was kind. "You need rest. It takes stamina to complete this rebirthing."

A red alert light started blinking on and off. Reacting swiftly, Erik vaulted over a padded stool trying to get to the console where an audible alarm was beginning to sound. Every person in the room went into overdrive. Erik's expert fingers turned a knob, guiding a prescribed injection of calcium down into the placenta. Relieved, he withdrew a packet of dehydrated tarragon from his shirt pocket. Sticking the contents into his mouth, he began to chew.

In the amniotic fluid the child's eyes closed. She slept.

Erik gave them a curt obligatory bow. "I'm going to get some fresh air."

Isidore looked at Thayer, "Help me into my office, please. We'll leave Nyah to reset the calibrations."

Outside Erik took a sad walk through the back meadow down to the shoreline of the shrinking lake. He listened to the lapping water and let the dreary light of an overcast sky help him bring events into perspective. These days his life was like that of a cook constantly opening an oven to check on the readiness of a roast. Perhaps he should go and gather some peas. Picking up several small stones, he sent them skipping across the murky water. The sound of a mournful wailing came up from a small island out in the center of the lake. The cry blew across the liquid surface and he knew its source. Out there, on that sandy patch that housed a few scraggly pines, rested a cleverly chiseled piece of granite about the size of a tombstone. In another life he'd poured his grief into carving that rock, designed it so the wind blowing through a funneling center hole created this sorrowful dirge. A sound fit to put a wife into a crypt. He'd cast his lot with that woman. Produced children.

Michael, his melancholy son, was an inspired sculptor. His works embodied the emotional perfections of celestial grace and beauty. But the joyless marble faces Michael fashioned were always full of remorse, like his pair of angels in the chapel – standing motionless, embracing without kissing. Erik's second son was Ariel, a doctor, a healer inspired by the pain of others to act on their behalf. It seems he'd spawned a number of well-intended physicians. And then came their last, Sarah, a goddess of sultry persuasion and strong-headed stubbornness.

If he understood Christine's journals correctly, nothing that happened between Julian's parents could have been averted. It was as if Genetic Sexual Attraction rose up to feast on their freedom of choice like a gremlin gorging on a hot meat pie.

Looking up the hill, he pictured the grounds as they were when he lived here as the grand imposter. Back then this was a peaceful geometric landscape dotted with pruned fruit trees and flowering bushes heavy with blossoms. Curving walkways marked with doublewide borders of riotous color. Asters, verbenas, and pink petunias...all backed with a variety of iris and thriving roses. Pleasant paths where a soul could meander toward fountains graced with nymphs and mermaids, statues standing like gracious hosts. Every alcove, surrounded by its own semi-circle of clipped junipers, created a small haven for reflective thought. The trees in autumn literally burst with wondrous color. Their foliage stretched over an expanse of forest spread further than the eye could see. Woods that teemed with small and large game: partridge, rabbit, deer and wild boar. The animals were gone now, eaten by another gremlin – the sprawl of civilization. He regretted bringing Christine back into a world lacking that kind of distinctive beauty. Hopefully, in resetting her brain she wouldn't miss what she could not remember.

Inside his office, Isidore poured himself a good stiff shot of one hundred proof Knob Creek bourbon. The tensions building in the lab were inevitable, so he let the alcohol warm his blood. When Thayer emerged from the restroom, Isidore was just finishing a phone call. "Erik believes that Christine is a constant he cannot do without. He doesn't understand the enormous emotional pressure he's laying on her shoulders. She will never be the exact duplicate of the original. I've reassigned Dillard. He's to guard the tank and keep Christine safe. It's time Torossian earned his keep by protecting Erik. Now that I'm committed to forming this child, our marvelous prodigy must have the patience to let me complete his prize. My ambition rushed the situation with Julian's DNA. I can't endure watching Erik speed pell-mell into mistakes, too."

"Tell me about Julian," Thayer thought this a good opportunity to address Isidore's health.

"Initially his disorder seemed idiopathic, but intuitions began to play within my mind. It was almost as if the Julian incorporated within my genes led me to where the problems lay. His mother ingested a poison during her pregnancy – the substance altered his genetics. Really, it's a blessing he never bore children. There was of course the facial deformity evidenced at birth. Then malformed proteins, attracted to the rich gray matter of his brain and central nervous system, accumulated as he grew. The effects started evidencing themselves at a young age. One of the first was a tremendous calcium buildup in his bones and teeth. Puberty, with its rocketing hormone levels, tipped the scales in the wrong direction." Isidore finished the bourbon. Thayer declined the proffered bottle, so

Isidore poured himself another. Under the influence of the alcohol he continued to reveal more of Julian's maliciousness. "He couldn't cope as tragedy after tragedy piled up. He accidentally killed his sweetheart, Sonia. What he did to her body after death is too wicked, too disgusting to describe. He was powerless to save himself from his own actions.

"After I damaged myself with those cursed injections, I practically ransacked the crypt. When I discovered Raoul's substitute, x-rays showed he had a re-ossified broken leg. I already knew that both Julian's legs were fractured at death. The injuries occurred when they fell into the oubliette. Julian pushed his grandfather. Michael pushed Julian, a son he failed to recognize. Did you know that Erik's blood is O negative? Christine's is A positive. All their descendants were A positive. Erik's identity was hidden even in blood type." He felt like waxing philosophically. "Julian was angry over losing Sonia. Primeval urges are not tamed by centuries of culture and the civilized rules dictated by society. Man's true colors eventually show themselves." He lifted the bottle poetically, "Restraint is easily washed away with a little alcohol. We must guard against upsetting the apple cart with Christine."

Worried, Thayer stared at his masked friend. Isidore's lab coat seemed to swaddle him in cloth. He'd grown so thin. Wisps of white hair floated in strips atop his head. The skin of his recently wondrous hands was wrinkled and dotted with brown age spots. "I think it's a bad decision to place Dillard between Erik and Christine. Erik won't be satisfied with a holographic image from two rooms away. Not when he's got the real thing gestating in that tank. Trying to control his passions won't end well for either of you."

"In the beginning of their relationship she didn't care much for him. She thought he was taxing, an inspired drillmaster sent from Heaven by her father to give her music lessons. When he actually abducted her, she was furious."

"Maybe you should limit your medicinal intake of alcohol."

"What? No recommendations for mild tranquilizers? Painkillers? Percocet perhaps?" Isidore scoffed. His voice trembling, he seemed almost another person with his next observation, "No one is forcing you into this alliance, Thayer Delaquois. Leave anytime you like...or stay... it's all the same to me. I personally find the dynamics of Erik's dilemma invigorating."

"Is that Julian speaking? If so, you can tell him his fondness for controversy isn't the least bit stimulating. In my entire medical career I've never encountered cases like these, but greed and revenge are very common motivations. And if Isidore happens to be listening, let him know that this isn't exactly the most conventional way to pass on an estate."

"True, but the possibilities now open to me are remarkably stunning."

"Let Erik work out his relationship with this new Christine. The mental stress you'll foster trying to block him…"

"Block me from what?" Erik stood quietly in the doorway, arms folded across his chest. "We're all under enormous stress."

Isidore eyed his protégé and asked, "Do you remember those female spirits that presided over the groves and forests in Greek mythology? Julian was very fond of his grandfather's stories regarding those creatures. He envisioned himself as their brother. Apparently he didn't grasp that those tree nymphs were governed by greater divinities. Artemis for one and Zeus above her. Through the dryads they punished humans who thoughtlessly harmed the trees."

"Fascinating," Erik said thoughtfully. "And what? You're like Zeus? Seeking propitiation?"

The great and mighty geneticist stretched his aching back. "Our cleverly engineered instruments tell all. Christine is like one of those trees. At this vulnerable state she could so easily wither, and I will protect my work," he declared self-righteously.

"How much of this is Julian speaking?" Even in his tormented state, Erik knew he needed to guard against Isidore's ruthless possessiveness. As Christine's maker he truly held all the master keys. Erik noticed Christine's journals stacked neatly on a back shelf. He'd confiscate them later; they should be with him, not Isidore. A new edge to their conflict was brewing. For the moment, he'd curtail his accusations.

"I know the difference between Julian and myself. The Weirdling hasn't taken over."

"Your health is deteriorating," Erik walked over to the desk and pushed the bottle away. He tried to sound like a concerned son talking to a benevolent father. "Whatever demons you're battling, you would do well to practice temperance. There are other ways to make yourself feel comfortable: a massage, a good movie, a sumptuous meal." *Thayer's blinding drugs!*

"Great sex," Isidore cut to a point of contention. He still had urges. Even shriveling, he wasn't sapless.

Dressed like another absurdly outfitted laboratory technician, Dillard entered the lab's main corridor. Isidore had summoned him. He came to the tank room and waited for Nyah to buzz him in. She sighed, telling him where to stand once he joined her. He waited with avid curiosity as she revealed the container's contents. At the unveiling of their Picasso, he let out a whistle of surprise.

Erik sensed it all – like a pleasant dream going horribly wrong. "Impertinent fool!" Bursting from the office he ran to his love. Aloof and flustered, he paced. "Dillard should not be admitted here. Revoke his clearance."

Dillard's mirthless smile stretched his crooked scar across his cheek. He insolently pulled out two brass creatures from his pocket and set them on a metal lip right in front of the vat. One was the scorpion and the other the grasshopper. "Want to know how I got these? Ask Dr. de Chagny."

Erik crumbled, wordless, to the floor.

Running through the open door, Thayer shoved Dillard aside trying to reach his patient. "Madness, this is madness. Insanity reigns supreme in this house."

Taking Erik under the arms, Dillard dragged him roughly from the room.

Out in the corridor, the Revenant waited before addressing Dillard in an edgy condescending tone that caused pain to auditory nerve endings. "Let me tell you something about insanity, Mr. Kelly." Torossian's intentional grating made the guard grind his teeth and cringe. "Madness can grip a mind in less than a minute. All it takes is that split second in which the stricken individual concedes that what his mind projects as reality, is indeed real...then sight, sound, all the other senses align to regulate a new interpretation of events. Truth evaporates. The individual seizes upon this new understanding to maintain some form of balance. He modifies dictated behavior. I'm a derivation and even I know this."

Dillard swooned. Letting go of Erik, he dropped to his knees, and with his head swimming, fell forward – slamming his face onto the floor.

The crunch of his nose re-fracturing sent a chill through Nyah and Thayer.

Still under the influence and content to let events play out, Isidore was nowhere in sight.

Thayer managed a modicum of courage. "All right, you've made your point, Revenant. I concede to your power, but you'll have to agree that Erik has a rather gloomy outlook for one about to be given such a tremendous gift. Christine is no longer a perilous hallucination; she is reality. Since he's unconscious…again…I cannot tell if he is perplexed, disoriented, or mad as a hatter that Dillard is supposed to guard her. Help me get him onto a stretcher, then I need to address Dillard's nose."

"No!" Torossian took protective hold of Erik. "Only my brother commands me now. Look at me, Doctor." Thayer stood frozen to the spot. "Heed my warning. An unparalleled agony will descend upon your brain if you interfere with me. Everything you touch, even the clothes brushing against your skin will cause you excruciating pain. As I disappear, argue that your eyes deceived you. I was never here."

The creature stretched out his arm and taking a yellowish-black keratotic nail, raked a smooth open cut down the center of Thayer's chin to the hyoid bone. "Ponder that in the mirror. The wound will need stitches, I think." A cold, vice-like hand compressed the good doctor's bilateral carotids. As soon as Thayer dissolved into unconsciousness, Torossian left – carrying away what was most precious to him.

22 *ENDURING A BLOOD FEST*

𝔄 lone and barefoot, the Shah's Magician stood on a stone ramp leading upward to an arena. Sharp rancid odors rising from the dungeons below assailed his deformed nasal passages. The stench of rotting flesh permeated the air – reeking, nauseatingly sweet. There was nothing on earth like the fetid smell of bacteria eating the decomposing body sugars of both human and animal flesh.

Stripped bare to the waist, the only garments allowed him were abbreviated baggy pants and a specially designed covering of twill he'd fashioned for his head. No helmet, no weapons. In preparation, Heerad had shaved and oiled his master's entire body. What a strange sensation to be minus every fleck of hair below his chin.

Shaking the muscles of his arms and legs to keep them loose, a genuine concern to guard his horrific face from exposure caused him to test, once again, the knots securing his headgear. Above all else, he dreaded revealing his face to the crowd assembling above. The modified black balaclava rested flat upon his skull. He'd built out the nose and ridge of the eyebrows to suggest normalcy. The covering opened in two rectangular bars at the eyes. Ties ran from his temples to the back of his head and from his mandible to his posterior neck, pulling the covering tight to facilitate vision in all directions. Extra cords, wound from under the chin and fastened at the crown, made doubly sure that the headgear could not be yanked off easily. The casing would have to be torn, and he had no intention of giving another combatant the opportunity to accost his head.

From the shadows at the bottom of the ramp Rakesh Mizoram appeared. He came to him on padded feet, bearing secrets. "Your opponent suffers attacks of excitement that drive him to murder violently. The court condemned him to decapitation tomorrow, but Khusrowshah has pleaded the man's case with the Shah. Claiming that the individual is stricken with bouts of cerebral congestion and deserves the right to win his freedom in battle."

"So I am forced to fight a condemned man? A criminal who has nothing to lose?"

"Such is often the custom." Rakesh rubbed heavy grease on the lateral surfaces of both Erik's forearms. "If he is victorious, he'll win a purse of gold, but the Court Physician is commanded to bore holes in the man's skull in an attempt to relieve the congestion. Where's the triumph in that? Courage, my scrawny assassin! You take into the arena the strongest of weapons, your mind. Ignore the jeers of the crowd and let your opponent teach you his weaknesses. Heavy betting is going on among those attending, speculation favors your adversary." From a dish Rakesh blew Indra's Kiss over the grease. "The fat will prevent the chemical from absorbing into you. Wipe the substance across his nose and lips if you feel the necessity. In less than a count of sixty, you will evaporate from his sight like water tossed on the sands of the desert. Put your hands atop your head, wiggling your open fingers and he'll perceive you as an antler-decked demon."

With contact that close, Erik pictured the man biting him. "And have you laid a wager?"

Rakesh grinned, his teeth a set of ivory. Apparently air redolent with decay did not affect the mystic's ability to utter contradictions. "I detest gambling, but have laid a small fortune on you!"

An enthusiastic threefold blast of trumpets, followed by an answering roll of drums, announced the appearance of the Shah. A minute later metal scrapped against metal and a circle of daylight opened above Erik's head. Leaving his student illuminated by the forlorn shaft, Rakesh backed a few feet away. Down the dusty beacon came a chain with a stirrup affixed to its end. He was to be lifted up and dropped into the arena.

"I'll see you when it's over," Rakesh whispered. "I know you will not disappoint."

Happy to escape the repugnant stench of the dungeons, Erik grabbed the chain and placed his foot within the slot. He was really in his element with odors, but this putrid funk required concerted vigilance not to vomit. Hauled upward, he heard one last directive from Rakesh. "Do not resist what inclinations come naturally to you."

What a contrast between the inhospitable world below and the stadium above. The arena was a dry and sandy circle, with stark twelve-foot walls encasing its floor. Two heavy iron doors, standing opposite each other, allowed access from alternate areas. The circular bleachers spiraling round above the wall's height were filled with colorfully dressed spectators. The entire stadium was shaded from the sun by long sheets of pale yellow cloth that rippled in the fickle afternoon breeze. The crowd cheered at the magician's arrival. The entertainment of combat in the Shah's utopia came at a dear cost. The jostling audience seemed totally unaware it sat above levels of filth and percolating contagion. Though the people in the stands could not detect the rot and ordure, Erik, who stood just above the massive decay, smelled little else.

A guard led the Royal Inquiline to a spot below the Shah. The regent sat in a special carpeted section, his first two sons to either side. A murmur of ascent rose from the crowd. Above these three men were two layers, the first of males and the second of women associated with the court. Every adult member of the royal family was there, clustered in their respective groups.

"Unleash the prisoner," declared the Shah.

Unleash? Erik refused to shift his feet or glance around uneasily. Above the Shah and to the right sat Prince Fazel's promised bride. Khusrowshah busied himself undressing his brother's intended with his eyes. The arrogant second in-succession did nothing to conceal the evil lodged within his heart. Erik marveled that a prince of such wealth would openly display this degree of rancorous jealousy. Khusrowshah's malignant ambitions to own everything his brother rightfully possessed enslaved him like a bitterly deceptive drug. Erik's eyes went quickly to the girl. Properly veiled and sitting with her handmaidens, she was delicate and feminine. Smallish head and shoulders, perfectly arched eyebrows framing a set of dark brown eyes, skin like alabaster. Tiered necklaces, studded with dozens of sparkling jewels, graced her upper chest. Acquiring Khusrowshah's gaze, the princess suddenly blushed – a bad sign in Erik's reckoning. She unwittingly returned the bold stare. In a few seconds, her eyes dropped demurely, but the damage had been done. She'd foolishly acknowledged the strength of the rival's interest.

The proposals of marriage were formally announced. The proclamations regarding the details of the unions signed and sealed, with all of Khusrowshah's protests held in abeyance to fester with time.

One of the heavy iron doors creaked opened and the throng cheered. Two heavily armored guards pulled a dual-chained, spike-collared prisoner over for the Shah's inspection. A wary burly combatant, the man had a leathery face permanently tanned from years of exposure to the sun. He was brought to stand twenty feet from Erik, his neck pulling at the guards' chains for show.

From the arena floor, Erik kept a cautious eye on his opponent.

The Shah raised his hand for silence. "We rejoice over the upcoming marriages of our two oldest sons. We declare that there are to be no more arguments, no more skirmishes, around our palace. We wish to maintain peace within our corridors. All disputes of a physical nature shall be brought to this forum and formally settled in the *Khunin Ziyafat* (Blood Fest). The rules of engagement are simple. No weapons of metal or stone. The stronger and more cunning shall prosper at the cost of the other's life. Do you vow to engage each other in a fight to the death?"

The contenders below each nodded their consent. A guard undid the opponent's collar.

"Begin," decreed the Shah.

Staying apart, the pair started circling like two confronting predators – a bull and a sleek cat – moving as if they were fascinated with the physical make-up of their opponent's body. Fighting weaponless meant they had only ingenuity and physical strength to master the other. So they searched for identifiable weaknesses that might dictate how the conflict should commence. The tall muscular Persian facing Erik glistened with the sheen of oil and sweat. The tips of his meaty fingers bore long dirty nails, bit into points and sharpened, no doubt, by dragging them against the stonewalls of his cell. The brute felt disappointed that his foe was so small and laughed boisterously. Erik, on the other hand, had to admit that the sheer girth of the man was formidable. Even though his own arms were long, it would be difficult to encapsulate the solid block of prodigious chest before him. Crushing his opponent's ribs was out of the question, unless he could somehow get him flat to the ground and stomp his full body weight onto the thorax.

The prisoner scowled, baring a nasty set of cracked teeth. With his face hidden by the head covering, Erik could offer no such threat. Instead he sought to gauge the man's intelligence. The roar of the crowd prohibited the audience hearing his words. "Our conflict is stupid. There is no quarrel between us. Let's work together and give them an exhibition until we tire."

The brawny combatant pounded his chest and shouted a fierce reply, audible to the audience. "The rules are to the death! Only one goes free with a hefty purse as reward."

Excitement rose within the crowd. Spurred on by their cheers, the prisoner centered his wrath and rushed at the Frenchman. Erik stood his ground, the working muscles in his face tightening behind the cloth mask.

I am brave and formidable, determined...let him come! The attacker swung a powerful fist. Erik easily ducked and dodged. In this close proximity to the man, he noted an offensive chemical effluvia, an invisible emanation, as if the gargantuan had sunk himself in camel dung before entering the ring. A vision of dancing dromedaries tied together in an untidy line and giggling like women sprang into Erik's mind. He shook his head, ordering his thoughts to stay focused. But a massive Bedouin with a two large tree trunks for arms appeared from inside a dilapidated tent. Howling and swaggering, the Arab tried to orchestrate the prancing animals into caravan-like order. With his mind reeling, Erik realized some undetermined amount of the hallucinogenic, Indra's Kiss, was seeping into his skin.

Angered that his blow missed, Erik's adversary roared in a voice fueled with uncontained fury. He charged again, striking almost blindly at his scrawny opponent. Dancing in and out of the windmill of blows, Erik sidestepped around the uncooperative camels and let the man expend some energy.

A couple of guards, standing at strategic points on the arena's walls, simultaneously emptied two baskets. As dozens of snakes and scorpions pelted the sandy floor, the crowd roared in shocked surprise. The Shah stood in alarm. He had not ordered this addition. Enthralled at the added mayhem, the crowd hollered and stomped its feet. Brazenly picking up a snake, the real Persian swung it round his head and launched it toward Erik.

Turning sideways and stepping backwards, the Frenchman failed to be a receptive target. Quickly kicking sand on the vermin closest to him, he watched in fascination as they responded by scurrying and slithering in all directions.

Disgusted with the infidel's preoccupation, the burly savage sauntered around the outer ring of the arena, fisted arms waving high above his head to gain the approbation of the crowd.

Standing with his head slightly bowed, Erik took stock of every imaginary creature around him. Only the circling Bedouin seemed credibly genuine. Maneuvering at a constant angle, he cautiously familiarized himself with the power charged moves of that being. He studied its gait, the manner in which each leg overlapped the other with a full brushing of the inner thighs. The Persian favored the right ankle and Erik guessed that at some point in the past the joint had suffered injury, possibly fracture.

Ignoring the deadly threats lying in the hot sand and inspired by the heckling spectators, the beast charged directly at him. Erik blocked out the shouting, the unholy curses, the jeers. He hated chaotic frantic crowds. They operated with only the basest emotions, letting the bizarre fascinate them past the point of reason. All he heard were the slow, laborious breaths of his advancing opponent – air moving heavily in and out, in and out – mouth open, spittle spraying with each exhalation. The ground shook with every thumping step.

No need to judge toro's finer points of attack; he had none. Under the effects of Indra's Kiss, Erik let himself be taken under the arms and lifted. A repulsive halitosis generating from the man's mouth dissuaded him from engaging in conversation. He concentrated. There was so much to be learned, especially from an adversary. Out of contempt, the Persian spit at the face of the head covering. In response, Erik slathered grease from his left forearm, then his right, across the flaring nostrils and wet fatty lips blowing air at him.

Carrying an awkward tangle of flailing arms and legs, the stampeding bull bore Erik's spine toward one of the iron doors. Erik's back hit the metal so hard his head bounced, the air rushed from his lungs in one swift *pahh-wahp*. The door and its frame actually rocked, the bolts affixed to the gussets threatening radical misalignment. Beneath the head covering, Erik's cranium absorbed the shock of a fiery rocket exploding within his skull. His lips opened wide in an initially ineffective attempt to inhale.

Still holding his captive up against the door, the opponent paused to enjoy the crowd's applause.

Engaging his foe's eyes, a primitive intuition suddenly struck Erik –
Survive! Rallying his strength, he twisted and relaxed within the man's
fingers. Fighting naked to the waist gave one the advantage of being
very slippery. Lifting his arms straight above his head, he slid out of
the oily grasp. Back on his feet, he experienced a nauseating vertigo.
Concussed, he tried to speed away, but not before the Persian grabbed the
head covering. Tugging on the posterior ties brought Erik to an abrupt
standstill. During the moment the headgear held in place, Erik took
both his fists and hit backward into the man's groin. Taking advantage of
a momentary release in pressure, Erik darted off. Ignoring the noxious
crowd, he moved to the opposite side of the arena. There he lingered
against the wall, trying to regain his equilibrium. The cost of that head
thump had given him what he needed to know: the key to a divisive
maneuver. The man lifted him leaning to the left, letting the stronger
ankle take the weight of both their bodies.

All his life Erik had tried to define himself within the context of a
miserable face. Deemed unworthy, he angrily but fatalistically agreed with
the dictum issued by virtually every soul who'd ever viewed him. That
concession allowed the terrible risk he'd just taken, but in getting plowed
he learned something surprising about himself. He had a specific reason
to live: All he could experience in the years (or minutes) ahead. Here
in the throes of battle he was ready to shed his first real layer of suicidal
self-deprecation and become an aggressor who defied reduction.

Determined to win, he contrived a way to make the bull rush at
him one last time. Knowing his adversary liked to be on the attack,
he bent forward and staggered a few steps – half-pretending he could
not overcome the trauma done his head. When the charge began, Erik
counted the steps and waited for a distance of fifteen feet before springing
into action. Seconds counted. Dropping into a ball, he rolled. Arriving
a few feet in front of the advancing Persian, he crouched and quickly
maintained balance by flapping his bent arms like the wings of a chick.
Straightening one leg, he swept his limb in an arc. Momentum worked
in his favor. Tripping his opponent, he forced the right foot and ankle to
take the full weight of the pounding charge.

Toppling forward, the combatant fell flat onto his stomach. It was
the criminal's turn to have his head bounced by a wiry Frenchman.
Stunned, he rolled to his back, amazed that he now faced the overhead

cloths rippling in the scant breeze. A terrible burning pain, akin to being speared with a sword, shot through his skull and all the way up his right leg.

Erik hovered for only a moment. His pulse slowed, his mind calmed, and he unleashed the monster. He jumped and coming down on the heel of his foot, broke the ankle. The snapping crunch of shattering small bones sent misery streaming through the opponent's body like a foul unstoppable bilge. In agony, the man's arms and shoulders floundered in the sand. Positioning himself at the fallen head, Erik jumped again. Leveraging the weight of his body, his feet were hammers, which as they landed fractured the humerus bones bilaterally.

With the loss of both upper extremities, the antagonist finally lay still.

Clearly enthralled with the inventive blitz, the crowd started screaming a singular chant. "Blood Fest! Blood Fest!"

Erik's eyes widened in astonishment. *In what manner do they expect me to comply with this demand?*

Listening to the repetitive phrase, the loser surrendered to the truth. He looked upward into the intelligence behind the spectacular amber eyes studying his injuries. It never occurred to him that this thin agile youth could best him. With his body quivering, he tried to breath inside the pain. *Defeated!* From the depths of some immense reserve he finally managed to speak, "They want you to end the battle with blood. Mire in the blood fest. Had I killed you, I would give them their required gore. They want open gaping wounds."

Beneath the head covering Erik winced.

Defiance gone, all strength dissipated, the fractured man rasped, "Living or dead, my body will be thrown to the dogs. Death at your hands is better than the mangling teeth of curs." He shuddered with pain. "Make the crowd fear you."

"You're telling me they hope for something more gruesome than this?" Erik responded dully.

"Give these decadents something to gnaw." Then he muttered strange words, even to a newborn killer's ears. "How do you want them to think of you?"

The silence of the crowd reflected a growing interest in what events were to follow. Fascinated, they could see the vanquished fighter was still alert enough to speak. To leave the act unfinished would prove the Frenchman really had no backbone at all.

Taking deadly aim, Erik punched the man in the throat, crushing his larynx.

Robbed of oxygen, the Persian struggled, fighting for that last morsel of air that never came. The black inky waters, that the Italians call *acqua passata* and the sons of Allah *âb edâme*, swept his brain into unconsciousness.

Crouched low to the ground, Erik wondered if he'd won by accident. *Why doesn't it feel like victory? What final act would suit this horde?* Oh how he loathed them, and longed to be loathed in return.

Suddenly he knew. Without hesitation he took his opponent's own finger nails and plunged them into the leathery abdominal skin. Ripping, tearing, digging into the viscera, he pulled out uncoiling lengths of intestines. Holding the fruit of disembowelment high for those above to view, he let the blood and excrement run down his arms to his elbows. This final act of carnage was all he could conjure to embarrass the inhumane hearts of these twisted royals. Women blanched and averted their eyes. Men sat aghast, their mouths left open. Even the Shah's stomach roiled at the sight.

Erik raised his face to the sky above the awnings. A long soulful cry issued from his throat – an excruciating quavering wail that screamed its way past their callous inured hearts to bang at Heaven's door in shame and supplication. Its notes carried the cadence of desperation and fear. Everyone in the audience froze, their throats mute, their eyes and ears fixed on the pathos demanding celestial attention. At last, the woe faded. Receded into its source emptied of hope. For a time the sound echoed through the amphitheater declaring that life and decency were finished. Mouths agape, the Persians listened to the emptiness until the snap and flutter of the cloth overhead rushed in to occupy the vast hollowness of the arena.

Then a whisper of comments raced like a wave through the stadium. What was he doing? Singing a dirge for his fallen opponent? Surely a shallow infidel would feel nothing of remorse killing a felon!

Flowers started to fall from the hands of the women. They tore off their jewelry and threw the pieces to the sandy floor. Following their example, men emptying their purses, sent the money sailing through the air to encircle the magician. Surrounded by this incongruous debris, Erik felt drained of emotion, more exhausted than he had ever been in his short life. Fatigue, like a great consuming undulation, overtook him.

Servants appeared to carry the corpse out on a litter. Too weak to walk, two guards hastened to take Erik beneath the arms and bring him – limp, toes dragging in the sand – to stand before the Shah. With his head throbbing unmercifully, Erik opted to remain mute. Even if asked, he'd refuse to offer justifications to this nation of cruel oglers. They were worse than the crowds who visited the gypsy camps. He wanted to retreat within himself, to shrink and be cocooned, safe from their infection.

"I proclaim Erik the victor," announced the Shah. "His deeds are worthy of record in the annals of my reign. They will be discussed for years." The Shah leaned forward, hands pressed down on a rail. "You continue to bring glory to this court. You are my champion."

The servants let go of Erik. He swayed dramatically. Squelching his desire to vomit at their feet, he swallowed his retort. "Sire," he replied. The dizziness was worsening; the people in the stands swam as if they were fish in a pond.

"Because you finished the battle properly, I call for a chest of gold coins to be brought to you. All that has been thrown onto the sand is yours as well."

Not accustomed to refusing gain he'd rightfully earned, Erik nodded and accepted the tribute being brought to him. "My pleasure is to serve you." One of the more compassionate guards sat him on the chest.

Seated beside the Shah, Khusrowshah's wrath crested like a rogue wave. Though he managed to keep his rage contained, his glare betrayed his malignant heart. He hadn't expected the magician to win. He'd chosen the largest, most experienced maniac in the jails for an opponent. A man who bragged he murdered people by tearing them limb from limb.

Above Khusrowshah one soft brown hand arose. The Shah's favorite daughter, the little Sultana, requested that they finally see the magician's face. Her father raised his hand to add emphasis to his edict, "I forbid it! No one is allowed to reveal his features. He earns his right to privacy with every passing day. The *Khunin Ziyafat* is concluded."

Assisted by guards and jail servants, Erik stayed in his spot on the chest as the throng meandered back to their apartments. The royals and their acquaintances would have much to discuss.

As the last spectator departed, the Daroga ordered another stretcher so that his friend might be taken to the policeman's personal quarters. There he proposed to personally supervise the care given to Erik. Away from the scrutinizing eyes of the public, the Daroga asked for water, towels, and soap to be brought them.

"You were foolish to take such a nasty knock on the head. Was there no other way?"

Erik expected the Daroga's grumblings over his ineptitude in the arena. "You actually think I preferred getting my head nearly crushed? I could think of no other way to test the strength of the right ankle. At least I won."

The Daroga snickered, "Yes, you endured, and you made a great deal of money for some people. The Captain of the Guard is so pleased over his winnings that he is willing to have you taught any form of combat you choose. There is even another Frenchman living in the city willing to teach you European swordsmanship. They have invited you to their homes the moment you are better and welcome you as a protégé. You will learn to handle a rapier, and I've order the Hindu guards to teach you the art of the Punjab lasso. It's a great honor for so many to instruct you."

Servants stood at the door with the needed items.

"His clothes are dirty and bloodied," directed the Daroga. "Wash him. Place my own robes on him and burn these rags, but do not touch his head. That is for him alone to address." As the men began to work, the Daroga commented, "The guards who threw the scorpions and the snakes into the pit have been handed to the torturers. They have not divulged on whose authority they acted, but we know it was Khusrowshah's sport."

Erik was sore and lacked the strength to resist the hands of those who pulled off his clothes. "They'll be executed for following their orders?"

The Daroga shrugged. "Since you were the victor, the Shah is very happy. He doesn't like to lose. He's telling everyone within earshot that you are a splendid addition to the palace. Smart, cagey, definitely entertaining."

"Cryptic, self-deprecating, and a genuine paradox since I managed with very little effort to get myself into the *Khunin Ziyafat*." Lifting his head from the pillow, Erik surveyed the damage done to his body. *Only bruises.*

"My spies tell me Khusrowshah is at this moment having something of a fit. We will keep these doors closed and locked," the Daroga's voice was full of warning. "His attempts to have you blamed for Fatima's demise failed, and now instead of dying in the ring, you've achieved acclaim."

"I hope I'm driving him mad."

"So far your efforts appear very successful, but he's a long way from vanquished."

After the servants finished, they left him to rest. Erik barely closed his eyes when he realized someone else approached. In the dim light of the room, he recognized the sad face of Soha Houri. "Have you come to visit my injuries?"

"I've brought Heerad to you. We've located a European toothbrush and here is mint water. And these..." she hesitated to hand him a small package. "These are an excellent kind of lozenge manufactured in Baghdad. They will help you relax and ease your pain so that when you awaken you will have clarity of thought."

He thanked her and took one of the lozenges. The strong taste of licorice laced with opiate entered his mouth. Though he craved sleep, he surreptitiously let the tablet slide to the pillow. He soon discovered that no position was comfortable with his head banging like a drum. He lay there motionless, the last shreds of any idealism he secretly nurtured peeling away as his brain replayed the battle. Almost grateful to the female who'd raised him so harshly, toughened him to withstand the test of ridicule, he finally drifted off.

Erik remained there for a week, enjoying a quiet alienation from these strange perplexing people. Strong gentle hands assisted him, bathing his body and respectfully leaving him to tend his head. Small exertions sapped his strength. The performance of even the simplest actions caused extreme weariness. Rakesh came and advised him to lie flat in a darkened room until the swelling in his brain went down. He was given only small meals and drinks. When the dizziness abated, he sat up slowly and started taking short walks around the room. He wasn't anxious to return to his own apartment, his quarters were sealed and guarded as his gold was taken there. Though his inner turmoil was acute, whatever feelings might be expressed through his eyes were extinguished. His gaze was emotionless and cold.

On the eighth day of his recuperation he sat quietly on an upholstered bench, his back leaning against the wall. It seemed the Daroga favored a more Western style of furniture. To his left stood a solid ash gaming table. A masterpiece of handcrafted wood, it's top was supported by the most magnificently twisted wrought iron legs. The Daroga sat there late at night over quiet cups of tea, conversing with him privately. They planned to have Erik take his next meal there.

His only true friend, if he could be called one, was Khalil. Their sense of mutual respect developed over time. Like a vine of dense ivy that conceals the structure lying beneath it, their common bond was what they held in secrecy. They saw each other several times a day now. They'd even developed a set of silent hand gestures.

The Daroga and Soha Houri entered. Pleasantly attired in an aqua robe, she took a seat on the bed opposite Erik. Wearing a more formal tunic-styled suit, the Daroga sat at the gaming table, his hands folded together on its top.

"Has something happened?" Erik asked expectantly. They both looked sadly resigned.

Two slaves entered the room, one with a tray of fruit and biscuits, the other with juice. Khalil pointed them to the table and impatiently dismissed the slaves. "No one is to annoy us! Shut the door." The servants backed away.

"We seek to confide in you, Magician." Soha Houri's voice was serious.

"My honest discretion is a small payment for your many kindnesses."

"As soon as you can depart in safety from the Shah, I want you to travel. See all the buildings, mosques, public places...everything that is worthy of notice in this land."

"I had planned to attend your wedding. My presence will be expected." To continue with the ritual niceties he should say something regarding her great beauty on that day, but why offer slanted words of congratulations?

Above an opaque veil, Soha Houri looked perturbed. Her eyes were rare and exotic, like shiny bronze-colored pearls. "The truth cannot be ignored." Her hands clasped both her knees. Determined. "It grieves me to tell you that I am burdened with a centuries old sorrow, one shared by many other females in this country. Royalty may not marry their sisters, but they may wed their cousins. Here women are bartered and traded. A vigilant father assures protection against harm for his daughters. Mine is dead, and as the sister of the Shah's chief investigator I must wed at the regent's discretion."

Erik had an inkling where this conversation was headed, "With your permission, I will retire to my bed and rest."

"Wait. I pray you hear me out. I intend to impose upon you. You are my brother's friend." From within her garments she produced a folded piece of lustrous fabric. "In my fingers lies a cerement of gold brocade fashioned with silver flowers I embroidered myself. It is to be the burial cover for my face. My religion forbids suicide. You will help me die. Then I will be washed clean, dressed in my finest garments, and go to Allah as a virgin, perhaps in Paradise to meet my true husband."

Erik's eyes went to the Daroga, anticipating a barrage of objections to come forth from his lips. Instead Khalil kept his hands folded, maintaining a conservative posture.

"You approve of her request?" Erik hissed in disbelief.

"If you could assist her, I would be grateful. Even though I'll miss her, she will not be Khusrowshah's victim."

Erik's head snapped back to Soha Houri. "Lady! I will do everything to console you, and will if possible, make you forget all your sufferings. Surely this is only a momentary affliction. No such disastrous intervention is required. If necessary, your brother and I will smuggle you out of the country."

With undisguised admiration, she declared, "Your offer confirms you possess a magnanimous soul, but it is not in the nature of husbands and masters to brook dissent. Believe me when I assert that the Shah would uncover the truth and take both your rash heads. He will view my fleeing as an act of rebellious disobedience, an insult to his son. He'll order his agents and Khusrowshah to search relentlessly for me. Every minute of every day, fear of being caught will afflict me. You are a death angel. Be my advocate!" Tears glistened in her eyes.

A poignant moment of disbelief passed before Erik could speak. "Great courage brought you to this space and time. If I am to be your friend, permit me again the favor of seeing your face."

With an air of natural grace, she removed her veil. "View my sincerity." The storm of emotionally charged tears he had expected to see fall never materialized. A pair of vacant eyes to equal his own stared back at him.

"Even if a husband excels in physical beauty, nothing guarantees his mind will match his outward appearance." She spoke with such eloquence, allowing the fire of earnestness to penetrate every word. "A woman hopes her husband will be affable and gentle. That he will be encouraging and engage her affections with patience – not forced submission. She prays for a man who will divorce himself from the prods and jests of other males. That he will not see her reservations as frivolous, but honor her as a child of God."

Proud and composed, she used brave words to paint a picture of her situation. "Khusrowshah will not be gallant when he takes me. He will slice the magnificent wedding clothes from my body; torture me as he did your young slave, Fatima. As his new wife I will be expected to show the court that I am blessed with good living and promote wise choices within my household. While privately, I am to submit to his perverse sexual tastes. Night after night, when he is firmly ensconced within me, I will cry with the pain of him. I know his irascible heart. I have known him all my life. Nothing less will suit. He delights in pain.

"These malevolent inclinations that come so naturally to him are absolutely repugnant to me. I could not hate him more if he was a hunchbacked demon with red eyes, crooked claws and a dozen horns protruding from his head. The instant his staff rises from his groin and he demands satisfaction I will loathe him with every fiber of my being. And though my mother, in a fit of ingrained subservience, would have gone down on both her knees...asking how she might humbly be of service, I will not! I will condemn my soul and slicing my wrists, let my arteries bleed upon the marriage bed before I'll let him rip apart my virginity."

Grateful to be masked and his emotions obscured, Erik had no idea how to respond. It was useless to solicit aid from the Daroga. Khalil stayed with his face cast downward. "Saying all this must be a great catharsis for you." *What a lame response, not a counter argument at all!*

She sensed his reluctance. "I mean to impose myself upon you... despair over my ill-fortune solidifies my resolve. You can free me. One way or another, this will be the day of my death."

The sheer redundancy of her pleas reinforced the truth. She meant every word. The unwavering strength of this woman held him like a spell. Awakening to her conviction, he vowed to learn the secret of such feminine resolve. His left eyebrow and forehead furrowed in a frown. Trying to pick one of the dozens of methods to destroy her, he realized the task was impossible. He had no idea how to choose the correct technique.

It was as if she read his mind. Soha Houri lifted the hem of her robe. Tucked in a sheath on the outside of her calf she carried a ritual knife. Pulling it forth, she let a tiny shaft of sunlight play upon the blade. "Don't hesitate to help me define my end. I am not acting recklessly. You are the Terror, the Phantom. Take this poniard and press it into my chest, here...," she pointed to the spot. "Don't act out of friendship for me or contempt for Khusrowshah. Act because it is your nature to do this."

She turned the dagger and held it out to him. On the hilt an artisan had etched a flying lion – his own damn knife! Ambidextrous, he reached out with the snow-white palm of his left hand.

Khalil cleared his throat.

Ah yes, etiquette demands I receive it with my right. "This will create another stunning affair within the palace. The prince will not be happy that he has forfeited a wife."

Soha Houri sighed deeply. "Good. Do not fear that I will haunt you, I am not given to narcistic regrets and have no plans to follow you around disturbing your thoughts with disembodied moaning and untenable remonstrations."

"Once you are in Paradise and at peace..." Khalil's words choked off in his throat. He rocked the heel of his hand against his forehead, unable to finish the thought.

"Maybe I should act first," Soha Houri stood, summoning her executioner with an open hand. "Heaven welcomes my approach."

Rising to his feet, the Persian nodded an affirmation that Erik should do this terrible thing.

After a contemplative stare, the executioner made a suggestion, "Perhaps the Lady would care for an opiate?" He stood, wrapping his hand around the dagger's grip.

"No," came her confident reply. "After this deed is completed, certain assumptions will be made concerning you and I. We must make it look like I plunged the knife, not you. It is enough that Allah knows the truth."

Khalil came to stand behind her. Looking sadly resolute, he took a small scroll from his pocket. Without taking her eyes from Erik, she reached up for the piece of parchment. Opening the scroll, she let it drop to the floor between them. "That is my declaration. In my own hand it states how much I detest this pre-ordained marriage. I have written that Khusrowshah is the very vilification of our nobler traits and that I refuse to be his wife. Stay steadfast when you explain how I took my life."

Erik knelt to help position the blade. As he tightened both his hands around the grip of the dagger, she took his hands in hers.

"Your icy skin horrifies me, yet it has great appeal," she bent toward him. "The coldness I perceive spreads through me like a wave of night. Here in this moment of truth, it is within your power to cast my requests aside or to allay my fears. Let these fingers I hold within my own grant swift peace." She stared into his upturned face. "Your eyes mystify and confound, but in their own strange way manage to flood contentment into my spirit. No trace of smile or frown betrays any hint of your intent. Here in this isolated union grant me some insight with which to gauge your thoughts."

"I will not leave you to the prince's defilements."

"Then I beg you...set me free. Let me rest." Silently she pressed the tip of the weapon to her dress and with his hands still enfolded in hers, spoke. "Give the blade its home." Her eyes were liquid, deep and trusting. "I obligate my brother with guarding your life and your affairs. Let all of Erik's needs be Khalil's primary and most valued concerns. Throughout time my soul blesses you both." Her eyes closed. For several quiet seconds their two sets of hands firmly held onto the dagger. She exhaled deeply and as the last bit of air escaped her lungs, she let go. In that cosmic instant he shoved the blade into her heart. Accepting the deliverance without resistance, her arms fell to her side. She slumped, limp upon the steel of the knife. The Daroga pressed her back into his arms.

Lifting her, Khalil laid her on the bed. Tears brimmed his eyes, spilling down upon his cheeks. "You have done her a great favor; released her to Heaven, still pure, before the prince can maul her. Please leave me to my goodbyes. I will come to you later."

Erik felt like an intruder, an alien in this room where he'd recuperated for the last week. He didn't belong. An unbridled vacancy consumed him. Every place he tread he was a stranger, and in this land a long line of bodies was stacking up behind him. At some point he must choose a different path.

He stepped forlornly into the outer room, realizing that in the aftermath of her death they would be awash in malicious accusations. The curious tongue waggers would have their next outlandish incident to gossip about. Private hushed conversations would breathe the scandal from one ear to the next. And though their tales would bear a sad grain of truth, the wrong person would be blamed for taking Soha Houri's life and the real culprit would walk free.

Rakesh Mizoram waited on the sofa. "You are braver than any man I have ever met…and greatly misunderstood."

In a few minutes, a calm and collected Khalil entered the room. Coming to them, the Daroga took and oath, "Before the patriarch of my family, the Magus Rakesh Mizoram, I swear to protect you, Erik. My constant devotion to you shall last through the archives of time." He took the dagger and slicing the skin of his palm, offered to seal the bargain in blood.

23 *A BIRTH WITHIN THE QUAGMIRE*

𝕿 he sharp smell of sulfur saturated Erik's nostrils. *Brimstone.* Pungent and demanding, he winced inwardly. *Someone's lit a match.* For a moment the spell of the vision continued to hold him. In that one dwindling flame, the drama of one woman's assisted suicide contrasted sharply against the sudden memory of another female, vibrant and alive, about to be reborn. He opened his eyes. Transitioning back into the present was becoming an easier, less disorienting trip. Isidore and Thayer were perched on either side of the bed.

"Neither of you smoke," he commented flatly.

"True," Isidore's eyes belied a brooding excitement. "What sets you into these altered states of consciousness is still to be determined, but apparently, after a time, a sharp smell can bring you back to the present."

Thayer tried to speak calmly. "You'll have to postpone telling me about this latest excursion. Christine has reached her former height. Isidore has successfully reversed the pseudo Progeria. She's in the capsule literally scintillating with energy."

"We need you there when she attempts her first independent respirations. She's liable to be a little panicky."

"I promise...no doom and gloom. Let me wash my face. I'll be downstairs directly."

In the lab she floated in a crystal clear liquid. There before him was the recognizable straight little nose, the brown wavy hair, the sweet chin, and the lips of his angel. "What's happened? Why is the fluid so clean?" Erik was anxious. Her eyes were open, inquisitive.

"We completely filtered out all the waste products," explained Nyah, closely monitoring levels within the amniotic soup. Once out, she can't go back in and the first air she'll breathe will have no impurities."

"Guard your emotions, Erik," cautioned Isidore. Remember to stay neutral. We'll watch her primary functions and let her vital signs dictate immediate needs. This initial transition will be critical. Everything will be different for her: the feel of gravity, trying to breathe against the resistance of her own alveoli, the sensation of air upon her skin."

"At what exact age are you removing Christine from the tank?" asked Dillard.

Erik was stunned. *He knows her name?*

"We'll give her organs a chance to equilibrate, then let her hormonal levels and bone development tell us what age she's at," Nyah was remarkably contained.

A stretcher, locked and ready, sat positioned beside the capsule. An injection of pitocin into the amniotic fluid caused the placenta to begin separating from the artificial umbilical cord. Dressed in a plastic suit, Dillard waited, ready to ease her out as Thayer cut the base of the capsule with a surgically precise Stryker saw. The fluid poured forth in a steady stream, flowing down into a drain on the floor.

There was no struggle against emergence, she passed through the opening feet first with a strange almost ballerina lift of her upper limbs. Delivered from the slimy goo right into Dillard's arms, he handled her with the greatest care possible. Laying her on the stretcher, he stepped back.

Now, with the spell of encapsulation broken, the reality of trying to breathe set in. Slightly cyanotic, she opened her mouth. Thayer rolled her onto her side, gently patting her between the scapulas while Isidore suctioned mucous from her throat.

Coughing, gag reflex intact, she took her first sticky wet breath. Heaving air into her lungs, the skin took on a healthier shade of pink. Her first tremulous little cries cut into Erik's gut. Thayer rolled her back and seated an oxygen mask over her nose and mouth. The doctors fixed a blood pressure cuff to her arm and drying her chest, placed cardiac electrodes in strategic places. Her eyes were open. She simple stared.

"This is one of the calmest births I've ever witnessed," Thayer smiled.

"Why doesn't she say something?" asked Dillard.

"She cannot talk," Erik said in wondrous understanding. "She needs the rudiments of an education. Despite what we've funneled to her..."

"Her mind isn't blank," finished Nyah, hugging Erik briefly. "But her psyche is fragile. We must be careful to make every perception of this world a positive one. Even now her nerve endings are fine tuning themselves." Nyah pointed to a series of waves on a scope. "Blood pressure and pulse are stable, Isidore. Respirations sixteen per minute and calming. Arterial blood oxygen saturation is one-hundred percent."

Christine's eyes shone with intelligent life. Her vision was rapidly adjusting to the more pronounced level of light. She ran her hands across her breasts, instinctively sensing something stirring within herself chemically. A small amount of blood appeared between her legs. Erik's nostrils twitched.

"Did we overshoot?" asked Thayer.

"What is created by man is never perfect," responded Isidore confidently.

Christine cried with the pain of her first menstrual cramp.

"Give her something," Erik demanded.

Isidore nodded. "Stay reserved. Don't raise your voice. Regardless of what little memory she may have of you from her gestation, she most certainly can sense agitation. Nyah, two milligrams of morphine please, before the umbilical cord separates completely. The bed scale indicates she's one hundred-ten pounds. Very nice."

"So what age is she?" Fascinated, Dillard had not left the room.

"Shut up and let us do our work. It's obvious she's right at pubescence," Thayer tried to intervene before male competition got out of hand.

"Actually, she's moving through pubescence rapidly," Nyah said, looking at a console. "By the look of bones along the longitudinal planes, I would gauge her age to be closer to fifteen."

"Fifteen," Dillard snickered. He could not stop himself from ogling. "The age of consent in France since 1945."

"Don't be stupid," reprimanded Isidore. "Mentally she's barely more than a fetus."

"She's a clone, as illegal a being as Erik," a miffed Dillard reminded him. "Conceived in a flask, without parents, gestated and brought into the world six months later."

Rage washed over Erik. His instincts told him that Dillard might be a traitor to the project. "Mind your place!"

Dillard issued a savvy humorless laugh. "It's hard to ignore a magnificent naked woman when she's lying right in front of you."

Spawn of Hell! He's picturing her lying beneath him, gasping with exhilaration during a vigorous intercourse. "Get her washed and covered,"

Erik ordered protectively. He walked up to Isidore and whispered a demand. "While she's sedated, cauterize her fallopian tubes, the misery of this disastrous lineage ends with us. And cut her hymen. I want her to know me as soon as possible."

Erik doesn't want another family! Isidore let the shock of those contrary dictates sink in. "All of you leave the room. I'll tolerate no more testosterone-based confrontations, regardless of how minor. I'll call when I need you to return."

With his shaky defenses crumbling, a bittersweet emotion constricted the walls of Erik's chest. *Separated already!* Now he found it difficult to take a deep breath. Bowing slightly, he followed Dillard from the room.

Isidore's attachment to Erik was entrenched and immovable within his heart. He'd raised the boy a full fifteen years, and despite Julian's deleterious influence, he was certain that Erik respected him. Basically, it was a desire to please this son that spurned him into creating Christine. Not the public exposure Erik threatened. It was this great affection that brought him to Erik's room several hours later.

Sitting on a chair in the dim shadows, Isidore asked the moody young man about the surprising requests he'd made in the birthing room.

Erik resisted explaining his decisions. "If I can't be with Christine right now, I want to be left alone. But knowing how she's faring would help to ease this band of apprehension constricting my chest."

"I'm afraid you're going to have to be a little patient. At the moment she's sleeping quietly."

The buzzer requesting entrance into Erik's room sounded. He nearly jumped out of his skin. "Has something happened?"

Isidore remained amazingly calm. "Everything's fine. I'm not an amoral man. I just don't have any ethical standards worth mentioning. You're a virgin, yes? You have no real experience with women?"

"I beg to differ," Erik pulled on the legs of his pants, freeing his crotch to make a point. "I have all the experience of one and a half lifetimes, enough talent to sustain me for the present."

Skeptical, Isidore offered what he believed was sound advice. "Nothing beats the real thing. I ordered a present for you. She's out in the hall, and she's without an STD." He rose to open the door.

Erik's eyes grew wide. "You brought in a prostitute? For practice?"

Isidore nodded. In waltzed a five-foot-two brunette wearing tight fitting midnight-blue stretch pants and a nearly transparent chiffon poncho that revealed a skimpy lace bra beneath. High-heeled shoes and jet-black chandelier earrings completed the outfit. She popped a wad of bubble gum between her teeth.

"This is the lovely Genevieve. Fresh from Paris, plus she has the added advantage that you cannot impregnate her."

The girl's tongue shoved the gum to the inside of her cheek. "Gonorrhea when I was fourteen. My fallopian tubes are blocked with scar tissue. Can't be undone." She popped her gum again.

Erik could not put a name on what he felt. He picked up a dagger and let it fly into a wall target.

The girl didn't even flinch, "That's impressive. Got great eyes."

"How could you, Isidore? You know perfectly well I only want Christine. Bringing her in here...sorry Mademoiselle...borders on punishment."

The prostitute eyed the bold defiant mouth, the aristocratic cheekbones, and clear skin of the tall good-looking male balking at the situation. She batted her eyelids, trying to flirt. "You don't have to be so testy. Doctor de Chagny didn't tell me about this other girl, but you can. I'll play Christine for you."

"Will you now? You're that talented that you can re-invent yourself?"

"Sure, customers want me to role-play all the time." She chomped on the gum.

Agitated, Erik stiffened his back and balled his fists. Looking straight to the ceiling, he vibrated his lips.

Isidore added helpfully, "You need some hands-on skills before we continue with our other experiment. There are logistics to intercourse."

Erik faced the girl with the sternest expression he could muster. "I'm an evil decadent man."

The girl held her ground, "Well...you're not the antichrist are you? There's not much you could request that would be reprehensible to me. Lets have sex so you get to know how."

"I already know how. Aptitude is not a problem."

"How is that possible?" Isidore reminded him.

"I remember."

"I need a drink," Isidore rubbed his forehead.

"You already drink too much. Your eyes are bloodshot from the level of alcohol you consume."

"Perhaps we could all have a drink," Genevieve suggested smoothly.

"Why don't I have a bottle sent up to the room?" The emphasis on Isidore's last syllable was oddly unnerving.

A powerful insight sped through Erik's mind...too quick to grasp... was it...hatred? No. Cynicism. Isidore believed nothing of value could be accomplished unless he orchestrated it. Erik wanted to grab the girl by her flowered chiffon shoulders and propel her from the room on her spiky heels.

"Be rational, Erik. What you think you know in your mind needs practice in the here and now. No man is so adroit that he can read a manual, look at some pictures, and know how to gain control of himself. Restraint and a slow pace are key components to pleasing a woman."

Erik sneered, "Advice from a man who has never wed?"

"You know it takes a great deal more than that to offend me."

"Listen, Monsieur," the girl's hands went to her hips. "Your lack of appreciation isn't very gallant. Maybe you should remember that your uncle," her thumb pointed toward Isidore, "has laid down a bundle to have me visit you. I'm not a street whore and I'm damn good at what I do."

Erik retreated to the drapes. He didn't want to be belligerent, didn't want to snarl and glower. He had to concede that in some respects Isidore was right. "Can you keep me from losing interest in you?"

"No cause for worry on that score," she smirked confidently. "I have skills, too...and a trunk just inside the front door. Amusing you is my priority."

Erik beckoned Isidore over to the curtains and started whispering earnestly. While the two men were tied up in discussion, the girl bent over a table looking at a pretty candy dish. Maybe she could filch the thing, but really, where would she conceal it in this skimpy outfit? "Hey, can I light a cigarette?"

"No," the two men shouted simultaneously and went back to their serious conversation.

"Don't get riled. I can smoke outside...after we do it...right?"

"Right," they answered in unison once again.

"You two been living together a long time? You're like stereo or something."

The comedy of the situation suddenly hit Erik. He scratched his head and started to laugh.

"What's so funny?" the girl retorted

"I'm afraid I have no idea," murmured Dr. de Chagny. "I suspect my nephew's laughter is generated by relief."

While the debate raged upstairs as to whether or not Erik should lose his current state of virginity, Thayer rested in Isidore's laboratory office, ready to begin Christine's basic mental assessment when she awoke. The plan was to keep her in the lab until she learned to walk and had the rudiments of communication. Then introduce her to her rooms upstairs. Overjoyed that the particulars surrounding the birth had gone so smoothly, the neuropsychiatrist crossed his arms in satisfaction. None of the disastrous events he feared had erupted. No one, not even Erik, had ruined anything. The overall condition of the entire planet had not worsened with her arrival. Knowledge of her presence among the living, though a momentous occasion upon the estate, ended at the guarded towers. Nothing in the world at large, not even the ripple of a rumor, was mentioned in the news about it.

In a nearby recuperation room, Christine slept in a serene absence of noise – vital signs stable. The young dark haired man before her mind's eye was perfect, perfect in every conceivable way and yet deeply flawed… flawed beyond repair…scarred so beautifully. Letting the serenity of his presence carry her, she stepped forward into a shaft of florescent light. She wore a long sleeved dress of jade green silk. She heard the rustle of her skirts as the crinolines swept smoothly along with her steps. Angling up to him with nimble grace, she let the man take in her scent.

"You are absolutely beautiful, you smell of lavender."

Lavender must be a good thing, right?

Quietly he asked, "I know you think it a burden, and I apologize… but I need your tactile response."

She did not move to touch his hand. She had no strength. *How very odd.*

"Do you know me? Recognize my face?" His voice held the memory of the silky fluid she'd swam in.

Angered that she lacked the ability to move and had an inclination toward nakedness, she willed the stuff encasing her body to disappear.

In response to her tart decision, the handsome man clapped his hand over his mouth to stifle his joy. Christine smiled, so glad that she could please him.

The speed with which she acquired knowledge startled everyone. Within the short span of a few weeks, she walked and fed herself. Though she said very little, she scored off the charts on every non-verbal intelligence test Thayer gave her. Erik watched her progress through a two-way mirror, a glass that so reminded him of the Opera House. Isidore decreed that during these initial phases he had to stay apart from her. When the time came, he would be granted the privilege of taking her into her rooms.

She liked to smile and when she did, her face and blue-green eyes lit up the entire room. The highlights of her wavy brown hair were ash, and her manner delicate and tentative. When she mastered simple requests, Isidore declared her fit to inhabit her former quarters. He instructed the others to remain in their places so that he might have the pleasure of escorting her from the lab.

Outside her newly refurbished quarters, Erik waited for his chance to participate in this milestone. When the elevator opened he stood there, unflustered that she failed to recognize him.

Isidore shook his head. *No introductions yet. She's nervous.*

With a great flourish, Erik turned the knob to her door. "*Magno cum gaudio*, with great joy I welcome you into your new world." Somehow that sounded all wrong, too flamboyant. He wanted to carry her over the threshold or dance with her, cradling her in his arms...a waltz perhaps. She obediently stepped inside. As Isidore passed, he asked, "May I teach her to dance? What's the next item on our list?"

Isidore walked over to a side table and poured himself a drink. His laconic answer was a short, "Dancing can't hurt."

She conducted herself about the sitting room with quiet decorum, looking sideways for Isidore's approval. She brightened when she saw that neither man frowned at her. Going over to a glass cabinet she studied the collection of ivory skulls. Shivering visibly, she recovered enough to speak. "Death?" she asked.

"Believe me, that is not death," answered Erik softly. "Only a representation of human..."

"Craniums," her interjection was a flat statement of fact. She moved to the small brass knobbed drawers of a vanity table dating from the 1700's. Done in black lacquer – the chinoiserie inlays of mother of pearl and traditional gilt paint added drama to the very old piece of furniture. Her fingers trailed over a silver handled hairbrush and hand mirror. She eyed the massive ancient four-poster bed, the soft folds of its canopy and the luxurious overstuffed red comforter with gold braid accenting its ruffles. "For a wedding?" she asked.

An intuitive guess? Erik marveled. He certainly hoped so. She was changing, evolving right before his eyes – such a glorious mystery. He was glad he'd turned down Genevieve.

A stack of chic fashion magazines sat on the nightstand for her to browse at her leisure. They planned to give her plenty of time to adjust to this chaotic world. Her eyes focused on an enormous cheval mirror encased within an inch-wide frame of symmetrical pewter roses and sprays of leaves. With naïve innocence she moved to the mirror and its botanical motif. Erik watched her eyes. She did not seek out her own reflection. Instead, as if she were fascinated with the objects, she scanned for the collection of miniature skulls now behind her.

His heart leapt, thrilled to see her seek out her former possessions. It was a miracle that they stirred something familiar within her. Though he did not dare to speak of it, he earnestly hoped that his own presence might be of importance. Did she have any idea they had overturned the laws of time to put her here in this very room? Restraint was proving difficult. He longed to stroke her hand, brush her hair, kiss those expectant lips of hers. *Patience, brother. Remember your rooms are adjacent.* Which was all too true. Aside from access through the main hallway, a *couloir etroit* (short passageway) and two locked doors were all that separated Christine's quarters from his. *What fun we will craft for each other.*

"Can you leave me alone with her for a few minutes, Erik?"

"Certainly, Isidore. I am indebted to you for the rest of my life. If there's nothing else you require of me, Mademoiselle." He bowed politely, his hand extending to the right in a very old-fashioned gesture, "With your permission, I'll seek your company in the morning." It was getting easier to incorporate his two personalities, one with the other in seamless precision.

In the morning he rose, showered and dressed carefully. Today he might have the satisfaction of a real encounter with Christine. Rushing through the first door of the *couloir etroit*, he came to the second, knocked politely and entered her rooms. Inside he found Dillard sitting on one of her chairs, hungrily wolfing down a croissant with cheese along with a cup of coffee. Christine, wearing a simple denim skirt and sweetheart sculpted top, stood to greet him. Dressed in khakis, Dillard followed suit. Undaunted by the guard, Erik somewhat nervously straightened the front of his black shirt. With his heart soaring, he offered, "Good morning, Mademoiselle."

During the night he'd imagined how she might respond. A dozen possibilities had occurred to him. Now he realized with chagrin that he might have to wait to hear her response. Patiently he repeated his words.

Her facial attributes, as lovely as they were, remained perfectly blank, without recognition or acknowledgement.

Keeping his tone low, he speedily rephrased, "Did you have a pleasant night?"

He repeated again, exaggerating his question in case his words had not registered within her brain. Still no answer, so he proceeded to explain. "I am offering you greetings and asking how you slept." Erik knew she wasn't on tranquilizers, so he assumed that in entering without permission, he'd wounded her sense of how the world should proceed. He decided to massage her fragile ego and took two steps forward to tentatively take her hand.

Dillard's imposing figure stepped into the space between them. "Excuse me, but I advise caution," Christine's bodyguard was firm. "I am instructed to protect her. Dr. de Chagny says she's still in something of a fragile state and is not to be touched. I take my orders from him alone."

"Would you care to resolve our differences with a fencing match? We have that wonderful gym downstairs, a perfectly adequate facility. I haven't spent the last half-year waiting to have you interfere with us trying to communicate. And you would look so lovely prostrate at the tip of my rapier…again."

"Unfortunately, I am not free to abandon my post and play foolish games with you. Perhaps another form of combat at a later hour?" Dillard maintained the space separating the couple; the significance of his presence sent a most effective nonverbal message.

Erik did not enjoy baring his soul. "I am suffering, you imbecile. I could throttle you for less provocation." The potential for disaster was building. "She and I need to get acquainted. Surely she has questions. Has she spoken in more than one sentence yet? Written anything?"

"She's speaking behind my back. That is to say when I'm not actually facing her, she's making little sounds, as if she has her own secret language."

"How very poetic." Still annoyed at being forced to take a backseat, he gave her an approving smile. Ripples of angry frustration, alternating with a desire to punch Dillard, washed over him. They evaporated when Christine leaned around the bodyguard and met Erik's deliberate gaze with curious interest.

Drawn into her blue-green eyes, Erik made an effort to address Dillard and keep her concentrating on him. Adjusting his tone to an even politeness, he said, "You are rather handy to keep around, Dillard Kelly. Making sure she stays safe, but certainly my small prompts are not detrimental. All I've done so far is to wish her good morning and try to help her focus by touching her hand."

He certainly did not want the conversation to sour, he had no idea how much Christine comprehended. None of them did. Looking at her practically glowing in front of him, he sent her a non-verbal message. *You are my wife, meant for me before time itself.* Careful to keep his speech optimistic, he directed his words to Dillard. "I applaud your conscientious attention to your duties. It would be a mistake for us to quarrel in front of her. She might feel confused, even compromised."

"She lacks the mental or physical strength to accept or refuse anyone," Dillard said gruffly.

"Then I'm dreadfully sorry. I mean no animosity." Why argue his case when Dillard couldn't possibly be with her twenty-four hours a day?

"At the moment a full frontal greeting is considered far too aggressive an approach, a most unsporting challenge. You didn't even wait for her permission to enter. Did you know that her skin is very sensitive to touch? She feels everything a hundred times more acutely than a normal person."

How dare this idiotic American tell me about Christine! Then again, what had her constitution gained from the electric stimulus? Had the genetics and the amniotic soup given her an inheritance they hadn't recognized until now? Almost embarrassed, the notion made the idea of not touching her, even in the mildest manner, more palatable.

Dillard raised his shoulders, expanding his chest. "Why don't you go back to your rooms?"

"Yes, at all costs we must avoid even the mildest negativity." *Lies! Malignant lies!* Whatever Dillard said here, Erik knew the man wanted Christine for himself. He could smell the desire on him. Masking his anger, Erik laughed. Lifting his chin, his head shook in little jerks.

"Is his mind raging?" Christine asked in the softest of all possible voices.

Dillard glanced at her and touched his temple in agreement.

Almost relieved to have them thinking he was insane, Erik regained his calm. Making his voice as smooth and melodic as the silk of a gray dove's wing, he declared, "Let me enlighten you with some facts, Dillard. Your interests in her do not coincide with mine. Make no mistake about who will mate with this young women standing behind you. Does the notion that she is mine upset you?"

The ex-Navy Seal set his booted feet further apart and crossed his arms over his chest.

Stomping out the door, Erik exploded, "Hell! I hope you and Christine enjoy her breakfast hour immensely. I'll meet with her for lunch."

At the sound of this volatile young man shouting her name, Christine bent her head toward her left shoulder. A great sadness overcame her, an almost indefinable feeling. Beneath her breath, she muttered almost inaudibly, "Angel?"

No narrowed minded, narcissistic, ex-commando, American idiot was meant to have Christine! Back in his own quarters, Erik plowed across his rooms like Ahab forging through the ragged waves on the deck of the *Pequod*. Bent for the depths of hell, he paused to pluck a glass of grapefruit juice off a silver tray. Downing the liquid in one swallow, he reached for a second. *"Merde!"* He was a ball of conflicting emotions: tailored politeness, modest arousal, and broiling jealousy laced with mercurial wrath.

"She's already spinning a web of sticky fibers, entangling my feelings. Standing off to the side, she pretends disinterest, while I roll around rattling a distress call...stuck in the filaments!" He dared not approach her before noon.

Lifting the dome off another tray, he eyed a piece of salmon wearing two poached eggs and some sliced tomato for a fashionable hat. The whole mess swam in a pond of Hollandaise sauce. A pot of coffee, warm and aromatic, sat plugged into an outlet. *Tempting but I'm in no mood!* He spun the dome by its handle several times, ordering his rage to abate. He needed to occupy his thoughts and relax. Reminding himself that Christine was still mentally a child, he sat rather indecorously on a chair. *Dillard's interference is only a hiccup!* Shunning self-recriminations, he placed his elbows on his knees and cradled his chin. Calling for his alternate self, he declared, "Let's have a conversation, shall we?" He felt an almost imperceptible change in air density and waited impatiently for the Voice.

"Don't feel like being alone? I take it the meeting didn't go so well."

"Essentially it was more of a non-meeting. It seems that privacy is going to be a very precious commodity."

"Tch, tch, tch," the disdainful response was delivered without a hint of needed sympathy. "I'm becoming a bit of an escapist's habit, but I don't mind. The best marriages are forged in the heart and sealed with the groins, not legal documents. You haven't won the girl yet. Why not forget about her for the moment? We have important issues to discuss."

"You speak with a certain repugnance toward matrimony and the way of men with women. Right now I'd like to throttle Dillard."

A crackling mirthless laughter followed. "I don't care for ceremonies, but all in good time. You are every bit the misanthrope I was. Anger doesn't gratify. The emotion wastes a tremendous amount of energy.

Revenge, however, is less draining, more tangible, and with a trophy or two...can be enjoyed over and over."

"Spoken like a true foul-hearted creature of the night," Erik felt immediate remorse for his words. "I realize that in our former life we grew up fast...because we had to," he conceded, "but you're not the one having to explain these recall episodes. Do you grasp the tenacity of these scientists? They're like piranha."

"You're the one opening your mouth. Learning to be a changeling, walking in two lives that move side by side is vital for you. My life is over – yours is just beginning. We are both autodidacts, but if you represent what I would have become had I a whole face...you're rather like a soppy wet rag."

Modern Erik stiffened. "Are you trying to atone for your sins by having me relive these encounters? Am I becoming a man by borrowing from your life?"

"Hmm. No...and no again. Your current life should not be burdened with my guilt, but knowing what I experienced in the past helps you make choices based on historical fact."

The former Erik appeared in the mirror dressed in a rather archaic set of clothes. He had a small lasso in his hands. Throwing it deftly, he snared a rat sitting on a rock. The animal squealed once then struggled frantically against the noose cutting off its air. "You must always avoid the clawing of a creature caught within the Punjab." The strangling rodent twisted, scratched, then hung eerily still. The Phantom rocked him like a pendulum.

"You want me to learn this technique?" Erik pointed to the rope. "To practice flicking my wrists and capturing objects?"

"The Hindu guards at the palace taught us a very useful skill. No sound, no blood. Long strips of catgut softened with oils and the loving caress of fingertips, then braided and knotted into a simple lariat." Scooping the creature into his gloved hand, the vision presented the weapon and its victim for proper viewing.

Fascinated, the student observed, "Very impressive, but more important to me is the knowledge of how to control these seizures. I brought you here this time, and we haven't been sucked into the past yet. Isidore ended one episode by striking a match. Could the smell of sulfur also act as a trigger?"

"We could try several things, see what hits the mark. First, tell me how I died. You'll have to say it, that way I can't suppress the knowledge."

"You're negotiating?"

"Negotiating in good faith, that in itself should count for something." Behind the mask he smirked.

"The swine flu pandemic of 1918 took you. It spread worldwide, killed one person in fifty. Worst pandemic in recorded history, more deadly than the Plague of the Black Death."

"How apropos for someone who strangled so many with the Punjab lasso to die suffocating – starved for air." He seemed reflective, "I don't remember trying to clear my airway of bloody froth." Staring at the ground, he paused for a moment. "It took time to develop communication with you. I feel compelled. Isidore is a taxing role model to follow: living in his special world of paranoia, generating his own brand of worldwide justice, surrounding you with luxury. Through your eyes I've been watching him work. He's a somewhat disjointed combination of two human beings. Whereas, you and I are a more streamlined composite; there is nothing capricious about us. I'm in your genes thanks to radioactive copper. If you think long enough, you'll register the reality."

The breathing article rushed to stand. "Copper, an integral trace element in every living mammal. One of the best conductors of heat and electricity...exhibits nearly identical behaviors in its radioactive and non-radioactive forms. Shamans and alchemists invented hundreds of simple formulas involving copper...the properties have been studied for centuries. Copper 62/64 is used as a positron emission radiotracer in medical imaging. If I'm not mistaken, a chelate with the ring structure of a metal ion is used to treat cancer in radiation therapy. Are you saying that I'm my own little memory tomography machine? Isidore has never thought to stick a Geiger counter on me. If the isotope is there, the effects might be countered by penicillamine or zinc acetate. Either works to bind copper, and zinc is quite common. It's in deodorants, breath-fresheners, acne lotion, and chewing gum." He had a sudden, unsolicited picture of the prostitute smacking her wad of bubble gum.

The semiopaque version in the mirror responded, "See! Paying close attention when Isidore and Nyah work in the lab pays off. De Chagny would have you dull and pointless. I quickened your theatrical attitude toward life, your love for decoration, and a particularly glorious sense of doom."

"Really? I should thank you. A life of rejection and assassination has added such balance to me...doesn't quite equate!"

"Yes it does. The sleek art of murder is an enviable skill to possess, especially when one considers that life is full of vermin. Your enemies are much closer than you think. Soon you'll be able to put out a sign: Rivals need not apply for a position within."

"Let's cut to the chase. How do I deliberately bring on a seizure?"

"Besides the chemistry, I think someone is helping you and the possibilities are limited. Start with your innate intuition about images." His words were as water babbling over stones, titillating musical sounds. "For now use the image of the Punjab. Go within yourself. Don't lurch. Don't speculate. Suspend all thought. Then in one physiological ideomotion, one unconscious response to an idea, you simply are the rope. It is an extension of you. The two of you act as one innate being, moving smoothly together."

Focusing on the rope as instructed, Erik forgot about abnormal electrical discharges in the brain and offered the lasso untainted adoration. When he felt the lariat yearning to uncoil for him, his cognizance transferred swiftly back to his apartment in the Shah's palace. He sat alone, an untouched tray of sliced oranges on a table. Alongside the fruit rested several nearly translucent porcelain bowls containing rice, curried lamb, and a yellow squash topped with a sprinkling of coconut. The rooms were the same, the only renovation the removal of Fatima's blood and the addition of a traditional Holy Kabba wall hanging, similar to those found in most Islamic homes. He knew instinctively that he continued to spend his nights sleeping in the walls, and that only Heerad and Reza were with him. The man's cooking, though well intended, wasn't very palatable.

"No offense, Heerad, but we cannot exist on a steady diet of glops of overcooked rice and tough-as-leather meat. Start sending to the kitchens for our meals." *Have I killed with the Punjab lasso? Ah yes, the incident in the harem.*

𝕹 otable only for its butchery, this was the era of Erik's bloody battles in the arena. Weekly conflicts that propelled his rise in popularity throughout the palace. No one successfully removed the wily Frenchman's headgear, and all who came against him fell to their deaths. Betting odds went from even to always in his favor, so the royalty and staff bet on how long it would take Erik to annihilate his opponent, how many maneuvers. The grim looking warrior-magician created an aura of mystery and dread about himself. He learned to limit his own injuries to those of bruises and sore muscles, an occasional cracked rib. At the end of one performance he dazzled them all by pulling a drugged snake from his mouth and allowing it to slither away unharmed. He accomplished this feat mimicking a sword swallower. Executing the entire fight with a collapsible leather tube run down his esophagus. His tongue, pressing the end of the container against the roof of his palate, kept the tube sealed tight during the contest. The feat amazed the Persians, even the acidic Khusrowshah.

After the battles the Frenchman retired to his private quarters, there to work on his drawings for a new summer palace. He planned to offer such an intricately compelling structure that its construction would distract the Shah from these months so marked by blood and murder. He labored against heavy intrigues that swirled through the palace corridors like the hot winds. The Shah contracted a painful case of gout, the same disease that destroyed his father. Part of eastern Persia remained under British influence, so the Royal House had appealed for added strength from the Russians. The residence now echoed with the quick sure step of these foreign agents and their native speaking interpreters. These Slavic ambassadors, along with the palace guards, bet heavily on the Royal Magician and won enormous sums.

During these volatile days, an incident of debauchery occurred within the Shah's select harem of concubines. Though it was strictly forbidden, some of these foreigners bribed the Chief of the Eunuchs for entrance to the women. The eunuch, urged on by some of the neglected more-verbal females, had not turned the foreigners away. In this palace sex seemed to be in season year round.

When reports of these secret liaisons reached the Captain of the Guards, the seasoned soldier took a small squad and kicked open the doors of the secluded section housing the concubines. Enraged, they beheaded the offending Chief of the Eunuchs. Any woman found with a man, the Captain also put to the scimitar. The male offenders were brought, bound hand and foot, before the Shah to be expelled from the land, disgraced. A stunning story swept through the palace like wildfire, one of an innocent girl lying atop another to have her life taken in place of her sister's. Heedless, the Captain's sword took both their heads in one fell swoop. While the carnage was cleared away and the area cleansed, the remaining concubines were moved to another section of the palace. In the aftermath of the turbulent massacre, many of the palace residents longed for an end to the violence and a time of peace.

Bitter, seething with frustration, Khusrowshah reluctantly postponed his thievery of the Shah's treasury. Making himself less conspicuous, he focused his ill-bred intentions elsewhere. But his mother, the Shah's second wife, continued stirring the pot. With a biting wit, she goaded her son. It was insane to remain without a promised bride, so incomplete. Khusrowshah should take revenge on the magician for helping end the life of Soha Houri. She even suggested that a boy be brought in from the streets, a child fair of face. That this sylph-like being be washed and dressed in silken nightclothes, then laid in the Frenchman's bed, so that the infidel might be discovered and shown to the Shah as a deviant.

An incensed Khusrowshah abraded his mother with scathing remarks. Yelling that he believed her to be a sorceress robbed of sight by demons for she soured every room she entered. Staring brazenly into the sightless eyes, he informed her that no child could be laid atop the trickster's covers. It was a well-known fact that Heerad slept on the floor outside the room's door and that night after night his master's bed went untouched. No one knew exactly where the illusive brother to the jinn slept. During the day Erik went nowhere without his slave and was never alone in the presence of another human being, except for the Shah. So for a time, Khusrowshah abandoned the defamation of his self-induced nemesis and turned his mind to scheming in other directions. Perhaps another calamitous upheaval within the concubines' quarters would provide the perfect distraction to pursue his brother's betrothed.

None of Khusrowshah's friends could say for certain whether the prince's abnormal attraction was born of arrogant jealousy or a genuine desire for the beautiful creature. Khusrowshah teetered on the edge of love and hate, attraction and disgust. Amine's cultural charm and essential beauty was maddening. He pictured them naked in a marriage chamber, her hair cascading around his head like a perfumed cloud, her mind overwhelmed with the urge to ease him with kisses. Delicate as two flower petals, those lips he craved descended upon him with unequivocal adoration. He pressed her to him and plucked the flower hidden between her thighs like an orchid drawn to his nose.

As he mired in these lurid thoughts, he also reasoned that no token of her affection would ever come to him. Worse yet, he feared reprisals. Should his tantalizing reflections ever be exposed, the damage of public ridicule would diminish his status as a potential ruler. A scoundrel brought out into the open, would suffer (at the very least) banishment at the Shah's decree.

Hard and bitter, with few running rivers and a dearth of shade trees except in the Caspian and western provinces, the life of an exile would dry out his vigor and he would wither. In the end, it was the very nature of this austere land that helped him execute the next chapter of his plan.

One of Khusrowshah's closest friends, Nasser Nabataea, was a crony who dallied on the fringes of their pranks. More a lover and a poet than an antagonist, Nasser always opted for telling stories about their raucous escapades rather than participating in the caustic acts. He deeply regretted the violation and death of the sweet maidservant Fatima and hated attending the conflicts held in the arena. It was to this affable friend that the vile prince now turned.

"It's come to my mother's attention, that you have caught the eye of one of the choicest remaining concubines, Bonafsheh to be precise."

In light of the recent incidents, Nasser's eyes widened in terror. "Then she is a very foolish woman. These days, females given to the Shah who connive for the strictly forbidden affections of other males are worse than simple-minded. They are crazed and hungering for death!" He circled his temples with his fingers. "Forfeiting breath for brief physical pleasures lacks reason."

Khusrowshah picked a banana from a bowl and proceeded to peel its skin. "Nevertheless, Bonafsheh has listened to your lively recollections and is disposed to experiencing you. With my father suffering and neglecting his women, her strong thighs long for you, Nasser." His tongue came forward, symbolically touching the fruit.

"Accommodating such longings costs too dearly. The Captain lurks in the hallways, just waiting for further invasions into the harem. Surely Bonafsheh's sister concubines are painfully aware what harvest these wanton affairs reap. They'd probably scream out with indignant rage at the slightest hint of wrong doing."

"What if you had the assistance and private sanctions of my mother? She has listened to Bonafsheh's petitions and is persuaded to help her. Your creative tales also stir the heart of the Shah's second wife. How many times has my mother told me that your rich poetry reanimates her soul? I have not fingers and toes enough to count, Nasser! Your stories gladden her day, and her need for encouragement is so easily understood, given the unbending severity of her son's present situation. The elaboration you add to our exploits helps her endure our degradation. She praises all that springs from your mouth and applauds your ability to bind our group in spirited comradery."

Khusrowshah felt no remorse whatsoever in sacrificing this friend. His growing lust and jealous desire for the Princess Amine motivated his illicit pursuit of her virginity. A press of angry guards, once again wrecking havoc within the harem, might afford him the perfect opportunity to spring a surprise visit on Amine. If someone uncovered his clandestine contact with the princess, he could offer a valid excuse for his presence. Thinking she might come to harm during another upset, he would simply claim a deep and abiding concern for her safety.

"Exactly how would we navigate this troubling channel of deception and meet Bonafsheh's needs?"

And with that one question Khusrowshah snared the stupid Nasser within his treachery.

Unknown to the plotters, the Captain of the Guard had no intention of creating another blood bath within the harem. Even though the strict performance of his duties earned the respect of his fellow soldiers, their wives and daughters abhorred his harsh treatment of the straying concubines. They compared the slaughter of women to the flagrant leniency given their foreign lovers, branded the Captain as excessively cruel, and whispered he merited a full reduction in rank. Not only was his reputation suffering, but lately his own wife refused to accompany him to their bed. With stinging accusations that effectively deflated his ardor, she labeled him a heartless butcher and fled to the home of her father, a tribal chief in the northern hills.

Human nature being what it is, the Captain knew that others would attempt to amuse themselves by consorting with the concubines, especially since they were housed in temporary chambers. Rather than set off a general alarm, he turned to the magician to help him guard the Shah's women. In return for a two-week reprieve from the arena, Erik quietly accepted the assignment. Bowing low, he promised to be as invisible as the wind and keep the Captain appraised.

Confident that no Persian woman would touch the infidel, the Captain directed Erik to the area of the concubines, gave him the power to slay intruders, and instructed him to secretly collect all the information he could. Hopefully the Shah's health would return soon.

The concubines' interim place of confinement provided very pleasant accommodations. The harem was reached through a magnificently tiled vestibule that led to a spacious courtyard surrounded by yet another open gallery communicating with a number of magnificent apartments. In the middle of the walkways the mouth of a large agate pitcher, as tall as a man, fed clear water to a pond lined with white marble. At the far end of the garden stood a sort of draped cabinet. Within this richly carved compartment sat a throne fashioned of Russian amber and supported by legs of polished ebony. The three walls encompassing the throne were set with reliefs hammered from Indian gold. These reliefs depicted every variety of flower known to grow in Persia. Their frames were studded with extraordinary diamonds of enormous size. Closing the cabinet's drapes created a very private space within the courtyard.

Thinking themselves deprived, even in these lavish new surroundings, the women strolled or lolled about in nearly transparent garments festooned with tiny bits of jewels and precious metals that shone brightly in the sun. Erik held little confidence in the fidelity of these severely affected females. From the rooftops he watched these strange birds of perfection. Supposedly unobtainable to everyone but the Shah, their very expensive upkeep spoke of a rich decadent history that not only condoned their existence, but supported it as well. One in particular caught his sharp eyes. Responding only when spoken to, she stayed apart from the others, keeping her thoughts remote and hidden. He watched her closely, thinking that if anyone in the troupe might engineer a secretive affair – this would be the female. She had an exceptionally curved, lean body and wide almond eyes of the deepest brown. Delicate sculpted eyebrows and velvet eyelashes, made heavy with mascara, framed those eyes. Known as Bonafsheh; she was the concubine who, for a chest of gold and the promise of an escort into freedom away from the Shah's realm, secretly agreed to entertain Nasser.

To Erik's way of thinking, the schemers weren't very subtle. Outside the concubines' courtyard, Khusrowshah and Nasser played dice with the guards and added opiate to their drinks. The watchmen were lax, believing that no one would brazenly attempt an assignation so soon after the recent fray. Alone, Nasser snuck into the *bâgh* (garden). He had been told to proceed to the cabinet and wait for Bonafsheh to seek him out. Pulling back an edge of the drape, he saw the girl already standing beside the amber and ebony throne. With a soft, almost sardonic laugh, she gestured him forward.

Turkish coffee and French almond liqueur sat on a small table beside a dish of washed and sweetened fruit. Nervous, he looked behind. Scanning the garden with squinted eyes, he tried to peer into the deepest shadows.

"Please, enter. Set aside your trepidation. The mistress has commanded the girls and all our slaves to retire. We may speak here in private, but shut the drape least *shêytan* (the devil) see an invitation to enter and cause disorder."

Nasser stepped inside. Letting the cloth fall behind him, he wondered how much feminine resistance he would have to overcome. "Many times at court I have noticed your rare beauty. I risk much to enjoy your company in private."

From the rooftop Erik dropped a rope and rappelled downward. Though he knew where the storyteller had gone, he uncovered his deformed nose. He let his discriminating senses take in the cool night air. The scent was easy to follow; with his eyes closed he could track the nascent footprint.

Bonafsheh lit a tiny brass covered Alhambra lamp; in the heat of the flame half moons and stars began to circle the space. She removed her veil and let him see the perfect fullness of her lips and refined chin. "I have drink, my Lord, and fruit. If you are inclined, my hands will carry the choicest pieces to your mouth until you are satisfied. And as you sate your appetite, I will say a thousand soft and tender things to you."

Thinking he hardly had to work to win the girl, he ignored the ominous silent warning of the Shah's throne. "'Tis not food which tempts my palette, but the willingness of the luscious woman who stands before me. You enchant all who behold you, Bonafsheh. Had I a room full of fragrant sandalwood furniture and a luxurious bed of silken sheets, I could not make love to you with more ardor than the increase I presently feel within my loins."

"Strip," she whispered.

Nasser obediently disrobed down to his European pointelle socks, and following her direction, laid himself upon the cushions.

"If you will permit me," she knelt near his chest and placed a succulent grape within his mouth. "Think of this as our own chamber."

Delighted, Nasser tasted the grape and asked, "What if I fall asleep here in this pleasantry? The hour is late."

"If you sleep, I promise to awaken you, to bring you back to my presence before any demon can invade your dreams with fear and distress."

Her perfumed hand gently rubbed the hair on his chest. He sucked in his breath and held it. He was experiencing a very obvious erection. Hungry to be saturated with her charms, he felt tempted to return the caresses Bonafsheh lavished upon him, but held back. Should he dare the liberty of sinning with this girl, one whom the Shah devoured with his eyes and royal manhood?

"How do you justify gratifying me when you hold the position you do?" he asked, choking. Her henna decorated hands had moved to his exposed crotch. She was very good at what she did.

"The Shah refused to give my father money for me, declaring my body should be presented as tribute. The man steals human flesh. We have the Sultana's permission to be here."

"Which amounts to nothing if we get caught. My stories please you so much that you would risk the wrath of the Captain and certain death?"

"Oh, yes," Bonafsheh whispered. "I am no longer myself, but am entirely at your disposal. You have full power to do with me as you please for it would give me the greatest happiness to submit."

"You strip," Nasser croaked like a happy frog. "Hurry."

Erik waited for the full commitment to the act, the actual moment of penetration. When Nasser rolled the girl to her back and started a frantic pumping of his hips, Erik initiated the soft yowling of a cat – making sure it came first from one corner of the cabinet, then another. So frenzied was Nasser's urge that at first he didn't hear. He wanted to howl with ecstasy, but was stopped when Bonafsheh clamped her hand across his mouth.

"Shh," she directed. "Slow down. A cat stands nearby and you will incite it."

Nasser paused his very un-poetic thrusting. Only fear caused him to reign in the stimulation. "No, it doesn't sound like an animal. It sounds like someone scraping something metallic."

He had the mental vision of the point of a blade dragging across stone. Scratching and bouncing off shiny marble, the sword's tip traveled through the blood of the fallen concubines, leaving a clotting crimson trail. His mind saw fingertips dripping with blood, heard the dying screams of girls trapped without hope. He sat up, almost paralyzed with fear. Alone and isolated, cutoff from Khusrowshah's aid he felt the presence of a powerful predatory beast prowling around outside, a being wanting to inflict a world of hurt. He thought he saw the sole of a boot pass along the bottom of the drape. As he tried to collect himself and focus, the menace disappeared.

Bonafsheh sat up. Sliding to the throne, the object of this night's unsanctioned tryst drew up her knees, wrapping her arms around them. Huddled on a cushion, she began to rock.

Red Chinese smoke filled the air inside the cabinet. With their vision clouded they couldn't see who or what threatened them. Nasser scrambled for his pants and his dagger.

"Faithless, disloyal subjects!" Terse cogent words came through the fog. "My first victim was afraid of the Roc. What do you fear, Nasser?"

"Nothing," answered the dissolute storyteller. Still naked he started to stand.

"Big mistake." The Punjab lasso came flying in to catch the man's throat.

Too late to raise his hand, Nasser recognized the moment the noose went around his neck. Dropping to his knees, he clawed frantically at the restraint. Erik stepped forward, revealing the identity of their attacker.

"Allah preserve us from this evil sorcerer!" Bonafsheh spat.

"Cover yourself, woman," Erik was careful to angle his head away from her and keep his directions concise. "There's more sex in here than in a French nunnery and that's saying something." He focused on his male captive, grateful that he only had to listen to the female speak. "Care to give her any advice, Nasser? Cat stole your tongue?"

"Your eccentricities have done me momentous harm," Bonafsheh cautiously grabbed her robe. "I gladly deny you the vision of my femininity." Deeply wary that an outsider could be merciful, she divulged, "Pity me, Sir. This hasty lover was my road back to freedom." Tears filled her eyes.

"Explain." Erik's long articulate fingers moved to the noose, loosening it enough for Nasser to draw in a painful breath. The throat of the *cavalier servente* was scorched and already swelling.

"I have sufficient control to restrain from associating with a mischievous man who carries nothing but lust in his pants," she slipped the robe over her head. "But as the proverb says: When the time is right, take up your hammock and run! So when I was offered freedom in exchange for entertaining this clown, I consented."

Erik frowned in mock consternation, letting his voice convey what his mask concealed. "It's my newly trained lariat that deserves pity. How very sad that the prince's neck is not within the noose. Instead, the rope's first kill shall be Khusrowshah's most foolish friend."

Realizing his end was near, renewed alarm flooded the kneeling paramour. With his throat too constricted to scream, he eyed Bonafsheh.

Sharpened by the recent fighting inside the arena, Erik watched Nasser's pupils widen. Instantly realizing the danger he was in, Erik tightened the rope just enough so as not to stop the heart of his prey. Turning left, he faced the concubine with her dagger raised high to strike. Faster than her, his long arm shot out. Steely fingers took hold of the girl's wrist, twisting the joint brutally. The blade hit the marble floor with a clang and Erik kicked the deadly fang away.

Bold and contemptuous, she sat upon the throne and bore the pain of her throbbing wrist in silence; crying out would only bring a horde of guards and indignant women down upon their heads.

Nasser was suddenly sickened. Reaching up to the noose, he loosened it and a projectile spray of vomit sailed forth from his mouth. A gross bilious smell filled the booth. "Hear me out!" he begged, wiping his mouth with his bare arm.

Until the repugnant smell offended him, Erik enjoyed playing with these two. The game afforded him an enormous sense of power. Bending toward Nasser, he swiftly bound the poet's wrists with a second piece of braided cord. "Stay on your knees, you idiot, and I'll listen for as long as I can tolerate this odor."

"These women can have anything they want," Nasser whined.

Erik stood in an attack stance, one booted foot before the other. Head tilted slightly to better appreciate the scene. "Obviously! Even you," he ridiculed.

"She granted me a fleeting pleasure! I am of high and noble birth and can't have my every whim granted. Look how flawed she is, beauty disguises the rot held within her heart. She values nothing."

"Ah, the culprit sings," Erik was amused. "Telling us his life is worth more than his partner's."

"She summoned me," Nasser's sour mouth repulsed him, but he plowed on. "In the inside pocket of my jacket is a note. Read it for yourself."

Still holding the end of the noose, Erik pulled out a small piece of parchment containing several lines written in script letters called *abjad*. Unable to decipher its message, he handed the scrap to Bonafsheh. "Read it!"

Her trembling fingers unrolled the tiny scroll. "It is not a love note written by my hand. It is a receipt for the purchase of three camels and two crates, one each of figs and dates...all from an Egyptian merchant named Waziri."

"Liar!" Nasser spat on the floor.

"Look," Bonafsheh pointed to the bottom of the script, "Waziri draws the sign of the *ankh* beside his name."

"It seems I've caught a rather dumb fox in the Shah's hen house. Into what imaginative world have you strayed, Nasser? I can't believe that she would call for you, bring you here to a place fraught with danger." He looked toward Bonafsheh, studying her closely. "This discourteous bore blames you for this liaison. Did you call for the services of this imbecile? Who initiated the contact?"

Bonafsheh crossed her arms over her breasts, "The *dovvom* Sultana."

"She is without honor," Nasser gasped. "Makes ungrateful, injurious reproaches against a great lady. Apply the rope to her throat and you will listen to truth gush from between her teeth!"

Erik remained on alert. "I have listened to your stories at court and I've never heard you sound so crazy, Nasser. Is the lack of oxygen depriving you of coherent thought? There is very little honor in the second Sultana."

Bonafsheh interjected quickly, "Please, Magician, don't be agitated. Nasser was my path to freedom outside these walls. He is culpable and wrong to accuse me."

"I'm not agitated in the least. Aside from the offensive smell, it's a rather a lovely night here in the garden. You need not blame each other. One would have to be an idiot not to learn of the subterfuge arcing like sparks through this palace. Is it not said: The one who speaks the least often possesses the greatest intelligence." Erik paused to hold up the rope, "My instructions are clear. End the life of the criminal who dares to enter the harem. Let me remind you, Nasser, you have done more than breach the doors. You are caught immodestly naked with your manhood and its fuzzy sack dangling about."

Bonafsheh snickered. "We have an avenger. Khusrowshah is nearly out of control with jealousy over the bride soon to be given Fazel, and now he has lost even the Daroga's sister as compensation."

From the floor Nasser added, "He has vowed revenge for the life of Soha Houri. I didn't maul Bonafsheh, but Khusrowshah tore at Fatima's body before killing your slave. If out of sheer maliciousness, he pressed her eyes from their sockets like grapes, what more will he do in retribution for this?"

A sharp uneasy pain knotted in Erik's chest. In answer to the returning vision of two innocent women lost, he instinctually shifted the position of his feet. Yet the crony had a valid point. No one knew if there were limits to Khusrowshah's evil. Where would the prince draw the line? Erik grew impatient, "You have not told me anything I do not already comprehend."

"Wait, Lord! I can trade valuable information for a minute of my life." Summoning a slip of courage, Nasser groveled, "Khusrowshah finds your repeated success exasperating. At every opportunity he inflames animosity toward you."

Erik was not in the least offended. He could leverage that animosity for all it was worth. Beneath his head covering his one existing nostril flared. Nasser reeked most unpleasantly.

"No crime of disrespect or thievery is beyond Khusrowshah," whispered Bonafsheh.

"You two are meddling in the snake charmer's basket. In trying to protect an asp that doesn't need protection, you'll suffer a nasty bite. A confrontation between Khusrowshah and myself is inevitable. Let this evil-hearted prince burn with hatred. I only pray he does not grow fickle to the cause. Let him become so enraged that he seeks me out… in the open or in secret. Either way would suffice." Erik prodded one of Nasser's knees with the toe of his boot. "Go on, let your mutinous mouth try to dissuade me. I assure you that Khusrowshah will learn all too quickly the price of unpunished transgressions. Too bad he's missed the failure of this deviation."

Nasser did an amazing thing. Instead of an impassioned plea, he rallied what little strength of character he had left. "Bonafsheh is the victim here. Let my admission of guilt sway your purpose, for it is the sad truth. I will not have my final words be those of dishonorable lies. I consider myself a cur. Offered a woman valued by the Shah himself, I leapt at the opportunity. Spare this girl. In the revelation of these misdeeds my mother will be disgraced, but I confess that I chose to guard the door while Fatima was defiled. I participated vicariously in that distasteful act. Tonight I realize with grim acceptance that my just end is near!" His shoulders slumped and he braced himself for the end he knew was about to come.

These people are almost beyond reason! They get their way in everything, even death. But this ignoble fellow participated in the rape and murder of Fatima. Erik pulled the catgut tight. Nasser's face turned a sickening purple-blue. The full weight of the storyteller's body fell face forward with a startling thud. Erik stuck his boot on the prominent vertebrae of the cervical spine. Using the leverage of weight and position, he snapped the neck bones.

Devastated, Bonafsheh realized she was not to be spared. Losing control, she sobbed, "Please. Please."

Erik reached down, retrieving his rope. "Given the chance to flee, where will you run?"

"With great speed I will head for the Caspian and there in its waters drown myself. My desire for freedom was foolish and unfounded."

"I'll spare you the expense of the trip." Erik grabbed her hands and tied them to the neck of her worthless lover.

Confiscating their daggers, he strode from the throne area toward the garden's gate and the office of the Captain of the Guard. Though these wretches deserved a thousand deaths, he'd chosen to give them only one. He left the unfaithful girl alive, to be brought before the Shah still breathing and hopefully still attached to the lifeless body of Nasser.

Squinting against the slender thread of sunlight shining through the curtains in his bedroom, Erik awoke face down on the carpet. Nauseous and unwell, he uncurled his fingers. Something soft and familiar lay beneath his left palm. With his head pounding, he sat up and without questioning the appearance of the object, flicked his wrist. The soft braid sailed through the air, catching nothing it returned obediently to his lap. He'd never forget these lessons. They were permanently ingrained within his exacting photographic memory. Raising a cool hand to his forehead, he tried to soothe the headache that pleaded to pump the gray matter free of his skull. Ignoring the pain, he rose and taking a lampshade off a lamp, tried the Punjab lasso again. This time the rope slid easily around the base of the bulb and when he pulled, the whole fixture came crashing to the floor.

He addressed the thing that felt so natural in his hand, praising it. "Compared to other weapons, none have the ability to sit so innocuous within my pocket. None have the strength, when blessed with the direction of my hand, to strike like a venomous snake!"

Smiling, he thought to call for aspirin and Arabian *Mariamia* sage tea to relieve his headache and settle the rolling cramps in his stomach. The wonderful magician who stimulated his mind with cinematic reruns gave him more than a weapon. He now had a plan forming – a plan to lay claim to Christine's heart.

"Sometimes a person has to find their past to know how to act," he waved to his reflection in the mirror.

Standing in the chateau's main kitchen, Kathryn Arlington listened to Erik's unusual requests. She kept her finger pushed down hard on the intercom button, "Are you sure you really want to try this tea? How do you know it can alleviate your symptoms? You've never been sick like this before. Maybe you've got the flu? I'm not even sure we stock anything like *Mariamia* tea."

She babbles interrogatives like Fatima. "Just check, will you? Send out if you have to…I'll wait."

25 ACTING OUT

C ooler winds from the north blew over the chateau that evening, dropping the temperature dramatically. With the house almost chilly, Erik sat on a wing chair in the southern salon. Alone and left to his own thoughts, he watched the flames of a crackling fire. How many times in his former life had he sat in this very chair, reading, listening to the wind and rain? He had no idea, but for the moment enjoyed a great peace. With the incessant drumming of the headache gone and his stomach eased into neutrality, a distant delicate sonata played in his head.

Like the small soft touches of stippled paint to a canvas, random thoughts came to entertain. *I know the secret ways of this house, how my ancestor vanished from corridors.* In the hall outside the library sat an intricately carved console table; its antique black varnish rubbed through to an underlying stain of red, its turned leg posts inlaid with brass striping. Above this table hung a rectangular mirror with segments of its silver frame woven as a basket. The mirror and table were special only for their age, but the panel they were affixed to was very important. The engineers hadn't found that tunnel – its entire expanse was intact. It traveled round the chamber of mirrors and from there to the bedroom he now occupied. He understood so many odd facts about that devilish chamber – deceptive reflections, multiple accesses – one need only appear to be in a particular place. Activating the gears to move the mirrors of the chamber was not difficult if he followed a series of simple procedures. His hands rested quietly on his thighs. He was in the zone, appreciating the fact that sentient man was a complex mixture of arrogance and trust...*so dupable...a spectator who easily allows that whatever his eyes behold is the only truth there is to be had.*

He heard Christine's buoyant footsteps as she walked past the arched entrance, Dillard in tow. *Damn! Where are they headed?* Two seconds later she was back. He didn't need to turn around to know she waited expectantly in the doorway. *Merde!* Standing politely, he turned to face the pair. Did he have any choice but to trust Isidore's motivations? He would happily volunteer to guard her if he thought he could stomach Isidore's refusal – again. She wore a cute little red oxford blouse with tiny black polka dots, straight-legged jeans, not too tight. Her blue green eyes were piercing. He bowed his head and shoulders in a somewhat solemn acknowledgement.

"You don't mind if we join you in here, do you?" Dillard asked calmly. "She actually requested this room." Erik's sparring partner held a black leather briefcase at his side.

"By all means, enter. The room is large enough to fit a crowd. Do you know me, Christine?"

"You're a doctor?" Her voice was like a soft silken scarf from some ritzy Parisian boutique.

He shook his head in a non-verbal answer. Her question was understandable. "I'm Erik de Chagny...Isidore's progeny."

"Isidore." Unable to draw the connection, her eyes shifted quickly to a pair of nineteenth century Dutch ginger jars resting on the mantle. Erik knew the jars were attractive, portraying an idyllic landscape set against a *soleil* yellow background scattered with blue birds. Was she toying with him by breaking eye contact or just uncertain? "You and I are not related by blood," he said a little too autocratically. Then added as an afterthought, "Sit anywhere you like."

Pleased at the dryness of his brow and palms, the steady beat of his own heart; he crossed his arms over his chest, ready to objectively view her progress. Paying strict attention to skeletal-muscular function, he watched her skitter to a comfortable sofa and plop down a little awkwardly. He wondered if this was some ungainly teenage phase. She hadn't noticed her magnificent harpsichord, and the instrument had recently been re-tuned. Unsure if he was happy or disappointed at the omission, he feigned indifference and looked at Dillard. The man set his briefcase on a coffee table and clicked open the lid. Withdrawing a fashion magazine, he handed it to Christine.

Erik studied the situation for a moment – privately hoping that he didn't have to endure seeing them touch. He might have been a scented room vaporizer swirling fragrance in the air for all they noticed him. *No physical contact, all right?* He noticed her fingers tremble as she brushed the glossy paper of the magazine. Her thumb and right index finger slid over the surface, drawing circles over photographs. *How deeply does she feel it? Her tactile sense might be so acute it borders on pain.* Time and practice had taught him how to control this perception so that he didn't need to parade around wearing cotton gloves. In his younger years he'd felt like one of those art dealers at an auction house. *Perhaps she's been offered a pair and refused them?*

Washing his face of emotion, he dropped his eyes deceptively. Took in her dainty ankles and the lovely pair of black Mary Jane's, then flung his butt into the chair and returned to his ruminations. Pretending there was nothing else in this garden of furniture and gaming tables worthy of his notice, he mentally honed in on her.

Perhaps Isidore's warning was materializing early. She showed not one iota of interest in him. *Have we created an indifferent Christine?* That predicament was simply not acceptable. Besides, without speaking to her, engaging her, how could he be confident of his own affection? *Has anyone considered that possibility? What if I haven't decided?* He knew one thing for certain. He didn't want Christine thinking of him as a brother or a distant cousin! *Why, just tell me why, I need to feel like seeking moral absolution just to meet with her? So unfair, Isidore! Go rot!*

Like a reclusive wolf, Erik peered out past the winged extension of the chair. The disconcerting thrill he hoped would shoot through Christine did not materialize. But there – plain as day – was the noxious curl of Dillard's upper lip. Doing nothing to conceal his outright 'drop-dead' message, Erik's face returned to view the flames. Love and fire bear a strong kinship, they both need to be fed, and this relationship was already guttering – spitting and choking for want of fuel. He sighed, *oh well.* She was free to bestow her favors where she chose. He consoled himself with imagining her fingers fondling the front of his shirt. Her movements were smooth, accurate...the pull of a newly freed placket and the cloth withdrew, exposing a portion of his chest. The tips of her fingers were cool, like dewdrops. His reaction to her touch – automatic arousal.

Sneaking furtive glances, Christine secretively scrutinized the dark brooding young man watching flames turn logs into ashes. The tall handsome creature that had stormed into her bedroom earlier that day hadn't come down to dinner. Now he sat before the fire so quiet and sullen. A brooding mysterious tower, withdrawn into his own world, he barely spoke. Somehow she knew his basic nature was to be aggravating and unpredictable, to taunt unmercifully and forgive only after the payment of satisfactory retribution. It was actually a good thing that he hadn't joined them for her first meal in the formal dining room. She'd sat before the silver candelabras (with their fancy bowls of intertwined leaves supporting tall smokeless tapers) mystified as to what fork to use. Awkward and clumsy, she tried repeatedly to tilt a flute of almond champagne to her mouth. Every time she managed to get the cold frosted glass to her lips, she'd spilled some down her front. She felt ridiculous. *Grace is important, just look at the fashion models on these pages.* The ultra-thin females were chic, aristocratic, proud of their sleek beauty and pouting sensual warmth. She had almost tripped just getting to the couch!

Erik continued to pry without speaking. He surveyed with senses other than his eyes, paying special attention to her bodyguard. Dillard evidenced more than a trace of possessiveness, but not like Khusrowshah – the *non compos mentis* author of so many torments. Still, he knew Dillard could get there. All men could. So far, the American tended to be very diplomatic, exemplary behavior except for what his eyes and subtle body language betrayed.

For his part, Dillard relished being close to Erik's intended: her tiny feet, the sweetness of her eyes, the smoothness of her skin, and those breasts! God, he enjoyed this assignment. He'd seen her naked. The vision of her floating in that vat of primordial soup was indelibly implanted in his brain. He re-lived the sight continuously. But for the moment, he sought only what recognition he needed in order to keep her attention focused on him. He hoped, with all earnestness, that his shrewd little glances told her loud-and-clear about the depth of his interest. He meant to have this girl, was determined to get inside her pants. He didn't know she'd always possessed a natural talent for trapping the attention of men.

Erik comprehended Dillard's sly unspoken undertow while Christine focused elsewhere. *How ironic that we are playing the same mad game as at the theater.* He mentally shoved Dillard and his intentions into a dank jail cell and concentrated on her. Craving insight into her thoughts, he followed their conversation closely, trying to telepathically get behind her eyes and see what she saw on the page. The initially cloudy picture cleared, the reception improving with concentration. *They're giving her more trendy magazines. Sure, why not? This is France the home of couture.* Some words were highlighted – subtle instruction.

In her mind, she struggled to imitate the poise of the girls in the magazine. Imaging how they walked with long leggy strides, their backs straight, heads held high. She laughed, and it was like music hanging on the air. Her intent eyes came to a section of very Goth-looking women. Apparently, she was considering coloring her hair blue and spiking it like one of the models. Erik almost chuckled until he realized she wanted to purchase a fringed black leather jacket with a death's head on the back and gleaming studs down the front. She didn't care for the strangely brimmed postman's leather cap created by a sophisticated milliner. The concoction struck him as funny too, but he kept his mirth bottled and corked. A not so easily accomplished feat when he suddenly realized she understood the sophisticated concept of buying and selling. *How wondrous! She knows the models are making a living, and she's curious about a lot of other things, so very bright.*

"Look," her fingers pointed to the model in the fringed jacket. "Bold."

"They are rather stark, making a rebellious statement." Dillard edged closer.

Absolutely unaware of appropriate personal space, she couldn't contain her enthusiasm. "I agree. Where do I get these clothes?"

Taking her friendly attitude as flirtatious, Dillard spoke with an instructional tone (one Erik had never heard him use before), "I have no idea. These women, women in general, have a power over men with their manner of dress...and undress. They are like goddesses."

"Like goddesses," Christine responded lightly.

Coquettish fraud, Erik thought skeptically. *You want to see him naked. For what purpose?* He let the horror of a possible 'why' escape consideration.

Dillard tried to add humor. "Women have made jogging a spectator sport, they cause car accidents all the time."

"What?" Christine was genuinely confused.

"I'll ask if I can take you out for a ride and I'll show you," Dillard added helpfully.

Erik winced. He should be the one to take her for a drive. How could he ever tolerate Dillard escorting her? *I'll kidnap her first! Stay a perfect gentleman, Dillard. I'll extract your teeth without anesthesia.*

As if to mock him, in the very next instant, Christine and Dillard shared an innocent, but not unnoticed touch of their hands.

Consumed with dark derision, Erik stood. With a respectful and surprisingly emphatic sweep of his hand, he bowed. "I bid you both, good night." *Why bother beginning a courtship if she's neutral toward me? And I am not jealous. No, I'm simply a male hawk needing to soar!* That was the last mental image he broadcasted as he exited the room.

Someone programmed him in an interesting fashion; he could take viewing quite a lot of amorous foreplay, but only up to a point. Then he'd explode and there would be all hell to pay. *Patience – I'll drive her mad with oceans of patience.* He stomped down the hallway and up the main stairs. Grounded by logic and reason, he was unprepared for the emotional turmoil caused by the interference of a second male in the romantic scenarios playing out in his mind. He lacked control, a decided downfall. He couldn't afford to let Christine see the amount of anger she stimulated, and he couldn't hide it. Her receptiveness to an expressive hand touching left him furious.

Dillard reacted to Erik's flight with open pleasure. Eagerly turning to Christine, he decided to advance his intentions. Taking her shoulders, he leaned forward to attempt a kiss. She frowned. With Erik out of the room she exhibited less enthusiasm. Her head actually reared back in defiant refusal.

"Take your paws off me. Manners!"

When did she learn to communicate so directly! Enraged, Dillard snapped at her. "Who are you to order me?" Still, he obligingly loosened his grip and when she actually snarled, dropped his hands into his lap. Licking his wounded pride, he went to brood in front of the fire.

Her angry resistance dissolved as quickly as it came. *Who am I?* Confused as to why the young man's exit accomplished such an uneasy response in her, her eyes traveled to Erik's vacant seat. She wondered how he managed to turn his emotions on and off. She'd felt him in her mind. Warm and comforting. That she would forever glance around doorways, peer through lab windows, hoping to see if he was there was exasperating. The fleeing young man should stay...engage her openly. Frustrated, she knew, despite his rare appearances, that he was always there...in the background. Waiting. Watching. She slouched, leaning her head over the arm of the couch to stare at the ceiling. She needed to remember something and couldn't quite lay claim to the slippery thought.

Shocked. Angered. Erik entered his room grinding emotions down into his gut, forcing the blades of the meat cutter to create chopped sirloin of his abrupt ridiculous behavior. He told himself he wasn't desperate. He just wanted to castrate Dillard, smother Christine with his mouth, and satisfy this demanding erection! He should go back down there, yank her into a locked room, and teach her how to smolder by ravaging her. She was meant for him! "Get some control!"

He tromped to the mirror, raised his right arm and with a fury welling upward, curled his fingers into a bowl of claws – calling forth his former self.

"We need to talk! Everything is different now – what went before is ancient history. She doesn't remember what we had, or if she does it's meaningless."

"Fatalist. You're upset because another male could find her alluring?"

"She's a seductress, a teaser."

"And you want her virtuous to what degree?" The older masked Erik materialized; sitting in a chair identical to the one modern Erik just occupied downstairs. His left leg casually bent over his right, ankle atop a knee. "You can't say that Isidore didn't warn you. Need I remind you that the original Christine went through a process? First, she had this adoration for the Angel of Music, then a disgusted rejection for the creature that lied and imprisoned her. Passion came with planned coaxing."

"How did you overcome her ambiguous phase? What steps did you take to win her? I have no intention of compounding the problems we had before."

In his mind he saw the older Erik breathe the answer, "Yes, you're overwrought...you want all the problems instantly resolved. Like in a movie or a one-hour television program? Pity that you have to endure a degree of torment to value her. The way has already occurred to you, but the details won't reveal themselves suddenly. No snap judgments. I need you wise and studious."

"Oh, pah...lease," he refused to hide the sarcasm, "don't hasten with advice. God forbid we get to the end product before it's time." Yet his passion was easing.

"You are not one of those readers who turns to the back of the book and scans the ending before the juicy middle has been sucked dry. You have willpower. Why don't you take their advice and go into Paris, see the sights for yourself? Kathryn will gladly accompany you. Go tell her to get dressed up. She'll curl her hair until it cascades around her head like a yellow waterfall," his fingers mimicked the action. "You'll go to a posh restaurant where they'll offer you iced water in a crystal glass and a fancy gold tasseled menu."

"I don't want to date Kathryn." The standing Erik squared his shoulders. "I refuse. I'll think of some other engrossing subject to pass the time. I'll recite from memory every model of Harley ever brought to market." He lowered his eyes, tapping his foot impatiently. "Christine! Ouch!" His fingertips rubbed circles on his burning temples. "No other pursuit will do."

"Oh, you're a regular fortress, but I can't fault you. Lending you my experiences has inherent inadequacies." Leaning back, the masked image put his hands behind his head. "This is a very old story. You can barely resist your urges. Minutes ago you weren't sure you wanted her, now you're positive you do. I think I liked you better when you didn't roller coaster through obsessions. Why not confront the facts of the situation head on? I had all the time in the world to court her, but your barely contained impulses have you itching to undo the front of that pretty red blouse and run your fingers down her chest between those blossoming breasts...headed straight for..."

"Who the hell are you to tell me what I want to do?"

"You could call me your monitored intuition, fragmented though I be. Since I've now been both alive and dead, I can honestly say that at least 'dead' leaves no gut-corroding urges. Whereas alive as a clone, seems to be fully invested with them." The incongruous reflection uncrossed his legs and leaned forward. "I find the sight of you groveling a bit disconcerting. Calm down and think. Since when did you ever back away from competition?"

"If I were more focused, I could come up with a way to keep Dillard from pursuing her. It's her flirting back that blocked my ability to reason, it made me sick. My problem is not controlling my own desires – it's controlling theirs."

Scornfully silent, the dark presence merely tented his fingers before his mouth.

"She's still transitioning…still a child," the newer version reasoned. "She likes Dillard's attentions. He jokes and makes her laugh. Her mental acuity is faulty, there's emotional instability. Perhaps occasional bursts of memory from the tank are frightening her. I haven't considered buying him off."

"Where do you suppose she is right now?"

"I don't know! I was so furious, I left her alone with that clown." Leveling his eyes at his counterpart, he considered the matter slowly. "She's desperate?" Modern Erik jumped to his own conclusion, "Well desperation is a precious waste of time."

"You're the clown. Feel her. Reach out." He practically shouted his next words, "WHERE is she?"

"On the roof! Getting ready to throw herself off!" He catapulted toward the door. "Where in hell's name is Dillard?"

"Dinner break," came the fading answer.

Nerves on hyper-alert, positive they faced a premature disastrous tragedy, he sprinted down the hallway straight for the door that opened to a steep switched-back set of stairs leading to the roof. *How did she even know how to get up there?* He opened the metal hatch and stepped out onto a precipitously slanted area of slate. A front was moving through; the air was deceptively clear, but would soon enough grow thick with rain clouds.

If I were a despondent girl where would I go? His eyes surveyed the roof and its series of solar panels. Nothing. He rounded a chimney and froze. There she was, irritatingly just in the periphery of his vision, a full thirty feet away and swaying. She'd taken a position right on the edge. She now wore a long white Chinese night coat…with an open-mouthed dragon embroidered on the back. The frog loops and knotted closures below the Mandarin collar on the garment's front offered little protection against the wind. *Who is buying these clothes for her?*

He walked in what he surmised were the same dusty footprints she took to get to the ledge. Anxious, he wondered how quickly he could reach her. For a chilled moment he feared she had the same suicidal behavior patterns as the original Christine. He had a distasteful glimmer of what Isidore and Thayer feared might happen. He searched his mind for a way to join their thoughts together, to be one great rollicking upheaval.

Her body wavered in the oncoming wind. Swiftly unfastening the front of the night coat, she let the sides billow out, facilitating her next movement. Her shoulders went back, her chest lifted. Arching her spine in a slow curve, she raised her arms and fanned open her fingers. She looked like a swan posturing its opened wings. *She means to fly off the roof, to be free! How do I exert some power of emotional balance between us?* He calculated the distance to reach her. She needed immediate help. *Let there be enough time!*

Intuitively he stepped up and took the same body posture as hers. *What an exquisite exhilaration standing before the precipice!* "Wild night for flying."

Fat raindrops began to pelt them. From the corner of his eye he saw her neck, pale and white, like a majestic bird about to lift in flight. "I like that outfit. No doubt the colors of the embroidery will run in the rain... might get ruined." His eyes traveled downward. She was stark naked and exquisite. Perfect breasts, two brown Mobe pearls for nipples, a flat quivering abdomen, patch of thick chocolate curls protecting the most secret wonder of her feminine form.

Luxuriating in this overwhelming new awareness of the wind, she said, "You don't need to attend this."

"Erik. My name is Erik, remember?" his tone was quiet. "Unless you plan on developing wings, we're much too close to an abrupt introduction with the flagstones below. I don't recommend making another forward movement."

Her eyes flitted nervously over to where he stood, handsome, neatly groomed, despite the wind disorganizing his black wavy hair. She scrunched her face. In the breeze she couldn't smell him, and she wanted to experience his scent. "Are you mocking me with that imitation?"

His mind was suddenly lost, twisting down some dark corridor cluttered with roped planks and ladders...*catwalks!* He followed the edge of her long dress, the brief glimpses of the heels and soles of leather shoes as she fled around a curving metal stairwell. *Upward, headed upward.* "I think we were on a roof together once before." His voice was hollow, detached.

"Yes. A roof. City lights as far as the eyes can see!" Feeling suddenly breathless, she dropped her arms and faced him. Contemplating the shallow area beneath his Adam's apple left her with inexpressible sentiments. Furrowing her brow, she bit her lower lip. It seemed that years of dread, decades of joy, infinite inexhaustible tensions flowed with every move this male took, and she had absolutely no idea why.

"You feared me," he echoed a simple statement of fact. "I wasn't attractive. Compared to the men in your magazines how do I stand the test of scrutiny now?" He swallowed hard, lowered his arms in defeat. He could fall, end the masquerade, stop the loneliness.

"Don't. There's no need to feel despair. You're not obligated to me."

Just having her sympathies eased him. "I can't tolerate you attempting to end yourself. I'm not sure what to do about it. We won't put you over our knee, we've never spanked anyone."

"Suffice it to say that I wouldn't like being bullied. Why did you follow me? And who is 'we'?"

Her queries should have made him indignant, instead he warmed to her. He took in the wild brown hair whipped to the side of her head like a pennant in the wind. Half her body was still delectably exposed.

She braced herself for a verbal onslaught, felt certain it was coming. The barrage she sensed issuing from him faded.

"I'm not going to bully you, Christine. 'We' is only me...*sarcastically acknowledging a psychotic splintered personality.* We'll face the reality of our situation when and if we can. Come." He cradled her elbow in his hand. "Let me walk you to your rooms. May I pay you another visit tomorrow morning?"

She was bewildered...and suddenly chilled.

26 *TELEPATHIC INSERTION*

alfway down the stairs, he turned to study her expression and tried to read her thoughts. Aggravated, he wondered why Isidore bothered to put a locater chip in her if no one was going to pay attention to it. He planned to upbraid Isidore as soon as he had her safe. He also thought to kiss her, but didn't want to frighten her after what they'd just experienced. Then he reminded himself that she seemed to feed on the dramatic. His mind was flying. *Why was she up there trying to harm herself?*

Her shoulders lifted, her hands traveling upward.

She wants to caress me! Wait…wait for it. No!

She started fastening the closures on her robe. *Recovering some modesty*, she sent the message not knowing if he received it.

Escorting her the rest of the way, he felt sure they were learning romance in the most backward of all manners. In the hallway outside her door, he rather lamely said, "You should rest. Sleep will help refresh your brain."

She raised her eyebrows in a question. "Will you come into my rooms a moment? There's something I want to show you."

Erik smiled thinly. He wouldn't mind jostling around with her, setting her off balance in that mythical world of ruffled red and gold pillows… teach her how to respond to him, but this wasn't the appropriate night. They needed to connect on a multitude of levels. Lord, how she spun him like a top, moving him from one unsettling apex right into the next. Once upon a time, in another life, surrounded by a grand sumptuous theater, she destroyed his soul. She'd taken his adoration, divisively enjoyed the flattery it represented, and unmercifully crucified his fragile heart. Withholding the affection she ungraciously claimed not to feel, she labeled him shy because he was ugly. She could be cruel. Still, she was so precious. The hope of igniting a tiny spark within her inched him closer. On the roof she'd almost destroyed herself. Worlds were colliding here – time and space compacting too rapidly, sucking the air from his lungs. Christine was a most welcomed obsession.

Despite her allure, the memory of their adversities helped him lean toward postponement. He'd invest the time. He was certain she needed him in ways she didn't comprehend yet.

"Who is this twit of a girl your thoughts are referring to?" she asked. "You pictured her on the roof and right now she's ripping out your heart."

His brain reeled. *She's prying into my head! Is she forging a stronger mental link between us or just nosey?* Studying her stoically, he ordered his mind to lock itself into a basement, an imagined storm cellar, anywhere she couldn't follow. His defensive blocking stopped her from reading his thoughts.

"You like to bluff at cards. It's a strategy." She was electrifying his senses. "You think I'm a clone? What's a clone?"

How did she pull that word from my mind? Yes, you are a clone, in every conceivable way the original Christine and more, much more. In a short whimsical maneuver he fingered the top closure of her damp night coat. The garment was old and soft. Had she found some aging things lying in a chest? *Will you be upset if I take my hand away?*

The young man standing in front of her was a convoluted paradox: exhilarating and charming, scary, one second attentive and the next – so cold. She looked up at him with dreamy eyes. "Somehow I know your touch would soothe every perplexity. Settle every question."

He raised an index finger, pointed it toward the ceiling then sent it straight down to his feet.

Her eyes comically, but obediently followed. Taking in the sight of his side buttoned, British leather boots, she waited.

"Do you mind?" His voice was like an aphrodisiac to her. "As much as I love these, I have got to get them off and relax awhile. I slept in them earlier and now it feels like I own a pair of expanding goblin feet." He kissed her forehead and walked away.

Frankly embarrassed, she blushed and entered her rooms alone.

Invited to share in freshly baked lasagna, Dillard sauntered into the hub of the chateau's security. Located in a steel-plated room off the north wing of the first floor, all the motion sensors, thermal imaging, and camera feeds played 24/7 into these central computers. Glancing to his left, he saw nothing unusual on the bank of twenty-eight monitors scanning the hallways and grounds. Nyah, Kathryn, Isidore, Thayer and John were all clustered around one corner monitor displaying a section of the upstairs corridors. Bent over they listened intently. John straightened and pointed to the pasta resting on a warming plate. A crusty loaf of garlic bread on a cutting board and a large bowl of spinach salad sat off to the side.

"Help yourself," John directed, then returned to whatever was holding their interest. "Take a break and enjoy."

"Everything all right? What's got all you guys stuck together like a group on Afghanistan night patrol?" Dillard laughed, rubbing his scar.

No one answered.

"I have to be proud of him, very inventive," whispered Isidore.

"He's not wasting time," Kathryn agreed. "Brilliantly self-motivated."

Dishing up a healthy portion, Dillard glanced around uneasily. His eyes fell on the locator signal from Erik's chip. It showed him moving down the hallway to his room. Christine was entering hers. In the maddening silence, Dillard licked his dry lips. *Oh, to hell with it.* He stuffed a fork full in his mouth. *Delicious.* "What's got you guys so preoccupied?" He tried to sound matter-of-fact, as if eating this meal was simply an expected obligation.

"Shh," said Nyah, "for once just be still and let us listen."

"We can construct magnificent roads and buildings that touch the sky, but we still haven't learned how to repair an impoverished heart," Kathryn observed seriously.

"Or have we?" mumbled Thayer. "I'm betting he's already formulating a plan."

"A shift in scenery might be all that's required," reasoned Isidore. He was happy to remind them, "He stole her once, perhaps he means to steal her again."

Dillard's back stiffened. "What did you say?"

In the pitch dark of his room Erik occupied a chair. The computer lights allowed him to see all he cared to observe at the moment. While she developed, he'd been allowed to remain close to her. Now they'd put Dillard in the way to keep him distant. The American was like a diligent cheerful beam of sunlight and Erik the cold unbending finger of night. *I will not give up, Christine.* Restless, he ordered his mind to focus on her. *There was a time when we danced through these rooms. An evening when you wore a dress of floral georgette that you couldn't take off fast enough.* He experienced everything so intensely, and speculated to what degree that might be happening for her. They weren't disparate entities; no, they shared a common bond. Both percolated in the same laboratory, both derivations of another life – long ended. Would it be enough, just for the moment, to comprehend what she felt?

He set his mind to wandering until he latched onto her very feminine channel of brainwaves. She slept, adrift in the beginning stages where slow eye movements occur, alpha waves appear, and little muscle jerks are common.

Mentally circling her room, he scanned the sights. There sat the Louis XVI half-moon bureau with its hand painted flowers and vintage ivory finish. Her bedspread, a sea of pomegranates set to a deeper background of red that reflected the art of ancient guilds, and flowed right up to her curly haired head. The ocean of fruit tended to her in a centuries-old promise of fertility and abundance. Erik's hormones surged. Beneath the zipper of his jeans, parts of him demanded liberation. All too conscious of his pressing desire, he knew he was staked and fettered to need. He wanted to arrange a ceremony, take his bride, his mate...and had no trouble admitting it. *She's a rhapsody that makes my skin tingle and my loins ache! How devilishly delightful! I would sign a pact with the head demon to win her. Wait, I already have and his name is Isidore de Chagny.*

Rolling to her left side, Christine threw an arm out over the covers. The vision of a pale-pink, bell-capped sleeve accented with tiers of scalloped lace swamped his mind with possibilities. Inspired by something so minutely feminine, an idea dawned. He had a way to stave off Dillard and provide enough time alone with her to make an indelible impression. Silently congratulating himself, he decided to invade her sleep – cause it to become fitful.

She sat up, ignoring her heavy-lidded eyes and their clamoring to remain closed. Drawing up her knees, she pressed her back into the headboard. Something was wrong. Making herself rigid, she waited. Her tired eyes lashed about and saw nothing unusual. *How foolish, here I am, weak with fatigue and guarded by nothing more than a soft pomegranate-*

decorated comforter. The clock on the mantle struck ten bells. *Not yet the witching hour,* she was probably safe. Her hand reached up. Pulling a chain she turned on the light. She surveyed the room and yanked the light off again.

More alert, she stayed poised, wary to release her vigil. Draped in darkness, with only the ambient outside lights streaming in through the open curtains, she studied the corners of the room. Stark shadows from a tall backyard oak danced in ghoul-like movements across the walls. In the near perfect stillness, the only sound was the faint moaning of the tree's limbs. She concentrated harder. No one walked the grounds, out on the road not even a single car passed by.

Her mind flashed in comprehension. *Was there a movement at the door leading to Erik's room?* She tensed. *Had it opened ever so slightly?* Nothing. A dry chastising snicker escaped her throat. A whiff of night blooming jasmine wafted in the air. What was its source? She pounded the coverlet with her fists. How long should she wait? She needed to sleep. Sinking back into the mound of confection surrounding her, she slammed the ends of two pillows across her face. *What ineffectual providers, these sirens of silken fluff.* Apparently she was still to suffer from Erik's neglect.

He thrived in this role of hunter. Respecting a safe distance, her honor thus far unquestioned and still intact, he eased a set of black-gloved fingers around the traveling side of the door. Out he came, curling round the lip, honing in on her in the dark. *Cold, remorseless stalker!* Something clicked inside his brain…a monk torn to shreds… left to decay at the bottom of an inky oubliette. He refused the image. *NOT NOW, NOT HERE.* His thoughts went crystal clear. He'd erased the picture as easily as switching a TV channel. A lone doubt called out for acknowledgement. *Not worthy! Yes worthy! Worthy in every aspect… and big time ready!*

She slipped from the covers to her feet. "You're here. Did you come to make sure I'm all right?" Amber eyes glinted in the near dark. Unnerving her.

Keeping a tight reign on his labile temper, he stepped to her. Pressing the back of her head with one gloved hand and clamping the other over her mouth, he whispered, "Speak to me only with your mind. Do you understand? There are sensors everywhere that can pick up the slightest sounds. I am positive we can accomplish communication telepathically, without speech. Climb into my head gently, I'll guard my thoughts for you."

She wasn't sure how to interpret that last announcement. Despite the intoxicating feel and glorious smell emitted by her captor, the words 'from corruption' had slipped in alongside 'guard'.

Sensing a sharp uneasiness clouding her acceptance, he let his forehead touch hers. A projection started. A run of almost painful electric shocks sparked and twisted within her brain. The serrated spikes cut new pathways downward from the crown of her head, through her core to her legs and feet. They didn't stop until she nodded in agreement. Pulling his hands away from her head, he went to steady her arms.

He slowly removed a glove and taking her trembling fingertips, held them with only the lightest touch. So fine was the sensation he generated, she could barely move from the disorientation, yet as his hand settled within her grasp the distorted impulse calmed.

When I left you at your door you wanted me to see something. What?

Her eyes widened in wonderment. She'd heard him…again! Soft and encouraging words spoken from inside her head, yet not her own. *There's an etching on the wall by the door entitled 'The Heart Inspired'. An angel with its wings outstretched, chest and face uplifted. I struck the same pose up on the roof trying to recall something this picture inspires in me. I can't remember. I wanted to ask if it evokes anything for you.*

He smiled, genuinely happy. *I created it. It's from an époque millennia away.*

She answered almost inaudibly: *Why have they made it so difficult to hold a private conversation?*

Letting go of her fingers, he explained: *You'd be surprised at the large company of people interested in everything we say and do. If they descended upon us, even as spectators, I'll never forgive them. Besides, their arrival would definitely interfere with my plans.* She was barefoot, the thought of her toes made him smile. *Do you trust me enough to take a trip in a mental dimension?* She nodded. *I want to be alone with you for a while, in a place where no one can listen in. They don't expect you to avoid the confines of the house so early in your life. Go into your bathroom, Christine. I'll wait here. Keep everything out of your head but me. You'll leave by a second door I will disclose. Go through that door and imagine a tunnel. You'll know what to do.* The rustle of her nightgown was her only response.

In the impenetrable blackness of the corridor, from a distance not too far away, his clear strong voice sung out to her. *Christine, Christine.* Sliding her hands along the walls to guide her, she swept her feet in slow arcs, gauging the angle and firmness of the ground beneath her feet. She traveled downward; somehow knowing she headed toward a lake. In the thick musty air, his voice carried across the acoustically perfect waters – a cascade of sounds so pleasant, so melodious, it stirred her heart. She could weep for the joy it brought.

Two simple words came to him when he finished. *More...please.* Yet he sensed her resistance to come further. Stretching out both his arms, he extended a fierce magnetic attraction. Willing her to him. Radiating across the water, his love filled the space between them. *Christine, sometimes a person has to let go to discover who they are.* The air above the water took on a misty delicate quality. He flexed his arms and singing in soothing tranquil tones willed her forward.

Cocooned within the spell of his mellow baritone, she felt her reluctance dissolve and her anticipations rise. Slowly she began to believe in the possibility of levitation – sailing beyond corporeal awareness. She tentatively wished herself upward and felt her feet rising off the shore, as if she could fly to him on nothing but air.

Once she started, Erik experienced a nearly indescribable joy.

No! The refusal itself planted her feet firmly back down on solid ground. *It is not time to float. You want me to surrender? Compromise myself?*

He paced the shore in agitation. *We were both compromised long before this and in ways you can't imagine, because Isidore hasn't bothered to explain them.*

She responded with a warning. *Isidore will admonish you for recklessness.*

No doubt he'll counsel me for rushing you. Shall I tell him that our almost intimate meeting was born of my zealousness? That you're not at fault because I brought you down here against your will? By the way, I have no idea if he cares past scientific curiosity. He's liable to say nothing beyond, 'Can I stick a probe into your cerebellum?' Ahead in the yawning blackness he considered how to bolster Christine's confidence. Why was she still hesitant to respond to the call of his mind? Her doubts trapped her. Nothing new, but knowing how to maneuver out of them in this lifetime was another predicament all together. In a veritable world it might be easier. *Ah, yes! Abbreviate the darkness.*

As if on cue, the level of light surrounding her gradually rose, dispelling the deepest shadows, distributing a sense of reassurance. The rocky outcrops above the phosphorescent bluish waters appeared as only dark humps. No longer threatening since she could delineate their character. The surface of the lake lying between them fluttered with tiny waves, sending up tendrils of mist. She shivered and the moisture rolled in, enveloping her like a comforting blanket.

Are you chilled, Christine? It's a warm breezeless night.

She began to move, allowing him the experience of a deep surge of satisfaction. Her nearing presence sent a sweet harmonious rush of heat between them. When he could see her, he curled his fingers in invitation, a powerful possessiveness settling over him.

As she descended, she asked: *How did you raise the light?*

Using only thought. He caught her engaging hand with a laugh and led her toward an even more isolated spot. *In the ocean of a laboratory vat, not too far from here, I emblazoned my voice upon your heart.*

I remember lustrous singing, she admitted grudgingly.

He spun around and abruptly clasped her about the waist, his thumbs pressing prime stimulus points in the oblique abdominal muscles situated beneath her ribs. The staged atmosphere reverted back to inky blackness.

The response to this profoundly insistent touch was unnerving. Little hitched gasps escaped her throat. A passion seemed to be exploding out of nowhere. In some enduring essential way she felt glued to him. Frightened of the emotional intensity, she clutched at his jacket.

You must trust me, he reassured. *We are out of earshot, outside their reach. Over here I've constructed a place for us. If you consent, we can be bound together on the softest bed of sand imaginable.*

Listening to the energy concealed within his breathing, she sensed him caught in lust. He was transferring the intensity of his need. *You mean to have between my legs?*

He frowned. *You think I'd jump to extremes? Don't always put the most animalistic interpretation possible on every impulse that passes between us. I know how to restrain myself and won't go anywhere you don't permit. Actually, I'll wait until you beg me to go there. I would never hurt you.*

True, but you might claim me before another can present a suit.

In agony he crawled deeper into her mind. *Look how you fit so perfectly in my arms.* He encircled her like a patient greedy boa constrictor, seeing what she would tolerate. He would labor most diligently to rediscover what lay beyond her resistance.

Trembling, she felt his lips come to rest upon the corner of her mouth. His breath sent little bursts of warmth cruising through her veins. An insistent tender tongue teased its way between her lips, brushing rhythmically against her teeth. Prodding gently, it seemed to ask for entrance into the depths of her mouth. He aroused feelings in her, ignited blatant hungers she could barely cope with, much less address. Still reluctant, she conceded that all these sensations felt rather delicious.

How quickly do you want me naked? Shocked that she'd asked such a question, she pulled away, pushing his chest roughly with the flat of her palms. *No!* She screamed inside his head.

He winced, acknowledging grimly: *Ok, now we know for sure that you can shout telepathically. Have some tact. No more vehement outcries. I'll go deaf. Come back into my arms, Christine. Learn to trust me. Shall we dance? Do you know what a waltz is yet?*

That strangely familiar perfume of night blooming jasmine drifted through the space between them. She came back to him, letting his arms encompass her.

Does this feel nice? He soothed: *Not threatening?* They moved with their own rhythm to a classical piece he supplied to the conscious awareness they were actively sharing.

You're not gruff or coarse, but you do seem to love moody scenes. You find this habitat stimulating?

He swayed with her, dancing slowly along a path, letting her decide where to place her feet. He longed to see her eyes filled with a love that refused to hide the baser desire to mate. But if those lovely doors to her soul mirrored only a core of honest curiosity, he'd settle for that.

How do I get off this island?

There's a small boat over there, but you won't need to row.
Rowing will be good for my arms, I think. I'm not very strong yet.
Open your eyes, Christine.

There was no mist – the air was clear and still. It was her brain that was foggy. She'd never left the chateau. She flipped on the light switch. Actually she'd never left the bathroom. Everything that happened occurred because Erik settled in her head…realistically visited her limbic system, the center for emotion and motivation.

Back in Security's central office, Dillard switched on a set of infrared thermal resolution cameras. Instantly revealing the location of the pair. Erik stood outside Christine's bathroom door and she just inside the *salle de bains.*

"They're standing, right? A door between them?" Dillard asked concerned. He didn't know if it was guilt or jealousy he was expressing.

"Hush, dammit! We let you join us, but you're such a bozo," John admonished.

"Yes, they're upright. They've been like that for ten minutes," Thayer noted with regret. "Glad I didn't make a bet on this."

"Sixteen year olds are fickle creatures," Nyah added appraising the situation. "We need to make her more inaccessible…make him want to install himself as her principal desire."

"You're playing matchmaker?" Dillard queried skeptically.

"Sometimes you're as thick as a chuck of wood," Kathryn rolled her eyes.

Dillard didn't even bother trying to sound civil. "I'll go up and check on her. Erik shouldn't be in her room." In two shakes of a dog's tail he could grab an automatic machinegun off a metal peg, go to the front of the house and spray bullets into the air. That would interrupt whatever the hell they were doing.

Christine returned to bed and slept like a child in her massive four-poster. But the rest of the night proved a long arduous journey for Erik. He lay there in a hypnagogic state demanding to know how a woman could be this complex. Sleep came eventually. Deep in the third level, where delta waves appear and dreaming is common, he experienced the most appalling vision to date. The question as to why the former Erik left

France had never actually been asked, he'd assumed that in that lifetime he'd simply run off to find the world. Though he empathized with his previous trials, he did not always understand the incentives. The two personalities had not completely converged, though the probability of full lucidity grew increasingly stronger with every passing day.

At four in the morning Erik awoke full of dread, feeling like he stood in snow and ice. Grabbing some clothes he made his way down to Isidore's room. Kneeling beside the sleeping figure, he quietly said, "Wake up old man, we need to talk."

Groggy eyed, a nearly chinless Isidore looked at Erik. "Hand me my mask. What's wrong?"

"When we were young you lied to us, told us our mother died of an amniotic embolus, that her demise could not be helped."

"You know the foundation for the lie, to place me as the sole person in charge of deciding how you should be raised. I had hoped that believing you'd been saved would make you feel special."

"When you raised your hand in that grand flourish of yours, exposing our genetic lineage…there was more you kept hidden, yes?"

Isidore was coming to full alertness. "Was it such a shock to learn that Nyah was the descendent of the Marchioness Pascale de Grasse? Nyah is as noble as her ancestor, she bravely courted my scientific mind and was willing to give her body to our experiments."

"To be honest, I think I intuitively guessed at the lie. On some level I knew my mother was still alive, and that in truth she was Nyah. You need to get up out of bed. I killed my mother."

A dull glassy-eyed look of grief spread across Isidore's eyes, "Nyah is dead?"

"No, not Nyah. Nyah never caused me harm. Some other woman… there were insults and abuse. Detrimental neglect. A distortion of personality."

"Such a morbid temperament you have. I assure you, the only mother that matters – though she has never directly declared her sentiments – is forever glad she brought you and Torossian into this world."

"Nevertheless, I've had a vivid, terrifying recollection. I don't feel any remorse or grief…just shock. I have to understand before I go any further."

Bewildered but resolute, Isidore ordered Erik to assist with getting his crotchety legs over the side of the mattress. "Perhaps the bodyguard staying so close is upsetting you in these early stages of your relationship with Christine. Where's my walker?"

"Brush your teeth," Erik declared flatly, sliding the walker to him.

Isidore hobbled toward the bathroom.

"I disgust myself," Erik waited by the dresser. "The intensity of my reactions during this last murder show me, quite clearly, that I was bankrupt of any moral compass. It's time for explicit honesty. I'm incorporating these recollections into my psyche, can they be controlled?"

"We had hoped that Christine's presence would dispel some of the more particularly disturbing aspects. That once all was known, these visions or regressions would become an aberrant phase you simply passed through on the way to maturity. Our original plan was to reveal everything we knew gradually, and in stages appropriate to what your young years might accept. Perhaps creating Christine has complicated the process, further distorting the entire time line."

"So the answer to my question is: We don't know if they can be controlled. There's a possibility that all my days and nights will be spent evading monsters from the past, monsters that chase me like ghouls bent on digging my grave."

"These memories are making you over-reactive, almost paranoid. Don't be so pessimistic, we have a secret weapon in Thayer Delaquois." Isidore punched a button on his bedside table.

A crisp masculine voice answered, "Yes, Sir."

"Send someone to Dr. Delaquois' rooms," Isidore directed. "Ask him to get up. Erik and I are going down to the lab."

27 ONE IS THE LOWLIEST NUMBER

$\mathfrak{R}$igid and anxious, Erik sat semi-reclined in an exam chair, not unlike those found in a dentist's office. Thayer walked around the room reading notes while Isidore sat anxiously perched on a chair. A microphone hung from the ceiling just over Erik's head. Thus far, all Delaquois had intravenously injected into him was a mild tranquilizer.

Wide-awake, Thayer closed his journal with a snap and promptly took a seat to Erik's right. He spoke with utter kindness, "You will see what is about to unfold as an informative tableau. If my hand touches yours, you will remember, above all else, that you are outside these events and not entangled in them. It is paramount in your mind that this is but the recollection of a journey, and as such cannot affect you. During the trip you will recount for us, outloud and in detail, what you see, but only as one observing a movie or flipping through the pages of a picture book. Staying relaxed, you'll move past your most recent years, directing yourself to proceed backwards to the upsetting period that concerns us tonight."

"The time I committed matricide. I think we should just say the word. I killed my mother."

"Yes, all right. Matricide. I've strapped your wrists for your own safety. Ketamine is a powerful psychotropic drug. You'll be dissociated from the lab's surroundings, but only for a short duration. There will be profound analgesia and perhaps some marked nystagmus, so keep you eyes closed. All your pharyngeal and laryngeal reflexes will remain intact. You'll be comfortable and tell us the story untroubled by the safety of this mild confinement."

Erik summoned the Revenant, ordering him to stay in the hall and be on guard for anything untoward. He nodded to Thayer who slowly injected the drug. At first, his mind sank into a dark cauldron of perplexity. Then he experienced a series of brilliant flashes – clear bubbles crowded with tiny pictures that burst around him like a 360 degree IMAX Theater. The dizzying kaleidoscopic effects of ketamine were nauseating – he needed to control this high-speed cinematography, learn to slow it down, to be both asleep and awake enough to focus his memory.

Thayer noted a mild rise in blood pressure and pulse. "You'll scan all the memories, paying particular attention to those that trouble or excite you," he suggested. "Identifying, then letting go of those that are not related to your biological mother. Take the story backwards, Erik. Where are you?"

Their marvelously adaptive patient began with a strange indifferent tinge to his voice. "A Sunday afternoon wedding – an entire night of celebration is planned. There's to be a picnic luncheon on the following day. I've expanded the library making more space for a classroom. There are dozens of books with armorial bindings on the shelves. I love those books. They are my friends."

Isidore nodded thoughtfully to Thayer, showing his agreement.

Erik continued, "I'm worried about the exposure of my true identity and concerned for my children. They are all so willful, but Sarah is particularly prone to error. Given to hedonism and constantly striving to control every situation. Why can't she be more like her mother and less like me? By early evening the ceremony is concluded. The household staff is bustling to serve the guests. Sarah and Michael have disappeared…free from supervision they are exploring other interests. I don't know it yet, but they've rendezvoused with a pirate."

"Further, Erik, go back further," directed Thayer.

"I've dug several channels, expanded the area of natural runoff and found an underground spring to feed another pond. I like to work in the water and the sludge, it makes me feel as though I'm of some benefit, but nothing expunges my crimes…not even building a chapel. We share a number of responsibilities and a good many secrets with the family of the Baron Castelot-Barbezac. Together we employ a number of charades to hide our activities. Jean has become famous for breeding superior horses. Our women have two houses on *Rue du Renard*. One is rebuilt. It stands across the street from the ballet studio. Several times a month the women go to Paris and stay in their townhouses for the weekend. Over the years an accumulation of sewing, furniture, household articles and clothes to outfit the children for the school year has built up. Clutter. But everyone is loathe to part with these properties since so much history has evolved there."

"Those houses are no longer standing," murmured Isidore. "The land sold decades ago."

Erik continued going backward. "After Imel's death we should have melted a heavy gold mask presented to me by the Shah. The money the gold brought could have paid the debts left by Raoul. But Christine will not hear of parting with the thing and I am secretly glad not to surrender ownership of an item that cost so dearly to acquire. So much life destroyed."

Isidore scratched a quick note to Thayer:

That mask is in the vault!

"And before *Rue du Renard?*" questioned the neuropsychiatrist.

"I'm fingering a jacket of black baize. I've learned to weather the cold in these dark caverns, to let rock and dirt encapsulate me. It takes patience to live this life of isolation. Louisa loved and caressed me, took me under her protection in my misfortune and held me safe from threat as much as possible. Dozens of inspiring ideas drive my music, but they cannot ease the close and ceaseless darkness that smothers me. I am buried alive. Like a drab little *segue* I must proceed to what follows without pause, my heart clamoring for *mezzo forte*. There is a potential *chanteuse*, a naïve girl who might be a wondrous concert songstress. Still a virgin, she does not know that Fate has intended her for me."

"Her name?" asked Thayer, knowing full well what would come forth next.

"Christine Daae."

"What holds you back from speaking your mind to her?" Thayer prompted, unaware that years were rapidly regressing for Erik.

"A good chain, each link forged strongly, holds the shackles on my wrists and ankles. Caged, I am taken to a prison. There to be whipped, perhaps beheaded. I can sense my doom. The better prince has forsaken his comfortable palace life, denounced his right of succession. I congratulate myself that at least the savage self-possessed brother will not inherit the throne. Scarce equanimity in that no real justice has been served."

Momentarily confused, Thayer frowned deeply. "Persia? Come forward in time, Erik. You've left the Middle East and returned to France. Without any sense of strain or want, you stand beside this other

Erik...outside of Rouen. Composed and passive, tell us what you see and all you feel."

"I'm hungry. I stole food for this final leg of the journey to avoid being seen. I am still imperfect, but I don't seem to care. I hate them all, the entire world. I know that love and acceptance will never happen. My life is a farce. It's taken some time to locate the house I seek, not because my memory is faulty, but because it's been six years. Some things have changed and it's winter now. The countryside is covered in snow and it's still falling. This is a wet backbreaking cold, it drenches and freezes me through to my very core.

"I've found the wrought iron fence that surrounds the house and followed the snow drift to an iron spike. Furred in rust, the spike acts as an anchor for a once pretty gate. Oxidation from lack of care is claiming it. Long rotted, ready to fall to the ground, the heavy snow locks the gate in place. In the center of the gate is the painted iron medallion of a white *fleur-de-lis*. The symbol of the lily sits in the center of a circular field of blue, etched with gold. At their midpoints the edges of the petals curl inward slightly. Strange that I should be so taken with this piece of iron trash. I feel no sentimental drivel for the thing; perhaps I am simply reluctant to look up. The house is set back into the property about an eighth of a mile. I can see it further down the path. There are no lights on inside, no smoke curls from the chimneys. I speculate that it might be empty and brace myself for what I shall discover. Using my gloved hands, I shove the gate through the fallen snow.

"I have come home, but expect no welcome. There stands the federal style house, exterior bricks painted gray, steep darker-slate roof. My eyes search for a familiar dormer window tucked under the eaves. I spot it all too quickly. Behind that window stands the attic where I spent my first years. Reared in isolation. The air is thin, frigid with cold. Dawn is coming. I head right, down the driveway that leads toward the front of the house. A susurrus sound fills the air around me – the barren skeletal branches of oaks not ten yards away rubbing together. Looking around I assure myself that the whispered rustling is only those barren frozen limbs. The gray sky above is heavy with clouds and the dismal snow still comes – like crystal tears mounting in piles upon the ground.

"At the juniper shrubs that stand before the somber walls of the main parlor, I stomp my feet to warm them. Glass crunches beneath the soles of my boots. What is this I wonder? Pieces of broken glass lay scattered all about. Someone's thrown a brown liquor bottle through the main front window. I kick the half-exposed bottleneck free of the ice that holds it.

"I gain entrance by picking the lock to the front door, and thus commit myself to trespassing. The parlor is to the right, all the furniture still there. A set of lace curtains blows inward with the snow. The shattered window has turned this section of the house into a block of ice. The effect is almost religious in force, the tomb of a frigid cuckold. Devoid of emotion I take in the compromised room. It's rather picturesque with its exposed rough-hewn ceiling beams and thick floorboards. Behind the couch and curio cabinets, a once burnished wainscoting rises four feet upward on the interior walls. On a side table sits a glass vase holding a bouquet of silk roses. Once a brilliant bloody red, the flowers have faded to a duller shade – like me, they are too late for dramatic transformation. Beside the vase, in a fancy crystal candy dish lays the remnants of a sad group of smoked cigarettes. Their pungent smoldering put to a final end. I walk over to them. Several cylinders are still rather long. I pick one up and let my nose travel down its side. Interesting, an Egyptian import.

"In the adjoining dining area, on a linen-covered table set for two, I find a dish of half-eaten *foie gras*, a stack of blinis ready to be served with dollops of crème fraiche and jarred peaches, a dish of Russian caviar, and some half-eaten shrimp. She lives well and serves her guest rather expensive specialties. I try to steady my hands, but they jitter from hunger. My current needs win out, so I feed myself on the frozen food she has not eaten. I know I need strength to view what sleeps in her bedroom.

"She didn't wake up until noon. I'm waiting in her room, a place I hate more than any dungeon. I've made the chamber as dark as possible and sit in a chair cloaked in shadows. She lays in an alcoholic stupor on the right-hand side of her bed, the body of her lover beside her. Grown heavier, she is nothing like the sylphlike woman she used to be. Earlier I restrained her wrists and ankles to the head and footboards, left her bare feet to stick out from beneath the covers. She was always a little pigeon-toed. But her lubricious skin is still soft from the ample use of creams and lotions.

"The lingering stench of sex and foul sweat pervades the air, making the hairs of my one good nostril curl. I know she rarely (if ever) experiences any kind of sexual euphoria. She performs the act as a perfunctory attempt to avoid loneliness.

"When she finally stirs, her eyelids flutter open. She lets vision help her sift through the dense miasma of groggy thinking. Lifting her head, she notices the dark atmosphere of the room. I've allowed for only a small ribbon of daylight to come through the window's drapes. Enough scant illumination to let her identify objects. With an odd comprehension, I see dust motes floating visibly in the air on that beam of morning light. Small tiny C-shaped pieces of dust that I imagine are cradles, each containing a microscopic child.

"She struggles against the strips of leather, twisting her wrists and ankles, fighting half-heartedly to get free. I know her joints are complaining, that she needs to move them, walk about. Frustrated, she smacks her tongue against the roof of her mouth. No doubt she feels like another drink would dampen the gnawing pain inside her head, but it has never been her practice to imbibe spirits until late afternoon. We are creatures who find it difficult to deviate from powerfully ingrained habits.

"'If only I'd won the game, this morning would be perfect,' she croaked with a dry throat.

"I wonder who she is addressing. *Ah*, the lover.

"'What? Not one note of sympathy for your Feigel-Evie?' She shoves him with her hip. The lecher's natural balding pattern was not dissimilar to a monk's tonsure, leaving the crown of his head exposed. He has grown a detestable shade of blue, but she hasn't noticed yet. Now I know for sure that her head is killing her.

"Losing energy, she pulls the ties less vigorously, still unaware that I've returned. Without a sound or hint of smirk on my face, I throw a knife. The blade whizzes past her temple, sinking itself with a *thwamp* into the burled cherry wood headboard. Unable to comprehend what has just happened, she lays still and tentatively sniffs the air. She frowns disdainfully at the aroma of bodies in need of soaps, and catches just a whiff of necrotic tissue. Lifting her head again, she looks toward her feet and notices the out of place cheval mirror set at the foot of her bed. I've placed it to cast her reflection back to her.

"With a tone scrubbed of all emotion, I remark, 'Your avid collection of lovers has always unsettled my nerves.'

"Initially shocked to hear my voice, her eyes dart about, eventually locking onto the corner where I sit angled behind the mirror. When I see how cleverly she's discerned me, my soul hardens. 'Hypocrete lecteur,' my voice is soft and sarcastic. 'According to Virgil: Time bears away all things. Except of course, the prodigal son.'

"She strains to keep her head up off the pillow, 'Apparently time brings them back as well! Is that you, Boy? Let me see your face. I gave birth to it. Has aging helped any? You're a young man now. Fourteen... fifteen?'

"I feel not a twinge of compunction to grant her the manifestation, so I keep my face in shadow. 'Yes, the prodigal son returns. And what was the given name of this good son? No one knows, because his mother didn't wish to grant him an appellation. She only called him Boy, Unworthy Boy.'

"'You sit so quietly. I heard that you'd gone with the Romani and become something of a gypsy thief. Why is it so cold in here? My toes are nearly bitten with frost.'

"'I boarded up the broken window downstairs. Did your lover win whatever game you two played, and throwing the bottle out the window, scoop you up to haul you to bed? The fireplaces gave up their dying embers hours ago. Sorry I didn't bank the wood to warm you up. I wanted to be as inconsiderate as your latest companion. Besides, after the hot sands of Persia the cold is refreshing.'

"'Move the mirror,' she commanded unceremoniously.

"I extend my arm, angling the glass so she can see both her lover and herself. Something perverse in me wants to needle her. 'An old expression states that there is no comfort at table unless there are at least two. Can you take in the pleasant view?'

"With a surprisingly dismissive expression, she admits, 'I need a bath.'

"I peek around the mirror with my normal left eye, keeping the other half of my face concealed. Her gaze reflects the vast emptiness in my own soul. 'What no witty repartee? Relax,' I direct condescendingly. 'Your stink creates its own brand of perfume.'

"'Lacertian Bucher,' she calls to her bedfellow. 'Wake up and help me untie these straps!'

"'Derelict woman, the lover beside you is dead! I didn't care for his pitted pock-scarred face. I hope he served you well as he cannot function now.'

"Her eyes grow round and rove the ceiling, avoiding acceptance of my words while she strives to gauge the amount of danger my presence poses. At last she looks at the gray donut-haired man. She tries to scream in disgust, but not a sound comes forth. The muscles in her larynx close down with fear.

"'No need to choke yourself. I haven't decided what shocking compensation I shall claim for all your scheming and abuse.'

"Waves of gathering panic wash over her. She jerks her head and sees my dagger, but knows she cannot quite reach it. I have placed it as a strategic tease. She wiggles and kicks. Yanking at the unforgiving leather that holds her wrists to the headboard, she stretches in a fruitless attempt to free her hands using her teeth. Then manages to produce a sort of strangled outcry. Acting the part of the menacing intruder, I approach as a black wraith from behind the mirror. Deliberately silent, eerie and forbidding – I move with the gliding tread I have been taught. Snatching two discarded stockings trailing down the front of the bureau, I ball one up and as she gains volume, place the sphere of undergarment within her gullet. I run the other around the back of her skull and tie it with a pretty bow beneath her nose to hold the wad in her mouth. 'Let me encourage the same degree of silence you demanded of me.' Staying detached, but dangerously close, I let my eyes blaze into hers. She kicks her feet, rocks her shoulders up and down, as if the futile gestures could chase me away! I try to reward her with my most magnetic smile, but I'm afraid my exaggerated attempt appears more like a sneer. She seems genuinely frightened.

"Standing there beside the bed, I remove my pocket watch. I loathe touching her with my hands; to me she is the infidel. But I order my fingers to travel to the base of her right thumb, and there I count the pulse of her radial artery. Her heart rate is accelerated. At last, I have her rapt attention. 'Yes, I have some new skills. A Persian proverb states: No man becomes clever without consulting a clever man. I have been with such a man, learned from such a man. I'm going to calm you by rubbing a salve containing an opiate into your palm.'

"After I apply the ointment, I wait a few minutes before passing my hand down over her forehead, closing her despondent eyes. 'Sleep, woman. Sleep. Enjoy your peevish dreams. You have a few hours before the drug wears off.'

"The next time she recovers her mental faculties, she is tied to a chair at the table. The inviting smell of freshly made coffee fills the air. The body of her dead lover is nowhere in sight.

"When I hear the legs of her chair scraping along the wooden floor I enter the dining room. I take a seat opposite the woman who robbed me of a childhood. 'We have some serious subjects to discuss.' Divorced of compassion, I keep my rage contained. I cannot allow anger to rule me. My calmness has alarmed her. She stares at my masked face with the wild eyes of a rabbit about to be butchered. 'It is the manner of men in the Middle East to shave their hair as a sign of grief. Take comfort in the sight of my curls still attached to my head. I want to tell you about a young woman I met. She had her whole life before her and longed for death because the Shah promised her to his cruelest son. She begged for my assistance. I didn't deserve the honor she conferred on me, but tried not to fail in the duties of an obliging executioner. This girl's character was so strong – rather than live a life of humiliation and degradation – she chose the silence of the grave. She had a name like a song: Soha Houri. Even you have a name, but I was not worthy of one. Was I a walking-talking afterbirth that you only called me Boy?'

"She deliberately slows her breathing, trying hard to maintain some semblance of control. I press on, 'Oh, I know I'm cheating, calling you to court without a warrant, but this is not a joke, life is unpredictable. I'm only being systematic – lining up the charges against you. Evil woman, your soul is more distorted than my own. Your thirst for alcohol and lovers never ended. Your inane bantering went on-and-on about how God laid too heavy a burden on you. What you claimed to endure sucked every glimmer of innocent happiness from my young mind. You ranted that the sight of me made you physically sick. Your profound, irrational unease at the appearance of my distorted face instilled such shame within me. I swear, the effect could not have been worse had you done me violence. Did you ever consider what your venomous words and rigorous isolation actually generated in me? Oh, you conjured such desperate feelings within my soul. What would a little pity, a little tenderness have cost you? In that pit of a chest that holds your heart there is not a drop of mother's love. In that cold void you spawned a man who surprises and violates the will of others without a qualm. Abominable witch! If you had beat me at least I would have thought you cared a little. But I wasn't worth even that exertion.'

"I push back my chair. 'Now, as a reward for not pestering me today, I've taken the trouble to prepare you a meal. You might consider it your last supper.' I reach up and untie the bow of the stocking in front of her lips. She uses her tongue to push the ball of fabric from her mouth.

"'Water, please,' she coughs out the words.

"'Coming right up,' I reply. Her kitchen has water in abundance. On its shelves I found clear glass jars of peaches, pears, and apples. She had taken the time to collect and prepare some of autumn's produce from the orchards in the area. There was also a wheel of cheese and bread, a bowl of dried cherries and another of black walnuts. I fetch not only her request, but also a bottle of port and a copper kettle with a potato and dried mutton stew I made while she slept. For some reason there were no carrots or turnips to be had.

"I feed her in silence. The stillness must be unnerving for she shivers and starts offering information. 'A group of architects and talented engineers are building a great theater in Paris, a grand Opera House to entertain people for centuries to come.'

"Furious, I put down the fork. She wants to compromise my retribution with chitchat! I stand behind her, looming over her chair. 'Shall we visit the attic?' A primitive guarding causes her muscles to tense. There is a fairly extensive library in another room, full of books and architectural scrolls scattered over a few pieces of gilded furniture. As a child, I was allowed to go in there during the early hours of morning, but prohibited from the parlor with its crimson oriental carpet and huge fireplace that spread such warmth. She forbade me any cheerful atmosphere where I might learn civility. The library and the hated upstairs attic were the only spaces I was permitted. Those two areas were all I really knew as a child. Since she believed that such an ugly example of Divine anger didn't deserve a formal education, I took great pains to teach myself to read. A quick intellect helped immensely.

"Apprehensive, she declares with rushing words, 'I don't want to go into the attic!'

"I free her from the chair, leaving her wrists tied, and practically drag her to a door that declares itself just a closet. 'Shall we look inside?' I taunt. 'Together we can reconstruct the path upward into purgatory!' The unfinished cubbyhole of exposed plaster and lath smells of dust and old things. Thirteen wooden stairs mark the ascension to my former home. 'I've written something original in prose for you, though I fear the piece is rather dreadful. You'll have to tell me if it suits your fancy. Do you promise to give it serious consideration?' I push her toward my old quarters, but she lets the steep incline of the stairs work against me. Using her full weight as a passive opposing force, she presents a challenge for me to overcome.

"'I could drug you again…to ease the horrors of this revelation, but I'm at the bottom of the Well of Kindness.' Sobbing hysterically, she manages to flee my grasp and my arm whips out to apprehend her. 'You lack grace and agility in those fancy heels. Let me assist you.'

"Leaning down, I pull off her shoes. Barefoot, the cold of the wooden floor sends a chill up her spine. 'A firmer grip to assist you, perhaps?' With me shoving her rump, she starts to crawl the ascent of the thirteen wooden stairs. I have a strange almost morbid thought that as a child I should have named them. I was neglectful.

"On the rough boards of the attic floor rests the ratty mattress I slept on. Beside the mattress is a rack for drying the sacks I wore over my head as a child and the two ragged sets of clothes she'd given me. I had no pillow, but where the pillow should have been sits a jar of coal tar – an unguent for chicken pox. When I was five, she ordered me to spread the salve on my body, never caring that I couldn't reach the pustules on my back. Today a single candle flame in a brass holder lights up the entire exposition. I sit her down on the mattress and place myself as an obstacle between her and the door. 'Ready?' I ask."

Since Erik continued to speak in the first person, Thayer took his hands, "Remember to describe the scene as if you are viewing it from the sidelines. You are emotionally distant as you relate what happens next and how she responds."

Erik sighed. "Pulling a paper from my jacket pocket, I proceed to read. Frowning at the dogged escape of my own sarcasm.

You swaddled me with your disgust,
Yet I thrived, bathed in derision.
Every boy regards his mother, hoping he will please.
You called me evil, seeing only my distortion,
And you had such a lovely face
To front your hollow soul.
Heart cast in iron,
bitter grievous wounds you etched.
Observe the truth, though I know you can't.
You robbed what's most precious,
A basic regard for life.
Tis the hand of vengeance that reaches to destroy you.
And it has no name, for you chose to give it none.

"'No negotiations!' I'm fuming. 'My final ultimatum is that you cease to breathe, become God's victim one last time.' Like a magician employing a card trick, I produce the Punjab lasso and cast it from my hand. Choking her, I feel such a release. Her fingers clutch the sleeves of my jacket in frenzied complaint. The braid actually sings at the silent screaming face growing cyanotic from want of air.

"'Don't have a spasm, not yet. Isn't this fun?' I am a tease. She sinks unconscious onto the filthy mattress, the Punjab still laced around her neck. How apropos, that she should end in stages here in the attic. A world upon itself, with its own set of macabre rules, and its history of a strange little boy with his head ritually stuck in a bag. I'd forgotten to inquire about the date of my birth. We never celebrated it.

"I become so agitated at my own irrational forgetfulness that I go to the rack. Taking the larger of the two small jackets, I begin ripping the fabric with my teeth. My distraught moaning and the tearing sound of the cloth wake her. Coughing and rubbing her neck, she rolls to her side. I throw the shreds of the garment in her face. 'Here, I don't need these anymore.' Still trying to breathe, she bats the tatters aside.

"I retrieve them like they were precious jewels and hang the sad remnants on the poles of the rack. 'You so carelessly discard what might well save your life.'

"'Don't care,' she rasps.

"I reach for the lasso and choke her again. Then I stand, waiting vacantly, as she regains consciousness a second time. I ask her for my birth date. When she does not reply, I re-introduce myself, 'I am your Angel of Death!' And speed her on to Satan.

"Pacing the attic, I chase away creeping admonitions. I am well beyond their reach. Angered into irrationality, I set the candle flame to the strips of old clothes. Inhaling the pungent smoke gives me a bizarre sense of relief. When the excruciating need for oxygen burns within my own lungs – a fundamental need to live becomes paramount. 'FIRE!' I yell as if someone in another room might hear me scream the word.

"I can hardly believe that in my rage and dismay, I have become the victim of my own disordered thinking. I've set fire to the attic. In a frenzy, I use the mattress to get the flames under control."

He grew silent and Thayer let him take a minute before saying, "Go on. Finish it."

"I buried her and her latest lover in the sub-straight of the basement where plinths of nearly black granite formed the lowest level of the foundation. With all my rankling ire spent, I left the house painfully aware that one is the lowliest number. Out on the path I paused to punch the back of the *fleur-de-lis* medallion off the gate and take it with me before vanishing into the snowy drifts. For years I banned her from my mind. Never again did I want her image to offend me. The trauma she wrecked within my soul did not resurrect itself until I fell in love with Christine. Years later I painted Feigel-Evie's exact likeness from memory and hung it on a wall in my office at the chateau."

In telling the tale young Erik grew stronger. His intellect accepting the memories quiescently harbored in his DNA. Laying claim to an important area of his former persona, he internally reconciled a number of inexplicable traits. He wanted more of the original Erik's resolve. The man was ruthless and remorseless, he could always follow through.

In the lab's examination room Erik's voice grew excited. The air crackled with an electrical charge. Small sparks actually arced from his fingertips. He ignored the pain. "I used to spend hours walking the roads of this estate. Letting the rain hammer my head as I tried vainly to recapture this memory of Feigel-Evie. I wanted to deal with its impact, but couldn't. She was the impetus for so much of my insanity. My inability to acknowledge her treatment and what I had done in response, were keys to the origin of my mental instability. The events that followed her barbarous rearing only compounded things. I killed my mother with a unique skill I learned in Persia. Here, pull the Punjab lasso from my jacket pocket. I have one, though I don't know how I managed to bring it with me from my last seizure."

Isidore ran his fingers through what little hair he had left. "You could have brought him out of this recollection in a more sangfroid state of mind, Thayer! He's too anxious...his blood pressure too elevated."

"It wasn't just matricide, it was retribution. Get this intravenous out of my arm," Erik bent forward, but was unable to reach the needle with his teeth. Outside the room Torossian stood ready, waiting for Erik to signal.

Delaquois managed to press Erik's shoulders back onto the chair.

"Calm yourself, son. I agree. *Cherchez la dame*, eh? It does seem that her negligence and abuse compounded your donor's psychosis. To some extent she was the catalyst behind his dreadful crimes, all those horrid acts he committed!"

"Dark and wanton tendencies fed the soul of that woman. My mission in returning to Rouen was to level accounts. But why did I suppress the memory of the murder and then nag myself the rest of my life, desperately trying to remember what I had done? I think I wanted to face the terror of it for Christine's sake. I was always building walls between us."

"I'll undo the straps if you can regain some composure," Thayer didn't reach for the buckles.

"Please, Dr. Delaquois. I am trying to calm myself and the ties are not helping. They make me feel trapped."

"You experience this man's pain so acutely. I have a proposal," Isidore thoughtfully rubbed his hands together. "Let's go find this house outside Rouen. If it's gone we'll look up the records. No son of mine should suffer the burden of such guilt. If this woman existed, and it seems she did, we'll find out how she died."

A clear nerve-shattering voice came from the doorway. "Woe to the woman who finds herself at the hands of one so dry of pity, so drained of soul. If there was any purity in that female, she showed no evidence of its existence." They turned to see the Revenant stretching out his hand. Under Torossian's bidding, Erik's restraints unbuckled. As soon as he was free, his brother ripped the IV from his vein.

"You persevered!" Torossian ground a fist against his own chest. "You would have given anything for three words of genuinely inspired love from those harsh uncaring lips."

"Yes, 'I love you' would have meant the world." Erik moved to embrace his brother.

Standing with his arms at his side, the Revenant growled in recognition and let himself be hugged. His chilled gray hands came to Erik's elbows. *I made the Punjab lasso and put it in your hand. You didn't bring it back. You wanted one and your visions showed me how.*

Erik winked then kissed the pale inhuman cheek. *Let it be our secret.*

"Don't go to Rouen. It's dangerous for you to be outside the chateau." Torossian bore the burden of some terrible dread.

Erik couldn't put his finger on the context of the apprehension; it was almost reverential. "I won't go broadcasting who I am, all right?"

"Could you two boys please look a tiny bit happier? Consider that I'm learning how to say 'yes' to all your demands." Isidore raised his hands in a gesture of acceptance. "We'll take a mini vacation and find this hag's house. I'll get some exercise, walk around a bit like we used to do back in the day. We'll be safe. I'll have two guards in the limosine with us."

"I cannot leave," the Revenant commented sadly. "The world is not ready for the strangeness of me."

"Then I will hate every moment apart from you and hurry back." Erik squeezed the nearly bloodless hands. "The past cheated both of us. These visions devour our shared thoughts like malignancies."

Isidore reflected for a moment before adding, "Your mind has been thrown into chaos trying to separate the reality of the present from what went before. These are not just troublesome shadows. They are fingers spreading upward from the Underworld, demanding you change and adapt."

Frowning intently, Thayer confirmed their decision. "Then we shall not continue to ignore the former Erik's current existence or any of his needs. We will go on this trip, face the past, and try to tie up some of these incongruous ends. The three components of your structured personalities, the Id, Superego, and Ego are crossing the known parameters of human awareness and are somehow melding together."

The Revenant's soul softened, Erik felt the change. Though his brother's face remained veiled and expressionless. *You want me to identify something? Acknowledge its existence. What?*

The mental question went unanswered.

28 RECRUDESCE

𝔍nside the bulletproof Rolls-Royce Silver Wraith limousine, Erik relived something of the angst and exhilaration he experienced during his earlier Paris escapade. Traveling to Rouen in this vehicle was Isidore's playful idea – he proclaimed it a more comfortable ride than a motorbike. Safer, too. They'd left John and Dillard behind to look after the women and guard the interior of the chateau. Two of the outside guards, one acting as chauffeur and the other as shotgun, sat sealed off in the front seat. The doctors anticipated the trip would take just over two hours given early morning traffic. Disguise was unnecessary, as no one would recognize a masked and crippled Isidore de Chagny. Besides, the geneticist intended to wait in the car, safely behind the nearly black windows, while Thayer and Erik searched the house that might contain the remains of Feigel-Evie.

Initially the passengers in the back were quiet. Thayer sat opposite Erik and Isidore, running his hand across the dark dove-gray leather interior. His eyes not focused on any particular object.

Erik watched pines and fir trees, several open fields blur past – letting the changing scenery confirm the quest's beginning. He was an avowed vehement knight setting forth on a crusade. Even though this trip to weed out some form of substantiating history felt akin to re-opening a raw sore, he didn't admit it, even to himself. At last, he could provide real proof that this other world existed. The appearance of the Punjab lasso hadn't impressed either doctor. They privately believed Erik found it, castoff in some long-forgotten drawer. He hadn't mentioned Torossian's confession.

Satisfied to be left to his personal thoughts, Erik turned his daydream to the new Christine and their nearly triumphant mental adventure. He respected that she didn't belong to him any more than he belonged to her. They both still had choices, but for now he chose to close his eyes in the self-indulgent preoccupation of intimate secrets.

How clever to have devised an underground home in such a forbidding place. The caverns were fraught with bone-chilling cold. Radiating from the stone, the frigid temperature permeated the air and threatened to stop the heart of anyone foolish enough to climb down after him. He'd traveled there many times in the recent months, undeterred by the invasive dark and the persistent fog that swirled across the lake. He often paused to listen to the tiny sounds of waves lapping at the shore, licking away at time, seeping through the years. The surface of the water glistened in the light of the lanterns he held high. Its depths an old familiar friend set with alarms against intruders. Bending to run his hand through the water, he reminded himself that his muscles and thoughts were one confluent being. He possessed total self-control, total confidence. Even Isidore and Thayer, with all their probes and tests, hadn't found this sanctuary of mind.

Content, he reviewed the details of Christine's recent visit. She did not comprehend the idea of passionate devotion to another person. Perhaps she was too new. It appeared he might have to work at this relationship. Did he value her enough to invest the energy? He considered his options. If he wanted her, he'd have to win her. The thought that he might be too inept to keep her interest rocked his confidence. Alarmed, he steadied his nerves. *No room for self-doubt.* Indulging an over-active imagination, he pictured the moist heavy tendrils of her hair floating about her head in the incubation tank. Her arms lifted upward to offer him a new home. *And after breakfast I left her in the library in the company of Nyah and that idiot Dillard...damn!*

"Up for some discussion?" Thayer's voice pierced Erik's blossoming consideration of pudenda. Christine dissolved, along with his apprehension over how best to please a female. He opened his eyes; ordering his voice to respond, "Proceed."

"I want to know if your current visions are following any chronological pattern?"

"At the moment, yes...hopefully that will continue. I'm being taught lessons. This last one took me back to France, but before that...Persia. The trip between the two countries has not been disclosed to me yet."

Thayer worried that Erik felt stalked, that the young man possessed his own genetic intruder doggedly distorting his life, purposefully robbing the boy of reality. Excising the embedded personality was tricky. Containment might be the best he could hope for, "What was your last known function in Persia?"

"Still a magician and an assassin in bold service to the Shah. I want to show him my architectural skills; I also fight in a sandy arena. I try not to think about the latter. No, that's not true. I compulsively think about all the aspects of my former life all the time. The next seizure will tell me if I'm back to following any kind of sequence." Erik paused. "A silken menacing finger is scraping the insides of my brain's gray matter. The catalyst floods my mind, lingers around corners, ready to trap me, damning this new life into one centered in the morbid past. All these images imprinted in my brain, haunt me. What key permits my ignoble deeds and the current me to be one and the same? Joined in an appropriate perspective in this place and this time period?"

Isidore's anxiety was straightforward. "So are you ready to stand face to face...opposite the reality of a segment of your history? What lies ahead in Rouen could be brutal."

Erik grimaced. "My fondest wish is for a definitive answer." He pictured himself standing before the house, shuddering at the grave truths it might protect. The severity of what he'd done was enough to drive him past the borders of sanity. *Control your fears; use discipline to restrict your impulses.* Apparently the older Erik was traveling with him. *Did you control yours?*

Thayer wrongly concluded that for the moment Erik wasn't fearful, just irritated. "Why did your former self choose residency in France? Why not Russia or Germany, or the Americas for that matter?"

With the passing of each day and the revelation of every undertaking, the older Erik regulated an increasingly firmer hold over the newer more innocent version. "Returning to my homeland, where people spoke my mother tongue, made sense. I am, after all, a child of this country... living here affords a degree of comfort." He skipped over the issue of his mother. "Fixing the theater's water problem, helping to build the structure, meeting Madame Giry were added benefits I hadn't counted on. They helped ease, but not erase my circumstances." Erik realized he was speaking in the first person. *I cannot stop being this Phantom! He is a powerful persona I created and wish to expound upon!* "His tortured soul existed. Everyone in the back of this vehicle knows he existed."

"He functioned in a somewhat murky past," Thayer commented wisely. "Some of what you envision might be invention or exaggeration."

"No addition to the truth matters. He really lived only through Christine. She helped define him as a person," countered Isidore. Caressing the head of his cane with his withering fingers, he added, "Such a strong attraction that the 2012 Christine still reaches out to own our Erik."

Listening to Isidore's defense of him, Erik smiled. "You don't see it yet, but she is an exceptional person. Despite their adversities, they were drawn to each other. I haven't told you, but my donor-self affixed an emollient to the base of his neck to draw her to him."

"Did he love her?" asked Thayer.

"If you mean did he suffer pain over her, was he willing to endure additional loss; then yes, he loved her." Erik sighed, pushing himself further back into the seat.

"Love bruises and cuts," advised Isidore. "It carries with it the risk of monumental loss."

"Why didn't he take her to the caverns sooner?" asked Thayer, intrigued.

Erik straightened. *He's referring to Leroux's book*, the inner voice informed him. "I imagine he wanted to, but restrained himself until she threatened to leave the theater with that pompous suitor."

"He feared his face would scare the underpants off her," Isidore fingered his mask for emphasis.

"When she took an interest in someone else, the heartache became too great a burden to bear," Erik agreed. "He stole her before she could abandon him and elope with her fine fellow, Raoul."

"Women!" Isidore smirked.

Erik decided to have some fun with them. Leaning forward with a purposefully twisted face, he set his hands like curled talons. "He came as a thief, first to enter her brain," he let out a short girlish squeal, "*Oouu!* Then to steal her body from her *petit-maitre* and erode her precious hopes. Angry at her fickle betrayals, the ghost turned up the heat and despoiled her hopes with the painful experience of abduction!"

"You've become the most verbally colorful patient I've ever had," laughed Thayer. Better to keep a degree of humor with all this. A red light over one of the windows blinked, inquiring if they wished to break and stretch their legs.

Cursed with the humid heaviness that precedes bad weather, they reached the outskirts of a town called Belbeuf. A storm front was moving in. They found a small apartment building occupying the most likely spot where the house would have stood. Erik sat staring at the concrete and glass structure, simultaneously disappointed and relieved. He had hoped to confront whatever insights the place of his first birth might offer.

"We'll go to the Hall of Records," suggested Isidore. "You can question someone there, then we'll take lunch in a nice restaurant."

"Persian food?" asked Erik. "I'm in the mood for minted tomatoes and broiled eggplant."

"Persian or Moroccan, whatever we can find."

"Bargain," Erik was suddenly relieved not to be exploring the dirt floor of a soggy basement.

In the middle of a busy weekday, the streets of Rouen were congested with traffic. The intersection where the Hall of Records stood boasted a peddler with a cart selling a variety of hot food – her voice boomed over the crowd hurrying to cross the busy streets. The female vendor eyed the handsome young man emerging from the limousine and hurrying up the granite stairs of the clustered administrative buildings. She tracked him all the way up the rather magisterial steps, losing him only when he and a shorter man sped through the heavy glass and metal doors. From a pole near the front columns whipped the regional flag of Upper-Normandy and the *Le Drapeau Tricolore* (French Tricolor), the national flag of France since 1790 and the French Revolution.

At an inside counter, Erik and Thayer located an attendant with wiry brown eyebrows and a hefty set of jowls. Dieting had loosened the flesh of the man's chin and the folds actually flapped as he spoke. "May I help you?"

"We need to find someone."

"Name?"

Erik hesitated. *What was her surname? Do I know it? She never married.* "Feigel-Evie Rossman." The appellation blurted from his mouth like he hurled it on a spear.

"Particulars? How long has she been missing?"

"She's not missing, she died over a hundred-fifty years ago."

A snicker twisted the clerk's mouth. The wrinkled aspects of his recently changing face took on the remarkable appearance of a dried crab apple. "Then you don't need to fill out a missing person's report with the police."

Thayer intervened, "Did we ask for one? Certainly you can punch up an address on that computer over there. Get us some information. There was a house off *Chemin de la Poterie* near Belbeuf. Gray painted bricks, a tight fitting gate rusting with age and neglect."

"Virtually every pre-war residence in that area was torn down and rebuilt decades ago."

Thayer grew stern, "We know that. We're interested in any records you might have regarding the previous house or the building that replaced it."

Erik was an old soul; he'd always been an old soul. Bending slightly, he rocked back and forth on the heels of his shoes, his arms laced across his chest. *No trace of her left to permeate the air. She breathed her last and disintegrated. Gone, ages ago...turned to dust.*

The phone beside the clerk's hand rang. He stuck the handset over his ear. "Yes, they're right here in front of me." He listened. "All right, that's acceptable. I'll assist them." He was obviously a man accustomed to obeying others.

Without explanation, he led them to an elevator. Apparently they would be permitted free access. Erik realized that Isidore must have called from the car and offered the man a sizable sum. No interesting project was too venal a chore; Isidore overcame every obstacle with money.

Inside the elevator the assistant punched a button for sublevel two. "We journey into the archives, Messieurs. I'll point you in the right direction when we get there."

"It seems we are to be in a basement after all," Thayer stayed close to Erik, actively controlling his phobia.

The doors swished open to a room jammed from floor to ceiling with alleys of metal shelves, each overflowing with stacks of journals and boxes. In the sallow light provided by strings of bare electric bulbs hooked to the ceiling, they stared at thousands of dusty records stored in the building's bowels.

"This should be fun," observed Erik.

"Crawling around in the past will prove itself an allergen-producing project," Thayer sounded indignant. "In the digital age…to have so much piled up, just taking space." Like the firing of a gun, a sneeze blasted forth from his mouth before he could draw a handkerchief. Stepping out of the elevator, he blew loudly to emphasize his distress. "Here's a distinct irony, us looking for a dead woman, when you've got one living and breathing at home…one you'd like to get to know better." He turned to the attendant. "Is the city government so broke it can't afford to assign an employee to scan all these records?" Back to Erik, "Did I mention I'm allergic to the excreta of dust mites?"

"Go right," directed the clerk. "I'll join you in a moment." With that the man went left.

"Go right! How far?" Thayer didn't sound amused. He received no answer to his question. Astonished at the man's gall, he murmured, "Go right, indeed! I'll deal with that imbecile later."

They walked down six rows and halted. "This is ridiculous," Thayer complained impatiently. "These stacks go on forever, this basement might easily join with those of other buildings. Swallow your pride and holler for this idiot. We need help to dig through this stuff."

Before Erik could blow on a referee's whistle borrowed from the chateau's gym, the assistant materialized out of the gloom behind them. "I've come back to help you," he announced matter-of-factly.

"You're not opposed to giving us more specific clues are you? Actually pointing us to the aisle containing documents for Belbeuf from around 1850?" Thayer slipped a roll of francs into the man's fingers.

The jowl wagging man clenched the money and didn't bother counting it. Manuvering a fold of his abdomen, he shoved the bills into a pants pocket.

They read in the musty stacks that in 1946 the bones of a male and a female were found buried in the cellar of a house during its demolition. Purchased by Jessup Bellisario in December of 1882, the land had never been resold. It still belonged to the Bellisario family. After WWII, Jessup's descendents operated a construction company struggling to re-establish itself after the Nazi occupation. With the government's permission, they'd built the apartments. Though Erik had no memory regarding the sale of this parcel, he was not surprised to discover that something remained to confirm the truth of his mother's demise. They put copies of the bill of sale and the original excavation reports in a Glassine envelope, and went out to tell Isidore what they'd uncovered.

For lunch they selected a small four-star Persian restaurant with adequate parking, and an easy to protect front and rear entrance. Elaborate mullioned glass windows graced the establishment called *Aladdin's Cherâgh*. The reception area of Aladdin's was nothing more than a space contained by a half-dozen leafy Lady Palms and a podium. Beyond the well-fed *Rhapis excelsa* rose the tinkling of silverware against porcelain, mingled with the murmur of quiet conversations. The aroma of savory Eastern spices filled the air with exotic smells. A thin gentleman, impeccably dressed in a black tuxedo, tailored to define his frame, approached them. The *maitre d'* twirled one end of a thin mustache with a thespian's panache. Dressed like a conscientious mortician, Erik instantly enjoyed the man's flare.

"Has the number of lunch-hour patrons dwindled?" Isidore inquired, speaking softly.

"*Oui*," responded the café au lait skinned Persian, ignoring the mask and walker.

Isidore reached into his jacket and with a gesture of pronounced largesse, withdrew an envelope. Why take unnecessary risks among the public? Handing it to the *maitre d'*, "I'd like to hire the restaurant for the next two hours, close it to new arrivals. Is this an acceptable sum?"

The host discretely scanned the amount placed within his hand and responded, "Of course, Monsieur." He walked to the glass door and flipped the open sign to *Closed*.

"Seat my party in a corner apart from those still dining. We have bodyguards outside these doors. They'll need to be fed as well."

Erik chided him by raising a couple of fingers. "To be specific, there are two bodyguards."

Isidore flashed him a look of piqued disapproval.

As they were shown to a table-for-four, a distinct silence spread across the already seated patrons. The total absence of sound filled the restaurant with an odd declaration: Strangers and an odd cripple to boot! Isidore's decrepit walk and masquerader's appearance called undo attention to them. Erik certainly didn't believe it was his own fine features. He pulled a chair out for Isidore, and after admiring the immaculate white linen tablecloth, boldly scanned the faces of the people so rudely glaring at them. Caught staring impolitely, they looked away – embarrassed. No one sat at the two tables nearest Isidore's party, and the number of clientele decreased dramatically over the next twenty minutes.

They sated their hunger by feasting on a seven-course meal seasoned with saffron, cinnamon, cloves, coriander, and nutmeg. After a desert of apple cake drizzled with almond glaze, Isidore asked Thayer to escort him to the restroom. It was then that a scrawny Persian in black pants and a neat (frankly oversized), white long-sleeved shirt walked up to Erik. "May I join you for a moment? Your server is on his break and I don't have much time." Without further ado, the man Erik thought to be a waiter pulled out the extra fourth chair and sat.

Erik set his coffee cup on its saucer. "Joining me without invitation is rather presumptuous behavior."

The man stuck out a bony hand. "I am Ebn Ali Khan – born from the world as a whole, I help with the directing and serving of people."

Erik shook the man's hand reluctantly. "Rather curious introduction."

"I enjoy the peculiar, especially when it comes spiced with a little added insight." Ebn could see that his comment left Erik intrigued so he continued. "Destiny is a tricky thing. Difficult to manipulate."

"Do I know you?" Wiping his mouth with a napkin colorfully embroidered with the stereotypical emblem of Aladdin's lamp, Erik looked into the man's eyes.

"I have a rather common face." The man had anything but a common face. His twinkling eyes were almost ebony black with shiny silver discs set behind the pupils. As if the retina were metallic and strangely reflective. "Some Europeans say that all Persians look alike to them."

At the sight of the man's bizarre eyes and the added inference of a racial slur, Erik set down his napkin, paying strict attention. His guest made a strange half-smile. *Is he congratulating himself?*

"Heroes are born in times of imminent threat, the greater the threat the mightier the hero." One of the Persian's hands lifted off the tablecloth, rose twelve inches and came back down. His fingers landed like five, straight, cylindrical rocket ships. "Stirred into action by predisposed instinct and the moment's need for survival, a young Herculean might unwittingly put himself in league with dark forces. Such an alliance could result in disaster. Either way, the warrior I'm referring to represents the lip of evolutionary change."

"Evolutionary? Nature doesn't vault over tried-and-true patterns that stabilize a species."

"Not without a little shove! Man's ancestors were here millions of years ago. Cro-Magnon shows up and in the span of mere centuries, takes over the planet and the Neanderthals die out. The oldest fossils of modern man, with his high intelligent forehead, were found right here in France. I'd say we're past due for some kind of evolutionary bender. But I concede that sometimes forces collide for the most inane reasons. If you've been raised in a hole – climb up and look about. I chose to descend into a hole, and after a time lifted myself above ground." He smiled that same half-smile again, this time broader, showing off some very white teeth. "We're similar, yes?" He paused as if he expected some form of insightful reply from Erik. When the Frenchman uttered nothing, the dark-skinned Persian frowned and continued. "When you look in the mirror, do you remind yourself that the image a man projects reflects only the surface of the package? The real substance, the core, waits to be teased out. The person before you might be your strongest ally or your greatest enemy. How would you know? If there's conflict, he might even be both. One should strive to understand. Comprehend the unseen. The reflection swings a double edged sword: lust in opposition to love, greed versus generosity, revenge and a hunger for acknowledgment in contrast to isolationism."

"So far, all the image has disclosed is that greed and lust serve nothing of permanence. I'll keep searching." Erik was looking intently at his new companion. A vague feeling that he somehow knew this uninvited guest struck an uneasy chord within him. "Answers come with time."

"And with experience," Ebn leaned forward, his voice lowered for emphasis. "You have a power you are not aware of – a magnetism that derails the hearts of men and women alike. Conduct this power carefully. The soul before you at any particular time may not be the soul you think it to be. It might teach you a great deal before you choose to alter it."

"Should love be the touchstone?" Erik whispered.

"Love is an unreliable standard. Some are incapable of the emotion. Certainly, loyalty proven through years of sacrifice would be a more reliable indicator. Look to that quality – dip your fingers into the possibility that it's there. Remember that your past teaches you what to value most – specifically how to be resilient." He tapped his fingers on the table in a digital display of mirth. "Someone very close to you has had the patience to wade through long periods of boredom by constructively occupying his thoughts and yours. Yes, I'd count him as an important and loyal comrade. He's teaching you that all the facets of your life matter, but resilience is of particular value. I'd say you were the perfect candidate."

"Candidate for what?"

"What does the world need? It needs a hero. Pay attention, please. This is where we opened. It wants for a Herculean with a smart ultra-intuitive mind that will not sacrifice humanity, or the world, for both to survive. Someone not afraid to call an evil person evil, and a good person just."

Erik held onto the edge of the table with both hands. "Someone who can decipher a thousand shades of gray instead of instantly calling a thing black or white?"

The little Persian sitting across from him nodded his head in agreement. "I think you've got it. Shall I fetch more coffee? Some fruit? The cook has ripened Philippine mangoes," he kissed the tips of his fingers. "Excellent!"

"Not yet," Erik was curious. "Are you some kind of guru?"

"Flattery is unnecessary." Ebn waved his hand. "Titles don't mean a rat's whisker to me." He paused, aware that in the restroom Isidore couldn't get his pants buckled. "We have time to continue this conversation for a few more minutes. What did you learn this week?"

"Something dreadful, matricide, though I cannot prove it occurred."

"Men are killing their mother planet and even though the proof shouts out enough evidence to shatter eardrums, not one soul steps forward to take direct responsibility. You are a totally unique individual. I think you should bask in your existence. Some women need to die, others to be saved in the most splendid manner possible. Fear oblivion – above all else – fear the oblivion of never really adding anything to the greater whole. Life on this planet has faced extinction five times before. On December twenty-first there will be a galactic alignment of astronomic proportions. Once in every 26,000 years our sun aligns with the dark center of the galaxy. The winter solstice of 2012 is marked as a time of traumatic renewal and we're not ready. Instead of preparing, the world's governments let their people die of famine, thirst, and disease. Powerful men, soaked in greed, do nothing while the planet hurls toward one of the most spectacular premieres ever witnessed."

The informative Persian grew quiet, seeking a level of inner communion. "The soul of your uncaring mother is resistant to purification. Forgiving herself, she could obtain the next level. Her journey is her own. She must be left to stumble. There is another woman, more interesting and struggling to comprehend a world that has been thrust upon her. Let the acceptance of this second woman, newly reborn, give you some of the answers. What you saw as an attempt to perish was an attempt to learn flight."

Erik's eyes grew larger. "That's very perceptive! You are some kind of gifted mentalist, a mystic!"

A gentle self-deriding smirk crossed the Persian's face, as if compliments, given few and far between, fell on disbelieving ears. "I think you should visit Rouen more often, the country around here inspires you."

"Do they serve buckwheat blinis with crème fraiche around here?" Erik's youthful stomach drove the question.

"Life on this globe is a wondrous thing, is it not? A miracle compared to all the barren gaseous planets floating in outer space."

"We try to ignore that and live on." Erik echoed a truism he'd once spouted at Thayer.

"So shall the Earth be left to struggle without a gladiator to defend her in the global arena? She is trying to give birth to the next new age."

Erik let the challenge slip by; something more pressing had his attention. With a guarded voice, he asked, "Is it possible that a friendship might endure time?"

"Certainly! Especially if the wiser friend had arbitrated its merits with the Universal Consciousness. Rather than risk being compromised by the shocked exuberance that predictably follows unexpected reunions, he might arrange for the parted companions to meet again accidentally, in some cordial manner. A restaurant would be nice. Observe." Ebn's hand moved swiftly across the tabletop and a dessert menu miraculously appeared. "Nice trick, eh?" The tiny personage mockingly rolled his eyes toward the ceiling and a knowing stirred within Erik. "At last! Your eyes grow clear with recognition. You hop centuries and find it surprising that my spirit hops over time and continents." He looked to the little hallway that led to the restrooms. Thayer and Isidore had just emerged.

Erik scolded himself. For a genius that scores off the upper limits of I.Q. tests, he should have recognized Rakesh immediately. He just hadn't expected to meet him in modern France at a lunch table. Erik followed his teacher's gaze and never saw him touch his fingertips to his forehead, mouth, and heart in a gesture of farewell. Thayer and Isidore saw only Erik at the table, no one else sat talking with their protégé.

On the way home, under the influence of a full stomach and the gentle rocking of the limousine, Isidore started to doze. Erik watched him, wondering what the scientist dreamed. Familiar doubts resurfaced – sores in recrudesce. Isidore's claim that he'd recreated his famous ancestor as a token for the disaster of wrecking himself with flawed DNA just didn't add up. The geneticist could clone anyone. His wealth bought unimaginable resources. *Did he seek some form of revenge for Julian? What goes around must come around.* Erik was sure that Isidore was not the individual Rakesh referred to: the loyal soul who had taught himself the art of patience. Leagues of dark forces lurked here. Could he reckon with the man who had brought him back? *If necessary, I can oppose his wishes. I'm as devious a demon as he is.*

Isidore picked up his head. "Do you want to visit the Paris Opera House on the way home? Inhale the air around the proscenium and the stage, investigate the orchestra pit?"

"There's no need," Erik's voice was pensive.

"You've never been to a theater performance." Isidore tested the waters.

"You're kidding, I've been to dozens. Backstage the performers strut around preening themselves like a wide variety of different-sized peacocks. Stretching their vocal chords – more to impress others than obtain a further degree of quality."

"Is that an example of memories occurring out of sequence?" Thayer asked.

Erik nodded. *I already know the caverns, all the passageways.* "The theater is no mystery to me. I won't learn anything new exploring like a boy scout." *I could find the underground chambers again, even though they lie shrewdly hidden behind stonewalls.* Reluctantly, Erik mulled over Ebn's words: *The greater the threat the greater the hero, drawn forth by the double-edged sword of life. Surely every boy wants to be a hero, but it's hard to identify a nebulous menace. What if the threat isn't Isidore, but this death-serum he invented?*

Erik realized what the Fates were trying to reunite. *How obvious could my mentor be?* He made a quick decision. "We need to go back to the restaurant."

"Did you forget something?" Thayer inquired.

"I want to hire that man who sat at the table with me. I know him."

Thayer raised an eyebrow. "What man? You think you need another *aide de camp*?"

Isidore gripped the head of his cane. "Don't ruin the end of the trip. I want to go home. If you don't care to see the Opera House, I had enough waiting while you rummaged through the *archives municipales*."

"Nothing's ruined," Erik said softly. He vacillated between trust and paranoid suspicion. "Thank you, Isidore, for traveling with me. I'm very grateful. Things are beginning to make more sense. To survive, a man needs physical and mental strength, a secure place to sleep, an income... *perhaps a rehash of a past he cannot alter.* France in the 1800's was a demanding place, but it presented nothing even close to the challenges I face today. Please turn the car around and head back to the restaurant. A man sat down at our table. At least let me find out how to contact him."

Isidore nodded mournfully and ordered the driver to return.

At *Aladdin's Cherâgh,* Erik impatiently popped the limousine's door lock and jumped to the curb. Skittering to a halt in time to fling the decorative front door open before bursting through it, he secretly feared they'd tell him no such man was ever there. Rakesh was such a trickster.

Instead, the *maitre d'* admitted seeing the gentleman. "No tie or jacket, very strange for our clientele, but it was the more casual mid-day meal. I assure you the man is not an employee, nor is he a regular customer. I have never seen him before today."

"But you did see him?" Erik pressed.

"*Le plus certainement,* this is not a room of enchantment. He said you'd be back to pick up your package."

"He left something for me? What?"

The *maitre d'* reached into a shelf beneath the podium and pulled out an object about the size of a brick. Covered in ordinary brown paper, it was tied with string. Inside the wrapping sat an ancient looking box of lignum vitae. Undoing the latch, Erik carefully lifted the lid and exposed several egg-shaped Mandragora roots.

"Do you recognize those?" the *maitre d'* asked.

"They are a form of nightshade the Arab's called Jinn's Eggs, because their wrinkled sinuate surfaces often resemble human bodies. They've been used in magic tricks and pagan rituals for centuries." The hallucinogenic alkaloid of Mandragora root composed one of the primary ingredients in the recipe for Indra's Kiss. A drug the illustrious Phantom later referred to as *Phantastica.*

Modern Erik had never mentioned Rakesh's special concoction to anyone. He stood there trembling in unyielding shivers, as if the air had lost all its warmth.

$\mathfrak{S}$afely back at the chateau, Erik propelled himself up the stairs to his rooms. Not a minute later Torossian entered, quietly locking the door behind him. Erik set Rakesh's gift on a side table and started rapidly yanking off his clothes, throwing one article after another onto the box.

"I'll get the news in a minute. I need a shower!" he announced. "My skin disgusts me."

"What I have to tell you can't wait," the Revenant countered. "Dillard, John and Kathryn left the chateau. Nyah watched Christine today, and I acted the part of covert sentinel."

"That's odd. Were they angry?" Erik marched into the *salle de bains* and turned on the water.

"No. After breakfast, they got into John's Volvo and drove out the front gate."

Adjusting the spray, Erik asked, "Dillard left the Harley?"

"Yes."

Erik stepped in, mulling over this new information. "I'll need another fencing partner and Christine is out a bodyguard unless we assign you to the task." Soaping up his chest he watched Torossian smirk in disinterest. "How's she doing by the way?"

"Remarkably. Physically stable. Lots of reading and working on language skills. She didn't seem to mind Dillard's disappearance, hasn't asked for him. She spent some time playing the piano and has discovered she owns a pleasant voice. She's still at it. There's something else."

Erik took a hand and wiped a circle of steam off the frosted glass. "What?"

The Revenant sat down on the tub, crossing his long legs – an ancient skeletal gentleman. "She's curious, unsure who you are. Wanted to know your age. Nyah told her you were sixteen, since that's the current age of our bodies."

Erik grabbed the shampoo and vigorously created a helmet of white suds for his head. "Everyone's got a story. She'll have to wait for the telling of ours. Today was interesting if nothing else. We can go over the particulars later. Humor me, please. Where is Isidore?"

"Started toward the lab, but he's hungry." He turned his head, scanning the mound of clothes covering the box of lignum vitae.

"I'll join him for a bite. Any perceptions?" Erik was asking if Torossian had a possible explanation for the disappearance of their employees, or if he'd picked up on any other disturbance.

In a vacuity of calm, Torossian played with him. "None. The most emotionally labile person in the house is Christine. I'll obey my cravings when I sense them." The Revenant used a nail to remove a tiny crustacean's scale forming on his neck. Like a lobster, he would digest it later. He stuck the piece of exoskeleton behind the healed edge of a flap he'd cut into his right cheek years ago. "My advice is to send her little presents and write poetic notes. She'd like to trail you around like a happy puppy, but she won't...something to do with feminine pride and the wherewithal to stand on her own two feet."

Erik was out and towel drying. He regretted that she had absolutely no memory of their former life together. Even if she remembered but was unsure, it would be better than the near total blank he had to deal with. Winning her might prove a steep uphill climb. He shook his head, envisioning the required training of a 'suitor'. Walking into his closet he chose a fresh pair of jeans and another black silk shirt. After dressing he emerged a new man. "I think I'd rather take than give."

"Her room?"

"Absolutely!"

The area around her bed held the fresh scent of bergamot and lavender – heady sweet fragrances. A jewelry box with a hand-carved floral bouquet for a lid held no keepsakes, no trinkets to show off. *God, she needs some new little treasures, stuff to reminisce over.* Continuing to peruse her room, he rounded a three-paneled dressing screen and went straight to an armoire with fancy solid brass mesh panels at its front. *Ah, rustic charm. When did Nyah order this piece of furniture?* He spread the armoire's doors apart and pulled open the top drawer. *Panties!* Second drawer. *Bras! Pretty bras!* He held one up. Third drawer. *Lovely satin and lace trimmed nighties!* He rifled through them. *Back to the panties.*

Christine stood in the doorway. Startled at his unexpected appearance in her room, she stayed in the entrance.

Hearing her breathing, he angled his head and made a naughty show of sniffing her underwear. Smiling broadly he lifted his chin. The girl in the doorway smelled like just picked mandarin oranges with a hint of crushed lilies. *God, she is intoxicating.*

She met his clear unflinching gaze with a chagrined resolute stare. "You seem fascinated with my belongings." Her voice carried more than a trace of indignation. "Explain yourself."

"Familiarity is everything," he teased.

"If I feel similarly inclined may I make equally intrusive inquiries of your underwear?"

"How very accommodating of you to contemplate such an offer," he responded almost absent-mindedly. "Will you have these on when you come to visit?" He held aloft a white thong and a matching lace bra. "They're not my favorite color." Smiling, he congratulated himself. He now knew every nightdress she owned. *There was that stretchy turquoise camisole thing with the little spaghetti straps. No doubt her nipples would look like two appealing peaks beneath that number.* He touched his temple to prevent sending her the image.

"You are occupying yourself with impolite entertainments," she stated flatly.

How clever to pick out the thought regardless. Is blocking an issue of timing? "How egregious are my sins?" he said, unsuccessfully repressing a grin. "Do you know the word 'egregious'?"

"Yes and your inspection of my personal items is totally unacceptable. What happens if I lock the door that leads to your rooms?"

"I'll try to pick the lock." *That should keep her unsettled.* Happy to jostle her, he pointed to the door with an index figure draped in her undergarments. "But just telling me to stay out would effectively negate any chance of me viewing you disrobed. Though to be honest, I think I'd prefer watching you sleep. Your face resonating in peaceful slumber is as equally provocative as you undressing." *Hope she buys that one.*

"I'm not accustomed to voyeurs." She stomped toward him. "Those are not playthings." She tried to snatch back her panties and bra.

Amused, he held them away from her with one hand. While his other hand, pressed against her upper chest, kept her flailing arms at bay. "Would this be an example of pragmatic strategy or fledgling ballet,

Cherie?" Mocking her, he pressed the crotch of her perfectly clean thong to his nose.

"Have you no scruples? Anything else you want to smell? What a disgusting unpredictable ferret you are!" *You're really a playful risky thrill.* She gave up and stopped trying to grab her highjacked possessions.

He laughed and the sound lifted her spirits to the rafters. Still teasing, his finger stroked the side of her cheek. His scheme was working. He watched her fake a flinch and knew he had her interest. "Skin so smooth, softer than an infant's bottom." He deliberately spoke in a hushed low voice, forcing her to attend to his words. "I know there's not a blemish on you...anywhere." *I could trail my fingers over you in the night with so light a touch you'd never know I was there. The Arabs say that some women hold such natural charm – they drive men straight to the brink of foolish peril.* This time he sent the message loud and clear, though he was sure his former self was supplying the needed knowledge to his conscious thought.

"Payment for your panties, Mademoiselle." He magically pulled a coin from her ear and set it in her hand. "I'm hungry, in need of food." He knew he'd never bother explaining himself, nor would he apologize for being such an outrageous thief. Operating on sheer gut reaction, he merely offered a dramatic bow, swept his hand with her panties and bra out to his side, and abruptly strode from the room – with the trusting hope she'd follow. She didn't.

Hastening to lock her doors, she busied herself arranging pillows on the bed, continually glancing over her shoulder to see if he'd return. His boldness unnerved her, but he hadn't really threatened; 'trying' to master the lock was more-or-less a compliment. *Do I want the thrill of being threatened? No. He provokes me,* and she realized how grievously disappointed she'd be if she couldn't upset him right back. Declaring herself free from further invasion, she went to the single drawer of a little inconspicuous Chinoiserie sewing table. Setting several yellowed photos aside, she pulled out a brown sepia-toned tintype. The aged item was a picture of Erik and herself standing beside a bride and groom, (the as yet unidentified Estella and Benjamin DeVille), on the latter's wedding day. Chewing her lower lip, she puzzled over her archaic dress and the tips of some funny looking satin pumps peeking out from under the hem of her gown. She paused to pass her hand over the ancient image, being careful not to allow the oils of her skin to touch it. She liked mysteries. Leaving the tintype face down and safe in the little drawer, she went to find a book, something interesting to read.

"You took your time getting down here." Isidore sat at a small table set in a corner of the kitchen, a modest spread of food set before him.

"What do you plan to investigate down in the lab? You're not going to scare up the ghosts of more past family members, are you?" Erik joked.

"You're in a good mood. No, I'm not a medium. I just want to check some data, decided to come in here first. You had more than a shower upstairs. What have you been up to?"

Erik slid his butt onto a chair. "After scrubbing myself perfectly clean, I stumbled – not so confidently – down the corridors of courtship." From his pocket he drew forth the trophies of lingerie and showed them to Isidore.

"She let you have these?" Isidore fingered the satin and lace appreciatively then released the items to the highwayman. "Bravo."

Leaving the underwear on the table to be admired, Erik started constructing a sandwich. Spreading mustard on Jewish rye and arranging sliced tomatoes, he answered, "No, she didn't let me have them. They're stolen, but I paid her. Real coin." He laughed in a short unbecoming snort. "She walked in on me. I think she's angry," he confided. "At the moment she has no use for burglars, so I'm taking a break from her."

"If she had no use for me – I think I would create one," retorted Isidore.

"I can't just dump my primordial urges on her all at once. I'm not libidinous."

"Oh, no...not much," Isidore fingered the top buttons of his vest. "Single minded, a touch stubborn, but definitely not driven by the urge to experience sex."

"Maybe I just wanted to test her resilience."

"A resilience that barely exists? Continue teaching yourself emotional endurance," encouraged Isidore, "you've a long way to go." He tapped the table, shaking his head. "At least you're engaging her, letting her know you find her attractive enough to tease. The only way to win is to jump into the game. Get your knees dirty. Advance in a zigzag of subtle offensive. Be patient."

Frowning, Erik stuffed the completed cheese and fresh ham sandwich into his mouth. He ignored the inward groan of a complaint. The former Erik was protesting his culinary choices. To assert exactly who was boss tonight, the modern version poured a small glass of *pastis* to wash down the sandwich.

"Rather ominous sign that Dillard, John, and Kathryn ditched us. What are we going to do if they don't return?"

"They're already barred from the estate. Tomorrow I'll address the headache of replacing them. Thayer tells me he knows some very good people. I trust him." Isidore yielded to hubris. "I believe that for tonight we're safe."

Erik chewed and thought for a moment. "Hire some detectives to find out what happened to them. Maybe they've been bought off, become turncoats." He leapfrogged subjects. "I think I should confess something. I regret that Christine has absolutely no memory of me. With that concession, I take full credit for my current state of unhappiness… and my mood swings."

Isidore nodded, "How very responsible of you. Remember, please, that we didn't create her on capricious whim. We made our choices with valid reasons."

"Do you have any tinctures that promote good luck? Some little blue glass beaker you might have forgotten about?" Erik chewed and swallowed, then almost as an afterthought added, "Should I be wary of loving? They say the sentiment can drive a person insane and I'm already hallucinating."

"The context of your ideation is unusual, but the basis seems sound. Centered in reality, even embellished, your recollections do not meet the criteria for delusion. I'm leaning more toward cognitive dissonance. Trust me. The conflicts resulting from incongruous attitudes held simultaneously will resolve with time and wherewithal. You've got the stamina, thanks to a resilient mind and an athletic body. Along with those attributes you're developing a sense of humor. A valuable quality that will stand in your favor. Don't underestimate your capacity to recover from misfortune – yet another laudable trait. I think you can tolerate the few knocks on the heart she might give you."

"How tightly drawn is the line separating insanity and rational thought? Because the barrier between the two seems a hair thin."

"Psychology is open to interpretation…in this case, our interpretation. Surely you, more than any living person, should understand that! Both Erik's are facets of the same core personality. I'm certain that neither of you need luck to navigate your course. You, my boy, already possess all the luck and good looks that the world has to offer. I've stacked the deck in your favor, remember? Keep in mind that the insanity love spawns is a marvelous spell. I speak from firsthand knowledge. Before Nyah, there was someone else, another extraordinarily intelligent person. She died on an emergency room stretcher years before you were reborn. All my talents couldn't save her. I never loved like that again, though I have indulged myself with feelings for Nyah. Let science be of assistance to you. We'll concoct a pheromone spray to attract Christine. What you mentioned in the limousine about a scented emollient made me consider the possibility. The chemicals secreted by animals, most especially insects, function as an irresistible…"

"Attraction to the opposite sex," interrupted Erik. "That might be a better option than the tactless act of exploding like a powder keg in the southern salon or conducting a panty raid because I don't know how to woo her." He stood, straightening his shirt, tucking its tails further down into his pants.

"You look perfect! But you ate too fast," Isidore protested. "Where are you off to now?"

"Thanks for your insights, Isidore. All your thoughts are appreciated. Torossian says that today she favored music, so I'm to the chapel to unearth my organ from its coverings." He paused to sit back down. "Thank you for the trip to Rouen." The younger de Chagny took one of his elder's frail hands in both his own. "Thank you for this life and for this second chance with Christine."

Isidore reached for a napkin to cover his eyes. "You are worth all my efforts," he sobbed quietly. "You're worried she might be fickle, but what could Dillard offer in comparison to you? We should remember Julian's motto: *Omnia mea mecum porto*."

"All that is mine, I carry with me."

"Take comfort in those words, son, and make her a part of you."

Erik entered the chapel in a saner, more hopeful state of mind. The structure was never intended to be a church, unless one judged quiet personal reflection and more secular gatherings as noteworthy criteria for sanctification. The place hosted one wedding in the 1800's despite the fact that there was no altar or vestry. Up front, the abbreviated chancel consisted of an odd series of three semi-circular asps.

Beneath the vaulted ribs of the Gothic ceiling, Erik moved with quick strides down the middle aisle. Coming to the principle intersection of the transept, he waved to Michael's statue of the two embracing, nearly kissing angels. Bounding up three simple steps brought him to the shrouded massive black and gold organ. Removing the layers of cloth, his first thought was to check the organ's tone. Struck by the remembrance of deprivation and loss, he turned abruptly and stared at the multi-pointed star centered on the floor before the pews – the hidden entrance to the crypt. Down there in the ebon blackness at the feet of the two angels, four bodies lay at rest. Once again in their coffins, only their DNA resided in the lab. He stood erect, respectfully saluted the deceased and with a grateful nod turned back to the keyboards.

Sitting on the bench, he tested the octaves and was pleased to find the instrument nearly in tune. He decided to play something light and airy. The cheerful notes of The Lost Lady Found, an English folk dance collected and orchestrated in Percy Grainger's Lincolnshire Posy filled the space of the chapel.

She did not come. Acknowledging that it might have been presumptuous to assume she'd miraculously appear uninvited in the chapel, Erik continued his private concert. In a vain attempt to decrease the gloom rising in his own spirit, his outlook became less benevolent, bolder. Instead of dissipating sadness, the music he produced followed his changing temperament. Transferring to another piece, Lord Melbourne A War Song, only deepened his depressive anger. It seemed easier, more apropos, to develop something of a passionate irrational temper. Put most frankly, the role of patient suitor sucked his manhood dry. *She may never want me*, he argued mentally. *Experiencing this kind of love is a self-induced poisoning!* He pictured her grasping for her captured underwear. *She is stunning, nearly irresistible.* He wanted to kiss her repeatedly, gently chew at her lips, but she wasn't a chocolate pudding to be had for the taking. Churning his hips on the bench, he hit some darker stanzas and went swiftly into a wild extemporaneous composition. *What a foolish assumption on my part...my gallant intention of restoring her to life. All the playful obstacles I might put in her way only serve to irritate her. She's always displeased with me.* "Well, that's giving into self-doubt," he argued outloud. Focusing on the music, he permitted a flood of memories from their past life, very emotional, very tender, to direct his fingers over the keys.

Silent and cautious, Christine listened from one of the bleachers in the choir asp to the far right. Every time his mind traveled to her specifically, she projected a stronger imprint of her presence into his mind. He was simply too absorbed to allow that she might have been here long before he arrived. She had the coin and the tintype to buy back her undergarments.

Walking into his asp, she imprudently let a sudden rush of anger take her. "Am I a prisoner here?"

He didn't skip a single note. Shoulders bent over the keyboards, he replied, "I am well acquainted with the historical grievance of women – it's justified. They've been used and abused like chattel. This chateau is not a place of bondage. You are free to leave, but it takes lots of those coins I pulled from your ear to live in the world out past the front gate." Melancholy thoughts seized his mind. Life was conspiring once again to rob him of her. Without a hint of reservation, he stopped the flow of the musical composition, and then as if it had no meaning whatsoever, mentally tossed the invisible staff sheets to the floor.

"That was wondrous music, deeply emotional. Made me want to cry."

He slid his booted legs around so that he faced her. His eyes opened wide in wonder – she wore the black fringed leather jacket from the magazine over a scoop necked T-shirt and straight legged jeans. Would she never cease to surprise him? "Did you know that the signs of the Zodiac are interspersed on the capitals in the nave of *Basilique Ste-Madeleine* in Vezelay? There, just as in this chapel, they represent the passage of time. The whole basilica of *Ste-Madeleine* is only a fraction smaller than Notre Dame in Paris. The church stands atop a high hill and was the rallying point that launched the knights of the Second and Third Crusades. Some very respected authorities consider it the most beautiful sight in Europe. I wholeheartedly agree with them." *From the depths of the Opera House caverns I so wanted to marry you in it. You were so important that I would have forged a bond between us before a God I don't believe in.*

"Sometimes you're very vague, at others more than blunt. Your music speaks of an enormous creativity, yet you waltz into my room like an unscrupulous brat. I may be naïve, but I know nothing compels you to come taunt me."

He visibly winced, fairly choking on the unpleasant state of confrontation that existed between them. *Will I ever master control of myself?*

"Does anyone really sleep in this house?" she asked.

"Thayer does. John, Kathryn, and Dillard did. Some of us are oddly altered and require very little sleep. Right now I'm wide-awake, not sleepy at all," he slid forward, puzzled but steady, anything but tired. "I miss Kathryn." *Can I make Christine jealous? I can't seem to shame her.* "Do you miss Dillard?"

"They may be back shortly." Christine sniffled. Bringing out a tissue to wipe her nose, she complained, "I hate everything about this place. It's too somber and old. I've looked out the windows, there's not a living flower anywhere. Only cut ones sitting in vases."

"Those cut flowers radiate a great deal of cheerfulness. There have been quite a number of funerals in this family, and we are constantly thankful that they are not here to offer tribute or accompany coffins in an effort to overcome the stench of death. You and I are not dead, Christine. We're revived."

She stepped closer, boldly wanting to touch his hands where they rested on his knees. "I don't understand the meaning. Revived?"

He sighed. "Of course you don't." *How do I explain this one? Our bodies are just over there...under the floor.* He changed the subject. "Isidore's lost loved ones and still grieves. We don't grow flowers." *It's too happy an occupation.* "We order them brought to us."

"Are you deliberately trying to provoke me? Are gardens forbidden?"

Extremely annoyed at his inability to appease her with a perfectly logical explanation, he retorted, "You are souring my creative mood!" He decided it must be an unhealthy state for a man to walk around with an almost constant erection. The ideal solution would be to relieve the pressure. "Your youthful innocence simultaneously whets an appetite and irks me," he blurted. Wondering at his inept choice of words, he honestly hoped they'd bring a tart response.

"I make you hungry, like a divertive dish of pudding. And I upset you because I'm...what...not quiet enough?"

She's sarcastic? "No. Pay careful attention to the details behind my words, follow the symbolism expressed in the phrases."

"Why be secretive? Don't conceal what troubles you." She studied him closely, peeking into his mind. "To be the child of a scientific genius is very difficult, add to that the thorn that you don't trust him."

"Don't sneak into my brain!"

"You sneak into my room!" She tamed her indignation. "Sorry. Repeat what you were thinking about arousal a minute ago." Her last request came in a pleasant studious voice.

"In a stirring musical composition there exists a living harmonic affinity – finding the affinity breathing within the stanzas of such a piece increases the listener's experience. The affinity elaborates the mood, creates the theme," he offered lamely. *I am a complete and total idiot! What the hell am I saying?* He could so easily gather her in his arms and let his body talk to her of delirium. "We are not perfect people," he conceded. "We're flesh and bone."

"You are as close to perfect as I've ever seen."

"Which isn't saying much," Erik replied.

"I'm seeing more than you think. I have strange snippets. I know where things are, and earlier today there were billowing clouds scudding on a blue sky. I lay on my back with someone's children around me, trying to imagine shapes in the clouds above. After that, there were strange glass balls floating on some bath water. Witches' orbs...said to trap ill-intentioned spirits within their webbed interiors." Her hands moved listlessly through the air. "Then I heard the jingling of bells on a horse drawn wagon, a conversation in the attic of a mausoleum about leaving this chateau, yet I chose to stay. I'm not sure, but I remember singing to you while I wore some very strange silk shorts with my breasts exposed."

"Pantaloons," he responded with a disillusioned nod. "A rich mezzo-soprano voice needs to be developed. As your instructor I rewarded myself with ogling. You're not supposed to have memories." Erik concentrated. Energizing his thoughts, he sent her a directive.

Christine automatically brushed her fingers through the long brown waves of her hair. "Why am I doing this? My hair is too long. I really want to cut it all off."

He exaggerated an exhale through some tightly pursed lips and didn't bother inhaling. Mounting desire nearly robbed him of anything but the perception of the female presence before him. *Wait a minute, who's doing the courting?* He took in a breath and laughed with *sotto voce.* He couldn't suppress such a profound degree of amusement. She'd turned the tables. Aroused him.

"See," she pointed at him. "Isidore is cold and gruesome, you're a happy person."

"And Isidore doesn't dance," Erik smiled. "I dance. Dancing is a big deal." Right on this very spot he could so smother her with kisses, widen her dimensions with his excessively high levels of testosterone. The desire for her was coming in waves, hurried powerful waves pulled to the shore by lunar attraction. Under her astonishing influence, they had no choice but to continue on, crash, wash the sand, and die – crash and die again, enveloping everything they could penetrate with...wet... salty sweet...

His ardor was very much like watching a movie and continually re-playing a single stimulating scene. He considered calling her closer, mesmerizing her. Under the spell he'd slip inside her without her knowledge or consent. He was getting stronger now. He could do it. *Honor her virtue,* he cautioned. *Don't operate solely for self-gratification.* The ability to censor himself while in this amorous state came as something of a surprise.

"You are in love with me, aren't you? So deeply that," the tips of her fingers came together and interlaced, "for one conjoined experience you'd give me freedom all over again."

What a provocative statement. "You are free to love whoever you choose," he said with a remarkably husky voice, one intended to imply that he meant the exact opposite.

"So very cynical. Even without gardens, I don't want to go searching. The house would be dull without me."

"True!" Embolden, he sent a strong nonverbal message: *Memories fill our souls, set our faces toward the past, and define who we were, not who we will be in the future. What corrupted us before will not corrupt us again. Don't be afraid. Come to me.*

"Will you kiss me if I come? Not mentally. Really kiss me. I can reward you with a sort of memento."

"What?" He swallowed his surprise.

"The coin you gave me upstairs...and this picture." From inside her leather jacket she produced two objects. In one palm she held the shiny disc, in the other sat the tintype.

He stood. Taking her payments, he stared at the tintype in disbelief. He set her presents lovingly on the organ. Choosing his position carefully, one arm wrapped around her back, the other went at an angle to hold her unrelentingly by the back of the head. *This one has to count.*

She had a vivid ecliptic memory. There one instant – gone the next. They stood at sunset, on this very spot, the colors streaming through the stained glass windows turning to deep shades of rose, royal blue, and yellow. Past and present merged. His lips touched hers, soaking her into him. His tongue traveled slowly passed her parting teeth, kissing her so deeply the passion almost stole her ability to reason. Her body softened, yielding to the demand this unspoken begging made upon her. He tasted delightful, felt so familiar. Here in his arms she was enjoying something divine and deeply satisfying. She could easily luxuriate in this act. When the fingers he'd intertwined in her hair finally relaxed, she pulled her head back.

"Every piece of marble, every slab of granite, every shade of color on these walls has a history and a story to tell, Erik. You worked on this chapel everyday for eighteen months...from sunrise until dusk."

"As I said, you're not supposed to have memories!" In a moment of almost comic relief, he twisted away from her, trying to conceal his great need before she perceived its girth. Clearing his throat, almost child-like, he ordered his body part to recede. He was very close to sweeping her off this dais.

"You paint confidence over my hesitation. Kiss me again. Inspire me."

Oh brother, how much of this can one enthusiastic teenager take? Master yourself. He kissed her more gently, letting his essence flow into her then ebb like the tide – out into a tranquil bay. After the kiss, he took her hand and walked her to the transept. Taking a B-B from his pocket, he showed her the tiny metal ball.

"Why did you salute this spot when you first entered?"

"Watch and listen." He set the B-B on one of the farthest points of the star, where a tiny hole lay chipped away. It disappeared. Clattering and rolling, the tiny sphere hit one marble step then the next. The finite sounds continued on for a full ten seconds before exiting reality all together.

"What's down there? Some kind of chamber? It sounds immense."

Speechless, he studied her eyes. Letting her reach for possibilities.

"Do I know what's below this floor? Is it some kind of bedroom?"

"You used to have a fetish for making love in the incipient nowhere of..."

"Crypts and mausoleums," she added with quick enthusiasm. "Death shall not own us!"

At the open door to the chapel the Revenant shifted, letting his presence be known. His haunted sightless eyes identified the spot where the young lord of the manor spoke with his lady. Christine stood riveted. She'd had a glimpse of the creature earlier in the day. His physical appearance didn't frighten her as much as the fact that she could not read the strange being's impenetrable mind.

"Thank you for your vigilance," Erik exaggerated his gratitude with a short bow. "No need to anguish over this meeting." He swept his arm around Christine's waist. "We're communicating nicely."

The chapel grew very quiet. Not a breeze, nor the sound of a groaning tree branch, disturbed the air, yet there was some form of intense communication between the two males. Christine could not track the message or its response. She looked from the visitor back to Erik. The latter stood frozen, staring with keen interest at the living thing that for all intents and purposes appeared devoid of life. The creature growled, the intense sound vibrating in a decibel almost too low to discern.

"This is Torossian. Please call him, the Revenant. He won't hurt you," Erik reassured her. "Just don't touch him without his permission. We need to walk you back into the house. There's a situation brewing down in the lab."

$\mathfrak{T}$roubled, Erik stepped from the locker room and entered the pristine world of the lab. Passing the data storage area, he came to Nyah's computer workroom and was surprised not to view her or the elderly geneticist. Mental imagery helped him locate Isidore in his personal office, sitting at his desk. Breathing with pursed lips like an asthmatic, the scientific wizard was intensely preoccupied with the details of some absorbing subject on his computer screen. He seemed unaware of his own dyspnea. From the doorway, Erik scrutinized his benefactor. Dressed all in white – mask, shirt, pants, and orthopedic shoes – he resembled a spooky modern day Dr. Frankenstein with a respiratory challenge. *Why didn't I detect this change in breathing during our snack? Is his deterioration rapid onset heart failure?*

There were other, more subtle, changes occurring; changes Erik hadn't taken the time to notice. The doctor was spiraling downward, growing painfully thin, perhaps from overwork and accumulated stress. Erik regretted leaving the kitchen so quickly. He should have stayed and monitored the man's protein intake, insisting they had dessert. *Isidore could certainly use the calories.*

"Has there been some kind of lab accident?" For the moment he avoided mentioning the disturbing respiratory pattern he was observing.

"More like an interesting breakthrough. Nyah's been studying peptides in organ recipients. There are documented cases where patients experienced something of the donor's memories. She looked at subjects where the mental acquisitions were permanent. Irreversible. The limbic system may not be the only clue to your vast storehouse of very specific history."

"That's interesting," Erik stayed just inside the doorway, trying to assess from that position all that was adrift. The familiar potter's rectangle of California sage was still in place, but not two feet from the doctor's left elbow rested a very dead Boston fern. Its long slender fronds reduced to tapering brown fingers, curled back upon themselves. "Why keep something so un-alive...?"

"In such a sterile environ?" Isidore finished. Multitasking did not diminish his level of concentration. His eyes remained focused on the screen's information. "Think I should stick it in a hatched enclosure? See if I can revive the thing? Well, I don't feel like doing that." After deliberately drawing in a few deeper breaths to facilitate speech, he continued. "I'm keeping my extinct *Nephrolepis exaltata Bostoniensis* to remind me how easily failure follows unbridled pride. How is Christine?"

"Unhappy that we don't have flower gardens brightening the atmosphere of the place. She's up in her room, probably plotting."

"Flowers?" Isidore finally looked up. Regaining a bit of stability by hooking his thumbs under the edge of the desk, he asked, "Do you think me ugly? Distorted?"

Erik noted the bluish tint to the fingernail beds. "Never. I used to label you a cantankerous headache, but now I'm certain you're not. You're more like changing barometric pressure as a storm front passes through. Today there will be severe attitude with record high temperament and an occasional unhappy outburst, followed by a cool demeanor, fairly cranky winds and a probable chance of intractable tantrums."

Isidore's eyes brightened. "How fortuitous for those on the ground that at the sight of Erik, the irascible energies built up in the cumulous cloud layer will disperse. The aberrant temperament will warm." Again he paused to blow out several exaggerated breaths and oxygenate his brain. "And in the aftermath of the dissipating front, rapidly developing cheerful periods of extended sanity will prevail. Ha! Here, have a look." He turned the computer screen so Erik could review it. The monitor was packed with complex biochemical formulas and nucleotide sequences; all so tiny they bore the appearance of cuneiform writing.

Without a qualm Erik came confidently closer. Months ago he'd been given access to all of Isidore's encrypted files. Before taking a seat, he picked up a few papers uncharacteristically strewn around the floor. After obediently scanning the screen, he studied Isidore's rheumy eyes. There were a few moments of intense stillness before the doctor spoke again.

"What is happening to me is a *fait accompli*. Malignant cancer. Spreading like an infection I can no longer fight off. I detect suppurative lymph nodes in several strategic areas of my body. There's not a trace of malignancy in Nyah, but we fear it will come." A rectus of pain shot through his intercostal muscles, eating its way downward deeper into his chest. "I now know the touch of pernicious evil. Its ultimate name is agony." To overcome an increasing shortness of breath he lifted the mask off his face. Exposing his decrepit features, he sat there taking in air with lips widely separated. It embarrassed him to reveal his still shrinking mandible with its folds of loose flesh covered in webs of spidery purple veinlets.

"You need additional oxygen. Let me get a tank. Do you know the primary site?"

"I have my suspicions. Go get the oxygen."

Erik left, returning promptly with a small portable tank and a nasal cannula. Positioning the cannula beneath Isidore's deformed nostrils, they adjusted the flow and in a few minutes Isidore's breathing was less labored.

"I don't have much time. This is what I get for mixing my DNA with that of a wolf in sheep's clothing. Julian's codes are too enmeshed in my system to reverse the disease." His fingers tapped the desktop for emphasis. "At all costs we must keep the part of me that is Julian extremely calm. He could act out at any time. I don't regret declining invitations to speak to the scientific community, what with my looks and..." He withdrew his shaking hands and placed them in his lap.

Wrestling with denial, Erik made a suggestion, "Let's do some tests. Study the problem and address a cure, if not a cure then a remission. Is there any of your original DNA left?"

"Yes, quite a lot."

"Then we'll inject you with it, order your cells back to normal and put the cancer into quiescence."

"We've tried that. My very first thoughts were to eradicate Julian's existence from my body. I used to hate what he did to me. Now I no longer have the strength to hate. I don't even have to tell him that I surrender – he's always listening. At this point, locking the gun between what teeth I have left and pulling the trigger would be most appropriate."

"Don't say that!"

Isidore sought to console his ward. "According to the Bible, seventy is the allotted age. I've come close enough. The outcome of Julian's reign was inevitable victory over his hasty imprudent host. Pharmaceutical companies offer remedies for everything from a sore throat and high blood pressure, to migraines and impotence, but they cannot cure this form of grief. This strikes too deep, right into the keys of cellular logistics, the very language of my cells has been irrevocably altered."

"You must live. Look at all you're triumphs. You actually made Christine and in an artificial womb."

"Indeed, there's an accomplishment to be proud of for awhile. If only the two of you would come to terms and agree to spend the rest of your days in serenity and safety at this chateau. I've provided for you financially. Use the abundant technology of this age to bring back the mansion's former grandeur. I'm leaving you all my wealth. You're the only one deserving of it, and I assure you it's substantial. Protect your health. Employ these great insights of yours to useful purpose and figure out how to reproduce. Remember that a duplicate does not experience the world in the same fashion as his donor organism. You are your own soul."

"Let's stop the lecture and for the present focus on you living to enjoy your wealth."

"My genes are too muddled. What an ironic tragedy that I'm unable to save myself. I cannot live on-and-on, but you can."

"Yes, you broke your own mandates with Christine and I. There will be no timed physiological death at the age of eighty two for us."

Isidore responded in a reedy voice, almost as if there were some kind of small obstruction in his throat. "Don't misunderstand. I'm not embracing death. This demise is intensely harrowing because it's happening to me, personally. My end is justifiably more painful than the global formula I ordered up for the rest of mankind. I've been criminally without honor my entire life."

"Just listening to you inhale and exhale is chilling," Erik extended his hand to count Isidore's pulse. "You're going to need all the help you can get," he said soberly. "How can such defeatism be coming from a man who won countless awards as a world renown scientist?"

Isidore's fingers brushed those of his son. The fine bones and prominent blue veins on the back of his hand were sharply accentuated in the tissue paper skin. "Shh," he directed. "Julian is very much alive in here – him and his confounding memories. Of course, his directives are nothing compared to the scale of those driving you. You're actually re-living your donor's life. Julian's divisive inclinations are projected as small bright pictures that splash onto the pitch-black television screen of my mind. Whether I want them blocked makes not a smattering of difference. Julian was grossly maladaptive. He should never have survived his birth, but even a struggling squash plant, when it's given the right fertilizer and enough moisture, can run riot and overrun the garden. Did you know that a monk repeatedly raped him? Really, those pictures are the worst. The entire priesthood should undergo castration as a mandatory criterion for taking the vows of ordination. You know they won't. But why keep a penis after swearing not to procreate? Emasculation would prove sincerity."

Erik leaned back in his chair, amazed at Isidore's directness. "I distrust everyone outside this compound. People operate for self-reward. They seek continual gratification. In breaking moral law they only fear getting caught. I've learned that what's done in secret needs to remain secret...a tricky business at best, especially in this age of digital-information. People say and do whatever they please. No one believes that they will offer retribution in this world or the next. Scientific advancement and the veneration of technology are the new world religions."

Isidore gave him what would account for a smile. "Spoken like a dues-paying member of the misanthropes. Comeuppance dawns for us all in one way or another. With our presumptive egos, Nyah and I thought we were alive at the dawn of a brand new genetic age. We thought like children! Now we could write volumes about what we didn't understand regarding that tiny cellular level that defines life. I've expended considerable energy compartmentalizing Julian's scurrilous antics, but his inherent baseness and depravity are invasive. He's the devil personified and reborn in me."

Erik countered surrender with a decisive truth. "Thwarting his impulses makes you the victor. He hasn't won! And there's no denying that in the process of change, both of us picked up some very interesting information. We've learned that genetic personalities are passed on virtually intact. Dominant traits are supposed to be influenced by environmental circumstance and personal choice. But it's almost as if Nature operates through some undisclosed backdoor, determined to unseat our authority and set us on a predetermined course. Initially duped, the genetically altered person experiences new deep-seated cravings that clamor to be met. Driven by want, they feel compelled to satisfy these exigent needs, so they undertake actions they believe are their own original thoughts. I suspect that it was Julian who really put you on the relentless quest to create me. Did he dictate the cloning? Did you ever hesitate?"

"Yes, to both questions. I really didn't want to go further, but felt forced, and there was Nyah enthusiastically offering to donate her eggs. In my own moral turpitude I didn't recognize the inherent dangers to you. I told myself that bringing you back was for me, when it was really to sate the part of me that is Julian." Isidore's eyes glassed over with incipient tearing. "I'm becoming so emotional. I don't think Julian ever really cried. He trained himself not to...there's a large component of me the wicked scoundrel can't acquire. All that matters now is keeping you sane, helping you outlast these episodic melodramas playing out in your head."

Erik waited patiently while Isidore wiped his face. "Didn't Thayer say that evil is all that negates life? Even in the Garden of Eden, God warned the two innocents, Adam and Eve, that to eat the fruit of the tree containing the knowledge of good and evil is to die. Imagine someone truly vile procuring the biological keys to live forever. Hitler for instance. He would have cloned thousands of copies of his 'perfect human' and waged a terrible destruction on the rest of mankind."

"Yet placed in more philanthropic hands, cloning may represent the last hope for the survival of a vast array of rare and endangered species." Isidore sounded almost remorseful. "Immortality has its drawbacks. God, Nature...whoever it was...the original intention was for humans to live longer than a single century. I've taken the first step to getting you back there. You'll have to guard your health and enjoy the coming decades without me."

"Even if Julian prompted your choice to re-invent me, I appreciate all your efforts. Giving you some solace brings greater purpose to my life. You sought to stop the teeming multitudes from overpopulating themselves out of clean air, food, and water. Your serum allows the more progressive governments to limit their citizens' length of life, affording them the finances to provide healthcare and alternate energy sources for homes and industry. Sure, there are problems all along the way, but they'll have to resolve them on their own. I intend to assist you. You and the almost extinct wild tigers have a lot in common – if we blink, you'll be gone. Let's focus on the task at hand and eradicate this cancer."

Isidore absent-mindedly scratched his shoulder. "Radioactive Iodine has some very specific isotopes. I-131 emits beta and gamma waves and decays with a half-life of eight days. The substance is a product of fission released in nuclear weapons tests and accidentally at Chernobyl. In medicine it's used for both diagnostics and therapeutics. Lower doses of I-131 treat overactive thyroids."

Erik moved to the next inherent thought, "You want to revisit its functions in overactive DNA? Let me get a wheelchair."

The doctor stood, "All right. We'll get some tests going. Bring you up to date. Let Nyah sleep for a while." Isidore was growing remarkably shorter. He glanced at Erik, "I'm similar to a melting glacier, yes? Your youthful bones are ossifying nicely, while mine are turning to dry sponge. I attribute the wasting to the disease. It feeds on calcium. Julian is alive – full of pain and misery – and so am I. Who knows, you and I are both suspicious and paranoid enough to stand a chance at developing an answer."

Erik and Isidore spent the next eight days in the lab together. Thayer visited frequently and Nyah was an almost constant companion. During that period the detectives, hired by Isidore, learned nothing of the fate of Kathryn Arlington and the two Kelly's. The trio had simply vanished. Isidore ordered Nyah to hire more guards and interview proper teachers for Christine. On the evening of the eighth day, Torossian appeared in the lab.

"Christine knows where you are and wonders why she can't see you. She grows increasingly curious," the creature reported flatly.

From a hospital bed at the back of the negative airflow, germ-free room, a dry chuckle escaped Isidore's thin lips. "What he means is that she grows restless for direct contact with you, Erik. No doubt she enjoyed your attentions." In pain, he ground his remaining teeth together and punched the button of an intravenous morphine drip for an additional dose.

Erik didn't even look up from the microscope where he studied Isidore's cancer cells. "I can't leave here. Isidore is going through some very difficult procedures. We're practically rebuilding his immune system.

For the moment his body is ungraciously declining a cure. Warding off errant infection has become another priority."

To emphasize the point, Nyah sanitized the space around Isidore with a smelly disinfectant spray. Everyone wore a surgical mask except their patient, who testily waved an arm at her to go away.

"Can't you keep Christine entertained?" Erik adjusted the magnification on the electron microscope. "*Qui facit per alium facit per se* – he who does a thing through an agent does it as himself. Play a game with her. Occupy her mind."

"You want me to play with her. If I do, I won't enjoy it."

"Thanks. I owe you a favor."

Up in her rooms, Christine scanned the creature. He looked like he needed interment, but didn't smell too bad. At least her fear of him had lessened. "Can't Erik come talk with me...just for a little while?"

Careful to quiet his voice and keep its sound from grating her nerves, he responded, "Not this evening, he's occupied with Isidore. He wants us to play a game. I'll teach you chess or backgammon."

"I looked up the word revenant on the internet."

"And?"

"It said a revenant is one who, considered dead, returns after a long absence. Stick out one of your hands," Christine requested politely. She placed a circlet of polished double-terminated quartz on his left wrist. "These stones are supposed to recharge psychic sensitivities, channel them back to your heart." She looked at the pale hollow face and the empty milky blue eyes. *He probably thinks my next request will be for a rutilant crystal ball.* Trying to conceal her disappointment at his lack of interest, she removed the bracelet and said apologetically, "Sorry. That probably wasn't rational thinking at its finest."

"The heart has nothing to do with psychic ability. The heart is a muscular organ that pumps blood."

"Still, it's considered the seat of emotion. I was speaking symbolically." The creature's lack of expression didn't deter her in the least. In the last eight days he'd been around quite frequently, sometimes shimmering in a corner like a living pool of spilled liquid.

"Humans often rationalize and retreat into superstitious folklore."

"True, but not very encouraging." The subject she really wanted to explore was romance. As he turned to give-up, she stopped him by offering to be more cooperative. "Stay. Please. Let's play a game. People learn a great deal through games. We could role-play. Perhaps have a rendezvous with a legendary figure. How about some mysterious personage from history?"

"For the intent of study."

Christine opened one of her fashion magazines. "My actual preference would be for a dark haired man." She flipped the pages rapidly. "Is there a hair anywhere on your body?" Without pausing for an answer, she continued her search. "Someone lean and graceful, with chiseled facial features and long delicate fingers. Granted, he's only a handsome male model in a women's magazine," she stifled a sigh and turned the copy of *La Mode Francaise* so the Revenant could take in the picture. She'd chosen the one that most favored Erik.

The Revenant glided his cold white hand across the page. "I can only see the object, the magazine. All else, any detail or bit of writing, is indiscernible unless it's raised."

"Like embossed?"

"Yes. Describe the male for me."

The model was demonstrating the stylish cut of a tailored jacket and pants. With an engaging smile across his face and one hand tucked into a trouser pocket, the jacket's lapel opened to expose a partially unbuttoned shirt and suggestive triangle of chest. "He's annoyingly unpleasant. Creepy actually."

"That's hard to accept. Shall I teach you the basics of transcendental communication?"

She flopped onto a chair, grateful for the company. "Proceed."

"This form of messaging cannot be expressed by a set of finite numbers in a mathematical operation. That's one reason why I excel at it. The sharing is done out of a purposeful intent. The mind decides to speak without opening the mouth, determines a recipient, and sends the message...sometimes an image."

"I've already experienced that."

"Accepted. But you haven't experienced *le cinéma de la mémoire*. Close your eyes."

She did as directed and felt him start to rub her forearms with his frigid fingertips. "I read about this type of massage, promotes circulation, and invigorates blood...**along** with psychic energy." She started to relax, knowing that she'd enjoy the experience more if Erik did the demonstrating.

With a level voice Torossian informed her, "I'm not touching you at all."

She opened her eyes. He'd actually flown backward, occupying a space some twenty feet away.

"Close your eyes again," he directed. "Have you read Leroux's book?"

"Yes, kind of jumps around a bit. In some ways, the masked phantom acts irrationally."

"Why did the reclusive Opera Ghost dress as Red Death for the ball?"

"I have no idea...because he was crazy and wanted people to fear him?"

"Not crazy. Explicit. Exact. He was telling everyone not to touch him. He couldn't bear their touch. So, he was death to them all."

"And death to that *chanteuse* if she dared to love anyone else but him."

Pleased, the Revenant stilled his body and tilted his face toward the ceiling.

Her arms slid quietly to her sides – a gesture suggestive of surrender. She was successfully making the transition. Opening up to prior experience. "I thought he was never coming back...that I would never see him again. Raoul told me the Ghost was dead. That was foolish. Death can't die. Death is the transformation, the passage...and Red Death is...the dreaded curse of small pox...he's..."

"Coming across the room." Dressed in red silk the Revenant strode to her. He looked like a masked musketeer, crimson cape swirling – trimmed in gold embroidery, plumed cap upon his head. On his face he wore the threatening death's head, made all the more fearful because he had not bothered to replace his milky blue discs with a set of normal eyes. With a great flourish he bowed and swept his arm out to his side. The whole maneuver was unsettling and familiar.

Her hands went defensively to her mouth to squelch a scream. "Already here, demanding my submission. Drinking up my freedom. Nothing moves but him. And what is he? Certainly not a rescuer! Oh, God! Can't breathe. Can't breathe!"

"You're getting plenty of air," the Revenant assured her. "Otherwise how could you be complaining? The game is afoot. Speak only with your mind."

All that was real to me is gone. Snuffed out. Suffocated for lack of oxygen. There's only him now. Only him.

He stood not two feet in front of her, elbows flexed, one hand upon the hilt of a sheathed sword, the other hooked in his black leather belt. *Though I appear as a dead person, I am not deceased. See for yourself.* He ripped open the front of his spectacular jacket, exposing his pale skin. He bent over her and taking her hand, let her feel the beating of a normal healthy heart. *I live through my love for you; you live through your love for me.*

She felt her energy dwindling, as if he sucked it through the hand he held pressed against his chest. *You seek me out. Your love totally alive, only hidden in the guise of death. Behind that covering you conceal something deemed too ugly for sight. What is it you keep secreted away? A part that makes you feel ashamed? What can I grant that you have not already taken? Acceptance?*

"You understand at last! All that you are is mine! All that I am is yours!"

Fiend! You cannot drain all of me. Weak and trembling, she had to preserve her still awakening sense of self. "Not this game, Torossian. It sours me with fear."

Red Death stepped back. "What then?"

"Let me choose another stratagem." A rectangular room of sand-colored walls rose up from the floor to surround them. Chests of glistening jewels and stacked bars of gold and silver lined the walls. A hot afternoon breeze blew through a gauzy single-layered drape covering the open doorway. A band of painted lotus flowers worked its way around the upper walls, as if some invisible artist labored furiously to add the picturesque border. Clay pots magically effloresced a variety of flowers: arum accentuated with the red petals of safflower, iris, cornflowers, and chamomile. Tall metal urns adorned with fuzzyheaded papyrus, palm fronds, red berries, and mint sprung up in the corners. The heady sweet fragrance of lilies began to fill the space. Added to the other scents, a floral perfume literally floated on the air of the chamber.

The Revenant saw it all and wondered: *If she can control this, what else could she control?*

Christine found the discovery of her new talents very satisfying. "We'll act out another story – Egypt in antiquity. War chariots were decorated with these flowers before leaving the city. You are Pharaoh, ruler of the upper and lower Nile. All things ancient now burst forth anew."

He braced, preparing to pit his will against hers. Since she wished to be master of the game, he'd let her think she controlled it – more out of curiosity than complacency. He was in for a surprise.

Around the base of her neck materialized the traditional wide semi-circular necklace, the *usekh*, of the pharaohs and their queens. Her body shimmered in a pleated diaphanous robe of silver. The sides of her garment were drawn to points attached to gold bangles at her wrists. So that when she raised her arms, she bore the translucent wings of Isis, the goddess who was mother to them all.

Together they inhabited another place in time, most certainly a militant period. His chest armor and spears rested on a stand. *Interesting.* Scanning downward, the Revenant saw his own body was naked save for a short white scarf held in place at his hip by a crocodile-shaped jeweled clasp. Since she left his garment opaque, he reasoned she had no idea what his genitalia looked like and could not express them.

You are a spectacular representation of Isis. He sent the message quietly so as not to jar her. *Obviously you were Pharaoh's favorite.*

From within an orange and black amphora, she cast a spray of sparkling gold dust that stayed suspended in the air, filling the space between them with bright twinkling specks. "Your elements evoke a powerful response in this Egyptian female."

Don't say it! Think it!

In response, her fingers flared into the floating gold dust, a remarkably artistic depiction of the sun's rays. *Will you call me to you?*

A thousand tiny beads of light began to radiate outward from his thorax, abdomen, and pelvis. An aura of opalescent turquoise and amethyst that registered in his brain as scores of tiny vibrating electrical sparks. Even stimulated, the Revenant maintained control of himself. She was an unheralded, powerful, and manipulative transmitter. Her projections intensified, reaching a level he was unprepared to resist. This was not learned; she was a natural. Gliding toward him in an array of golden light – the sighting of a celestial goddess – the Revenant reckoned himself captured in her delusion.

She moved around him as a circling comet, trailing a stream of brilliant fiery particles. *Peace and satisfaction are still to be squeezed from life;* she hummed the thought as one would a familiar song. Halting in front of him, she applied a gentle effleurage to his abdomen, all the while reveling in her strengths. Continuing the persuasive massage with one hand, she pushed him toward a canopied bed with the other. Bidding him lay atop the covers, her adaptive hands reached under his short loincloth. Gently, persistently, she fingered an area she asked him to picture. Her lips opened. Extending a willing tongue, she pressed something firm into her mouth.

The Revenant's body responded with a violent accelerating desire. Leaning back into the pillows, he wished for death at that moment. *To die defined by this act!* But he didn't know if he could die, encased in a body with such a slow metabolic rate.

She swung her legs across his pelvis and eased herself onto the area of cloth covering his penis, a soft moan escaping her lips. *Now is the time of the guardian,* she said. *Accept me.*

What did you say? He made every possible effort to focus.

The guardian is here, Lord. Make ready. Make ready, she repeated softly, hoping he would comply and let her ride the lightening.

His hands went to his face. Feeling his skin, he reassured himself that he was not wet with sweat. He had no active sweat glands, no need for them, as his body temperature was normally so low. He passed his clawed fingertips over his lips, defining their borders. The labella were thin and dry, and he wondered if she might resign herself to kissing them.

What is wrong? Return your mind to me, or have you more onanistic tendencies?

The Revenant rolled her onto her back. *I feel your stimulus like nothing I've ever experienced before…thanks be to the god Amun-Ra.*

She spread her legs, her vital feminine enclosure still shrouded by the lustrous fabric of her dress. *Bolt the door with a brace and come back to me.*

Phwrump. *It's done. Where do you want me?*

Her hand went to her own crotch, stroking playfully. *Here. Don't hesitate. Be exacting. Make me pay the price for sending you away a hundred times.*

Torossian froze, guarding his thoughts from invasion. *Ah, she slipped,* but he was drawn into her web. *Open your legs. Yes, a little wider.*

She hitched up the bottom of her garment, rolling her hips so that she was almost, but not quite exposed. Her arms reached upward to receive him. *Like this? I want to know the reality of sex. Tonight there will be comfort.*

He leaned over her, hiding his thoughts. Supporting his weight with his hands, he went no further. *I am leaving. Ending the game. I'll come back later.*

"Stay!" She spoke outloud and it sounded like the racket of thunder rolling through storm clouds after so much silence. "When you return I'll only insist that we try again. I can be very persistent. This isn't about Erik. It's about you."

Despite her persuasive tone, the Revenant knew in an instant that she lied. He possessed feelings. He could be as emotionally bruised and lonely as everyone else. It wasn't him capturing all her fantasies – it was his brother. "Even though I do not carry a fast-beating heart and a bounding pulse, I am not dead and can be hurt."

"Leave me!"

Still in the raiment of an Egyptian apparition, he lifted himself off her body and receded into a corner.

She sat up, fearing that someone would knock at the door and scold her. She would send whoever came to badger her away. Angry with herself, she had to admit that she wanted Erik, only Erik crawling inside her. The ancient chamber, with all its floral sweetness and treasure, disappeared. Without a word, she got up and went into the *salle de bains*.

In a moment Torossian heard the shower running. Music was playing, an old rock group called Fleetwood Mac. Left without completion, he briefly considered joining her in the water. His sharp ears detected her crying. Some lessons needed to be learned alone. *I'm going back to the lab.* This was not the day, nor the hour, for her to be physical with any male.

He went out, carefully closing the door behind him. Passing silently down the hallway, he debated telling Erik about her considerable talents. Smirking internally, he opted to leave his sibling only partially forewarned. Brothers had a prickly non-negotiable right to annoy each other. The fact that Erik had dictated a game earned him the special privilege of discovering, on his own, what degree of dissatisfaction her powers brought.

31 NEEDLED AND PRICKED

𝔍n the waning hours of afternoon sunlight, a series of pearl gray stratus clouds stretched across the sky above the chateau. Generated by the declining heat, the sunset birthed an incarnadine sky that resembled ashen skin smeared with blood. Sitting on the chateau's roof, Christine watched this strange transformation take hold of the sky and slowly begin to fade. Five levels below, down in the laboratory, Erik viewed a miracle of his own through the microscope. In the sample of blood held fast by two glass slides, Isidore's malignant cells evidenced the first signs of destabilization. The nuclei were losing cohesive durability. Too soon to guaranty a turning point in the disease, Erik took courage and looked up to smile. The few souls clustered together in the room latched onto the tentative hope of a possible remission.

"My boy has the wisdom of the ages," Isidore declared, despite the fact that the cure proved more agonizing than the disease.

Thayer gazed through the eyepiece. "We're a long way from the end, but for the time being, guarded expectation is not unwarranted."

Fueled by a temporary state of elation, Isidore found the strength to do a scuttling kind of walk around his sickbed. In the short span of nine days his stamina had dwindled remarkably. His constitution, now wasted into enfeeblement, was punctuated by periods of great fatigue and waves of pain.

The eminent geneticist halted, a single thought giving him sudden pleasure. "As an unfulfilled father, I was driven to create life…that I might acknowledge my own progeny. What a gift to see my son peer into the savagery of cells, so chaotic they devour their own blood supply, and have him restore healing."

"Let's get you back into bed," suggested Erik. "We have more tests to run and the cure is not assured. All we've done is head the apostate devils in the right direction. They can't multiply, and very soon they'll be facing self-destruction. Showering commendations on us is premature." Isidore's legs were so frail Erik could toss them single handedly onto the sheets.

"Nonsense," Isidore offered no physical resistance. "Modesty serves no purpose! As your patient I applaud your talents. In this crazy perplexity of a dual personality your individual summits were briefly indiscernible. The former Erik just temporarily upset the applecart by playing so powerful a role in your ideation. Obviously only a momentary setback given what's hidden within your genetic code."

Thayer was on the other side of the bed, adjusting the flow of a blue-tinted intravenous. "Can you reconcile the two men within you, Erik? The man you are and the man you have been? Tell this cranky old gentleman that you can, lie to him if you have to, or he'll postpone resting to continue heaping accolades on your head."

"I already embrace the more constructive components of my former self." Growing within him was a sincere gratitude for Isidore bringing him back to the land of the living. "In many ways he was the better person."

"Better or more experienced?" asked Thayer.

"More alive...more alive in a thousand ways." Erik raised the bedrail, locking it in place. "By the time he reached my current age, he'd done a lot. Isolated and alone, he opened his mind to learning. His analytical brain always sought answers. Even as an assassin he strove for practical and sustainable *(actually more entertaining)* eradications. He had to kill the Royal Treasurer twice, but didn't falter in the task."

"From what I understand he never tamed his rebellious nature," Isidore reached for a glass with a straw. "Water, please."

"I'll pour fresh for you," Thayer raised the spout of a pitcher to the glass. "You need to rest a few minutes, then I'll prep you for a lumbar puncture. To pass the time while we wait I'd like to discuss the Revenant."

Isidore set the glass down on the over-the-bed table. "Still curious about our novel humanoid? What wondrous, monstrous things are hidden in the womb! Even there Erik's genetics were powerful. We heard only one heartbeat, sonograms revealed only one fetus. I've always suspected that Erik projected himself in the form of an accretion – a twin. We thought the creature born dead...poor scraggly thing that emerged after a healthy crying boy. No heartbeat, no pulse. We left it there on the counter to study at some later point and focused on our robust baby. Upon delivery Torossian weighed five pounds, twenty-four inches crown to heel. You can imagine our shock when, without a sound, this long angular being moved its limbs. Some force we did not comprehend enlivened the second male."

Erik heaved a sigh, "Wouldn't you rather talk about something else to pass the time?"

"No. Why does he wear that skeletal rib cage over his jacket?"

Erik put down his pencil and cracked his knuckles. For some reason the act felt very pleasing. "He considers himself kin to the Grim Reaper and is especially fond of that section in Leroux's book where the Opera Ghost dresses as Red Death." Thayer's eyebrows raised in astonishment. Erik snickered, "Well, he nearly stopped your heart in the crypt."

"In the first twenty-four hours of their lives," Isidore redirected the topic, "our amazement that Torossian managed to live only intensified. Yet there he was...a new undefined existence. His cardiac muscle contracted once every thirty seconds, always proceeded by a short shallow breath. His body temperature was and still is only seventy-six degrees. His vision is not acute; he cannot discern printed words, but perceives anything with dimension to the most astonishing degree of accuracy. Erik put someone in the womb with him, as if he (who actually cares little for worldly possessions) was storing up the loot of a brother."

"I didn't create Torossian," Erik sounded irritated.

"But it wasn't us," insisted Isidore. "If we move in concert past the dead cerulean eyes of your saurian brother, and accept his nature for what it is...then frankly, we must declare that he is some remarkable offshoot of your natural DNA. Is he an example of where our species might be a half million years from now?"

Erik was becoming uneasy. "He doesn't like conversations, especially when they center on him. He knows his voice makes people jittery, so he barely speaks, period. Prefers telepathy and image transference."

"*Natura non facit saltum* – nature makes no such leap," asserted Thayer.

"Go ahead, wallow in erroneous self-deception. The argument that life makes no such leap is superfluous given that the creature already walks around," scoffed Isidore. "He's virtually allergic to sunlight, and I might add that above anything else, he prefers Erik's company. For years they trusted no one but each other. Even if Erik denies it, I know the truth."

"What does he eat?" countered Thayer's bruised ego. Though the creature's outward appearance was that of strength, Delaquois found Torossian's chalky-white skin and the cadaverous hollows of his face nauseating and wondered what nourishment sustained such an anemic being.

Almost as if he knew they were discussing him, the Revenant spared Isidore answering the question by entering the room.

Given the recently acquired and extremely unflattering scar on his chin and upper neck, Thayer kept his distance.

Devoid of warmth or any note of cordiality, the glaucous creature moved toward Erik. Taking a position near his brother, there followed a long moment of silence.

Erik nodded and as a courtesy spoke outloud – in distinct sentences as the thoughts were delivered. "Yes, I can control my hot headed temper. What is it you want to say?" There was no need to look into the clouded glacial eyes, nothing registered there. "He wants me to announce that our DNA is different. In utero my fetus expunged itself of code it couldn't stabilize. The redundancy caused him. He wants to remind you that not every problem is meant to be solved. It's appropriate that some aspects remain a mystery. Both of us incorporated our donor's DNA, but in the split and regeneration, I kept most of the ingrained memories. He absorbed very little of them. The growth spurts of childhood prevented remembering past life right away. Our hidden natures developed over time…with maturity. Put into the simplest terms, the condition is like peeling an orange. Remove the rind and what do you have? The sweet inner fruit, each section of which still forms the entirety of what matters. The former Erik is filling in the blanks, telling me what he, no… correction…what we have done." Erik studied his brother. "I am given to understand that I'm in a chilly unpleasant schoolroom. The trick is to remain serene, protect my current mentation, and provide this Phantom with the friendly invitation of allowing him to express the whole of our former life."

"I doubt that it's really that simple," Thayer cautioned.

The two dichotomous individuals ignored the statement, continuing in private conversation.

Console Christine? asked Erik. *Provide her with a degree of comfort? Why? Did something happen during your games?* As the creature backed out of the room, beckoning him to follow, Erik's head tilted, a frown creasing his brow. A few seconds later, like a proud chanticleer, the budding oncologist asked to be excused for a while.

Upstairs in his room, Erik walked to the foot of his bed and rolled back the edge of a thick Chinese carpet. "I am the *dam dar ashegh* – the trap door lover." Slipping the edge of a pocketknife into a groove in the flooring, he lifted upward. Removing a slender section of floorboard, revealed a metal ring. Pulling the ring tightened a length of well-oiled cable attached to a pulley. He listened to the catch release, then pushed on the flooring. An eighteen-inch square dropped downward a mere three inches. Riding on brackets, the square slid easily into a pocket, revealing the top of a smooth metal dome three feet below. "Greetings, patient friend," he murmured. Dropping abdomen-first onto the center of the dome, he spread out his legs to evenly distribute body weight. He pushed a bar and the center of the dome opened. Hanging onto the lever like a monkey, he stayed suspended in the empty space below before dropping quietly onto a circular wooden platform. He stood in the center of a chamber completely lined with mirrors.

Turning around confidently, arms slightly flared – elbows bent, he looked at himself in the dim light dispersed from a phosphorescent green ball about the size of a grapefruit. Walking to a panel, he spun it on a pivot. He was there – he was gone – he was back again. "Was I ever here?" Amused, he feigned wonderment. He wanted to regain a sense of the Phantom, to bathe in his temperament before approaching Christine. "Somewhere in Persia I built an entire palace with a special room very similar to this one. Though I haven't remembered the particulars of that phase, I will eventually. Rakesh wants me to influence the world. I'm not so sure I want to change what the Fates are prescribing, just rattle the intriguing Miss Daae."

The catoptric chamber had a series of small rectangular windows so the eyes of spectators could view the inner space. Several nearly imperceptible apertures allowed focused beams of light to travel in any number of different directions. Left unmonitored, the application of light raised the temperature inside the chamber to uncomfortable levels. The inner wooden dais could rotate or be left stationary. If needed, the outer six-sided wall of mirrors expanded to eight sides with the simple addition of two sliding panels. The dais and outer wall rotated independent of each other. A dizzying experience for anyone parked at the center. Each turntable operated on a series of gears that were set into motion with a gentle shove. Engaging several sets of powerful magnets perpetuated the motion. The turntables spun until the operator separated the banks of magnets. The application of several soft brake pads brought the spinning to a welcomed halt.

Erik stood there, concentrating. Dressed in a white full-sleeved vineyard shirt, buttoned at the cuffs, well-worn straight-legged jeans, and black boots, he wanted the sense of his former feelings. *I've neglected you, Christine. Forgive me, t'was of necessity.* Even as a clone he had all the emotions and perceptions of any normal person. Armed with that knowledge, he plunged forward, soaking in the character of the man who built the chamber. *In the theater, life presented me with a paradox. I never expected to discover love. Working out that truth often ran contrary to the dictates of my own common sense.*

He flashed on a now familiar mental picture. Like cached memory in a computer, the scene played out. He'd left a fire blazing in the hearth of his underground home. In the theater above he walked, dressed as Red Death through one congested lounge into the next. Endless knots of partygoers, arrayed in bright costumes of repeating motifs, surrounded him: soldiers, fairies, animals, and funny game pieces of chessmen and dominoes. The scents of mandarin, tuberose, jasmine and bergamot filled the air. From space to space, repeating on and on, endless music played in the background. He was watching for her, always watching for her...even from the casement windows of theatric scenery, where he scanned the magnificently decked revelers chatting and dancing below. Hidden in the props of fake Castilian balconies he listened to promises being made, favors granted in hushed giggles.

Beneath the light of an antique chandelier, amid the romantic glow of thirty candles, the girl he hunted appeared. *La belle Mademoiselle* emerged – gowned in obsidian black brocade, décolletage trimmed in midnight lace, the arms of the dress the sheerest black chiffon. Over her eyes she wore a mask of feathers trimmed in double layers of gathered black tulle. He recognized the ease with which she moved, ever the leggy ballerina. He waited for her to pass. Then dragged her aside to speak from the depths of his burgeoning fervor. He let the dolorous sobbing of his anguished soul decry the net of love she'd thrown so callously about him! For he was emptied of reason, filled with the bitter poison of her... all because love would not release its hold, and she was without the slightest ounce of mercy. *I will have more than insipid approbation!*

When he grew calm, the lovesick sleuth climbed a rope and re-entered his upstairs bedroom in the chateau. At midnight, with his thoughts gathered, he traversed the *couloir etroit*, easily picked the lock, and went into her chambers to watch her sleep. Two dim lights softly illuminated the damsel's room, an area made perfect simply because she occupied it. The bathroom door stood ajar. Inside on a tiny wooden table, not too far from a porcelain bathtub with heavy ball and claw feet, burned a small stained glass lamp. Intended, no doubt, to light her way lest she stumble. He clicked it off.

Near her bed sat a heavy wing chair, its head and arms covered with crocheted antimacassars. On a button-tufted ottoman that rolled on silent rubber wheels, he found a novel and a volume of an encyclopedia she'd been reading. She was at R. And the work of fiction was something new, an American sequel to <u>The Phantom of the Opera</u>. He shrugged. *It's all right. Speculation about our fate was inevitable.* He flipped through the pages. At the theater, Christine had overturned the sanctuary of his perverse and lonely life. Not this time. He'd brought her into this century and now she owed a debt to the Opera Ghost. He set the novel down. He found the interest spawned by one of his former careers very odd. The critics of these authors caviled unnecessarily, haranguing over frivolous trivial faults in the works of others similarly intrigued with the Phantom. They should know that he had been a great many things to any number of people. *Difficult to schmush such a character into any particular cookie-cutter mold.*

Eyeing Christine's stereo, he moved to look over her music collection. She'd been ordering on line from Amazon. *Shall we dance, my sweet? To what?* He flipped through the CD's, reading their labels. An eclectic collection, all of it meant to inspire an enthusiasm for motion. Everything from fiery salsa to sultry flamenco, hip-hop, even Western line dancing. *She always adored flittering about, rhythmically waving her arms. She taught our children.* His thoughts clouded.

He angled leisurely over to her bed. Her breathing was peaceful and regular, her mind miles away in dreams. The center of the headboard was a carved wooden heraldic shield of a lion couchant, its head held high. Proud.

What a miracle she is! Just having her alive presented such a pleasure. Even asleep she managed to invade the remotest corners of his heart. *Such an alluring enchantress with the waves of her brown hair cresting the pillows.* Quickened by the train of his thoughts a dynamic drive took over. Every non-somatic germ cell in his body lusted for her. He bent his will back upon itself, forcing his passion into constraint.

I didn't feel alive until you were here, now...standing two feet from you, I feel alone all over again. Every time I manage to touch you, I die inside. The sensation is startling. Before your birth, I only existed. Now I am both alive and undone. I don't understand. Torossian is a block of strength and you managed to affect him. What motivations drive you? Do you have a need to be coy, or is it that you crave experience? I had hoped that this time there would be no rivals, only your will to overcome. Grant me a time and a place to experience you for myself and I'll share you, even as I shared you with Raoul.

He watched the right carotid artery pulsate in her neck. She lay on her side, her right arm bent across her chest. Intense and brazen, he divided the space of air, the obstruction of separate thoughts, even the decades of time between them and lifted away the comforter and the sheet. She lay there in a lavender lace-embellished nightgown – the bottom half hiked up about her hips. The right knee flexed, the leg draped forward. He could smell the perfumed cream upon her skin. Still in REM, she rotated to her back; right arm left delicately trailing across her breasts.

Moody and pensive, he unplugged the only nightlight left, a small shell arrangement in a jack on a floorboard near the bed. The absence of light penetrating the room made the blackness complete. He sank backward until he touched the outer wall, imagined himself a lonely Phantom coming into her presence to slither about in the darkness.

Here we are, once again in the flesh, able to behold each other. How much time passed unattended in our first lives? How much wasted time – spent as if we had a never-ending supply of minutes to lavish about? When truthfully, all we had was a constantly diminishing pittance. The thief of time unraveled our lives once before and stole all we had left. Now another thief, one motivated by scientific curiosity, awakens us from sleep. Shall we idle away the minutes as we did before? As if it matters little how much we squander?

With his eyes fully adjusted, he crept forward. Lifting the nightgown, he viewed the quivering flesh of her abdomen and exposed *mons veneris*. Reassuring himself that he could not impregnate her, he remembered when their first son lay secreted there within that womb. Growing safely right where he'd planted his seed between her legs.

He so wanted to touch her, lie within her, think of nothing else but her and what it felt like to lovingly penetrate the gates of glory. *Little cosset, how I would pet and pamper you.* Letting his fingers ripple in the air above her flesh, traveling over an imaginary keyboard, he played a sonata over her body. Though he did not touch her, the warmth of her skin beneath his opened palms was a soothing comfort, an aromatic balm.

Swimming in his music her mind was stirring. She tumbled about on oceanic waves of *concerto grosso* cellos accompanied by piano. Before he thought to stop himself, her eyes opened.

Withdrawing his hands as if they'd been slapped, he stepped back.

The fact that Erik had managed, undetected, to stand beside her once again served to both thrill and mortify. *Why does this man wield such power?* In the dark, only his bright liquid amber eyes were speaking, and they were saying volumes. She admired his totally immobile pose – and simultaneously wanted to insult, tease, and cradle him within her arms.

"Pardon me for not observing the appropriate courting rituals," his voice had the saturating rush of a warm Caribbean breeze, "but we are in a rather unique set of circumstances."

Her hand fumbled around beneath her pillow searching for an object inadvertently left on the side table.

"Are you looking for this?" he asked through his teeth, growing testy. He clicked the flashlight on, letting the upturned beam cast his features into a sharp macabre relief, practically daring her to scream. "I had hoped to wait for morning, but finding myself free, decided to pay a visit. Actresses have a long history of entertaining fans in their private dressing rooms. You like romantic adventures. Tales where Tutankhamen pays you homage and satisfies your needs." He clicked the light off and in silence relaxed his frame against the wing chair. "You're not the only one who can beam commands into the heads of other people."

His words bit into her brain. She eyed him furiously, "You frightened me! And the games I play with my guardian are none of your business." Nevertheless, she couldn't deny the guilt she felt for using Torossian so boldly.

"I could try to ease your apprehension, but I doubt the validity of your fear. Given to histrionics, Christine?" He lowered his voice. "You're always watching to see if I'll appear. And once you spot me, your eyes follow me about. Care to explain why?"

"All right, I'll admit that I'm attracted…and a little awkward at expressing my affinity. Consider the merits of taking me under your tutelage." She sat up, straightening her nightgown and yanking a pillow to her back so she could press herself comfortably against the headboard.

He studied her, contemplating the consequences of acting on her request without saying another damn word.

"Unexpected petition? Unprepared to act? There's more, Erik. You said that I'm not supposed to have memories. You didn't do such a great job of erasing me. I can trump you, I'm certain that you secretly hoped that I **would** have memories."

"I don't think we could have predicted the outcome, but had to try."

"We? Define 'we' later. I know that you and I danced together, rolled around in this bed, played with babies. The whole room breathes of you."

In as even-tempered a response as he could manage, "Yes, many times…I took you in my arms many times…for the cotillion, quadrille, the waltz. I'm not sure where this is going."

"And you sang to me?"

"Yes, in the most sonorous fashion I could project – from corridors, behind screens, out in the wide open spaces. What I lacked in looks, I tried to make up for in impressive vocal style and physical agility." He came again to stand beside the bed and postulated how far he dared go with her in the next minute, the next hour, the next century.

She flipped on the lamp. She'd taken the covers back, covered her lavender laced chest all the way up to her chin.

A damn vault! He couldn't help but broadcast the announcement.

The door to the main hallway opened and a strange panther-like creature honed onto the four-poster. From low in the back of its throat, it issued a threat, warning Erik against advancing further.

How prosaic, Torossian is projecting a more menacing change in shape. "Thank you, wonderful impression of Reza. Good of you to grant me admittance. You keep your vigil well."

From the entrance, the Revenant's paw became more human. Delivering an offensive hand gesture, he made it clear he didn't like her sleep disturbed.

"I only came to watch her breathe." *And compose some abominable music over her abdomen.* Erik's mind captured the aspects of the scene from the different angles it presented – a perfect triangle. The Revenant framed by the doorway, Christine in her bed, and the instigator unmasked and threatened back into temporary obscurity. He suddenly realized how Khusrowshah had become richer and richer. He and his allies secreted money and jewels in a cooperative tri-pointed *mise-en-scène*. They'd been doing it for years. He blinked playfully.

Incredulous and a bit irritated, Christine blurted, "Stop fretting! It's putting creases in your forehead."

"If you do nothing else tonight, forgive my addictive behavior. You're like a designer drug." He turned to leave.

"Your overconfidence is driving me mad – get out! Both of you get out! You're disturbing my rest."

He stopped and reflected a moment. Her explosive admonition was rather off cue, given late. He was already on his unrepentant way out. Pleased, he turned to face her. She'd let the covers slide to her lap. Her body language was betraying her real intent. That angry sounding voice was just melodramatic acting. He stiffened. "Shall I take my perfect face and leave, or stay and give you your first lesson in sexual congress?"

She stood, letting the covers fall to the floor. "Wait. Don't go. We were married?"

"Of a sort."

"How? When?"

He was moved. There were tears, wistful tears, filling the basins of her lower eyelids. *What answer do I supply? What inadequate response?* "It's a long story. It didn't happen in the *Basilique Ste-Madeleine*. Tomorrow.

Take a walk with me at dusk and we'll talk." He fled to the comfort of his own quarters to regroup.

Waving the Revenant out, she pulled a purple chenille robe over her shoulders and shoved her feet into a pair of fuzzy slippers. Summoning her indignation, she followed him down the short hall. She'd never had the nerve to walk into his rooms and felt a degree of pleasure when she found the knob rotating in her hands. *Unlocked!*

"Not tomorrow. Tonight." Her tone was lyrical, evocative, and very earnest.

Wiping his face with a wet towel, he poked his head around the corner of his bathroom. The only real light in the room came from a spectacular one hundred gallon saltwater fish tank. A school of bright clown fish swimming around a reef encrusted with sea anemone caught her eye. Set at waist height on a special cabinet, the internal lights sent a series of colorful prisms across the walls and furnishings of the room. A relatively new acquirement, the staff kept the tank immaculately clean; there was not a hint of algae. The soft bubbling of the air system was rather pacifying.

"You followed? Those flowers are for you," he pointed to an arrangement on his desk. In a tall vase sat an order from a florist: two dozen vibrant long stem red roses graced with delicate bunches of paniculate baby's breath. He wanted to present them to her...to solicit a sentimental response, but vetoed the idea of hauling them into her room in the middle of the night. "They arrived late."

Huh? Now there's a limpid, ineffectual excuse, an inner voice chastised him.

At the sight of the flowers her eyebrows raised with surprise. She fixed her gaze on him. "You entered my room, entertained yourself at my expense and failed to mention that flowers had arrived for me? I accept bribes."

"You're welcome." Regaining a bit of confidence, he strode into the room and sat down on a small sofa upholstered with a detailed Aubusson rooster pattern. With the act of crossing his legs and dramatically throwing his arms over the back of the custom-contoured settee, he proclaimed himself ruler of the roost in his own domain.

"What is the matter with you?"

"I told you. *Mon état c'est vous* (my condition is you)." He let those words sink in. "It's late, would you like to have a seat? Something to drink? An apology for picking your lock?" *What a strange puffy robe-thing she is wearing, it doesn't flatter her shape.* He made himself focus. *Why is she in here?* He mulled over the possibilities, deciding not to make the mistake that this counter-intrusion defined any degree of authentic acceptance.

She sat on a chair opposite him. "You wander around without any regard for my privacy. Obliging me to deal with your crudeness."

Her words stung. He gave her an alpine cold stare.

"I too have a hunger inside me." She conceded a point.

"Oh, you don't know the definition of hunger. I could make you hungry, ravenous. You have hot spots."

"Hot spots?"

"Yes, well defined areas that make you feel needy...aroused. I could show them to you. Not one hour ago I..." With a sly smile crossing his lips, he stood to tower over her. Delicately lifting her chin, he said, "If I insist on showing you, will you run for cover? Flee down a hole like a wild little rabbit who has detected the whiff of the hunter?"

"Why is it you can't sleep?" She avoided answering.

"I don't know. Maybe I'm afraid you'll disappear."

"You've never been afraid of anything."

He wondered what he had done to convince her that was true. "I'm not anxious about my life here in this chateau. But there is one thing that drives me to distraction." He retook his seat. "The thought that I'll wake up again and it will be another day without you in the world."

She sat in the strange light of the fish tank, barely able to accept the depth of his words. "What were those days like? Before you put me in the tank to develop?" She nodded toward the fish.

She remembers the infernal tank! So much for cyclic voltage! "I had a lot of nightmares, strange adventures I didn't want to mull over, yet seemed unable to forget."

"That's happening to me."

Erik felt like he was grasping at straws, trying to understand how much was intuition and how much she really knew. "Electric shock, we periodically reset your brain with a low voltage current."

"You tried to drive away the ghosts?"

"Ghosts?" He leaned forward, elbows to his thighs, hands clasped.

"Yes, they slip into my mind, specter-like videos without explanatory memos. I started telling you about them in the chapel."

"Do they upset you?"

She shook her head to indicate the negative. "Not always."

"Tell me one thing you know about us."

"I can't – nothing sticks," she tapped her forehead.

Like Torossian, Erik knew every time she lied. "That's not true."

"All right. I just don't know what to make of it. There's a vivid impression of dozens of rats looking down at me from the walls, and you are inching your way among them. I don't know if that's a memory or a reoccurring invention of my mind."

"How old are you?"

"I'm not sure. I don't look down at myself. I'm watching you."

"Close your eyes. Don't look at the rats or me. Can you see your hands?"

"I have breasts...and...a wedding ring!"

"Do you know that if you loved me for five minutes, those would be the most exquisite five minutes of my life. I swear, rubbing my body against yours, a fireball would burst forth within me, and a great sensation of peace descend into my brain. I would hug you...grateful beyond words for the solace."

Christine studied his face, relishing his sincerity. "What a shrewd cajoler. You just persuaded me to forsake the rabbit hole."

His eyebrows rose, obviously pleased. "What next?"

Her eyes of blue-green tourmaline sent a plaintive message. "When people are riddled with doubts and lack explanations they embrace every kind of superstitious talisman imaginable. They fear that even a minor calamity is an omen that death itself lurks at the door. Perhaps for me, it's just a matter of plucking away the remnants of our past by getting some answers."

"I want to talk to you about Isidore," he dared to broach another subject aching in his heart. "He's ill. Cancer. I can't imagine the world without him. After so many years of self-imposed exile, he deserves to experience a sense of family. You can help with that."

She wanted the conversation back along its former lines. "You're helping to cure him, aren't you? You started to tell me what you did an hour ago."

Erik clutched the carved wood arm of the settee, anger shooting through him. *She has no appreciation for Isidore's gift of life, not a shred of empathy for his disease!*

She hadn't noticed his change in attitude. In the shadows she'd caught a glimpse of an amazing wall of masks. Flipping on a light to illuminate the two-dozen altered faces; her eyes ran from a silver feathered Venetian concoction to a plain white kidskin, then on to that of a laughing skull shrouded in a black hood. A sense of dread started choking her. She barely focused on one before another drew her attention. Her hands shook in fine uncontrolled twitches. "The name, what is his name? He plagues me, mocks me...would suck love from me with a passion as unruly and hot as...as...a fireball!"

She froze, arrested by a cloudy fog bank that for one moment seemed to grant the dim recognition of a pair of adoring eyes set within a hideously deformed face. "Phantom," she whispered in fearful reverence. "The detestable Opera Ghost." Pale with terror she confronted Erik. "You've come for me again. Why don't you put on your mask so I can really remember!"

"You want a performance?" He barked, springing from his chair.

Taking her wrist in his cold vice-like grip, he unceremoniously removed her from her seat. "Consider that before this re-enactment, you were never abrasively dragged against your will, never forced to descend jagged musty tunnels. Never pleaded with a repulsive abductor who locked you in rooms that had become your cage! Never shrieked at the top of your lungs, demanding to be set free after listening to the love-starved confessions ranted by a monster trying to dote over every glance you made, every word you uttered!"

32 *TACKLING THE MONSTER*

*N*atural grace doesn't exist and is often a misspoken phrase. Fluid movements under pressure must be learned and practiced. Christine tripped to the right, then went left as he jerked her through the door. Her own feet were in her way; at one point she actually hopped sideways. Hauled down the corridor like cargo, her left arm got twisted, but she offered no complaint.

Erik ignored her grimace, rudely declaring, "You're impatience to experience the truly macabre allows you free admittance! Let me escort you to real terror."

Out of the shadows the Revenant surged forward. Erik paused in his vitriolic rant to shove her into a position behind him and deal with his brother.

Imprisoned within his rough grasp, she stumbled to a halt like a wild out-of-control marionette. "Back off, Torossian. I asked for this!" She sounded like a judge hammering down a gavel.

In reaction to her gutsy command the rescuer bowed and got out of the way, tracking captor and captive as they steamrolled toward the elevator.

"This isn't like children scouting for Easter eggs," Erik shoved her knuckles onto the button. "You no longer set the pace. Your abductor sets it for you." The bell sounded announcing the arrival of the car. Barely clearing the elevator door as it started to open, he literally hoisted her into the metal cubicle.

"Stay!" he shouted at Torossian like he commanded a dog. "She desperately needs to be taught a lesson about life and gratitude." Then back at her. "Oh, I don't mind the unceasing competition. You can have them line up like toy soldiers, but things may end poorly for your squad! I would have auctioned my entire kingdom of rats for you." He spared her another yank forward and punched the button for the basement himself.

She dared a look into his stormy face. His jaw was set, his expression fierce and unforgiving. In defense, she lowered her eyes.

"How many times did you look at me and not see me, Christine? I was there in the mirror, the corners, the shadows…with my sad eyes waiting to be summoned like a neglected mongrel. You never hid yourself in dark obscurity so people couldn't see you. Never wanted to hold someone so close to your chest that you choked on the need." The elevator landed smoothly at the bottom floor, and his grip tightened as he wrenched her into the dusty basement. "I am a despicable fiend who hates all others and violates their will as I please. Shall I savor every inch of you here on the stone floor?" He projected the figure of a frenzied black-draped Phantom into her mind.

"I was wrong to goad you into proving your authority. I admit it – you're stronger. I'm ready to listen", she bargained. "You don't have to do this."

He punched in the code to enter the lab. "I refuse to smother my feelings any longer!" His fury was still escalating. "Tonight you may have one full-blown experience, one more unsavory chaotic episode to add to the amalgam of your life! Though I promise, you'll be expending a great deal of energy trying to heal from the interesting effects of this." He shoved her into the waiting area, through the locker room, and on into the lab proper.

When he again latched onto her wrist, she dragged her feet in resistance. "Your temper is a parasitic lichen erupting on a tree. An unpleasant match to the bleeding nodules that at one time held a vague resemblance to a face!"

That stung. "Have a care, women! I am the perfect center of a swirling emotional hurricane." The door to Isidore's sickroom swooshed open. "Don't be alarmed – there's no smell quite like this, rotting flesh actually walking on the hoof!"

How did things go so awry? She'd hoped for the stage of a glorious theater and here she was thrust into a lab. His vigorous push sent her lurching into the room. He pinched her shoulder, and as she drew in a breath to yell, "Ouch!" a pungent reeking funk hit her like a hurling train. Unable to stop an involuntary retching, she swooned, knees buckling beneath her.

Erik caught her round the waist before she sank completely to the floor.

From his bed Isidore stared in disbelief.

Nyah stood at a medicinal work cabinet, in her hands she held a syringe with the needle stuck in a vial ready to aspirate. "Erik, what are you doing? She's only a child."

"She is a disgrace and needs indoctrination into our gruesome little family," Erik bristled. "How is a man to survive the erratic whims of her agendas? She ordered the thrill of the Opera Ghost's tentacles reaching up from the muck to unsettle her."

"Help her to a chair," directed Isidore. "I take it you're having your first argument?"

Erik gladly complied with the order, doing nothing to hide his belligerence.

A disconcerted Nyah interjected, "Erik, neither of you have masks or gloves."

"Shut up, Nyah," ordered Isidore. "It's all right. There isn't a shred of DNA in this lab that isn't covered and redundantly protected. Crack an ammonia inhalant and stick it under her nose."

At the sharp knife-like sniff of the chemical, Christine's head jerked upward, re-alerted to a stench that made a person want to slam their head into a stone revetment. "What is that smell?!"

Manipulating the electric controls, Isidore raised the head of his bed before addressing her. "I apologize for the stench. That smell is the necrotic tissue sloughing off me. A primary malignancy, followed by a metastases has overtaken this shell of a body I'm housed in. This is my sickroom, located in a place of unlimited possibilities. Here in this realm of science, past lives can be reborn and lived again in current time."

Erik leaned against the wall, arms defiantly set across his chest. "She's impatient to know the truth."

Despite his debilitation, Isidore's eyes twinkled, happy that the weight of the surprise should fall to him, the unscrupulous shriveled gnome. "There is a set of facts you must digest, my girl. I recommend chewing slowly. Absorb them as you would a story, then apply the tale to yourself. You are here because we reproduced the tiniest part of a biological chain, links of code that define your body."

Embarrassed at her spinning emotions and nauseous state, her reply was more cryptic than she intended. "You made me…like a piece of jewelry?"

"You are a copy of the necklace. Men have been reproducing and altering jewelry for eons. The links we used for you are called DNA, manipulated since the days when the great Louis Pasteur walked the *Ecole Normale Superieure*." He spoke with the authority that was his right. "I'm also a man of some repute. You were not brought into this century on impulse, or for mercurial sport. You are most valuable, especially to Erik. He would have no other."

"In a word, I am a shitty clone."

"Don't say the word 'clone' like it implies sub-human! You are a living breathing woman with vigorous health and a mind of your own. Your obviously self-serving enough to swear." Isidore had a wealth of argument to deflect her rebellion. "This life is a separate experience you will create for yourself. How much of your former existence you incorporate into today's universe is a tangle you must also sort out. Whatever your preferences, there is no denying that you are here breathing among us. You will change all our lives for the better or the worse. Your choice, but understand that no one will expect you to be perfect." Lowering his voice to a growl, he ordered, "Show her the tank, Erik."

Christine's facial expression changed from one of annoyance to eager interest.

Erik opened the door and silently bowed to his two misshapen creators.

"When you have a minute," Nyah interjected almost playfully, "we purchased a present for you, Erik. It's just outside the gate of the north courtyard. Waiting for your approval."

"Thank you. Whatever it is, I'll treasure it." He wiggled his index finger in a come-hither gesture. "Follow me!"

Since he was more polite and not manhandling her, Christine dutifully trailed his shirttails. At first she seemed a little disappointed in the vessel that had contained her during gestation. She remarked, almost annoyed, "Great. How imaginative. It is like your fish tank upstairs, only busted. You grew me like an aquatic specimen."

"In some aspects, except that this was a very ingenious container. It's empty now because it no longer contains the most precious jewel on the planet."

Taken aback, she scrutinized his face, trying to gauge his temperament. "Can we go outside for awhile? Negotiate a truce on neutral ground?"

"Your capricious streak is showing," he tapped the tip of her nose. "Let me tell Isidore so he doesn't think we're sneaking away to amuse ourselves with anything but resolving our differences." He hoped the statement might reassure her.

They took the elevator to the first floor, grabbed a canvas field jacket off a coat rack for Christine, and entered the kitchen. From an eight-foot steel refrigerator Erik grabbed a cold bottle of water and slipped it into her pocket. Patting the object in place, he asked, "Shall we take a turn about the mansion?"

"What an odd way to say: Let's take a walk."

He steered her queerly attired body toward the kitchen door and the backside of the chateau. "Be careful outside. Pay strict attention and stay by my side. There are some pits with barbed wire. Six to be exact."

She took his hand. It was remarkably cool and dry. "Could you ever trust me again?"

Ignoring the question, he entered the code onto the keypad and swung the door open. A rush of night air greeted them. "Good thing you're wearing a coat."

He led her, more graciously this time, down the walkway. The lowest balustrades off the northern patios were to their right. They overlooked the back meadow where the grass had just been mowed.

"Why are there twelve foot walls and enormous lights around the place? I see them from every window."

"Since my earliest childhood the grounds have been like this. Isidore is a very famous man. He's done some things that have upset quite a number of people. There have been threats made against his life." He emphasized the word 'threats'. Coming to a stop, senses on alert, Erik breathed in the fragrance of the recent trimming. Crushing a blade between his thumb and index finger, he rolled the sweet smell near his nostrils. *Edifying.*

He watched as she mimicked him with another chopped stem. Her nose curled in distaste, the smell of ammonia and decaying flesh still stuck in her nares.

Glad in a somewhat perverse way, he scanned the terrain. "Nature grows on you. Too bad we're reduced to this. There used to be an impeccably manicured garden here. Now there are only a few closely pruned evergreen shrubs, a couple of benches, and this soft Gramineae leading down the hill to a shrinking lake."

Slipping her hand around his elbow, "Let's stroll down there. What has Isidore done to make people hate him? Are there armies of unhappy clones?"

"No. You and I are the only two. It's a little complicated. Involves world politics and you're only at R in the encyclopedia."

"Did we ever gather rhubarb and chard from the kitchen garden?"

"Probably," he resigned himself to a limited rehash of the past. "There were two weddings here in the 1800's. One with bright orange and yellow nasturtiums, and every other orange flower they could come up with."

"Colorful."

"I think I miss the trees the most. A stone archway on the southeast corner of the house leads to the chapel where some ancient oaks still stand. You must have seen them. Despite Isidore's paranoia about safety, he couldn't bear to chop them down."

"I'm glad we came outside. Perplexities seem less overwhelming in this setting. I can picture delphinium in every imaginable shade of blue out here."

"And roses, lots of roses. Their heady scent hung like a perfume in the air, especially after rainstorms. The formal garden was not as ostentatious as some, it leaned a tad toward domesticated countryside. It fanned out in five carefully planned ever-widening sections; each graced with statuary, parterres, and water fountains. Everything was turned to face the focal point of your bedroom windows. A geometric design that acted like a theater applauding you with flowers and Nature."

Down the contour of the long rolling meadow she kept her steps in stride with his. "We played games in the gardens?"

"A form of Hide-and-Seek, very entertaining. The logistics of building a laboratory beneath this area forced the engineers to sacrifice the ornamental plants and trees. Isidore wanted to pursue his field of science privately. He over-compensated by keeping the inside of the mansion as untouched as possible. We don't even take our meals on the terraces anymore. Missed opportunities, so regrettable."

"People used to enjoy the warmer weather? Yes! They ate in embroidered gowns and tailored suits with bouffant hair piled atop their heads. Foods swimming in high-cholesterol sauces while they listened to the breeze and chirping birds in the bushes."

He shook his head in wonder. She was such an odd mixture of then and now. "Today you might need a bulletproof vest to accomplish such a simple pleasure."

In a few minutes they arrived at the lake's shore. A still visible moon blessed the water's surface with a thousand coruscating diamonds. A small boathouse, enveloped by a cluster of pine trees, stood closed and locked behind them. Looking out across the water, they saw the sandy island surrounded by its court of rocks and reeds. The lone oasis still managed to support a few pine trees of its own. Before morning a fine mist would rise up off the lake to tenderly blanket the landscape. With luck the mist would accumulate into a gentle fog and add some moisture to the dearth of vegetation.

After a respectful moment, Erik sighed, "There's still duck and geese out here in the fall."

"Where are our former bodies?" She had to face reality sometime.

"Try to put that question from your mind. The grave is silent, Christine, but you are no longer mute...and neither am I."

"Our children?" She clutched her left breast to calm a racing heart.

"All long dead. Our great-great-grandchildren walk the earth as elderly people. Isidore is one of them. The rest are estranged from us."

"So he is biologically related to us. The scientist is not our father, but our descendant?"

Erik nodded. Water was the perfect metaphor. He swept his hand in a symbolic arc. "On a lake of rippling time, our second son was Ariel, our grandson Rupert...his son was Lowell, and Lowell was Isidore's father."

"And you stand, a dark tower at the beginning and in the end."

"I didn't cook this fiasco. Isidore did, but he is extremely ill. We lack the luxury of years to criticize his choices." *Why burden her with the knowledge of Julian, and the fact that there will be no more descendents? She's not even curious about Torossian's origins...still too early in the process.* "If the cancer cannot be contained and atrophied, this historical chapter will play out very soon." He turned his back to her and kicked the sand to locate a few stones.

"You're trying to accomplish a cure?"

"We've tagged radioisotopes with a poison that has a particular affinity for the malignant cells and infused them into Isidore's bloodstream. The concoction also carries a genetic command that tells the nuclei of the carcinoma they cannot reproduce. Painful as hell, considering the cancer has metastasized to his bones, but it is working." He began skipping stones across the water.

She knew he needed time to think, so she walked up to the pines. Keeping her eyes on him, she was grateful not to see the frown creasing his face. "So you were restless and dissatisfied, you brought me back for what? Company? How did you accomplish getting me in the tank?"

He angled sideways and strategically tossed one stone to chase another. Bending over he counted the number of skips. *A measly four each. Ugh!* He did a one-eighty to rocket the next from his left hand. "Be reasonable, all right? This is a very romantic spot. Why not surrender to the ambiance?" His control this time was excellent – the stone skipped eight times before sinking. Not his record, but it would do. He turned to follow her into the pines.

She clung to one of the lowest branches, swinging outward, expanding her chest. The movement opened the oversized jacket and the purple robe, pulling the lavender nightgown tight across her breasts.

He sent his mind into the zone, zeroing in on her thoughts. *Sprouts, fresh from their roots, seek sunshine and attention. Just so, I sought you... my muse, my nourishment.*

She looked up. Startled. Unable to see him, but sure he was very close, hiding behind some tree trunk.

Erik pressed his back against the rough bark. Smiling with satisfaction, he ran a hand through his stock of thick leonine curls. He really needed a haircut. He checked – she was trying to locate him by peering into his mind.

He increased the telepathic channel. *I reached across time for you. Cloning didn't change our attraction for each other, if anything it's heightened.*

"Am I your subject? You're hands are shaking."

Unaware, he checked. *Merde, they are.* He crouched, sticking them on the ground for balance. He reasoned that he looked something like Reza – on the prowl.

Why now? She thought the question, trying to distract him. There were only so many places he could be.

I needed time to grow, time to remember and miss you. And no, you are not my subordinate. I swear it.

As a silent wraith, she came to stand before him. Less afraid, she confided, "I'm remembering more and more all the time. Tell me everything. Please! Abandon reluctance and reeducate me."

He stood. *You are very skilled, a psychic natural.* Embarrassed, he looked down and started a perfunctory dusting-off of his knees. "Acting on impulse is not the wisest course of action. It might seem like I enjoy circumventing forethought and jumping before measuring consequences, but upstairs you disintegrated my self-control like a mad wizard. I apologize. Sincerely."

Leaning forward, she clutched the front of his shirt.

"Do you want to kiss?" he wondered hopefully.

"In autumn big-bowled roses were still in bloom, a profusion of hardy pinkish white cyclamens carpeted large areas of the grounds." Her eyes were searching his. The pupils were dilated, unguarded. "See there are memories. Upstairs...those masks started to open a terrifying door."

He placed his hands over hers. "Try to remember the flowers and dismiss the demon who stole you. I remember the animals: sloppy tongued dogs, sleek wide-eyed cats with litters of fat-bellied kittens, imperial horses, henhouses, cages of rabbits. On the outlying farms, cows for milk and beef, rambunctious goats, and flocks of sheep we sheared every spring."

She strained to make out the details flowing in his mind. "I can see you studying a crow. He's cawing over a hole in a decaying tree he's raided for grubs and worms. The land could be revived again, at least in part."

"Honestly, picturing things as they were, or as they might be again, doesn't make me feel any better." He wanted to tell her about the precipice he negotiated, the threatening catastrophe of personal identity looming ahead. The Phantom was strong, perhaps too strong.

"There used to be a banqueting pavilion. You built that pavilion! Where is the thing?" She turned her head and stared in the direction of the chapel.

He answered her with the picture of another empty space of simple grass and brush just east of the giant oaks.

"The pavilion is gone?" At a loss to grasp the enormity of the situation, she let go of his shirt. Her hands drifted rather indelicately to her sides. "I'm a shell. A piece of something that used to be full of life." She sounded incredibly morose.

Reasoning that females enjoy men of wisdom, but prefer men of decisive action, he issued an order, "Come back to me at once." He caught her in a kiss. His lips warm and full, demanding she pay attention. His tongue searched her mouth, imploring her for intimacy. He suddenly let go, sidestepping away. She hadn't responded.

Despite the delicious chill running down her spine, she stayed frozen.

"Do you know what buckram is?" he asked dryly.

"Yes, it's a stiffly finished fabric used to interline garments. Why?"

"I have a dose of it within me." He referred to the unheralded thickening in his loins. *Sixteen is a difficult age, a constant battle over control. Is that a blush around her neck? Well, that will be an impediment!* Seconds ticked past – an agonizing eternity.

"What do you have in mind?" she asked.

"Some really heavy petting before I escort you back to the house. Kissing and hugging that doesn't quite bring us to the act of uniting, despite a luscious overwhelming arousal!" He sent the picture to her mind. "Before this night comes to an end," he added as an afterthought.

"Why me? Paris must be full of women."

"Because I need **you**. You burn within my heart, a constant hope. You are my full and complete soul mate. My beloved." *There, it's out. You drive me nuts.*

"Can we afford to be intimate again?" Her mouth felt like cotton.

"Are you referring to money or procreation, as in babies? In either case, we're safe."

"Were we good together or did we create a string of tragedies?"

"We had some very wretched moments and some rather glorious experiences that actually broke the sound barrier." With an eye toward a preemptive pause, he pulled the bottle of water from her pocket and cracked it open. "Here, relieve your thirst and purge your thoughts."

While she drank, he continued to enlighten her. "You should know that I don't favor uncertain outcomes, and that I usually don't exaggerate other than to make a point." He set his hand poetically over his heart. "I'm not just making-due with you. You are not a simulation, every inch of you is very real."

She handed the bottle back to him, "Drink?"

After taking a swallow he screwed the cap back on. *At least she's not nervous about sharing germs. Maybe she doesn't know about bacteria.*

"I do know about bacteria...and I might know something of the mistakes we made two centuries ago. You craved me and I rejected you. That's the scary abduction part. Then after we separated, I discovered I wanted you back because I selfishly felt a bank-vault's worth of regret over throwing you away."

"Don't do that. No guilt! Why be hard on yourself? People naturally spurn deformity, doesn't matter if it's congenital or the result of an accident. They're especially unforgiving when a ghastly distortion is sprung upon them. It seems they equate a twisted body with evil and weakness. The ugly are luckless victims disowned by Fate. Only the perfect are worthy of association. Darwin. We are indebted to Isidore de Chagny and must anchor ourselves in this place, this century."

"You deserved better treatment."

"Apparently I never lost hope. When the original Christine distanced herself from me, I brought her back through music."

"And kidnapping...just to thrust defiant rage in her face, you stole her right off the Opera House stage."

"Mistakes. Cruel mistakes. But we managed to restore the balance. If we could do so again the really great sex would be an energizing factor for both of us."

She straightened, hands going to her hips. "What chicanery to bring me back!"

"What would you have me do? I can't erase what's done. You may have it all, the best of me, the worst of me...you just sampled a taste of that up in my room. I have genuine feelings for you, a wellspring of untapped passion. There's also this: I am incapable of permanently walking away from you."

She looked at him suddenly fascinated. "Take me to our dead bodies."

"I made that same request of Isidore with almost those exact words. He and I were at odds, and I forced him."

"Well that was foolhardy. He could probably flip a switch and disintegrate you."

"Have you been watching science fiction movies? Isidore and I declared an armistice over the decision to make you. There is so much to enjoy in this world, we could stay together and help each other to see with new eyes."

The duality of touring the world and still taking care of Isidore confused her. She thought he was joking. "Do you plan to bring the full weight of your considerable talents to breakdown my will power again? Give me some advantage with which to resist you! You can't win every argument."

Admonishing himself to be patient, he tensed and took in a frustrated breath. "You have several advantages. One is the fact that we did have children together. I will always honor you as their mother."

She waited, considering the statement. "That was another century, another lifetime."

"True, but I wanted you very badly then, and I want you just as badly now."

A vision of Christmas tree branches festooned with bows and ornaments appeared to her. "Did you send me that picture?"

"No," he breathed guiltily.

"Yes you did. You don't have as much control over projection as you think. I'm not your best-ever Christmas present." She waved her fingers delicately in front of his face. "Our bodies are in the chapel. I feel obligated to see them. Mine and yours."

Inside the door, at the back of the nave, Erik brought up some soft respectful lighting. She walked down the center aisle in her fluffy slippers and bizarre costume, repeating, "Hello? Hello?" Just to hear the pronounced echoing that followed, and for once Erik trailed after her. "Great acoustics."

Before completing the process of opening the crypt, he hesitated. "Are you sure you want to go down there? The *crypticus* is a place of secrets and death, not life and never-ending love. I'm not trying to be melodramatic, just honest. Don't try to re-live the first Christine's life, be yourself."

She made a defining circle with her index finger, a non-verbal 'open it up'. As the bat-like teeth separated, she peered in. "What are those gears for?"

"They prevent slippage. The entrance doesn't close until you tell it to shut." Together they descended the short flight of marble steps. "We're in the ante chamber. I'll tell you who rests in these first two sarcophagi later." Erik dutifully disengaged the lock to the posterior section.

It was easy to pick out the dead Christine's sarcophagus. A trefoil, an endless tri-cornered Celtic knot depicting eternity, was carved into the base at its foot. She ran her fingers over the relief. "Celtic knots?"

"Not all the Celtic realms were confined to Britain and Ireland. Case in point: Brittany, where you spent a large part of your childhood, is today part of northern France."

"I thought you said this wasn't a place of endless love. Everything in here seems to speak of *amour sans extrémité.*" A moment of eerie calm descended in the space between them. "You think it's morbid to want to see my former body. Yet you did exactly that, correct?"

"*Et lux in tenebris lucet.* The light shines in the darkness. We've been dead over nine decades."

"How did I die?"

"Isidore said congestive heart failure took you."

"What did it feel like interring me?"

"I am saddled with those memories. Why should you know more sadness? We are both in the springtime of our lives. You are ripe and I'm practically high on breathing the air that has just left your lungs." He glided in a small semi-circle around to her posterior. Pressing her back into him, he whispered into her ear, "Am I speaking plainly enough? Do you understand me? Do you know what I need?"

"Not always, but I get that you are alive and above ground…and I am too."

"Technically not true. In this tomb we are below ground level." He rubbed his body against hers in a suggestive, non-threatening manner.

She put her hands over his, curling into him. *Push, push your way through my misgivings,* she sent the thought with care. Even though she seemed amiable to being touched, he fought a tremendous urge to continue fondling her there in the semi-darkness.

Within the embrace of his arms she turned to face him. Before she could hug him, he drew back, and her hands landed on his chest. He knew she wanted to unbutton his shirt and see if he had hair, actually she wanted to view his entire body.

"You always had a rather gross affinity for making-out in tombs."

"You're not in conflict over losing the original? You said I'm enough, right? After we prove the truth of that statement, I want these bodies cremated and any of that DNA jewelry stuff that's stored in the lab destroyed."

"I swear to have it done. We'll live on as ourselves."

She smiled. "Two doves simultaneously freed and entrapped."

Relieved that he could so easily please her, he felt himself grow hard again.

"What is that?" she shyly pointed toward his crotch.

"Thirst, unsatisfied thirst. My body wants your attentions."

"Guide my hands," she whispered. "I want to feel this."

Opening the palms of her hands, he pushed them steadily downward. "The inner turmoil I feel is not from setting the old Christine aside. It's from wanting every inch of you." As her fingers tentatively explored the girth of him, he knew how much he hurt inside. He was very vulnerable to the softness of her voice, the physical stimulation of her movements. Leaning forward, he brushed his cheek against hers. Sensing her fears receding, he whispered, "Please, don't stop. I love you. I'm sorry if I frightened you."

No longer combative, he relished the manner in which she pressed her forehead to his chest, the exploration of her hands as she tried to assess his agony. He took a locket of her hair and played with the silk of it. Passing his fingers over her temples, he massaged in circles. She copied the movement below. Seeking the base of her skull, he tilted her face upward to him. His hands encompassed the entire back of her head. Now his thumbs insistently rubbed the flesh of her ears. He reminded himself that she was essentially still a virgin and small in comparison to his size. His thumbs made their way across the front of her chin. "I could kiss you again and again...take liberties...but I've vowed not to taste your womanhood without your full consent. So either withdraw your hands or suffer what comes next."

He'd let her response direct his course of action. He'd been without her a long time, he was randy, his nerves strung out, but he could still postpone the knowing if he believed the culminating act an inevitable certainty.

"You're thinking you'll cause pain in a secret place, one already cut open between my legs. Your worried that I'm too tiny and you don't want to inflict another emotional scar."

"Do you want to know the depth of the darkness surrounding me? In our previous lives you were engaged to Raoul for a whole month while you wore my wedding ring. I abducted you because I was jealous. I couldn't allow you to run away with him. In my zeal, I had to have you before any other, had to be first into that secret place. Now I'm guilty all over again. Right after we birthed you, Isidore cut away a piece of flesh to make it easier for my first visit."

Her lips puckered, she intended to plant a consoling kiss on his cheek. In response he ran his finger across their scrunched up heart-shaped surface. The distraction succeeded and the moment they softened he took them with his own. He had every intention of seducing her, hot and heavy, right here on the floor of this dreadful sepulcher. "Ahuh," he moaned. "I am in heaven again, brought to a plane of ecstasy."

"Enough of words – let touch and the reaction to touch speak for the both of us." Hungry for him, she sucked his tongue, hard.

My idol, my queen! Mentally he checked that his fingernails were cut, hands clean. Nothing impure should touch her when he slowly slid a finger inside her to test for readiness. *How do I know I should do that?* He lifted up the hem of the robe and the nightgown underneath, letting his hands seek out the small curves at the base of her buttocks. He pressed into the sides of her gluteus muscles, seeking invitation. She separated her legs. One tense finger probed, slipped inside. *Mine to claim. You're moist and feel like warm silk.*

The stimulus he offered was profound. She dropped the last of her reluctance. In an unexpected display of sensuosity, she lifted a leg and wrapped it around his hip. She sent the uncomplicated straightforward idea of his erect penis searching for her with the fierce inexhaustible energy of a flame – one fed by an endless supply of fuel. *Completed P in the encyclopedia a week ago.*

She unzipped him, allowing passion out the gate, inciting a riot of emotion.

They were made in the shallows of endless time for this act. They arched hungrily into each other. Swimming in an ocean of amplified arousal, they tried to absorb all the reality at once.

Erik was fast losing restraint. Having his tongue sucked out of his head in the midst of all this heavy breathing, with her riding up and down on his finger was driving him crazy. Very soon he would be forged into one white-hot shaft of crystallized desire and drive himself home. Otherwise, what was the point? He sensed the foot that bore her weight rising up on tiptoe trying to affect a better angle.

Yes! Sometimes I think I see your mind melding right into my own. Luxuriating in the sound and feel of a stormy wind literally tearing the foam off the crests of erotic waves, they rode higher and higher. He picked her up and set her on the edge of her own sarcophagus. *Blasphemy?*

Here – right on the verge of claiming her, declaring her his consort for all time – he suddenly pulled away. Tilting his head to the right, he paused, straining to reiterate a bizarre vibration he'd just picked up. Listening, reaching out with every super-sensitized nerve ending he possessed, he caught it. Faint, at a great distance...two people, no, three were screaming at the top of their lungs. A second later a loud alarm wailed across the compound. One continuous unnerving horn that shattered the mood and drowned the screams into oblivion.

"What's that?" Frightened, she drew his muscled shoulders closer for protection.

His eyes narrowed, "Someone has successfully breached the outer walls and a very loyal employee just died trying to alert us."

She leaned back, flexing her head backwards so that she spoke to the ceiling. "I wish you'd breached me!" Then quickly lowering her face, "Someone's dead?"

He separated from her, swiftly corralling his exposed equipment. "We're being attacked. Stay right here. You're safe in this tomb. I have to find Isidore and Nyah. Keep sharp and be aware that very few people know how to enter this subterranean chamber."

"You're going to close me in? Next to our dead bodies?"

"For safety's sake. I don't know where the intruders are, and I don't want to drag you around, especially if there's shooting. Guns – a G word." He zippered carefully, not everything was cooperating.

"Will I have enough oxygen? Can I trust that you'll come back for me before it runs out?"

"Yes. Have faith – you have my love entire." He kissed her, momentarily lost his bearings, and started stuttering. "Blast this menace…I'll bet it's the Life Liberationists…we were so close…five more minutes…five more minutes and we would have been sealed. Don't fret, I will come back for you!" He vaulted up the stairs.

Even though she was confused, she obediently stayed in place. "I think I know what an abruptly emptied oil drum feels like."

Before closing the crypt, he blew her another kiss. "I meant every word I said!"

In the pitch black of the underground chamber Christine heard the brief sound of receding footsteps echoing off the stones above her head. Seconds ticked by. Several muffled bursts of exceedingly rapid popping noises brought every muscle in her body to rigid attention.

She didn't remember the sound of firecrackers, much less the release of automatic weapons.

33 *EENIE, MEENIE, MINEY, GO*

€ rik was gone. Though the effect of his ardor and the smell of him were all over her. She sniffed her palms. *Still here.* Left alone in a total absence of light, Christine found the racing of her mind nearly unbearable. All was silence. *Anyone there? Hello! Entombed in a room of death, not a friend in sight!* There wasn't a slender thread of light to help her see. *Think! There are advantages to an underground shelter,* she rationalized. *I'm safe from fires, bombs, bullets.* She slid to her feet. Placing her hands on the sarcophagus, she felt her way to the angel's face. *So like my own!* Smacking both her hands over her mouth, she suppressed a scream. *What if Erik is dead and no one knows I'm in here?* Her ears detected the quiet sliding of stone and the brief rush of air changing the pressure within the crypt. Something dangerous and deceptive lurked not too far off.

The Revenant sensed her frozen in place, saturated with dread. It took only a second to analyze the situation. Her heart was responding to a flood of catecholamines secreted into her blood stream. Accelerating rapidly to an almost inefficient rate, sheer primordial instincts told her to prepare for fight-or-flight, but trepidation held her paralyzed. *How odd that in this instance, her adrenals are the seat of emotion.*

"You are safer with me," he whispered in the softest tone his grating voice would allow. She appeared to have gone deaf as well as immobile from fear. He came forward and deliberately laid his hand over her left breast. Beneath his touch her heart was calming: *one-hundred fifty…one-hundred…seventy-eight beats per minute.* "Nicely done! There's another way out of here." He took her hand and led her to the mouth of the tunnel.

"You plan on moving me? Erik said not to leave. What if he risks getting hurt to come back?" She received no answer, mental or otherwise. "All right. In view of our ongoing relationship, I think it's about time I know your whole given name."

"Torossian is all there is," he replied simply. "Erik will always be able to locate me."

Outside the temperature must have dropped dramatically over the last half hour. The mists were thickening into gray soup. Erik hadn't expected to hear erratic shooting when he emerged from the chapel, the ancient oaks proved a welcomed cover. The deafening tonal quality of the automated alarms hurt his ears and vibrated his chest like a penetrating shriek. Unable to block the noise, he rubbed his hands across his uncomfortable ears. Resigning himself to the noxious stimulus, he entered the chateau through the only functional southern entrance. Once inside, he sprinted down a corridor only to find room after room empty. Near the kitchen he perceived a high level of endocrine secretions lingering in the air. The small number of staff still in the house at this late hour had experienced real terror. They'd fled, hopefully to safety. His knotted stomach rolled. The ounce of emesis that entered his mouth was nothing but water and bile. *Idiot!* The words of the Magus came to him: *Banish fear!* He hurriedly wiped his mouth with the cuff of his shirt. *Fear is my enemy, not these invaders touting their technological weapons.*

His first thought upon entering Security Central was to assess the situation by viewing the monitors. Two cameras had already been knocked out. Thermal imaging showed the walls had been breached in the far northwest corner of the estate by three agile entities. The outer-wall klieg lamps were still on except for that corner. Decommissioning them, along with the motion sensors, hadn't tripped the alarm – the guards in the main tower had accomplished the feat. Now he was sure these were terrorists. He punched several buttons and happily silenced the deafening *basso profundo* of the air horns.

Turning on the speaker to the Panic Room off the kitchen, he asked, "Who is in there?"

"All the night staff," answered the cook. "Joseph, Anton, and myself. We jumped into the shelter the moment we heard the siren."

"Stay there," Erik directed. "Your room has its own air supply and a generator for lights. The moment the alarm sounded the police were called, so help is on the way." With his mouth tightened grimly, he opened the line to the lab's Panic Room. "Isidore?"

"Here," came the feeble reply. "Thayer went home before the alarm, but Nyah is with me. We brought in a portable oxygen tank and some morphine. We're settled for the duration, despite Nyah's nervousness and my palpitations. Where is Christine?"

"In the crypt," confided Erik.

"Couldn't you take her anyplace else on your first walk?" Nyah's voice sounded shaky.

"This is not the time for courtship guidelines. She's safe. I heard gunfire a few minutes ago. The house staff is in the bunker off the kitchen. I think we're in the first wave of an assault."

Isidore hurried to assert, "Even if they blow the house apart they can't hurt us, and we're insured. No one but our employees knows the locations of these hidden rooms."

Erik eyed the speaker with disbelief. "We've placed a great deal of confidence in them. Bargained on their loyalty, but people are unpredictable. Money and fanatical ideation buy deceit. Our newest hires are barely proven. Stay suspicious. Trust no one. A traitor may have surrendered the keys to the kingdom."

"Yes," answered Isidore. "There may well be turncoats among them. We'll question everyone afterwards."

"How many intruders?" queried Nyah.

"I have no idea. Three came over the wall in the northwest corner. Their job might be to let in others. The downstairs is deserted. I'm going to stay above ground and make a nuisance of myself. I'll disconnect the electricity and put the house in darkness. That should even the score a little…if they're not wearing night vision goggles."

"I agree with turning off the electricity, but you confronting them is totally unacceptable." Isidore was anxious and a little dyspneic. "Come down here to us. They can't get in, Erik. They don't know the codes were changed the day the Kelly boys and Kathryn disappeared. The police are coming, and our guards are armed."

"Oh, save your breath," Nyah urged. "He intends to hunt."

"Stay safe," Erik eyed the steel walls around him. Pushing on the corner of one panel, he exposed the electrical cables and terminations. He manually pulled out the cords – one by one. Every electrical appliance shuddered to a halt – every light switch went defunct. Erik slipped quietly out the door. He knew instinctively that this battle would not last long. Outcomes would be decided within the next fifteen to twenty minutes.

When he opened the delivery gate of the northern courtyard, he found his present – parked poetically on the very spot where he'd defied Isidore with a Parisian escapade. A brand new metallic-bronze V-rod Muscle Harley Davidson sat waiting, large red bows attached to both handle grips. The fuel tank registered full, keys in the ignition. He rolled it inside the courtyard. Not that he could guarantee its safety, but it might prove useful before the night was over.

The mists surrounding the northern fountain and blanketing the front meadow were settling low to the ground, partially obscuring his view. He could hear the dogs penned up near the garages barking wildly in their kennels. *Why hasn't someone had the presence of mind to set them free to harass the intruders?* The dogs were suddenly silent. Not even a yelp as they died. *Poison gas? How brave you are to kill confined dogs!*

He thought to double-back and check on Christine. A second later, the explicit concussive sound of an explosion ripped apart the atmosphere. The guardhouse and garages blew up in a visual feast to the eyes, flames soaring, pieces of metal and wood flying fifty feet upward. In the next breath, an expanding wave of compressed air pinned him to the wall and blew the windows inward on that end of the mansion. The blast seared the side of the fountain and the trunks of a few newly planted saplings, stylizing them with angled strokes similar to those produced by an artist's brush. Righting himself, Erik heard some sporadic machinegun fire followed by the explosion of a grenade.

They mean business blowing structures to bits. Unpredictable randomness? No…there's a plan. His ears were audibly ringing.

Testing his balance, he shook his head, trying to regain his hearing. At least the heat had temporarily cleared the fog. A prickling sensation crept over the back of his neck. He paid strict attention to the warning. A sinister shape, wielding a semi-automatic weapon hooked to a black nylon shoulder strap, was zigzagging up the hill, pausing at points to crouch before proceeding toward the chateau. *It's possible he means to simply walk through the courtyard.*

Erik's face took on an expression of stoic concentration. Keeping the known threat in front of him, he snake walked like an assassin – right shoulder and leg followed by left shoulder and leg – backward to the fountain. Feeling the base of the low outer wall against his calf, he slid under the cool water. On his side, he curled his torso around the fountain's base like the letter C. Keeping his eyes trained on the surface, he knew he was vulnerable but had to take the risk.

The flicker of a shadow passed over the fountain's pedestal. Erik rose up from the water like a venomous asp, the Persian dagger with the flying lion already in hand. He was only wet, not cold. No need to lock his teeth, they didn't chatter. Stepping out, he spun low in a very familiar circle and slashed the man's hamstrings. The invader looked down as if to consider the severity of his wound, then tried to lurch forward, but even one staggering step was prohibited. As the man crumbled to his knees, Erik swiftly slit his throat. *Always silence them!*

Rolling the man to his back, Erik yanked off the headgear. The face was no one he recognized, but the fellow had flaming red hair. He watched impassively while the trespassing terrorist's mouth trembled. Desperately striving to inhale, blood bubbled out from the open wound in his throat.

Erik picked up the man's ComDev and following the prompts, flipped through the menu. There were eight contacts in this fellow's group. Erik reasoned that an additional two or three might be off grounds if someone else was orchestrating the attack. Erik stuck the earpiece in his ear and slapped the microphone into place. He bent his head, listening.

"Red Dog. Red Dog, this is Blackheart. Are you there? I can't see you."

The thought that someone might be scanning the area of the fountain with a telescopic lens sent an appropriate chill down Erik's spine. He stayed low and responded. "This is Red Dog. Sorry. Nervous. Tripped and fell."

"Did you achieve round-out-one?"

The small courtyard and driveway surrounding the fountain was circular. Erik leapt to the obvious conclusion. "Affirmative," he answered and held his breath.

"Wait at round-out-one. Repeat: wait at round-out-one. We'll meet in ten after main gate secured."

"Affirmative," Erik answered brusquely. *Ah, invaders in a cluster – how entertaining.* Staying low at the fountain's outer wall, he stripped his victim. After donning his entire black latex uniform and Kevlar vest, he commandeered the equipment. *Good, now I have guns!* He ran his hand down the burnished steel of the rifle. *A long sleek snake that bites.*

Though he didn't know it, the DPMS Panther .308 semi-automatic rifle was a precision tool, the current weapon of choice for marksmen around the free world. In the hands of an expert, the weapon's discharge was flawless, deadly accurate. Taking a chance, he hoisted the body over the ledge and settled it into the fountain's water. Red bloody spume bubbled up to the surface. *Oh well, nothing to be done about that.* Reaching down into some blood pooled in the abbreviated flowerbed, he smeared mud on his face and the backs of his hands.

He made a decision to head toward the roof and its more strategic view – perhaps to pick them off. Waving his hand impatiently in case he was being observed, he veered off the walkway and dove into some bushes near the gate. Back inside he walked through chunks of broken glass, window framing, and bits of plaster. He treaded carefully, remembering that the most important weapon he carried was lodged in his skull: his ingenuity and the stubborn will to divest the intruders of their potential, not to mention the mental home-turf advantage.

Outside the lab's doors, Torossian and Christine halted. "I've left something important upstairs." A profound sentimentality over the few photos she'd discovered motivated her statement. Retrieving them from the drawer of the sewing table mattered, they were the only proofs she'd managed to scrounge that her former life and loves existed.

The Revenant held onto her elbow, arresting her. "Allow me to follow. I'll guard you."

"Where's Erik?"

The creature angled his head from left to right, his mind searching for active mental channels around them. "Can't tell. He's blocked his thoughts."

"I thought you said you could always locate each other. Go find him, make sure he's all right. Tell him I love him, will always love him. I'll meet you right back here in ten minutes."

Torossian led her to a narrow set of stairs, "Be quick."

She hurried up the flights and was shortly in her room. Maneuvering in the dark like a cat, she located the pictures and hugged them to her chest like precious old friends. Behind her the bedroom door hinges made an eerie and unexpected creaking. *Someone's opening the door!* She fled down the short corridor between her room and Erik's. Frantically scanning the area, she grabbed the first thing at hand – a can of compressed air off the computer desk. She darted into a closet where he stored paper, ink cartridges, and dozens of music CD's. Running her hand over the cedar board wainscoting, she came up against the shelves with the stacks of Erik's supplies.

Not a minute later a tall black clad commando opened the door of her hiding place and popped up the extended tubes of his night vision goggles. "Cramped quarters...very nice." The sinister unmistakable drawl belonged to Dillard.

She gave an involuntary yelp as one of his mitts pinned her against the shelving.

Tightening the fingers of his other hand to chop her in the larynx, he raised his arm, but suddenly felt her body soften. Complimenting his profound influence on women, he relaxed his threatening posture. "Sorry," he murmured apologetically. "It's me, Dillard." His hands rested on her shoulders.

She played dumb. "Naughty boy, your outfit is hardly couture and a flaring temper certainly doesn't recommend you." She smiled, letting the can's top fall onto the reams of paper behind her. "For a moment I thought I was going to experience a nasty knock to the throat."

He grinned, wondering how she knew his exact intentions. "Obviously I'm pleased to have snagged you so easily. Are you not screaming because everyone's locked in the Panic Rooms or because you're happy to see me?"

Neutralize the threat, neutralize the threat, the thought rose up as a cherished mantra. She let her empty hand brush across the area of his crotch. "I cried out because I was startled, but I'm not afraid. What if I decided to come along with you?"

"I was hoping for a warm welcome the next time I saw you."

"Sneaking around these rooms, armed to the teeth is a little disconcerting. Are you part of a ring of dangerous thieves and cutthroats?"

His amusement dissolved. "I'm the captain of a unit sent on a mission," he leveled his voice, he meant to impress her. "My combat experience makes me the logical choice to lead. Do you comprehend?" Compared to what she'd known of him, he sounded alien, like someone accustomed to issuing orders.

"You make decisions and offer direction," she tried to sound naive. "How many on your team?"

"Strike force," he corrected. "Eight total." Dillard sped to a more urgent point of contention. "Have they changed the codes to enter the lab?"

"I don't know, and I don't have the current ones," for emphasis she lightly pounded his chest with a spirited fist. "When they want to test me I'm always brought there."

"Lively, if not a little dramatic. You've always had a certain appeal. It's not part of our contract, but you're leaving here with me."

"Do you know the song: I Bumped Into a Burning Ring of Fire?"

Dillard immediately thought to amend her error. The real title was a Johnny Cash classic. Just as he opened his mouth to speak, she brought the upside-down can of air to his face.

Spraying his throat with a brain-freezing squirt, she jested, "Fire away! The label says the contents contain a bitterant to discourage inhalant abuse!"

Wheezing audibly, Dillard stepped back and tried to speak. Choking, he was unable to move his mangled tongue or throat.

She took advantage of the moment with a solidly placed kick to his privates. "Sorry, I can't extend the kind of attention you desire," she cooed. "You may recall that I was intended for another purpose altogether."

Up on the roof, Erik cautiously eased around the east facing solar panels toward the western side of the house. Taking in the view of the grounds below, he noted two attackers cutting across the front meadow. Dressed exactly like the one resting in the fountain, he reasoned this was Blackheart and a third associate. The pair neatly skirted two pits of concertina wire. Coming to the main entrance, the villains paused to send a crisp fusillade of bullets across the chateau's front door. Probably to scare anyone hiding in the foyer into drawing back within the house. He watched their AR-15 tactical carbines with Colt 4x20 scopes fire without a single failure to feed. A stream of empty casings ejected to the right of their weapons, about a yard from their feet. With this display of aggression, he feared they meant to kill the entire household. *If we survive this assault, Isidore will retreat like a turtle. Probably decide one can never be vigilant enough and refuse to leave the lab ever again.* He

wondered if he could convince Isidore that bullet holes only added to
the history of the place. From behind a pediment he watched the two
assailants clear the corner of the house, heading toward the fountain.
Hustling to the northern edge of the roof, he watched their dual pronged
arrival at round-out-one.

Just as he was considering how to fire the gun and pick them off, he
heard Torossian speak behind him. "Lovely costume, a little tight." He
came to the edge to share viewing the two attackers as they searched for
their comrade through their scopes. "Need I remind you that I like my
steaks *saignant* (rare)?"

His brother preferred everything that went into his mouth uncooked.
Without looking up, Erik retorted, "You can't eat them. There will be
police here – eventually."

Store some of the meat? Torossian never got excited.

*Negative. Resign yourself to it. The authorities will want to account for
bodies.* "We need to buy some time. Want to let loose some chaos of our
own? The recoil of firing this gun might knock me flat on my butt," he
exaggerated. "So let's knock one of the crested pediments to the ground
to distract them. Then as they cluster, I'll drop a tiny grenade between
them."

"You just don't like the sound of gunfire. You never have."

"Isidore won't mind if we need to destroy a little of the historical
house protecting ourselves."

"A house is a house. No doubt the blast will cause another change in
air density. That was aggravating."

Erik nodded and raised a finger to wait a second. In his ear he heard,
"Converge on round-out-one in twenty seconds. Blackheart out." They'd
switched from French to English; this Blackheart fellow now spoke with
a distinct Bostonian accent.

Together Erik and the Revenant shoved the pediment. The marble
object wobbled and teetered, they needed it to go over.

Torossian shot Erik a mental image to look upward. Overhead was
a parachutist, heading toward the roof – a second wave.

With one mighty kick, Erik finally sent the object toppling. Pulling
the pin from the grenade, he let it fly. In the ensuing blast the bodies of
their enemies flew into the air like rag dolls.

"That's three confirmed down. I estimate a maximum of around eight, probably six on the grounds with one or two in a getaway vehicle. We're going to have to pick off the rest. The first wave probably secured the front and provided a diversion to allow this airborne assault to approach unhindered."

Let's get them to run around a little. The thought amused Torossian, but only slightly. *Might as well enjoy the night if the three invaders on the ground were only a ruse for the one parachuting onto the roof.* Torossian swayed right, then left, back to right: *eenie, meenie, miney...*

"Go!" Signaling for his brother to head left, Erik sprinted back toward the solar panels.

They separated, easily flowing in two different directions. The Revenant parted with a fading placid mental message. *Look, flyboy has barely any wind to cope with.*

The parachutist must have seen the grenade explosion, but was unable to retard his arrival on deck. Apparently the fellow knew the roof, he was going to drop right next to the metal hatch so he could retreat downstairs. Armed with an Uzi strapped to his chest, the intruder touched down and immediately went to release the clips attaching the chute. Deliberately slowing his heart, Erik stepped out from behind a vent and raised his gun to feign firing the weapon. The black commando ducked and rolled, drew a pistol from a breast pocket and aimed at Erik.

The instant before he fired, Torossian smoothly yanked a pipe off one of the solar panels. As the trespasser spun toward the noise coming from behind him, the Revenant swung the pipe like a baseball bat, hitting the man full in the chest. Stopped cold, their uninvited guest went flying backward. Torossian moved swifter than the eye could register and lifting him, stood him back on his feet. With his sternum cracked free of his ribs and his breath taken away, the man staggered, dizzy – the gun dropping harmlessly from his hand.

"Nice. Where did you learn that trick?" Erik lowered his weapon.

Torossian calmly reached over and with truculent grace, grabbed the back of the assailant's neck in a paralyzing hold. Whipping off his prey's black ski mask and goggles, he exposed a completely shaven head and wide-open mouth. The man favored a cue ball silently screaming. Baring some rather savage teeth, Torossian bit brutally into the man's left carotid artery. Not intended as any cruel form of punishment, the Revenant was simply feeding – content.

"We don't have time for you to dine on blood sausage," Erik commented mockingly. Though he sensed the Night Creature had not fed. Torossian never ate for sport, so Erik waited.

"Let me know when you're finished."

With a thud the body dropped alongside the unused gun. *Didn't drain him*, Torossian delicately wiped his mouth with a white linen handkerchief.

"Well, toss him off the roof to break him up a bit. Better yet, here's a grenade. Pull the pin and stick it in his pocket; he'll scorch and flay as he falls. No, you can't stick him in the kitchen's meat locker. What about the prying eyes of the police? Don't involve anyone else in this meal. Stay alert. We may have traitors."

Torossian knelt down, intending to comply, but found himself still hungry.

At the sound of some rather hideous slavering, Erik started toward the roof's exit. "That makes four eliminated. Evening the numbers is obviously the most practical approach. I'm to the crypt."

Sailing down the stairs, Erik halted at the bottom. Closer to Christine, he registered her declaring war against Dillard. Her intent to fight him triggered a signal in his brain as loud as the noxious alarm. Turning the corner of their corridor, he watched for movement, then lowered his head and listened. *Silence.* He sped toward his bedroom.

Cracking the door, he heard her speak. "Sorry we have to sacrifice tonight's treachery." She grew sarcastic, "And I am still a novice, so this might be messy."

"Everything under control?" Erik inquired off-handedly. Waltzing over to the curtains to let in what little light there was to be gleaned, he turned to find the love of his two lives straddling Dillard's abdomen. She was preparing to re-break his nose with the can of compressed air. His anger over her joining the fight was forgotten when he assessed her position of dominance.

He beamed fondly at her. "Hold, Mademoiselle. I salute your very determined spirit, but I need a brief word with him."

Dillard was still in the throes of agony over having his privates solidly kicked.

Erik squatted beside them. "I thought you were safe in the crypt. I told you to wait there."

Christine didn't take her eyes away from her victim. "Did I agree? Don't worry, I'm holding onto every little thought that I had about making love with you."

Dillard's tearful eyes grew stormier.

Erik responded so calmly that he might have had hours to appreciate the party going on all around them. "When did you conclude that running about unprotected in your night dress was appropriate?"

"You didn't count on Torossian's awareness of my predicament. I think he actually experienced some of my of dread."

"I am no longer amused. On the roof he didn't mention moving you."

Christine smiled smugly. "Perhaps he felt he didn't have to report in." She eyed his clothing. "With concentration one can achieve a great deal. How'd you get one of their outfits?"

"Ingenious mobility." He focused his attention on Dillard. "Bested again, my friend, and by a female. You and John were not exactly honest about your extra curricular activities on your job apps. You seemed so happy executing your duties, when you were really someone else indeed. Did you watch and record everything like good little spies?" He teasingly tweaked Dillard's nose and Christine pushed his hand away.

"Mine!" she countered possessively. "He made the mistake of thinking I was the weakest link in the chain, and might divulge the newest codes to the laboratory." She paused. "Why are none of the lights working?"

"I shut off the chateau's main supply of electricity." He wiped a tear off the outer canthus of Dillard's right eye. "My, you are in a state, Dillard. Shall I call for paramedics?"

Dillard smirked and managed to rasp, "You don't have time for jests."

Erik stroked his fingertips across Dillard's forehead, edging not so gently into his mind. "You were the first to land on the roof. Not two teams of attackers, but three. Frontal wave, assault from the sky, and... the eastern backside? All with the same operative gear you're wearing. And the total number of attackers is?" Erik's voice became the mellowest Christine had heard thus far. "Come on, you know you can't hold your thoughts still. Seven! The eighth waits in the getaway van."

Trying to talk, Dillard scrunched up his swollen acid-distorted lips, "Three crack teams, one driver. You can't save de Chagny."

Erik was ready to move, but didn't. He realized the intruders' plan was flawed with some drastic oversights. Not only had they underestimated the advantage of defending the home court, but they hadn't planned on what Torossian, Erik, and Christine could accomplish. "Why attack us, you were a friend?" he asked truly puzzled.

"You're so clever and you can't figure it out? A worldwide campaign of genocide conducted on the aged. Our most experienced minds are lost thanks to your geneticist."

"Revenge? Not the atrocity of re-creating his ancestors?" He watched Dillard shake his head negatively. "So the plan is to assail the front and the roof in succession, while the covert arm sneaks up on the laboratory from the side of the lake." He was learning more about strategy all the time.

Wordless, Dillard made the sign of the cross over his head, chest, and shoulders. He pressed his cheek to the floor and using his tongue, freed a small plastic capsule stuck to the inside of his mouth. He bit the slender vial, cracking it with his strong teeth. Entering his blood stream through the thousand minute capillaries beds in his mouth, the poison rushed toward his brain. Once there, the toxin depressed the primordial respiratory center in three unalterable heartbeats.

Erik swiftly took Christine under the shoulders and lifted her off the corpse. "You really look lovely dominating Dillard, but it's unpleasant business watching a former friend commit suicide."

"This attack isn't over," Christine sat on the floor crossed legged. She pulled out Dillard's semi automatic handgun, studying it. "Let's you and I orchestrate the finale together."

In his gravest tone, he replied, "The discussion over us fighting alongside each other is not happening. Don't broach the subject again. The game of life and death is afoot here...too dangerous for an inexperienced female." He looked at the can of compressed air. "Even an inventive one. I need to move to the basement levels, the last wave may be the worst."

"Don't jump to conclusions." She set the gun in her lap. "You need my help. Right now you're thinking that there's two moving toward the lab and they need to be dispatched. I heard an explosion a few minutes ago."

"Hmm," he stroked her lovely cheek. "Torossian and I had to blow the place up a bit." He suddenly realized that the second grenade, the one he'd given his sibling, hadn't gone off. As if on cue he heard the explosion, it rattled the windows.

Still determined, she removed his hand from her face. "Don't coddle me, and don't pretend we have any semblance of a regular relationship. In two lifetimes we've never had one." Deciding to play the cards dealt to her, she continued, "Need I remind you that the final arm is too close to Isidore and Nyah for comfort? I'm going with you. Besides, our bodies aren't cremated yet and there's DNA these fools could steal. Torossian would take me!" she teased. Picking up the semi automatic, she pressed a button. The clip of bullets unexpectedly fell out.

"You are extremely depressing. Let's not make a routine of arguing, all right? Constant disagreements lack practicality and a certain sense of *esprit de corps*. I'm willing to wager a sizable sum that the Revenant made it his business to know you were unfairly saddled with apprehension down in the crypt. Endangering you further doesn't fit in with his motivation."

She shrugged, tried to count the number of bullets, but couldn't. Then checking the open slot in the gun, re-inserted the clip of ammunition. "He told me he has no other name but Torossian. That puts me in the confidence of the inner circle. With this I can be a more formidable menace." She waved the pistol in the air. Searching for a target, she settled on the fish tank.

"Only if you take the safety off." He reached over to show her. "Here."

"Did it ever occur to you that I might bring some fresh assets to the fight? I have talents, and I **do** remember how to sneak around efficiently," she stated rather tartly. "Once upon a time, in a beautiful archaic Opera House, someone very proficient taught me the art of dodging in and out of shadows."

He flinched at the harshness of her reprimand.

"Yes, you," she drove home her argument.

"You can't put on Dillard's outfit. He's too big."

"Cut off what's too long."

He arched an inquiring brow and standing, offered her his hand. "Strip, woman! Who could resist this? I haven't seen you totally naked since the tank!"

ℐℱitting her commando's outfit took too short a time to suit him. As he prolonged the struggle to zip her up, he asked, "I'm wondering if the primary objective of these intruders is to kidnap Isidore, not kill him. Force him to try and undo things."

With her hands on her hips, she pulled down on the latex and made herself rigid to give him better traction. "They might also be interested in money. Isn't Isidore wealthy? In the crypt you sensed something was about to happen right before the alarm."

"The air changed." *We'll talk about creepy preternatural hearing later.* "Did you know that you used to pull that bell cord over there to summon a dumbwaiter?"

"Well he's not coming now, is he?" She adjusted the side seams.

Erik sighed. "I'm talking about a device to help us leave the room. I don't have a rope long enough to make a dead man's knot and allow us to scale down the outside wall like mountaineers. In the year 1900 we installed a small lift so meals and other essentials could be hauled from the first floor up to us. We had an affinity for our bedrooms. I think I enjoyed those days." He spun her around checking her outfit. "Like two specters we're going to access that mini elevator and use it to sneak downstairs. I don't know why, but there are no guards in the house. It's deserted except for the enemy. I'll go first, so I can punch out the panel closing off the opening in the kitchen. A little tricky, I'll have to use my legs because it's currently behind a refrigerator." He moved to the wall to examine the rectangular piece of cherry wood covering the dumbwaiter.

"We may have to improvise something," she said while waiting. "Let's review our weapons."

With the panel off, he faced her. Pulling down on the rope to bring up the box, he listened intently for telltale squeaks. Growing impatient, the long white fingers of his opposite hand gave her a tight circular wave of permission. "Go on."

"We have daggers, two guns apiece – the ones with the scopes and the short ones with the clips that fall out too easily. In my room there are some long slender hat pins and a bottle of acetone, that's nail polish remover."

"Go get them."

When she returned, he was already stationed inside the dumb waiter. Out from the hole his hand sounded for hers.

She grabbed it and gave him a squeeze. "As soon as you can disengage yourself send the carriage straight back for me," she directed.

He withdrew his hand, stuck the thumb straight up in agreement, and softly shut the metal door. Downstairs he pressed himself against the box for leverage and gently, like a kitten kneading, rocked-pushed the back of the appliance forward. He cleared a very adequate space and slid out over a countertop. He had the decidedly lame urge to disassemble the dumb waiter's pulley and keep her out of the fray. With the realization that she'd probably stay angry for months, he reached in and sent the lift to retrieve her. Walking the refrigerator out to give her more space, he barely had time to regret his actions when she swung right through the damn opening.

Landing gracefully on both feet like some feminine super-heroine, she stood there in an almost lyrical pose, gazing at him intently. "I read about swinging exercises and using door ledges to gain leverage in one of my magazines."

"Uh-huh, right." They made their way quietly down into the basements.

With their backs easing along the walls, letting their crawling fingers guide them in the pitch black, they came to the area leading to the lab's entrance. Down the hall, working in the light of two battery-operated beacon lamps, two ski-masked assailants were zeroed in on the digital locks of the pneumatic doors – obviously trying a multitude of codes to open them. Erik sank flat to the floor and raised his head only slightly to watch. As Christine joined him in this supine position, he placed his index finger to his lips to signal silence.

The taller one is muscular like Dillard, but he's got a bigger gun, she whispered mentally.

Erik suppressed his mirth at her choice of words. *No need for admiration. He's a Life Liberationist with a grenade launcher.*

He assumed these last two marauders knew of the explosions and death of their comrades. They worked without speaking a single word into their ComDevs.

The second commando was remarkably shorter and thinner than the other. Together they had an oddly familiar proportionate ratio. Tension over their failure to gain entrance was increasing. Frustrated, the smaller person gasped and backed up. Lifting a Beretta semi-automatic pistol, he or she threatened to shoot bullets into the keypad.

The taller one finally spoke. "Wait. If we can't breach the door we can blast the lab's entrance completely shut. Make it so they have to drill through rock and steel to get in there. They'll be like minors stuck down a hole. By the time they're rescued they may have died from lack of oxygen."

Something about the timber of the smaller one's gasp caught Erik's attention. *A savvy Kathryn! Still partnered with John!*

The male knelt down and opening a petard took out the explosive that would so efficiently decimate this area of basement and seal in the contents of the lab. His partner squared off in surveillance.

The pair's aggressiveness troubled Erik. Nothing they did during their employment betrayed this level of hostility. It irked him that he could be so easily duped. Blind ignorance was not an asset to be fostered. Then pragmatics took over. Without verbiage, Erik informed Christine: *They'll leave before the blast and so must we. In such a tight space the force will blow out our eardrums!*

We can run to the crypt! But I can do more than just lay here listening, Christine sent the thought.

Erik gestured for her to continue.

Christine attempted to make her explanation as clear and succinct as possible. *I can project an image into their brains that will confuse them. One problem – I can't maintain the delusion for long in a person who is not a trained receiver. I suspect you know that Torossian is a powerful receiver and a gifted sender as well.*

How ingenious! He had time for one worshipful glance. *Can you mess with their minds long enough to alter their responses? Make them so dependent on your projection they don't realize what they're doing?*

She nodded, taking pride in the fact that he actually needed her help and would be grateful.

Erik pulled off his headgear. *After I have the bomb, we'll run for the stairs and let them see us. Force them to come and chase us around a bit. Stay close.*

Christine threw the lyric: *Lets get this party started* into the loud speaker of Erik's brain, then focused her attention on the pair in the corridor. She reversed the image, so that the wall was the door…and the door the wall. Next she dissolved the case, making it appear like the floor, and offered the male a replica with which to work.

Erik watched with undiluted curiosity as John set the imaginary explosive on the imaginary door. *He'll need a fuse next.*

Christine complied.

I'm going! He planted a quick air-kiss near her temple for luck, and ordered: *Stay put and don't get shot.* Gingerly picking his way forward, he marveled at how calmly they worked on the opposite wall. They were so engrossed in the vision Christine sketched for their minds, so totally unaware of his close proximity, that Erik plucked the real explosive from the petard and hugged the brick to his chest without detection. Christine boldly tiptoed up behind him. Giving her an oblique look of inquiry, he was unable to maneuver around her. The demolitionist turned.

Just as John's hand went to rest against the real door in a thinking stance, Christine's hands brought both Erik and herself into a stooped position. *I could sense that he was about to touch you. Good thing I moved, huh? He has no idea we're here, but would have found the sensation of hitting an invisible object a rather unexplainable experience.*

Bent over, Erik avoided John and headed for the stairs. *I have to admit that I like this version of you. Disobedience suits. What do they think we are?*

Walking backwards so she could stay focused on her subjects, Christine kept the performance going and answered: *Nothing – air. I'm still developing my talents.* She turned and breaking into a run, headed for their exit route.

At the foot of the steps Erik spoke outloud. "Thanks for sharing. We've enjoyed traveling with you and trust we'll get to visit later."

Startled, the two intruders looked down the corridor then at their handiwork, amazed to find they had not set a charge at all.

With his foot on the first step, Erik lifted up the brick of plastic explosive and waved to their visitors. Christine giggled. As they ran up the stairs, he chastised her. "Risking our lives is not funny."

"You sticking it in their faces was humorous."

"I'm not trying to amuse you."

They vanished before Kathryn or John could think of an appropriate retort.

Freed from the treacherous confines of the narrow stairs, they broke into a sprint and entered the kitchen. After stashing the explosive in a cereal cabinet, they hit the hallway to make for the closest exit point – the northern entrance. The sickening hum of a bullet whizzing passed their heads, followed by the distinct sound of a ricochet, hastened their steps. At the door to the courtyard, a very angry Christine whirled about. With an ear-piercing shriek and a forceful thrust of her hands outward, every lovely piece of furniture still standing in the hall sailed toward their pursuers.

She propelled the items with such strength that it astonished Erik. He had not thought her capable of such power. "You're a veritable Roman ballistae of chaos."

"I'm not injecting myself too much into the fight, am I?"

"Not at all," he flung the door wide. "I don't know what I'd do without you." They couldn't span the courtyard fast enough.

"Can we use the Harley?" she shouted.

"Too noisy, too easy to track with a scope. Nice present, huh? I hope we live long enough to ride it."

"Maybe we can drive these two apart. Get them to separate, even create a crossfire." They cleared the gate, briefly scanning the dismal damage done to the fountain area.

"This way," he suggested heading toward the front northwest corner. *If I hadn't exploded a grenade beside the fountain, I could have introduced you to the first casualty of the war. For a while he floated in the fountain's pool, an agile swimmer even in death.* It still bothered him that none of their employed guards were anywhere to be seen. He spun her into a small stand of sculpted bushes. For the moment they were safely concealed. Hopefully long enough to gather their thoughts and form a plan.

Their two pursuers appeared outside the delivery gate. John signaled Kathryn that he would launch a search in the front of the chateau and she should head toward the back.

As soon as John went around the corner, Erik stood with his hands straight up in surrender. With a dawning horror, Christine realized Kathryn was turning to put him right in her line of fire.

What are you doing? She's already spotted you!

Not a problem, Erik reassured her. *At the wiggle of my fingers, make her trip on an imaginary log.* He brazenly walked toward Kathryn, putting Christine squarely at his back.

There might be another problem, I'm a little drained.

Erik froze. *You never said anything about depleted powers.*

I did. I told you I couldn't keep the ruse going for long.

Erik felt an unpleasant wave of nausea.

Marching forward, Kathryn kept him centered in the scope of her weapon. "Isidore will pay good money for you. He might even trade himself." Kathryn stopped with the delivery gate about fifteen feet to her left. She couldn't possibly miss even if he ran pell-mell for his life.

Erik moved in an arc, drawing her aim from Christine's spot. He started to laugh. *Shoot your gun into the air, Christine. Draw John into this.*

"What's so funny, simpleton?" Tracking him, Kathryn hadn't lowered her sight.

Where's the safety? I can't see a thing in here.

Erik continued laughing. *Don't panic, feel for it.* He sent her a mental picture of the semi automatic.

A bloodied Torossian strolled around the northeast corner of the chateau and paused. With his hands in his pockets, feet casually crossed, he stood with his left shoulder leaning against the building. He cranked his gravely unnerving voice up an octave. "I don't know whether to join you in laughing or curse you for foolishness. You do have gall! She's got a gun pointed right at you."

Erik realized they'd created a perfect dilemma. Kathryn would have to choose which one to shoot first. John's arrival in the mix would only complicate the scenario, lower their odds of survival.

Kathryn started to experience a sobering chill of dread across the back of her neck. She turned to view the Revenant through her scope.

She'd never seen the thing before. Her eyes took in the black liquid dripping from his chin, the strange vest of ribs and sternum encircling his torso; it too was smeared in what could only be blood.

Christine's gun suddenly went off. Everyone but Torossian jumped. Not two seconds later Christine stood up and John was back. Startled into turning toward the direction of her partner, Kathryn had a momentary flash of confusion. Erik and John were dressed alike, same height, same body build. She fired, missing John completely. Her partner, mistaken for an adversary, started to run straight for the road leading to the cemetery.

Facing Kathryn, Christine headed sideways for Erik.

Erik lowered his arms to watch the turkey shoot and weighed the serious possibility that he'd miscalculated – their getaway van was actually parked in the family graveyard.

Kathryn's dilemma was obvious: Bring the fleeing 'Erik' to a halt. She fired again, and missed again. Torossian disappeared.

There's always the risk that she might actually hit him, Erik sped the message to Christine. *Maybe I should go take her gun.*

Can I punch her in the mouth?

So unladylike.

I've made her think he is you.

Thank you for recovering your abilities so quickly.

Kathryn shot a third time.

No door prize, yet! Erik wondered what criteria her team had used to qualify her for this mission. This branch of the Life Liberationists was inept.

"Look there," Christine pointed with a single digit.

A hundred yards away, the man Erik knew to be John skidded to a halt and swiveled, taking aim with his *Flechette*.

"He's got a dragon!" Christine shouted. "He's angry. Her last bullet sheared his right thigh."

"Practice makes perfect. What's he got?!" Erik questioned.

"I see a dragon's fierce eyes with wings and talons!"

"Talons? Shit! Get down!"

With a boom and a spray of sparks, the speeding trill of a tremendous hollow roar resounded in their ears. The dragon creature swooped down upon them, barely missing their heads as they sprawled flat on the ground. Impaling itself with slotted prongs into the outer wall of the delivery court, the grenades in the projectile were set to go off at any second.

"Cover your ears," ordered Erik. "Brace." From the corner of his eye he saw Kathryn abandon her wide-legged stance and lunge in a running attempt to distance her body from the gate.

The explosion flashed in a stunning display of rockets. Splintered pieces of wood and the already battered wall surged skyward. Still in her night vision goggles, the searing light blinded Kathryn as if someone cracked a roadside flare right in front of her eyes. She too went airborne, insufferable heat biting into her. She landed on her abdomen and rolled to put out the fire melting the suit onto her skin.

Out through the rising smoke, over the remains of the wall's foundation, came a spiraling gas-ignited motorcycle.

Stretching out her hands, Kathryn scrambled to get away before the soaring metal rogue hit ground. Quickly losing vertical momentum, the heavy vehicle came crashing down. The front bumper stove-in Kathryn's skull, and the whole assemblage bounced and tumbled toward Erik and Christine. He jumped up, flinging himself onto Christine's back to create a shield. The steaming metal object came to rest not a foot from their heads. Bits of stone and mortar rained down upon them. Little skittering daggers that stabbed Erik's latex outfit and pelted the grass and dirt, shaping hundreds of miniature craters.

Shocked, Christine lay perfectly still. As the shower concluded, Erik's hands searched her head, back, and limbs, offering thanks that she appeared unharmed in any way.

"This group is in desperate need of stress therapy!" The smoke was making her cough. "They should stop overreacting with big nasty grenade launchers and get a life!"

"All done in the name of murdering science," Erik replied, as his eyes searched for John. He was nowhere in sight.

"Is it safe to get up? Do you realize that you just saved my life?"

Finally, approaching from a distance, the sound of police sirens reached them.

"Our other company is arriving," Erik stood. He looked toward John's cemetery escape route and decided the risk involved in following wasn't worth it.

Christine's eyes lit up with curious enthusiasm. She wrinkled her nose, "It stinks of sulfur and gun power, charred everything! I hope this is the last of it."

"I predict this isn't the end. The fanatics don't have their prize geneticist."

"Let's discuss future tactics inside. We have to alert Isidore that the police are coming, and we have to hide like that rabbit you mentioned a thousand years ago."

"Yes, the authorities can't be allowed to question us. If they discover he's created clones, they won't be sitting down over tea and politely toasted bread to congratulate him. They'll seize his work, run invasive tests on us...and he won't survive imprisonment."

"You could employ your humor and point toward Nyah's uterus. I could show them my birthing tank." She threw her arm across Erik's shoulder. Together the two limped toward the house and Security Central to turn on the electricity.

Erik entered the lab alone. In a couple of minutes he appeared in the reception area with Nyah and a heavily robed Isidore. "I told them the assault is over. That the intruders came over the northwest wall, landed on the roof, and snuck up from the lake in three separate teams...and that you, our latest addition to the family, saved the day." He winked at her.

Holding her nose, Christine's free hand came upward in dismissal, "And now the police are at the main gate."

Isidore straightened a large filtration mask over the bottom two-thirds of his face. "At long last the authorities arrive. That makes everything so much better. You two hide here in the lab. Take over the Panic Room and seal the door for the duration. I'll have Nyah wheel me out front where I can deal with the officials."

"Are you up to that much exertion?" Erik was already reaching for Christine's hand.

"What exertion? I'll be in this chair and the stench alone will back them up a respectable distance." Nyah headed him toward the elevators. "We're safe because of your extraordinary abilities. You accomplished a great deal of good tonight."

At the moment, Erik did not appreciate the gifts of Christine's strange capacities or his own complex genius. He was too absorbed in getting them out of sight.

Positioned at the top of the mansion's front steps, Isidore and Nyah watched the huddle of police cars, with their colorful rotating lights, clustered just outside the main gate. They appeared to be experiencing difficulty getting the opening mechanism to work. After a minor explosion rocked the metal frontage, an armored assault vehicle plowed through, separating the two sides. A moment later a stream of cars and vans flowed inward, following each other in a parade. The renewed blare of their sirens as they proceeded up the entrance road was disconcerting and unnecessary, now that the action was over. *So much for maintaining home security*, thought Isidore. In a few minutes there would be the additional bedlam of police teams searching everywhere, sticking their noses about, asking questions.

As vehicles parked, Isidore and Nyah waved. Officers started jumping out, weapons drawn, spreading like a viral infection. A captain in charge of the response unit was the first to approach and introduce himself.

From behind the wheelchair Nyah addressed him, "Please stay several steps below the doctor. He's in a fragile state, masked for his health, so you'll have to be brief with him." The outside air helped to dissipate the smell.

The officer actually saluted. "Who in France does not know of this man's great work? We apologize for the delay getting in. A number of your guards are in the tower at the main gate, dead, overcome with some form of gas then shot. We've taken immediate measures to cordon off the estate, Doctor de Chagny. Are there any injuries? Did the criminals escape with anything?"

"The intruders took nothing that I know of, though they did cause some damage. They appeared to have acted in the manor of The Three Stooges – blowing themselves up. Please feel free to climb all over the house...discretely mind you. The lab of course is off limits, nothing happened down there."

The captain nodded. "I will keep my men in line while we conduct a thorough investigation. The State of France stands at your service."

Isidore added, "When you've concluded your surveillance and things calm down, we'll explore the possibilities of what happened out here. Right now we need to get a few staff members out of a Panic Room off the kitchen."

Erik hustled Christine into a steel plated room containing nothing but a few chairs and a small metal desk with a modernistic phone.

"No doubt the police will want to search the lab," she sounded tired and displeased.

He double locked the security door. With a push of one button on a keypad, a steel wall came silently down over the side adjacent to the corridor. Camouflaging this section as just the backend of the lab. "Let's see them try to find this."

"Where are we?"

"The lab's Panic Room."

"So we just exchanged places with Isidore and Nyah? Does he keep some alcohol in here?"

"I would hardly discredit the notion. No need to pack a suitcase or bring anything, we're like hamsters in a well-provisioned cage." In the drawer of the desk he found a bottle of Kentucky Bourbon, a bottle of Codeine and another of Phenobarbital, several ampules of morphine and the syringes needed to administer it. "Here's strong liquor and pain medicine. Food, drink, and everything else we need to survive for more than a week are stored in hidden wall cabinets." He went to a panel and brought down a concealed hinged bed. On the opposite wall he opened the door to a heated shower, and ended by showing her a refrigerator stocked with food and water. "All the comforts of home." He went to take her in his arms. "You were magnificent."

"We are not getting physical without sleep and a shower...shower first."

His eyebrows went up in elated surprise. "And here I thought I'd have to coax you, little minx." He gently ushered her to the shower, showing her how to obtain towels, soap, clean surgical scrubs and disposable slippers. "You may go first."

After his shower, he emerged with a towel wrapped around his loins, using another to dry his hair. He discovered her sitting at the desk already dressed in comfortable scrubs. She'd located a comb from somewhere and was finishing untangling her mass of wavy hair.

"Christine. Beautiful and wicked…and oh so talented." He pulled the comb away from her hand and ran his fingers into her thick brown curls. Her hair was like soft rich silk. He lifted a lock and pressed it to his lips. Her tresses smelled of lavender scented shampoo. He smiled. Some traits remained firmly implanted. Heat within his frame was localizing. "There are fierce yearnings burning within me." He started combing some of the ends. "My need for you has echoed through my soul through two life times. Just to touch you I have followed Isidore's path and become a peddler of flesh."

She gave a short snicker. "I've seen something of your yearnings and experienced your moods as well: anger, petulance, jealousy. Frankly, what does happy look like?"

Sweeping away the towel wrapped around his hips, he demonstrated the full measure of happy. "I'm practically gleeful." Lifting her up into his arms, he carried her to the nearby bed.

She looked rather serious for a woman who was about to be worshipped. "Will you allow me to chart my own path?"

"Of course," he set her down. "Only the most independent thinking women, those who have courage to back their ideas with action, make their way into my life." He pulled the sheet over her and slid his body into the bed. "Comfortable?"

"Practice patience and get some sleep," her lashes fluttered.

He moaned in frustration. "I mean to have you."

"You'd better believe you will…nothing will seem right until you do. But I won't enjoy the romance without some rest."

He wondered what Rakesh, a man steeped in common sense and the wisdom of the ages, would think of her eloquent powers – they took a person's breath away. *He'd probably be convinced my new consort was some form of sorceress. Great mysteries don't give up their secrets easily. I'd love to test her fascinating talents.*

"Later."

He rested a hand on her abdomen. "If our existence cannot be kept secret, there's a better than even chance our prestigious inheritance will lay in ruin in the very near future. There won't be anything to offer you except the remembrance of a past love. Perhaps you will allow me to register an impression before destiny scripts the next segment of our history."

"Can I trust you to get some sleep?" She was tired and her voice sounded more irritated than she intended.

"We're finally together in the same bed and we're delaying the next logical step? I'll comply with whatever you wish, but I may not be able to hold back for long. I have a tremendous urge to possess you. Unfortunately for me, knowing your body without your complete consent would dishonor my vow."

"You'd like me to think that I'm bound to you, but the reality is you are seriously indentured to me. Is there an emergency exit from this room? Something besides the only entrance I've seen?"

He ordered his hand to stay still. It wanted to travel, caress her. "I'm not telling."

Her eyes were closed, her voice barely a whisper. "I want to know everything. Like where does Torossian sleep?"

His fingers went to her *mons veneris*, lightly stroking. In a minute he'd be investigating heaven.

"Stop it!" She rolled away from him. "Torossian cares for you deeply. I'm curious about him."

He kissed her exposed earlobe. "He has no use for a conventional bedroom anymore. If anything, Torossian has blurred the medical definition of death. When he sleeps he has practically no pulse at all, no respiration, his body takes on whatever temperature is in the air or furnishings around him. He's a walking anti-testament to scientific understanding, a true phenomenon." He pressed the tip of his erection against her buttocks and felt her tighten. "All right, my eagerness is beyond your tolerance. I'll postpone showing you what we feel like together until we've slept." He curled up to her backside. "My Royal Member is very disappointed." His arm tightened possessively around her middle.

When his breathing changed and his fingers jerked in the first involuntary movements of sleep, she knew she'd won. *How lovely*, she followed close behind.

The police caused less of an uproar than Isidore anticipated. The inquisition he feared never materialized, as the captain kept all inquiries to an authoritative minimum. A damage assessment of the grounds proved that the rest of the guards were somehow taken captive and blown up in the garage along with the dogs. Until Isidore could replace his security staff and repair the gate, the police announced they would protect the compound's perimeter. The French government was adamant about sheltering their world-renowned geneticist. The authorities blocked all wireless signals and radio frequency transmissions coming into the estate, creating a military-like buffer zone to shield their scientist from further threat. The news media were told that nothing serious occurred; a simple leak in a gas line had caused several minor explosions. No one was hurt.

bscure neon-blue lights pulsated in one-second intervals across a steel wall in the Panic Room. Christine's bleary eyes opened wider trying to discern the source. Sleeping soundly for a prolonged period of time and awakening to an unfamiliar metal box proved somewhat disorienting. The secure chamber was in sleep-mode, hence the near absence of light. Forcing herself to focus, her eyes searched the walls and shadowed corners. The room didn't seem to have a clock, but the large digital display on the face of the neoteric phone was the source of the strange blue light. Though she couldn't see it, the same LED readout registered the date, time, ambient room temperature, and a simple one-word description of the local weather.

She rose, used the facilities, and drank a bottle of water. Standing beside the bed, she studied the magnificent creature sleeping on his back. *Wise, generous, and benevolent – if not stubborn, secretive, and outrageously authoritative!* Her fingers hovered over his lips – imaging a kiss. Her attraction to him was profound. She knew this source of masculinity, full of warmth, could easily retreat behind the safety of an emotionless curtain. Placing her hands on her breasts, she pictured his mouth reclaiming them. She wondered how experienced he was, not recognizing that he carried the wealth of his prior lifetime with him.

Retrieving a second bottle of water, she dropped several Phenobarbital tablets into the container and added a half-dozen Codeines for good measure. If she fell back to sleep, she didn't want him waking and leaving without her. She wanted him near, waiting for deliverance together. Meanwhile, she could play with him.

Slipping free of the bottoms of the surgical scrubs, she crept back into the bed. Inclined to draw him from his dreams, she rolled to her side and smelled him, saturating herself with wonder and anticipation.

"What?" He spoke through the emotionless fog of sleep.

"Nothing, I was just enjoying the clean scent of your flesh." No need to undress him, he still lay naked beneath the sheets. To stimulate desire, she massaged the area over his sternum, rubbing her fingers up and down over the inner sides of his pectorals. No reaction. So she took her fingers and ran them up the skin of his inner thigh until they rested almost at the base of his scrotum. Leaving her hand relaxed between his legs, she contemplated further exploration. She sought the uppermost edges of his mound of soft black genital curls. Stroking softly, she began to explore, to browse this strange scepter that had not so long ago offered its imperial attentions while she combed her hair. Beneath her tentative touches his manhood was growing thick, extending its length and taking on a rigid excellence.

Erik offered no resistance, but volunteered no inducement of his own. His body was passive. His eyes, like his brain, remained closed, as if he concentrated on some private movie in the theater of drowsy awakening. His physical reaction told her that on some level he sensed the persuasion of her touch, but she couldn't judge if he had strayed back into sleep. Whatever perceptions he experienced, his thoughts remained veiled...until he sucked in a breath through his teeth.

Smiling, she knew his awareness lay focused on the path where she beckoned. Quietly congratulating herself, she continued.

Beneath the sheets the regal staff had grown glorious, creamy juices squeezed forth from the tip in readiness. His willpower to resist waned, his arterial blood was singing. "Thank you for making yourself available to me, Christine." He uttered the words sincerely, delighted by the clucking noises her mouth produced in response to his gratitude.

She had a question that required an immediate answer. "Do you love me?"

"I don't remember a time when I didn't love you. I want you like air." The sedate pace, the almost languid stimulus her fondling offered over his erection, indicated she was not in a rush. He knew that women experienced a degree of fear prior to their first coitus. There was time to let her satisfy her curiosity about this strange organ dancing to her encouragement. He could so easily fall back to sleep, except that every once in a while she reached the tip and tapped gently with her thumb. The distraction was jolting him more awake with every performance.

When she enfolded the shaft within her whole hand and slid down to the base, he turned toward her. Nuzzling into the hollow of her neck, he asked, "Do you understand the weight of what you're doing?"

She tensed and though she didn't remove her hand, her doubts caused her to hesitate. *Am I about to cross a line?* "What should I comprehend?"

"You're locked in this strange room with me. No little deadbolt key can let you out. Only a code and you don't know the sequence. There's no withdrawal, no hope for escape…only commitment to what you've started."

He lifted up the bottom of her amusing shirt and saw, with his own eyes, the totally feminine form that awaited his intrusion. He looked into her eyes. *Soft and accepting.*

Her hand reached upward, curling around his upper arm to prompt him further. "Go on. The air in this room is cool and you've exposed me. My body will stay warm if you embrace me." His lack of response was maddening.

"I will not have at you like you're some toy I've been presented. You're a human being, a person deserving respect."

"Well that's something!"

His hand encircled hers and he kissed her fingertips. Bringing her pliable digits back to the tip of his organ, he ran them down the side again. "Tighten, relax, tighten, relax," he instructed. "This is no little response, but take your time. There are hours ahead to heighten the experience for both of us." He pulled the sheet up over her shoulders. "I am not going to hurt you. You've been prepared."

He took her hand off him and maintaining control, guided her fingers to her own abdomen. Tensing his fingers over hers, he drew small circles right then left, almost arriving at her *mons pubis*. Sending her a picture of plunging gently in and out of her inviting passage, he continued to assist her with fondling herself. The hooded troubadour waiting to be touched was surprisingly hypersensitive the first time her fingers brushed against it.

"Loving yourself will help you respond to me. Learn your body and mine."

When she operated without his guidance, he started caressing her breasts. Tenderly circling her nipples, inviting her closer. As she pressed against him, he whispered in her ear, "How delicious to have you not as a memory, not a dream…the real authentic you."

His versatile hands swept around to her scapula, pinning her to him. "You've never had a single day of illness, so you won't understand this. I'm sick with love. I've risen from the ashes to reclaim something of my life. Hope dawned the day a tiny clump of cells sprang into existence beneath a microscope. Wanting you eats me alive from the inside out."

The depth of her response was genuine. Amazed and delighted that she did not retreat, he let her advance on him once again, stoking the fires burning deep within his groin. As his pelvis began to rock against her, she slid his erection into the triangular space below her vestibule. Letting the stimulus ignite the blaze within their bodies, she whispered, "Don't hug me so tightly. You're too strong. I cannot breathe."

He turned away and rising, stood beside the bed. "Sorry...too excited. I'll go use the bathroom." He gave her a brief nod.

When he returned, he opened the bottle of water she'd left on the desk, but took only one swallow. He'd grown flaccid and noticed her eyeing his genitals. "Still interested? Shall we renew hope?"

"This is not how I pictured events. I thought we would attend a theater performance, then have dinner in a restaurant. You would be in a tuxedo and I would wear a delicate organza appliquéd with cinnamon roses, perhaps some pearls, definitely a plunging neckline. Something that hinted at the couture of the 1870's, when provocative sophistication, not the excess exposure of skin, drew the eyes of appreciative males."

"And would I reach across the table and hold your hand by candlelight? Suggestively assail your fingers with little rhythmic pressures applied to their tips?"

"Your solicitations would not go unnoticed, but I wouldn't tease or coyly pretend skittishness – too insincere and boring. I'd let my eyes and parted lips speak for me." She watched as he set the water down and brushed his hand across his lower abdomen. This simple gesture recalled his knight-errant to its previous amorous eagerness. "Oh!" she declared with apprehensive surprise. "Your body seems keen to the task ...of..."

"Shh," his hand went to his lips, then moved through the air in a short gentle arc as if to comfort her. "Patience. I'd like you to lose all your inhibitions, banish every sense of restraint, let every passing impulse rule you...your id unleashed and free." From a drawer in the wall he produced a tube. "Lidocaine in a water soluble gel. Our first experience will be virtually without pain for you." With calm certainty he moved toward the bed.

Still standing, he let his hand trail lightly up and down the front of her neck from her chin to the edge of the sheet. Delicious tantalization. What emotional distance remained between them was dissolving. When she issued a little moan of gratitude, he laid beside her.

Pressing her breasts toward his mouth, she offered her brown nipples surrounded by their delicate areolas. She waited in expectation, groaning audibly when he took one with his tongue and lips. She spread her legs, inviting exploration. Amazed and satisfied, he re-discovered the depths of her acceptance.

An enduring surge of desire conquered the last of her apprehensions. "I don't require food or water, I want you...over and over until they rescue us," her voice reflected the vibrant seeds of expectation blooming within her soul.

His right hand, laden with the gel, moved to the dark landscape waiting in the hollow of her crotch. Gently separating the petals of the rose, he was astonished to find her opening-up like one of those well attended flowers they used to nurture in the gardens. Fingering the plump margins, he meticulously applied the anesthetic. As he stroked and marked the entrance to her vault, a single finger explored its way inside.

She wiggled, letting an expectant splash of electricity wash her pelvis in warmth. When a second finger joined the first, she thrust her hips upward – the hub of her female pleasure pleading for its right to be touched. In response, he took his mouth and kissing his way down her abdomen, greeted the hooded seeker. Sucking, licking, making friendly overtures, he trained her reactions to increase in steps while sliding his fingers in and out. Firmly pulling the sides of the vault apart, he stretched all that he would soon command.

Her body literally shivered with contained emotion. She could definitely stand more of this. Freed into the pleasure of enjoying her own sensuosity, she was on fire, a brilliant comet screaming through space – burning and twirling.

"Don't attain the pinnacle yet, these feelings are to be relished," he directed.

A 'please-don't-stop-this' moan escaped her lips. Her genitals were engorged. The center of tiny shocks that rocketed sparks up her spine and down her limbs. She took the fingers of his right hand, still moist from her, and placed them in her mouth. Licking and sucking, she exuberantly acknowledged her own taste. "I want you!" Kicking her legs in a restrained tantrum, she took his hips and guided him on top of her body. When he settled between her legs, she wrapped her limbs around his back and waist, presenting an almost irresistible invitation to enter the passage. "Still yours," she breathed the words.

Several times he let the end of his penis probe her exposed folds, glide along the sides, and return in nearly unthinkable allurement.

Trembling and weak, she entreated, "How long shall I be held prisoner by a spectral tool? Help me! In the tank, every time you imagined making love to me I could see the pictures in your mind. Your cravings were driving me mad and this is worse. Join us!" She snaked her hand downward and began to stroke his sack.

He listened to her plea, testing her readiness by letting his penis wait at the entrance to the sacred portal. The incitement nearly shattered all control. She moaned and pressed his buttocks toward her. The last of restraint departed. He thrust himself within her, never noticing that he tore out a little skin, the better portion of her virginity, as he went. Isidore had not honored Erik's rash requests. He sensed her pelvis rotating, allowing his presence to fill her. Finally ensconced within, he murmured, "Breathe, Christine. Don't hold your breath. Breathe on my cheek, my neck, my shoulders. Let me feel you dynamic and alive." Maintaining a steady deliberate cadence, he helped her concentrate on the act. Helped her rise and fix on a summit of ecstasy, then fall away. "Don't climax. Ease down." He tried to stair-step their advance.

Little whimpers were coming up from her throat; little inarticulate declarations that she thirsted for more. "I love you, Erik."

He found a delicious gratification between her legs, a meticulous carefully applied heat that equaled his own. He gazed down at her, a whirling storm of sexual fire burning to and fro beneath him. "There will never be another like you."

She clutched at his back, her nails digging into the skin between his scapula and spine. "I love you in a fashion I cannot explain with words."

"Then let your mind tell me."

Down the hall in Isidore's office stood the twelve-foot high virtual reality screens; employing proprietary high-definition imaging, they displayed more than just the immediate outside. With the selection of different channels, pictures of enormous panoramic vistas came into view – absorbing, breathtaking realism. She didn't need them. Cradling his head in her hands, she sent the fire into the forest, the smell of smoke, the clarity of plumes heading out over windswept waves, the taste of salt, and the song of the crashing crests straight into his brain.

"You are really too much...a surreal temptress that eats away at a lover's brain and leaves reality nothing but a blur of indecisive shapes. Everything pales against the backdrop of this." He was joined to her, fused, internally melded. In retaliation he eased forward, pulled out quickly and repeated the movement. The rhythmic absence and return of pleasure had the strange effect of making her hungrier; she wanted him back, time and again.

"This is crazy. How could someone want more every three seconds? What are you doing to me?"

"I'm cooking a recipe for orgasm." He drove in as deeply as possible. The shaft withdrew, waited for her desire to mount. Then returned and returned again.

An exultation of seismic proportions rose up from the ocean's floor to swallow her whole. Her fingers clutched him. Even the palms of her hands were tingling. An excited screaming could not be contained any longer, for she was coming undone in a shower of meteoric stars cast across the sky at the stimulus on her G point. "Oh...to feel love like this! Erik!" She was panting, sweating. "What if my heart can't last?"

"Then we die together in ecstasy."

Jubilant, she was growing dizzy. The entire right side of her body felt numb as he possessively suck-kissed her deeply on the neck and shoulders.

"You're heart is fine. I think you're overreacting," he rumbled the complaint into her ear.

"Am I?" She shifted her pelvis downward and slid a dainty finger into his sphincter.

Not anticipating the maneuver, he froze – every muscle in his body a steel cord trembling with delight. Her finger circled gently. He thought he would die within the insistent licking flames. Her free hand swept downward over the enticing crack of his buttocks, opening and closing, repeatedly. Just when he thought he regained control of the sequence! "Oh, Christine!" He dared not move, but felt compelled. "Would you have protection from a fire-breathing dragon who worships you? The safety of an obtainable shore versus a jarring immolation? I am about to explode within you. What purpose does this challenge of yours serve? Trust me...you do not have to be the master."

"I promise you will pay for every predicament you place me in. The dominant role is to my benefit."

When she rocked her hips, he moaned – almost undone. If he refused to move, she maintained the rhythm, knowing he was close to exaltation. "The stimulus is too great!" He pleaded, but she rocked her pelvis over and over. Determined, he tried to hang on, but she resorted to some form of milking him with her pelvic muscles. Squeeze and release, squeeze and release, just as he'd taught her.

Now the little gasping exclamations were his own. In a rash leap of hope, he stretched out on top of her, his arms spread wide as if he soared through the sky. The wind raged against him, pushing the fear of losing restraint aside. What a jaunt, he sailed and swooped – dove from the sky into the liquid flames of the woman beneath him.

"You are not master of every situation," she whispered, "acceptance ends the pain. Unleash yourself. Let go."

He curled over her, freed. A thousand light years ahead he would still talk of this orgasm. His surrender was complete. Even as he raged against it, she saw fit to join him, swelling in and out of a fevered crackling bliss. Endorphins rushed through their blood streams. A chorus of celestial voices rose as wave upon declining wave pitched itself against the conflagration on the shores of their bodies, washing their souls with a smokeless, glistening peace.

"Could I become a habit of yours?" She wanted to dance, to squish the sand beneath her toes and chase after him giggling – twirling, splashing water, running into his arms.

He caressed her lovingly to his chest. "I'd like that very much."

She kissed the corner of his mouth. "Drink of me, swallow me. Let this be my home, for I want no other."

Wet with perspiration and the fragrant creams manufactured by their bodies, they lay curled in each other's embrace, drifting for several minutes.

"When can we do it again?" She kissed his throat.

"Are you ready so soon?"

"Yes."

"Then I did not satisfy?"

"Because you did satisfy me, I want you all the more. What are your recommendations? How do I close your mind to anything else but another union?"

He rolled over and pointed to an organ standing erect and proud. "Can you kiss here?"

She knelt beside him. "With my body or my mouth?"

He grinned wickedly.

Her mouth covered his genitals, and he responded so quickly it bordered on pain. Alive, vigorous, with his penis again in a rock-solid posture, every muscle in his body grew taut, begging for her continued touch. His body was pulsating, rolling, wailing with gratitude. In matters of passion she was so generous with her favors. "Name your price, woman. I must have you."

"What knowledge am I missing?" She resumed her sucking kisses.

"Stop! Stop! It's too much." He eased her off. "In our previous life you did not remain a virgin long – I had to possess you before Raoul. In the theater I told you that I had to be your first, so I stole you, seduced you. I didn't tell you that I gambled, bet on myself...exploited every fact I knew about you and coaxed you into surrender. What do you think of me now?"

She studied his worried expression. "I think you were and still are an explicit thunderstruck lover who waits for no one."

"A lover who does his homework. I studied you. You strive for perfection as much as I. You like to prepare...and normally don't like to rush. I learned it excites you to the point of delirium when I breathe into your ear, kiss your neck, blindfold you and play games. You enjoy the thrill."

Aroused by his words, she straddled him, wrapping his hips and thighs with her legs. Hooking his staff with her fingers, she guiding him within and sank downward. With her body she told him how happy she was to have him reestablish his dominance. "Be that rampant lover once again."

Latching onto her hips, he looked at the woman above him with wonder. There was no end to her. Hidden within the private confines of the Panic Room, he sought a steady stream of paradise by repeatedly lifting her and letting her lower herself.

After a period of time, she extended her legs to maintain balance and pulled him upward into a sitting position. In silent acceptance, he rose to have her cradle his head in her arms. Welcoming the mutual warmth, they rocked rhythmically back and forth. She placed her mouth over his; letting his tongue probe as his hands roamed the rest of her.

Caressing her breasts, he started kissing all that his mouth could reach. An orchestra was playing in his head, the timbrels resounding in response to a flare of horns, the roll of deep-throated drums gave way to a symphonic harmony of strings. His ardor built, his solicitous caresses declaring she render immediate and total submission of her will. He so wanted to push continuously into the silken pink channel, to love her for an hour without climaxing. Erik rolled her onto her back. His hands moved to her buttocks, tightening the receptacle of her pelvis for the pleasurable waves he intended to ply downward into her.

She grabbed his upper arms, urging the maestro to renew the excitement. In a dark menacing voice she told him she wanted him inside her again, "Must have you." When he paused in playful refusal, shifting to lift away, she pulled her knees up toward her shoulders. Stretching to let him in as far as he could go, she purred, "Take me, Bright Angel. Since we've formed this alliance, I make no pretense that I want you – all of you."

"Concentrate only on me. Consider nothing else, Christine." At last their cheeks came together. His facial skin was rough, bristling with whiskers. She relished the coarse scratchy irritation.

When she moaned softly, waiting to be devoured by the dragon, his hands slipped again to her buttocks, uplifting home. He entered as the king. Pumping vigorously, side to side, back and forth, with powerful strokes. Relentlessly sampling all that she had to offer.

When his body rose and fell back against her, she arched into him, dragging the sheath of her clitoris against his pelvic bone and wiry hair to excite frenzy.

Resolving not to orgasm, no matter what she did, he set his mouth upon her, tasting their co-mingled sweat. And when they grew dry, he reached for the lubricant so as not to excoriate her before they ran through a series of titillating pinnacles together. She giggled in wicked appreciation. Begging for relief from the ache he kept rebuilding in her pelvis, she bit the base of her own thumb to submit and allow him to call the pace. Together they gave themselves over to the euphoric storm, not once, but several times. With each episode they entered the thrall, elating in the exquisite state of complete absorption. Knowing, learning – stamping the other deep into their souls.

In the final lingering phases, the *finis coronat opus* of their personal symphony, when she sensed her energy waning, she uttered, "You are a blessed person, an intense presence...unique in every way. From my first cognitive moments floating in the primordial ocean of the tank, when I heard you speak...so distant and foreboding, so sweet...I was smitten. I don't remember anyone else, but you. You're magnetism is all encompassing. I am drawn to you..."

He paused inside her, just as large as before. "Go on."

"Hmm, it's difficult to think. Your attraction is so complete, it dissolves inhibitions." A stunning teardrop slid down her cheek. "You are erotica incarnate, Eros, the divine impulse channeling into the core of me." Her lips parted. She gasped.

He felt her breath as the brush of a feather. He caught the tear with his tongue, taking the pearl into his mouth, savoring the taste of salt and honey in all its sweetness. His lips traveled over her face, kissing her in a dozen tender places. She drifted off to sleep. Sated at last.

Releasing his hold of her, he smiled. They'd climaxed not to the point of pain, but to exhaustion – like intense energetic children who rally at their games a half-dozen times until they finally drop. What he achieved with her, he could never obtain with another. He rose from the bed to check the time; the phone read 2:05 am. He didn't notice the the date - had no idea, not the slightest comprehension, that they'd slept a whole day and into the next night. He drank the rest of the water and went to wash.

Feeling lightheaded when he emerged, he thought to go outside and get some fresh air – invigorate his brain cells. He dressed quietly, happy that there were no coins or key chains in any pockets to jingle as he lifted the scrub pants.

Barefoot, stumbling toward the bed, without any idea he'd been drugged, he glanced at her. Assuring himself she slept the sublime sleep of the well loved, he grabbed Isidore's bottle of bourbon, punched in the proper exit code and the outer wall responded. He paused to drink; the liquor was smooth and sent a wave of heat through his blood. Wanting to feel the nighttime air on his skin, he closed the door with a hush and pictured the tunnel leading to the chapel. He planned to be absent from her just long enough to take in the cool fresh air. Then he'd come back, wake her out of sleep, and do her again if she was willing.

Saturated with sedatives and endorphins, overjoyed with bliss, a few minutes later he breathed in the air of the dark, starless, indigo night. He thought to walk down to the lake, and for a change, spend some time obsessing about the future instead of the past. The new Erik was liberated from the shadowy hounding of his predecessor. They weren't one persona. He drank again. *I'm free of the Phantom's weaknesses, free of his facial deformity.* He loved a Christine that lived in the here and now. This female was an even greater challenge. Arms held wide, he spun in a circle. His aspirations soared. He thought to find the cure for the infection of cancer, and show the scientific community the origin of the problem. *They haven't viewed it as a cellular infection...and malignancy is all of that...and more! People will die of coronary artery disease, but not cancer. They'll have their eighty-two years in astounding health, then before the torment of real body failure commences...* Click. "Goodnight and we'll close the garden gate." The words were slurred. *How odd.*

He could feel himself walking down a gentle slope; he must be in the meadow. *We're so close to guaranteeing a profound degree of health right up to the end.* He wandered down the hill, but where was the lake? *Someone moved the lake?* Amused and groggy, he stopped and swallowed another ounce of bourbon. *At least some things remain the same!* He kissed the bottle, and in a whisper asked the container, "I'm I a husband now?"

The Phantom's scoffing voice replied: *Not without me.*

Erik stepped forward, offering the bottle. He didn't see the hole, didn't spot the smallest of glimmers coming off the dozens of razor-sharp edges attached to the roll of concertina wire within it.

His right foot went unexpectedly down into empty space. In the first disorienting twelve inches of air, his initial thought was simply: *Damn!* An instant later, his whole body jolted forward, thrown awkwardly off balance. Panic overwhelmed him as dozens of scalpel blades sliced into his face and body. His fingers released the bottle. He adjusted his head one minor degree and felt an eyebrow sliced away – arms, thighs, palms, and chest were ripping open. Feeling himself bleed, he couldn't imagine where he'd landed. He intended to go to the shoreline. Where was he? Even the locks of his hair held him solidly in place.

His brain recovered almost instantly, sending a rush of catcholamines to reenergize his muscles and heighten his perceptions – readying him for fight-or-flight.

No! He refused to let shock rule the moment. He calmed his analytical mind, ordered his thoughts to evaluate what was digging into his flesh from so many points. Something was pinching into the area of his right iliac crest, while something else, quite painful, had his penis! The softened hum of a car's hydrogen-powered engine told him where he was. His breath hitched in a deep sense of alarm. He hadn't gone east, he'd gone west. He didn't move, realizing the horror of his error. He angled his face left – he had no choice. An excruciating finger of pain was shooting through his cheek directly into the bony floor of his ocular orbit. In doing so he sacrificed the cartilage and skin of his nose. *Better to have sight and no nose.* Even if he could slowly extract himself, he'd leave a blood trail for the police to follow. *Hemorrhaging from several hundred deep cuts, I'll resemble a tall dripping red candle. Something fit for a witch's ceremony,* his brain fired angrily. *At least the damage is superficial, done to the meat of me.* He knew he had both his eyes; he was looking into the pitch of the hole. *Nothing major has been lost. Well, almost nothing.* He couldn't see them, but he was certain he'd cut his privates.

Physical shock was taking over. Trying to channel the greater wealth of blood to preserve his major organs, the muscles of his limbs recoiled in a spontaneous reflexive contraction. He winced. The more he moved the more entangled he became.

Pinned, trapped, he cursed the very act of living. Every ounce of him wanted to retreat in time, to take back that single instant when he stood unknowing at the edge of the pit. *Stay strong! Sort through this! Take an inventory of body parts!*

Enraged his mind lashed out. *I will murder Isidore for this...bleed him dry!* He choked back a sob. "Hear me!" A tiny sharp scalpel took the middle of his upper lip. *I am not an inferior copy. Not just a clone of the original. I am Erik. I have a soul. I feel its presence. I breathe and want. I know that life flows within me. Even if the Fates are abandoning me, I have the good sense to cry!*

But he couldn't cry. He barely dared to blink.

36   *HEARTLESS, HELPLESS*

Ranting served no useful purpose. He could exsanguinate before thinking up a plan. Accepting that he was unmercifully ensnared in the pit, he turned the nerve endings of his body to stone. *I am not powerless!* A sense of the unreal started creeping in — numbing the despondency. The cool night air worked in his favor. Slowing his heart, he calculated that he weighed one hundred sixty-four pounds. How long before the five or so quarts, approximately eleven pints of blood dripped out of him? *Estimated time to unconsciousness?* His brain flew over the mathematics. *Without knowing the exact number of wounds...not calculable.* Accepting the situation, he tried to estimate the pit's dimensions. He'd been in holes before. *The past is never really finished messing with one's current life.* His face and body lay on wire. His hands were open, resting on metal edges, fingers curled. He imagined he looked something like a mountain climber holding on for dear life. His feet didn't touch anything solid, nor did the crown of his head. Since he was six feet one and still growing, the diameter of the circular pit must be greater than his height. He remembered that most of the traps were not more than five feet deep.

He could stand up! *And sacrifice what?* Facing down, he couldn't see where the free concertina blades were set. All the accumulated knowledge in the universe regarding the science of angles wouldn't help evade the multiple hazards. With chagrin, he acknowledged the totality of what had hold of him. He was impaled on a ball of evil wire. He tried to insulate his mind, to gauge the threat of the situation versus his only recourse for extraction.

*Where **does** Torossian sleep?* He wasn't sure these days. Resisting the urge to thrash, he took his mind into deep meditation. From this barren empty silence he sent the strongest telepathic message he could, never doubting that his exceptionally strange fraternal twin would hear.

Torossian rescue me, he pleaded. *Don't pass this off as a game. Desperate situation...I'll die if you don't recover me.* He ended with a powerful picture of his predicament.

Weak and despairing, he hypnotized himself just as a strange current passed through his body. Not like electricity, the deeper stages of shock are acidic phenomena. He felt his internal pH ticking lower, lower – filling his head with an alarm he immediately sought to abandon. To avoid compounding the acidosis, he sent himself into a deep velvety blackness. Allowing the total absence of everything to consume him.

In the ashes and blackened beams of the main guardhouse, Torossian rose from his bed. He enjoyed the feel of charcoal, but Erik's pain compelled him upward. *Where?* He demanded. All he could tell was that Erik was mentally floating in some dismal abyss.

Don't know. Erik's mental voice was nothing but a faint hollow whisper. *Damaged.*

For the first time, Torossian experienced trepidation. Erik was beseeching his intervention, and he had no idea in which direction his precious kinsman lay. Crouching at the sound of patrolling policemen, he turned his head from right to left. Listening, sniffing the breeze. *Send a picture!* Nothing came back. **E R I K!** He broadcasted the name like a microwave tower would send out a circular beacon. *Cannot sense you. Send a picture!* Torossian saw a grave filled with slashing daggers, hundreds of daggers – *no, not daggers* – blades, small sharp blades and coils of thin snaking steel. The Night Creature unfurled his arms and bending over, dug his gnarled fingers into the soil. Relying on an ancient form of illumination, he bared his teeth and from low in the back of his throat, sent forth a fierce growl. Letting the vibration travel through the molecules of dirt, he listened ignoring anything as dense as metal or stone. *Fifty paces, a hundred paces, two hundred.* The sound wave was fading before it hit the softer density of familiar muscle and bone. The anomalous brother tore through the space between them.

The Revenant stood on the edge of the pit; a charred aluminum garbage can tucked under one of his arms. The unholy desecration of Erik's body staked on the wire and the steady flow of blood pooling in the base of the pit was an horrific revelation. With his arm he crushed the can toward his chest, decreasing the internal space just enough to allow him room to fit inside. *In two lifetimes you've never been dull. This abominable wire cannot be snipped, held in a tense coil it will spring wildly. You must be extracted by hand.*

Erik raised the middle finger of his right hand in assent. *Come, my brother. Free me!*

Torossian slid the can down the side of the hole, displacing both the wire and Erik – worsening the severity of the injuries. *Where have you been?* As if he didn't know.

Drinking of Christine, making love, she couldn't resist my relentless advances.

Lowering himself into the can, operating from the empty space created beside Erik, Torossian directed, *Stay limp. There's no way for me to find any kind of purchase on this sinister ball. It's doing what it was meant to do.* Trying not to slice his own hands, he lifted Erik's right arm. Some of the wire stuck to the flesh. The dual rows of stainless steel razors were set 24mm apart, each blade had the appearance of an open-ended stubby T that could not only slice, but hook a person as well. Using his fingers and his teeth, Torossian disengaged the razors, one by one. When the limb was free, he slipped the trashcan's lid beneath it. Erik made not a single sound of protest.

Working quickly, Torossian bent back sections of the wire and moved Erik bit by bit over to him. To pass the time Torossian informed him, *No body is monitoring the locater chip inside you. The police are using their own surveillance until security is brought back into order. I've listened, they're happy – making tons of overtime. Once you're disengaged, I won't be able to rummage through the wire for bits of you.* Working on the face, he could see the nose and right eyebrow were lost, the cheekbone below the eye exposed.

Concertina wire! A haunting frightful sight ripped Christine's sleep apart. She sat bolt upright. *Erik!* Stunned she rushed to the door of the Panic Room. *Awake? Walking around! Torossian, where is he?* She pounded on the only exit from her claustrophobic realm. *There must be some other way to get out of here! What if there was an earthquake?!*

From the pit Torossian sighed. *She is awake. Knows you strayed. Wants to grab a flare, run outside, snap the thing and coat the area in sputtering red light. Don't be so fitful, Christine. He is not dead. The pits of wire are deliberate traps. There are no signs warning him to proceed with caution.*

She pressed her back against the unyielding door. *The devastation done to his body is extensive. I see it.* She threw some clothes on.

Working on the chest, Torossian hissed a mental order that drove her back. She'd never heard him use such a frightening tone. *Don't rope me into a corner! You must not draw attention to me. If the police discover us, I'll be forced to vanish...too many uncomfortable explanations. Call Isidore and Nyah...we need an operating table. Tell Nyah if she has to come out and identify him, he's in the pit west of the chapel.*

She ran to the phone and with great relief heard Isidore's frail voice on the other end. Christine's beseeching screech almost deafened the man.

At the sound of her wailing, Torossian only shrugged. *Think she'd ever do the same for me?* People were approaching. *No time for particulars. Must move.* He swiftly hoisted his wayward brother over his shoulder and onto the grass. Erik lay prone on his abdomen much like he had on the wire. After tossing the lid out like a Frisbee, the Revenant jumped to the rim of the can, balanced briefly and leapt to level ground. Crouching low, he shoved Erik's limp figure over. *Your abdomen and anterior legs look raked.* He caught his still bleeding brother up into his arms.

Drifting in and out of consciousness, Erik jerked spastically. Limp, bent at the groin, he was only vaguely aware that he was being carried toward the chapel thanks to his brother's immense strength.

They sped through the door not a moment too soon. Behind them two police officers, patrolling the front of the house, turned a corner of the chateau ´ – the beams of their flashlights chaotically scanning the area.

In the lab, the hopeful look in Isidore's eyes faded when he viewed the injuries. "Sliced to ribbons!" The scientist directed Torossian to set Erik on the surgical table. Isidore issued orders with strident respirations, the adrenaline-fueled excitement nearly closing his already deformed throat. "We are becoming an arena of freaks."

In his confusion, Erik heard the sound of voices splashing through the air. The words were indiscernible, soft, like the fluttering wings of bats. People whispering in hushed phrases, cutting off his clothes, scrubbing his skin with something very cold. *Iodine.* No one laughed. A laugh might have indicated he wasn't too badly cut up, just messy. A needle pricked the upper surface of his left hand. *Another diabolical intravenous.*

Isidore operated for three hours. In the end, the accident cost Erik a tremendous loss of blood and a nose, the tips of three fingers, an eyebrow, and multiple deep wounds over his front – from forehead to feet. Preparing an area for recovery in the Panic Room, the geneticist regretted ever enmeshing himself and the lives of others into the world of altered DNA. The dabbling ultimately brought nothing but disasters.

For the remainder of that horrific night and for several days following Christine stayed in another laboratory room, where she was told to wait patiently. She couldn't visit Erik, even though she persistently asked and constantly wrote him notes. Isidore collected all her encouraging little epistles, telling her that reading them would be suspended until Erik regained full consciousness.

Dressed in the normative lab outfit, she eventually managed to finagle enough freedom to stand outside their patient's room. The door was closed and locked, the wall a solid sheet of metal. She knew in her heart that whatever the outcome of Erik's condition, the accident would complicate their relationship. Somehow she had to make him see that nothing mattered except their love.

Isidore approached her from behind, gliding silently in his wheelchair. "My dear child, he's not ready to see you. He's heavily sedated."

"Don't send me away," Christine urged. "Let me sit beside him."

"I've medicated him to prevent movement. Pulling at the stitches will only complicate the next round of extensive reconstructive surgery." He didn't mention the rampant staphylococcal infection. Apparently members of the police force were urinating and spitting in the pits.

"How bad is he?" She clung to whatever shred of hope he could offer.

"Erik is extensively bandaged. He knows his mental and physical conditions are grave. There isn't an area on his anterior surface that's not affected in some way. At the moment, his facial attributes are hellacious. Scarring will be extensive and require a great deal of correction. He will, no doubt, go through many stages trying to adjust. Melancholy will be the least of his problems."

"Will he recover?"

"I have confidence in him, and confidence is certainly a precious commodity at the moment. One in which he needs to reinvest, for I will be gone soon. The cancer will reclaim me." Isidore's guilt prompted a backhanded apology. "It was never my intent to bring you into such calamity."

"Don't." She silenced him by pressing her fingertips to the artificial lips of his mask, and dutifully returned to her own area.

Inside the Panic Room, Erik lolled through semi-conscious states of inertia. Even in periods of transient wakefulness, the fever left him lethargic. He'd never had an elevated temperature, but understood that bacteria were eating him. Surrendering to the inevitable, he settled into a rather predictable pattern of sleep dotted with brief periods of angry denial. The will to overcome self-inflicted mortification had not surfaced.

The absence of certain body parts was a disconcerting plague. Since what was left of his nostrils was packed with tight fitting rolls of cotton, he breathed through his mouth, making his oral cavity as dry as the Maranjab desert of Iran. Sips of water and the occasional applications of foul tasting glycerin swabs did nothing to appease his parched throat. Ice chips helped, but coupled with the fluids Isidore pumped into him intravenously, he wanted to pee like a racehorse. And there were stitches on his newly redefined genitals, tight stitches that constricted most painfully.

Stressed, vexed with his injuries, he welcomed the effects of the languorous drugs. They helped postpone discovering if he'd actually managed to castrate himself. Every cognizant thought only brought more questions regarding what was left of his manhood and his handsome features. He could almost define the edge of every cut, the border of every area fighting to heal with granulation.

Wafting in and out of varying states of mental frustration, he forced his body to relax, sent his mind down inky ribbons of dream states. One in particular reoccurred with consistent frequency. Since the attack, Thayer had conveniently disappeared, so he couldn't ask the good psychiatrist to interpret for him, though he could almost guess at the vision's meaning. Sheets of wind-driven rain drummed against his hooded head, telescoping his view. Before him he saw a grave surrounded by a growing puddle of water. Each clear celestial tear hit the surface, splashing upward in a cascading circular funnel. As the funnel returned to join the greater whole, the water turned a crimson red. The puddle was becoming a pool of blood that was suddenly lying beneath him. He closed his eyes and ordered the soggy grave to leave, but the rain of blood continued – it was his life that was departing, his future dripping out.

He tried to crawl aboard a ship, to meet Raoul and sail off into weightless oblivion with the Count and his older brother Philippe. The fact that he had irreparably marred himself seemed all too fitting.

Then the smell of suppuration and the itch of discharging pus would return him to the Panic Room. Semi-awake, he'd mentally line up sturdy lacquered wood easels, fill them with baroque gilt frames, and review all the Impressionistic French paintings he'd ever seen. Sheltered by a parasol, Christine walked leisurely beside him. They'd been on a picnic near a creek – stretched out on a red-checkered tablecloth decorated with a bunch of purple lilacs and co-attended by garnet feathered chickens. As they walked, he pointed to the lush tones of earth and woodland, the glorious bounties of fruits and flowers set to canvas with such artistic exuberance. Their brief stroll came to an abrupt end. Time seemed an urgent pressing issue. They moved within the limited demanding borders of cleverly calculated hours, minutes, and seconds. He pulled a vintage pocket watch from his vest. Pushing a button, the cover of the housing flipped open. They needed to leave. Through this preoccupation, the distant howl of a train whistle called to remind him: She had to return to Raoul. Despair comes in all shades...mostly gray, swirling funnels of gray that unexplainably transformed to a pond of crimson red.

Awake again. Lying on his back. Unable to move for fear he'd tear some set of stitches on the carnage of his face or carriage. *Rot! The poisonous process of becoming loathsome and impure.* The rank, fetid smell of his own festering flesh hit the couple-of-dozen sensors left high up at the back of his palate and nares. Through the un-bandaged areas of his posterior forearms he felt the nubby patterns of a comforter. He tried to erase the present, to regress and go backwards, rejoin his former life. The man without a face was better than the man completely butchered. A ribbon of gray cement appeared before him. Carefully counting the cracks in the sidewalk, he walked beside her once again and the colorful elaborate paintings reappeared.

Sharp overhead lights snapped on, then dimmed. "You'll need this. Might help with the disorientation." Isidore gave him the little wedding ring that was on the right pinky finger of his corpse. "Christine issued specific instructions for us to retrieve it."

Erik remembered viewing his dead body. An antique figure in a French museum-crypt. Time slowed interminably. His mind didn't want to resurface and confront the present, but it was impossible not to flow with the current. "This is insane. How can I be alive in two places?" A cacophony of screams rose into his ears. He tried to raise his hands to his temples, but layers of gauze held him fast. "Too much information for my brain to unscramble!" Within the tangled confluence of time and space he wanted to reject the present and reclaim only the past. He wanted to wander unimpeded within the degree of certainty his old life provided.

Frustrated, he sent an untouched cup of custard flying off the over-the-bed table. Isidore stood somewhere near the right side of his head. "My eyes?"

"Untouched. I've removed the coverings. I want you to adjust to the increased stimulus of light. You can open them when you like."

"How many days?"

"Four twenty-four hour periods thus far. The infection is resolving. Your temperature is back to normal, leukocyte count within expected parameters."

He felt Isidore's soft fingers examining the bandages on his right thigh. Strips of Neosporin saturated scrim stuck to him in places. He so wanted to scratch.

"Penis?"

"You still have one, though it's circumcised now, and stitched where it was nearly severed. I'm fairly sure it will still function, but I don't recommend touching it for a while. Very clever your telepathic message to Torossian. Bolted him right into action. You couldn't tell him exactly where to go because...?"

"Didn't know anything except a pit on a downward slope."

"Along with this ring I just presented you, Christine proposes I let her in for a visit. She only asks several dozen times a day."

"Not yet," he justified himself with a reference to the smell. "She'll start bawling." Secretly, he wished she would. *Someone should grieve over this.*

"I'm afraid it's too late to deny her entrance. She's standing at the door."

Erik's crusted eyes struggled to open. Her blurred silhouette gradually came into focus. Clothed in a jacketed dress of muted gold and black velvet that came just to her knees, the scalloped paisleys of the lustrous fabric reminded him of Persia. He found it a strange inexplicable outfit for the lab, until he realized she was projecting the eye-catching ensemble for his benefit. Her calm stance did nothing to hide the alarm etched across her face. She was wondering how badly scarred he would be, and thinking this might possibly spell the end of their budding relationship.

Isidore nodded to her, suggesting he wished to excuse himself. But as he rolled past Christine, she whispered, "Stay. You brought me to something weirder than any stage performance."

Erik's ears went on alert. With some effort he guarded his thoughts. *What did she just say?* Alongside her spoken request, the word 'betrayal' flashed in her mind. *How did she betray me?*

She came over to the side of the bed. "It's so quiet in here, would you like some music?" Hidden in the background of her mind he teased out the guilt over what she'd done with the Phenobarbital and Codeine.

He remained aloof, not responding.

Uncomfortable, she babbled on. "Actually there is very little quiet. Practically every corner of the world is full of sounds. People ignore them." She drummed her fingers on the bedrail, stopping when she thought that it might disturb his concentration. She could hear a deep beating sound coming from within him, the steady rhythmic pounding of a sad and violent heart – in mourning. "You don't need to talk, but if you feel like a conversation choose any subject."

He sensed that she wanted to kiss him, to make the physical and emotional distance between them evaporate, as before when they'd made love. "Nothing comes to mind." The sarcasm in his voice revealed only the edge of his bitterness.

"Then I'll settle for standing near you."

Erik's stormy eyes stared, fuming beneath the head bandages.

She could see the tears he shed internally, alarming tears…of blood. "Take one small step toward wanting me and we can make a future together," she reassured. "Whatever your needs, we'll invent solutions."

"You think me such a simple creature."

She leaned toward him. Areas of flesh, deprived of circulation and eaten by bacteria, would need debriding. A polluting smell suffocated the air. Christine tried to ignore it. "Shall I kiss the bandages? There's only one smallish hole. What lips you may, or may not have are unreachable behind the strips of gauze."

How accurately she had guessed one of his most frustrating new dilemmas. Her wanting to avail herself of his face placed him momentarily in a quandary. She curled completely forward with the agility of a cat and kissed a barren area of eyelid. "Growth can be very painful, Erik. Things coming to fruition too rapidly can hurt. They lack the gift of appreciation that living through an ordeal bestows." She was trying to tell him she wanted him to heal, that his recuperation had priority. Next to that, formalizing their union was an equally important consideration. Somehow her aspirations lacked conviction.

Here, in his nearly moribund state, he experienced a rapid hard erection that stung unbearably as it pulled against the stitches. Despite his wounds, she stimulated him to such a degree that his body offered up itself. He ground his teeth together. Apparently he still had all of them.

She was suddenly dabbing a handkerchief to her eyes. "The path down some cliffs is very steep. Are you ready?"

"For what?" His voice was low and contained.

"To make babies. Isidore wants grandchildren and I want to begin again, relearn you. Familiarize myself with your touch and merge the two of us into a partnership." She didn't want to tell him that she saw their former children all the time now. She was flooded with the visions of their faces and wanted to cry constantly. Ariel's wedding to Grace, the summer when Michael and Sarah took off and returned with little presents for everyone. She'd been living on hope and memories during his isolation.

"We cannot have others," he stated flatly. "Making love will bear no fruit."

She put her hand on her abdomen, questioning her own anatomy. "I want us to resume where we left off."

"But so much has happened since then. Who do you think I am? The Voice? The Angel of Music? I'm a man, a killer with abundant natural talent and a fixed determination. I'm not out in the world torturing people at this very moment because I've suffered an unusual setback." He tried to vocalize the rising crescendo of his thoughts, to drive her clean out of the room. "This is a man conceived **twice** in *kryptos* (secret)."

"On my sincerest oath, I swear to you that I want a ceremony and a marriage license," she blurted.

"We were cooked in a lab and don't need a marriage license."

"Oh, my love!" She grasped the bedrails, refusing to let him retreat behind the stench of reeking bandages and mauled history. All she wanted was to firmly implant within his mind the unwelcomed knowledge that she loved him with fierce devoted passion. Regardless. "Time and patience can heal your injuries!"

His half-hearted shove to send her packing had no effect. When he answered, his voice was less like thunder, more akin to the former Erik. It lent itself to the sound of water running over rocks held fast within a stream. His neck was uncut, his throat undamaged. Coming first into the wire, his face had born the brunt of ruin. He still had vocal control. "How can I appeal to you?"

"You have always held an extraordinary purity in my eyes. A blazing light burns within you. An angel on fire that rises from the ashes, ready to obey the divine components of his nature. That alone supercedes deformity."

"With me comes pain, brutal pain."

"Then I shall be the protectress, the gentle goddess formed of song, offering an ever-widening procession of blessing. You are the intelligent high-minded god who treads on ahead, bearing all my hopes, carrying all my love. Knowing me, forgiving me. You define what I would die for and what makes life worth living."

"You could poison me with intravenous potassium chloride and have Isidore make you a new Erik."

"No, the bodies in the crypt were removed yesterday for cremation and I helped Nyah destroy all the samples of our DNA in the lab. You and I have become a rather endangered species."

He didn't bother to remind her that they were walking cesspools of all the DNA they would ever need. Every cell bore an entire sample of their genetics. Her visit had done one helpful thing. He'd reached the conclusion that he wanted to live, even deformed. Given the permission to heal itself, his immune system roared into high gear. "Leave me."

When the door closed, Torossian stepped out of the bathroom. Punching in the code, he sealed the outside wall. Since the night of the incident he'd never left Erik's side, possessively demanding that every treatment be explained to him. There were no cameras in the Panic Room. They had complete privacy. Torossian acknowledged his brother with a rare smile and the low mental howl of a wolf. He sensed the decision to heal and the ensuing internal changes already beginning within Erik's body. "You've begun the process." Torossian hesitated, "We could wait."

This was a crucial moment. Erik raised a bandaged hand. "You have the mirror?"

Torossian had unscrewed the thing from the bathroom wall. "Big step. Angled and at a distance, right?"

"You won't run?"

"Change is an unalterable dictum of the universe. Everything is in a state of flux. I'm not going anywhere without you. To exist apart is impossible since your mind's projections are a jailor rattling keys in front of my cage."

Erik steadied his nerves. "All right, let's see my face first."

Torossian rested the mirror on the back of a metal lab chair. "You think eight feet enough to cushion the blow?"

"I need to control what I'm about to look at somehow. Help me unwrap my head."

The creature washed his hands and started unraveling the yards of gauze. When he finished he stepped back, waiting patiently for Erik to take in the view. "A partial mask will not do. It must be a whole one. Isidore will never re-clone you. Too attached to what he raised, too proud."

Erik's eyes remained closed. "I can't go through this again. The first Erik is somewhere in the basement of my soul – locked up, madly trying to kick his way out. Things with Christine are ill defined. For one night she felt like Heaven, now she defines Hell itself."

Reluctantly, Erik peered slowly at the silvered glass. An unstoppable rocket of anger fired upward. He screamed so loud the sound raised the slender almost invisible hairs on Torossian's forearms – they'd taken forever to grow. He was suddenly rather proud of them and their feat of standing straight up. "When you were young you played in all kinds of masks. They are all there on your bedroom wall. You were quite cynical then, even with regular lips and a nose. Maybe you were preparing yourself."

The face was a disaster, but so poetic. "This is ironic. The people in the Opera House always exaggerated my looks. Now I am a monster! But I clearly remember swimming naked in a mephitic black lake... feeling very free to be without the mask. Not a monster to myself."

Torossian left the mirror in place and pulled over another seat, folding his long body onto it. "There are no extraneous bacteria in the air. I think we can safely afford to leave you exposed for a few minutes. Let you grow accustomed to your features. The swelling will recede, the scabs will soften and fall away." He crossed his arms over his chest and watched as Erik sadly bowed his head. "Some people trot around desperately trying to project a pleasant face. Cosmetics, hair, practiced smiles. The sins they fail to hide in their manufactured faces are gruesome." He set his thumb and index finger on his chin, fingering a non-existent goatee. How Erik felt about the future mattered a great deal to him. "Did you know that in the middle of searching for your dead body, when Nyah and Isidore were growing painfully deformed, they took a break? For a short time they renewed their love affair – a last token of intimacy."

"How do you know that?"

"Certainly not from Nyah, I respect her too much. I picked it out of Isidore's head. I can connect with him, but not as deeply as I can with you." With a settled familiarity he touched one of Erik's undamaged fingers – the Revenant wasn't happy or unhappy, just sincere. "In an old quarry, not too far from here, there's a scrubby pine tree growing a full thirty feet off the ground. Its base is set between some shelves of weathered limestone. More than half the tree's primary roots are exposed because there's no dirt available to anchor them. It's quite a sight, this tenacious tree with its twisted roots lying open to the air. You and I are like that tree. Alien to the setting, yet still affixed to the side of the landscape, still alive despite the ugliness that's exposed to the world. Sometimes at night I sit and study that tree, thinking about who I am... longing to understand."

Erik looked at him in disbelief. This was more than Torossian had ever spoken outloud. "The tree still has the limestone to accept its intrusion. The quarry doesn't totally reject it."

"It's as if the stones are curious over the demented pine. They're playing with the tree, not giving it due space. There's a small grotto at the base of the slope. Workers used to take shelter there when it rained. The site produced stone for the construction of this estate. Some oddly hewn blocks still lay scattered about, half-chiseled. They were left abandoned on the quarry's floor. They cracked and someone judged them unfit. Up the hillside is a clearing where a hunter's cottage once stood...we hid a baby there."

"What are you saying?"

"Who decides what is suitable and what is not? In most cases, changes from altered DNA happen slowly, not quickly. In a normal human body an entire re-synthesis completes itself every seven years – every living cell is less than eighty-four months old. At sixteen we've done that twice and I think we are still evolving. I don't want to develop as that tree – not understanding the precariousness of our roots. It was my will to have our donor come back. Providence put him on the Earth in the 1800's...Isidore did the creating this time."

Totally intrigued, Erik lay in the bed staring at him. "Go on."

"I am the trigger that brings the Phantom back into your existence. Not Nyah, not any chemical smell or random taste. I brought him to you and left the door open for both of us to learn. For better or worse, I added to us."

"Even when I called him?"

"My brain has to assist. You, me, him...the three components work in conjunction to get him here and you back there."

"Do you see the events?"

He actually sighed, taking in enough oxygen for the next three minutes. "Once the visions start in earnest, but only through your mind."

"Do you feel them...touch, taste...as I do?"

"Just the visual projection...and there's sound, but no sense of touch or smell. I cannot experience what's in your mouth. Still, I get the gist. I had no idea we killed Feigel-Evie until our original self disclosed it." He rested his elbows on the arms of the chair, rubbing his hands on the cold metal. He was behaving more humanly all the time.

Erik lowered his face again, speaking toward the sheets. "You consummate thief. I thought I had some form of neurotic hysteria, a split personality, except that I could remember and retain events and information after the seizures. So, you entered my head and on a cellular level opened memories and started events rolling like a..."

"High definition movie. Not a thief, a key – a key into the occasion of a past life. Nature has a very dark side. We need to understand its characteristics."

"Thayer Delaquois would call this a *folie a deux*, the presence of the same delusion in two persons closely associated with one another. What would you call it?"

"A very real, very ubiquitous gift."

"If I could have anything, I'd wish for a set of eyes in the back of my head to protect me from you!"

"Could be done. First we'd have to construct some kind of bony cavity to support your new eyes." Torossian actually smacked a knee.

"What's so amusing?"

"You could buy a dog and get almost the same effect, but why block the beacon I initiate? When you encounter and overcome what our original self confronted, you no longer retreat from their threat. Knowing the details of what you did makes you bold. It feeds internal strengths. Your wit and courage sharpen."

"True. Very true." Erik lifted his chin and Torossian stuck a piece of ice on his intact pink tongue. "I don't want to divest myself of him or you. We have to coexist. What he experienced we shall both know."

"Good. We'll be one totally connected unique being." Torossian waited. "What now?"

"Khusrowshah. I want to know, how the conflict ended."

"If I send you to him will you eat when you return?"

Erik closed his eyes and leaned back into the pillows. His left fingers rose in assent. "Agreed."

37 *ENIGMA*

ute, Erik waited for what he hoped might be his last trip into the past. A scratchy sound of static reached his ears, loud, annoying, as if Torossian reset the link to a satellite radio channel and was adjusting. When the meaningless repetition cleared, life in the present ground to a halt, swiftly transitioning backwards into the past. Erik no longer smelled the stench in the Panic Room. Persia was reclaiming him with the distinct smell of spiced lambs roasting on spits and the murmuring of a crowd in a massive courtyard.

Looking up, he saw a dozen colorfully dressed servants standing on balconies. Working simultaneously, they released hundreds of doves from a series of golden cages. The birds needed no coaxing to spread their wings and take to rapid flight. Upward they climbed, freed into an already hot morning sky. Over the painted terra cotta tiles of sloped roofs they careened and tightened their formation. Their primary instinct – to speed as far away as possible from the palace into the peace of a less congested countryside. To the sound of flutes and timbrels, happy children danced about, laughing, singing, waving good-byes to the doves – unaware that in the dirt outside these royal walls other little ones starved because their regent lacked the thinnest thread of concern.

This was Fazel's wedding day – the anticipated highlight of the season.

During the final culminating weeks of the royal engagement, the Shah's eldest declared the great acceptability of Amine in all the traditional manners. Every day his servants carted gifts to her apartment, criers walked about spouting blessings for the couple and announcing an endless stream of feasts and parties heralding the event. Yesterday the bride and groom had gone in separate processionals for their ritual bathing, massaging, and the elaborate application of henna designs to their hands and feet. Inside the palace, everywhere one turned, attendants and those directly associated with the wedding party wore bright yellow to indicate extreme happiness, and orange as a clairvoyant prediction of prosperity, not only for the pair, but for the entire country. Anyone not wearing the appropriate colors was reminded of their duties with the sting of a switch taken to their legs.

Privately, Erik considered the entire flock a horde of superstitious fools.

For the actual wedding, the couple declared their love for each other by dressing in crimson red. Pearls and diamonds accented their collars and cuffs. At the ceremony they sat in separate rooms. If they leaned back and strained, they could barely see each other through an archway. Three times the *imam* went from one room to the other, asking them individually if they wished to marry and entered the marital contract of their own free will. Honoring tradition, Amine replied only through her father. He, of course, only replied in the affirmative at the third and final inquiry. Satisfied, the *imam* brought Amine a golden pomegranate to hold in her hand, then led her to sit beside her new husband. On the floor before them stretched an elaborate cloth covered in candies and presents. At the end of this cloth stood a gold-framed mirror set between two elaborate candelabras, prepared so that the couple might view themselves for the first time as husband and wife while listening to the *imam* recite prayers and readings.

At the conclusion of the holy words, a score of musicians picked up their instruments and started playing delicate happy tunes. Four of the bride's female relatives stepped forward with a white pashmina shawl. Identifying the bride and groom with protection and purity, they held the garment above the heads of the newlyweds. Other ladies, carrying festive cones of sugar, danced elegantly around the group. To glad shouts and acclamations from those gathered, sugar was sprinkled atop the shawl, symbolically raining sweetness down upon Fazel and Amine. Guests formed a queue to offer their well wishes and lay silk scarves containing candies and decorated baskets filled to the brim with precious stones before the couple. When the cloth spread out on the floor could hold no more, tables running alongside the walls began filling up.

Bottles of French champagne were uncorked and with the popping, the celebration began in earnest. Several dozen singers joined the musicians, filling the rooms with a great harmonious concert to delight the ears of family and friends. Brightly outfitted slaves shuttled food to tables already laden with a rich variety of meats, fruits, vegetables, and sweets. Servants went from group to group, delivering platters of food adorned with peacock feathers, pouring juice and wine from golden pitchers whose handles trailed garlands of flowers all the way to the floor. Amid rounds of applause, trays laden with the delicacy of ice-cold sherbets were passed to waiting diners.

Outside in the clear windless air the doves were long gone and little dirty children sucked their thumbs in want.

Heedless, the festivities carried on. Male poets walked from room to room reciting love poems and skilled jesters exaggerated their buffoonery. Talented females danced for the congregated caliphs and khans – all clustered with their allies in specifically designated dining areas. Boisterous laughter and overstated gestures indicated the various groups were obviously pleased. As an infidel, Erik was not allowed to perform, only to observe from the back of the rooms. Since he held such contempt for their ostentatious behavior, this suited him. At least they weren't hypocrites; they never ceased to flaunt their wealth. The darkly clad magician had the honor of masterminding the pyrotechnic fireworks to be displayed later after the sunset. Until this segment of the entertainments, he only watched and listened.

Before twilight cast a gloom within the joyful halls, servants lit torcheres and chandeliers containing hundreds of candles, so that the rooms were bright as day. With the coming of the stars the dulcet tones of musical instruments gradually changed to more invigorating ballads. Female slaves, dressed in shimmering costumes, hit tambourines to the heels of their hands, elbows, and knees as they pranced around more luridly. The ensuing outbursts of laughter grew louder and more encouraging. Erik glided around the back of the halls like a ghost on a mission. Holding himself apart from the caliginous mental trance cast by the ballads, performers, and opiate laced incense; he secretly kept his eyes on Khusrowshah.

Inherent contradictions ran like subtle currents just beneath the surface of this royal wedding. The evil hearted prince sat with his friends, greedily watching Amine and the presents showered down upon his brother's bride. During the celebration there was no opportunity to impose upon her. His chance, bold and fraught with risk, would miraculously manifest itself when she retired.

Khusrowshah schemed to sexually educate Amine prior to his older brother's arrival in the wedding chamber. Though his ideas contrasted sharply to the time-tested morality of Islamic law and the ethics of royal decorum, they were very human. Waiting patiently as the evening droned on, the unrestrained sentimentality and molasses-like antidotes offered to the couple by those in attendance, grated the nerves of the needy Khusrowshah. Soaked in lechery and avarice, he made little effort to conceal a digging motion he presented to the friends gathered at his table. Accompanying the movements with disgusting shoveling sounds, he tried to convey the idea that he would soon bury the couples' joy.

Beneath his breath, Erik hissed at the brazenness. As the daughter of the principle Khan of the northern cities, it was more fitting that Amine be the bride of the oldest son. How unfortunate that Prince Fazel Soroush was not transported with love. Amine's beauty did nothing to stir his affections. He longed for an intelligent wife, one with whom he could debate the sacred and secular laws. Amine failed to inspire, despite her physical appeal. But he was a dutiful son and planned to engage her as an honorable husband.

When one of the city's judges approached to offer congratulations, the groom's patient and encouraging smile fueled Khusrowshah's nefarious intentions almost past bearing. Scowling, he studied Amine closely. To the sound of lighthearted flutes and beating drums, he rose and came to stand before the bride. "I have written my good wishes." Producing a small scroll from his inside cloak, he placed the note within her hands. "With your permission."

Amine, you do not burn with love for the one who delights in legal speeches. I know you fear that this night, and every night hereafter, Fazel will leave your passion unrequited. Let your husband's brother assure you that all your anxieties may be put to rest. You are possessed of elegance and have the power to please. Fazel will employ gentleness and conduct himself with meritorious demeanor. Should he neglect all that simmers within you, my swift wings will carry you to newer heights.

Keeping her head bowed, the princess slid the note with its veiled threat into her pocket. At her lack of acknowledgement, Khusrowshah stormed from the room. These inexplicable reactions bothered no one except Erik. The Frenchman recognized the symptoms of a young man about to become a tempest. Unable to follow the retreating royal, he had no choice but to hurry to the courtyard. The hour to address the fireworks with their flash of cascading lights and resounding booms was upon him. Ten minutes later a series of trumpet blasts signaled the couple to turn around in their seats and walk to a large open latticed window. The breathtaking exhibition lasted twenty minutes.

With the glorious display concluded, Amine excused herself from her husband to say her goodbyes to her parents. The pleasure of bringing herself to good account for Prince Fazel bore the hopeful reward of a long and happy life, but failed to wing her steps from the room. Given her parents' blessings, she still was not ready to become a woman.

The bride moved to an exit with a small entourage of her handmaidens. Noticeably quiet guests stood aside, allowing the group of sedate but congenial women to conduct their mistress to her husband's apartments. Amine kept her resolve strong; she knew Fazel's ardor was non-existent. She indulged not a single amorous vision of his passion reaching heights that deprived her of her senses. Holding her breath, back stiffened, she entered the wedding chamber. She was but thirteen years old.

Perfumed lamps of aloe-wood fixed with ambergris and placed on golden stands highlighted the furnishings of the splendid room. Cast in this mellow glow of light, she saw that the walls and ceiling were entirely covered in plates of gold set with large emeralds at their corners. Nearly translucent green Cahara marble swirled across the floor.

"My husband has excellent taste," she murmured in prescribed appreciation.

In the center of the room stood an immense canopied bed, draped in sectioned curtains of the most vivid colors. Purple for intuition and spirituality, deep indigo for the strength of wisdom, blue to expound communication and tranquility, and deep green to reflect prosperity and healing. All about were tables with gold and silver bowls filled with intermixed bouquets of roses, jasmine, violets, and carnations. The entire chamber was a perfumed box to delight the senses.

One of the handmaidens drew back the purple drape and gestured for Amine to look. Atop the bed sat a tray with presents from her husband. Her eyes flashed on a pair of extraordinary long-tailed silver pheasants sitting alongside an ivory handled brush, comb, and mirror. On a piece of red velvet rested a gold chain and a pendant. In the center of the Rococo-styled openwork setting rested a brilliant fifty-carat black opal, shining with every color in the rainbow. Beside the tray were the marital cushions to lift the pelvis of the new princess – for it was hoped she would conceive this very night and produce a male heir to the throne.

She sighed, resigning herself to her fate. Not once had Fazel whispered tender words of love or encouragement to her. Almost thankful that the man did not declare empty sentiments, she retired to a screened-in area that acted as a dressing closet. In the golden light her women prepared her. They lifted off her clothes, rubbed her quivering body with primrose oil containing specs of gold, and combed the lustrous black hair that fell to her waist. When the fragrant oil set, they drew a gossamer red silk caftan over her body and draped her head in a dyed-to-match veil studded with hundreds of tiny white seed pearls. Then she was served a series of small cups of tea containing Siberian ginseng, red clover, black cohosh, and Chaste Tree berries – all thought to stimulate secretions and promote fertility.

After setting in place the translucent *niqab* that served to cover her nose and mouth, her handmaids led her to the bed and helped her position herself. None could stay with her. She would await alone the arrival of her spouse. Her women would not appear again until morning to examine the sheets and report to the Shah their findings. With quiet gestures she sent her servants away.

The last to leave whispered to her mistress, "Blessed be Allah."

"Allah be praised," Amine responded. Pure, untainted, free of the depravity and influences of the apostate world, she sat on her bed – practically venerated for her virtue.

Patiently awaiting the sound of music that would announce the procession of males accompanying Fazel, she steadied her nerves by forcing deep breaths down into her lungs. *Would his intrusions hurt?* She'd been warned they would. She prepared by divorcing herself from emotion and instructing her muscles to relax.

In the gnawing silence, she strained to hear the ancient tunes mingled with the voices of singers raised together in a loud harmonious entourage. *Nothing!* She congratulated herself with some heady realities. Should she produce a son, he would be a future king. She imagined a strong intelligent young man, ready to defend his kingdom, full of compassion and warmth. Blowing out a breath, she ballooned her veil and went back to controlling her fears about copulation. The realization that she might actually grow weary remaining so stationary and fall to sleep, made her laugh. The amusements would not conclude until dawn and the parties were scheduled to go on for another week. She was totally unaware that Khusrowshah's cronies occupied the groom with every conceivable distraction to delay his approach.

At that very moment Fazel insisted on taking his repose, "Good friends, my duties await!"

Khusrowshah's cohorts zoomed in to entice the groom with a particularly talented Egyptian dancer – successfully detaining the prince again. Expounding on the dancer's undeniable merits, they boasted that the female contorted to accomplish what few others could do, by bending over backwards and touching, first the crown of her head, then her full face to the floor. This ploy proved too tempting. Politely setting aside his waiting bride, Fazel feigned mortification and fell into the trap. Excited and garrulous to the extreme, Khusrowshah's confederates congratulated Fazel on his choice and brought out the tantalizing female from Cairo.

The curtains of the marital bed were designed for privacy. Closed, they not only concealed the occupants, but also obscured from sight the contents of the room. Thus adding the advantage of heightening curiosity by not allowing the marital couple to view each other until that last moment when the groom's hand drew back the drape.

Hidden secretly in a louvered closet, Khusrowshah experienced the perverse excitement that compelled him to perform so many of his crimes. The pleasure of watching Amine undressed and lovingly prepared, sent dusky shivers of anticipation snaking down his spine. Stepping out, he stole quickly about. Assuring himself that no one else waited in the room.

The heavy breathing of someone standing outside the curtain sent an alarm through Amine. "Who's there?" she asked, genuinely frightened when no reply was offered. In the next moment a small brass scorpion, followed by a similar grasshopper, flew in through the corner of the drapes to land before her. Confused, Amine picked them up.

"Learn to distinguish me from my brother."

She recognized the voice and instantly felt almost irrational. Like these insects, she too had been plopped, unannounced, onto a bizarre field of battle.

"I have come early to service you," the disembodied voice taunted.

Trickling tendrils of fear swept over Amine. A split second before the intruder revealed himself, her precarious position registered. She kicked out a leg and prepared to rise. Too late, the edge of a curtain parted.

Veiled in black, the villain addressed her. "Pride. You should at least know the name of the fickle sin that makes you guilty. I'm sick to death of your little innuendos, your vague illusions that you may or may not want me." Her lack of enthusiasm to his overture meant nothing to him.

The contents of her stomach roiled, forcing the turbulent bilious taste of honey cake into her throat. Lamely she asked, "Why are you here, Lord?"

There was no coaxing, no consideration of her arousal – he had no time. The riotous thief ripped the sheer veils off her head and face, grabbing her long black hair. Twisting his fingers into the scented curls, he jerked her to her feet. "You are wondering if your husband will arrive in time to save you. What has happened to delay him? All my associates are working to give me a few minutes with you. Had we been introduced to each other a year ago, before negotiations started, you would have preferred me to Fazel." He hocked up phlegm and spit the clog to the side of her jeweled, henna painted feet. "Sorceress!"

Amine froze with wretched understanding. His breath reeked of wine. Before her terrified gaze Khusrowshah's eyes sparked with anger and lust. In response she cried out the only word that came to her. "Deceiver!" Scratching at his face, she tried to push away from her assailant, but his restraint held.

Astonished that she would dare to fight off a pure blood prince, her newly acquired brother-in-law barked, "Do not speak!" Punching her with all the brute force he commanded, he hit so hard and so accurately that he broke her jaw. Without a moment's hesitation, he let her fall to the floor to experience the shearing spasms of pain that followed.

Withdrawing a copy of Erik's dagger from his belt, he slit the nuptial tunic up the front. Teasing her briefly with the tip of the knife, he executed a straight quick slash across the skin above her breasts. Carving a line from shoulder to shoulder, he marked her as his property.

With her fractured mandible and cracked teeth sending jolts of jagged pain into her brain, she offered no further resistance.

He untied the sash of his pants and let the leggings fall about his ankles. His manhood, solid and ready, throbbed to his touch. "Perish the thought that my older brother should have your flower first. It would be such a mournful shame to waste such a precious piece of skin on him."

She swallowed her own blood and whimpering, held her jaw in a desperate attempt to comfort the shattered bone.

"Stop! Stop!" the malicious prince mimicked her unspoken plea. "I shall congratulate Fazel on providing me with such a perfect opportunity. He threw his body on top of hers.

"Why," she could barely choke the word.

"Why am I doing this? I thought it obvious. Shall I call out 'rape' when you seem huddled on a fence, undecided as to which way you should flop?" The head of his penis poked around between her legs searching for the sight. "I desire you and declare that the attraction evidenced by my body has a more pressing right than my unavailable brother." *I don't know if I'm capable of honoring anything anymore.* "You don't love Fazel. You're fascinated with the French magician." She winced at the chilling sarcasm in his words. "Your eyes follow him around the room and it's not fear that prompts you to track him. You haven't said it, but all your sly little peeks declare you are attracted to him and his mysteries." His fingers went to her nipples, pinching them until she screamed with silent agony. "I shall have more than left over morsels, Amine. More than the little teasing flirts you offer from a distance."

He located her virginity. "I'm afraid the trick's played on you – the damage is about to begin." His determined eyes hardened. Blasting forward, heedless of his position on her anatomy, he sealed her firmly to him.

Gasping, Amine's lips parted. Unable to move her jaw in protest, she raked her nails down his back. She had not expected such a rigorous proceeding. Summoning all her strength, she shoved at his shoulders making every effort to free herself from his clutches. Under the multitude of blows he delivered to the sides of her chest, she quickly quieted and suffered without relief the staggering humiliation he metered out. Resigned to her fate, she closed her eyes and suffered the indignities he perpetrated on her person without further complaint.

A relentless, rhythmic power laid claim to the core of Khusrowshah. He vowed to prolong the experience, show Amine the prowess of a real male. Just as he surrendered to the overwhelming drive consuming him, he arched his back and grunted as if he were in pain. *No! What is this? I cannot bring conclusion!* He felt his body shying within her. Orgasm was not to be achieved. *Sorry pitiable shaft!* His disappointment caused an immediate deflation of his libido. He had hoped for a more pleasurable release, now he was robbed. The great satisfaction of despoiling his brother's bride would have to be enough.

Shrinking rapidly, he exited the gaping bloody hole that had become her pathway. As soon as he was outside her, he mentally wanted her again, despite the reality of the situation. His milky substance drained without force from the tip of his lax organ. He took her by the ankles and bending her knees toward her shoulders, lifted her pelvis so that he might pour something of himself into her.

At last! Amine heard the sounds of the groom's wedding procession as it passed through the pergola and advanced toward the chamber. With her body bruised and wracked with pain, unable to sob, she looked at the pathetic male instrument that had just introduced her to the world of womanhood. The ghastly ordeal was over. Now in a voice that sounded brittle and disinterested, but was very controlled, she uttered through teeth clenched shut, "I divorce you. I divorce you. I divorce you."

Pushing off her, Khusrowshah stared at the fallen woman in disgust. Utilizing Islamic law she had formally undone his claim. He wanted to roar but dared not make a noise. Concealed by his black veil, he grinned wickedly. Happily attending to a need just to smell her, he moved the lower veil aside. The scent of her perfume and his sexual hunt saturated the air. Tearing a sleeve off the nuptial tunic, he rolled it up and thrust it in her tormented mouth as a gag. Then to restrict any further outcry, he took a long silk scarf from his neck and wrapping it beneath her chin, forcefully tied a knot on the crown of her head.

Standing, he dropped the duplicate of Erik's dagger on the floor, several feet from her head. *At least the blame will fall upon that arrogant magician. I should take her troublesome eyes. Look how they burn with indignation. No time.* With the music gaining in loudness, he offered her an unrepentant salute and fled the room.

Stained and used, Amine reacted by squeezing her eyes shut. Tears spilled from the corners. Rolling onto her abdomen, she managed to crawl a foot on the floor. How to conceal her nakedness and shame? A stiff arm reached for a small rug to pull over her buttocks. No success. Straining for the leg of a little table, her fingers curled around the hilt of the dagger. She sat up with great effort, blood flowing from her chest wound and the corners of her mouth. Ruined, she reflected briefly upon her options. There was no hope, no consolation. Her position could not be restored. She would be removed, branded as used goods, and banished from court, possibly the country. Choosing to end her life, she realized she could not allow Khusrowshah such an easy victory. Justice demanded more. The French magician had not raped her.

Bracing herself for a final bloody ceremony, she dipped her index finger into the stinging gash across her chest. Her own fluids would reveal Khusrowshah's deceit and seal his fate. Urging her shaky fingers forward, she wrote the miscreant's grim name upon the marble floor.

Channeling her thoughts into one intractable beam of hatred, she convinced herself that she had enough energy to act. Her grateful fingers clasped the dagger's hilt. The gag muffled her short prayer for forgiveness. Listening for the music that announced the procession bearing her new husband, she guessed they walked very close to the door. An additional slow banging added a steady rhythmic note to the music in her ears. The drumming did not come from the wedding party, but from her own sad heart.

At the door, surrounded by his men and her handmaidens, her husband stood in resigned anticipation. He wondered if they would both enjoy this night and took a moment to mentally prepare.

With both her hands Amine lifted the knife, extending her arms out as far as she could reach. Her eyes caught the descending glint of the welcomed dagger, not to harm, but to cut her free of shame and defilement. She plunged the knife into her heart just as the door opened. The last thing she heard was the beautiful melody coming to an abrupt halt.

A haunting crash of dropped instruments echoed through the chamber, as Prince Fazel fainted, crumpling into a heap on the floor.

Cries of shock filled the corridor, rippling like a wave down the procession. The line stood paralyzed, with those at the rear of the small congregation wondering what had happened. Then the very floor vibrated as a dozen hurried footsteps pounded their way forward into the room.

Fazel's best friends knelt to revive the prince. Standing beside the body, several of Amine's brothers began screaming and wailing, rending their garments and tearing at their hair. In a profound state of grief, one of Amine's first cousins stumbled from the room. With the assistance of two of the servants he returned to the celebrators. He entered the halls with his braided locks of hair and his clothes disheveled, his thoughts in disarray. Weeping uncontrollably, he informed the Shah and everyone present of the shameful rape, the courageous suicide, and Fazel's faint into unconsciousness.

Still seated on the same cushions he'd occupied when Fazel's escort left, the Shah received this heartbreaking report with the greatest astonishment. "This cannot be true! It is an impudent falsehood. The mere utterance of such words causes us the greatest affliction."

Confused at the Shah's degree of calmness, indeed the lack of sympathy experienced by everyone in the entire room, the cousin remained immobile for several seconds. He was incapable of answering. Then, broken and sobbing, he drifted disoriented and whacked his forehead into a column. He lay on the floor dazed, uncomprehending, another victim to the incident.

In the nuptial bedchamber, Fazel's associates lifted him onto the bed. When the groom regained coherence, a chilling almost-inhuman scream issued from his mouth. He dragged himself to the edge of the bed to view his bride. No one had touched Amine. It was obvious what had befallen the princess. Fazel melted into tears, bewailing his forlorn state with renewed cries of anguish, "Deliver my good wife from this distasteful condition! What demonic scoundrel has brazenly maimed this child? As the night is long, most evil-hearted soul, I assure you that you will soon be just as dead." In anguish, the prince receded into the array of pillows. A throng of people continued gathering in the room.

Grief, carried by the sound of high keening wails, swept through the palace like a tidal wave. For a considerable length of time pandemonium reigned in all quarters. Those of calmer heads, more involved with formalities, sent for the Daroga and the Captain of the Guard to assess the abhorrent situation. Fazel's dismay was so excessive that he remained for some time among those clustered in the chamber. No one could convince him to move to other, more pleasant quarters.

Within a few short minutes the Daroga and the Captain entered. Careful to maintain their professionalism, they considered the deplorable condition of the bride. Speaking softly to the prince, the Captain informed Fazel, "We can barely find the words to express our dismay regarding this irreparable loss. Today we have all sustained the worst disaster. All our sympathies are with you, Lord."

Leaning in, the Daroga advised him. "Let these others escort you from this room and comfort you," his hand gestured toward the crowd. "Do not give the villain another gift. We have determined that the rapist wished to point the finger of guilt at Erik." The crying and murmuring in the room hushed briefly. "The dagger is a copy of one I gave him. But brave Amine has, with her own blood, followed the unwavering truths spoken by the Holy Prophet. In a courageous declaration, she had the good sense to write the name of the man who attacked her. All his depraved calculations shall fail. With your permission, we go now to inform the Shah and await his instructions."

A stunned Fazel nodded gravely. Those in attendance covered the face of Princess Amine with a piece of fine satin, wrapped her in an embroidered silk blanket, and turned her feet toward Mecca. As these proceedings took place, confirmation reached the Shah. Accompanied by his closest bodyguards, the regent went immediately to Amine's parents to deliver the crushing news.

Poorly disguised as a shorter version of Erik, Khusrowshah hurried down a servant's corridor toward the kitchens serving this section of the palace. Before reaching the first set of guards, he confidently stripped off the magician's outfit and with broad threatening gestures, ordered the men out of his way. Scurrying past the cooking stations and ovens, he intended to take a route down to the cisterns below the structure.

Returning to the palace by way of the kitchens, Erik could see by the chaotic mob of people that something terrible was afoot. *How could a wedding night have gone so awry?* In the din and shouting that composed the better part of the confusion, he learned Fazel had arrived too late to the nuptial room to save the princess from rape, and that Amine had written, in the crimson of her own blood, a name on the floor just before taking her life. Speculation was rife. Men and women alike were throwing pots and pans about, threatening to break the neck of the unclean culprit. Erik knew he had to locate the Daroga. The historically proven result of such angry disorganized crowds was the punishment and death of the wrong people.

A young boy, wide-eyed and hiding near the side of a stove, caught Erik's eye. At the timid beckoning of the child's finger, Erik approached and squatted down. From his pocket he withdrew a hefty pouch of coin. Bribes always disclosed secrets. After placing the payment in the boy's hand, the lad moved aside to reveal he sat on a set of black clothes and veils identical to those Erik wore.

The boy's whisper was so faint, Erik had to press the lad's lips almost to his ear. "I found these on the stairs after Prince Khusrowshah ran through here. I thought his appearance strange."

Grabbing the garments, Erik responded, "Point the way." He held his disgust within, understanding with great accuracy the prince's ignoble intent. Dressed to look like Erik, Khusrowshah had once again tried to frame him for a frightful crime. He set his will to locating the royal and administering his own brand of justice.

The char boy took him to a door then wiggled free and disappeared into the dysfunctional crowd. Erik eyed the iron knob. Fingering the upper outline of the escutcheon plate, he had an uncanny sense of the felon straining to hear through the keyhole. *Does Khusrowshah wait just on the other side of this door, shielded from sight? Reluctant to withdraw before knowing what news is spreading?*

Closing his eyelids, Erik prepared his vision for the dark. He mulled over the chilling possibility, sensing the malevolent presence ease away. *The best way to catch a rat is to bait a trap, but one must know where to place the enticement. Otherwise the prompt to give up secrecy will fail. True concealment is priceless.* He withdrew his dagger. Turning the knob, he eased the door open just a crack, knowing full well a slender ribbon of light would shine in the dark like a beacon. Entering quickly, he closed the door behind him. In the black he heard the soft footfalls of a man, receding like a crab down the curving stairs. Erik's conclusions were correct. A phosphorescent ball rested inside his cloak pocket, should he need to illuminate the route. Timing the faint steps with his own, he set his hand to gliding down the wall, showing him how best to advance. Khusrowshah was close, hoping to use the confusion so inherent in such a tragedy. But the waterways were not so vast that Erik could not overtake him.

Behind him the door opened wide, flooding the stone passageway with light. Erik froze, an opportunity forever lost.

"Sir!" the deep voice of an adult male addressed him. "The Daroga sends word: The Shah requests your presence at once." Erik's golden eyes peered down the snaking tunnel one last time before turning to face the cook.

In the immediate hour following the crime, the Shah acted with a swift authoritative hand. With little rhyme or reason, he impulsively ordered all of Amine's attendants summarily beheaded. Within minutes the command was executed. Khusrowshah's weak-kneed confederates were rounded up and brought before the throne. Trembling with fear, for the sniveling nobles knew of the beheadings, they broke trust with their prince. Prostrating themselves in misery, they confessed to the lesser crime of delaying the groom from his marital duties. The Shah decried their wanton acts, "Your insolence, your very diligence to the task, shows you are not friends to this throne! For aiding in the insurmountable grief of an entire kingdom, you are banned, not only from this palace, but from any inch of Persian soil – without hope of future reconciliation to your mortified kinsmen."

Khusrowshah's mother was dragged to the dungeons and imprisoned.

The victim's body was moved to a draped bier in a small stateroom. Prince Fazel shut himself up in his quarters to grieve that he had not loved the tender Amine above all things. Professional mourners dusted their faces with layers of ash and powdered charcoal; they painted lampblack on their cheeks. Sitting in circles at various hallway corners, they cried out memorized eulogies: "Kind and even tempered, unaffected by her wealth, the sweet Amine had the greatest degree of docility. Lovely beyond comparison, she approached with enthusiastic zeal every service given to her undertaking." On-and-on they droned for hours, working in shifts.

The Shah's craftiest assassin, found his regent reclining on a sofa. Two servants waving peacock-feathered fans stirred the air above their distraught ruler, while several wives knelt beside him – striving to lighten the weight of such terrible grief by massaging his fingers and toes. When Erik rose from the floor, the Shah ordered, "Come. Let us go see her."

Sickened with the affairs of his household, the Shah was carried on a sort of sofa-litter, past conclaves of sooty-faced mourners, to the stateroom holding the corpse. Erik followed.

Left alone for the first time since the news, the Shah allowed a brief self-deprecating grimace to claim his face. "Monetary tribute will not be paid to the girl's father, for it is obvious she died by her own hand. The Qur'an expressly forbids suicide." The Shah got up and paced around the shrouded body. "I cannot accept this, yet I must. Two dozen of her kinsmen, crazed with grief, tell me that as soon as she is buried – which must take place this very day – they want Khusrowshah's head on a spike. 'Let us stay and help you,' they scream. 'We have no other family duties more demanding than to travel the countryside and rid the world of this despicable wretch.' Their demands for a just revenge draw me back into the world of reality. This innocent child has paid for all the years I looked away and ignored my son's wicked acts."

Erik memorized the context of the small room, marveling that it had been organized so quickly. Surrounded by flowers and burning incense, Amine lay only hours from her burial. From multiple gold hooks in the ceiling hung long braided cords with Islamic ornaments. These spun like prismatic discs: on one side, the sayings of Mohamed and on the other those of Allah. In this land of prayer rugs and tasseled prayer beads, people – even royalty – were always prepared for death. He would make sure Khusrowshah had none of these tokens.

A rather plainly embroidered death veil covered Amine's face. With the Shah's permission, an emotionally distant Erik lifted the shroud to observe her injuries. Khusrowshah's motivation was beyond comprehension. Viewing the corpse brought back the sharp images of Fatima and Soha Houri. *Three virtuous women lost.*

"Great good and great evil exist side by side in this land, just as in all others." The Shah pronounced the wisdom solemnly. Retuning to his sofa, he sounded resigned. "In Heaven, Allah may choose to regenerate her with a purifying power. A vibrant and renewed Amine will once again delight and beguile the eye." His hand went to his chest. "If men cannot practice restraint, they must meet the ends which our laws dictate.

In this unbridled destructiveness Khusrowshah has made an onerous mistake. Two thousand gold coins will expiate your guilt as my avenging angel. I want to know that the whining little coward entreated you for mercy, and that you offered him a balm of sorts." The ruler gave the non-verbal message of slicing a hand across his throat. With that malicious gesture, he ordered the capture and death of his precious second son. "I don't want to see Khusrowshah ever again."

With his hands folded respectfully below his waist, Erik went to his knees and nodded. "The man has fled the palace. Though the guards seek him diligently, I doubt they will find him."

"It is already rumored that he runs toward the eastern regions and on into China, or that he makes for some seacoast harbor where a ship might send him to Europe."

"Such linear thinking is predictable."

"I guessed that you would think otherwise. Regardless, I shall dispatch couriers in all directions to alert the people that he is a criminal wanted for capital offenses. I trust that I send the most ruthless of men to seek him, one who will let his darkest nature rule."

Erik touched his forehead, mouth, and heart before prostrating on the floor.

"Keep your oath inviolate," whispered the Shah. "Call for my servants. I want to be taken to Fazel."

Erik hastened to the Daroga, through him to obtain funds and needed supplies.

Khalil was exceptionally tense and worried. "My father observed with the greatest exactness the moment of my birth. Consulting the most knowledgeable astrologers concerning my destiny, he learned that I would one day leave this country never to return. The thought of that departure no longer pains me. If the heavens know my fate, then all is of-a-fashion already fixed and remains only to be acted upon."

"Therefore, fear profits nothing."

"Exactly. Long ago I made suitable plans for the day of my exile." He asked a rhetorical question, the answer clearly evident. "The Shah wants you to catch Khusrowshah, bring him proof of his son's death?" The Daroga picked up a book. "It says in First Samuel," he opened to the already marked page. "Behold, Dagon had fallen face downward on the ground before the ark of the Lord, and the head of Dagon and both his hands were lying cut off upon the threshold; only the trunk of Dagon was left to him." He shut the book with a decisive clap. "I believe that the mighty Dagon's bloated pride prevented him from anticipating the end of his reign of misery."

38 *MERRY, MERRY QUITE CONTRARY*

Obligatory farewells were made to Rakesh and Heerad. Blessings and wishes for a speedy return received. Resolved to the hunt, even if it took a year, Erik departed before Amine was in the ground. He traveled on horseback, northwest, directly opposite the two logical routes the Shah had suggested. He reasoned that Khusrowshah would not leave the country; the prince would stay in close proximity to the treasure he had accumulated. He'd wait, then under one guise or another retrieve his wealth. Perhaps with time, plenty of time, he could pay enough tribute to ferret his way back into the court.

Several days were spent questioning people in a gradually widening circle of the outlying towns. Chasing the prince proved almost challenging. Challenging until he learned of an odd dervish, a wandering mystic who renounced the pursuits of this world, but did not dance or beg, yet rode a phenomenal horse. With three days head start the desperate run towards the mountains began.

On the ancient plains, with the rocky foothills just ahead, the sun shone as a white-hot ball in an orange sky. Whipped upward by early morning winds, thick clouds of dust floated in the air, the dust of centuries. The bones and crumbling detritus of ages past, civilizations long dead, but not forgotten. No, never forgotten in this unbending land of the *Parsua*.

Erik came to a fork marked by an unusually carved stele. The inscriptions spoke of two vastly different routes leading through the summits. One, a well-maintained road for caravans, the other a more direct but treacherous path. Because Khusrowshah traveled alone, Erik was obliged to search in the more promising, if not more arduous direction. He waited patiently until dusk to cross into the lower elevations of the Elburz Sierra. Traveling at night, avoiding the heat of the day and the monasteries of the hagi, he could make better time and close the distance between a hunter and his prey.

As the sun set on the fifth day, Erik sat with his back to a stone looking down on the arid expanse beneath him. His horse stood tethered nearby. All the brooks they'd crossed were dry. In spring these channels were thunderous with life-preserving water, but not in this season. Their banks were as barren as the desert sands below. So the animal drank from the same water bags Erik drew from.

Watching the last of the heated air swirl in eddies over the nearly uninhabitable dunes, Erik welcomed the obscurity of the emerging night. He knew the darkness as an old and trusted friend. There was no bleakness or chaos in the enveloping folds of lengthening shadows. Events were actually clearer to him in the absence of light. He struck no fire; his advance up the trail would keep his blood flowing in the gathering chill. Down the face of the cliffs, off in the distance, he spied a twinkling light. Up on his feet, with telescope in hand, he viewed a few skeletal palms suffering from lack of water and a lone campfire burning. He was being followed. Apparently one lone party planned to make the climb behind him.

Two evenings later, beneath a stark white moon in an inky black sky, Erik rounded a peak and came to a small inn situated in an isolated spot. Outside, in the scattered patches of rustling dry grass, he discovered the place was just as parched as every other. Desperately in need of rain and melting snows, one small well still managed to function. Resting his horse in a cluster of creaking Camelthorn acacia, he stole forward and quietly filled his water bags. All the while his gaze swept cautiously back and forth over the façades of the buildings: a main house, a compact square annex, and a stable.

After watering the horse, he rested against a nearby boulder, studying the inn. One lone torch marked the front door, casting a twelve-foot pool of light around the step. All the rest remained in the achromatic shadow of silvered moonlight. Out from the front door came a porter. Hauling a pannier upon his shoulders, he headed straight for the stable.

Setting a brisk pace, timing his steps to the constant bark of a lone vigilant dog, Erik entered the structure several seconds after the man. Staying out of discernable sight, he coughed softly. The elderly laborer dropped his burden and turned.

"Do not fear me. I seek information. Has the inn a newly arrived traveler?" A small bag of coin thudded to the ground at the servant's sandaled feet.

Picking up the pouch, the man answered, "Last night a man arrived. Brave to venture forth in so arid a season. He stays in a room in the annex building my master prepared for overflow guests. His horse is tied behind; he requires it be kept close. This is his basket. I am to fill it with feed for the animal. He plans to leave at daybreak."

How convenient. Apparently the prince was willing to give up two nights camping on the trail for a bed indoors. Sending this man to fill the pannier meant he would settle for even the meager semblance of pampered living. Erik summoned every degree of control he possessed not to end the hunt too quickly. "Who else is about?"

"Only the owner, Shirin Mehdi, and his wife Neda. My family lives further up, shepherding goats."

"Good porter, I will speak to Shirin Mehdi and double the amount in that pouch if you can find an excuse to return to your people tonight. Take that noisy dog with you."

Huddled inside his room, Khusrowshah tried to relax within the darkened confines of a wretched chamber. He found every distant sound a cause for fright and the absence of noise even more alarming. Every squeak in a floorboard, every stomp of his horse's hoof or complaining neigh spooked him. Rebellious, even unto himself, he judged these fears as obnoxious weakness. Drinking wine and smoking opiate through the small hookah he'd brought with him did nothing of value to calm his nerves. *And that dog! That dog yaps incessantly!* He envisioned running over its neck with a cartwheel. The brown mongrel's eyes bulging from its skull like wine grapes squished from their peels. Snickering, the picture of rendering such sadistic pain pleased him, made him feel powerful and cruel – so very close to what he experienced as sexual motivation. Hearing the sound of footsteps outside jarred him from his reverie. *Relax. Only that befuddled porter!* He gulped from the jug of wine and sucked in more of the rich smoke.

A howling dry wind began to lash at the buildings, confirming for Erik the idea they should be left alone. No one need hear Khusrowshah's screams. He approached the front door with the servant alongside him. Tapping the wood with a single knuckle, he challenged the owner to open up.

Shirin Mehdi was bald with a long straight nose set above a set of telltale-reddened nostrils. The dust irritated his sinuses, and he'd been blowing vigorously. Coming around from behind him was the aforementioned Neda. Generous in girth for one so short, the cleft-chinned wife looked rather like a quarrelsome Pomeranian. Taken by surprise, they soaked up the vision of a tall black-veiled man standing on their stoop. The stranger's every movement suggested restrained power, from the top of his plumed helmet to the sheathed scimitar at his side.

With a gloved hand Erik gestured them out.

Casting their eyes about in fright, they stepped forward as a unit. "Greetings wanderer. The name of God is ineffable – not to be uttered," croaked the husband.

"Peace be upon this house," responded Erik. "I request that you read a document." Breaking the seal of the Shah, he placed the scroll in the man's hands.

With dampened palms the owner read the warrant, his illiterate pugnacious wife for once totally silent at his side.

From a satchel Erik withdrew three pouches of coin. "I require that for an appropriate sum, you travel in haste up the mountain to your porter's people. Return the day after tomorrow."

The owner handed back the document. "The man you seek is alone, enjoying his privacy. Apparently he's developed a fondness for the product of the grape and the soothing poppy. We are away at your command, Sir."

A few minutes later, Erik moved slowly around the already aging painted walls of the annex room, heels kept close to the baseboards. Like two smoldering amber coals, his eyes took in the sight of Khusrowshah sitting on the armed chair beside the bed. Drunk and nearly stuporous, the prince's head lolled awkwardly. A fire burned deep within Erik's gut. He cared little if Khusrowshah was repentant or unrepentant; the royal had soaked in the view of his last horrified victim. The fugitive was so soundly drugged that his head bent forward almost to his knees, drool poured in a long sticky trickle from his mouth. Erik restrained a laugh. This would be a much easier kill than he imagined. Studying the prosaic human nearly falling off the chair, Erik thought: *You are as dull and ordinary as a mule, so predictable, lured by every worldly comfort. And oh, what terror will awaken you.*

Out from the shadows he emerged and lifting Khusrowshah by his armpits, laid the runaway on the bed. *Am I not an excellent detective?* He opened the prince's eyelids. From deep within the alcohol and drug induced fog, Khusrowshah's brain appeared dazed, unappreciative of his predicament. He saw nothing of his captor. His paranoid mind sent forth not the slightest scribbled message of alarm.

"We must improvise some very special contraption to define your extinction." Erik's bony fingers closed like a vice, hog-tying the limp wrists and ankles in place.

Leaving the prince to his coma, he knew he had several undisturbed hours to prepare. He would make do with whatever supplies were present within these buildings. It would take whoever followed until morning to catch up. Providing Erik all the time he desired to apply his inventiveness and experiment. He skillfully jimmied the lock to the storeroom. Digging his hands around in the fine curled wood shavings of a crate, he discovered several fragile items packed in excelsior to prevent their cracking in transit.

The lethargy and respite, the amnesic effects provided by the intoxicating substances were wearing off. Khusrowshah's body felt like lead and his head hurt. Within this jagged unpleasant awakening, he could almost sense a strong presence around him. A black menace that was no less threatening because it stood so perfectly still. A soft mocking laughter, issued out of the still incomprehensible area lying somewhere beyond his head, came uninvited to his ears.

"Comfortable?"

His eyelids were crusted shut. Raising his brows, stretching the muscles of his face, he had to fight to open them one at a time. Straining to focus, squinting, he saw someone put a snake, no two snakes, on his chest. The asps uncoiled, their heads swaying slightly. They threatened, as twins, by flickering their forked tongues. Knowing they would, of their nature, seek the warmth of his exhausted lead-like body, his eyes closed. He was too tired to be vigilant.

He felt a tickling sensation move up his chest and heard again that taunting voice.

"Do the groans of the dead echo in your dreams?"

He sucked in a breath. Could he possibly be so stupid as to have fallen into the hands of the magician? The mental fog dissipated as in a flash of recognition his doubts dispersed. These were not snakes on his chest. It was Erik gliding a pair of ropes. His eyes sprung open as two grain-hooks were thrust beneath his collarbones and grappled into place. Rivers of burning excruciating lava nearly drove him back into unconsciousness.

A ratcheting sound broke into the fire storm, something growing tighter. Tighter. Above his head, fastened to the ceiling he saw three pulleys, three ropes. Pain poured like molten stone from his upper chest down his torso and back. Naked, hauled upward on the two ropes attached to the hooks, he was brought to stand erect on the footrail of the bed. The third rope was fastened to a noose around his neck. Gripping with his toes to maintain balance, he wobbled precariously on the balls of his feet. The noxious stimulus parading through his body was so acute, so exquisite, that he bit into his own tongue. Blood flowed out over his lips, the taste of heme penetrating his mouth.

"Does this type of torture suit you?" Erik sat in a chair with one leg crossed over the other – the ends of all three ropes in his placid hands.

Khusrowshah opened his eyes wide. Before him was an ungodly horror of all too realistic detail. A three-fold picture that deceived the visual senses...an illusion...or a painting...that he might, with effort, blink out of existence.

"Mercies of Allah!" His neck veins distended with rage.

"Must I explain everything to you?" Erik spoke with a tone so devoid of emotion he might have been a disinterested parent dealing with a wiggling inattentive child. "The three mirrors cannot keep what they receive. They simply must give back what they are shown. Look closely and you will know your own dread as the consequences unfold. Were I to add three more mirrors, you could view yourself from behind as well, but these were all the crate held."

He paused as Khusrowshah focused on a physical reality far too alarming for his brain to grasp. Not only was his loathsome reflection securely hooked and noosed, but his ankles were tied together and his wrists restrained behind his back.

"What, no beaming smile of greeting for our reunion? And you've sought my attentions so ardently."

Khusrowshah's eyes burned from dehydration. Ignoring the question, he squirmed. Realizing, almost too late to recover, that his balance on the footboard depended on a concerted degree of concentration.

With a cold unsettling gaze, Erik intoned the divisive truth. "The indignations you've so freely lavished on others have been difficult to ignore. Your father and the rest of the court have viewed your accomplishments with intense interest. Were you all agog when you saw Amine in her bridal clothes? Eager beyond control when you took in the sight of her waiting on your brother's wedding bed? She didn't tap her jeweled toe impatiently waiting for you, did she? Do you think you left her scarred? Shamed beyond redemption? Surely you know she took her life. Fixed in your own selfishness, you never bothered to cultivate a real friendship with her or Soha Houri."

"You will pay with your life for this outrage! I'll see you drawn and quartered. Help! Help!" Refusing to look into Erik's fiendish eyes, Khusrowshah rallied. Trying to keep his shoulders and hips from twisting, tentatively measuring the physical limits, he hoped the innkeeper would come.

"We are alone, fine Prince. No one can hear you. No one. I paid them to leave." Erik's own threats were delivered with frightening calm. "Besides, you will not live long enough to see my end. You are a derelict, sick with an intolerable disease. Fortunately, the only hope for recovery is me. I am the cure."

"My father would never hold a blood prince culpable."

Erik frowned reproachfully. Standing tall, he punched his fist into Khusrowshah's abdomen.

Thrown backwards as his air was taken, the noose tightened and the hooks took on the attributes of two red-hot pokers. Biting, gnawing, they seared into his flesh.

Containing his derision, Erik corrected his captive's posture by manipulating the ropes attached to the hooks. "If you're not more pious, I'll let your feet drop and increase your suffering. I am under royal command."

Khusrowshah sucked in several hungry breaths. "Who are you to lecture me about royal commands? Surely my father will retract his warrant and forgive me."

"Since you wish to concern yourself with pardons, who do you think sent me? The Shah demands his orders be fulfilled, and the Shah is to be pleased."

The prince didn't appear to understand. "My father would never authorize my death. I am second in line to the throne."

"Unlucky birth order for you, fortuitous providence for the rest of the kingdom." Erik steadied the ropes and held the prince erect. "Don't be so fidgety. You're greedy to find your gravitational center...a normal enough motivation. But I've never met anyone as impatient and as mentally disordered as you. Soon enough the third son will be promoted to the position of number two."

"I am not a lunatic. I have my faculties. How dare you mutilate an Islamic Prince anointed by Allah!"

"Apparently, Allah has sent me to punish your undeserving hide." He gradually tightened the rope of the noose.

"Wait! I have much to offer. We could flee together."

Erik answered with droll relief, "Ah, at last. You are concerned for my well-being. How deeply touching."

"You're jealous!" He blurted the accusation.

"I admit that social acceptance is an issue," Erik crooked his head; studying his bluish victim inside a rectangle he created with his thumbs and index fingers. "But that doesn't mean I am consumed with envy. You might say that you're an absurd painting held in a beautifully engineered frame. And I am," he gestured toward the three ropes, "the nail that holds you firmly to the wall. Anymore meaningless offers before we part company?"

"Why didn't you challenge me to a duel in the style of the Europeans?"

With cool detachment, Erik shook his head. "You want fair play? You who doled out cruelty to the innocent? I don't care about the gentleman's code, and I don't care that you come from royal bloodlines. You're a vile addition to the earth. Everyone will be better off without you."

"No need to negotiate. I volunteer to fornicate with the demon!"

This was interesting. "What demon? I'm not familiar with any demon and I'm certainly not in awe of it."

"Then let my death pour a thousand of its curses onto you."

Was the fool baiting him? Erik strode with a menacing slowness back and forth in front of the footboard. Halting every once in awhile, he pulled softly on one rope or another, just to renew Khusrowshah's agony. Logical thought won out. He drew a pouch from his pocket. "This simple leather bag contains two very special objects – a scorpion and a grasshopper. Shall we bring them back into play?" With a misdirection of his hand, Erik produced a golden ring. With it, he tapped the back of the grasshopper. Nothing happened. "Wait...wait for it." Slowly a small scroll issued from between the wings of the grasshopper. "There may still be choices, yes?" He unrolled the scroll. "The grasshopper says that you shall be raised to the ceiling by the noose unless you select the scorpion. The latter calls for further special treatment."

"Grasshopper," Khusrowshah whispered.

Erik pulled the noose tight, crushing the villain's throat, denying him air. In the throes of dying the villain's body twisted and twitched. The magician relaxed the rope just to hear the stertorous respirations return. Cracking an ammonia inhalant, he brought Khusrowshah's mind back from delirium. Setting the base of the cold toes back on the footboard, he waited.

The royal burst into tears like a little girl.

Reaching upward, Erik slapped his cheek; demanding testily, "Stop blubbering!" He wiped the tears with the sleeve of Amine's nuptial dress, the same one that had been wadded and stuck into her mouth. "Recognize this? Perhaps I'll start a rumor that your ghost still obsesses over her. That you roam about the land, alone, wailing for her forgiveness."

Erik frowned and steadied the prince's swaying body. "I really can't explain why I felt compelled to bring you back, except that I plan to be most unkind to you. In comparison, I was rather gracious to your friend, Nasser. Before you leave this life and enter the next, I want to admit you were a rather lame animal to track and a ninny for stopping here. So glad you did. Image my surprise when the notorious sadist skidded to a halt before me so he could sleep in a bed." Erik pulled all three ropes and the prince's toes lifted off the footboard.

This time the bloodied tongue protruded sloppily from between the swollen blue lips. The body hung there limp, but still had a pulse.

"No, no, no. Don't die yet. Come back and enjoy your body's final performance...the last fundamental act of preservation during death." He lowered Khusrowshah all the way down onto the bed. "The primordial brain orders the vessels of the arms and legs to constrict, sending the bulk of oxygen depleted blood to the vital organs. Preserving them as long as possible. The limbs grow very cold and cyanotic, but the brain and its crepuscular ability to hear are the very last to depart." To help the royal regain consciousness and experience dying, Erik grabbed some pillows and raised the legs above the level of the heart.

Whispering directly into a purplish-blue ear, Erik teased, "Listen as I coax your warped brain into miserable awareness. You now reside in a place that is dead to the living and still too living to be welcomed by the dead. You lay between two worlds, unable to enjoy the conveniences of the first or capitulate to the merits of the second. When I sensed you hiding behind that kitchen door, I knew I would have to root you out. Had you traveled to Eritrea I would have tracked you without rest, hounded you from your deepest burrow."

"Be sensible," Khusrowshah rasped. "There's a vast treasure. Free me. I'll pay you handsomely."

Erik had developed an engaging, theatrical, if not ominous way of delivering his rehearsed lines. His audiences could almost palpate, with some genuine sense of foreboding, the unforgiving blackheart that stayed just beneath the surface of everything the magician said or did while performing. "Sorry to culminate negotiations. I have taken an oath inviolate to affect an agonizing death for you. The *imams* teach that envy, greed, and lust are painfully accurate prognosticators of a violent end. Unless you have some protective jinn stuck in your pocket…oh, I forgot, your currently minus your pockets…all the known elements in the world cannot get you to your treasure in time."

The strange unbendable truth of the words, the final clarity of their meaning, raked across Khusrowshah's brain. He surrendered to the near mystical presence leaning over him. The Angel of Death was beckoning and he recognized a nearly euphoric peace. "Dying is not so bad. Did you know that women are entranced by you?"

Taken off-guard, Erik leaned back. The tone and cadence of his next words held more than a hint of intense mockery. "How stupid you are to view their curiosity as romantic attraction. They are appalled and terrified, not magnetized."

"In the secret crypts of every woman's eyes dwells a lie – they hide the gate to the Netherworld between their legs."

To the end...to the very end...a salacious rouge! A lecherous cockroach! "Can you anticipate the next calamity?" leered Erik. "Let me draw you a picture. You have lived long enough to see yourself emasculated!"

Hooked and hauled upward to his feet by the collarbones for one final time, a terrorized Khusrowshah screamed against the claws that held him.

"Witness justice!" Erik stabilized the ropes. "You who plot so coyly, the culmination of your life is defined by what you have chosen to do. You are undone!"

Desperate, Khusrowshah threw out one last contemptuous jeer. "Did you like the living-bride I left you? Your sightless defiled Fatima?"

Stunned, Erik embraced the storm. He now had the wherewithal to perform the surgery. "All your evil machinations cannot protect you from my wrath. You were an insidious nightmare for Fatima, Soha Houri, and Amine. Go from this world a neutered beast, haughty enemy of their peace!" With that pronouncement, he castrated the prince, forcing him to view the gaping hole. Then broke both his kneecaps so he could no longer support his own weight and let the drop end him.

Finally divested of his convoluted plots, Khusrowshah's gaze dulled with a lack of feeling. His dead pupils dilated into sightlessness.

Unflinching, remarkably serene, Erik stood there looking at the body. It was almost inane how accustomed he was growing to grisly sights. Eyes nearly as vacant as Khusrowshah's stared at the mess of humanity hanging before him. Erik could not call forth a single emotion and wondered that he felt nothing at all. He doubted he would ever feel anything again. *What proof to offer the Shah of Khusrowshah's death? Something obvious.* Since he knew someone from the court was coming, and had his suspicions regarding the portent of their arrival, he maneuvered the body so that it lay facedown before the mirrors – not unlike the description of Dagon in the Holy Text.

Then he sat on the chair to await his own pursuers.

"Hello, Daroga. I've been expecting you." He watched with satisfaction as a very dusty Khalil took in the grisly sight of the ropes and positioned mirrors. "Dagon has fallen. Robbed of his life."

"Along with a few other tidbits," Khalil pointed to the genitals. "Please, spare me the lurid details until we are safely on the road." Several of the royal guards were entering behind the Daroga. "Hold," Khalil directed with sobering directness. "Come, Erik. Let's talk in the other room."

Once they'd settled in the dining area, Khalil continued. "You have done the kingdom a great service. Khusrowshah was an intolerable evil, completely malignant. Now his life is destroyed, just as he destroyed others."

Erik watched as the men walked back and forth with several large metal containers. "Justice and honor are marketable commodities and I am for hire. What proof will you take of his death?"

"Certainly not the appendage I would prefer. I've ordered his ears. They'll bring them out to me presently." The Daroga leaned in. "I recommend we share a celebratory drink." Khalil's eyes were sad, unbelievably full of regret. He looked to Erik in silence. They both knew that Erik might have to die.

In that intuitive moment Erik felt closer to Khalil than at any point in the past. "I am happy to pay with my life for the privilege of destroying him. Please, pour."

The Daroga filled two glasses. "How very decent of you!" He made no secret of adding a powder to the one he set before Erik. "With luck you will live a long time. The rules for men are not the same as those for nobility. You followed the Shah's orders, but murdered a prince of the realm. A genuine dilemma."

Erik flashed on the image of a millstone hung around his neck. He knew the window sashes were well oiled; he'd done it himself. He could bolt. Instead he lifted his glass. "In thanksgiving and to the rewards of success." He drank, scarcely able to set the cup on the table before the drug commenced its effect. "With one hand you congratulate me and with the other...arrest me."

The pungent odor of kerosene soaking into wood and furnishings spread through the air. "Since Khusrowshah will not comply and combust spontaneously, I will perform my own *auto-da-fe* (burning of a heretic)," the Daroga spoke without a hint of a boast. "If we fire this place into oblivion. Very few will suspect the truth."

Erik rocked sideways, threatening to topple from the chair. "You would deprive the innkeeper of his livelihood?"

Khalil's hands reached forward, guiding him to the floor. "I'll pay him most generously. He'll live out his days in comfort."

A deputy passing through the room scoffed and went to kick Erik in the side.

The Daroga was transported with rage. In one fluid movement Khalil was on his feet, dagger in hand. "Dog! Touch him and I will slit your throat. Your blood can mingle with what already decorates the next room."

Sensing the Daroga threatened without reservation, the guard kept his eyes on the dagger's tip and raised his hands above his shoulders. "This infidel killed a prince of the land."

"Wait outside by the cage," the Daroga seethed. "Send in two others less moronic than yourself."

Swimming in the effects of the powder, Erik opened his mouth, but was unable to utter anything coherent. The Daroga knelt beside him.

"I have to burn Khusrowshah's body so that Amine's male relatives will not dig it up and defile it. Take comfort in the vengeance you delivered for Fatima, Soha Houri, and Amine." Khalil looked deep into the magician's eyes and saw the flood of sad images hit the banks of his soul. He took his friend's fingers. "They are lost, but you avenged them. You avenged us all."

The Daroga had the guards lift Erik gently into the cage and waited while they covered the bars with drapes. "On the trip back, no one is to touch any part of him. How many weapons did you remove from him?"

The guards snapped to attention. "The scimitar, four knives, and two of the finest, most carefully made Punjab lassos we have ever seen."

"Befits a master of the garrote, yes?" The Daroga went to mount his horse. Behind him the flames consuming the inn leapt high into the air. Following the wind, the thick smoke curled up along the mountainside.

On the descent back to the plains, they stopped as soon as Erik woke.

"Allah, forgive me! I am to bring you back to the Shah caged and in chains," confessed the Daroga. "But you will not suffer on my account. Within the confines of these bars, you shall ride upon a *toshak* (mattress) of comfort."

Erik angrily kicked the bars with his boots. "Will the Shah give me the *bastinado*, have me beaten senseless? Order my body decapitated and left outside the city walls to be devoured by vultures?"

"You are the Shah's favorite, but the Commander of the Faithful finds himself in the awkward position of rewarding you and showing the disgruntled crowds that he has not forgotten you killed his son."

"Even though he sent me to do it? His every whim has been my command." Erik raised his shackled wrists to show the Daroga the fearful image of his restraint. "Why do you permit this reproach? You of all people! I have been diligent on your behalf. Only the hypocritical self-righteous can be offended now. This entire country lacks any degree of genuine kindness."

"You need to urinate," the Daroga replied knowingly. He ordered Erik taken from the cage and walked around the cart. When he was relieved and returned to his mobile prison, the Daroga continued. "We will eat soon. These guards and I will attend to all your needs. Do not allow despair the pleasure of dining on your heart. Purge the cannibalism from you. These are vulgar times and royalty has few words to justify their way of life to the public. I may have apprehended you, but I have not forgotten my vow to Soha Houri. We shall find a way to cool the political climate and quell even the most volatile complaints."

They were brought cups of water and fruit. Before drinking, Erik lifted the liquid, silently questioning the Daroga.

"It's not drugged."

Erik swallowed. His throat was as dry as the ground around them. "There's a city in Spain where they open bullpens and let the beasts chase after men in the streets. I think the participants relish the risk, the thrill they might be gored."

"I've heard of the city, Pamplona." The Daroga watched the men build a fire.

"I'm not of their ilk."

"Be sensible, you cannot return a hero. As we enter the city let the crowds see you as a captive. Once we are inside the palace, I will expend all my time and energy negotiating the terms of your release."

"Public abuse is unacceptable."

"By the beard of the prophet, I said I'd help you! The people can't throw flowers. They must see your face. Following these commands sickens me. That first evening, when I found you entertaining crowds for the gypsies, was the happiest of my life. I am still your advocate and will continue to intercede on your behalf in every thinkable way."

"The price of this betrayal will be a forfeiture of something most terrible."

"Give me time, Erik. Don't let this be a defining moment in our friendship."

"Time is no ally to me. Nothing will diminish the degradation of my face as you drag this cage among the crowds."

Taken through the streets of the city, a resolute and silent Erik bore the humiliating jeers of the people. The common populace proved no different than any other group of gawkers found anywhere throughout Europe. Hungry for a brief relief from life's boredoms, anxious to see something unusual, they stood and watched as the enclosure with the exposed face of the Shah's Magician went past.

Taken to the dungeons, his face thankfully covered, he found himself placed in a prison cell with one tiny window secured with stanchions. In the small amount of light traveling through the iron bars, Erik spied a metal ring fastened to a trapdoor in the middle of the floor.

"Your accommodations come on two levels," explained the Daroga. "The stairs below that door wind down into the earth. They lead to a small cistern filled with water where you may wash and drink."

Still shackled, an exhausted and veiled Erik lay face down upon the basalt floor. The penetrating cold of the igneous stone felt refreshing. For three days he languished in the dungeon. When the Daroga returned, he found the cell empty and the trap door closed. After opening the trapdoor, the Persian set himself on a small chest he'd brought with him. From this perch he addressed the embouchure of the black hole.

"Have you been properly fed?" No answer. "I do not deserve your silence." He waited; feet spread apart, hands hanging limply. "I take that back. You are correct. For being the instrument of your public disgrace, I am not worthy of conversation. And I am lower than a filthy dog for leaving you in a dank cell with a boring hole." The Daroga rubbed his bleary eyes. "Just listen. I haven't slept in days…and I haven't been upstairs reveling at parties. I've deployed every resource I possess with diligent vigor, met every *contretemps* this wayward court has to offer. I'm frazzled, but have successfully negotiated the terms of your release. There will be no torture."

Out from the hole came an empty set of unfastened wrist shackles. They landed on the stone floor with a chain-rattling thud. They were closely followed by the metal leg restraints.

"Well! Freeing yourself must have taken all of two minutes. It's a wonder you didn't unlock the door and saunter down the corridor with a swagger." Still no response. The Daroga put his hand to the level of his eyes and peered into the void. Up from the blackness came a polished piece of stone the size of a large grapefruit. The Daroga reached out with his free hand and caught a sphere of slick iridescent feldspar. "You've been mining?" In shock he held the translucent stone up to the light with both hands.

Erik couldn't resist playing with him. His unveiled head was the next item to appear. "The guards feed me extras for the stones. How has the Shah reconciled the contradiction of condemning me and praising me?"

The Daroga stared at Erik. It was most disconcerting to deal with a disembodied gargoyle. He couldn't see the shoulders. "Allah has blessed the faithful," he stammered. "I have been totally devoted to nothing other than your survival. No perplexity in this universe can alter my attachment to you. I'm a victim of the times in which I'm reared."

"That claim is false. Keep the labradorite as a memento. There's a whole deposit of it and some brilliant blue-violet pyroxene crystals down here."

"How'd you make this so smooth?" Khalil pumped the ball into the air.

"Ground pumice and water. I'm not the first soul stuck here with time to kill. The balls were more than two-thirds complete when I found them."

"It is wisely written in our books: If you bring something, you shall return with something; if you bring nothing, you shall carry nothing away."

Erik's hand appeared. He set a French hurricane lamp, with finely polished glass and brass fittings, on the floor.

To Khalil it appeared that the scrappy survivor crawling up out of the earth brought their two worlds colliding together with bizarre finesse. "The lamp is from the guards?"

Erik nodded. Sitting on the edge, he folded his arms across his chest. He was dirtier than Khalil had ever seen him, a veritable gopher.

"You've been treated well?"

"I am as you see me."

"You've made remarkably good use of your accommodations," Khalil observed.

"The most enchanting lavish apartment cannot afford delight when one is detained against his will."

"But we have persevered. I'm sitting on a chest of gold coins, which belongs to you I might add. Here." The Daroga handed Erik a sack of Turkish gold sequins.

"Persia lacks trees. If I am to be released, I'm going home where I can view branches of lush foliage and let my ears bask in the words of my native tongue."

The Daroga smoothly switched to French. "It would be imprudent to return there just yet. I fear you have no choice but to stay. The *Shabbe Baraat* (Night of Forgiveness) approaches. In honor of the time, the Shah has condemned the slaying of his son and officially declared you pardoned. Your contrition is to be evidenced by diligently laboring to build him a new palace. You are to make it one of the most beautiful structures in Persia with all the treacherous passageways your diagrams proposed. Here is your scimitar and dagger."

Erik's booted foot pushed the weapons away.

"Don't!" exhorted Khalil. "You must go armed to meet your crew, an appearance of strength will speak well of you. Remember that to die is the inevitable destiny of all men. The Shah is fickle. He may consider that you harbor some hidden resentment for the degradation and confinement he inflicted on you. If there comes a time when we must ferret you out of this country, I will give you the name of the secret nautical society that will help you. Under the guise of religious institutions, they lodge sailors and smugglers. I will follow after you, so stay alive."

"So you would thicken the plot with predictions? Think Daroga, if I were to leave here, how would you know where to look for me?"

"My enterprising nose will find you. I recommend avoiding caravans. Make your way to the busiest docks in Bandar-e Pahlavi and look for fishermen setting out on boats bearing a symbol I will show you. We'll make their nets heavier with an unusual catch."

Erik smirked.

"Don't let this experience damage your spirit. You are alive, and you are still the secret favorite of the Shah. This is but a pittance of the fortune he bestows upon you. We must secure your money in a private place. Draw on its increasing sums as you see fit."

"If it were possible, I would – by some willful work of magic – lift these walls and cast them beyond Mount Caucasus. For now, I consider myself fortunate to avoid further penalty. When the time comes, I will listen to your more practical means of escape."

The Daroga stood and offered Erik his hand. "Come then. We go instantly to bathe. Your helmet is polished and new clothes await you. I'll introduce you to your crew of engineers and workers. Tomorrow we depart to move about the kingdom, pick a suitable spot for the new palace, and begin to gather your supplies. We will further develop our code of secretive speech. If necessary, we will use only eye movements for the other to perceive a devious communication. We shall not veer from our tasks until the appropriate moment. Should either of us encounter disaster, let the same fate befall the other."

Erik rose, slid his dirty hand around to the back of the Daroga's neck, and pressed their foreheads together. "Do not break our pact. We are brethren, bent upon the same road, the same pursuits."

In the still hot air high above the palace, a raven, a mystical messenger of the Otherworld, spread its wings and soared across the sky. This time it was no accident, no encounter with revulsion or the pleading cry of weariness that brought Erik back to himself. With a deep reflexive sigh he recognized the creature sitting beside his bed in the Panic Room.

"Khalil." The name was barely audible, a word sent out in a short joyful breath to vibrate through the air between them.

"Please," the being leaned forward, hands hanging limply between his knees. "I've been given the name Torossian and prefer the moniker of Revenant."

"Loyal brother. Then and now, whatever place we go, you have always been concerned for my safety. To awaken to such knowledge!" He sucked in a breath and closed his eyes, not wanting to cry with so much damage done his face. Looking from the present backwards into the past, he could see how critical was the bond between them. Every vision had helped define it, even the use of mirrors to confront Khusrowshah and Feigel-Evie. The pre-electric world and this one of laser beams and satellite-uplinks were merged together, a continuous tale.

"Why?" Erik could barely speak, so momentous was the knowledge dawning in his brain.

"Our souls traveled together, even after death. Soha Houri named me the guardian; the deal was sealed in blood. The tree in the quarry gave me the answer. Dragged into remembrance, I had to awaken you for to my great sorrow you never recognized me. Change is often violent. I don't look the same, but I have great powers. I swear I didn't know about your mother. I was as shocked and horrified as you."

"I am one very stubborn son-of-a-bitch. Some of our behavioral patterns need to be re-cemented, others left broken to lie in the dust. I see the references now, choices made over and over creating nearly impregnable personality traits. I forced Christine here, too!" Dismay riddled his voice.

"If we are masters of our own fates, she deserves an opportunity to choose hers."

"Isidore and Thayer will never understand. Two souls...both born out of a former existence...brought forward in time yet beset by obligation...loyal to their pact."

Torossian leaned back in his chair. "We are so unwholesome. Where shall we seek definition of self? In the tenacious remnants of shadows?"

"Those remains are beyond price! Yes, we're to the shadows with all haste."

Isidore's private green parlor was blessedly quiet. Christine pushed the wheelchair bearing the aged geneticist over the threshold, onto the classic patterns of a thick Persian carpet. She tried to study the coveted heirloom, the richly articulated floral motifs intricately hand woven of pure wool yarns in beige and olive, with red accents. They were moving from room to room, turning on lights as they went. Over a late lunch she'd volunteered to take on the role of head of the household. With the construction crews busily working to repair the north wing, Isidore was showing her the entirety of the chateau, giving her the keys to their sanctuary.

Isidore cleared his throat. "As you can see, even though the furnishings are somewhat faded, each parlor was a room decorated with a distinct color. Only slightly askew, we've tried to carry their history into this century as meticulously as possible."

She paused by a couch covered with a sheet. Gently removing the cloth, she revealed a wood trimmed settee that had at one time been the deep blue-green of the Mediterranean. She picked up a pillow. A colorful needlepoint depicted a group of hens pecking away at acorns and flowers. Their busy activity framed in a wreath of oak leaves.

"My mother stitched that with her own hands. God rest her in peace." He had no idea he spoke an ancient Hebraic blessing ferreted into the family by an imposter named Jacob Klein in the 1700's. The source of so many family traditions was unknown. Buried with the dead.

Christine ran her hand over the tiny stitches. "The dissymmetry in the rooms adds to their charm. There should be more of you and Nyah in them."

Isidore nodded. "A proud and lasting heritage nestles under all these sheets. In the late nineteenth century, the Indian city of Agra became famous for its floral-patterned carpets. Intricate Tree of Life designs captured the fancy of artisans for decades. In the next room is a priceless antique carpet in a mellow range of yellows, browns, and burgundy."

Her eyes grew distant, as if she recalled the room in its former condition. Too accurate a memory, she grimaced, still emotionally unprepared for this strange state of affairs she found herself in. "The transcendent mind redefines reality. Everything I observe needs reinterpretation."

Isidore sat watching her, genuinely impressed with her progress.

"Could one energetic night with a man get a female pregnant?" she queried.

Isidore's eyes clouded. *Rabbits.* "It's possible, but highly unlikely."

"I know for a fact he doesn't want children. He'll call," she said hopefully. "He needs medical attention."

Isidore didn't want to fan her hopes. "He has access to a great deal of money held under complete anonymity, and Torossian has dug the locater chip from his back. Can you sense anything about him?"

"For the present Erik has closed off his mind. I can't reach him telepathically. How could he leave?" Her fist pounded the pillow, raising a bit of dust into the air. She vigorously rubbed her nose to keep from sneezing. It was twilight. Outside the wind was picking up. Rain was on the way. Nature was commiserating with the loss at the de Chagny mansion. Christine felt abandoned. Here she was, adult body with adult drives, inexperienced and inept.

"I miss him with every breath and I'm furious that I'm not his priority. I know he's tormented; his previous history and his injured body revolt him. But how could he go away without a single word? His absence creates such a vacuum, and to take Torossian with him!" The remedy was to stay busy. Sprucing up the chateau was all she could think of at the moment. "I proved once before that I could love him, given half the chance I'll prove it again."

"You've come full circle, have you not? The crux of the matter is not whether you can be with him, but is he desirous of facing life with you now that he's mauled?"

She let the sarcasm drip from her voice. "I'm not some ostentatious piece of finery left clinging to one of the walls."

"In his heart he knows you exist, and you don't have to merely endure without him. This is a new phase for Erik. There are multiple problems. He's learning how to merge himself with his donor. So must you. In his defense, reconciling the ideation of his two personalities takes precedence. Give him time."

"I want to be a part of the solution."

Behind his mask Isidore mourned in private. "Be grateful. He's sparing you a great deal of heartache."

"What a life I've inherited! All satisfaction lived in one stupendous night. I've landed in the twenty-first century with both feet on the ground, ready to run, with a strong unwavering allegiance to a man who has run off."

"Perhaps all is not revealed."

She gazed at him through shiny tears. "I appreciate your sympathies," she murmured. She longed for the gentle prison of Erik's arms, the feel of him deep within her. More than that, she wanted to shake him, lecture him sternly about leaving. Vowing to help heal the house and wait, she started to pace back and forth across the rugs.

Erik's eyes examined a copse of struggling elms. The sun had fallen below the horizon, dark storm clouds threatened rain. They planned to move only at dusk and during the night, two shadows clinging to trees and the sides of buildings. He'd discovered that he was very much like a small number of people who deliberately attached themselves to dangerous situations. They were magnets drawn into arenas where their lives were ultimately put at risk. He hadn't figured out exactly what attracted him to peril. Deeper purposes he hoped.

Stepping off a dirt utility road into some rolling weeds, they headed for the elms. *Nothing like the golden sands of Persia.* They were at the east end of runway 08-left, Charles de Gaulle airport – their bodies shook with every booming acceleration of a jumbo jet lifting off the tarmac. The countryside surrounding them was a patchwork of emerald pastures edged with hedgerows and low stonewalls, small orchards, and homes clustered too near the airport. They would formulate their next moves from this vantage point.

Trying to ignore the massive hole within his spirit, Erik feigned fascination with the lights and planes. He already missed those little disapproving clucks Christine made with her tongue, and worried if Isidore was too much for Nyah to cope with. Torossian settled near the base of a tree and occupied himself with eating an apple – forever fond of anything raw.

The roar of another plane engine bounced and echoed off the advancing clouds. Departures hastening to beat the storm. Erik threw his hands up toward the sky. *What shall I do about who I am? What can I do if destiny has issued a different decree than what Isidore planned? Perhaps I can pass myself off as an infectious victim in search of rehabilitation.*

Reading his mind, Torossian shrugged and bit into the apple again. He had faith they'd decide what to do next very soon.

Erik hesitated, clearly annoyed before opening the disposable cellular phone to dial the chateau's number. His eyes narrowed – convinced that one call to reassure them would not be enough. Hollowing out his heart to fill it up again would take time. He listened carefully to Isidore's voice saying 'hello'. "It's me."

"Ah, the infamous *me*."

"How are you?"

"Still in remission."

"And Nyah? Please give her my love." He couldn't get himself to ask about Christine yet.

Isidore tried wheeling stealthfully toward the door, away from the stalking Christine. "I'm delighted to learn that *sub specie aeternitatis* (from eternity's point of view), you've decided to explore the world." Isidore lowered his voice, "So you plan to merge the two lifetimes?"

"I'm working on it," Erik responded tersely. "I couldn't stay there any longer. Even disfigured, there's a whole world for me to see."

"The accounts in Switzerland are set up for you. You have the numbers memorized?"

"Yes."

"I don't want you to worry over money. You have access to limitless sums. The interest alone will replenish whatever you withdraw."

The Revenant paused in his chewing. Aloof, like a mystic who'd endured long abstinences and only just now returned from a suspended state of near death, he stared at Erik.

"I apologize for the strangeness of my departure. Tell Christine I couldn't saddle her with the horror of this mutilation."

"She's fuming, yanking at her clothes, walking around muttering under her breath during conversations. You'll have to keep your mind guarded."

"She'll calm down eventually. I'm not going to be reporting in."

"I'm aware that you keep some secrets a very long time. Besides, I can't abide speculation…find it maddening. Let's stick with the facts when you're ready to share them."

Fascinated, Christine stomped over to Isidore's wheelchair. With both hands to her mouth she stifled a shriek of joy, but couldn't block the simultaneous flush of tears. "Tell him I know he was prowling the medical library before he left."

"I heard her. I was hoping to speak only with you. I don't want her to know that I watched her earlier." He crushed a piece of paper and thrust the crumbled ball into the pocket of his hooded leather coat. "I don't want her worship. Let her have her own life."

Abruptly changing the subject, Isidore interjected, "I'm working with a very discrete lawyer to draw up the necessary documents for you to inherit the estate. He's also working on legal papers for both you and Christine. Torossian needs to remain a well-kept secret." Silence was the response on the other end. "One more pertinent matter," Isidore sensed Erik listening. "You might be able to make use of your accident. Even the normal psyche is divided between the self that interacts with the world and the alternate dream-self. Might help in gluing the whole."

Erik's voice was very low, "I'll consider your information, but the quest to restore equilibrium is mine alone."

"No doubt you'll be heroic as you resolve the conflict. I understand why you can't let me help you sort through this tragedy."

"Ensure Christine's happiness. See that she improves herself and wants for nothing."

"What she wants is you, my boy. You're most courageous to venture forth on your own. You've formed a design of course. Haven't acted too rashly?"

"I've resigned myself to what has to be done. I can ill afford to draw attention to myself and fling embarrassment down on your head."

"I am grateful. Not sure I can teach myself not to worry about you."

"You'll learn. I have figured you out, Isidore. You're an angel, a warrior *par excellence*."

"Not a devil living on a lake of brimstone?" A tear blossomed in the corner of Isidore's left eye. He looked at Christine and sighed. Signaling for her to come closer and share the phone with him. Touching his ear, he indicated he meant for her to only listen. "Why?"

"Because you know we're composed of the same material that makes up the stars, a truly noble fact. Tell Christine I'm sorry that I can't give her back what we once had."

"Not sure that will compute satisfactorily. She will be kept safe... until a wandering wind breathes the secret you have returned. Good luck, Erik. You are still my finest creation."

"Luck will have nothing to do with it." A brisk wind forced him to turn his back to the rushing air so he could continue speaking into the phone.

The Night Creature brushed aside a paper that flew up and landed on his face. Torossian rather liked the ambient sounds of wind and rain, along with the blast of the airplanes. There was a wondrous copulation of aesthetics and mechanical utility produced in every roar. *Remember, Erik, we must survive, to declare our autonomy even if science has no working definition for us.*

Erik lowered the phone from his mouth. *I won't disappoint you. Our new life might just exceed all your current expectations.* He didn't need to tell Torossian how dead he felt internally.

Without a thought for her dignity, Christine yanked the portable phone from Isidore's hand. "You're breaking my heart, Erik! I am not angry – emotionally crippled maybe, but not angry."

Isidore shook his head. This tactic was fruitless.

Erik registered her petulant ill humor. She was flying in four directions at once. "Be careful, Christine. Don't let yourself turn into the Queen of Ice."

"Me? Icy? Who has forgotten what we shared, denied us almost every worldly pleasure worth having? You, Erik...not me!" Pride made begging absolutely out of the question. "I'm not going to try and find you!" She lied.

"Good! Don't! Define your life however you like and let me define mine. Mine doesn't have to make sense to you, it has to make sense to me." Click. The line was dead. *What right does she have to remind me of things I am choosing to forget?*

Christine stared at the phone in disbelief. With gestures of expressive grief, she scraped her fingertips over the buttons on the phone, as if she wished to speed over the circuit boards and be fused within the molecules of technology.

Isidore silently admired her ability to feel. *How fortunate to be so alive.* Without consoling her, he turned the chair to leave the room. It was troubling that no one could locate Thayer Delaquois. But down in Isidore's laboratory vault sat all his computers and equipment – ready to pry into the tiny world of life's composite structures. All the little glass jars lining the walls brimming with treasures more valuable than gold or platinum.

Blinded by frustration, Christine balled her fists and hollered. "Why didn't you **order** him home?"

Isidore paused; he was just as grieved as she. "Calm yourself. A thousand Arabian nights may be all he needs. Surely you can give him that – you possess generosity."

"Where is he?"

"The airport, I think. The noise of airplanes was rather nerve wracking."

"If he doesn't leave the country, I think I know where he will go." Christine's voice was evidencing more control. "We have to find him."

Isidore maneuvered the chair so he faced her. "I think he would be one step ahead of every move we made, and it's a very big world."

Part of her wanted to be contained in that uterus-thing down in the basement...with the handsome creature taunting her. Another part wanted to bolt through the front gate in a mad search. The last bit told her to stay still, very still. She believed she might have conceived. Her nipples were extremely tender. That possibility alone should be enough to keep her from gallivanting off. *Come home when you're ready, Erik. When you've succeeded in this crazy quest.*

Nyah stood in the doorway. She spoke with all the sound intuition of a mother. "Maybe you'd have more insight if you asked yourself what he fears. I think he'll conquer his greatest phobias first. He can't be a man to you until he's met the criteria within himself. Before these seizures burdened him, he developed a rigorous regimen of self-discipline. Knowing Erik, he will struggle with what he perceives as weakness. He doesn't want to rein-in his anger; he wants to expend it, to use its energies as a driving force to grind away at whatever life is throwing at him. He'll emerge a polished stone that dazzles the eyes of the beholder."

"I don't want to discredit your suggestions, Nyah." Christine was ready to beg. "But Erik's independence is unnerving. All right, he wants to be a man...and I want to be a woman." She pounded a fist into the palm of her hand, suddenly struck with an insight. For a moment, she was unable to utter a word. "When you die, Isidore, will Erik come back and take your place?"

"Perhaps. At this point you know as much as I."

"When he returns will he expect me to be patient and kind?"

"He expects you to be happy. Erik is carrying a very heavy rock. When the weight grows too burdensome, he'll put it down to rest, but he will always pick it back up again...for only with his very last breath will the rock be taken from him."

"Congratulate me, I might be pregnant!"

Astonished, Nyah shot Isidore a cryptic glance.

Christine extended her hands, palms open. "How much money do I have access to?"

"My sweet child, funds are limitless. I am the richest geneticist in the world."

"I want you to show me his last opera. We shall produce it and draw him to us." She went abruptly to the window. "Listen, Erik. The girl you loved in another lifetime still lives. She loves you in any form you take. You produce a maddening effect on everything that surrounds you and you've left me aching. Scoundrel!"

A sneer crossed Isidore's face. Her bravado, for all its worthy intensity, betrayed a selfish hunger.

Still seated at the base of the tree, Torossian tried to shield her from hope. He sent her the clear picture of a candle on a windowsill, its flame flickering. *Put out the light, Christine. We're leaving France. Erik isn't ready.*

A sheen of water filled her eyes. If he could, Torossian would like to touch those tears. Life was proving a dissatisfying infernal place. He'd never tasted tears, but he couldn't touch her; she wasn't his.

An airport employee driving a cart around the back end of runway 08-left reported that he gave a young man, wearing a plain mask over a bandaged face, a lift to the charter flight terminal. When questioned, the man was adamant that his passenger was alone.

Here begins

ᛒᚩ **The Disciples of the Night** ᚳᛟ

13392218R00343

Made in the USA
Lexington, KY
28 January 2012